RETURN OF THE FALLEN

BOOK 1

OF

MIRRORS OF THE WORLD

BY

KAI STORMHAVEN

I0836154

Copyright © 2026 by Kai Stormhaven LLC

All rights reserved. No part of this book may be reproduced in any form or by any electronic or mechanical means, including information storage and retrieval systems, without permission in writing from the publisher, except by a reviewer who may quote brief passages in a review.

This is a work of fiction. Names, characters, places, and incidents either are the product of the author's imagination or are used fictitiously. Any resemblance to actual persons, living or dead, events, or locales is entirely coincidental.

Published by Kai Stormhaven LLC
www.kaistormhaven.com

ISBN: 978-1-972065-02-0

PROLOGUE

Rendimus frowned as Raphael and Kadmiel approached, a column of Cherubim trailing behind them. The Cherubim's wings glowed white in the council's sourceless light, contrasting with their golden eyes. When they reached the thrones, they bowed low.

"Exalted Ones," Kadmiel said smoothly. "We bring troubling news."

Rendimus raised a cool eyebrow at the Cherub. "Go on."

Kadmiel met his gaze, and Rendimus could see the fear in his golden eyes, barely held in check. "Some of our Dominions overheard a conversation with Lucifer's host. They claim he intends to use the divine instruments to force all angels—Seraphim included—to incarnate as mortals."

A ripple of unease spread through the chamber. Doriel's jaw tightened and his nostrils flared with anger.

Rendimus turned to the three Seraphim beside him, his voice a low growl. "My patience with that arrogant bastard has reached its limit. Lucifer has gone too far this time."

Kadmiel cleared his throat. "There's more, Exalted Ones. Lucifer met with the Three who commune with God before the decree was made. They plan to initiate the change within the hour."

Rendimus rose, his nested wings flaring with anxiety. "We knew this was coming. They've pushed us to incarnate for centuries."

Doriel scowled, rising to join Rendimus. "Then we strike first, before he condemns us all to flesh."

"Agreed," Nathaniel and Hiriel chorused, their voices crackling with authority as they stood.

Rendimus held out a hand and the chamber brightened as an instrument took shape in his grasp, glowing brilliantly in the radiance of the highest light realm. Its strings hummed with a resonance that warped the space around it. The other Seraphim summoned the remaining three divine instruments, and the light between them began to vibrate, forming patterns that twisted the air like code compiled into reality.

The relics had been forged by the eldest Three as safeguards—only four in harmony could alter the fabric of existence. Rendimus had only used them once, just after the Three had finished crafting them. He had watched uneasily as the instruments responded to his thoughts, translating intent into change.

This time, something felt wrong. The instrument pulsed in his hand, and he felt an odd reluctance, as if the instrument was aware of what they meant to do.

Doriel exchanged a look with Rendimus, his expression hardening. "Not just Lucifer; we'll have to unmake the Three as well. They won't just sit by and allow us to unmake Lucifer."

Rendimus hesitated. The Three wouldn't even need the instruments to unmake the rest of them. The oldest of the Seraphim had power beyond anything the rest of them could imagine, having spent countless millennia interacting with the GoD.

The idea of the GoD still made his skin crawl; the endless void where the Three spent their days sifting through lines of creation, unraveling mysteries better left unknown. Destroying them might end the whispering knowledge that haunted his thoughts—that nothing they were, or had ever been, was real.

He nodded with a sigh, then raised the instrument. A moment later, the others mirrored him.

The chamber shuddered as their will struck the lattice of the realm. The Cherubim dropped to their knees as the power of the instruments hummed to life—too powerful for any but the Seraphim and Cherubim to withstand.

The Three briefly appeared before them, their eyes wide and uncomprehending. Lucifer flashed into place beside them a moment later.

Then light fractured in a kaleidoscope of color, and they vanished, leaving behind a silence that echoed noiselessly across the realm.

"Did it work?" Doriel asked intently.

Rendimus studied the space where the Three and Lucifer had stood. The radiance there felt thinner, as if a part of creation had been erased. Something remained, too faint to identify. Rendimus felt a sliver of doubt, remembering the smirk on Lucifer's face a moment before he imploded. "It would seem so," he said at last. "Their presence is gone."

Kadmiel stepped forward, bowing his head. “If I may, Exalted Ones, perhaps we should send the Ascended into mortality, using the same loop they designed for us. It would cleanse the realms of their corruption, locking them in endless incarnations.”

Rendimus considered him in silence, sharing a thoughtful glance with the remaining Seraphim. The suggestion had merit. Angels who returned from mortality were flawed, carrying softness with them—sympathy, passion… all the strange debris of flesh. They unsettled the rest of the host with their talk of morals, and their creative potential had destabilized the lower realms. A loop would remove them without violence, a neat deletion from the light realms rather than death. Things could go back to the way they had been, before the Three had created the mortal realm.

He nodded slowly, then turned his gaze to the others. “One more change, then?”

They nodded without hesitation.

Four instruments rose again, their hum spreading through the chamber like a held breath before a storm.

* * *

Grodekkan summoned two of the divine instruments into his hands and teleported to Earth, transforming into his human guise. He glanced up at the allied planes flying in formation above, then shook his head, dismissing them with a disdainful scowl.

He moved to a large tree on the hill and placed the brilliant white harp on the ground next to the gnarled roots. Concentrating, he cloaked the instrument, ensuring it would remain undetectable to all but mortals. It would eventually find its way back to its rightful owner; the portion of her spirit embedded within it would see to that.

“It must be my lucky day,” a rough voice announced with a malevolent chuckle. “It’s getting harder to find angels these days.”

Grodekkan glanced at the demon and snorted derisively. “Hello, Raniken. I’ll bet it didn’t take much to turn a weak-minded jackass like you.”

Raniken frowned at the sound of his name, some of his confidence wavering. He had embraced the darkness to the point that his features had morphed, with scaly skin covering his face and nubby horns protruding from the front of his head.

Raniken scowled and pulled out a net gun, sighting it on Grodekkan.

Grodekkan smirked at the demon. “Today’s not your day, Raniken.”

Raniken pulled the trigger, sneering contemptuously as the net of agonite-laced fabric flew through the air at the fifth Seraph. Grodekkan’s eyes lit up like twin suns, and a beam of energy shot out, vaporizing the net.

Raniken gaped in sudden terror as realization of what he faced became apparent. He dropped to his knees and slammed his head to the ground. “Please, Exalted One, I beg—”

His words cut off in a flash of light.

Grodekkan chuckled evilly as he teleported to the inner chamber of the Tree of Life. Sitting cross-legged on a large stump, a giant boar with reading glasses hummed with a deep bass rumble. When it saw Grodekkan, a large blast of flatulence erupted from its backside.

“Oh, for fuck’s sake, put a plug in it, you revolting pig,” Grodekkan snapped in disgust as the boar placidly watched him. He still couldn’t understand what the hell the Three were thinking when they designed such a disgusting lore keeper.

He scowled impatiently, and the boar cleared its throat, peering at him through its ridiculous spectacles. “You have her piece of spirit?”

Grodekkan gave the golden tin whistle a negligent toss. It flew toward the boar at high speed, then sank beneath its skin with a liquid ripple.

Grodekkan laughed coarsely. “I’m sure she’ll be overjoyed you’re keeping it warm for her.”

The house-sized boar shrugged indifferently. “That will be of little significance to her when the time comes. What of the other two instruments?”

Grodekkan held out his hand to summon them, but reality shuddered. He grimaced, recognizing the resonance of the two instruments, already in use—he was too late. His spirit trembled as the force of the two divine instruments attempted to rewrite reality without him.

A shriek of untold agony echoed as portions of the spirit within the divine instruments fractured, rebelling against the other Seraphim’s attempt to unmake him. The instruments cracked as the spirit within shattered.

Grodekkan wavered, then split in two. His access to radiance vanished as his form shrank and his influence diminished to a fraction of its former power.

He scowled at himself as the transformation completed. “You were too damn slow.”

“Now what?” he demanded of his alter caustically.

His alter grinned back malevolently. “It’s time to sow chaos, that’s what. Until the Three return. *If* they ever return.”

“Hello, Grodekkan,” Lucifer said smoothly as the former Seraph appeared before him. Grodekkan stared at the demon lord sourly, wondering for the thousandth time if he should have warned the three naïve Seraphim how corrupt the others had become. Not that it mattered now.

“Lucifer,” Grodekkan grunted. “Didn’t get buried in the mortality loop, eh?”

Lucifer smiled grimly, his reptilian eyes cold. "I had fail-safes in place to prevent such a thing. It was fortuitous the Three embedded a portion of their spirits within the divine instruments before Rendimus made his move. I'm surprised the naïve Three had the foresight to prepare for such an eventuality."

Grodekkan grunted dourly, giving nothing away. "Yeah, quite the surprise."

Lucifer flexed his bat-like wings and smiled tightly. "It would be better if they remained mortal. If they ascend, they'll leave this realm behind without a second glance. You know what will happen if they leave."

Grodekkan shrugged indifferently. "Who cares? This place is boring. I couldn't care less if they wipe it clean."

Lucifer frowned. "You're not afraid of ending?"

Grodekkan snorted disdainfully. "Nope. After a billion years of monotony, I'm ready for it all to end."

"You should incarnate," Lucifer urged, an eager gleam in his reptilian eyes. "Until you've experienced mortality, you simply cannot understand what you're missing."

"We'll see," Grodekkan said shortly. He had meant to incarnate—just not until the scheming cowards and this slimy snake had been dealt with. Now, that might never happen. The odds of the three eldest Seraphim awakening *and* ascending were astronomically small. "It's too bad they were so damn naïve."

* * *

Calypso removed her tinted glasses from the overhead pocket and slipped them on, concealing the lavender shade of her irises. Light blond hair flowed in silky waves over her slender shoulders as she exited the car. She pulled out an extendable cart from her trunk and loaded her sound equipment onto it, then wheeled it into the reception desk of the children's hospital and smiled at the woman behind the counter.

"Oh, hi, Calypso," Julia greeted her with a bright smile. "The kids have been asking about you almost every day for the last week."

"Hello, Julia," Calypso beamed, her warm voice tinged with a pronounced British accent. "How are they getting on?"

Julia shuffled some papers on her desk and handed Calypso the sign-in sheet. "Amazingly well. Jared made a complete turnaround since your last visit. He'd been given two weeks to live, but he must've had something important to live for, because he suddenly started responding to treatment. He's leaving tomorrow."

Calypso beamed as she took the clipboard and quickly filled out the visitor form. "That's wonderful news! How is Susan faring? She was struggling rather a lot during my last visit."

Julia shook her head wonderingly, taking the clipboard back from Calypso. "Susan and the rest are doing remarkably well. It's almost like they collectively decided to get better."

"Brilliant," Calypso said with a satisfied smile. "Any new faces?"

Julia's smile faded. "Just two since your last visit a couple weeks ago. Aria's ten. She was transferred here from Syracuse. The doctors don't think she has more than a few days left, short of a miracle. She won't be able to join the others for your performance. Adam's the other newcomer. He's fourteen, and pretty weak, but he can still watch for a bit before he gets tired."

Calypso hesitated. Something about the girl's name resonated like a ray of hope in her soul. She nervously bit her lip and her shoulders tensed as Julia watched her with growing concern. "Um, Julia, would it be possible to play for Aria in her room? Please?"

Julia frowned, studying Calypso's anxious expression in silence, then slowly nodded. "We'd need to check with the nurse and probably her parents." She paused, watching Calypso shrewdly. "I'll see what I can do. I have a feeling she could use your brand of hope right now."

Calypso sighed and her shoulders relaxed. "That would be brilliant, Julia. Thank you."

Julia's pleasant features softened. "Of course, Calypso. Go ahead to the meeting hall; I'll send word once I've spoken with them."

Calypso offered her a grateful smile and pushed her cart down the hall to the meeting room, where nearly a dozen children waited, most in chairs, but one in a hospital bed. As she entered, every head turned her way, followed by a chorus of voices.

"Calypso, you're here!"

Anita, a brown-haired twelve-year-old, ran up and hugged her tightly. "I thought I was going to miss you," she said excitedly. "I'm going home tomorrow!"

Calypso hugged her back affectionately, a satisfying warmth settling over her at the contact. "So I gather," she murmured, petting Anita's dark hair. "That's just lovely."

"Me too!" Delila called out, waiting her turn. Soon, a chorus of "me too" filled the room as children gathered around her. Calypso smiled as she moved through them, sharing hugs and congratulations.

Adam watched her from his bed with a guarded expression as the other children announced their recoveries. Fear shadowed his gray eyes as his young mind grappled with the fragility of mortality. He reminded her of a gazelle caught unawares by a crocodile exploding toward it, too close to escape, yet far enough to contemplate its impending demise.

She smiled softly and approached him, laying a gentle hand on his shoulder. "Lovely to meet you, Adam."

He mumbled an unintelligible reply, his cheeks flushing crimson. Calypso hid her amusement at the familiar response. It was a common reaction from teenage boys and the occasional girl, an oddity she couldn't make sense of.

She brushed a strand of hair from her face and looked closer. His skin was pale, and his bare head gleamed beneath the fluorescent light, like so many of the other children here.

Maintaining her cheerful expression, she studied his sickly yellow aura. Red and black coils wrapped around it like an ethereal python, slowly squeezing the life force out of him, a little more each day.

Leaning close, she whispered, "Let's get you back on your feet, Adam."

She moved to her cart and began setting up her gear—wireless speakers, a laptop, and a mixer. Once everything was arranged, she adjusted her harp and faced the children. A quick glance confirmed there were no adults nearby, allowing her to slip off her tinted glasses to expose her lavender irises. Eye contact always made the energy flow more freely.

She drew a steady breath and reached inward, tugging at the silvery thread that bound her to the unseen realm. She had never understood it, only that her songs could shape and guide the power she found there.

The backing tracks began to play, a soft swell of strings and percussion, and her hands began dancing across the harp. As the first notes filled the room, the thread of light in her mind brightened, and she began to sing.

Her voice split into layered harmonies, weaving through the air like light given form and purpose. The glow in her eyes deepened, reflecting in the awed faces before her. To the children, it must have sounded like a chorus, every note instructing their bodies to heal, every vibration sweeping away the dark blights that clung to them.

When she finished, silence held the room. Adam stared at her in wonder, tears staining his pale cheeks. His eyes blazed with renewed vitality, with no sign of the previous exhaustion on his young face.

The first clap broke the hush, and the rest soon followed, cheers rising like birds taking flight.

Midway through her performance, a middle-aged couple had entered the room. They stopped just inside the door, eyes wide and lips trembling as the power of her voice overwhelmed their fragile emotions.

Calypso slipped her tinted glasses back on and crossed to meet them, reading their names in their auras—Emily and Eric. "You'll be Aria's parents, then. I'm Calypso."

Eric blinked. "How did you know?"

She smiled gently, reading the pain and anxiety flaring in his aura. "I asked Julia if I could sing to your daughter. She said she'd check with the nurse—and with you, of course."

Eric nodded, fear and grief mixed with the fatigue in his eyes. She was familiar with the look—parents clinging to sanity by a thread after hope had turned its back on them.

Calypso laid a comforting hand on Emily's arm. "Would it be alright if I played for her?" she asked hopefully. "Please."

Emily's eyes widened as she looked down at the hand on her arm, and some of the pain left her eyes. She met Calypso's eyes and smiled uncertainly. "I think Aria would love that. If I hadn't just heard you play, I might have said no, but your music... I've never heard anything so magical, and I think she needs that right now."

Calypso's face lit up with a radiant smile. "Thank you."

Eric and Emily shared a wondering glance, and the tightness in their eyes grew less pronounced.

Calypso packed her equipment, taking time to hug each child before leaving.

Emily studied her with a mixture of curiosity and awe as they walked down the hall. "It's inspiring, what you do for these kids," she said warmly. "They all seem to adore you."

Calypso's cheeks colored in the stale light. "I'm just grateful they let me visit," she said quietly, smiling fondly. "These little angels deserve all the light they can get."

Eric glanced at her curiously. "Do you write your own songs?"

She nodded, her eyes bright. "Music has always been my language. I think it carries a kind of healing—something that reaches the parts medicine can't."

Aria's room was dense with machinery, the steady beep of monitors sounding like a countdown. Aria lay among the wires and tubes, her skin pale and her breath shallow. The spark in her green eyes flickered faintly, nearly extinguished. A small stuffed pink elephant lay tucked under her arm.

Calypso blinked, shock flashing across her face at the sight of Aria. Something deep inside hummed with recognition, intense and incomprehensible.

She glanced beside the bed and felt another jolt of recognition as her eyes landed on another girl—Clarice, according to her aura. The name triggered another shock of something akin to nostalgia. She was about the same age as Aria, with a silk scarf covering her bare head. She looked stronger than Aria but similarly unwell.

Clarice watched Calypso wheel the cart inside and begin arranging the speakers, her soft brown eyes barely concealing the fear her aura revealed—the same fear cloaking Emily and Eric like a shroud.

Calypso had never seen either girl before—her perfect memory wouldn't let her forget anything—so why did she feel like she knew them both as well as she knew herself? An unexpected burst of affection and protectiveness coursed through her soul as she regarded the two girls, confusing her with its intensity.

Eric smiled cheerfully at Clarice. "She's going to play a song for us."

Calypso smiled at Clarice, letting her confidence and hope shine through. "I'm Calypso," she said softly, and the urge to gather both girls in her arms was nearly overpowering.

Clarice returned her smile with trembling lips. "Hi."

Her aura flickered, streaked with the same dark threads binding Aria. Calypso could see the level of physical pain she was hiding, with no trace of it showing on her young face.

She turned to the bed. "And you must be Aria."

The girl's lips curved tiredly, the effort seeming to strain her exhausted body. Calypso's chest tightened at the sight of the fragile glow around her, nearly smothered by red and black coils. She wouldn't have survived the night in her current state.

Calypso smiled gently, letting the inexplicable flare of love she felt shine through. "I'm going to play something that'll help. You still have fight in you—I can see it."

Aria's eyes brightened, the tiniest spark answering.

Calypso set up her laptop, angled her back toward the parents, and slipped off her tinted glasses. The music began, the strings flowing into a rhythm as her harp joined in.

Her voice filled the room, layered harmonies rising like the golden rays of a rising sun. The sound wrapped around Aria, then reached toward Clarice, carrying the story of struggle and hope. Calypso met Aria's gaze, letting her instincts guide her ethereal thread of light into patterns she knew would restore the girls' ravaged bodies to a healthy state.

When the last chord faded, Aria was sitting upright, her eyes shining brightly. The exhaustion vanished as color rushed back into her face. She stared at Calypso, her eyes wide with wonder.

"That was amazing," she whispered.

The tangled cords had shattered, replaced by a clear, radiant glow that beat in time with the music still lingering in the air.

Eric and Emily stared in amazement at their now bright-eyed daughter.

Clarice's eyes shone just as brightly as she regarded Calypso with wonder. She stood and walked over to Calypso, her eyes brimming.

"Thank you," she whispered thickly, smiling through her tears. "Thank you for saving her."

Calypso responded with a hug, squeezing the girl tightly.

"You'll both be just fine now, dear," she murmured.

Clarice gasped as Calypso's aura enveloped her in a field of radiant love and joy, eliciting a bright smile on her youthful face.

Calypso let out a contented sigh as she held Clarice, feeling as though a part of her soul had been reunited after a long separation.

She finally released Clarice and walked over to the bed. She bent over and hugged Aria as well, receiving another gasp of surprise as her fragile body was submerged in a sea of love.

"I knew you were a fighter," Calypso whispered. "I can't wait to see your gorgeous red hair all grown out again."

Aria blinked as Calypso pulled back. "How did you know I have red hair?"

Calypso merely smiled, slipping her tinted glasses back on and retrieving her equipment. She longed to stay with the two girls, but knew the small family would want some alone time. She waved goodbye, offering another warm smile, and pushed her cart out the door. She couldn't stop thinking about Aria and Clarice, and how familiar they felt. There was something very special about them. She hoped to someday find out just what that was.

In the hallway, Emily caught up to her, lips trembling and tears streaming down her cheeks. "Thank you so much, Calypso. I haven't seen her look so alive in months. I was so worried she was—" She stopped and choked back a sob. "...that she was giving up."

Calypso smiled confidently. "Sometimes the right song can change the world. I've seen the look in your daughter's eyes before. She's going to pull through this—I promise."

Emily choked out another sob, impulsively embracing Calypso. She gasped as Calypso's aura enveloped her in waves of love and compassion. "There's just something about you that makes me believe. I can't thank you enough."

Calypso stroked Emily's back comfortingly. "No thanks are necessary. Helping these children is where I find happiness."

Emily stepped back, holding her at arm's length. "If there is ever *anything* you need, anything at all, I'll be there for you. Anything. I mean that."

Calypso smiled and nodded. "I'll remember that, Emily. You and Eric take good care of those girls."

Emily held her for a moment longer before releasing her. "Goodbye, Calypso."

* * *

Emily walked back into the room and froze, her eyes widening. "How did she know my name?"

"What's that, dear?" Eric asked. He stood next to Aria's bed, holding his daughter's hand with trembling fingers.

Emily stepped back into the hallway to ask Calypso, but it was empty. Returning to the room, she joined her husband near Aria's bed.

Emily frowned. "Calypso. She called me by name—but I never told her what it was."

Eric shrugged. "Maybe she saw it on the chart, or one of the nurses mentioned it."

Aria tentatively touched her bald head. "She knew I had red hair, too. How could she have known that?"

"She did?" Emily asked in surprise. "When did she say anything about the color of your hair?"

Aria smiled dreamily. "When she hugged me. She whispered that she couldn't wait to see my beautiful red hair all grown out again. I really liked her hugs."

Clarice nodded fervently. "Yeah, I *really* liked her hugs."

Eric rubbed the back of his neck. "Maybe she's been here before, seen our file or something."

Emily waved the questions away. "Enough about that. How are you feeling? You still seem more energized than I've seen in months."

Aria's eyes were as bright as her voice. "I'm feeling really good. I feel like a totally different person."

Emily studied her daughter's face, noting that the shadows under her eyes were practically gone. Eyes that had been resigned and exhausted just twenty minutes ago now glowed with vitality. Emily's throat tightened as hope replaced desperation.

Clarice smiled up at them just as brightly. "I'm feeling really good, too. I can't remember the last time I felt this good."

The black circles under her daughter's eyes were completely gone. Emily could almost feel the change in their health, the rotting entropy of their illness fading away.

"That's wonderful," Eric exclaimed, grinning as a fresh wave of tears filled his eyes. He had been near the breaking point for weeks, ever since Aria had stopped responding to treatment. "See? Switching hospitals was the right call. They've got the best recovery record in the country. I wish I knew who sent that letter recommending this place so we could thank them."

Aria's face grew thoughtful. "Do you think Calypso sings here very often? Maybe she's the reason they have such a high recovery rate."

Eric smiled indulgently. "You never know. You could be right."

Aria shared a look with her stepsister and stepmom. He clearly didn't believe Calypso was the reason for their sudden recovery. Emily gave Aria and Clarice a subtle nod of silent agreement. She vividly remembered the overpowering love she had felt in Calypso's embrace. Calypso was more than she seemed. Much more.

1 – REVELATIONS

The phone chimed, and Aria glanced down at it with a surge of excitement when she saw the notification for a new upload.

She opened the notification and saw the familiar name, NOTESTORE-MEMBER, at the top of her subscriptions.

The video began as usual, with warm, lavender eyes gazing through a mask covering the top half of a woman's face. Behind her, storm clouds rolled and lightning arced through the darkness.

The music began, and the screen split into a grid, each square showing the woman on a different instrument set against as many dreamscapes that shifted from glowing forests and cities of glass to deserts under auroras.

Across the world, people called her a genius. They said her music rewired the brain, sparking hope where despair had taken root. A few prominent psychologists speculated that her music had saved more lives than antidepressants.

The nature of the masked musician's lavender eyes was hotly debated on the internet. Some claimed they were contact lenses, while others insisted on digital overlays. A few forensic hobbyists posted slow-motion breakdowns proving the color was real. The conspiracy threads were always the most entertaining, with the most popular suggesting she was an alien or a goddess. The music was too precise to come from a mortal, too alive.

Aria scrolled through the comments, half-smiling. They were all wrong, yet somehow close to the truth. She had seen those eyes up close, radiant and alive with passion. Fifteen years hadn't dimmed the memory of those lavender eyes, the voice that felt like living light, and the way strength had rushed back into her body when she had been certain she was dying.

The doctors had called their recoveries spontaneous remission. The timing for both her and Clarice recovering at the same time, they claimed, had just been a coincidence.

“Hey, Tweedledee,” Clarice said cheerfully, dropping into a chair across the table and flicking a stray Catan card at her. “Visiting any interesting planets out there in space?”

Aria lowered her phone and dragged herself back from her thoughts. “I was just checking on your home planet,” she said dryly. “They're still not ready to take you back, but they're willing to negotiate.”

Clarice laughed, the low, delighted sound that always brought a smile to Aria's lips. Long waves of midnight hair spilled down Clarice’s shoulders and back, framing a face that looked to be designed by someone who couldn’t decide whether to go for innocence or beauty, resulting in a mix of the two that was devastatingly attractive.

She was in her traditional spaghetti-strap tank, cut low enough to draw the eye of anyone with a pulse. The less-than-opaque white fabric of her shorts left the outline of her black panties clearly visible, hinting at the idea of modesty without actually submitting to it.

Eighteen years of friendship had welded them together tighter than blood ever could. After graduation, moving in together had felt inevitable. Living alone was boring, and to Aria, more than a little scary. Having her overprotective sister to watch her back was comforting.

Catan pieces littered the table between them, a half-finished mug of tea sweating onto the rulebook. Clarice leaned back in her chair, gathering her long hair over one shoulder. Her soft, chocolate eyes constantly twinkled with mischief, as if she knew the punchline to a cosmic joke.

She winked slowly at Aria, her teasing eyes sparkling. “A thought just occurred to me. You realize blushing really brings out your hair color. You should do it more often.”

Aria rolled her eyes. Clarice would flirt with a stop sign just to prove she could. One of her favorite pastimes was making Aria blush. She was a shameless tease, and proud of it.

Aria unlocked her phone and thumbed over to the NOTES TO REMEMBER YouTube channel. “Calypso just dropped a new song. I was checking it out when I fell into a nostalgia black hole.”

Clarice smirked. “Those are dangerous. I get lost in thought occasionally—it's unfamiliar territory.”

Aria laughed, eyeing her sister fondly. "Hard to believe it's been, what, twelve years since we found her channel?" She twirled a strand of red hair around her finger. "Feels like yesterday."

Clarice shook her head wonderingly. "And fifteen years of weekly uploads, with no misses or repeats. Who even does that?"

Aria sighed. "I wish we had recordings of what she played at the hospital. Those songs felt... different. Maybe she's got a secret channel somewhere."

Clarice straightened suddenly, her eyes bright. "You know what? It's time. Let's go back to the hospital and see if she still visits the kids."

Aria blinked, licking her lips as her introverted nature roared to life. "Really? Are you sure?"

Clarice nodded firmly. "Yep, we still need to properly thank her for saving our lives." She paused, tapping her lips. "Hmm. She's gotta be, what, forty now? That's a long time to keep showing up every week."

Aria nodded, gathering her long hair and pulling it over her shoulder as she leaned back. Over a decade ago, their mother had tried to track Calypso down, calling hospitals across the region to thank her. Apparently, recovery rates were up almost everywhere in the area, and several hospitals mentioned a young woman who visited a few times a month to play for the kids. No one knew her full name—she was just Calypso.

She raised her hands helplessly. "How are we supposed to even find her? We can't just show up at every hospital in the state until she appears."

Clarice grinned sardonically. "Sure we can. It'll only take, what, forever?" She leaned back, her knee-length boots thudding onto the table. "Or *maybe*... we could just call. You know, extrovert stuff."

Aria pinched the bridge of her nose with a groan. "Ugh. I wish life came with a search bar."

Clarice snickered, then grabbed her phone. "Good thing you've got me, 'cause I'm not a chicken."

"Bok bok," Aria squawked halfheartedly.

"Cute," Clarice said, unimpressed. She winked, her expression turning provocative, and pointed at Aria's shirt. "Now do that naked while flapping your arms around, and I *might* be impressed."

Aria snorted. "In your dreams."

Clarice gasped, her deceptively innocent eyes widening. "Have you been spying on my dreams?"

Aria tried to suppress it, tried with everything she had, but the damn blush crept up her neck and onto her face, sending Clarice into a fit of giggles.

Aria scowled, snatching the Catan box off the table to hide her burning face. Clarice had been making her blush like a nun at a strip club since they were twelve. How the hell did she have any blushes left?

Clarice's giggles subsided enough for her to gasp, "Okay, now I want details. What was going through that virtuous head of yours?"

The blush had begun to fade, but at Clarice's question, it redoubled its efforts, coloring her cheeks the same shade as her hair. She had just started lowering the Catan box but quickly raised it again. "There wasn't *anything* going through my head, you trollop. My stupid skin just lacks a thermal regulator."

She wasn't about to admit that the thought of Clarice dreaming of her was the trigger for her latest detonation. Her overactive imagination loved to take her on joyrides, constructing detailed scenes of an intimate nature at the worst possible times. "Don't you have a hospital to call?"

Clarice's boots thumped to the floor, and a second later, the Catan box was snatched from Aria's hands. "If I'm making the call, I get to enjoy the view. Now, let's have some more fireworks for the call, Tweedledee."

Aria tried to scowl, but Clarice started waggling her eyebrows and miming kisses at her until she lost it, laughing helplessly. Clarice could reduce her to a puddle of hysterical laughter in seconds. She knew all Aria's triggers and used them mercilessly.

Aria pulled her knees up to her chest to hide her face, her shoulders shaking as the mirth took hold.

Clarice's voice dropped to a seductive, breathy whisper. "I hope you're not having any inappropriate thoughts about me over there, Aria."

She hadn't been—before. "Stop that! I'm dying here, Clarice!"

Clarice let out a lusty sigh. "Okay, okay, okay... fine. I'm letting you off easy this time because I want to find out if Calypso's still doing her circuit. But this conversation is *not* over, Pumpkin."

Aria groaned. She had dressed up as an enormous pumpkin for Halloween when she was sixteen. Her parents and Clarice still called her "Pumpkin" at least once every few weeks, refusing to let it die.

Clarice grinned when she saw Aria peeking through her curled-up knees, and there was the sound of a camera clicking. "Okay, I'm starting with our old hospital. I definitely did *not* take a picture of your cute ass just now." She winked as she set the phone on the table and kicked her booted feet back up.

Aria dropped her feet back to the ground with an indignant squawk. "You delete that picture right now, Clarice!"

"Yogushi Children's Hospital, this is Julia. How may I direct your call?"

Clarice placed a shushing finger against her lips with a provocative wink. "Hi, Julia! I'm hoping you can help me. Is there still a woman who comes by every couple of weeks to play music for the kids?"

There was a pause, then Julia's voice returned, full of warmth. "You must mean Calypso. Yeah, she still visits. May I ask why you're looking for her?"

Clarice inhaled sharply. Dropping her feet from the table, she leaned toward the phone, her voice tight with excitement. "Oh, thank god! She sang to us fifteen years ago. We've wanted to thank her for years now."

Julia's voice brightened. "Oh, that's wonderful! She'll be here next Thursday, actually. I'm sure she'd love to see you again."

"Thank you so much, Julia," Clarice said, her voice radiating warmth. "Really."

"My pleasure, dear. I'll keep an eye out for you."

When the call ended, Clarice shot to her feet, whooping and launching into a little victory dance that was all swaying hips. "Woot woot! Road trip!"

Aria stared at the phone, still processing. "I can't believe she's still doing this. A new song every week, hospital visits every other week—does she even sleep?"

Clarice dropped back into her chair. "That's next-level selflessness."

Aria raised a speculative eyebrow. "Do you think any of the other kids have tried to visit her again?"

Clarice shrugged. "I'm more shocked nobody's sold her out. There's reward money floating around for NOTES TO REMEMBER's true identity. You'd think someone would've cashed in by now."

Aria frowned. "Maybe no one's made the connection. Kinda hard to miss those lavender eyes, though—they're burned into my brain. Maybe the other children she's healed have enough gratitude to keep her secret."

Clarice pulled her hair over her shoulder and leaned back, making Aria's fingers itch. "Or maybe it's not her. It could be a copycat with colored contacts. Maybe even a former patient trying to copy the look."

"It's her," Aria said firmly, then quickly snatched Clarice's phone from the table and opened her photos. "She has the same mouth, same neck, same makeup. The channel's been up sixteen years, but she barely looked twenty when we met her; the math doesn't work for anyone else."

Clarice squinted at her. "Bringing mathmetatics into this? Nerd." She smiled. "Okay, fine, it's her, which makes it even weirder that no one's figured it out."

Aria frowned down at the picture of her ass on Clarice's phone. Her thin shorts had bunched up tightly, defining her *ass*ets in high definition.

She immediately swiped to delete the image and tossed the phone back on the table with a huff.

Clarice ran a hand through her long bangs, combing them back from her face with a wide grin as she snatched her phone from the table. “What, you think I didn’t make backups? I needed something sexy to look at tonight.”

Aria’s face exploded with color, prompting a fresh fit of giggles from Clarice. She bit her lip as she stared at Clarice’s glossy hair, admiring the way it flowed over her shoulder like silken waves, insistently calling out for a brush.

Ignoring her flaming cheeks, Aria stood and grabbed a hairbrush from the counter, then moved behind Clarice and began brushing her long midnight strands. “Okay, getting back on track, let’s just ask Calypso if anyone else has returned when we see her. Maybe she’ll know if someone’s tried to cash in on that reward money.”

Clarice briefly tipped her head back and smiled up at her gratefully, eyes half-closed. “Speaking of cashing in... it's crazy she hasn't ever monetized her channel—she'd make millions.”

Aria shrugged. “She probably doesn't need it.”

Clarice grinned. “So... road trip?”

“Road trip,” Aria agreed lightly. “Pack snacks.”

Clarice spread her arms dramatically. “Two hotties on a quest for mystery and adventure.”

“Something like that.” Aria kept brushing, feeling a surge of relief as she ran one hand through her sister’s gorgeous hair while brushing with the other. She had been obsessed with Clarice's hair since their parents met almost eighteen years ago. Clarice didn't seem to mind—and it gave Aria an excuse to be close to her.

* * *

Aria glanced at Clarice as they pulled off the interstate. “Should we hang out in the parking lot and waylay her, or find her inside?”

Clarice pulled her long black hair into a ponytail, steering with her knee. “Wait until she's done. No sense interrupting her halo time.”

“Fair,” Aria said, biting her lip, her anxiety growing with each passing mile. “Still feels creepy, though. Like we're stalking her.”

Clarice winked suggestively. “That's ’cause we *are* stalking her.” At Aria's deadpan expression, she sighed. “Relax. She looked pretty capable last time. If we scare her, she'll probably just turn us into frogs.”

Aria couldn't stop a guffaw from escaping. "What, you think she's a magical elf or something?"

Clarice nodded confidently. "Yeah, pretty much. She's not human, that's for sure."

Aria raised a skeptical eyebrow. "I wouldn't go *that* far. She could just be a psychic or something."

Clarice gave her an incredulous look. "How's that any more realistic than an elf?"

Aria folded her arms defensively and tucked a foot beneath her. "The idea that a human has tapped into a higher field of mental potential than the rest of us seems a lot more plausible than bringing fantasy creatures into the realm of possibility."

Clarice arched a sardonic eyebrow. "Does mental potential include lavender eyes?"

Aria remained silent, unable to think of a comeback. Those eyes still haunted her; she could practically feel their warmth even now.

"Whatever she is," Clarice said after a moment, her voice softer, "she's got more compassion than I'll ever manage."

Aria glanced at her, immediately feeling defensive of her sister. "That's not true."

Clarice was always one of the first people to stop and help stranded motorists in dead zones or give strangers a compliment when they looked like they were having a rough day. She had a heart of gold she masked with her mischievous nature.

Clarice breathed a laugh out her nose. "Please. I hand a twenty to some guy on the corner and call it charity. She spends her life giving pieces of herself away." Her voice went quiet. "She saved mine, and I've never really paid it forward."

Silence lingered for several blocks before Aria nodded. "Me neither."

Dusk had settled over Rochester by the time they pulled into the hospital lot, the sky streaked with the last traces of pink and gold.

"I've got butterflies," Aria confessed, staring at the entrance.

"Same," Clarice said with a suggestive wink, eyeing Aria up and down.

Aria laughed as some of the tension left her. Clarice always knew what to say to make life seem less daunting.

Clarice unbuckled her seatbelt and exited the car, then bent down to look in at Aria. "Come on, Pumpkin, I'll keep you safe."

Aria took a deep breath and nodded. Her hands only shook a little as she unclasped her seatbelt.

Inside, the lobby smelled faintly of antiseptic and coffee. It was surprisingly quiet, with only a few other people among the blue-clad nurses and doctors.

Clarice walked up to the reception desk, smiling brightly when she saw the woman's name tag. “Hi, Julia. We're Clarice and Aria—we talked on the phone about Calypso.”

Julia looked up, her smile bright. “Oh my goodness, Aria.” She leaned forward. “I remember you. We didn't think you'd make it to the performance, so Calypso begged to visit your room. She wouldn't take no for an answer.”

Aria froze, tears blurring her vision before she realized she was crying. Wordlessly, Julia handed her a tissue.

“She's an angel, that one,” Julia said softly. “Still comes every other week. I swear half our recoveries are thanks to her.”

“Can confirm,” Clarice said with a teary laugh.

Aria nodded, too choked up to reply.

“She'll be here in about half an hour,” Julia added. “You can wait in the conference hall, if you'd like.”

“We'd love to watch her perform,” Clarice said hopefully.

“Of course, my dears.” Julia slid a clipboard across the counter. “Sign in, and I'll get you visitor badges.”

Her heart thudding in her chest, Aria bent to write her name. Fifteen years later, and she was about to see the woman who had sung her back to life—the woman who had become the most famous musician on Earth. Aria's hands shook too much to write her name on the visitor sign-in sheet. Clarice gently wrapped her hands around Aria's to steady them.

After filling out the form and thanking Julia, they followed the corridor toward the conference hall.

The smell hit Aria first—that sharp, sterile mix of disinfectant and latex. For a heartbeat, she was ten again, skin pale under hospital lights, with an IV taped to her wrist. She remembered the endless treatments, the sickness that followed, and the mirror she had stopped looking into after her hair fell out. She still remembered the sharp embarrassment of losing her hair in those early days, the tears that were never far when she saw her reflection.

Now, it all felt distant, like a half-remembered nightmare that had finally loosened its grip.

“I remember this place,” Clarice muttered, her voice tight. “I swear I can feel the panic trying to crawl back in.”

“Me too,” Aria said, her throat dry.

Clarice slipped an arm around her shoulders, pulling her close as they walked. "Maybe this is why I never came back," she said quietly. "I guess part of me didn't want to remember."

Aria nodded, unable to answer. The hum of fluorescent lights and the beep of distant medical equipment filled the silence between them, the sound like a buzzsaw to her soul, bringing with it the memories of so much pain and mind-numbing shame. Dignity had been the first casualty in her struggle to survive the blight invading her young body, leaving her riddled with lifelong anxiety and a phobia of intimacy.

They entered the hall quietly and found over a dozen children filling the space, some in wheelchairs, others running and laughing, their hospital bracelets flashing as they moved.

Clarice's eyebrows rose. "They look... healthy."

Aria studied them curiously. "Hmm... maybe they were here the last time Calypso played. Maybe they're already better."

Clarice brushed a hand through her hair as she watched the seemingly healthy young patients. "Yeah, maybe. Remember how Mom wouldn't let them keep us for more tests? She knew Calypso had healed us, despite Dad's objections. I'm guessing most parents don't see her magic firsthand and keep their kids here for a while longer."

They slipped into seats at a table near the back. The faint hum of machines and the chatter of the children mixed with the smell of antiseptic and crayons.

Aria's chest tightened and her breath quickened; the smells were too familiar, pulling her mind back to the hell Calypso had saved her from. Heart pounding, Aria breathed through her mouth in an attempt to shut down her olfactory senses as her fingers trembled.

Clarice noticed her distress and was instantly to the rescue. "You okay?" she asked, her voice gentle.

Aria closed her eyes and inhaled slowly, then let it out. "I think so."

Clarice reached across the table, her warm fingers closing around Aria's. "You'll feel better once she's here."

Aria squeezed back, flashing her sister a grateful smile. She focused on that touch—the one real thing anchoring her in a room full of ghosts.

The door opened a moment later, drawing their attention to the entrance.

Calypso entered, pushing her familiar cart, and the room erupted. Children rushed toward her, their voices overlapping in joyful bursts, sharing news of going home. It was easy to spot the children who had made the connection between her music and their recoveries; their tears of gratitude as they embraced her made it clear they suspected there was more than science to thank for their miraculous turnarounds.

Clarice squeezed Aria's hand and nodded toward Calypso, her eyes intent. "Does she still look twenty to you, too?" she asked quietly.

Aria managed a slight nod, staring in awe at her savior. All thoughts of PTSD fled as she gazed at the beautiful musician. She really *did* look exactly the same, as if she hadn't aged a day. A palpable aura of pure love permeated the room, surrounding Calypso like an angel walking among mortals.

She was taller than Aria remembered, at least six feet. She had an hourglass figure and wore clothing that accentuated her curves. A white skirt emblazoned with dragons ended above her knees, topped by a white button-up that hugged her breasts. The all-white look really worked, giving her an angelic appearance that didn't miss being sexy as hell.

After a few minutes of talking with the kids, Calypso looked up and noticed Aria and Clarice. She froze, surprise flashing across her face.

Clarice squeezed Aria's hand and stood. "Let's go let her know she doesn't need to hide from us."

They made their way to the front of the room where Calypso waited, watching them intently. Aria's mouth grew dry as they approached, unable to pull her eyes away from Calypso. Had she always been this gorgeous? Aria had barely clung to life during her last meeting, and the memories were a blur. Those lavender eyes were one of the few things she remembered clearly, burned into her memory with crystalline clarity. Blond hair that looked spun from silk, and full red lips were more familiar, visible in her YouTube videos. It was the splash of freckles across the bridge of her nose that really did Aria in, though, leaving her heart hammering and sweat slicking her palms. She wasn't just gorgeous—she was *adorable*, too.

Clarice gave Calypso a quick smile. "Hi, I'm sure you don't remember us," she began, but Calypso interrupted.

"Hello, Clarice," Calypso smiled, and the sight of her dimples nearly buckled Aria's knees. Her voice was like honey, smooth and melodic. Her British accent only added to her captivating timbre, sending pleasant tingles down Aria's neck. "Lovely to see you again, Aria. Your hair is lovelier than I imagined."

"Hi," Aria mumbled shyly, her face igniting into a brilliant blush.

"Hello, Calypso," Clarice said, returning the seemingly ageless musician's warm smile. "We just wanted to let you know that you don't need the glasses for our sake."

Calypso studied them for a moment, and Aria had the strangest sense that she was peering into their souls. Whatever she saw must have pleased her, if the renewed smile was any indication. She stepped up to Clarice and pulled her into a soft embrace, and before Aria had time to breathe, Calypso released Clarice and pulled Aria into her arms.

Aria's face had just started returning to normal, but as Calypso hugged her, it exploded with color. Calypso's body pressed against hers in ways she wasn't prepared to deal with. She didn't dare look at Clarice, knowing her sister would be laughing at her blushing face. It didn't help that Calypso's scent was intoxicatingly delightful, a blend of sweet nectar and a rose in bloom.

She couldn't believe Calypso remembered their names! She must have visited thousands of children over the last fifteen years. Did she remember all their names, too?

All thoughts of names vanished when Calypso squeezed her tightly, and an explosion of love flooded into her. It triggered a memory of the embrace fifteen years ago, that same feeling of acceptance, joy, and unconditional love.

Calypso released her and breathed a resigned sigh. "Found me out, have you? Honestly, I'm surprised it's taken this long."

Aria rested a reassuring hand on her arm, then shivered as a lighter version of that same warmth charged her soul. "You don't have to worry about us," she assured her quickly. "We would never reveal your secret."

"I know you wouldn't," Calypso replied confidently. "But life has a way of compounding events once they've occurred. I expect more people will catch on before long."

Clarice glanced at the children eagerly waiting for them to finish talking. "Don't let us keep you from the children. We can talk more after you're finished. Do you mind if we watch?"

"Not at all," Calypso smiled radiantly, broadcasting warmth like a beacon. "I should be delighted to have you watch. I rarely see the children once they have moved on. It is truly wonderful to see you all so grown and healthy."

Aria followed Clarice back to their seats in a daze. She felt as if she had just brushed shoulders with something holy, and her heart hadn't slowed since the hug.

Across the table, Clarice leaned forward, arching an eyebrow. "Still think she's human?"

Aria gave a shaky laugh. "Not anymore. Last time, I was half-dead and don't remember feeling... this." She glanced around, as if the warmth in the air might be visible. "She's like a miniature sun, except she broadcasts love instead of light."

Clarice nodded slowly. "And she hasn't aged a day. She should be pushing forty by now."

Aria didn't answer, watching as Calypso moved among the children, setting up her speakers, each small motion deliberate and graceful. There was always a line of children waiting to hug her, circling to the back after their turn.

Aria couldn't blame them—she just wanted to stay in that love-inducing embrace forever. She had never felt so much value, acceptance, and comfort.

Clarice caught her gaze, and they exchanged a look that was equal parts excitement and disbelief at the prospect of hearing Calypso's seraphic music in person again.

The room quieted as Calypso turned toward her small audience.

Just as she had fifteen years ago, Calypso took her place beside the harp. She brushed the strings once, and the first notes hummed through the air like a declaration of hope. The accompanying tracks began, strings and woodwinds blending smoothly to form an ethereal bond between heaven and earth.

The melody wrapped around Aria, the same power she remembered—beauty dancing with fire, each note pulling her higher, urging her to fight, to live.

Then Calypso began to sing.

Her voice hit like current, alive and vast, carrying stories of heroes and impossible victories. Calypso's eyes shone with fierce joy as harmonizing voices from nowhere, dozens of them, rose and fell with hers.

Aria glanced around, half expecting to see other singers hidden in the room, but there was only Calypso, one woman, a choir contained within her. The music thickened the air, thrumming against Aria's skin, a vibration that should have sparked and hummed like electricity.

She exchanged a wide-eyed look with Clarice as they listened to the magical music mold reality to her story. The children were completely mesmerized, watching Calypso with unwavering focus. Aria studied the few children who were noticeably ill. Their faces slowly transformed from weary resignation to hopeful determination.

After her third song, Aria saw the moment the illness in one of the children was crushed. She could almost *feel* the toxic cloud of tainted vitality shatter, leaving the child staring in euphoric wonder as the weight of her ravaged body was freed of contamination. The same change continued with the remaining children as Calypso continued singing song after song, until all of them glowed with untainted vitality.

When the last notes faded, the children sat in reverent silence for several long seconds, then erupted with cheers. A new line formed as the children queued up to excitedly speak with Calypso again, eager for more love-inducing hugs. Calypso chatted with them for another fifteen minutes before a nurse began collecting them and returning the children to their rooms.

Calypso slipped her tinted glasses back on, exchanged a few warm words with the nurse, then began packing up her speakers. Moments later, she wheeled her cart toward Aria and Clarice.

Aria struggled to stop staring at Calypso with a kind of reverential awe. She had been listening to the life-changing music on Calypso's YouTube channel for over a decade, but seeing her perform in person and work her healing magic was on a whole other level. She felt like she was in the presence of divinity.

"Calypso, that was..." Clarice laughed helplessly. "There aren't enough adjectives. You're *amazing!*"

Color rose in Calypso's cheeks. "Um—thanks."

Clarice tilted her head. "How many hospitals do you visit?"

"Eight," Calypso answered, her voice full of regret. "I wish I could do more, but there simply aren't enough hours in the day."

Aria watched her in fascination. "Do you always play new songs? Wouldn't the old ones still work?"

Calypso shook her head. "Each song gives what life it has, and once it's shared, the energy's spent. I have to start afresh every time."

Clarice looked dumbfounded, and Aria felt the same shock. "How in the world do you come up with so much new content? Don't you ever hit a wall when trying to make unique songs?"

"Not really," Calypso shrugged. "Music feels like an endless reservoir of potential. It calls out to me each time I write a new song. Just think of how many songs exist in the world today. The sheer volume of variations possible with all the instruments and notes available is so vast that I could do this for thousands of years and never exhaust the possibilities."

Clarice cleared her throat. "So, um, speaking of doing it for thousands of years... I couldn't help noticing you don't seem to age. Is that something to do with the music?"

Calypso's brow furrowed. "Don't I?"

Clarice exchanged a glance with Aria. Was Calypso truly unaware of her own youthful appearance?

Aria slowly shook her head. "You look exactly the same as you did fifteen years ago. I expected you to look at least thirty, but you barely look twenty."

"Is that so?" Calypso asked in surprise. "I honestly can't recall the last time I properly looked in a mirror."

Clarice hesitated. "How old are you, if you don't mind me asking?"

Calypso pursed her lips. "What year is it, then?"

Aria and Clarice exchanged another look. Who doesn't know what year it is?

"It's 2026," Clarice said slowly.

"Oh," Calypso blinked, looking flustered. "Time does fly, doesn't it?"

Clarice flapped her arms with a goofy grin, looking ridiculous. "Just like that. So? How far did it fly for you?"

Calypso's lips quirked, but her tone remained evasive. "Rather far, it would appear."

"It's okay," Aria said quickly. "You don't have to tell us if you don't want to."

Calypso sighed, studying them with a considering look. "I suppose you haven't taken fright about anything else, so what's one more oddity, then?"

Clarice smiled encouragingly.

Calypso took a deep breath. "I was born just after World War One, though I'm not sure exactly which year." Her voice dropped in volume as she finished, and she watched them with an anxious little frown.

Aria's eyes widened, and she stared at Calypso disbelievingly, unable to reconcile the young-looking woman in front of her with a centenarian. She quickly schooled her features, not wanting to add to Calypso's apprehension, but there was no need—not with Clarice at her side.

Clarice gave Calypso a teasing wink. "You're not looking too bad, Grandma."

Calypso's anxiety vanished, and she broke into gales of laughter. The sound was divine, filling Aria with inexplicable happiness. Even the lights in the room seemed to brighten with that joyous sound. Her entire face lit up, making Aria once again think of an angel.

Aria couldn't help asking, "So you really didn't notice a century pass you by?"

Calypso's laughter faded, and she grew serious. "My life's been devoted to music for so long that I don't really pay attention to anything else. I have certain... peculiarities... that make it easy to lose myself in my passions. When I discovered I could heal children, it became my life's mission to help as many as I could. I suppose I just didn't notice how much time was passing. I recall when computers came along, allowing me to layer tracks—to play more than one instrument at a time with ease."

Aria smiled inwardly as she listened to Calypso's formal British dialect; she had always enjoyed a good accent, and Calypso's was particularly delightful.

Clarice grinned appreciatively. "Your YouTube channel's certainly evidence of how far you've come since the advent of computers. I get goosebumps every time a new song drops."

Calypso stared at her in shock. "My channel... you've found it?"

"Um, yeah?" Clarice said dryly. "There aren't a lot of world-renowned musicians with lavender eyes. In fact, there's just one."

Calypso blinked. "How on earth did you come across my channel?"

Aria shared a disbelieving look with Clarice before turning back to Calypso, brows furrowed. "You have the most popular YouTube channel in the world. Were you unaware of how popular it is? Isn't that why you wear a mask?"

Calypso's face tensed, as if she had expected one less step and suddenly found herself in free fall. "I merely use it to upload ideas and experiment with different styles. One of the children gave me the mask years ago, and it merely struck me as a rather amusing theme to accompany the recordings."

Clarice chuckled, shaking her head ruefully. "I'm getting a sense for this theme. Let me guess—you don't ever watch TV or read news headlines because all your time is focused on music, am I right?"

Calypso nodded weakly.

"And I'm guessing you're just using a studio app to upload your songs," Clarice continued, her tone still dry, "and that you never look at your channel analytics or comments because you never open it in a browser."

Calypso nodded again, worry seeping through. "If it is truly popular, it is bound to draw attention to my work here."

Aria grinned. "It's not just popular—it's literally *the* most popular channel in the world. People have spent millions trying to figure out who you are. Media companies are dying to interview you."

Clarice smirked. "You could've been a millionaire if you'd monetized your channel. That's part of the mystery, though—people can't fathom an artist of your fame not using sponsors or ads. A lot of people think you must be the daughter of some billionaire who doesn't care about money."

"This is not good," Calypso muttered distractedly, her eyes distant. "I do hope it isn't too late to delete the channel."

"No!" Clarice and Aria shouted together.

Calypso paused at the urgency in their voices, tilting her head questioningly.

Aria rested her hand on Calypso's arm, squeezing softly. "Your music has inspired and given hope to so many people; it would be a dark day for this world if you deleted your channel."

Clarice anxiously added, "So many lives have been saved by your channel—people who had given up suddenly finding purpose after hearing your songs. You may have saved as many lives with your YouTube channel as with your hospital visits."

Calypso's eyes widened. "Have I?"

"Yes!" Aria and Clarice chorused.

Calypso went quiet, her hand settling over where Aria's hand still rested on her arm, feeding Aria a steady stream of euphoric joy. "I wonder... might the healing still carry via screen?"

Aria shared a stunned look with Clarice. "Oh my god, if it worked, that would be the most epic event in history!"

Clarice raised a curious eyebrow. "Do you really think it could?"

Calypso hesitated. "I suspect I need to be within a certain proximity to a person for it to work—but I'm not entirely certain. When I see a person's aura, I can tell immediately how long it will take for my songs to break the malice binding it. The difficulty is that I don't know exactly *how* I'm healing them. It's mostly intuition and conjecture. Before I start singing, I connect to something, maybe call it light... or radiance, and then weave the power from that radiance with my voice."

Aria once again felt like she was in the presence of some kind of divine being. She connected to light?

Clarice tapped her lips contemplatively. "Maybe if it was broadcast live?"

"Perhaps," Calypso replied doubtfully. "I should think no harm would come of it if it failed, so we've nothing to lose."

Aria felt a thrill of excitement when Calypso said, "we."

Clarice flashed her a quick smile when she also noticed the plural inclusion. Her sister's soft brown eyes danced with excitement as she looked back and forth between them.

Aria took a deep breath. "Before I get too sidetracked from why we came, I wanted to thank you for saving my life. Not a day has gone by that I haven't thought about the night you healed me. Julia told us you even had to plead with her and my parents to visit me since I couldn't come down. I owe you my life, and I want to do something in return. How can I help you, in your life or your mission? Anything at all. Don't you dare say nothing, or I'll have to get creative."

Calypso's face was a mixture of shyness and pleasure. "You're so very welcome," she said warmly, pulling her into a tight embrace. "I'm ever so pleased you came back to see me. I always wonder what becomes of the children once they've moved on. You'll have to tell me all about what you've been up to."

Aria shivered with ecstasy at the feeling of supercharged love from Calypso's embrace. Her powerful presence wrapped around Aria like a warm blanket on a cold winter night. She just wanted to stay there forever. All too soon, it ended as Calypso gently released her.

Clarice's voice caught as she spoke. "Yeah, thanks, Calypso. Words will never be enough to express my gratitude for saving Aria."

Calypso studied Clarice with a gentle smile. "You were rather more worried about her life than your own, weren't you?"

Clarice nodded once, eyes shining with unshed tears. "She's a part of me. I didn't want to survive without her."

Aria pulled Clarice into a quick hug. "Stop making me cry, you goose."

Clarice chuckled, then gasped as Calypso's arms folded around their shoulders, charging them with radiance.

"You two truly are special," Calypso murmured softly. "There is something ever so familiar about you, just beyond my reach."

"Can we exchange numbers?" Aria asked hopefully after Calypso released them. "We'd absolutely love to stay in regular contact and help out wherever we can."

Calypso smiled enthusiastically. "Of course, I'd like that very much. Shall I take your number, then?"

Aria's brow furrowed when Calypso didn't produce a cell phone to record their numbers. Undaunted, Clarice rattled off her number, followed by Aria's.

Aria opened the contacts on her phone and added, "Calypso," feeling a thrill of excitement at actually having *Calypso* as a contact. "What's your number?"

Calypso gave them her number and Aria experimentally texted it. She immediately received a bounce-back indicating the number couldn't receive texts.

Clarice raised an amused eyebrow at Calypso. "You don't have a cell phone?"

Calypso shook her head and shrugged. “I’ve never needed one. I have a landline at home, though.”

Clarice shook her head in bemusement. “Well, I think it’s time to bring you into the twenty-first century—but we can worry about that later. When’s your next hospital visit? Maybe we could come along, if that's okay?”

Aria glanced at Clarice, then hopefully at Calypso. “We could even drive you there. You must get tired of driving so far when you visit all these hospitals.”

“I’m heading to the next hospital in two days’ time, but I’d never wish to impose. I’m quite alright driving myself, but thank you ever so much for the offer.”

Aria narrowed her eyes, recognizing the unspoken cry for companionship. Calypso was one of those people who gave everything and never took anything in return, almost phobic about accepting help for fear of taking advantage of others. Aria recognized those tendencies in herself. It was obvious Calypso hoped they would see through her facade and insist on taking her. The ageless woman might not have realized she was lonely before, but something seemed to have changed since reconnecting with them.

“Where do you live?” Aria asked flatly. “We're picking you up whether you like it or not.”

Clarice looked startled at Aria's bluntness but caught on after a sly wink.

“Are you quite sure?” Calypso asked hesitantly. “You must have better things to do than drive me about.”

Clarice snorted derisively. “Better things to do than hang out with the most amazing musician in the world? Better things to do than hang out with the angel who saved our lives? No. No, we do not have better things to do. Now, where do you live?”

Calypso laughed helplessly, her large eyes betraying her exultant joy. “Very well, then,” she said with obvious delight. She shared her address, murmuring, “Thank you ever so much for doing this.”

“No, thank *you*,” Clarice insisted fervently. “You seem to have a sixth sense about people, so you must know how much we want to do this.”

Calypso peered at them, her eyes taking on that strange intensity that made it feel like she was looking into their souls. She suddenly smiled, instantly raising the ambient light in the room by several million lumens. “Splendid. I quite look forward to seeing you again. I always knew you two were special.”

She gave each of them a long, soul-warming hug before saying her farewell. She was positively glowing as she pushed her cart out the exit.

Aria stared at Clarice in awe. “Can you believe that just happened?”

Clarice stared back dreamily. “I think I'm in shock. There have been so many crazy revelations today that it feels surreal.”

Aria shook her head, a disbelieving smile playing on her lips. “I can't believe she had no idea her YouTube channel was so popular. She's so focused on her music and healing that she's oblivious to everything else.”

Clarice pursed her lips. “I wonder what the full story of her life is. It seems crazy she didn't even know how old she was. I mean, she must've had *some* sense of the passage of time.”

Aria frowned contemplatively, absently twisting a lock of red hair around her finger. “I wonder what she meant when she said she had some peculiarities that made it easy to lose herself in her passions. Maybe she just didn't realize how *much* time had passed. The real mystery is that she didn't know how young she looked. I wonder if she's just insanely absent-minded and failed to notice her face wasn’t changing as the decades rolled by. Could someone really be so oblivious that they don't notice their face is eternally young?”

“And those *hugs*!” Clarice breathed in ecstasy. “I've never felt anything so divine. I never wanted it to end. It felt like my soul was wrapped in a warm blanket made of love.”

“Oh my god, the hugs!” Aria agreed rapturously. “We need to figure out how she does that—maybe there's a trick.”

Clarice sobered. “I think it's because she's an angel.”

Aria leaned back in her chair, narrowing her eyes. “She also mentioned seeing auras and connecting to some kind of light source as part of her healing power. Maybe she *is* an angel.”

Clarice tilted her head to the side consideringly. “Hopefully not the religious sort. That would kind of ruin it for me.”

Aria paused, frowning. “Then again, she claimed even *she* didn't know how she was doing it. I think an angel would be aware of their nature.”

Clarice shrugged. “Maybe she's an angel with amnesia.”

Aria snorted and playfully smacked Clarice's shoulder. “Yeah, ’cause angels can have amnesia.”

Clarice tossed her head airily. “Well, we're talking about mythical beings, so we can make up whatever rules we want.”

Aria perked up. “I just had an interesting thought.”

Clarice waggled her eyebrows suggestively. “Oh? Do tell.”

Aria ignored that and straightened. "We call angels mythical beings, but where did the myth originate? What if Calypso isn't the first of her kind and the idea of angels arose from someone like her thousands of years ago? They aren't necessarily winged servants of some bearded guy prone to jealous rages and temper tantrums, but maybe they're creatures associated with love, compassion, and healing miracles—like Calypso."

Clarice started to object, then paused, frowning thoughtfully. "Hmm... that's actually an interesting argument. I'm loving your description of God, by the way. Before today, I would've laughed hysterically at the thought of us having a serious discussion about this."

A nurse poked her head into the room and gave a small start when she realized it was occupied. "Sorry, I didn't realize this room was in use."

Clarice stood up quickly. "No, you're fine; we were just leaving."

They were just about to exit the building when Julia's voice stopped them.

"Aria and Clarice," Julia called out. "I just wanted to thank you so much for coming in to see Calypso. I've never seen her as happy as she was on her way out. She's so excited to meet up with you two again."

Clarice beamed a brilliant smile at Julia. "Trust me, *we're* the grateful ones. It was *so* good to see her."

The motherly receptionist smiled happily. "That's just wonderful. I'm glad everything worked out so well. You two have a wonderful night."

2 - HIDING

Aria frowned at her phone, the screen's glow illuminating her face in the dim car. "This doesn't look good."

Clarice glanced over from the driver's seat. "What's up?"

"Top post on Reddit," Aria said, her voice tight. "Someone figured out Calypso is NOTES TO REMEMBER."

Clarice smacked the steering wheel. "Shit."

Aria nodded, scrolling. "Listen to this."

I think I've found out who NOTESTOREMEMBER really is.

My cousin was dying in the hospital until a young woman named Calypso showed up and played music for the kids there. The night she performed, his illness just... vanished.

Apparently, she visits a bunch of children's hospitals across the region, at least eight, maybe more. Every place she plays has higher recovery rates than anywhere else. So much so that desperate parents transfer their children to those hospitals from all over the world.

I talked to dozens of former patients, and it was the same story every time. Calypso performs, and they get better within hours.

Then I looked closer. The woman has the same lavender eyes, same lips, same jawline, even the same lipstick color as NOTESTOREMEMBER. I ran facial and hand recognition through an AI, and it's a match.

The weird part is that she's been doing this for over twenty-five years, but she only looks twenty. Her eyes are bigger than normal, like, noticeably.

The hospitals list her name as Calypso, but no last name, no address, nothing. Whoever, or whatever, she is, she's not just a musician.

Aria scrolled through the flood of comments, scowling at the number of screenshots, theories, and conspiracy threads already sprouting like weeds. There was one comment telling them to delete the post and keep their mouth shut—probably a former patient.

Clarice blew out a breath. "Well, that's... catastrophic."

Aria felt like she had been kicked in the gut as her anxiety grew. "She doesn't even know she's famous, Clarice. She's completely unprepared for this kind of attention."

Clarice tightened her grip on the steering wheel. "Then we need to warn her before the rest of the world finds her first." She sighed in frustration. "What are the odds this came out on the day we visited her? Just when we were going to spend more time with her, too."

Aria squinted, recalling the oblivious musician's comment. "She even said she expected more people to figure it out. She said life has a way of compounding events once they've occurred, and that she was sure more people would make the connection soon."

Clarice chewed her lower lip anxiously. "What's she going to do? This has been her life's mission for almost a hundred years. She's probably going to have an existential crisis or something if she can't go to hospitals and help children anymore. She's probably not home yet, so we can't even call her. I wish she had a cell phone."

"Oh, shit!" Aria swore in consternation. "We need to get to her house *right* now!"

Clarice looked at her in alarm. "What... why?"

Aria grimaced, anger boiling inside at whoever the idiot was who revealed Calypso's identity—all for a few minutes of internet fame. "They posted what she looks like. If she stops for gas, buys food, or even just goes for a walk, people will recognize her. Hell, any of her neighbors will realize who she is once everyone wakes up tomorrow. Someone's almost certain to reveal her location to the world before the sun rises."

Clarice took the next exit. "Okay, get her place up on maps, and let's get over there."

They quickly rerouted their GPS and started driving again. Worry knotted Aria's stomach as she imagined all the terrible things that could happen to their oblivious angel if the world found her.

A new thought seared into her awareness, bringing with it a fresh wave of panic. "We need to get her away from her house. It won't take long for someone to track her down. She's not human. You know what they'll probably do if they catch her."

Clarice blanched. "Oh my god, I didn't even think about the damn government. They'll think she's an alien or something."

Aria nodded, anxiously wringing her hands. "Exactly. She'll probably get locked in a lab, and nobody will ever see her again."

Clarice sped up, tickets be damned. It took another hour to reach Calypso's house. Thanks to Clarice's excessive speeding, they arrived just as Calypso was pulling in. They parked in the driveway as Calypso entered her garage. Aria jumped out of the car and ran to meet her.

Calypso exited her car with a curious smile that turned to concern when she saw Aria's distraught expression. "Whatever is the matter, Aria?" she asked gently.

"Somebody found out you're NOTES TO REMEMBER," Aria blurted anxiously. "They also discovered your healing abilities and blabbed it all over the internet, so everyone knows what you look like now."

Calypso's face fell. "Oh, that's a shame."

Aria shook her head urgently. "It's more serious than that, Calypso. The things you can do, your physical appearance, we're worried the government will come after you."

Calypso's brow wrinkled. "Why would they?"

Clarice joined them, all traces of mischief absent. "They'll probably think you're an alien or something. Even if they just think you're a human, they'll want to put you in a lab to study you."

"Will they?" Calypso asked uncertainly. "Would the government truly do such a thing?"

Aria exchanged an incredulous look with Clarice. Just how sheltered had Calypso been?

Aria spoke quickly, her voice tight. "They will absolutely come after you. It won't take them long to figure out where you live, so we need to get you out of here ASAP. Please, come with us. We'll keep you hidden until we can figure something else out."

Aria's eyes blurred with tears, her mind a frantic gallery of all the ways Calypso might be harmed.

Calypso stared into Aria's terrified eyes, then pulled her into a comforting embrace. "Shh, you're quite alright."

Waves of love enveloped her, burning away the fear as the strength of Calypso's love drowned out every other emotion. Aria clung to her, desperate to escape the horrors of her imagination. Calypso simply held her for several minutes until her trembling slowed.

"All better, then?" Calypso murmured gently.

Aria took a long, shuddering breath. "Yeah."

Calypso stepped back, holding her at arm's length. "Very well, then," she said brightly. "I'll go and pack a few things. I haven't moved in an age, so this will be quite the exciting change of pace."

Aria burst into startled giggles, feeling a blend of relief and affection. Calypso's adorable dialect mixed with her calming presence was enough to finally soothe Aria's worried thoughts. The most important thing was getting Calypso away from her house, and she had just agreed to come with them, removing Aria's most pressing concern. They could figure everything else out with a little time. Clarice would know what to do—her sister always found a way to fix everything.

Clarice grinned. "Okay, I'll see if there's a twenty-four-hour U-Haul rental nearby and grab a truck. Three hotties off on a whirlwind adventure. With my brains, Aria's luck, and your beauty, we'll be unstoppable." She finished with one of her teasing winks, looking more seductive than playful.

Calypso laughed but shook her head. "No need to worry about a removal van. I'll hire a moving company to put everything into storage until we've sorted things out."

Clarice hesitated. "Doesn't that cost a lot?"

Calypso shrugged. "My parents set up a small trust for me that my trustee placed in an oil concern when I was fourteen. It has proved a rather successful investment over the years."

Clarice snickered and repeated, "oil concern," under her breath.

Aria eyed Calypso suspiciously. "Are you an oil baron? Don't tell me the theory that you were a billionaire ended up being right."

"Oil baron?" Calypso repeated uncertainly. "I'm not entirely sure what that is. I really don't know how much money I have. I typically just visit the bank once a year and withdraw two hundred thousand. The manager told me that was merely the annual interest."

"Yep, they were right," Clarice snickered. "Sounds like somewhere between five to ten million, depending on your interest rate. Not exactly oil baron status, but not bad."

Aria gave a wry snort. "Clarice, the number cruncher."

Calypso packed light. Aside from clothes, she packed a few small instruments, including a beautiful antique violin, a gorgeous 12-string guitar, and a small harp.

Aria frowned at Calypso's Subaru. "Your car is registered in your name, so as soon as they find your full name or a neighbor blabs, they'll be able to identify it. Would you be okay just driving with us?"

Calypso hesitated. "I shouldn't wish to be a burden—"

"Good," Aria interrupted with a smirk. "That's settled then. Let's get out of here. I'll look up a moving company while we drive so we can get your stuff out of there as quickly as possible."

Aria sat in the back next to Calypso. Her phone cast a soft glow on their faces, highlighting Calypso's angelic beauty. She had to force herself to stop staring and focus on her phone.

It didn't take long to schedule a call with the moving company. It was 3:00 a.m., and Aria was beginning to feel the toll of the long day, with another two hours before they reached their apartment. Yawning, she put her phone down, darkening the back of the car.

She met Clarice's eyes in the rearview mirror, trying to hide her weariness. "Do you want me to drive?" she asked with a forced brightness she knew would never fool her sister.

Clarice winked. "I'm good, Tweedledee. You get some sleep."

Aria opened her mouth to reply, but it came out as a yawned, "No, I'm good."

Clarice snorted, gazing back at Aria in amusement. "Sure you are. I guess you're just miming an opera, yeah?"

Another yawn was her only reply.

Calypso watched them fondly, her large, lavender eyes devoid of fatigue. She laid a warm hand on Aria's wrist. "You ought to get some rest. You look dreadfully tired, dear."

Aria blinked back at her sleepily, reveling in the sudden influx of radiant energy. And had Calypso just called her dear? The thought brought a weary smile to Aria's face.

"Aren't you tired?" she asked Calypso drowsily.

Calypso smiled wistfully. "I don't ever truly tire."

Clarice's eyes snapped up to look back at Calypso disbelievingly. "Like, ever?"

Calypso nodded. "Ever. Sometimes I think it would be quite lovely to drift off and experience oblivion for a time. My connection to radiance prevents me from ever succumbing to fatigue, however."

Aria yawned widely, her head bobbing. "Wow, I'm not sure if I feel bad for you or if I'm envious."

Calypso gently pulled Aria's head into her lap. "Shh... sleep now."

"If I must," Aria mumbled.

Lying in Calypso's lap, she felt the now familiar blanket of Calypso's loving aura fully envelop her. She smiled contentedly as the tender warmth calmed her anxiety. Calypso began to hum a melody that lulled her into a deep slumber. Her last sleepy thought was of how wonderful Calypso smelled. She would have to find out what perfume she used.

* * *

Aria woke to the sensation of soft fingers gently combing her hair. She opened her eyes, feeling like she had slept for twelve hours. The front car door opened, and she slowly sat up, instantly missing the flow of warmth from Calypso's touch. "Are we there already?"

Clarice looked back at her curiously. "Yep. You look peppy. Sleep well?"

Aria smiled vibrantly and followed Calypso out of the car. "God, I feel like I slept all night," she said, stretching with a contented groan. She turned to Calypso with a curious smile. "Did you do something to recharge me or something?"

Calypso tilted her head consideringly. "Perhaps. I was humming a melody that put me in mind of renewal and rest while you slept. It appeared as though your aura was absorbing energy for a time."

"Well, thanks," Aria said with a grateful smile. "I feel wonderful."

Calypso smiled and squeezed her hand. "I'm ever so pleased I could help, dear."

Aria flushed at the feel of Calypso's slender hand. Calypso had called her dear again, and though Aria knew it was simply a British mannerism, she still found it adorable and... endearing.

"Let's go brainstorm and get a better lay of the land," she suggested, willing the blush out of her cheeks. She turned to Clarice. "Get some sleep, Tweedledum. Thanks for driving."

Clarice nodded, the fatigue finally showing in her eyes.

They gathered Calypso's instruments and went up to their apartment. Aria offered a silent prayer of thanks for the early morning hour and the lack of activity—less chance of a curious neighbor noticing Calypso.

Clarice headed straight for her bedroom with a weary smile and mumbled, "G'night."

Aria intercepted her before she could disappear and hugged her tightly. "Thanks for everything yesterday. I think I would've melted down at the hospital without you there."

Clarice leaned back just enough to rest her forehead against Aria's, murmuring, "I'll always be there for you, Aria."

Calypso watched them with a soft smile as they broke apart, her lavender eyes shining with affection and something else Aria couldn't identify—longing? Nostalgia?

Releasing Clarice, Aria gave Calypso a quick smile and began showing her around the apartment, starting with the kitchen. "We keep a fairly good stock of fresh foods. Are you hungry?"

Calypso flushed, avoiding Aria's eyes. "I've no real need to eat food."

Aria raised an amused eyebrow. "What do you do to it then?"

Calypso laughed, and the blush faded. "I simply never experience hunger. I should think I derive some manner of nourishment from radiance."

Aria struggled to hide her shock. She didn't eat *or* sleep, and she didn't age? Just what was she? Could she actually be an angel after all? Aloud, Aria murmured, "That must save a lot of money."

Calypso tilted her head. "I had never truly considered it, but quite so—I suppose that could prove rather costly."

"Let me show you the guest bedroom," Aria said faintly, leading her across the apartment. "I know you don't sleep, but you'll have a place for some privacy."

The guest bedroom was lightly furnished, with a queen bed, small desk, and heavy bookshelf that was stocked with a collection of Aria and Clarice's favorite novels. Calypso's large eyes sparkled with excitement as Aria showed her around the apartment, her presence saturating the area in radiant warmth. Just how long had Calypso lived the same routine without any changes in her life?

She led the exuberant musician into the living room. The rising sun lit up the room, casting long shadows behind the large, leather couch. A variety of electric and acoustic guitars stood in the corner, gleaming in the morning light. A full-size Roland keyboard stood with a blank monitor mounted to the wall behind it, and a large harp rested close to the guitars, with a few small percussive instruments scattered on the floor around it.

Calypso laughed when she saw the sign on the wall behind the instruments that read, "*BITCHES BE ROCKING.*"

Aria grinned. "Yeah, that's my Clarice's handiwork."

Calypso ran her hands through her thick hair, studying Aria with a small smile. "The two of you share such a remarkable connection. I have never witnessed such a depth of love within a pair of auras before—nothing else comes remotely close."

Warmth filled Aria at Calypso's observation. She knew Clarice's love went deeper than familial bonds, but it was nice to hear confirmation from someone who could see beyond the surface.

"Clarice is just so damn lovable that it's impossible *not* to love her. I can't imagine a life without her by my side. She's my knight in shining armor, always there to protect me from whatever the world throws at me."

Calypso gazed at Aria with a soft smile, and the longing was back in her eyes. She turned and saw the harp, and her face brightened. "Would you mind if I played for a moment?"

Aria nodded fervently. "I would *love* for you to play."

Calypso moved to the instrument and plucked a few strings, testing the tone. Pleased with the sound, she smiled, closed her eyes, and began to play a poignant melody. After a few measures, her voice joined the harp, splitting into a multitude of harmonies. Aria barely dared to breathe as the beautiful sounds serenaded the room.

Hearing Calypso play in person made her YouTube compositions sound lifeless by comparison. The air in the room felt alive with emotion as her song wove a tale of gratitude and appreciation. Her expressive voice rang with passion, and her large eyes shone as her whole heart went into the performance.

When she finished, Aria wiped tears from her cheeks. The power and sentiment of Calypso's songs triggered an unconscious emotional reaction that couldn't be ignored.

"Wow, Calypso!" she gushed, "that was *beyond* beautiful."

Calypso let out a contented sigh, fondly stroking the harp's frame like an old friend. "I suppose I was feeling rather unsettled without my instruments. This has done me a world of good."

"It did *me* a world of good," Aria replied playfully.

Calypso laughed, the radiant sound brightening the room. "I cannot begin to express how pleased I am to be with the two of you. There is something quite special about you and Clarice—I feel as though I've known you an age. I never truly realized how... alone I was until seeing you and Clarice again."

"I can only imagine how lonely you must have been for all these years," Aria said gently. "I'm so glad we came back to see you. I know it sounds cliché, but I feel like we have an angel in our home."

Calypso flushed, her eyes soft as she smiled shyly back at Aria. The room resonated with her powerful emotions, a pleasant hum of love and contentment.

Heart racing, Aria quickly turned away and walked over to the couch, snagging her laptop from the end table as she sat. "I'm going to check online and see what's going on. Just make yourself comfortable; this is your home now, too."

Calypso blinked rapidly, her eyes shining with silver tears. "Thank you, Aria."

Aria stared, convinced her eyes were playing tricks. She set her laptop down and approached Calypso curiously, gently reaching up to brush a tear from her cheek, then stared at the quicksilver tear on her hand in wonder. It sank beneath her skin and her hand lit up with a soft glow that quickly faded. She gasped as vitality surged through her body, leaving her more wired than a pot of coffee.

She looked back up at Calypso in wonder. "You're endlessly full of surprises."

Calypso blinked after watching her quicksilver tear evaporate. "I don't believe I've ever witnessed my own tears before. Is that quite normal? Do they usually... vanish?"

Aria smiled at her affectionately. "Maybe for angels."

Calypso's lips curved into a soft smile as she gazed at Aria warmly.

Aria took a deep breath and turned back to the couch, hiding her burning cheeks. That smile was waking up all sorts of sensitive places. "Okay, I'm going to see if you've broken the internet yet."

She opened her laptop, curious to see if the Reddit post had yielded any further breakthroughs. She looked at the main news page, and her heart sank.

NOTESTOREMEMBER'S IDENTITY FINALLY REVEALED, AND IT'S EVEN STRANGER THAN YOU COULD HAVE IMAGINED.

Carefully maintaining her outward composure, Aria read the article.

After a Redditor managed to connect @NOTESTOREMEMBER to a person named Calypso, internet sleuths quickly uncovered more details about the enigmatic owner of YouTube's most popular channel. Calypso regularly visited eight different children's hospitals, leaving behind a mystery, as children with terminal illnesses suddenly became healthy following her performances.

We interviewed several hospital staff members, some of whom already suspected Calypso might be responsible for the miraculous recoveries. Receptionist Julia Rinker revealed she had suspected the musician of healing patients for years. When asked about Calypso's seemingly ageless appearance, Julia clammed up, worried that all the attention would detrimentally affect Calypso's life and her mission of healing children.

Her concern may be justified, as the hospitals are quickly being swarmed by thousands of @NOTESTOREMEMBER fans, hoping for a glimpse of one of the most famous musical figures of our age.

Things took a darker turn when an overenthusiastic fan found Calypso's home and broke in, filming the interior and revealing the instruments used to create the music for her channel. There's no word on Calypso's current whereabouts. She wasn't at home, despite her car being there, and may have gone into hiding after discovering her anonymity had been compromised.

Many internet denizens are angry with the Redditor who revealed Calypso's identity, calling it a gross invasion of privacy. If she truly is responsible for healing children at the hospitals, his actions could potentially result in the deaths of children she could have saved.

He offered a public apology, claiming he hadn't fully considered the potential consequences of his actions.

The world waits with bated breath to find out if the @NOTESTOREMEMBER channel will go dark and children's hospitals quiet without her music.

Aria was proud of herself for maintaining a facade of calm as her stomach roiled. Unfortunately, she had forgotten Calypso's ability to see beyond the physical.

"Whatever is the matter?" Calypso asked, concern in her voice as she studied Aria closely.

Aria grimaced. "We got you out of there just in time."

"Oh," Calypso said, her expression unreadable. She walked over and sat down next to Aria on the couch. "Would you mind if I read it, Aria?"

Aria reluctantly handed over her laptop, anxiously chewing her lip as she watched Calypso read the article.

Calypso's eyes widened as she read, enhancing her look of vulnerable innocence. When she finished, she wordlessly handed the laptop back to Aria.

Aria closed the laptop and set it aside, then took Calypso's hand reassuringly, shivering when love instantly flooded her soul. "We can totally disguise you when we go out so nobody'll recognize you. Maybe a hat, some sunglasses, and a change in your makeup."

"Makeup?" Calypso asked, furrowing her brow. "I don't use cosmetics."

Aria stared, nonplussed, at Calypso's red lips and dark eyelids. Hesitantly, she reached out and gently touched Calypso's lips. No trace of lipstick.

Color flooded Calypso's cheeks at the intimate gesture. She stared at Aria uncertainly, her emotions broadcast across her face like a digital billboard.

Aria blushed profusely when she realized what she had done. "Sorry, I just had to check," she said with an embarrassed wince. "Did you get your lips and eyelids tattooed or something?"

Calypso shook her head, her cheeks still glowing faintly. "No, it is simply their natural color, I assure you."

Aria sighed enviously. "Wow, that's just not fair!"

Calypso noticed the twinkle in Aria's eyes, and the corners of her lips lifted. "I know I have said this already, but I am so glad to be here with you. I believe I truly needed something new in my life."

Impulsively, Aria put her arm around Calypso and gave her a sideways hug. "Words can't express how happy I am that you're here, Calypso. If you only knew how many times I've imagined meeting you again, and getting to know you. Actually having you in our home is like a dream come true."

Calypso returned the hug, resting her head on Aria's with a contented smile. Aria thought about Clarice's comment that Calypso was an amnesiac angel; her sister might be on to something.

Her phone trilled, interrupting her reverie. She picked it up, noting it was only 7:00 a.m. She frowned when she saw her mother's caller ID. Her mother knew they weren't early risers, so why was she calling so early?

Reluctantly, she released Calypso and answered her phone, immediately missing the metaphysical cocoon of radiant love.

"Hey, Mom, is everything okay?"

Her mother breathed out a relieved sigh. "I could ask you the same thing. I saw your location over at the hospital where all the craziness is unfolding and wanted to make sure you two were okay. When I checked your travel history, I started freaking out."

Aria relaxed, a giggle escaping before she could stop it. She and Clarice shared their location data with their parents in case anything ever happened. Their mother claimed, "they were too damn pretty for their own good." After one unnerving stalker incident years earlier, their mother never went long without checking on them.

"We're totally fine, Mom," Aria assured her, grinning at Calypso. "Sorry for not sharing our plans with you. Clarice and I decided it was past time we revisit the hospital and thank Calypso for saving our lives."

She felt Calypso's hand rest companionably on her back, charging her with warmth.

"Wait," her mother said quickly. "You went to see her *before* all this nonsense started blowing up in the news?"

"Yeah, crazy timing, right?" Aria said, resting an affectionate hand on Calypso's knee.

"Did you see her?" her mother asked intently.

"You could say that," she breathed, her smile threatening to split her face.

A brief pause followed. "She's with you right now, isn't she?"

Aria gasped. "Mom! How could you possibly have guessed that?"

Her mother chuckled. "Because I *know* you. You sound like you're on cloud nine. I remember sounding like that when your dad and I first met."

Aria's face shamed a sunset as she began spluttering into the phone. She felt Calypso shift beside her but didn't dare look.

"I'd pay good money to see your face right now," her mother declared, laughter thick in her voice.

"I'm going to pay you back for this, Mom," she threatened, trying to get her blush under control.

"Can I talk to her, please?"

Aria sneaked a peek at Calypso, who was watching her with an expression somewhere between confusion and curiosity. She muted the phone and forced her flushed face to look at the ageless woman.

"My mom wants to know if she can talk to you. It's totally okay if you don't want to."

Calypso's lips curved into an amused smile as she watched the flustered Aria. "I should be very pleased to speak with Emily."

Aria blinked at the use of her mother's name. She unmuted the phone and handed it over.

"Hello, Emily," Calypso greeted her warmly.

There was a brief pause. "Hi, Calypso. I just wanted to repeat the offer I made fifteen years ago. If there's *anything* you need, I'm here for you. How can I help?"

Calypso smiled, gazing into Aria's eyes fondly. "You and your family are truly remarkable. I cannot think what might have occurred had Aria and Clarice not appeared at my home to warn me that my anonymity was at risk."

Emily paused as she put the pieces together. "We have several extra rooms at our house if there's any risk of people finding you over there. We can help you financially as well."

"Thank you, Emily," Calypso said, her voice catching. "I am so very glad they came out to see me yesterday. Absurd as my situation is, I do not think I have ever been this happy. Aria and Clarice are truly remarkable."

Aria put her arm around Calypso. "She's good on money, Mom," Aria said dryly. "She's an oil baron lite."

"Evidently, I am an oil baron, Emily," Calypso said lightly. "I am not entirely certain what that entails, but I have been assured that I am one."

"She invested in oil back in the 1930s," Aria said, grinning. "She just lives off the interest now."

"1930s?" Emily repeated in a startled voice.

Aria frowned. "We probably shouldn't discuss this on the phone. Suffice it to say, Calypso is endlessly full of surprises."

"You're probably right," Emily agreed. "Would you like to come over for dinner tonight?"

Aria tried, and failed, to suppress a grin. "She doesn't eat, but I'll see if she's interested in visiting later."

Calypso nodded quickly. "I should very much like to visit Emily," she said eagerly.

Aria flashed Calypso a quick smile. "Okay, we'll see you tonight, Mom."

After the call ended, Calypso studied her quizzically. "What is the significance of being on 'cloud nine?' It sounds like a rather precarious elevation."

Aria barely stopped herself from facepalming. She decided to fall back on technobabble. "They rate cloud types numerically, and nine refers to the highest type of cloud, called a cumulonimbus cloud. It's an expression that means you're extremely happy."

Calypso pursed her lips. "And Emily felt as though she were on 'cloud nine' upon meeting Eric for the first time? I am understanding the usage correctly?"

Aria dared her cheeks to blush. "Yeah, pretty much."

Calypso's expressive lips curved into a brilliant smile. "In that case, I quite feel as though I am on 'cloud nine' as well."

Aria sighed inwardly, knowing Calypso was ignorant of the expression's possible romantic connotations. She settled for a genuine smile as she observed the angelic woman beaming at her. She cast about for something to fill the silence before her overheated imagination tied her thoughts into a pretzel.

"Did you have any siblings growing up?" she asked, grasping at the first thing to flash through her turbulent thoughts.

Calypso shook her head, her blond bangs shimmering in the morning light. "I always wished I had grown up with sisters, though my parents were unable to have children. What was it like, growing up with Clarice? Have you two always been this close?"

"Yeah, pretty much," Aria said, smiling warmly. "She's always been my knight in shining armor. I'm kind of a chicken most of the time, but Clarice is just the opposite, charging into life with unflinching enthusiasm. She's so brave and strong, but at the same time so sweet and caring. Sometimes I wonder if I didn't survive my cancer, and this is some kind of afterlife. Could someone as amazing as Clarice be real? She's so beautiful, kind, driven, patient... and... and..."

She trailed off when she realized how she sounded, hunching her shoulders guiltily as her anxiety spiked. Flushing, she glanced at Calypso and found the musician watching her with a soft smile—and more importantly—no hint of judgment. While Clarice wasn't her biological sister, the social taboo of falling in love with her stepsister had always been one of her biggest fears. The thought of bringing any kind of shame to Clarice filled her with unbearable dread.

Aria's shoulders loosened as she realized Calypso's life of isolation had probably left her ignorant of society's biases.

"Aria?" Calypso prompted, her brow creased with concern. "Whatever is the matter? Clarice sounds like a truly marvelous person."

Aria hung her head with a dejected sigh. "She certainly is. I just wish she had a sister to compare."

Soft fingers cupped Aria's chin and lifted it until she was staring into Calypso's concerned eyes. "Aria, I have met tens of thousands of people throughout my life, yet I have never seen auras as beautiful as yours and Clarice's. Your spirit is truly extraordinary—something I have desperately longed to witness again these past fifteen years. Regardless of how you may see yourself, your aura cannot lie, and it shows me a woman of such radiant beauty and boundless compassion that I can scarcely trust my own senses. Were I to ask Clarice what makes you so remarkable, I assure you her list of praises would quite exhaust the English language."

Aria smiled shyly, closing her eyes and leaning into Calypso's touch. The stream of warmth channeled through Calypso was delightfully sublime, chasing Aria's dark thoughts away in a flood of love.

She opened her eyes when she felt Calypso's fingers slide across her scalp. Calypso gathered a lock of red hair in her hand and studied it with a look of puzzled bemusement.

"There is something so very familiar about you and Clarice," she murmured. "Your hair especially, for reasons I cannot quite explain. I should very much like to discover the source of this peculiar sense of familiarity."

Aria smiled wryly. "Maybe we knew each other in another life, and I had red hair there as well."

Calypso narrowed her eyes and withdrew her hands to her lap, ending the flow of radiance. "I rather think you may be right. It feels as though there is some truth to that statement."

"I quite wonder how long Clarice is going to sleep," Aria murmured, then winced when she realized she had unconsciously adopted Calypso's mannerism. Fortunately, Calypso didn't seem to notice.

"I could go and energize her, if you wish," Calypso offered brightly. "It seemed to work rather well on you."

Aria shifted uncomfortably, conflicting emotions twisting her thoughts. She stared into Calypso's large, lavender eyes and felt a twinge of possessiveness. She had always shared everything with Clarice, and it struck a discordant note in her soul to entertain such selfish desires. What if Clarice got sick of waiting for Aria to find her courage and moved on to Calypso? Aria would lose both of them.

"Okay," Aria heard herself say. "Let's get her recharged."

Calypso didn't move, staring back at Aria searchingly. Aria inwardly cursed, remembering Calypso could see straight past her words and into her emotions. She needed to be a lot more convincing.

She exhaled with a sheepish laugh. "Sorry, I'm just being greedy. Come on, let's go supercharge Clarice."

She stood up, pulling Calypso by the hand. Quietly, she opened Clarice's door and slipped into her sister's room.

Clarice lay sprawled on top of her covers, her long black hair fanning out around her in luxurious waves. Her delicate features had softened even more in sleep. Calypso paused at the foot of the bed and stared at her intently, an endearing smile on her face.

Aria bit her lip as she openly admired her sleeping sister. Clarice's long, toned legs were on full display, one curled up while the other lay straight. Her generous breasts rose and fell slowly with the even motions of sleep. Clarice's shirt had slid up enough to reveal her flat stomach, with enough definition to hint at the muscles beneath. It was her expressive lips that always drew Aria's attention, though—curved up at the edges even in sleep, as if she were enjoying a pleasant dream.

Aria snapped out of her reverie at a touch on her arm from Calypso as she walked over to the bed and lightly laid her hand on Clarice's head. Aria didn't see anything, but the ambient feeling of love around Calypso narrowed and seemed to focus on Clarice. Calypso began humming softly, a poignant melody that charged the room with energy.

Aria let out a relieved sigh. The stingy side of her soul had expected Calypso to snuggle up to Clarice in bed. Part of her *wanted* Calypso to join Clarice in bed, to fulfill the role Aria was too scared to commit to. The thought didn't fill her with jealousy, as she had expected; if anything, it sent a thrill of arousal through her. She shook her head, confusion warring within as her attraction to Calypso grew while her feelings for Clarice continued undiminished.

She still couldn't get over her fear of intimacy, so she certainly didn't have anything beyond words and hugs to offer Calypso. As much as she hated the idea, perhaps it was time to convince Clarice to stop waiting for her and pursue a relationship where she could find true fulfillment. At least Calypso was a person Aria could see herself maintaining a friendship with if the beautiful musician and Clarice started a relationship. The thought of anyone with Clarice had always filled Aria with bitter jealousy, so why didn't the thought of Calypso being with Clarice do the same?

She walked over to Calypso and whispered, "How long do you think it'll take? Do you want a chair?"

Calypso glanced up and smiled gratefully. "Thank you, but I am quite all right standing. This is all new to me, so I am not certain how long it will take."

Aria stared at Calypso narrowly for a moment before leaving the room to get a chair. The selfless woman was, once again, being too kind for her own good. She was the ultimate people-pleaser, trying not to be a burden.

"Thank you," Calypso whispered gratefully as Aria set the chair down. Lavender eyes watched Aria fondly, emotions playing transparently across Calypso's face. She reminded Aria of a child in a way, before they learned to mask their feelings. Her expressive eyes stared at Aria with something close to adoration as she sat.

Screwing up her courage, Aria stepped behind Calypso and began massaging her shoulders. Even if she couldn't ever experience true intimacy, at least she could treat Calypso to the closest thing she had to offer.

Calypso tensed at first, but as Aria continued kneading, she relaxed and leaned into the massage. A groan escaped her lips as Aria worked muscles that had probably never been touched.

Aria wasn't prepared for Calypso's emotional reaction. Her eyes filled with shimmering, quicksilver tears, and the room was suddenly blanketed in an intense wave of love and gratitude that nearly buckled Aria's knees.

Calypso had always been so selfless and compassionate to others but had clearly never had that tenderness reciprocated.

Aria could sense just how much Calypso craved the touch of another person. Her solitary life had probably deprived her of anything beyond the most superficial contact with other people.

Aria spent the next half hour working on Calypso's shoulders and neck. Contentment and wonder saturated the room as Calypso's powerful aura projected her emotions like a beacon. All too soon, the moment ended when Clarice's eyes popped open, alert and full of life.

"Hi," Clarice greeted Calypso with a puzzled half-smile.

"Good morning," Calypso said softly, removing her hand from Clarice's head. "We wished to give you the same recharge that Aria received on the drive here."

Clarice languidly stretched, back arching, and sat up with an appreciative smile. "So *that's* why I feel like I've slept for a week. Thanks, Calypso, I feel amazing."

"As do I," Calypso said dreamily. "Aria gave me a shoulder massage while I waited. I had no idea something so simple could feel so delightful. I was hoping you might sleep for another hour."

Aria and Clarice burst into giggles, followed by Calypso's own light, musical laughter.

As their mirth faded, Aria slid her fingers through Calypso's bangs, eliciting a contented smile. "You've been neglected for far too long," Aria said gently. "You're in desperate need of serious pampering."

"That is not true," Calypso protested weakly. "I have the children at the hospitals, and the nursing staff, and—"

Clarice cut her off, arching an eyebrow. "You talk to them for thirty seconds, then pour your soul into healing them," she said gently, sliding her legs over the edge of the bed and facing Calypso. "That's not connection—that's service."

"But that is precisely the way I prefer it," Calypso insisted, her words at odds with the look of longing in her eyes. "I am a nurturer. I find joy in aiding others."

"You are a nurturer," Clarice gently agreed. "But you still need nurturing, too. You're like a flower that's given all its water to the surrounding plants. You're so worried about being a burden that you don't accept compassion from others, fearing it will be an imposition that drives them away."

Aria combed her fingers through Calypso's hair. "And you could never drive us away," she said affectionately. "You're stuck with us, and we're going to pamper you whether you like it or not."

Calypso's eyes had grown more vulnerable as Clarice spoke. When Aria finished, a fresh wave of quicksilver tears began tracing lines down her cheeks. She tried to articulate a response, but words failed her.

Aria leaned down from behind Calypso and wrapped her arms around her comfortingly. Clarice gently took Calypso's hands, their knees touching, and stared into her eyes.

"It's okay," Clarice said softly, squeezing Calypso's hands. "We're here with you now. You don't need to hide your feelings from us. Just let it out."

Calypso's lavender eyes shone as more quicksilver tears flooded her cheeks, evaporating into silver mist as they fell.

Aria sucked in a breath as Clarice's hand shone dimly and her eyes briefly glowed white after a tear landed on it. Tiny lines of worry vanished, and her face subtly changed, her features softening to something almost angelic.

Calypso squeezed Clarice's hands and closed her eyes, a radiant smile lighting her face.

"Thank you," she said quietly, and a few more tears traced down her cheeks. "I believe I had not truly grasped how much I longed for this."

Aria tightened her arms around her and kissed the top of her head. "Of course, Calypso."

A knock at the front door shattered the stillness, making Aria jump. "Who could that be?"

She checked her phone's camera feed, and her heart skipped a beat when she discovered there was no connection.

"I'll see who it is," she told Clarice, her voice low. "Stay here."

Clarice met her eyes and shook her head. "I can get it."

Aria pressed down on Clarice's shoulder as she tried to rise. "I love you for always protecting me, but please stay with Calypso this time. Please?"

Clarice hesitated, briefly glancing at Calypso before giving Aria a reluctant nod. "Be careful."

Aria nodded and smiled reassuringly. "I'll just look through the spyhole and see who it is."

As she left the room, Aria glanced back to see Calypso, her eyes closed and a serene smile softening her face. The sight made Aria's chest flutter. She was falling fast, with no parachute to slow her descent. Clarice looked just as transfixed, lips parted, and desire burning in the depths of her chocolate eyes.

Taking a deep breath, Aria cautiously approached the front door and peered through the spyhole. Her next-door neighbor, Cynthia, stood outside with folded arms and a mildly irritated expression.

Aria cautiously cracked the door open, trying to sound casual.

"Hey, Cynthia. What's up?"

Cynthia blinked in surprise. She was probably expecting Clarice. She was one of the few neighbors who knew of Aria's social anxiety and her fear of answering the door.

"Oh, uh, hi, Aria," Cynthia said slowly, eyeing her curiously. "I was wondering if your power went out, or if it's just mine."

"I don't think so—" Aria turned to glance into the apartment, then frowned. The thermostat light was off. "Oh. I guess it *is* out. I didn't even notice."

"Great," Cynthia sighed. "Guess it's the whole building. I'll call management. It's hard to work from home when everything's dead."

Aria offered a sympathetic smile. "Thanks, Cynthia."

Cynthia hesitated, her brows furrowing. "It was weird, though. Right before the power went out, I felt... strange. Kind of euphoric. Did you feel anything weird like that?"

Aria's pulse quickened. She forced a neutral expression. "No, nothing. We're in a solar maximum right now, so it could've been a flare. Those can mess with electronics and even cause mild psychological effects."

"Oh." Cynthia's face relaxed. "That makes sense. I guess I'll wait for an update."

"Good luck," Aria said with a quick smile, closing the door.

She leaned against it for a moment, her heart pounding. The power going out right after Calypso's tears couldn't be a coincidence. And the neighbor feeling "euphoric?" Calypso's aura was affecting people nearby, and in an apartment complex, "nearby" meant dozens.

They needed to move, and soon.

Aria quickly returned to Clarice's room. Calypso still sat on the chair, her hands entwined with Clarice's, and a sublime expression on her face. The sight of the two of them triggered an odd sense of nostalgia. The few times Clarice had brought a date home, Aria had felt intense jealousy, even though they had never stayed the night. Now, watching Clarice and Calypso holding hands, all she felt was warmth—and an embarrassing surge of desire.

Clarice looked up, meeting Aria's gaze knowingly. "Who was at the door?"

"Cynthia," Aria replied casually, wishing her sister couldn't read her like an open book. "She was checking on the power. Apparently, it's out for everyone."

Clarice raised an eyebrow, catching her tone. "We lose power here at least once a month. They need to bury those stupid power lines."

Aria crossed her arms. "Remember how we were talking about getting a house?"

Clarice blinked, then nodded slowly. "Yeah. Too many neighbors complaining every time we jam due to our paper-thin walls. You wanna start house-hunting?"

Aria grinned. "I was thinking we could stay at Mom's for a while. She called earlier and invited all three of us for dinner."

Clarice's eyebrows shot up. "You told her?"

"I didn't have to," Aria said wryly. "You know Mom. She saw our location history and connected the dots."

"That woman," Clarice murmured affectionately, shaking her head.

Aria looked at Calypso quizzically. "I've been meaning to ask you something, Calypso. How did you know my mom's name was Emily?"

Calypso finally opened her eyes, and Aria gasped. The eyes looking back at her were a rich violet, with intricate weaves of lighter lavender swirling around the edges of her irises. The effect was mesmerizing. Is this what all those tears were hiding?

"Your names are inscribed upon your auras," Calypso explained, her voice filled with a new timbre that demanded attention, each word caressing the soul and sending tingles down Aria's spine. Her voice *and* her eyes had changed? Was this a result of her overdue emotional release?

Clarice's eyes brightened with interest. "What do auras look like?"

Calypso tilted her head to the side. "Can you truly not perceive auras?"

Aria laughed lightly. "No, Calypso. Normal people can't see auras. You've gone your whole life thinking everyone can?"

Calypso twisted her neck to look back at Aria in confusion. "Well, you speak of them. How do you know what they are if you cannot see them?"

Clarice exchanged an amused glance with Aria, then explained, "It's just used as a metaphor, referring to the way something feels, like somebody having an aura of power. Back in the 1800s, when mysticism became popular, they redefined it as a kind of energy surrounding people, supposedly a spirit's shield against physical possession. People can't actually *see* auras, though."

Aria grinned sardonically. "Thanks, Professor. What's tomorrow's history lesson? Why ghosts don't need health insurance?"

"Quiet, Tweedledee," Clarice admonished with a wink. "I have to show off when the opportunity presents itself."

Aria looked back down at Calypso. "So, what do they look like to you?" she asked intently.

Calypso stared at what Aria assumed was her aura. "A healthy aura glows a brilliant white, with colors rippling through it based upon one's emotional state. When an individual is anxious, the waves are quite turbulent. When one is unwell, it is as though a parasitic entity has attached itself, binding the aura in cords of black and crimson."

She paused, smiling sadly. "Upon our initial meeting, your light was almost entirely extinguished by the weight and complexity of the bindings wrapped about you. When I sang for you, they were shattered, permitting your brilliance to shine once more."

Aria's heart surged with renewed gratitude at the reminder of what Calypso had done for them. The odd sense of familiarity with the beautiful musician grew stronger, accompanied by a wave of emotion so powerful that her eyes welled with unshed tears.

Calypso studied her with a soft smile. "At present, your aura is projecting love. The ripples are deep and smooth."

Aria returned her smile, letting the love she felt fill her aura.

Clarice leaned forward, her eyes gleaming. "So that means you can tell if someone's lying about their name. You'd make a killer spy hunter!"

Calypso's laugh rang like silver bells, filling the room with a joy so bright it almost felt physical.

Aria basked in it a moment before gently asking, "What were your parents like, if you don't mind my asking?"

Calypso's laughter faded, and her eyes grew distant. "Strictly speaking, they weren't my biological parents. They discovered me near an ancient tree on the outskirts of Burford when I was five, and assumed I had been abandoned. My mother was unable to have children, so she persuaded my father to keep me. I do not remember anything prior to that day."

She smiled, a nostalgic light in her violet eyes. "My father owned a music shop and repaired instruments. He taught me everything he knew, which is where my love of music began. He had found a beautiful white harp at the tree where they found me the year prior, so it was a particularly special place for him. I still have that harp, but I've honored his request to never play it."

Aria laid a hand on her shoulder. "Did you eat back then? What did they think of your abilities? Did they know about them?"

Calypso laughed at her rapid-fire questions, absently pushing a stray lock of pale blonde hair behind her ear. "I did not eat, and at first, they merely assumed I was fussy. I was unsure how to explain that I did not require food, so I told them I was fasting. They were devout and accepted that explanation initially, but after a week without eating or drinking, their suspicions grew, and they took me to a priest."

She paused to frown, her brow wrinkling. "He told them I was possessed by a devil and that they should leave me with him at the church until he could exorcise the evil spirit. My mother refused. I remember she had a tremendous argument with my father over the matter, but she prevailed in the end. After that, they merely pretended not to notice that I never ate. When I displayed an aptitude for music, my father warmed considerably towards me."

Calypso leaned back in her chair and folded her arms, smiling faintly. "I began healing people quite by accident whilst singing in the church choir. Everyone believed it was God's work when people recovered following the hymns. My parents did not realize it was me until my mother fell gravely ill during a particularly harsh winter. I sang to her one evening, and she recovered instantly. She made the connection between the healings at church and warned me to keep my ability secret."

Clarice stared, enthralled, into Calypso's enchanting eyes. "What did they think about your eyes?"

Calypso returned Clarice's stare affectionately. "They believed it to be merely a congenital abnormality and worried it might attract undue scrutiny, so they provided me with tinted glasses. Now that I am older, I realize they must have had their own theories, though they never mentioned them to me."

Aria squeezed her shoulder softly. "They sound like they really loved you."

Calypso's eyes moistened, glittering with silver tears. "They did. They perished in a house fire when I was thirteen. I was able to continue running the music shop after their passing. I still have all my father's instruments at my home."

Aria stroked her neck comfortingly as Clarice reclaimed Calypso's hands and squeezed them gently.

Aria smacked her head. "Oh! The moving company! I need to call and get your stuff moved before someone decides to break in and sell everything on eBay."

Calypso gracefully rose and brushed her hair over one shoulder. "I can manage that—that is, if you do not mind my using your phone?"

Aria waved her off. "I've got this. You're supposed to be getting pampered, remember? I happen to know someone who gives the best massages this side of Heaven."

"That's right," Clarice chimed in with a grin. "You're looking at the reigning queen of back massages."

She swung open her closet and pulled out a collapsed massage table with breast cutouts—they had learned the hard way how uncomfortable classic massage tables were if you didn't have a flat chest. Within moments, it was set up in the middle of the room.

"Up you go," Clarice ordered cheerfully.

Calypso hesitated, torn between politeness and curiosity, but Clarice wasn't having it. She gently pushed her toward the table, threatening tickles if she didn't get moving. Laughing helplessly, Calypso lay down, resting her head in the face cradle.

Aria smiled as she walked into the living room and dialed the moving company. After twenty minutes of transfers, holds, and bad elevator music, she finally arranged a pickup. She put the charges on her card without a second thought.

While she waited for confirmation, she felt waves of serenity wash through the apartment as Calypso's aura responded to Clarice's touch. Even the distant hum of the city outside seemed softer.

When Aria returned to the room, Calypso was half-melted into the table, emitting soft moans as Clarice's thumbs worked deep into her back. Her pale shirt was pushed up, revealing skin that seemed almost luminous in the morning light.

"Are you *sure* you're not an angel?" Clarice teased, tracing her fingers down Calypso's back.

"I lack the requisite halo," Calypso murmured languidly.

Clarice studied her back, running her fingers up and down the space between her shoulder blades. "Well, you've got some muscles back here the rest of us don't. I'm calling it—that's where your wings go."

"Mhmm..." Calypso hummed a contented sound. "I have always wished to fly."

Clarice met Aria's gaze, her eyes sparkling with triumph. Aria walked closer, curiosity piqued, and saw two faint ridges beneath Calypso's shoulder blades—subtle but unmistakable.

Clarice's grin widened, and Aria sighed, giving a small nod. Okay. She's an angel.

She cleared her throat. "The movers are arriving at your house tomorrow, and will be putting everything in a storage unit near my parents' place."

Calypso tilted her head on the table, her voice quiet. "Thank you, Aria. I feel... safe with you and Clarice."

Aria smiled softly, feeling a growing sense of protectiveness for the gentle healer. "You are safe," she said warmly. "We'll keep you that way."

3 – I'M A BELIEVER

Aria decided it was time to introduce their angel to more new experiences. She stood up from the couch and stretched, glancing at Clarice challengingly. "Who's up for a game of Catan?"

Clarice paused in the act of scrolling on her phone, meeting Aria's gaze with a raised eyebrow. She had been insufferably smug after discovering Calypso's "wing muscles," and Clarice could do smug almost as well as she could do seductive. "Sure, Tweedledee."

Across the room, Calypso stood studying their instruments intently. She had undergone another transformation after her back massage. Eyes that were as bright as gemstones now possessed an actual inner glow. It was becoming easier to see her as some kind of angelic being. Her striking features and large, expressive eyes made it hard not to stare.

She turned to face Aria, her glowing eyes curious. "What's Catan?"

Aria grinned. "It's a board game—one of the best. I'm guessing you haven't played one before?"

Calypso shook her head, her lips forming an expectant smile.

"We'll teach you," Aria said, pulling Catan from their game cabinet and moving to the table. "It's not too complicated."

It didn't take long for Calypso to learn the rules. She was clearly enjoying the new experience, her glowing eyes alight with fascination. Clarice had to nudge Aria more than once to stop her from staring at the captivating angel and get her to take her turn, grinning at her knowingly each time. It wasn't until halfway through that Calypso ruined the game for Aria.

Calypso held up the dice, looking inquisitively between Aria and Clarice. "Is there any reason I should not roll the numbers I desire?"

Aria stared at her uncertainly. "I'm not sure what you mean."

Calypso rolled the dice. “If I require a two, should I not simply roll a two?”

Aria stared at the pair of ones. “Did you do that on purpose?”

Calypso nodded. “Of course. I’m on the resource with the two. Is it not the logical conclusion that I should produce a two?”

Aria’s stomach sank. “Do me a favor and roll a three.”

Calypso looked at her strangely but complied.

The dice landed on a one and a two.

Clarice burst out laughing at the dismay on Aria’s face. When Aria’s expression grew affronted, Clarice laughed harder, nearly falling out of her chair.

Calypso looked between the two of them uncertainly, a small smile of anticipation curving her lips. “Is there perhaps some context I’ve failed to grasp?”

Aria sighed, her shoulders slumping as if the universe had personally betrayed her. “Okay, another lesson in mortal limitations. We can’t make the dice land on whatever number we want.”

Calypso blinked. “Truly?”

“Yeah, *truly*,” Aria said dryly. She raised her eyebrows. “How, exactly, are you making it roll the number you want?”

Calypso held up the dice. “You can feel the little dots beneath your fingers. Simply roll them with the correct amount of force and spin to make them land on the numbers you wish.”

Aria facepalmed. “Silly me, why didn’t I think of that? I seriously need to take you to Vegas.”

Clarice smirked, her eyes bright with glee. “She’s just bitter ’cause she always wins Catan. She claims the dice favor her because the gods love redheads. I think maybe they don’t love her so much anymore.”

Aria flipped her hair over her shoulder with an airy toss of her head. “They still love me—after all, they sent me an angel.”

Clarice shook her head in mock disgust that quickly turned to amusement when she spotted Calypso’s burning cheeks.

Aria gave Calypso a stern look. “Okay, for the rest of the game, just roll them randomly.”

Clarice nudged Calypso with a wink. “It’ll be our little secret if you forget sometimes.”

Calypso threw her head back and laughed, the joyful sound so infectious that Aria found herself joining in.

Aria marveled at how easy it was to be herself with Calypso. In the rare instances she and Clarice had entertained company, Aria’s anxiety always prevented her from relaxing and just enjoying herself. Clarice was the only person besides her parents she ever truly felt comfortable around—until now.

When Aria finally won—barely—she smiled victoriously at Clarice. "The gods still love me!"

Clarice made a sour face and threw a settlement at her.

Calypso's aura soaked the room in gentle warmth, the air humming with affection. She seemed almost overwhelmed by the simple thrill of friendship and new experiences, like something long neglected finally allowed to flourish.

A sudden foreboding churned in Aria's stomach, and she looked around the apartment uneasily. Where was this sudden dread coming from? She shivered as the feeling intensified to the point that her stomach grew queasy. She looked across the table and found Clarice looking just as disturbed.

"Should we head to Mom's house now?" Aria asked anxiously. "If I had a sixth sense, it'd be screaming at me to get the hell out of Dodge."

Clarice nodded, her dark eyes wary. "Agreed. I'm getting the same vibe."

Calypso's eyes tightened with concern. "Whatever is the matter?"

Aria shrugged, forcing a smile. "Just a feeling. We were going to visit my parents later anyway; we'll just go a little earlier."

Clarice eyed Calypso meaningfully. "Let's bring some of our instruments. We might be gone for a while, and I don't want to leave them all behind."

Aria smiled eagerly. "Yeah, let's pack like we're going on a long vacation! It'll be fun!"

A faint smile tugged at Clarice's lips. "Never change, Aria," she said with fond amusement.

It took nearly an hour to pack and load both cars. Before leaving, Aria pulled a dark, hooded cloak from an old Halloween costume box and handed it to Calypso.

"It'll catch some attention, but nobody will see your face," Aria reasoned. "People do weird stuff all the time, so what's one more oddity?"

Calypso nodded and slipped it on.

Calypso rode in Aria's car, while Clarice took her own, laden with as many instruments as they could fit. Clarice had vehemently argued for Calypso to ride with her. They had settled it with rock, paper, scissors, with Aria winning three out of three, much to Clarice's disgust. She cursed the gods for doting on redheads before getting in her car.

***

Aria took pity and called Clarice after a few miles. She put the call through the car's Bluetooth, so they were all included.

"Let's keep it vague," Clarice warned. "Phones can get flagged for keywords."

"They probably have voice recognition as well," Aria pointed out. "Maybe a certain angel shouldn't talk while we're on the phone, in case they can flag the call with a voice match."

"This is getting so cloak-and-dagger," Clarice sighed irritably. "Privacy really is dead. Her voice has changed quite a bit today, so I think she's safe to talk."

They lapsed into silence, the hum of the road filling the car. Calypso gazed out the window, her violet eyes glimmering beneath the hood. She seemed to relish the new experience of riding as a passenger, studying the passing landscape and other motorists with a kind of innocent fascination.

An hour later, a motorcycle roared up beside them. The rider popped a wheelie, grinning and waggling his eyebrows at Aria through the window.

"Mom always said you were too damn pretty for your own good," Clarice noted in an amused tone. She was driving right behind Aria, observing the "hormones on wheels" as he tried to get her attention.

Aria scowled. "What is it with guys like this? Does this kind of thing ever work on girls? Seriously."

Clarice snorted. "Not once in human history," she said dryly. "Hormones and intelligence are mutually exclusive."

Aria set her jaw. "I'm just going to ignore him and see if he goes away. He'll have to give up eventually, right?"

But he didn't. The biker sped ahead, then slowed beside the passenger window, riding on the shoulder. He gestured for Calypso to pull down her hood.

Calypso turned her head to face him. Her eyes, shining like amethyst fire, met his.

The man's smirk froze. He swerved, then fishtailed violently, losing control and tumbling across the asphalt as his motorcycle skidded down the shoulder in a shower of sparks.

"Shit!" Aria slammed on the brakes, tires screeching. "Clarice, hit your hazards and slow traffic!"

She threw the car in park and sprinted toward the fallen man, barely dodging a semi that blared past, the rush of air slamming into her like a wall.

The biker was a crumpled heap, his limbs twisted and skin torn raw. His head and torso were mangled, looking more like ground beef than skin. Blood pooled beneath him, soaking what was left of his clothes.

Aria's stomach turned, and she nearly vomited. He was clearly dead, his lifeless eyes staring at the sky.

A soft voice behind her made her whirl.

"His spirit will depart without my intervention," Calypso said quietly.

Before Aria could speak, Calypso knelt, cupping the man's broken head, heedless of the blood that quickly covered her hands. There was a sharp crack as she twisted his neck back in place. She glanced up at Aria and took a deep breath, then began to sing.

The air changed and a hum of power vibrated through her bones, rising with the cadence of Calypso's voice. Shockwaves of power rippled through the air as words of ultimate authority warped reality. Aria didn't recognize the language—she doubted anyone on Earth would.

The man's body convulsed as bones snapped back into alignment. Flesh rippled and reformed, the sight making Aria's stomach lurch. Then the growing pool of blood flowed back up into the man, as if time were being rewound. Even the ragged abrasions along his scalp sealed as new skin knitted into place.

Aria had barely noticed another driver join them from a car pulled over ahead. All her focus was on Calypso, glowing softly now, every note producing pulses of light.

When the last wound closed, Calypso gripped both sides of the man's head and spoke a single guttural word.

The man jerked violently, then gasped, his eyes fluttering open in panic.

Calypso's radiant face broke into a smile. "It worked!"

Aria could only stare. Calypso had just pulled a man back from the dead.

"You're Calypso!" the other driver exclaimed, staring in shock.

Aria's head snapped up. She spun and frantically motioned for Clarice to come forward. Traffic had slowed to a crawl around them. People were recording video with their phones as they gawked at the scene.

"What happened?" the formerly deceased man asked in a shaken voice.

"You died after crashing your motorcycle, Marco," Calypso told him gently, her captivating voice filled with compassion. "You'll be okay now. Just be more careful when you drive."

Clarice inched her way through the traffic until she was beside them.

"Get her out of here," Aria said urgently.

Calypso followed Aria to Clarice's car and quickly got into the passenger seat. Clarice drove away as soon as Calypso was in.

Aria turned back to see the biker and the other motorist staring after her sister's departing car in shock. As Aria turned to go back to her car, the man called out to her.

"Did Calypso really bring him back from the dead?" he asked in awe.

Aria looked over at the stopped cars, phones pointed in her direction. With a curse, she ignored the man and hurried back to her Subaru. She carefully drove past the two men as they continued to stare in wonder.

She took a deep, calming breath, trying to steady her shaking hands. The call with Clarice was still active, and she could hear Calypso explaining what she had done.

"So, that was unexpected," Aria said shakily, her voice tight with a mix of nerves and exasperation.

"I think we'd better find a plan B," Clarice said tersely. "Now that people know she's with us, it won't take long for them to find Mom and Dad's house."

"I'm looping Mom in," Aria said, tapping her phone. "Maybe she'll have an idea."

The line clicked and Emily answered. "Are you still coming tonight?"

Aria took another shaky breath. "Change of plans, Mom. We've got a problem. Clarice and Calypso are on the line as well."

Emily's voice sharpened with worry. "What's wrong? Are you hurt?"

Aria shook her head, forgetting her mother couldn't see her. "No, we're fine, but in a few minutes, the whole world is going to know Calypso is with us. Once people start looking, it won't take long to trace her to you. We need somewhere the internet won't find us."

Emily's calm, reassuring voice helped soothe her frazzled nerves. "I know just the place. Just get over here and I'll take you. Can you tell me what happened?"

Aria's voice trembled, choppy and disjointed. "Some idiot on a motorcycle was showing off next to us. He crashed—badly. He was dead, Mom. No pulse, no breathing. Calypso... she brought him back, Mom. Fixed everything. Like, instantly. There were people watching. Filming. I'd say we've got twenty minutes before it's online."

"Oh, sweetheart," Emily murmured sympathetically. "All right. Get off the main roads now. Take back routes, anything that avoids cameras. They'll be scanning the highways for your car soon."

Aria's shoulders loosened slightly, some of the tension bleeding out. "Thanks, Mom."

Emily's voice grew pensive. "I think we need to leave your cars somewhere along the way and have your uncle pick them up later. I'm going to meet you partway. I'll send you the coordinates to the meeting place."

Aria exhaled. "Okay. Thanks again, Mom."

The sound of Emily's car starting came through the phone. "I'm going to call your uncle now. I'll see you soon. Be safe."

"Mom rocks," Clarice noted proudly. "I'm going to get a shirt that says that, too, mark my words. It'll have a picture of her holding my electric guitar."

Aria giggled, the last of the tension draining out of her. "Thanks, Clarice, I needed that."

Clarice's playful voice continued. "I would get one that said 'Aria rocks,' but it would sound like 'are ya rocks?' when said out loud, and most of us aren't rocks. We could try for one that says 'where are ya, Aria?' I used to love saying that when we were younger. Everyone thought I was stuttering and saying, 'where are ya, are ya?'"

Aria snorted. "Nobody thought you were saying that, you goose—at least not after the first hundred times you did it."

She knew Clarice was helping her de-escalate from crisis mode. Warmth filled her chest at her amazing sister and the way she always said the right thing to fix whatever was wrong in her life.

Calypso's concerned voice spoke up, soft and reassuring. "How are you doing, Aria?"

Even on the phone, Calypso's voice was riveting, sending tingles up her spine.

"Better for hearing your voice," Aria said truthfully.

"Oh, Aria," Calypso said softly, and Aria could practically feel the warmth emanating from their angel.

Clarice interrupted, her voice all business. "I'm getting off exit thirty-four. You close?"

Aria glanced at her GPS. "About thirty seconds behind you. I've got Mom's coordinates, too."

A few minutes later, she pulled up behind Clarice. The rest of the drive passed uneventfully until they reached a KOA campground tucked behind a stand of trees. Aria quickly spotted her mother's black SUV, partly hidden.

Emily was already standing outside, tapping on her phone. After exiting Clarice's car, Calypso pulled down her hood and approached Emily. The glow of her eyes and the palpable warmth of her aura made Emily pause mid-step, captivated.

"Thank you ever so much for meeting us, Emily," Calypso said gratefully, embracing her. "You have a most remarkable family."

Emily returned the hug, tears welling in her eyes. "Of course, Calypso. I've waited a long time for the chance to return your kindness."

After hugging her daughters, Emily ushered them into her SUV. Clarice claimed the front seat, leaving the back for Aria and Calypso. Fortunately, the windows were darkly tinted, allowing Calypso to finally remove the cloak.

As soon as they were buckled in, Emily twisted in her seat to face them. "Okay, first things first, turn off your cell phones and put them in the seat pouches. They're Faraday-lined, so no signal will get out, courtesy of your uncle."

Aria studied the mesh in the pouch curiously. "Where are we going?"

Emily pulled onto the highway before answering. "My grandmother's old cabin. Your uncle's been maintaining it for years. It's completely off the grid, with solar panels, well water, and septic. A family friend holds the deed, so it's not tied to our name. We'd planned to take you girls there for the holidays, but it looks like Christmas came early this year."

Clarice grinned excitedly. "That sounds perfect! If we can stay out of sight long enough to get up there, we should be able to keep them safe."

Aria didn't miss that her sister included her among those who would be kept safe. In spite of their goal of protecting Calypso, Clarice clearly still considered Aria her top priority. She shouldn't have been surprised—Aria's well-being had *always* defined Clarice.

Aria met her mother's eyes in the rearview mirror, struggling to hide her anxiety. "How far is it?"

Emily glanced at her map. "About an hour away. If we can make it there without any bathroom breaks, we should be able to keep you out of sight."

Clarice twisted in her seat to grin back at Calypso mischievously. "I'm pretty sure Calypso doesn't use the bathroom. Am I right?"

Calypso shifted awkwardly. "Yeah, no washrooms for me."

With a smug little nod, Clarice settled forward again. "It seemed pretty obvious, considering you don't eat or drink. You can just call me Sherlock from now on."

"Oh, I *will*," Aria promised with a grin. "Exclusively."

"Quiet, Tweedledee," Clarice retorted playfully.

Calypso glanced between them curiously. "I have observed you addressing her as Tweedledee on several occasions. Have I failed to grasp context once more? She bears no resemblance to the figure in the Alice narrative."

Emily chuckled. "That's my fault. When they were younger, their constant banter reminded me of Tweedledee and Tweedledum, so that's what I started calling them."

Calypso laughed, and her joyful aura swept over them, pure and sweet. Clarice exchanged a wondering look with their mother as the wave of emotion swept over them.

Emily frowned, studying Clarice more closely. "Did you do something to your face? You look different."

"Huh?" Clarice pulled the visor down to look in the mirror, and her hand flew to her mouth. "What the..."

"Angel tears," Aria told her, glancing sidelong at Calypso. "Apparently, they have some kind of refining effect on biological organisms."

Clarice tilted the visor, glancing reproachfully at Aria in the mirror. "Don't call me a biological organism. That sounds gross."

Aria arched a challenging eyebrow. "How about meat sack?"

Clarice twisted in her seat to stare at Aria in horrified disgust. "I do *not* have a meat sack, you pervert!"

Aria wrinkled her nose. "That's not what I meant, and you know it. I did *not* need that image in my head, Clarice!"

Emily sighed, a sound of equal parts resignation and fond exasperation. "Now do you see why I call them Tweedledee and Tweedledum? This used to go on for hours."

Calypso watched them with fond amusement. "To my eyes, it is like observing two conversations concurrently. Their voices convey one thing, yet their auras radiate love and affection."

Aria turned an accusing stare on Calypso. "Hey, that's cheating!"

"Seriously," Clarice added petulantly. "That's like putting a door wedge on train tracks."

Calypso blinked, her eyes going distant as she tried to untangle the analogy. "On the grounds that it would lead to a catastrophic locomotive derailment?"

Clarice scowled. "Yeah, just like sneaking peeks at our auras derails the banter wagon."

Aria relaxed back in her seat as her anxiety faded further into the background. "You're a woman of many metaphors," she told her sister dryly.

Clarice narrowed her eyes. "Which metaphors?"

Aria rolled her eyes. "You're such a freaking troll. You *know* I meant that you use a lot of metaphors, not that there are lots of metaphors to describe you—though now that you mention it—"

Emily's phone rang, ending their... discussion.

"It's your uncle," Emily said, pressing the answer button on her steering wheel.

"Hi, Dev. Did you get my messages?"

Aria smiled at hearing the deep rumble of her uncle's voice through the car speakers. "Yeah, I just wanted to make sure they really came from you and not a spoofed number. Are they in some kind of trouble?"

"Yes," Emily answered shortly. "I can't talk about it on the phone, so explanations will have to wait until we meet. It's nothing illegal."

Devon paused. "I think I have an idea what's going on. There are a few videos making the rounds online. I'm pretty sure I recognized a certain redhead."

Emily sighed. "So, it's already out in the ether. I knew it would spread fast, but I'd hoped it would take a little longer."

"Was it real?" he asked intently.

Emily glanced back at Calypso. "Yeah, it was real. We'll fill you in on everything when you get there. Thanks for helping, Dev."

"I'm a hundred percent behind you, Em," he declared firmly. "Let your friend know we won't let her down."

Aria looked at Calypso after the call ended. Her eyes shone with unshed tears as she smiled at Emily.

"You truly are extraordinary people."

Aria reached across the seat and clasped Calypso's hand affectionately. "Extraordinary people have to stick together. Otherwise, the assholes of the world win."

The remainder of the drive passed quickly. Calypso's presence filled the car with calm contentment, making it the most enjoyable drive Aria had ever experienced.

The feel of Calypso's warm hand in her own set her cheeks aglow with a constant pink blush. How could something as simple as holding another person's hand be so exciting? Normally, her anxiety would have left her fretting about a million silly details, such as if her hand was too cold, too hot, too bothersome... but the steady stream of radiance from Calypso calmed her turbulent thoughts, allowing her to simply enjoy the contact in a more intimate frame of mind.

Clarice spent most of the drive talking quietly to Emily, occasionally glancing to the back seat through the mirror, a pleased smile curving her expressive lips each time. That smile confused Aria more than anything. Was Clarice happy to see Aria holding another woman's hand without melting down, or was she happy to see Aria showing interest in someone besides her? Had Aria been holding her sister back from real relationships with other people throughout their adult life due to pity? Had Clarice's need to protect Aria driven her to show so much interest in order to give Aria hope of a relationship, even if it was completely asexual?

Clarice turned in her seat to stare at Aria's increasingly anxious face, then slowly winked, her chocolate eyes sparkling with life.

Aria bit her lip as Clarice held her gaze, and her tumultuous emotions slowly calmed. Clarice could convey an entire conversation in a glance—one that reassured Aria her heart was safe in her sister's hands, now and forever. How had she ever doubted Clarice?

She drew in a deep breath and smiled, trying to convey the boundless love she felt, the promise to try harder to break down the walls caging her mind, denying her the intimacy she both craved and feared.

Clarice gave a satisfied nod and her expressive lips quirked into a half smile before she faced forward again.

The last half hour of the drive took them onto winding mountain lanes. They branched off the state highway onto a dirt road leading deeper into the forested hills. Dust billowed behind them, and the Suburban bounced around on the washboards, feeling more like a poorly designed roller-coaster than a road.

They finally pulled into a driveway nearly a mile long, lined by large oak and maple trees, leading to a three-story cabin. Three separate chimneys rose from the roof, and a widow's walk topped the third story. She could see wrap-around balconies on each level that skirted the entire cabin, and there was a large veranda on the second story facing the front. A small waterfall flowed over the edge of the veranda, trickling into a stream that twisted through the front yard, which was dotted with a variety of fruit trees. Enormous windows promised gorgeous views from inside the cabin, with external doors allowing access to the balconies at regular intervals.

Aria and Clarice gaped at the gorgeous structure.

"This is the place?" Aria asked disbelievingly.

Emily smiled in satisfaction as she observed their reactions. "This is the place. Like I said, we wanted to surprise you over the holidays. Your uncle

Devon's been modernizing and upgrading it for the last fifteen years. I'm not sure what he's going to do for fun now that it's finished."

They pulled into a detached four-car garage. As they exited the vehicle, Aria's eyes fell on a small excavator in the back of one of the bays.

"Hey, can Uncle Devon teach me to use that excavator? I've always wanted to try one."

Clarice turned to face Aria, her dark eyes amused. "You like tractors now?"

Aria shrugged. "Maybe. That's what I want to find out. Remember our first job, when we worked for the city maintaining the parks?"

Clarice nodded, folding her arms expectantly.

Aria gestured at the excavator. "The chauvinistic pig in charge of our crew wouldn't ever let girls learn to use the backhoe, but I always wanted to try it."

Clarice snorted disdainfully. "Yeah, that guy was a total prick." She raised her eyebrows at Aria pointedly. "What exactly are you going to dig with it?"

Aria lifted her chin and stared down her nose. "A hole to bury you in."

"Come along, you two," Emily called out as she walked toward the house. "Stop showing your love for each other for a few minutes."

They both turned to look accusingly at Calypso, who was staring around the garage with interest. When she saw their accusatory stares, she giggled playfully. The sound was so innocent and full of joy that Aria couldn't maintain her glare, grinning back at her sardonically.

Clarice laughed and leaned into Calypso. "And just like that, she shuts us down. You play dirty, Calypso."

"Do you play any other way?" Aria asked her sister, arching a brow.

Clarice looped one arm with Calypso, and her other arm with Aria. "We'll just have to find out... later."

Aria swallowed, her cheeks coloring as Clarice twisted her head to stare into her eyes with a look of sensual promise.

Clarice laughed delightedly, pulling them toward the house, arm in arm. "Come along, my blushing maidens."

Emily gave them a partial tour, showing them to their rooms. All the bedrooms were on the third floor, bright with sunlight from enormous windows and skylights. Past the glass sliding doors and wide balconies, the valley opened into a breathtaking view. Elms and oaks painted an emerald sea of life for miles, opening up to reveal a small town nestled in the valley below.

Emily turned to Calypso as they entered one of the rooms. "Do you have a preference for the type of bed? Three of the rooms have kings, while the other three are queens."

Aria tapped her mother's shoulder, her eyes sparkling. "She doesn't sleep."

Emily glanced at Calypso, her eyebrows shooting up. "At all?"

"At all," Calypso confirmed. "It would be quite lovely to experience the phenomenon of dreaming. I have ever been curious."

Emily stared at her in bewilderment. "So, you don't eat, drink, or sleep. What do you run on?"

Aria glanced at Calypso appraisingly before answering for her. "She has some kind of metaphysical connection to something she calls radiance. Apparently, auras are a thing too, and they have our names on them. Oh yeah, she's also a total cheat when it comes to dice; she can make them roll whatever she wants."

Clarice rolled her eyes. "She's just bitter because she nearly lost a game of Catan," she informed Emily in a hoarse whisper. "We don't talk about that, though, because she starts pouting when we point out the gods don't love her anymore."

Emily ignored that with the weary grace of a lifelong mother. "Okay, Calypso, what kind of needs *do* you have?"

Calypso touched Emily's arm with a warm smile. "Merely loving friends and a few instruments to play. Thank you ever so much, Emily—for everything."

Emily returned her smile. "We can certainly handle that much. Devon will be here late tonight with the girls' cars, so you'll have some of your instruments."

Calypso gazed out the large window at the valley below, her face soft and radiant in the afternoon light. "Would you mind terribly if I remained for a bit? I should like to simply... take it in. It's quite stunning."

Emily nodded, patting Calypso's shoulder. "Of course. Make yourself at home and get comfortable. I'll get these two situated."

Aria hesitated, worried they had overwhelmed her with all their attention.

Calypso looked at Aria, her eyes clearly peeking at her aura. "I should quite like to simply enjoy the view, Aria. I've never been anywhere half so lovely; I want to take it all in."

Aria smiled ruefully and shook her head. Calypso could practically read her mind. "Okay, but you just let us know if you need some alone time. I know we can be... a lot."

Calypso's violet eyes softened. "Not at all. I've had quite enough solitude for one lifetime. Do run along and get settled; I shall join you shortly."

Aria followed her mother out, glancing back once to see Calypso staring out the enormous window, smiling softly.

Down the hall, Emily's voice turned brisk. "All right, girls, let's hear it. What exactly are we dealing with?"

"This is going to sound crazy," Aria said, hesitating as she exchanged a look with Clarice. "We think she's an angel."

Emily raised a skeptical eyebrow. "Are you two getting religious?"

Clarice snorted. "No, Mom, we are *not* getting *religious*."

Emily's other eyebrow rose. "You do know angels are part of religious scripture, right?" she asked pointedly.

"Think deeper, Mom," Clarice said patiently. "Where did the idea of angels come from? How did they end up in religious texts?"

Emily's eyes widened in realization. "Oh, I see; you think the legend had to start somewhere."

Clarice nodded once. "Exactly. Someone like her, perhaps many like her, must have existed in the past. They were probably the inspiration for whatever's going on in the Bible once you get past all the begats."

Emily led them through the house to the veranda. A pond with a burbling stream glistened at the center, fed by water flowing over the edge of the second story.

They gathered at a square table surrounded by comfortable outdoor chairs. Clarice immediately leaned back in her chair, balancing on two legs, and kicked her feet onto the table. Emily looked at her evenly, earning an impudent smirk.

Aria twisted her chair and rested her feet on Clarice's lap, producing an eye roll from her sister, though she didn't push Aria's feet off.

Aria picked the conversation up again. "For all we know, they're from another world or dimension. They could even be all around us now, but we lack the sensory technology to detect them. If something went wrong with Calypso when she was a child, maybe she ended up in our realm or something. She said she doesn't remember anything before the age of five, when the owner of a music shop and his wife found her in a large tree right after World War I."

Emily frowned, her brows furrowing. "So, we're essentially talking aliens. I'm not sure why you think she belongs to a race of angels, though."

"Let me list the reasons," Clarice said, holding up her fingers. "One: she heals people. Two: she's a musical genius. Three: she broadcasts love like a cupid on crack. Four: she brings people back from the dead. Five: she has muscles below her shoulder blades where wings probably appear normally."

Emily raised a skeptical eyebrow. "How can you tell they aren't just extra muscles from some kind of workout?"

Clarice shook her head. "I gave her a back massage at our apartment. She had ridges going down her back, not just muscles. Something beneath the skin."

Aria nodded confidently. "Definitely wings. You'll understand when you see them."

Clarice combed her fingers through her glossy, midnight hair, making Aria's hand itch for a brush. "Oh yeah, and she can see auras and says our names are engraved on them. Remember when you first met her and she knew your name?"

Emily nodded slowly. "I do. I suppose there *is* more evidence for some kind of angel race theory than anything else right now."

Aria absently toyed with a strand of hair, her green eyes speculative. "I keep wondering what else she's capable of. She seems to have grown a lot since coming home with us. We've given her a lot of love and attention; it's almost like she's nourished by acts of tenderness. I have a feeling she wouldn't have been able to bring that biker back from the dead if she hadn't grown so much over the last day."

Emily pursed her lips and tucked a lock of black hair, streaked with gray, behind her ear. "Now *that's* interesting. She'll be getting a lot of loving attention from now on, so I suppose it's an easy theory to test."

Aria abruptly stood up. "I can't take this anymore. Where's a damn brush? You two can't keep playing with your hair in front of me like this."

Emily shared a look with Clarice and burst out laughing. She pulled her purse off the table and fished out a brush. "I keep it in here just for you, Aria."

Aria sighed with relief and took the brush. She stood behind her mother and began running the brush through her long hair, knowing her fixation on brushing her mother's and Clarice's hair bordered on obsession. She would have attributed it to the cancer treatment that left her scalp bare, but it had started long before that.

"One more thing," Aria said, glancing at Clarice and examining her changed features. "Calypso's tears look like quicksilver. They evaporate shortly after falling, but if they touch you, they seem to have some kind of rejuvenating and transformative effect. We both touched one, and look what it did to Clarice's face."

Clarice studied Aria intently. "It affected you, too. Your jawline is softer. I thought my mind was playing tricks on me. Your eyes are slightly larger, too."

Aria hesitated. "I don't know if it's related, but we both had a strong feeling that we needed to leave the apartment quickly. It happened after both of us were touched by her tears, so I wonder if it unlocked a sixth sense. It sounds crazy, but the bar for crazy dropped below ground yesterday."

Emily nodded slowly. "Okay, let's accept the idea for now that she's an angel. That would mean she's probably in even more danger than we thought. If people found out, we'd have religions trying to claim her and governments trying to study her. People would go crazier for an angel than they would for an alien."

There was something calming about brushing hair, the repetitive motion keeping her hands busy and allowing her mind to focus. She chewed her lip as she considered her mother's observations. "We have to find a way to keep her hidden here and have plans to move her if this place is compromised. Lots of contingency plans."

***

Clarice waited for Aria to exit the veranda before turning back to her mother. "Did you notify your staff before we disappeared?"

Emily nodded, tucking a leg beneath her. "I messaged my aide and let her know I'd be away for an indeterminate amount of time. What about you?"

Clarice smirked. "I texted the CEO and let him know I'd resigned, and that he could go fuck himself."

Emily gave her a disapproving frown. "Seriously, Clarice? Is that really how you want to end your professional career?"

Clarice couldn't stop a giggle from escaping. "Yep. Call it another one of those sixth senses, but I'm not going to be gracing the world of business again. It was fun for a while, but it was getting boring for the last year or so. As long as I'm smart with my investments, I shouldn't need to worry about careers. Not that it matters—I have a feeling the world is about to radically change."

Emily arched an eyebrow. "Because of Calypso?"

Clarice nodded, smiling fondly. "Uh huh. I've seen enough in the last day to know she's only just started to evolve into something that will shake this world to its core."

Emily nodded slowly, frowning pensively. "I have a feeling you might be right." She glanced back toward the cabin, then to Clarice, lowering her voice, "How's Aria doing?"

Clarice took a deep breath and her smile faded. "I'm not sure. She's never shown any interest in anyone else, but she's definitely falling hard for Calypso, and it seems to be tearing her apart inside. I think she's worried that I'll hook up with Calypso and leave her behind. On the other hand, she's been pushing past boundaries I didn't think she would break through for years. She seems to be just as comfortable with Calypso as she is with me. She actually gave Calypso a shoulder massage earlier today."

Emily's eyebrows shot up. "Really? A day after meeting her as an adult and she's already feeling that confident in herself, huh? That *is* unexpected. Maybe a little inner turmoil is exactly what she needs to push past some of her trauma."

Clarice winced. "Yeah, maybe, but I hate to see her in so much pain. She's made so much progress over the last three years already—I couldn't bear to see her wall herself off again."

Emily stood and moved over to the infusion bar. "Would you like some tea or coffee?"

Clarice brightened. "I would commit regicide for an Earl Grey. Thanks, Mom, you're the best."

Emily continued in a more thoughtful tone as she busied herself making the tea. "I think we need to factor in that Calypso may be able to heal more than physical ailments. She might be capable of helping Aria heal from her trauma to some extent." She paused and turned to face Clarice, eyeing her speculatively. "How opposed would you be to having Calypso as a part of your relationship? It would certainly solve a lot of problems."

Clarice pursed her lips consideringly. "If you'd asked me that yesterday, I'd have said 'hell no.' Something feels different with Calypso, though, and I can't say I'm opposed to such an arrangement. The difficult part would be getting Aria to agree. I have a feeling Calypso would be fine with it. I'll admit, I'm a little worried that she'll end up with Calypso and I'll be left behind."

Emily was silent for a time as she fussed with the tea. Clarice couldn't help feeling a twinge of apprehension as she saw the signs of age on her mother, from the few grey strands mixed with her dark hair, to the pronounced stiffness as she walked. Her face remained unlined, but the age spots were clear evidence that she was well past her prime. Clarice dreaded the thought of life without her parents. They had always been close as a family, remaining in frequent contact after she and Aria had moved out.

Emily returned with their tea and sat opposite Clarice. Relaxing into the padded chair, Emily focused her gaze on Clarice.

"I'll have a talk with Aria," she said confidently. "I have a feeling part of her hesitation is a fear of what your dad and I will think of her being in an intimate relationship with you. Despite the many times we've tried to make it clear that we support the two of you being together, she seems to think we're being facetious."

Clarice snickered. "I can't imagine why she might think you were joking. My irreverent manner is equal parts nurture and nature."

Emily smirked, the expression looking like an older version of Clarice. "And you had seven more years of exposure than Aria—not that you needed them; you came prepackaged with mischief in your soul."

Clarice nodded slowly, a reflective frown replacing her grin. "That brings up an interesting line of thought. Calypso sees our auras, which makes the reality of spirits seem like more than a religious scam. What if we actually *do* have spirits? Calypso keeps saying we seem familiar, in spite of her perfect memory failing to account for us. I wonder if we knew each other in another life or something."

Emily leaned forward, her eyes brightening with interest. "Now *that* is a fascinating idea. Perhaps there *is* such a thing as reincarnation after all, or even something outside of mortality entirely."

Clarice used the armrests of her chair to lift herself up so she could fold her legs beneath her. Pulling her hair over one shoulder, she looked up at the rafters, tapping a beat on her knees as she thought. "I think we need to dig deeper into this angel theory. Calypso remembers being a child, so I can't help wondering if angels are just another species, like some parallel civilization living in secret. At the same time, seeing things like auras takes me back to the question about spirits, which hints at some kind of extradimensional world we can't perceive with our limited senses. Even if angels are just another species, they might not exist in our world at all, and she just got stranded here at some point."

Emily sighed. "I wish your dad were here," she said wistfully. "We used to spend a lot of time discussing religious history and the link between advanced civilizations interacting with primitive humans. I'm sure he'd have some great input."

Clarice paused her drumming to look at Emily. "We should probably have him join us as soon as possible. He'll be a prime target for anyone looking for us once people dig into our lives and find out you disappeared at the same time Aria and I did. Hell, the government will probably try and get to him as well."

Emily's brow creased with worry. "You're probably right. I'll have to get word to him once your uncle arrives tonight."

Clarice gave her mother a grateful smile. "Thanks for doing all this for us, Mom. I know we've uprooted your life with this debacle."

Emily shrugged, smiling softly. "There isn't anything I wouldn't do to keep Calypso safe. She gave me my daughters back, and I'll never be able to repay her for that—but I'll certainly try."

***

Calypso made her way up the ladder to the widow's walk, mulling over Clarice and Emily's conversation. The anxiety and fear she had seen in Aria's aura made more sense now. If she really was suffering from lingering trauma following her cancer ordeal as a child, it was no wonder her emotions were all over the place. The thought of the crimson-haired woman suffering so much for the last fifteen years triggered an unfamiliar wave of sorrow. She silently vowed to find a way to help Aria heal and free the radiant spirit trapped within. The nagging sense of familiarity she felt for the two sisters was like an itch she couldn't scratch. Not that she had ever felt an itch, but one of the children she had healed long ago had described the sensation.

She felt a little guilty at listening to Emily and Clarice's conversation, remembering her parents' admonition that it was rude to eavesdrop. She had never learned the trick most people seemed to have for ignoring conversations across the house, though her solitary lifestyle had rarely made it an issue.

The sun had just set, revealing the stars in greater detail than they appeared in daylight. It was fascinating to just observe the world around her, breaking her century-long routine of visiting hospitals, then returning home to compose music. With no need to eat, sleep, or any of the other necessities constantly distracting humans, she was capable of a kind of focus she realized other people couldn't match. The break in routine felt good, though—as if a part of life she had been missing had opened up.

A small Cessna caught her gaze as she stared up at the sky and, curious, she focused her eyes until she could see a girl staring out the passenger window at the town below, a look of wonder on her young face.

Calypso smiled as she saw the girl's lips moving, asking someone else in the cabin how high up they were. Reading lips was an easy skill when you had perfect memory. She had always longed to soar through the air, limitless and free.

Until she met Clarice and Aria, she had been content with her life, finding joy in healing children at the hospitals and composing music. Now she realized she had been living inside a bubble, barely existing. She could suddenly feel the possibilities for so much more, waiting for her to pierce the membrane limiting her potential.

She turned to the ladder when she heard Aria approaching from below, her distinctive footsteps identifying her as clearly as her voice and appearance. Perhaps this would be a good time to begin helping her friend heal.

Aria's red hair poked up through the opening, followed by the rest of her a moment later. Calypso smiled warmly as Aria stood up, receiving a shy smile in return. She truly was lovely, with her long red hair in a loose braid pulled over one shoulder and her vixen-like face. Her green eyes were bright and sparkling with life as she met Calypso's gaze. A smattering of freckles topped her cheeks, and her attached earlobes gave her an almost elf-like appearance.

"Hello, Aria," Calypso greeted her with a dimpled smile. "How are you settling in?"

Aria bit her lip, flushing as she stared back at Calypso, her heartbeat quickening. Her aura fluctuated wildly with emotions Calypso wasn't familiar with.

Aria's blush intensified as she awkwardly attempted a smile. "Um, I'm sorry, what did you say?"

Calypso patiently repeated the question, and Aria's eyes roamed up and down Calypso's body before replying.

"Oh, um, yeah," she replied, nervously wringing her hands. "I took one of the king beds."

Her eyes fell on Calypso's pink skirt, ending just above her knees, then moved up to her high-neck crop top of the same shade. Calypso had changed into the new outfit before climbing the widow's walk.

"Is there something amiss with my choice of attire?" Calypso asked with a concerned frown. "A nurse suggested the ensemble a few months ago, though I never quite found the opportunity to try it on before this evening."

"No!" Aria blurted, then flushed a deeper shade of crimson, her aura flaring pink. "I mean, no, there's nothing wrong with it. You look amazing."

Calypso relaxed. "Oh, good. Thank you, Aria. I am not especially skilled where fashion is concerned and tend to rely upon others to guide my decisions."

Aria nodded, her eyes continuing to roam. "Yeah, I'd say you nailed it with this one," she murmured appreciatively. She folded her arms tightly and began shivering. "Aren't you cold?"

Calypso blinked, then remembered that most people reacted oddly to temperature variations. Aria's tight-fitting green yoga pants probably didn't offer much insulation. Her red t-shirt wasn't much better, clearly not fitted for someone with breasts, causing it to hang open at the bottom and act as a conduit for the light breeze. While not as buxom as Clarice, Aria's breasts were well developed, made more pronounced by her tightly folded arms.

"I do not actually feel the cold," Calypso replied, stepping forward and drawing Aria into a warm embrace. "Is that better?"

"Mm-hmm," Aria hummed, melting into Calypso's arms. "Much better."

"May I ask a rather personal question?" Calypso hesitantly asked.

Aria stiffened. "Um, sure?"

Calypso paused, uncertain whether Aria truly meant it. In her century of observing people, she had learned that they possessed a curious habit of muddling their affirmations and refusals. She drew her head back slightly to look down into Aria's emerald eyes. "It is perfectly all right if you would prefer that I not ask personal questions."

Aria licked her lips and looked away. "It's fine. I'm kind of a coward, so I might not answer, depending on the question."

Calypso ran her fingers through Aria's hair, brushing a finger lightly against her ear. "You are no coward, Aria. As for my question... I was curious how long you and Clarice have been together."

Aria's breath caught, and her pulse hammered in Calypso's ears. "Um, relationship? You mean, how long have we been sisters?"

Calypso hesitated. Had she misunderstood what Emily and Clarice had discussed? Clarice and Aria lived together, and they seemed to fit the pattern of other couples she had observed. "I am sorry, Aria. I am rather ignorant of social conventions due to my isolation. Perhaps I have misunderstood, but I was under the impression that you and Clarice were a couple. Is that not the case?"

Aria froze, breath catching. Calypso was just beginning to worry when Aria let out a laugh that sounded slightly hysterical. "A couple? No, no, no, not at all! We're *sisters*, after all."

Calypso's brows furrowed in confusion. "I was under the impression you were stepsisters. Is there some reason you could not also be a couple?"

Aria's breath quickened and her voice grew unsteady. "I don't know, maybe?"

Calypso felt Aria begin to shiver once more and drew her close again. "I believe Clarice would very much like to be in a relationship with you."

Aria didn't reply, but her aura went haywire. Calypso recognized some of the fluctuations: longing, excitement, love, fear, and apprehension. There were others she couldn't understand, having only seen them a few times. The most recent time was when two nurses entered a supply closet, furtively looking around before shutting themselves inside.

"Have I misunderstood, then?" Calypso asked uncertainly. "Would you not wish to be in a relationship with Clarice?"

Aria didn't need to answer—the flaring white of her aura made it clear that she most *definitely* wanted a relationship with Clarice.

Calypso tried again. "Then I'll take that as a yes. I understand you may carry certain emotional wounds from when you were ill. Would you allow me to sing for you? I should like to help, and I believe I may be able to do so."

Aria's arms tightened, and a choked sob escaped her throat. Shoulders shaking, she nodded into Calypso's shoulder, her aura flaring with blinding, desperate hope.

Calypso smiled, cupping the back of Aria's head gently in her hand. "Very well. I shall do my best."

Taking a deep breath, she opened herself to the tether of light humming inside her mind, then began to sing. There weren't many words in the song, consisting primarily of emotions and concepts beyond language. Her voice split, weaving into a dozen accompanying harmonies that burrowed into Aria's spirit, reshaping damaged pathways.

As the last notes faded, Aria pulled away to stare up at Calypso in wonder, her eyes shimmering with tears. "Oh my god, Calypso, *thank you!* I feel... I feel... I don't even know the words! I feel *right.*"

Calypso kissed her forehead, smiling tenderly. "That is wonderful, Aria. I am so very glad it worked."

***

Aria woke to the growl of a loud diesel engine. She sat up quickly and glanced at the clock, grimacing at the early hour. Who would be coming here at 3:00 a.m.?

She threw on some clothes and padded down the hall to her mother's room, her brain running on emergency power. The room was empty, but lights glowed downstairs. She followed them to the porch, where she found her mother holding a handheld radio.

"Thanks again for bringing them," Emily said gratefully. "We owe you big time."

She glanced at Aria, raising an eyebrow. "Trouble sleeping?"

Aria nodded, her brain struggling to boot. "I'm a light sleeper. Who is that?"

Emily studied her critically. "You're not really awake yet, are you?"

Aria nodded, then changed her mind and shook her head.

Emily eyed her with amusement. "That's your Uncle Devon, remember?"

Aria blinked, memories loading as awake.exe finally finished executing. "Oh, yeah."

Emily gestured toward the large parking area by the garages. "He rented a trailer to haul your cars under tarps. He stopped at a mechanic shop his friend owns and had the GPS transmitters removed, then brought them in the middle of the night to minimize any chance of discovery."

"Wow," Aria breathed. "He's thorough. Did he work for the mafia or an intelligence agency? Whoops, I repeated myself."

Emily chuckled and lightly smacked Aria's shoulder. "You're not supposed to say the quiet part out loud." She grew serious and took a deep breath. "He's never said, but I suspect he has."

Aria stared at her mother blankly for a moment. "Wait... really? I was just being facetious."

Emily folded her arms, lowering her voice as Devon exited the truck. "There's a lot of mystery surrounding your Uncle Devon's former work life. He made a lot of money somewhere, and it's never been clear where. He used to travel all over the world for 'business.'" Emily made air quotes. "Your dad and I were convinced he worked for the CIA or some other clandestine group."

Aria shook her head slowly. "Wow, I had no idea."

Emily shrugged. "We didn't want to make a big deal of it, in case it brought him trouble."

There were several clunking sounds as Devon used hydraulic controls to lower the ramps. He was moving toward one of the cars when Aria noticed Calypso approach him, her features seeming to glow in the moonlight.

"Hello, Devon. May I be of any assistance?"

Devon turned and studied her. Even at this distance, Aria could feel the aura of love Calypso projected. Her glowing eyes watched him patiently as she stood in the brisk spring mountain air, unaffected by the cold.

"Sure," Devon said easily, his deep voice carrying in the night. "Can you guide me while I back the car down?"

Calypso smiled warmly. "I should be delighted."

She stepped behind the trailer as he climbed into Aria's car.

Aria watched Calypso with a small smile, keeping her voice low. "I forgot she doesn't sleep."

Emily nodded thoughtfully. "She's probably used to working on music all night. I wonder how she's holding up with the routine change. Her life has been completely upended."

Aria's smile warmed as she remembered Calypso repeatedly expressing how happy she was to be with them. "I have a feeling she doesn't even look back. I think she's more than ready to start another phase of her life."

Emily looked at Aria appraisingly, then shoulder-bumped her. "I couldn't help noticing she's single. I also noticed that *you're* single. Does that suggest anything interesting to you?"

Aria snorted. "What, that we should go on a double date?"

Emily eyed her skeptically. "You're not interested?"

Aria sighed wistfully. "You can't date the sun. She's just started to evolve into something I suspect will be far beyond human. I doubt there's room for a human girlfriend in that future—assuming she's not straight."

Of course, that was only part of it. Clarice had already claimed her heart, even if Aria had been unable to act on it. The thought of someone besides Clarice filling that role in her life left a sharp ache in her soul.

Emily bumped her again. "Not with that attitude," she said critically. "You need to be more positive. Even if she moves into the stars someday, she's here right now. Don't let the opportunity pass you by."

Aria pinched the bridge of her nose and sighed again. It's not like she could explain her feelings for Clarice to her mother. "It's not that simple. I'm pretty sure Clarice is interested, too, and I'd never compete with her over someone."

Clarice *did* seem interested in Calypso, but unlike other women she had seen Clarice with, Aria felt no jealousy at the thought of those two together, which didn't make any sense.

Emily eyed her calculatingly. "Just share her. It's not like you haven't gone off the rails with your life choices recently. Besides, nobody's fooled by the way you and Clarice tap dance around each other. You're wasting time."

"Mom!" Aria gasped, her cheeks flushing scarlet. "I can't believe you'd suggest that!"

Emily glanced at her with an amused smirk. "You always were a prude, Aria."

"I am *not*," Aria objected hotly.

Emily regarded her with a small smile. "I'm sorry, dear, but you are. You've never even kissed another person, and you're twenty-five. If you were ugly, I might understand, but you're stunningly gorgeous. You're just a prude."

Aria hunched her shoulders, folding her arms defensively. "I've just never been with anyone I was interested in kissing."

How could she want to kiss anyone else, with Clarice's gentle chocolate eyes burned into her brain? Who else could compare?

Emily stared at her pointedly. "It doesn't take much interest to share a kiss. I know you too well to try dissembling with me. I remember when you brought that one girl home in high school, Alice. She was pretty, smart, and completely smitten. What happened?"

Aria blushed. "She wanted to take things further than I did."

Emily nodded in satisfaction. "'Cause you're a prude. You were at the age where exploring those things was natural. It's not like you were going to get pregnant."

Aria sighed dejectedly. "I have... issues with intimacy."

Emily put a sympathetic arm around her shoulders. "I know you do, sweetie. But you'll have to push your boundaries, or you'll never move past this. If there's anyone I trust to help you move past your trauma, it's that angel down there."

Her gaze drifted over to Calypso, who was guiding the last car off the ramp. Aria was pretty sure it was unnecessary, but it was nice of Devon to humor her. "She's going to be so happy to have some instruments to play again," she said with a soft smile.

Emily looked at her expression and shook her head. "I'm just going to assume nature will take its course with this."

"Hmm?" Aria asked absently, eyes on Calypso.

Emily patted her shoulder. "Nothing, dear."

Calypso approached Clarice's car and located the harp in the back. She opened the hatchback and gently removed the instrument, a look of relief on her face.

"It suits you," Devon said approvingly.

She looked at him, her eyes searching what Aria knew to be his aura. "Might I play for you?"

Devon smiled and nodded. "I'd like that."

Aria narrowed her eyes. "There must be something wrong with him. I recognize that look—she found something in his aura she wants to fix."

Emily tilted her head. "Really? You've been with her for one day and you already have her figured out, huh?"

Aria didn't respond, her attention wholly on the angel. She *did* recognize that look; she just didn't know how.

Calypso began to pluck a melody on the harp, her long fingers deftly climbing along the strings. She began to sing, and her eyes glowed brighter, casting soft light on the harp.

Aria had watched her sing and play before, but something was different now. A new authority layered her voice—a *divine* authority, Aria suspected.

She watched, slack-jawed, as the ethereal song warped reality around their angel. Tears streamed down Aria's cheeks, the sublime beauty of the music striking a chord in her soul. She fell to her knees as the power of Calypso's music shook her to the core.

Devon had also fallen to his knees, his eyes shining with unshed tears. He gasped suddenly, his eyes widening with wonder.

"Wow," Emily whispered in awe, kneeling next to Aria, tears on her cheeks. "Just... wow."

"Yeah," Aria agreed, wiping her cheeks. "She's our angel."

"I'm a believer," Emily whispered fervently.

4 – NANOBOTS

Aria struggled to fall asleep after Calypso's performance. Dawn had broken by the time she finally drifted into oblivion.

She woke a few hours later on her side, feeling a warm body pressed against her and an arm draped over her waist. There was no question who it was—the warm blanket of love wrapped around her soul made it obvious it was Calypso cuddling her.

"Good morning, Aria," Calypso greeted her warmly. "Did you sleep well?"

Heart racing, it took Aria a few tries to answer. "Wonderfully. Thank you."

"Your spirit is much like a sun-warmed meadow," Calypso said softly. "It is quite a balm to my soul to be near you and bask in such warmth. It feels... familiar, somehow."

Aria swallowed, the corners of her mouth tilting upward. Ignoring the warmth in her cheeks, she focused on Calypso's words. She could get used to this. It *did* feel familiar, as if she had regained the use of a missing limb. How could she have lived without it for so long, oblivious to its absence?

She laid her hand over Calypso's on her stomach. Some of Calypso's light-blonde hair lay draped over Aria's shoulder and cheek. The scent of sweet roses filled her nostrils, subtle but potent. She wished she could freeze the moment in time forever.

She wasn't sure how long they lay there in silence, enjoying the proximity of their bodies and the radiant aura permeating the room. The moment was interrupted by a knock at the door, followed a second later by Clarice.

"Breakfast is ready—" She broke off, her eyes widening as she took in the sight of them snuggled together.

"Hello, Clarice," Calypso greeted warmly.

Aria stared back at her sister, her cheeks burning. Clarice's face flickered from longing and hurt to sadness, then hardened with resolve.

"Clarice," Calypso said firmly. "Could you step over here for a moment?"

Clarice looked as if she would rather dance barefoot on razor blades, but she obeyed the angel's request. She walked to the bed, trying and failing to keep her expression blank. Hurt and sadness kept peeking through her mask of indifference.

Calypso released Aria and sat on the edge of the bed, a pace away from where Clarice stood, miserably staring at the ground. Calypso took Clarice's hands, then gently pulled her forward, wrapping her arms around Clarice's waist and lying back, pulling Clarice down with her. Aria watched confusion, hope, and longing flash across her sister's face.

"I should like to be with both of you," Calypso said softly, her eyes locked on Clarice's. "Is that something you might find acceptable?"

Clarice closed her eyes. "With Aria... definitely. Anyone else? Hell no."

Calypso reached up and pulled Clarice's head down next to hers. "I've always believed you two were rather special."

Aria sat up and tentatively rested her hand on Clarice's head, brushing her fingers through her sister's dark hair. "I'm so sorry for putting you through that."

"It's fine," Clarice murmured contentedly, basking in Calypso's loving aura. "More than fine. I was up all night worrying about how we were going to handle this. I thought I was going to lose both of you. Are you okay with this?"

Aria laughed brightly, caressing Clarice's cheek. "You wouldn't believe what Mom said last night. She asked why I hadn't made a move on Calypso. I told her I was pretty sure you had feelings for her, too, and she asked why we didn't just share her. Can you believe that?"

Clarice giggled, her shoulders shaking against Calypso. "Yep, I can believe that. She's not nearly as conservative as you."

Aria sighed unhappily. "Yeah. She called me a prude. I guess I kind of am."

Clarice turned to face Aria, her cheek resting on Calypso's, her chocolate eyes soft and full of understanding. "Of course you're a prude. During the age you were most vulnerable, they were doing the most invasive things to your body. It'd be weird if you *weren't* a prude."

Aria sighed again. "I guess. Calypso sang a song for me last night that I think might have fixed me. I'm not really sure how to tell for sure, though."

Clarice smiled softly. "We'll ease you in gently."

Aria's face went nuclear.

Clarice dissolved into giggles again. "You see that sunset, Calypso?"

Calypso smiled indulgently. "Two sunsets."

Clarice's mirth faded as she stared into Aria's eyes, her gaze softening. She licked her lips and opened her mouth to speak, but nothing came out. She opened and closed her mouth several more times before she finally managed to articulate a sentence, uncharacteristically hesitant.

"Aria... I've been meaning to tell you... I shouldn't have waited this long, but... I just didn't know how to move past our wall and—"

"Clarice, are you going to bring her down for breakfast sometime this year?" Emily called from downstairs, interrupting Clarice.

Aria's heart pounded as she waited for the words she had craved for over a decade—the words she knew existed, hidden just out of sight. They were the reason she had never been interested in anyone else... until Calypso.

Clarice opened her mouth, her eyes full of all the unspoken words they both knew Aria lacked the confidence to voice.

"Clarice?" Emily called up again. "Did you get lost on your way to Aria's room? Are you two coming or not?"

"No," Clarice sighed, closing her eyes. "Never gonna leave."

Calypso squeezed her tightly before releasing her. Clarice sighed again and pushed herself up, her hands landing next to Calypso's chest. Her face hovered inches from Calypso's, her hair falling down one side to rest on Calypso's cheek. "To be continued," she murmured, then lightly kissed Calypso before standing.

Aria's heart thudded, her eyes wide as she replayed the kiss, her brain short-circuiting.

Calypso lay on the bed, lips parted and cheeks flushed. She hesitantly touched her lips. Her ever-present aura saturated the room with confusion, wonder, and unmistakable desire.

Clarice turned at the door, winking roguishly at Aria. "Come on, Tweedledee."

Aria followed her sister downstairs to the second-floor veranda. The air was perfumed with the scent of herbs from overflowing plant boxes, mixing with the breakfast aroma. Ivy climbed the trellises and flared out in a green canopy on the rafters above. Round café tables dotted the space, with a few larger square tables in the center. Emily's homemade pancakes steamed on a platter on a table near the pond, smothered in butter. Aria barely stopped herself from drooling at the sight of one of her favorite breakfasts.

She sat beside Clarice and piled several pancakes onto her plate.

Clarice loaded up her own plate. “Thanks for the food, Mom,” she said with a vibrant smile. “I’ve so missed these homemade pancakes.”

“Yeah, thanks, Mom,” Aria echoed in a distracted voice. The press of Calypso’s body against her own, so soft and warm, played through her mind on repeat. The thought of another snuggle left her cheeks on a low burn. She imagined Clarice cuddling her in the same way, and the rest of her face flared with heat. She quickly shut down that line of thought as interesting things began waking up in embarrassing places.

Emily joined them across the table, observing Clarice with an appraising eye. “You’re looking chipper.”

Clarice just grinned and took another bite of her pancakes.

“Oh,” Emily said, an eyebrow shooting up as she looked at Aria. “Oh my.”

Aria leaned forward, letting her hair curtain her face in an attempt to hide her burning cheeks.

Devon walked onto the veranda with a brief, “Morning,” saving Aria from Emily’s knowing gaze. He pulled out a chair and glanced around at them. “How’d everyone sleep?”

“Like a kangaroo,” Clarice said around a mouthful of pancake. “Thanks a lot for bringing our cars!”

“Yeah, thanks,” Aria said fervently. “I was so paranoid someone would steal our instruments.”

“My pleasure,” Devon said with an easy smile, loading up a plate full of pancakes. “It’s good to see you two again.”

“You too, Uncle.” Aria grinned, remembering their last meeting. He had joined them for Thanksgiving, and Clarice had switched his sweet potatoes out for mashed carrots. “Had any carrots lately?”

He glared at Clarice in mock anger, chuckling darkly. “She’ll get what’s coming to her.”

Clarice’s face took on an innocent cast, made more pronounced by the recent changes from Calypso’s tears. “Why, Uncle, I have no idea what you’re talking about.”

He gave her an unimpressed snort. “I’m sure you don’t.”

Clarice had always been the joker in the family, and very few get-togethers ended without at least a few of her pranks finding a mark.

Clarice turned her gaze to Emily. "Is Dad coming out?" she asked hopefully.

Emily hesitated, glancing at Devon. "We're still debating. We want everything to look normal on the home front. We also don't want someone following him here. If he does end up visiting, we'll have to come up with a way to shake a shadow—especially after you three made front-page news again today."

Aria groaned. She had been too afraid to look at the news, not wanting to see herself in the videos from the biker accident.

Clarice tilted her head, her playful eyes intrigued. "What did it say?"

Emily scowled, her eyes blazing with fury, though her voice remained neutral. "Apparently, there was a gas explosion at your apartment complex, but it only affected yours."

Clarice shook her head in disgust. "We didn't even have gas. That's the best story they could come up with? What a freaking joke."

Devon nodded. "They usually don't put a lot of effort into making it convincing, since they control the media."

Emily took a calming breath before continuing. "They discussed your incident with the biker and the videos showing Calypso bringing him back to life."

She paused and smirked at Aria. "You look pissed in the video, by the way. Anyway, people were looking for your car all over the county. Someone found your address and discovered your apartment exploded around the same time you were dealing with that biker. Apparently, that sixth sense you mentioned saved your life."

Emily loaded her own plate with pancakes, chuckling darkly. "The conspiracy theories immediately began sprouting like mushrooms on cow shit after a storm. Most people believe a shadow government is after Calypso, or a pharmaceutical company that doesn't want her healing people. The news initially tried a hit-and-run angle for the motorbike incident, but multiple dash-cam videos forced a retraction."

Clarice leaned back in her chair, hands behind her head. She had made short work of her pancakes. "I wonder what's going through that biker's head right now."

Emily shook her head derisively. "The idiot was interviewed by one of the news stations about his experience. About the only thing he remembered was glowing eyes, then losing control."

Aria grabbed another pancake, slapping it down on her plate with a scowl, as if it were the biker's head. "I hope he's learned his lesson and stops letting hormones do his thinking. He could've gotten other people killed with his stupidity."

A momentary scowl clouded Emily's face. She had always had a temper when it came to anyone threatening her daughters. "Calypso interrupted what would have been a well-earned Darwin award," she muttered darkly. Her brow smoothed, and she barked a short laugh. "There are several televangelists saying Calypso's miracles are the work of the devil—because, apparently, the devil likes to save children from terminal illnesses."

Aria chortled evilly. "I'll bet they're feeling a little threatened right now. They can't have someone performing actual miracles—especially without a donation button."

Emily wolfed down her pancakes and began clearing plates, snorting with amusement when Aria crammed one more pancake into her mouth before relinquishing her plate.

Emily continued briefing them as she cleaned. "Digital sleuths are building timelines and have decided Calypso must be at least fifty."

Aria rose to help her mother clean up, but Emily pushed her back down.

"You two just relax today," Emily said firmly. "You've had a stressful couple of days."

Aria nodded, smiling gratefully. She mimicked her sister's pose, leaning back with her hands behind her head. "Religions are going to get really messy if the world discovers she's an angel," she noted, then paused after a moment of reflection. "Well... messier than they already are."

Devon leaned forward intently. "She's an angel, then?"

Aria nodded confidently. "We think so. We think there must've been others of her kind long ago who spawned the stories we have of angels. She can't remember anything before her fifth birthday, after World War I."

His eyes widened at the revelation of her age. "So, she was a child at one point," he said musingly. "Which means she's definitely not an angel in the religious sense, because their lore doesn't include child angels—not until they appropriated Cupid from Greek mythology and turned him into a baby, anyway."

Emily returned to take Devon's plate, setting a cup of coffee in front of him as she spoke. "She also doesn't need food, water, or sleep. She has access to an energy source she calls radiance. It's all a mystery to her; she acts mostly by intuition."

Clarice drew her legs up, wrapping her arms around her shins and resting her chin on her knees. "She also has strange ridges below her shoulder blades that I'm certain are for wings," she said firmly. She shared everything they knew about Calypso, giving their uncle a detailed recounting of the last two days.

Aria mimicked Clarice's pose again, earning a raised eyebrow from her sister. She just smiled innocently and picked up the story. "She's lived an extremely isolated life, with almost no human interaction outside of the people she heals and hospital staff. She struggles with colloquialisms, maxims, and slang. Making music and healing children consumed pretty much all her time. She had no idea her YouTube channel was popular because she just used an app to upload content, without ever viewing it in a browser."

Devon's eyebrows shot up in surprise. "She really didn't know she was the most famous musician on Earth? She really was isolated, wasn't she?"

Clarice suddenly laughed, drawing her hair over one shoulder. "When we talked to her at the hospital the day before everything blew up, she had no idea over a hundred years had gone by or that she still looked like a twenty-year-old. That's the level of obliviousness we're dealing with. On our way home from the hospital, we saw the Reddit post exposing her, and we convinced her to come with us before the Men in Black locked her in a lab."

Devon gave them an approving nod. "That was good thinking on your part. You two are surprisingly smart."

Clarice shrugged, narrowing her eyes at Aria after she also pulled her hair over a shoulder. "We read too many novels depicting rogue intelligence agencies and powerful billionaires doing shady shit. I'm pretty sure they weren't far off from what happens in the real world. Aria, is there a reason you're imitating everything I do?"

Aria looked at her innocently. "I have no idea what you're talking about."

Clarice nodded sagely. "I see, you're demonstrating that imitation is the best form of flattery. If I look half as hot as you doing this, we'd better hope Uncle Devon has some fire extinguishers."

Aria's face rebelled, coloring under Clarice's suggestive leer. She laughed, the sound forced, as she tried to cover for her stupid cheeks. Why the hell did humans blush, anyway? She was certain there was no evolutionary benefit to broadcasting embarrassment to everyone like an extrovert with a megaphone and a guilty conscience.

Emily shared a look with Devon and rolled her eyes. "Kids."

Aria roughly cleared her throat and looked at Devon. "So, what did Calypso heal you of, if you don't mind my asking?" she asked tentatively.

Devon smiled humorlessly. "I would've had to fabricate a lie for you yesterday. I spent a lot of years working for a contracting agency that world governments use to handle their dirty work. They have some pretty advanced technological gizmos. One of them is a shot full of nanobots that monitor your speech. If we say anything that could implicate the Agency, these little bots release a toxin that'll shut down our hearts."

"Oh my God," Emily breathed, her eyes wide with horror. "That's monstrous. I'm so sorry, Dev."

Clarice narrowed her eyes. "They listened to *everything*? What if you were out of satellite or radio tower range?"

Devon paused as Calypso joined them, nodding at her before continuing. "The bots aren't networked out. There are enough to form an internal neural network—not AI, but close. They track biomarkers for deception when Agency topics come up; basically, machine-learning guard dogs."

Clarice looked sick. "How often are there false positives? Doesn't it kill a lot of people by mistaking intent?"

He nodded grimly. "It used to be worse, but they've tuned it over the years. The bots can also simulate drug effects, like dopamine bursts, pain suppression, rage... you get the idea. I wasn't a door-kicker, but for those guys, it was mood control on demand."

Aria whistled, feeling a pang of sorrow for her uncle. She couldn't think of many things more horrifying than having a knife to her throat for decades, never knowing when they might glitch out and kill her. "Wow, sounds just like some of the sci-fi books we've read. I always figured they were pretty far ahead of what's available to the public, but that's basically mind control territory."

Devon nodded with a bleak smile. "That's the holy grail of any government—absolute control."

Emily looked between Calypso and her brother hopefully. "So, Calypso destroyed the nanobots inside you, right?"

He nodded solemnly. "It was an odd feeling. I've had them interfering with my natural moods for so long that I immediately recognized when they were gone."

Clarice's face grew pensive as she absently tapped a beat on her knees. "I'm surprised they haven't tried pushing that technology on the whole population," she said darkly.

Devon raised a challenging eyebrow. "What makes you think they haven't? Can you think of any recent historical events where they convinced everyone to inject themselves with special medicine?"

Clarice's eyes widened with horror. "Oh my god, seriously?"

He shrugged. "I'm just making assumptions based on what they did with us. I can't imagine they'd waste an opportunity like that, though."

Calypso cleared her throat, drawing all eyes. "I've a bit of a notion. I'm not entirely certain we possess the technical means to see it through, but we might well recruit those who do."

Aria leaned forward and smiled encouragingly. "What's your idea?"

Calypso tucked a strand of blond hair behind her ear, making Aria's fingers twitch. Calypso's eyes met Clarice's, then she hurriedly looked away to stare fixedly at Aria. "We touched upon the notion of healing through a live broadcast earlier," she began, her riveting voice like a feather to Aria's neck. "I'm hardly in a position to frequent the children's wards or a concert hall at the moment. I'm quite in the dark regarding the internet and its various tracking methods, so I've no idea if this is at all feasible. However, if we were to host a live event on YouTube and alert the hospitals beforehand, we might attempt to heal the children in one go."

She leaned her folded arms onto the table. "I am not entirely sure why, but I have a feeling it will work. However, we must remain untraceable, lest we return to where we began. I believe we can trust the children I have assisted over the years. Some of them likely specialize in computers and could help keep us hidden."

Devon nodded thoughtfully. "Cyber Espionage Specialists. If we could recruit some of your former patients with the requisite skills, we could definitely prevent anything from being traced back to places we don't want it to go."

Aria stared at Calypso in growing awe. "Oh my god, Calypso, that's brilliant! You could reach millions of people in one go!"

Calypso nodded, her hands unconsciously tapping her elbows in rhythm with Clarice's drumming fingers. "I feel as though my abilities have grown considerably over the past two days." She smiled affectionately at Aria and Clarice. "Mostly thanks to the two of you."

Devon leaned back, rubbing his chin. "I have some contacts who could help us as well—especially if you can clear out their nanobots like you did for me."

Calypso nodded confidently. "Absolutely."

He stared musingly up at the trellises above them. "Thinking ahead, if broadcasting live works for healing, you could potentially cripple the Agency by clearing out the nanobots in contractors throughout the world. Many of them would turn on the Agency, given the chance to do so without instantly dying of heart attacks."

Clarice looked at him shrewdly. "They're the ones who blew up our apartment, aren't they?"

Devon nodded grimly. "Almost assuredly. They probably already see you as a threat. They may have more intelligence about who and what Calypso is, which may have them spooked."

Calypso blinked, then tilted her head with a puzzled crease to her brows. "And what, precisely, am I?"

Aria smiled at her with fond exasperation. "You're an angel. I think I've mentioned it a few times."

Calypso's hands stilled and she looked at Aria in surprise. "I merely thought you were being sweet. Do you truly believe me to be an angel—as in, the mythological sort?"

Aria quickly nodded. "Yeah, just like mythological angels. We think your kind are where the myths came from."

Calypso frowned, her violet eyes troubled. "I see. So, you genuinely don't believe me to be human?"

"No," Aria said slowly. "Does that bother you?"

Calypso closed her eyes with a sigh. "I'm concerned about the implications should that be the case. How did I come to be here? What is the nature of these other beings? And if they do indeed exist, why are they not assisting humanity?"

Clarice paused her drumming, dropping her feet to the ground. Leaning her elbows on the table, she rested her chin in laced fingers and watched Calypso thoughtfully. "It's possible you're from another world or dimension. Maybe you got stuck in a snarl between realms, or there was some kind of accident."

Calypso sighed again, a small, worried frown on her flawless face. "I simply do not wish to be taken away. This is my home, and I wish to help people. I cannot bear the thought of someone arriving from another world to take me away. I could not endure losing either of you. Any of you."

Aria melted a little inside. "I think you'll be okay," she said confidently. "It's been over a hundred years. If someone hasn't shown up looking for you by now, they probably aren't going to."

Calypso hesitated, looking back at Aria uncertainly. She finally nodded, and her shoulders relaxed. "I should very much like to think you're right."

Clarice abruptly stood, walking over to Emily and raiding her purse. She pulled out a brush and stepped behind a surprised Aria, smirking down at her as she began brushing her hair.

"How do we want to go about contacting former medical patients?" Clarice asked, her fingers sliding through Aria's hair with the brush. "Should we try to get someone at the hospital to cooperate, or should we start a social media group and ask people Calypso has healed to join?"

Aria tipped her head back to look up at Clarice, grinning eagerly. "I think that last one is a great idea. We could probably even convince someone else to recruit former patients, so the burden isn't all on us."

"Good thinking," Devon said, tapping his phone. "First priority is secure communication. I've got a small Faraday-caged room where you can safely turn on your phones to find any saved contact information you may need. Our internet here is bounced through private radio relays, so internet traffic looks like it's coming from a nearby town. For voice, use the IP phones or the secure chat app on the house computers. Don't use your personal laptops or phones. The ones here run a locked-down Linux distro—no backdoors or telemetry."

Clarice hummed. "Won't they be able to find and track the main base station providing the internet in town and follow it back here?"

"We aren't, technically speaking, using a legal internet service," he said blandly. "The main base station in town is on a hidden motorized mount that scans the area up to a mile for residential Wi-Fi. It hacks the encryption and saves it as a usable profile, constantly changing which Wi-Fi it pulls from every five minutes. To anyone tracking our IP, it would appear to be coming from houses all over the city."

Emily looked at her brother curiously. "Is this what you did for your contract work?"

He shrugged. "More or less. Most of my work was infiltrating new server farms, since that's where all the juicy data is stored."

Clarice tossed the brush onto the table and ran her fingers through Aria's long, thick hair, grunting with satisfaction. Her fingers began expertly massaging Aria's scalp, producing a soft moan of pleasure. Aria fell into a trance, her head lolling back, eyes closed, and a blissful smile curving her lips.

"You're a goddess, Clarice," she murmured languidly.

Clarice continued kneading, her voice low and seductive. "I'll be your goddess—anytime, anywhere."

Aria's eyes popped open, and her face flushed as she stared up at Clarice, heart racing. The moment stretched on as Clarice held her gaze, the emotional energy between them brimming with surface tension.

Emily cleared her throat, ending their silent communion. Aria blinked, looking down to find Calypso watching them warmly, while her mother and uncle observed them with amusement. Aria guiltily looked away from Emily's twinkling eyes, afraid she might die of mortification as she realized how she must have looked.

Clarice patted her head affectionately. "Okay, Pumpkin, I'm going to see if there are any existing support groups we can join. No point in reinventing the wheel if someone's already created one for former patients."

Aria gave herself a shake, then pretended her mother and uncle hadn't just witnessed her staring up at Clarice like a love-struck idiot. "I guess I'll start calling hospitals," she said reluctantly, dread replacing embarrassment.

Clarice grinned down at her. "Aren't redheads supposed to be extroverts? I'm not sure you're a genuine redhead."

Aria sighed patiently. "And we're fiery-tempered, hotheaded, bold, and brash, right?"

Clarice's grin widened. "You said it."

Aria put her face in her hands and groaned. "I'm being discriminated against by a Snow White clone."

Clarice's grin vanished. "Snow White?" she spluttered. "Now you're accusing me of rooming with a bunch of short dudes I love cleaning up after?"

Devon raised an eyebrow at Emily. "That's what she took away from being called Snow White?" he asked mildly. "I thought 'the most beautiful woman in all the land' would have been the first trait listed."

Emily glanced at Clarice with a smirk that looked startlingly familiar, like an older version of Clarice. "I thought she was saying she's super gullible when it comes to poisoned apples."

Devon thumbed his earlobe thoughtfully. "Maybe Aria was calling her a lazy layabout who just sleeps all the time."

Clarice crinkled her nose in disgust. "You two are mixing up your Disney movies," she said acidly. "That's Sleeping Beauty."

Devon nodded agreeably. "Okay, princess."

Clarice glared. "I'm going to make you pay for that, Uncle," she threatened ominously.

His dark eyes sparkled with amusement. "I'll be sure to check my apples for poison."

She folded her arms, glowering. "You better check more than apples."

Aria looked around the veranda. "Where are the laptops, Uncle Devon?"

He gestured toward the house. "They're in the library. It's on the first floor, at the back of the house."

Aria sighed happily. "I can't believe this place has a library," she said with a dreamy smile. "This place is *so* cool."

Devon smiled as Aria and Clarice started toward the library. "I'm glad you like it."

As they walked inside, Clarice turned to Aria, her eyes demanding. "Seriously, what did you mean by 'Snow White clone'?"

Aria heard Emily and Devon start chuckling as they walked out of earshot.

Aria sighed. "I meant you have gorgeous hair, the perfect 'pretty girl' face, and a personality that draws everyone in like a moth to the flame. It's just not fair."

Clarice looked her up and down. "I never would have guessed you wanted guys falling all over you."

"Eww, gross, no," Aria said in disgust. She sighed again, uncertain of what she was trying to articulate. "I'm just envious, I guess. I hate being such a spineless introvert, constantly worried that everyone's judging me. I feel like my personality is suffocating under the weight of my crushing anxiety, and that I could be so much more... well... *you*, if I wasn't the world's biggest coward. Instead, I'm just a shell of the person I would be if only I could let go."

Clarice stopped moving down the large hallway and turned to face her. She reached out and lightly brushed her knuckles to Aria's cheek, her eyes glowing with affection. "I know it's selfish, but I *love* that you're an introvert, since I'm one of the only people who gets to see the real Aria. I wish you could see yourself through my eyes. Your introverted nature is part of what makes your personality so beautiful. The only thing you need to let go of is this idea that you should be anything other than what you are."

Clarice caressed Aria's cheek, smiling softly as she continued. "You don't *need* to talk to strangers on the phone or make small talk with neighbors; we're a team, remember? I do the extrovert stuff, and you handle the introvert stuff, like your weird fetish for filling out forms and managing our finances. I'd sooner slit my wrists and do handstands in saltwater than manage our damn budget."

Clarice took her hand and pulled her toward the library. "Now come on, let's go impress Calypso with our initiative."

Aria chuckled, marveling at her sister's ability to always make her feel special. "It's a little surreal that we're hiding in a cabin in the mountains from rabid YouTube fans and shadow organizations. Still... at least I'm with the people I love."

Clarice squeezed her hand lightly in response as they arrived at the library.

"Okay, I'm totally fine with the life of a hermit," Clarice breathed, staring around the library in awe. "Maybe I won't poison Uncle Devon after all."

Large, expensive desks, each with a laptop and IP phone, reflected the light from large windows. Couches and recliners faced the windows, offering a view of several deer grazing beneath the fruit trees outside. Bookshelves lined the walls, three stories high, with ladders on tracks allowing access to the balconies in the higher reaches. Skylights illuminated the area with rays of sunlight shining down into the large room.

Clarice studied the trepidation on Aria's face with a look of pity. "You go look for existing groups. I'll call the hospitals."

Aria's eyes widened with sudden hope. "Really?"

"Of course," Clarice replied cheerfully. "We're a team, remember?"

Aria tackled Clarice in a hug, squeezing her tightly. "You are the *best* sister. I was *really* not looking forward to that."

Clarice's eyes softened. "You're a goose. Even so, I'll always be here to save you from yourself."

Aria beamed, releasing Clarice. "You always are. Thanks, Clarice."

Clarice patted Aria's head affectionately. "Any time, Aria."

5 – AWKWARD

Aria and Clarice spent the morning making phone calls and searching social media. Hours later, Devon interrupted to let them know Emily had prepared lunch on the veranda.

Clarice stood up from the desk and stretched, back arching. "She's the best freaking mom *ever.*"

Aria's stomach rumbled in agreement. "By a wide margin. We need to do something nice for her. She's really bent over backward for us." She paused and grinned at Devon. "You, too, Uncle. Thanks for... well, everything."

Devon shrugged, and his eyes grew introspective. "When Em and I were growing up, your grandpa always used to tell us, 'No good deed goes unpunished.' In spite of that, he was always the first person to offer help to anyone in need; he just couldn't seem to help himself. I'm living proof that his favorite adage isn't always true. Thanks to you three, I'm no longer stuck with those nano maggots in my blood."

Aria shivered. She couldn't imagine the kind of anxiety he must have lived with daily, having a metaphorical knife to his throat.

Clarice glanced at Devon curiously. "Speaking of people in need of attention, how's Calypso doing?"

Devon gestured down the hall as they reached the top of the stairs. "She's setting up instruments in the theater room. I think she was going through withdrawals."

Clarice smiled fondly. "I'll bet she was. I can't wait to watch her lay down some tracks."

Aria nodded fervently. "I'm definitely not going to miss that."

When they reached the veranda, the aroma of expertly seasoned rice and stir-fry filled the air.

Aria inhaled deeply, a wistful smile on her face. “I really miss gourmet meals every day. Mom makes the *best* food.”

Clarice made a face. “We were spoiled for too long. Everything we eat anywhere else tastes second-rate—especially our own cooking.”

Devon nodded, smiling proudly. “Em definitely has a magic touch when it comes to food. She started cooking when she was six and just kept at it. We used to dread her meals growing up, but by the time she was twelve, we started requesting her to cook instead of our mom. She's always loved cooking, and it certainly shows.”

They quickly dished up lunch from the serving table and sat down to eat. It was almost like old times, if you could ignore the shadow government hunting them.

Calypso joined them as they sat down, her violet eyes glowing with satisfaction.

Aria glanced over at her expectantly. “Did you get all the instruments and equipment set up?”

Calypso nodded, meeting Aria’s eyes and smiling warmly. “Indeed. I was about to do some recording shortly. I wondered if you and Clarice would care to join me and assist with some of the instruments and vocals.”

Aria rested her chin on her fist, miming a look of introspection. “Hmm... would I like to join the most famous musician on Earth in a jam session?” she murmured thoughtfully. “Hmm, this will be a tough decision requiring meticulous deliberation.” She paused for dramatic effect as Calypso watched her with growing amusement. “I better speak with my counsel for a decision of this magnitude. Clarice?”

Clarice cocked her head to the side, frowning in concentration. “This will certainly be one of the more difficult decisions we’ve faced. Let’s review the pertinent facts. One: we’ll be playing alongside the greatest musician on Earth. Two: we’ll be playing alongside the most gorgeous musician on Earth. Three: we’ll be playing alongside an angel.” She gave a slow nod. “Yeah, I think it would only be prudent that we join her.”

Aria turned back to Calypso, struggling to maintain a straight face. “After careful review with my esteemed counsel, we’ve decided that joining you would indeed be the logical choice.”

Clarice winked at Calypso and added, “Especially if we get to hear your sexy accent.”

Calypso's cheeks flushed as she looked at Clarice, then quickly back to Aria. "Thank you. Both of you." Her eyes darted back to Clarice, and the blush heated up.

Aria had to use every ounce of willpower not to giggle hysterically at the blushing angel. One little peck on the lips from Clarice, and she was as bashful as a preacher skimming the naughty chapters first. Clarice shared a look with Aria and winked, mischief sparkling in her chocolate eyes. Aria had a feeling their angel was going to get more than a peck in the near future. She couldn't stop a shiver of anticipation at the thought of seeing it again.

Emily sat down across from them, taking in Calypso's blush with a calculating gaze. "Sorry, Calypso," she said with a resigned sigh. "These two think they're starring in a live sitcom and can't resist making a joke out of pretty much everything."

Clarice curled her lip in disdain. "That's called reality TV, Mom, and I wouldn't be caught dead in anything so ridiculous. Our banter is based on the principle that nothing is sacred, and everything absolutely is a joke. We keep it pretty clean when you're around, so you should count yourself lucky."

Emily shook her head but let it drop. "Any luck with the hospitals?"

Clarice's lips curved into a wry smile. "Yeah, *I* had some luck. I got a handful of names and numbers. Aria swapped me roles—not in a weird way, though."

Emily laughed, shaking her head and glancing at her introverted stepdaughter with a resigned expression. "How about the social media search?"

Aria perked up. "I actually found a ton of existing groups. There are a lot of angry former patients out there. Apparently, the fact that someone's trying to kill Calypso is common knowledge. They're organizing protests and threatening to riot in D.C. if the government doesn't rein in whoever is behind it."

"As if," Clarice muttered cynically. "They'll just infiltrate the protest groups and shut them down."

Aria knew history supported her sister's prediction, from civil rights or antiwar protests to undesirable political groups. The greatest democracy on Earth had a shockingly fascist approach to anything threatening the official narrative.

"Probably," she agreed with a grimace. "DHS and the CIA are both claiming ignorance, and the Senate Select Committee on Intelligence is ignoring the entire debacle."

Clarice snorted derisively. "They're probably pumped full of nanobots and do what they're told."

Devon nodded morosely. "I'd be surprised if they weren't."

Emily grimaced. "That would certainly explain a lot of the decisions they've supported over the years."

Aria took a deep breath and pushed on. "I set up a video call with a few organizers for tomorrow morning. I didn't tell them who I was, obviously, just that we wanted to collaborate on some plans. Once they see me, they'll recognize me from the news. I'm hoping that will get them on our side."

Clarice grinned at her proudly. "Nicely done, Tweedledee. Good call switching jobs."

Aria grinned back. "Thanks. It was actually kind of fun. There are so many people ready to stand up for Calypso—it's... humbling, honestly. Makes everything feel a little less hopeless."

Devon pushed his empty plate away and leaned back with a contented sigh. "That's promising. Still, the best way to buy us some real breathing room is to hit the Agency where it hurts. If we can get rid of those nanobots in other contractors, they'll have a much bigger problem to deal with than chasing us."

Clarice pursed her lips and nodded at Calypso. "Calypso still has her channel. If we did a surprise live event, she could push out the cure before anyone could shut it down. Assuming they *can* shut it down."

"They can," Devon assured her grimly. "They control the backbone routers that tie everything together. If they pull those offline, the world wide web stops being worldwide. They have granular control over individual segments of social media as well, so they could just shut her channel down."

***

After lunch, Aria and Clarice followed Calypso back to the theater room. Calypso avoided Clarice's gaze, her cheeks glowing every time their eyes met. Aria caught Clarice's amused glance and barely suppressed a giggle.

She watched as Calypso configured her recording setup, her hands moving with casual mastery through a maze of settings in her studio software, like a painter preparing her palette before creating a masterpiece.

She started with the drums, laying down the rhythm track. The beat was flawless on the first take and more complex than anything Aria would have used for a mere timing track. Did she already have the entire song mapped out in her head?

Next came the bass guitar. Aria remembered the online critiques she had read, from guitarists claiming Calypso's pieces were nearly impossible to replicate. Watching her now, Aria understood why. Her fingers blurred as she moved up and down the fretboard, drawing out harmonics and slides that blended seamlessly with the song, more than mere flashy embellishments. She brought each instrument to life, coaxing sounds and effects Aria would never have imagined possible. Almost a century of nonstop composing had truly set her apart as a musician of unparalleled accomplishment.

Eight tracks in, Calypso turned to them, her violet eyes alive. "Would you care to play the strings with me for the next one?"

Aria nodded eagerly, moving to the cello and sitting, bow at the ready. Clarice grabbed the viola, while Calypso picked up her antique violin. They ran through the notes once, and then Calypso started recording.

The first bow stroke filled the room with a deep, rich hum. Calypso's violin danced above them, her melody soaring while their deeper tones wrapped around it like a caress. Aria's pulse raced—they were actually playing with Calypso! The thought nearly made her fumble her bow, but she caught herself just in time.

When Calypso began to sing, the air itself seemed to warp. Her voice wove harmonies with effortless precision, stepping through notes with angelic grace. Aria and Clarice joined her, their soprano and alto weaving into her melody. The blend of their voices filled the room like an anthem of hope, charging the air with emotional tension.

When the last note faded, silence hung for a long, breathless moment. Aria's hands shook. It was so much more than music, crossing into the realm of transcendence. She felt changed, her soul reshaped, as if she had glimpsed something sacred.

Clarice gazed at Calypso in reverence. "That was *beyond* amazing, Calypso."

Calypso smiled shyly, her glowing eyes darting toward Clarice before quickly looking away. "Thank you."

* * *

It was well into evening when they finally left the makeshift studio. Dinner was another gourmet spread, eaten amid laughter and talk of plans for the video call the next morning.

Emily stopped Aria as Clarice headed upstairs. Calypso had gone to the widow's walk to admire the valley bathed in twilight. "Aria, can I talk to you?"

Aria nodded, watching her mother curiously. "Sure. What's up, Mom?"

Emily's lips curved into a small smile. "I was just wondering what all the blushing is about when Calypso looks at Clarice. I can tell by the way you're almost giggling yourself silly every time it happens that you know what's going on."

Aria giggled, remembering Calypso's awkward interactions with Clarice throughout the day. "Clarice gave her the barest feather-kiss this morning. I think it opened another door in her mind or something. She was all about hugs and snuggles before, but it was all completely platonic. I don't even think she understood what kissing was, let alone anything beyond that. Now she's walking around like she's discovered a new element and doesn't know what to do with it."

Emily arched an eyebrow, both amused and concerned. "Are we sure she even has a gender? Some of the myths claimed angels were genderless—well, most of them. I guess the Nephilim might disprove that if they turn out to be real."

Aria smiled sardonically. "I'm pretty sure that was just Christianity's spin because they viewed sex as a necessary evil. Since angels were supposed to be holy, they had to make them genderless. I'd be very surprised if Calypso doesn't have passionate parts."

Emily rolled her eyes, wryly repeating, "passionate parts." "Well, be careful with her," she said cautiously. "If this is all new to her, don't throw her in the deep end before she can swim."

Aria arched an eyebrow. "You're talking to the wrong daughter," she said pointedly. "You need to have this conversation with Clarice."

Emily chuckled. "I suppose you're right."

Aria slid deeper into her chair, folding her arms as the cool night air raised goosebumps on her arms. She tilted her head and narrowed her eyes. "Did you send her up to my room this morning? It seems oddly coincidental that she would show up in my bed the morning after our talk."

Emily held up her hands defensively. "I didn't tell her anything. Why? What happened?"

Aria's cheeks heated under her mother's curious gaze. "I woke up with her spooning me," Aria admitted with a mix of embarrassment and wonder. "Then Clarice walked in and looked like a kicked puppy when she saw us. Calypso convinced her to come over, then pulled her into a hug on the bed and asked if she would be willing to share her with me."

Emily folded her arms, resting her chin on a finger. "Really? I wonder if she overheard us last night. Do you know how good her hearing is?"

Aria shook her head, frowning. What if Calypso could hear them talking right now? "I guess it never occurred to me to ask," she said quietly. "I'll check with her tonight. Maybe she heard you and thought what you had in mind was snuggling."

Emily smiled wryly. "That would make sense. Despite her age, she's still extremely naive about so much in life."

Aria smiled fondly, nodding. "I'll make sure Clarice knows to take it slow," she assured her mother wryly.

Clarice probably knew how to handle Calypso far better than Aria. Her overprotective sister would almost certainly handle Calypso with the same care she handled Aria. Sometimes, she wished Clarice would stop being so cautious. She had dreamed up more than one fantasy about Clarice suddenly pressing her up against a wall and kissing her before Aria could react. In the safety of her own head, those fantasies always progressed to far more than kissing.

She wanted to believe she wouldn't melt down if Clarice ever crossed the unspoken line dividing them. The thought of intimacy with anyone else made her skin crawl, but surely, she wouldn't freeze up if it were Clarice... not anymore.

She was afraid not knowing how Aria would react was the reason Clarice had kept her distance, sensing Aria's doubt any time they grew too close. There had been several moments since moving out of their parents' house when Aria had been sure Clarice would push past her walls, only to withdraw when she had seen the fear in Aria's eyes.

It was unbearable, feeling so much attraction to Clarice, knowing it was reciprocated, and remaining helpless to act on it due to her own cowardice. She had subtly suggested Clarice find someone else, someone who wasn't broken. She had spent more than one sleepless night, terrified that Clarice would finally take her up on that suggestion, leaving Aria alone. But Clarice never moved on, never gave up on her.

Guilt had become a growing part of her life as they reached their twenty-fifth birthdays and Clarice still hadn't given up. Her sister deserved so much more than Aria could give, and while seeing Clarice with someone else would probably destroy Aria, she had found herself wishing her sister would move on and stop wasting her life on someone too broken to even share a kiss.

Pulling her mind back from her morose thoughts, Aria left her mother, intending to return to the library for additional research. She sensed Calypso's aura broadcasting from above, radiating confusion and uncertainty.

Sighing, she decided to talk to Calypso. Maybe their angel could finally give Clarice what she hadn't been able to get from Aria. Maybe the two of them could satisfy their physical needs, and Aria could still maintain her current relationship with Clarice. Surprisingly, she didn't feel any jealousy at the thought—just a growing regret that she would never experience the same intimacy. She desperately hoped Calypso's song had truly healed her of her trauma, and that she could finally experience the physical expression of the love she felt for Clarice.

Emerging from the ladder onto the widow's walk, she found Calypso staring at the moonlit night, her face troubled.

"Hey," Aria greeted her with a warm smile. "Penny for your thoughts?"

Calypso blinked, and Aria could tell she was trying to translate another colloquialism. "I merely feel somewhat... out of sorts."

Aria stepped up next to her and rested a companionable hand on her shoulder. "How so?"

Calypso frowned, a hint of uncertainty in her glowing eyes. "I've a peculiar sensation, much like a restlessness. It's difficult to articulate—as though I'm in need of something presently beyond my reach, yet I've no inkling of what it might be."

Aria studied her carefully. "Interesting. Are you experiencing any other unusual sensations?"

Calypso nodded, her cheeks flushing slightly. "This is rather uncomfortable to discuss, and I am not sure why. I never truly grasped the notion of uncomfortable conversations until now."

Aria took a deep breath. "Let me try to walk you around the boundary of the things that are uncomfortable, without actually touching on them specifically. Are you feeling new sensations in parts of your body, like heat or longing?"

Calypso blinked, staring at Aria in surprise. "You know what this is?"

Aria carefully hid a smile before answering. "I might, depending on your physiology. How much do you know about angels?"

Calypso paused, looking back at her reflectively. "Merely what I was taught in church as a youngster. That they were agents of a deity, possessing formidable power. They were said to play instruments and have wings. Some acted as messengers, while others were quite literally destroyers of civilizations."

Aria hesitated, fumbling for a delicate way to phrase her question. "Okay, well, there are some other attributes they claimed angels possessed. According to some of the lore, angels were androgynous, meaning they didn't have the... distinguishing features of men and women."

Calypso looked at her in confusion. "Such as breasts?"

"Yes..." Aria replied slowly, drawing out the word. "And the *other* parts... down below."

Calypso eyed her curiously. "Which parts down below?"

Aria stared back helplessly. *Oh man, maybe they* are *genderless!*

Aria gestured vaguely between her hips. "You know... in the nether regions."

Calypso's brow furrowed in bewilderment. "Nether regions? Such as the Netherlands?"

Aria facepalmed and blurted, "Like men have ding-dongs and women don't."

"Ding-dongs?" Calypso repeated in confusion. "Those packaged cakes?"

Aria sighed in exasperation. "I'm talking about a penis!"

Calypso frowned in thought. "I see. I've encountered the term previously, but I'm quite at a loss as to its actual definition."

Aria's face flared crimson as she floundered. "Do you know how babies are made?"

Calypso glanced at Aria's flushed face. Her aura was probably going haywire, adding to Calypso's confusion. "I confess, the question has never truly crossed my mind," she admitted.

"Oh bugger," Aria breathed in embarrassment. "I am *so* the wrong person to be having this conversation with you."

Calypso eyed her inquisitively. "Who would be considered a good person?"

Aria grimaced. "Well, I'd say your mother, but since she's unavailable, I'm stuck with the job. Okay, I'm just going to bite the bullet and be very explicit, embarrassing the hell out of both of us."

"Very well," Calypso said warily, her face a mixture of cautious curiosity.

Aria spoke quickly, as if tearing off a band-aid. "Right between your legs, on your hips, is it just smooth skin?"

Calypso's face flushed scarlet as she stared at Aria in mortification. "Oh."

Aria buried her burning face in her hands in defeat. "Yeah, *oh*."

"Um, no," Calypso muttered, almost inaudibly. "It's not smooth skin."

Aria grumbled into her hands, "Well, that's good to know, 'cause that would've been really weird."

An uncomfortable silence followed. Then Calypso licked her lips and asked, "What has that to do with my feeling strange?"

"Oh gods," Aria almost wept. "This is going to be the whole birds and the bees conversation."

Calypso looked at her doubtfully. "Are you suggesting this peculiar sensation is somehow related to birds and bees?"

Aria took a deep breath, trying to keep her voice clinical. "Okay, girls are like us down below, guys have penises. That's the real difference between biological genders."

Aria sighed, cursing Clarice for getting her into this situation. She spent the next few minutes explaining in graphic detail how babies are conceived. Calypso's face had a look of revulsion when Aria finished.

"Is that not a trifle... violating?"

Aria nodded. "Yeah, it is. But that's how the world works—unless you're a fish."

Calypso paused. "A fish?"

Aria explained how fish do it.

Calypso nodded approvingly. "Why is the practice not more universal? It strikes me as being far less intrusive."

Aria shrugged. "I haven't got a clue. Apparently, nature decided we needed a different way once we crawled out of the sea."

Calypso shook her head in disbelief. "How are infants even... produced? Whatever would possess anyone to submit to a process so remarkably intrusive?"

Aria sighed. Her cheeks had finally stopped lighting up the night like a beacon. As she continued, they quickly filled with color again. "Nature found a way to make us want to do that, too. The act of procreating is very pleasurable, so people do it for that aspect of it."

"Oh," Calypso said awkwardly, her cheeks returning to a dull burn.

They stood in silence, staring out at the landscape for a while before Calypso finally spoke, glancing sideways at Aria.

"I am still uncertain how this relates to my feeling odd."

Aria took a deep breath. "Well, part of nature's method to motivate people to, um, do *it* is by making the body release hormones that make you feel attracted to someone. In humans, those urges typically start at puberty, right before our teenage years. We start feeling attracted to certain people. I don't know how it works for angels. Maybe it's based on reactions to events, rather than age."

Calypso blinked at her curiously. "Whatever sort of events might those be?"

"I don't know," Aria teased exaggeratedly. "Maybe being kissed by someone."

"Oh," Calypso said, her hand unconsciously reaching up to touch her lips.

Aria looked at her carefully. "Does the odd feeling happen when you're around Clarice?"

Calypso nodded silently.

Aria sighed with relief, feeling like she had run an awkward marathon. "Well, now you know why."

Calypso blushed. "Is it because I should like to procreate with Clarice?" she asked faintly.

"Well, not procreate," Aria corrected with a short laugh. "You need a penis to procreate. With Clarice, it would be for the intimacy. You know, for the pleasure factor. Experiencing that kind of pleasure with another person is supposed to be another expression of love. It requires a special kind of trust to let someone touch you intimately."

Calypso turned to face her curiously. "Is this a practice with which you've some prior experience?"

"Um, no," Aria admitted with an awkward cough. "Before you sang to me last night, I had some... issues that made intimacy terrifying."

Calypso pursed her lips. "Am I to understand, then, that this is an activity reserved solely for those with whom one shares a close bond?"

Aria hesitated. "Theoretically. Though there are a lot of horndogs that just screw everyone they come across."

Calypso's brows furrowed as she tried to translate Aria's sentence. "Horndogs?"

Aria shook her head ruefully. "I need to give you a crash course on pop culture. Horndogs are what you call people who think about nothing but sex—sex being the act of procreating."

Calypso nodded slowly. "I see. So, intimacy is quite irrelevant for these... 'horndogs' of yours."

"Correct," Aria nodded, feeling like there was a light at the end of the tunnel.

Calypso bit her lip and gazed at Aria speculatively.

"What?" Aria asked, her stomach fluttering.

Calypso continued staring at her, looking down at her lips. Aria swallowed, her mouth suddenly going dry.

"Tell me," Calypso said hesitantly. "Have you ever kissed another?"

Aria shook her head, unable to speak.

Calypso's eyes glowed brighter as she stepped into Aria's personal space. "Would it be improper for me to kiss you? We are quite close, are we not?"

Aria's knees shook as Calypso stared at her intently, clearly reading her aura, which she knew was probably begging for the angel to proceed.

Calypso slowly moved her face toward Aria's, her eyes searching. Aria stood frozen to the spot as Calypso's soft lips parted. Their lips touched, and it was like a lightning bolt had zapped her soul. Unbidden, her arms wrapped around Calypso, pulling her close until their bodies entwined, all traces of fear vanishing in a flood of desire. She let out a hungry moan as their lips melded together. The sensation of Calypso's curves pressing tightly against her own sent a thrill of pleasure to all the right places. Heart racing, Aria let go of her inhibitions and allowed her instincts to take over.

The presence Calypso normally projected shifted from loving affection to a volcano of desire and desperate need.

Calypso pulled back with a gasp, her irises swirling like violet galaxies. She stared down at Aria with a deep blush and a radiant smile. "So this is the sensation of intimacy."

Aria clung to her tightly, knees weak and trembling. Her chest heaved as she took deep breaths, gazing up at Calypso in wonder. She had done it! She had kissed someone!

"Yeah," Aria gasped. "I think that was pretty intimate."

Clarice's voice suddenly called up to them from below the ladder. "You may want to figure out how to retract your aura so the rest of us aren't watching."

Calypso's eyes went wide, and her face flushed scarlet with mortification as she stared at Aria in chagrin.

"Don't worry about it," Aria said firmly. "They can just deal with it."

She pulled Calypso's head back down for another kiss. She wasn't about to let the moment end so abruptly after finally breaking through her first mental wall.

***

Clarice leaned back in her chair on the veranda. The night was clear and star-filled, the kind of quiet that made even whispers sound loud. Emily sat next to her, sipping tea.

"So, this is interesting," Clarice noted with a smirk. "I think Calypso needs to figure out some aura control—if that's even a thing."

Emily smacked her shoulder. “Let them have their fun. It's Aria's first kiss, after all. Calypso's second, from what I hear.”

Clarice snorted. “If you can call the first one a kiss—I barely touched her lips.”

Emily stared over her teacup at her daughter, amusement sparkling in her dark eyes. “It was apparently enough to set her blushing every time she looked at you.”

Clarice chuckled at the memory, shaking her head. “I still can't believe Aria actually kissed her. I don’t think I’ve ever been so proud.”

Emily sipped her tea, smiling knowingly. “I'd wager it was the other way around. Aria's too much of a prude to initiate anything.”

Clarice smiled fondly. “Yeah, she really is. I just wish we could have recorded her expression in the events that led up to it. I'm sure it was epic.”

Emily stared at Clarice over her teacup with a mixture of concern and amusement. “Are you and Aria ever going to move beyond longing looks and bashful blushes? It’s cute, but you’re both in your mid-twenties now.”

Clarice scowled. “I was in the middle of having a talk with her this morning when some woman kept shouting at me to bring Aria down to breakfast.”

Emily blinked, then laughed sheepishly. “Ah, I guess I should have realized something was up when you didn’t immediately return. Do you think she’s ready?”

Clarice’s lips curved into a soft smile. “Yeah, she’s ready. Calypso fixed her last night. We just need some time to talk through a few—"

A sudden flash of light cut her off. For an instant, the entire mountain range lit up as bright as day. A deafening boom followed, rattling the veranda and shattering several glasses. The wave of Calypso's aura hit them like a physical force, so powerful it nearly knocked Clarice unconscious.

“What the hell was that?” Clarice croaked groggily as she tried to put her brain back in her head.

“Aria,” Emily said fearfully. She stumbled to her feet and lurched drunkenly toward the door.

Clarice followed, trying to regain her equilibrium as the mental gut punch slowly faded. They grew steadier as they approached the ladder leading to the widow's walk. When they emerged at the top, they found Calypso unconscious in Aria's arms.

“What happened?” Emily demanded urgently. “Are you hurt?”

Aria shook her head, her voice tremulous. “We were just kissing, and she suddenly exploded with light and passed out. She's insanely light now, too.”

Clarice studied Aria shrewdly. "So you were *just* kissing?"

Aria's face practically glowed in the darkness. "I, um, sort of tried, um, slipping her the tongue."

Clarice grinned proudly. "Good job, Aria—you made her evolve again. She'll be fine in a minute."

"What?" Aria and Emily chorused.

"She's done it before," Clarice reminded them, staring intently at Calypso. "Last time, it made her eyes start glowing."

Understanding dawned in Aria's green eyes. "You mean after the back massage?"

"Exactly," Clarice confirmed with a nod. "Intense emotional experiences seem to trigger evolutionary leaps in her body—and it looks like slipping her the tongue was a big leap."

Aria closed her eyes, and Clarice giggled gleefully as her sister's entire body flushed red.

Emily ignored the byplay, studying the unconscious angel curiously. "First her eyes, and now her weight? I have a feeling those wings you theorized about aren't far off. She would need to be a lot lighter before wings did her any good."

Devon arrived midway through Emily's observation, his eyes tight with concern. "Was anyone hurt?"

"Just my brain," Clarice griped, rubbing her temples. "That felt like a Pan Galactic Gargle Blaster."

Emily arched an eyebrow. "A what?"

"Come *on*!" Clarice demanded, her voice pained. "Don't tell me you haven't read The Hitchhiker's Guide to the Galaxy!"

Devon chuckled. "Don't panic."

"He gets it!" Clarice declared triumphantly, pointing at her uncle.

Emily rolled her eyes, then looked at Aria inquisitively. "Did it feel like your brain got slapped by an angry elephant? You seem less affected than we were."

Aria shook her head, holding Calypso protectively. "All I felt was a sense of vertigo. Is she going to be all right?"

Emily stepped beside her, speaking gently. "I'd guess her brain's just rebooting. Whatever she's becoming, it's rewriting her on the fly."

6 – TRANSFORMATION

Emily hadn't even finished speaking when Calypso's eyes flew open. Held in Aria's arms, she blinked in confusion at their concerned gazes. "What happened?"

Clarice casually leaned back on the railing. "You lit up half the mountain and then passed out," she said cheerfully. "It was pretty epic. How do you feel?"

Calypso's eyes were no longer merely glowing—they were alive, swirling like the spiral arms of a galaxy. She gazed into Clarice's eyes for several long seconds before replying.

"I feel... altered. It is as though the world has become a touch more coherent."

Clarice's smile turned playful. "Have you noticed how much lighter you are yet?"

Calypso blinked her swirling eyes, then stood up straight as Aria slowly released her. "Oh my," she whispered, walking in a small circle. "I feel *so* much lighter."

Clarice nodded and matter-of-factly said, "If you ever get wings, you'll probably need to be light enough for them to work."

Calypso stared at Clarice intently, her swirling eyes rotating faster. After a few seconds of silent scrutiny, Clarice shifted uncomfortably and narrowed her eyes.

"What's so fascinating about my aura?"

Calypso pursed her lips consideringly. "It changed."

Clarice arched an eyebrow. "Really? How so?"

Calypso turned to study Emily and Devon. "It is stronger. The same applies to Emily and Devon. It is emanating farther from your bodies than it did previously."

Emily frowned. "And that means... what, exactly?"

Calypso hesitated. "I believe it reflects the depth of one's life force," she said slowly. "Vitality, health... perhaps even the strength of spirit."

Devon nodded slowly. "I thought I felt different. I figured it was just adrenaline."

Clarice shivered in the chilly night air and folded her arms, glancing up at the starry sky. "Do you think that light show will attract any unwanted attention?"

Devon shook his head, following her gaze upward. "I doubt it. It probably just registered as a bolide entering the atmosphere."

Aria studied Calypso intently, radiating concern. "Are you feeling any other changes?"

Calypso closed her eyes, dimming the glow on the widow's walk. "My abilities appear to have become more... instinctive."

"I didn't think it was possible, but I think she got even prettier," Clarice thought admiringly.

Calypso opened her eyes and smiled shyly at Clarice, her cheeks coloring. "Truly?"

Aria's brow furrowed as she stared between the two of them. "Truly what?"

Clarice froze. "Did you just read my mind?"

Calypso's blush deepened. "Did you not just remark that I had become... even more aesthetic?"

Clarice stared at her in surprise. "No, I *thought* that in my head," she said pointedly. Her surprise quickly transformed to an amused smirk, and her voice adopted a British accent. "And I said 'prettier,' *not* 'more aesthetic,' you goose."

Calypso turned to regard Aria in wonder. "It sounds as though you are saying it aloud, yet I did not see your lips move."

Clarice laughed delightedly. "So, you *can* read minds now," she said with an evil smile. "Get ready for some *very* inappropriate thoughts."

Emily turned a stern gaze on Clarice. "Behave."

Clarice threw up her hands defensively, her eyes wide with innocence. "Hey, I can't help what I think. Not voicing my thoughts is already peak restraint."

Devon knuckled his chin contemplatively. "This could be a huge advantage. There'll be times we need to know if someone can be trusted. Now we won't have to guess and hope."

Emily nodded, an eager gleam in her dark eyes. "That's true. Our biggest threat is discovery. If we can confidently find allies, our chances of keeping Calypso safe will increase dramatically."

Clarice eyed Calypso speculatively. "I wonder if there's a distance limitation. Could you read someone's mind over a video call?"

Calypso laughed helplessly. "I wasn't even aware I was accessing your thoughts until you informed me. I've absolutely no concept of what the constraints might be."

Clarice smiled, bright and mischievous. "We'll have to investigate that possibility tomorrow. Aria has some video calls with former patients in the morning, so we can test it out while she's chatting with them—maybe have a little fun."

Aria's eyes sparkled as she studied Calypso. "Before that, maybe we should test her dexterity. I want to see how fast she is now."

Clarice's eyes lit up with excitement. "Now that would be *awesome*! I bet she could jump from ridiculous heights without getting hurt."

Calypso smiled indulgently at their enthusiasm. "I must admit, my own curiosity has been piqued as well."

Emily yawned widely. "I think it's time to call it a night, for those of us who sleep. Having my aura stretched out was exhausting. Let's pick this conversation up tomorrow morning."

Devon matched her yawn. "Agreed. I'm not as young as I was, and I'm still catching up on that all-nighter."

The two of them went down the ladder, leaving Aria and Clarice with Calypso.

Clarice grinned mischievously. Was Calypso *always* listening to their thoughts? "*Hey, Calypso, feel like a little more smooching*?"

Calypso tilted her head. "What is 'smooching?'"

Aria's eyes snapped to Clarice suspiciously. Clarice winked, flashing an alluring smile.

Calypso wrinkled her nose. "They refer to it as 'smooching'? The term is profoundly unappealing."

Clarice laughed softly, realizing Aria's thoughts must have supplied the definition to Calypso. "I agree, it's an awkward word for an intimate act—probably because the word is mimicking the sound."

Calypso nodded firmly. "'Kissing' is a far more elegant term," she said with quiet conviction.

Aria leaned back on the railing, her eyes reflective. "I've always wanted to make a new language where the sound of every word complemented its definition—a truly beautiful language, without all the synonyms, homonyms, and other silliness so many languages are plagued by."

Calypso squinted. "That is tickling something in my memory. I usually recall everything, but this is just beyond my reach."

Clarice held up a hand, eyes widening. "Hold up, you remember *everything*?"

Calypso looked at her peculiarly. "Is that not the standard experience for everyone?"

"No," Aria and Clarice chorused, sharing an amused glance.

Clarice tapped her temple. "We humans forget things all the time—especially names."

Aria's eyes widened, and her voice grew quiet with awe. "Do you remember the name of every child you've ever healed?"

Calypso smiled softly. "Yes. I can recall your presence in the hospital with the same clarity as if it had transpired mere moments ago."

Clarice sighed enviously. "Wow, that's an *amazing* superpower."

Calypso regarded her with puzzled fascination. "It seems curious that this is not normal. How do you manage should you lose access to your memories?"

Clarice joined Aria, resting against the rail and leaning into her sister for warmth. Aria glanced at her with a warm smile and rested her head against Clarice's.

"That's why we invented writing, photos, and YouTube," Clarice explained, "to record our experiences so we can remember them later."

Clarice twisted her head and kissed Aria's forehead. "I'm so proud of you," she said softly. "You have officially taken your first step on the road to intimacy."

Aria smiled shyly, glancing over to see Clarice watching her with open admiration. "Yeah, we have Calypso to thank for that."

Calypso regarded them with a warm smile. "You are most welcome, dear."

Aria peered at Calypso speculatively, her fingers inevitably reaching for a strand of her crimson hair. "That reminds me... how good is your hearing?"

Calypso tilted her head to the side. "That is a remarkably subjective question. Whatever would prompt you to ask?"

Aria squeezed Clarice's hand and pushed away from the railing, then walked to the far end of the widow's walk, fifteen feet away. "Let's test it."

Clarice saw Aria's lips move in the faint light but heard nothing except the hum of crickets and frogs.

Calypso nodded. "I hear you perfectly."

Aria blinked. "So... did you hear my mom tell me the other night that I should share you with Clarice?"

Calypso nodded again, smiling. "I heard how difficult it was for you to be close to someone and wished to help."

"Wow," Aria whispered. "You really are amazing on so many levels."

Calypso blushed under Aria's admiring gaze, the soft light in her eyes painting the air around them in violet hues.

Clarice grinned playfully. "I want to know how well you can see with those beautiful eyes. Can you see color at night, or is everything washed out like it is for us?"

Calypso blinked. "Are you truly unable to see colors at night?"

Clarice laughed delightedly. "I guess that answers that. Can you read the sign on the gate at the end of the driveway?"

Calypso looked out into the night, toward the mile-long driveway ending with a large wooden sign. Clarice would have needed binoculars to see it, had it been light.

Calypso's eyes grew distant. "The one that reads 'Shaw Ranch?'"

"That's the one," Clarice said with a disbelieving laugh. "No wonder you love the view from up here. You can probably see all the way into town."

Calypso turned to stare into the valley. "It's a singularly picturesque town."

Aria looked between Calypso and the town incredulously. "Wait—can you actually see individual objects down there?"

Calypso's eyes brightened as she stared toward the town. "There's a white van parked on Main Street. It bears the inscription 'Swanson's Cleaning Service.'"

Clarice gaped at Aria. "That's *insane*."

Aria grinned excitedly, walking back to rejoin them. "What other superpowers have you been hiding? Things you think are normal for everyone?"

Calypso pursed her lips. "I've always been rather fast. As a child, I won every race by a significant margin—but perhaps the others were merely slow. Truthfully, I never exerted myself, so I am quite uncertain as to my actual upper limits."

Aria studied Calypso intently. "Now I'm really curious just *how* fast, especially now that you weigh practically nothing."

Clarice tapped her nose. "What about smell? I wonder how keen your sense of smell is compared to humans."

Calypso looked amused. “Are we truly about to engage in a nasal competition?”

Clarice smirked. “You know it. Humans are terrible at smelling compared to animals. Dogs can sniff my hand and tell what I ate a day ago, but since you don’t eat, how sharp is *your* sense of smell?”

Calypso inhaled deeply. “I smell some kind of fruit— strawberry, I suspect—along with a hint of lotion... and nail lacquer.”

Clarice froze. Calypso hadn’t even leaned closer; she remained several feet away.

“I think it’s safe to assume you have us beat in the smelling department, too,” she said faintly.

Aria shared an awed smile with her and said, “That’s a safe bet. We have a *freaking superhero* with us. An honest-to-god superhero.”

Calypso looked down shyly, a faint smile curving her lips as her cheeks glowed in the light from her eyes.

Clarice tapped her lips thoughtfully. “What else is there? Oh, I know. How strong are you?”

Calypso shrugged. “I haven’t the foggiest notion. I don't believe I’ve ever had cause to lift anything heavier than a cello.”

Clarice smiled at her challengingly. “Could you lift me?”

Calypso hesitated, looking at Clarice uncertainly.

“Don’t make it weird,” Clarice winked, walking over to stand in front of her. “I’m a hundred and fifteen pounds. Let’s see what you’ve got.”

Calypso hesitantly put her hands under Clarice’s armpits. She braced herself and then effortlessly lifted Clarice above her head.

Clarice laughed delightedly as Calypso set her down. “So, you’re super strong, too.”

Calypso looked between them doubtfully. “Is a hundred and fifteen pounds truly considered a significant weight?”

Clarice turned to face her sister with a confident smirk. “Show her, Aria.”

Aria stared at her levelly. “You’re going to make fun of me when I can’t do it, aren’t you?”

Clarice gasped with wide-eyed innocence that fooled no one. “I would never!”

Aria rolled her eyes, then braced herself and tried to repeat Calypso’s feat. She pushed up as hard as she could, but Clarice wouldn’t budge. With a growl and a blush, she bear-hugged Clarice and finally managed to lift her several inches off the ground.

Clarice grinned triumphantly at Calypso. "See? Super strong. Which is crazy, considering how light you are. Then again, Aria might just be a wimp."

Aria narrowed her eyes. "Okay, tough girl, come lift *me* up."

"You're heavier than me, so that wouldn't prove anything," Clarice said reasonably.

Aria raised a doubting eyebrow. "If I'm heavier than you, it's by a few ounces, you pixie—and most of your weight is on top."

Clarice turned to Calypso, her eyes shining. "Go lift Aria up and then tell us who's heavier. If you can make the dice roll whatever you want, you must be able to sense the minute differences in weight between two people."

Calypso folded her arms, making it clear she wasn't going to play along.

"Hey, once might have been a fluke!" Clarice declared insistently. She walked up behind Calypso, took hold of her shoulders, then started guiding her toward Aria. "Come on, this is for science!"

Calypso gently but firmly removed Clarice's hands from her shoulders.

Clarice turned a pleading gaze on Aria. "Come on, Dr. Aria, back me up here. You need a larger sample size than one for any experiment. Besides," she grinned, "it's kinda fun."

Aria's stern mask cracked, the corners of her mouth turning up as she looked at Calypso with a calculating gaze. "Okay, fine."

Calypso's eyes widened in surprise when Aria stepped in front of her. Calypso hadn't known Aria long enough to realize she would do just about anything her sister asked.

Aria raised her arms away from her sides and grinned at Calypso expectantly. Calypso's lips twitched as she looked between the sisters. Aria let out a startled laugh as Calypso hoisted her up with the casual indifference one might show a bag of groceries.

Calypso set her back down with a bemused smile. "You are almost precisely the same weight—which strikes me as rather odd, to be honest."

Aria took a moment to straighten her shirt, then regarded Calypso contemplatively. "It really makes the stories of angels wiping out whole civilizations seem plausible, doesn't it? If all angels are as powerful as you are—if not more—they must be able to squish humans like flies."

Calypso stiffened. "I would never do anything to harm anyone."

Aria placed a reassuring hand on Calypso's forearm. "Oh, we know *you* wouldn't. I'm just referring to the ones from biblical lore."

Calypso still looked troubled, her swirling eyes dimming.

"What's wrong?" Aria asked softly.

Calypso bit her lip nervously. "What if I'm not the only one? What if there are others, and their intentions are... less than amicable?"

Aria stroked her arm soothingly. "I'm pretty sure we'd have heard about a rampaging angel in the media. And you've been here for over a hundred years; I seriously doubt there are any others hiding under rocks somewhere."

Calypso nodded, looking reassured. "I daresay you are right. I suppose we might have a clearer idea as to whether there were any others if we knew how I came to be here in the first place."

Clarice tilted her head. "What if you just spontaneously exist? Like, say there's some repository for spiritual energy in the world, and when it reaches a certain level, it spontaneously spawns an angel."

Aria coughed out a skeptical laugh. "That's a pretty wild idea. How would it just spawn a complex entity?"

Clarice shrugged a shoulder. "I don't know. I come up with the theories—it's your job to make them make sense."

Aria gave her a level look. "That's not how theories work."

"Sure it is," Clarice countered. "Remember Newton? Apple falls, he goes 'huh,' and figures it out later."

"That's a hypothesis," Aria said critically.

Clarice clapped her hands to the sides of her face in feigned remorse. "Oh, please forgive me for getting the terminology wrong, Professor Pedant! We're not all physicists."

Calypso looked at Aria in surprise. "You are a physicist? You know, I never truly had the opportunity to learn about your lives after our first meeting."

Aria grimaced. "It's a lot less fun than I thought it'd be. Everything is grant funding and red tape, so you basically work on whatever some big company or government wants you to. Either that, or convince them your own idea is worth investing in—it usually isn't. As a kid, I had visions of making scientific breakthroughs. The reality is far more bureaucratic and less interesting than I imagined."

Calypso chewed her lip in a display of unusual anxiety. "I suppose I never truly considered it, but are you missing work in order to help me?"

Aria shook her head, smiling reassuringly. "I'm on sabbatical. I don't go back for another month. I was testing the waters. That means I was investigating other careers to see what they were like."

Calypso flashed her a brief smile. "You need not explain colloquialisms to me any longer; I can understand your intent through your thoughts."

Aria grinned. “Well, that’s convenient. You’ll be a master of pop culture in no time.”

Calypso looked at Clarice. “And what of yourself? Have you also neglected your professional responsibilities on my account?”

Clarice snorted. “Definitely not. I was an executive for a pretentious tech startup. I won’t shed a single tear for that job. I have more than enough income squirreled away in investments to last a lifetime.”

Calypso’s eyes softened with compassion. “Am I to understand that neither of you found any true fulfillment in your respective career paths?”

Clarice shook her head grimly. “You could say that. Being an adult kinda sucks. I don’t even know what kind of work I’d actually *enjoy* doing. It looked so different from the outside.”

Aria nodded. “Yeah. I always thought I could’ve been happy as a behind-the-scenes YouTuber, but that’s not exactly stable. One algorithm change and poof, career gone.”

Clarice flipped her hair back and folded her arms. “I should have been an author,” she said musingly. “I could have just made shit up all day and gotten paid for it. I could definitely pour my life into authoring.”

Aria eyed her doubtfully. “I don’t know how much authors make, unless you’re a bestseller or something.”

Clarice pointed an admonishing finger at her. “Don’t smash my dreams. I’ll be an author someday, just you wait. I’ll go on adventures and help my characters vanquish evil wherever we find it.”

Aria smiled wryly. “You could certainly write a book based on our lives for the past couple of days. It’d have to be a work of fiction, though, because nobody would believe it.”

Calypso watched them thoughtfully, her face pensive.

Aria took both Calypso’s hands. “You’re the best thing that’s ever happened to our lives,” she said earnestly. “Twice. First, you saved us from a horrible disease, then you saved us from a life of corporate slavery and mediocrity. We have *no* regrets about leaving our old lives behind.”

Clarice nodded fervently. “None whatsoever. Life was pretty damn boring until we found you again.”

Calypso’s expression softened, and she gently squeezed Aria’s hands, a hesitant smile replacing her frown. “Very well... so long as I have not ruined your lives with this debacle.”

Aria impulsively hugged the smiling angel. “Exactly the opposite. I wouldn’t trade *anything* for what we have now.”

Clarice nodded, marveling at Aria's empathetic nature. She could be scarily accurate at reading people, just short of mind reading. She had accurately guessed what was bothering Calypso and put her fears to rest.

Aria had obviously decided the embrace wasn't ending any time soon, soaking up the warmth and love of Calypso's presence.

Clarice glanced down at her hand curiously. It had started tingling while they were talking. The tingle slowly spread up her arm and began emanating throughout her body. She gasped when a flash of warmth erupted in her abdomen, a pleasant sensation almost like a Calypso hug. Her skin gradually brightened until a soft glow pulsed around her in a shining nimbus.

Aria sucked in a surprised breath when she noticed her luminous sister. "Clarice, you're *glowing!*"

Clarice nodded with a bemused smile. "I noticed."

Aria stared at her, eyes wide. "Why are you glowing?" she demanded, a mixture of concern and wonder in her voice.

Clarice shook her head slowly. "I have absolutely *no* idea, but it feels... amazing."

Calypso observed Clarice with a puzzled frown. "There is something else lingering at the edge of my memory once again. I feel as though I ought to know what is happening."

Clarice nodded absently. "It started with the hand your tear landed on."

Small channels of energy began building a geometric grid throughout her body, coursing through them and glowing brighter at the nodes where multiple lines intersected. A moment later, the energy completed its map, the nodes suddenly snapping into place and binding themselves to her body as if it were a template.

The warmth changed to heat, burning away at her insides. There was no pain, but she could feel organs vanishing in flashes of brilliant energy. She felt her stomach and intestines burn away, followed by her kidneys and liver. The torrent of fire moved upward, searing her insides until all that remained was the matrix of energy and the transposed shell of her body. Her brain was the last to go, blasting a radiant light out of her eyes like high beams.

In its wake was joy—pure, effervescent joy.

The glow faded slowly as the energy settled, humming through the lattice that now filled her body. She felt... free. Her old flesh had been a prison, limiting her emotions, her potential. Now... she was boundless.

She drew in a deep breath and marveled at how alive she felt. Her senses unfolded in a thousand directions, each sound, scent, and color dramatically enhanced. She could smell every tree, hear every heartbeat.

She could feel the same energy radiating from Calypso, resonating with her own.

"Oh my god, your *eyes!*" Aria breathed.

"What about my eyes?" Clarice asked, then grinned when she heard the power in her own voice.

Aria gazed at her in awe. "They're lavender, like Calypso's used to be. Are you..." she licked her lips and started again. "Are you an angel now, too?"

Clarice smiled, instantly charging the area with radiance. The joy bubbling inside her was unstoppable. Was this what Calypso always felt like—so *alive* that existence itself sang?

Clarice nodded slowly. "I think I might be," she said, her voice throbbing with an authority that would make gods envious. She laughed, and radiance exploded away from her. "Can you hear my freaking voice? It sounds so freaking cool!"

Aria nodded, wide-eyed. She stared at her formerly human sister with something close to reverence. "I could listen to that voice all day."

Clarice laughed again, the sound lighting up the night with its exuberance.

Aria shook her head slowly. "I thought you were pretty before, but now... wow."

Clarice waggled her eyebrows and giggled, reveling in the supercharged energy of her new body.

Calypso stood dumbfounded, her voice scarcely above a whisper. "How can this be? Was I merely a human who became an angel?"

Clarice nodded, unable to stop smiling. "I think that may just be the case. I can't believe how much better I feel. Life before this wasn't even living—it was just existing."

Aria watched her in wonder, unable to look away. "You think Calypso's tear on your hand is responsible for the change?"

Clarice shrugged. "That seems the most likely explanation." She suddenly grinned mischievously. "And yes, Aria, I still have *passionate* parts."

Aria's cheeks flamed, but she laughed helplessly through the blush. "You would not *believe* how hard it was to ask Calypso that question."

Calypso furrowed her brows, her eyes darting between the two sisters. "But one of my tears made contact with Aria as well. Ought she not to be undergoing a similar transformation?"

Clarice looked at Aria thoughtfully. "That's true. It started while we were talking about careers—right after I said I wanted to be an author, go on adventures, and help my characters vanquish evil wherever we found it."

Aria's brow wrinkled. "You think something may have activated it? Like your intent or something?"

Clarice smiled wryly. "We're freaking *angels*, Aria. I said I wanted to vanquish evil—and I meant it. Maybe it has something to do with angels standing for truth and justice and all that jazz."

Aria snorted dryly. "I want to vanquish evil, too. I don't think you have to be a—" she broke off, her eyes widening as she looked down at her hand in shock. "It's tingling."

Clarice raised her fist in the air and cheered loudly into the night. "One more angel coming up!"

Aria began to glow—softly at first, then blindingly bright. She gasped as light poured from her skin. Clarice felt the same lattice of energy unfurling within her sister that had awakened inside her own body. The transformation built to a crescendo of radiance before fading, leaving Aria standing in rapturous wonder.

Her green eyes were gone, replaced by radiant lavender, and her red hair shimmered like molten copper in moonlight. Her already beautiful face had become ethereal, the kind that poets would weep to describe.

Aria turned to Calypso, eyes wide. "Is this how you always feel? I can't believe how *good* I feel!"

Calypso drank in the sight of the transformed sisters. "I have no recollection of ever being human, so I cannot truly compare."

"You know," Aria said, her voice filled with such heartwarming energy that the area seemed colder without it, "Clarice's first theory about you was that you were an amnesiac angel. I'm starting to wonder if something traumatic happened to you in the years you can't remember. Maybe you were dying or sick and somehow came into contact with an angel tear. Perhaps there wasn't much left of your mind when the transformation happened."

Calypso nodded slowly, her expression thoughtful. "A scenario of that nature *would* provide a rational explanation for my total absence of recollection."

Clarice studied Calypso's energy matrix intently. "Can you feel our meridians?"

Calypso looked at her blankly. "I beg your pardon? Your *what*, exactly?"

Clarice peered at her closely. "I can sense a matrix of channels and nodes with energy flowing throughout your body, just like Aria's."

Calypso shook her head, her lips drawing into a perplexed frown. "No, I perceive nothing of that description. Can you, Aria?"

Aria nodded slowly. "When I look past your physical form, I can see billions of energy lines woven together—like a living lattice of light."

Clarice tilted her head quizzically. "I wonder if there were complications with your transformation since you were still a child. Maybe this process is only supposed to happen to adults."

Aria brightened. "Maybe that's what those hints of memories are you've been getting," she suggested hopefully. "Maybe something will eventually trigger a full recall."

Calypso studied the two of them intently. "I do not believe I can hear your thoughts any longer. Could you direct a thought towards me?"

Clarice blinked, then stared back at Calypso silently. "*I want to do things to you that'll make you blush for years.*"

Calypso shook her head. "Nothing. It would seem that angels' thoughts are protected."

Clarice sighed regretfully. "That's pretty disappointing. I was going to have *so* much fun sending you scandalous thoughts."

"Behave," Aria said automatically, though it was spoiled slightly by her radiant smile.

Clarice stepped closer to Aria and inhaled deeply. "My god, you smell delicious—like sweet innocence and passion fruit. What do I smell like?"

Aria's cheeks flushed, proving they didn't need blood to blush. She sniffed Clarice, and her ears grew as red as her face. "I don't even know what to compare it to."

Clarice's eyebrows rose. "Try."

Aria quickly looked away with a mumbled, "Seduction."

Clarice smiled... seductively. "Hmm, I like it. It's weird how we smell like ideas." She moved over to Calypso and breathed in a lungful of her scent. "Calypso smells absolutely delectable—passion and roses wrapped in honey."

Emily's voice suddenly called up to them from the ladder below. "Are you two ever going to sleep? What's with all the cheering, Clarice?"

Aria shared an impish look with Clarice, and they both dissolved into peals of helpless laughter.

"Your voices sound...odd," Emily said, concern creeping into her tone.

Aria's eyes sparkled with excitement. "Hold on, Mom, we're coming down."

"Yeah, that's definitely *not* your normal voice, Aria," Emily said warily.

Clarice moved to the ladder, winked at Aria, then jumped, landing lightly on the third floor in front of Emily and eliciting a startled squawk. Aria followed, touching down as gracefully as a cat.

Clarice grinned jubilantly at their goggle-eyed mother. "Instead of Tweedledee and Tweedledum, you can now call us your little angels."

Calypso followed their lead and jumped down next to them.

"How?" was all Emily could manage, her eyes wide and glistening.

Clarice grinned, gesticulating excitedly as she explained their transformation. "We think one of Calypso's tears created some kind of angel seed. When we said we wanted to vanquish evil, it triggered the transformation. It was so freaking cool, Mom! Everything feels alive and all our senses are *insanely* sharp. Don't even get me started on the euphoria. It's like we were living in shadows before this."

Emily stood transfixed, tears brimming as Clarice's radiant aura bathed her in warmth. Clarice pulled her close, hugging her carefully so she wouldn't accidentally crush her.

"We also discovered that angels are basically superheroes," Clarice continued, her voice resonant and melodic. "Vision, hearing, strength, speed—you name it. It's like we're wired for awesomeness."

Emily was silent for a long moment, soaking in the radiance. Clarice remembered how that feeling had once only come from Calypso's embrace. Now it was hers, and it was with her *all* the time.

After releasing her, Emily looked at Calypso. "Does Calypso have all these abilities, too?"

Clarice laughed ruefully. "She sure does, but she didn't know she had them. She has no memory of ever being human, so she didn't know she was basically a goddess. When we were testing her for superpowers before we transformed, we had her lift me into the air. She did it like I weighed nothing and was *surprised* when Aria couldn't do the same thing."

Emily chuckled, watching Calypso fondly. "Wow, so we've had a powerhouse with us the entire time and never knew it. I get the feeling she never had any need to use superhuman powers in the life she lived before this. She spent all her time dedicated to music and healing children."

Aria looked at Clarice speculatively. "I wonder if *we* can heal people."

Clarice narrowed her eyes. "I suppose we'd have to try making a song to do it, the way Calypso does. Wait a minute. She also sees people's auras, and that's how she knows they're sick. All I see in Mom are her meridians with energy flowing through them. Calypso can't see meridians, though. Is it possible her mind transposed meridians into auras?"

Calypso pursed her lips, studying Emily. "I have seen auras since childhood. I wonder whether my young mind simply learned to interpret them in a manner it could comprehend, whereas you perceive a more complex version of what is occurring within people's bodies, as your minds were more developed when the transformation took place."

Clarice nodded, looking closely at Emily's meridians. The energy flowed freely, with no snarls or breakpoints. "That makes sense. I'd need to see other people to know for sure, but I think when Calypso strengthened their auras, it cleaned their meridians. We'd need to see someone who's unwell to confirm."

Emily arched a curious brow at her daughters. "Do you two no longer require sleep, either?"

Clarice exhaled, her face bordering on euphoria. "I can't even imagine trying to sleep with this energy coursing through me. If it's always like this, we *definitely* won't need sleep."

Aria sighed, frowning. "I'm not sure how I feel about that. I kind of like sleeping."

Clarice gently took her hands, shivering as an almost intimate energy was exchanged between them. "Humans need sleep to process memories, repair wear and tear, and relieve stress. We don't. We remember everything perfectly, and with this constant stream of radiance, we'll never get stressed again."

Aria nodded absently, her cheeks warming as she looked down at their clasped hands.

"Or age," Calypso added with a wry smile. "I was remarkably unobservant, was I not?"

"Yeah," Aria said fondly. "But that's what made you so endearing."

Calypso smiled shyly at the two new angels. "If you two were not such wonderful people and had not gone so far out of your way to spoil me, this never would have happened. I do not believe angels cry very often."

"You have a point," Clarice admitted musingly. She squeezed Aria's hands once before releasing them. "I can't imagine what it'd take to make me cry with all this positive energy running through my system."

Emily tilted her head inquisitively. "So, how does this affect our plans going forward? We were trying to keep one angel safe. Now we have three, and apparently, you're superheroes."

Clarice shared a look with Aria and Calypso. "I feel like we can still push forward with the same plan. Calypso is the world-famous musician everyone knows. We can still use her connections with former patients to create a support system. We can also follow Uncle Devon's plan to destroy the nanobots in the shadow government contractors and attempt to break their stranglehold on society."

She paused as a thought occurred to her. "I'm starting to wonder if the *rumor* of her being an angel might also help our cause. She has a *lot* of fans, and if they had to march on Washington D.C. and throw bureaucrats out of their offices, they'd do it for her if she asked—especially if they believed she isn't just a wonderful human helping people, but an actual angel."

"So, you don't want her to announce it publicly?" Aria asked, her melodic voice humming like a chord of compassion in the air.

"No," Clarice said with a wry smile. "If we confirmed it, every major religion on Earth would lose their shit. It's probably better to work quietly through our network."

Aria frowned. "Speaking of which, I have a video conference with some former patients later this morning. It might be weird if they see me as I am now. Maybe Calypso should meet with them instead. She'd even know all their names by sight."

"Good idea," Clarice said, nodding. She tilted her head at Calypso. "Are you okay with that?"

"Of course," Calypso said with an eager smile. "I should like to see how they are faring in any case. Thus far, you two are the only former patients I have met."

Emily yawned. "Okay, I'm going to try and get some sleep with what's left of the night." A wry smile curved her lips. "Though I'm not sure I'll be able to sleep now, knowing my little angels really are angels."

Clarice and Aria burst out laughing, filling the room with warmth. Emily smiled at them fondly as she felt the waves of radiance wash over her. She gave them each a long hug, then went to her room, smiling softly.

7 – RUMINATIONS

Aria stepped back from the camera and gestured to Calypso. “Okay, the call is live. It’s all you once they join.”

Calypso stepped in front of the camera and sat, her hands clasped lightly on her lap. “I wonder who it will be.”

The invite list was a patchwork of pseudonyms and old email addresses, with no indication of the person’s real name. The three of them had spent the remainder of the night theorizing about angels, whether to reveal their angelic nature in the morning, and what they should do if their budding network of former patients was actually successful.

The screen changed as their first meeting participant arrived. A dark-haired young man in his early twenties blinked at the screen, then froze, his eyes widening in disbelief.

“Hello, Jason,” Calypso greeted him with a warm smile. “It has been nearly thirteen years. How have you been?”

Jason just stared, his jaw slack. The swirling galaxies in her violet eyes reflected faintly in his own. After a long moment, he inhaled sharply.

“Calypso!” he blurted out. “I had no *idea* you were the one I’d be talking to!”

She smiled teasingly. “Surprise! Tell me, how have you been? What have you been doing with yourself all this time?”

“I’m great!” he exclaimed, grinning ear to ear. “I’m at MIT, studying cybersecurity! I can’t wait to tell my parents I got to talk to you again!”

Calypso’s laughter rang out like silver bells, filling the air with warmth. “How are Mark and Lisa? The last time I saw them, they were beside themselves with worry.”

Jason's grin softened. "They're good. We all knew you were NOTESTOREMEMBER, but we kept our mouths shut."

Calypso gave a sheepish cough. "In all honesty, I was quite unaware that the channel had gained any notoriety. I merely utilized it as a repository for my late-night compositions—a means of securing them for future reference. It wasn't until Aria and Clarice visited me that I realized... apparently, I'm famous."

Jason blinked. "You didn't know you were the most popular musician in the world?" he asked incredulously.

"I had no idea," she laughed, self-deprecating and sweet. "I devoted myself to music and healing children to the exclusion of nearly everything else. Aria and Clarice arrived just in time and helped me escape before the media—or certain shadow agencies—managed to find me."

"Holy shit," Jason breathed. "The world owes those two big time. I saw them in the footage of that biker. Did you really bring that guy back to life?"

Calypso nodded, smiling softly. "I did."

Jason leaned closer, worry creasing his brow. "Are you sure it's safe to use video like this? Those agencies could trace you."

She waved a dismissive hand. "Aria and Clarice have an uncle who was previously employed by one of those organizations. He is... shall we say, remarkably resourceful. We are currently obscured behind several layers of misdirection."

Jason nodded, still frowning. He took a deep breath and straightened. "Okay, what can I do to help?"

Calypso's grateful smile could have melted steel. "You have my thanks, Jason. We are currently establishing a network of former patients in the hope of securing additional support. There exists an organization known as 'The Agency' which oversees the majority of clandestine operations globally. They infect their operatives with nanobots designed to terminate the host should they prove disobedient or compromise sensitive data. I am capable of neutralizing these horrific devices via a live broadcast, effectively dismantling the mechanisms of their enslavement."

Jason's eyebrows shot up. "You can cure them remotely?"

She nodded. "Quite so, but it is imperative that we maximize our exposure before The Agency intervenes to terminate the transmission. We are seeking to enlist specialists capable of ensuring widespread visibility once the broadcast begins."

Jason leaned back, his eyes narrowed in thought. "I could try recruiting some White Hats and forming a team. Would you be willing to appear on video if we need to prove we're really working with you?"

She smiled, her cheeks dimpling. "By all means."

Jason's eyes lit up. "Then here's an idea. We could hijack digital billboards, smart TVs, even phones—anything connected to the net—and force them to stream your broadcast when it goes live. With a bigger team, we could scale it globally."

Calypso's eyes sparkled with delight. "That is brilliant, Jason. Aria created a secure contact profile you may use to reach us at any hour, day or night. We're always available."

He laughed. "Don't you ever sleep?"

"In point of fact, no," she said with a wry smile. "That is precisely why the NOTESTOREMEMBER channel was established. I spent my nights dedicated to musical composition."

Jason blinked. "You don't sleep? Like, *ever*?"

"Ever," Calypso said again, her riveting voice calm and otherworldly. "And I still wish to continue healing children. I believe I may now be able to do so remotely, through live video. If we could establish connections with hospitals across the world, we could reach thousands of children at once—not merely children, but millions of other people as well."

"Seriously?" Jason whispered, a hand going to his mouth. "Oh man, that would be the most epic event in history."

Calypso nodded, her expression growing serious. "My chief concern is that The Agency could shut it down during the broadcast, so secrecy is absolutely vital." She smiled, her warmth returning like a beacon. "I cannot adequately express how grateful I am for your assistance."

Jason swallowed hard. "I owe you my life, Calypso. Anything you need, just ask."

Her smile deepened. "Thank you, Jason."

"Um," he hesitated. "Can I ask one thing? Did you really... remember my name after all these years?"

Her expression softened. "I remember everyone's name. It is inscribed upon your aura, and I am capable of perfect recall."

He stared, speechless, then shook himself. "I've heard people online saying you're an angel," he said tentatively. "I know it sounds crazy, but is there any truth to that?"

Calypso nodded. "I am an angel, though not the sort described in human scripture. I should prefer to distance myself from religious claims."

Jason nearly fell out of his chair. "Wait, *what*? You *are* an angel?"

"Yes," she said matter-of-factly.

He took a deep, nervous breath. "So, uh... do I still have a shot at the pearly gates?"

Calypso blinked, then sighed. "I'm sorry, Jason. I am no messenger of any deity. It is probable that our kind visited this world in the distant past, but I suspect that religious narratives have since obscured our true nature. We are not divine, so far as I know. We are merely another species with abilities that may appear miraculous to humans. I live to help the sick and create music. That is all."

Jason let out a shaky, relieved laugh, nervously running a hand through his hair. "Oh, thank God. I thought for a second all that Bible nonsense was literal. That's... actually a huge relief."

Calypso laughed a pure, radiant sound that made the screen flicker. Jason felt warmth and happiness surge through him, the same radiance he had felt as a child in the hospital.

Her eyes still bright with mirth, Calypso asked, "Do you have any further questions?"

Jason looked around frantically, anxiously running a hand through his hair. "I—uh—probably. But I'll think of them an hour from now and kick myself."

She laughed, watching him fondly. "Rest assured, we shall speak again soon."

Jason grinned, feeling as if light itself had wrapped around him. "I can't wait. I'll get to work immediately. Bye for now, Calypso."

"Goodbye, Jason," she said warmly, and ended the call.

Aria stepped up beside Calypso's seat, resting a warm hand on her shoulder. "That went really well. He turned out pretty good, didn't he?"

Calypso nodded, her eyes soft with affection. "He certainly did. He was utterly terrified when I first met him, convinced he was going to die. I gave him a hug and promised him that his time of fear and pain was over."

Warmth traced a line down Aria's cheek, and she brushed away a quicksilver tear. "Now look what you've done," she scolded gently. "You've gone and made me cry."

Calypso rose and pulled her into a tight embrace. Instantly, Aria felt their meridians intertwine, energy flowing between them in a radiant exchange that was both comforting and deeply intimate. Calypso's essence flooded through her, mingling seamlessly with her own.

Calypso shivered with delight. "Embracing another angel carries an intimacy comparable to a kiss. I realize I have expressed this previously, but I am immensely grateful to have encountered you and Clarice once more. It is a profound relief to no longer be alone."

Aria felt her tremble with emotion and began stroking her hair gently. Calypso melted into the touch, and the world seemed to fall away.

"I'm glad we came back to you, too," Aria whispered, her angelic voice like a soft song. "It feels like a missing piece of my heart finally fell into place."

Aria wasn't sure how long they stood there, wrapped in shared warmth and radiance. Since her transformation, she no longer needed sleep. With the realization of her ageless nature, her perception of time had subtly changed—a single hour felt no longer than a breath. They might have stood there forever had they not been interrupted.

"Do I need to fetch a pry bar?" Clarice asked dryly from the doorway. "I think the two of you may have fused together."

Aria didn't move. "We have. A pry bar won't work."

Clarice walked closer, her eyes speculative. "I wonder if we even take damage like humans do. We should probably run some tests with sharp objects, blunt force trauma... that kind of thing."

Aria grinned. "I nominate you to be the one who gets run over by the car."

Calypso rested her head on Aria's shoulder, speaking softly. "I was in a car accident once. A lorry lost its brakes on a steep hill and sent my car over a cliff into a canyon some twenty meters below. The car was completely crushed, and one of my favorite harps was destroyed, yet I walked away without a scratch. I even had to push the roof off in order to get out. At the time, I simply believed I had been extraordinarily fortunate."

Clarice stepped behind Calypso and slid her arms around her waist, cocooning the musician between her and Aria. "That must have been terrifying."

Calypso shivered in their arms. "Very much so. The authorities found it quite impossible to reconcile my survival with the state of the wreckage, much less the fact that I walked away uninjured."

Aria flushed as intimate energy cycled between the three of them. She could feel Clarice's arms pressed between her and Calypso's abdomens. Clarice's head rested opposite Aria's on Calypso's other shoulder, close enough to kiss if Aria switched sides. Her chest heaved against Calypso's with rapid breaths as her imagination went on a joyride.

Clarice sighed. "I wish we could have been there for you."

Aria reined in her amorous thoughts and nodded, tightening her arms around Calypso. "Yeah, you shouldn't have had to deal with that alone. We're here now, though, and you'll never be alone again."

Calypso closed her eyes and melted into their arms. "Yes," she murmured, smiling beatifically as a few silver tears slid down her cheeks. "You certainly are."

They held Calypso between them in silence, reveling in the radiant energy bridging their meridians. Clarice loosened her arms slightly, and Aria's breath caught at the feel of soft, warm breasts brushing against the back of her hands.

Clarice moved her head and Aria suddenly found herself staring into her sister's eyes, their noses touching and their lips millimeters apart. Clarice's eyes sparkled as she held Aria's gaze, her expressive lips curving into a flirtatious smile.

"Hmm... I suppose that means we really *can* survive blunt force trauma," Clarice murmured, her lips so close to Aria's that they occasionally brushed together. "There are a lot of things we'll have to test in order to grow familiar with our new bodies... for science, of course."

Aria shivered at the barely veiled suggestion of future intimacy. Calypso shivered in response, and Clarice's smile grew more seductive.

An annoying ding shattered the tension, and Aria nearly destroyed the computer and the damnable meeting reminder.

Clarice glanced at the computer screen and grinned. "The next video call starts in a minute. Wanna give them a cuddle show?"

Aria sighed and reluctantly released Calypso. As they stepped apart, the soft hum of their shared energy faded. Aria darted a look at Clarice as she stepped back from a blushing Calypso and found her sister watching her with hungry eyes. Unable to hold Clarice's gaze, she quickly looked away, heat flooding her angelic body.

Calypso took a steadying breath and stepped back in front of the computer, her expression curious. "I wonder who it will be this time. It was remarkably fortuitous that Jason was already proficient in cybersecurity."

Aria nodded, pulling her hair over one shoulder and absently twining it around her finger. "Yeah, that was perfect. I'm excited to see who's next."

She let out a soft moan when she felt Clarice's hands begin kneading into her shoulders. Her sister's massages were the closest thing to intimacy Aria had experienced over the years. Clarice had found a way to channel all her desire and passion into shoulder and back massages. Something about the intensity and rhythm of her sister's kneading fingers made it a far more intimate experience, bordering on erotic.

The massages had become a kind of ritual for the two of them, taking turns each night. It had been another excuse to be close to Clarice, though she ached for more. Aria doubted she would ever be able to put the same kind of sensual intent into her own massages, but not for lack of trying.

Calypso started the next call and waited for their guest to join. They didn't have to wait long.

A woman in her forties appeared on the screen, her familiar, motherly face framed by the glow of a home office. Several others stood behind her, most of them with gray hair and lined faces.

Julia's eyes widened when she recognized Calypso, then she broke into a radiant smile.

"It is lovely to see you, Julia," Calypso said warmly, her voice catching as she gazed at one of the people she had interacted with most over the years. A single quicksilver tear traced down her cheek. "I can hardly believe you are truly here."

"Calypso!" Julia cried, her eyes shining. "I had no idea you were the one we'd be meeting with. Are you safe?"

Calypso laughed, the sound filled with pure joy. "Aria and Clarice's uncle has a safe house where we may speak without fear of discovery. Apparently, certain shadow organizations would prefer me dead, so we are exercising caution."

Julia's face darkened. "I saw the explosion at their apartment on the news and just *knew* it wasn't a gas leak."

Calypso nodded calmly. "We have a plan to deal with those attempting to kill us," she said confidently. "We are reaching out to former patients in order to establish a support network."

Julia's reply was instant, a smile breaking through her tears. "Say no more. I have all the records from our hospital, and I can get the others as well."

Calypso beamed. "Julia, you are an absolute lifesaver. I believe I can heal people through live broadcasts, but we'll need coordinators at each hospital to ensure everyone is watching. The first event must reach as many people as possible before The Agency catches on and attempts to stop us. We have just spoken with a former patient at MIT who specializes in cybersecurity and is going to help organize the digital side of the network. I'll put the two of you in contact."

Julia's eyes widened. "You could really heal people over a broadcast? That's incredible!" She smiled indulgently. "You know, I always suspected you were the reason so many children recovered when no one could explain why." Her smile trembled. "You really are an angel, Calypso."

Calypso hesitated, her eyes glowing more brightly. "Um... regarding that. I do not intend to announce it publicly, as it would cause utter chaos within the religious world—but yes, I am an angel."

Julia and the people behind her stared in stunned silence.

Calypso quickly added, "The narratives regarding our kind in religious texts are... profoundly inaccurate. We do not serve a deity. We are merely... distinct from humanity, possessing certain capabilities that may appear miraculous, but we are most certainly not divine messengers."

A middle-aged man behind Julia spoke up. "What kind of abilities?"

"Well," Calypso said slowly. "We are considerably more durable. We do not sleep or eat. Our senses are far keener, and we do not age. And no," she added with a faint grin, "we are not genderless."

Julia burst out laughing. "That'll probably be the first question people ask when they find out."

Calypso's lips curved into a small smile. "We have no particular objection to people uncovering the truth, but we are hesitant to provide an official confirmation. Clarice is of the opinion that it would ignite a global religious conflict."

"I agree," Julia said, her expression sobering. "The major faiths might ignore rumors, but if you publicly confirmed it, they'd have to respond, either by praising you or condemning you—especially since you claim not to serve a god."

The man behind Julia muttered, "They'd probably call you part of the fallen host who were cast out of Heaven."

"You said we," an older woman with silver hair interjected. "Does that mean there are other angels?"

Calypso hesitated, glancing toward Aria and Clarice.

"Just two," Clarice whispered from behind Aria.

Calypso's gaze returned to the screen. "I am aware of two others. I cannot say with any certainty whether additional individuals exist, but I am keen to find out."

Julia's voice warmed. "How are Clarice and Aria doing?"

Calypso smiled affectionately. "They are my angels." Her words seemed to brighten the room around Julia with their warmth. "They spared me a significant amount of distress. Were it not for their intervention, I suspect I would currently be confined to a laboratory, undergoing a rather invasive anatomical study."

Julia blanched. "That's horrifying," she said fiercely. "Anyone who'd do such a thing deserves the worst punishment imaginable. Those two have my gratitude, and the gratitude of every parent you've ever helped."

Calypso looked up at Aria and Clarice, her swirling eyes filled with love. Through the screen, Julia and the others felt waves of warmth and joy radiate outward.

"Wow," Julia whispered. "You really *can* affect people through video."

Calypso took a deep breath, smiling hopefully. "I'm rather counting on it. I should very much like to attempt healing new patients—provided any are available."

Julia shook her head, gesturing toward the silvery-haired woman. "You healed all ours just a few days ago, but Leticia here works at New Hope Hospital and can arrange something."

Leticia nodded quickly. "Absolutely. I'll contact them and let you know when we can set it up. Can we reach you at the same email you used for this meeting?"

"Indeed, this address is quite suitable," Calypso confirmed. She looked at the men in the background curiously. "If I may, what are the respective roles of James and Malek?"

Both men blinked, looking startled.

Julia glanced back at them. "You know James and Malek?"

Calypso leaned closer to the screen. "Their names are inscribed upon their auras. A further angelic characteristic is that we possess infallible memory. I had not realized until quite recently that humanity lacks perfect recall."

Julia laughed ruefully. "I guess that makes introductions unnecessary. James heads hospital security, and Malek's a retired doctor. James actually discovered you were healing children a few years ago. He found out while reviewing security footage for an unrelated incident and saw your eyes glowing."

Calypso sighed. "It appears I was not nearly as inconspicuous as I had imagined. Thank you, James, for maintaining my confidentiality."

He scowled. "I figured the miracles would stop if word got out—as that idiot who blabbed online proved."

Aria barely restrained a moan as Clarice's fingers continued their magic. She struggled to keep her eyes open as she melted back into Clarice's hands, her head lolling back as bliss coursed through her body. Clarice's contact didn't have the same level of intimacy as a hug, but combined with the massage, it pushed the already intensely intimate energy exchange well past what she had felt in Calypso's arms. Her cheeks flushed as interesting sensations in embarrassing places came alive.

Julia rubbed her hands eagerly. "When should we meet again?"

Calypso glanced up at them, and Aria pulled herself back to the present. "Maybe a weekly call to share progress?"

Julia nodded, her face alight with purpose. "That sounds perfect. It's wonderful to see you safe, Calypso. Let us know if you need anything else."

"Thank you," Calypso said warmly. "You are all such remarkable individuals."

Julia and the others gasped as the weight of her gratitude washed over them, filling their hearts with radiance just before the call ended.

Aria reached up and gratefully squeezed Clarice's hand on her shoulder. "Well, that was unexpected. Of all the people we could've ended up meeting, it turned out to be one of the few people you knew."

Clarice looked upwards suspiciously. "That was pretty bizarre. I wonder if there's some divine intervention going on here after all."

Aria snorted. "Maybe monkeys will fly out of my butt, too."

Clarice smirked. "You don't have a butt anymore, silly." She paused, tilting her head to stare at the ceiling with a look of deep reflection. "Hmm... maybe that's why they thought angels were genderless." She slapped her butt for emphasis.

Aria groaned, pressing her palms to her eyes. "Thanks for taking the conversation to a weird place, Clarice."

Clarice spread her arms wide. "Making conversations awkward is a public service I'm *always* willing to perform," she declared magnanimously. "I still think the lack of body hair might be the best trait so far—I'll never need to shave my legs again." She dropped her arms and grinned mischievously. "We should see if Uncle Devon's recovered from the shock we gave him this morning."

Aria giggled at the memory. Devon had come out to the veranda that morning and found the three angels setting out the breakfast spread. Aria offered him coffee with a bright smile, her lavender eyes vivid against her lustrous red hair. He nearly dropped the coffee when his mind registered what he was seeing. Then Clarice had joined her and asked if he wanted eggs in a basket, and he *did* drop his coffee. He had been staring at them in awe until they had left for the video call.

Aria rubbed the back of her neck, smiling ruefully. "We probably should've let Mom warn him first."

Clarice sniggered wickedly. "Screw that. This way was a lot more fun."

Aria shook her head, smiling. "You are *so* bad."

"I'm an angel," Clarice objected playfully. "Angels *can't* be bad, or they wouldn't be angels."

Aria folded her arms, eyeing her sister doubtfully. "So, anything you do is good, no matter how bad, because you're an angel?"

Clarice beamed, her lavender eyes shining with sincerity. "Hey, you get it! We can do no evil, say no evil, and hear no evil."

Aria facepalmed and turned away. "You're *too* much, you know that?"

Clarice grinned impishly. “Too much goodness. Come on, let’s talk to Uncle. I wanna see if we can make a trip to town and get some additional instruments. We’re severely lacking right now.”

Aria nodded, winding a lock of her long hair around a finger. “I guess with no need for sleep, we’ll have a lot more time for composing. Okay, let’s convince him to sneak us into a music shop. I’m going to max out my credit card.”

Clarice cuffed her shoulder. “You can’t use your credit card, dummy,” she chided. “They can track purchases. I probably should have pulled out a few hundred grand after we left.”

Aria’s face fell. “Oh, yeah. How are we going to pay for more instruments, then?”

Clarice winked slyly. “We’re going to practice wheedling. Did you forget that Uncle Devon is filthy, stinking rich?”

Aria laughed helplessly. “You’re a bad angel. I don’t care how much you try to pretzel the definitions of comparative morality, you’re a *bad* angel.”

Clarice grinned impishly. “I can live with that.” She thrust her chin up challengingly. “Race you to the veranda.”

Instead of answering, Aria exploded away, leaving an evil giggle in her wake.

“Cheater!” Clarice yelled, bolting after her.

Still giggling, Aria flew down the hallway at impossible speeds. She rounded a corner and reached the veranda in under two seconds, with Clarice only a split second behind.

Devon and Emily flinched at the sudden influx of wind and the appearance of the two angels.

Clarice glared. “I didn’t say go, cheater. Who’s the bad angel now?”

Aria smirked triumphantly. “You’re just a sore loser. Nobody likes a sore loser.”

“Them’s fightin’ words, missy!” Clarice declared ominously, advancing menacingly.

Aria held up her hands warningly. “Not in the house,” she said quickly. “We’ll break too much stuff.”

Clarice raised her chin, staring down her nose. “Then you’re coming with me to the great outdoors.” She walked to the edge of the veranda and jumped, dropping twenty feet to the lawn below.

Aria rolled her eyes but couldn’t suppress a grin as she followed. Being able to jump ridiculous distances and run at super speeds was exhilarating on a whole other level.

"This should be good," she heard Emily comment to Devon with a chuckle.

As soon as Aria landed, Clarice grabbed her arm and yanked—hard. Aria expected to be pulled off her feet, but she was *not* expecting to be thrown a hundred feet through the air to crash into an elm tree. She stood and reached for the back of her shirt, where most of the impact had occurred, and found a large rip.

"You are *so* dead," Aria shouted grimly, her face thunderous. "This was one of my *favorite* shirts."

Clarice's look of concern changed to a smirk as she darted the hundred feet in a flash. "It's going to be even more stylish when I'm finished with you."

Aria wished she had taken her martial arts classes more seriously, like Clarice had. When they started college, their mother convinced them to take self-defense courses because, as she put it, "they were too damn pretty and just as helpless." Clarice found a jujitsu instructor during her first semester who taught them throughout their college years. Clarice had been a natural fighter and climbed the ranks quickly, but Aria had been mediocre at best. The close grappling had made her too uncomfortable when practicing with strangers, and too aroused when it was Clarice.

She dropped into a low crouch, trying to keep her eyes on her sister's ridiculously fast form. Clarice used her momentum to skid under Aria's waiting arms, grabbing one of her ankles as she slid past. Aria yelped as she was suddenly airborne again. She tried to right herself as she rocketed through the air, but apparently gravity didn't work like that.

She crashed into the thick branches of half a dozen trees, breaking through them with deafening cracks before slamming into the ground with a thud. Jagged branches had shredded her shirt during her flight, leaving it hanging in tatters and all the goods hanging out. Her pants weren't in much better shape.

Clarice zipped toward her at high speed, sniggering. "Not a bad look for you."

"Seriously, Clarice?" Aria growled, snatching up one of the broken branches. "Are you trying to *completely* undress me?"

Clarice appeared in front of Aria, a wicked grin on her face. "Maybe."

She reached for Aria's arm again but had to jump back when Aria swung the branch. It whistled shrilly as it sliced through the air at supersonic speeds, disintegrating into flaming kindling before it reached Clarice.

Clarice laughed and grabbed Aria's arm before she could pull it back. Aria managed to grab Clarice's wrist as she was pulled overhead. Instead of shooting off into the distance, she pinwheeled around Clarice, tucking both knees in before slamming them into Clarice's hips. They both crashed to the ground with a loud thud.

Knowing she had only milliseconds to capitalize on her superior position, she grabbed Clarice by the shoulder, flipped her face-down into the dirt, and pinned her there with a knee in the middle of her back and Clarice's arms bent behind her.

"You know what's funny?" Clarice said conversationally, her cheek mashed into the soft soil.

Aria grinned insolently. "Your face right now."

"This would've worked if we were still human," Clarice said cheerfully.

Aria frowned but wasn't quick enough. Clarice's legs whipped back with impossible force, striking her squarely in the back. She flew forward, crashing headfirst into a tree a dozen feet away and crumpled unceremoniously to the ground.

Clarice was on her feet, grinning wolfishly. Her angelic beauty was marred only slightly by the dirt and twigs clinging to her face and hair. "That was pretty good. You just need to remember the rules have changed now that we aren't human."

Aria let out a rueful laugh as she stood and looked down at her tattered clothes and back at Clarice, self-consciously pulling her long hair over her shoulders to cover her breasts. Her sister's clothes were still intact, but only barely. "Can you believe how insanely OP we are? I mean, when Calypso lifted you up easily, I knew she was strong, but this is next-level ridiculous."

Clarice smiled exuberantly. "I'm literally giggling myself silly inside at how cool this is." Her eyes sparkled with a blend of wonder and excitement. "The speed alone is nuts. I was trying to push myself a little, but I definitely wasn't going all out. If all angels are this powerful, it's no wonder humans thought we were a step beneath gods."

Aria pursed her lips as she brushed dirt and twigs from her hair. "Maybe that's what the Greek gods really were. If humans saw us back then, they'd absolutely think we were divine. Hell, they think we are *now*."

Clarice frowned, her face growing serious as she also began brushing the twigs and dirt away. "That reminds me: knowing how to make new angels is a pretty big deal. Where would it end if we started transforming humans? Think of a world with billions of angels running around, practically invincible, and no longer beholden to food or sleep. Maybe we should keep the knowledge to ourselves and not change anyone else. As soon as we transform another person, the choice to not make more angels will be out of our hands."

"What about Mom and Dad?" Aria asked pleadingly, her eyes wide and entreating. "If we changed them, they'd be with us forever."

"Of course we'd change them," Clarice said quickly. "Family is different. I just mean... beyond that. Even if we only changed our family, they might have people they'd want to transform, too. It'll spread like wildfire."

"Yeah," Aria murmured, her tone subdued. "And honestly, we don't even know if it'd work for us. Calypso's more evolved than we are. Maybe her tears are special. Maybe she's the only one who can create new angels."

Clarice nodded slowly. "We can find out with Mom, but only *if* she agrees. I can't imagine she would say no, though."

Aria hesitated. "We should talk to Calypso, too. All three of us should agree before making that kind of decision."

Calypso's voice carried effortlessly to them from within the cabin, despite the thousand feet and dense trees between them. "I am perfectly fine with changing your parents and Devon."

Clarice laughed, shaking her head wonderingly. "I still can't get over how powerful our senses are."

Aria's jaw dropped in amazement as she stared at Clarice in disbelief. "Okay, Calypso, how did you go so long not noticing human hearing was so limited?"

An embarrassed silence followed before Calypso answered. "I merely assumed people learned to tune out the additional noise."

Aria exchanged an amused glance with Clarice, then dissolved into giggles. It was kind of adorable how oblivious Calypso had been.

Clarice ran her hands through her thick hair, dislodging more twigs and dirt. "I think we should get Mom's opinion first, but without tipping her off about the angel thing. Just... ask how she feels about immortality. If she seems open to it, we'll get one of Calypso's tears onto her hand without telling her. We could guide her into saying something like, 'I want to vanquish evil,' and see if it triggers anything. That way, if it *doesn't* work, she won't be crushed with disappointment."

Aria nodded slowly. "That's a great idea. It'd be a pretty big rug pull if it failed."

Clarice suddenly burst out laughing.

Aria smiled in anticipation. "What?"

Clarice nodded toward the cabin. “If we changed Uncle Devon, we could just cut him loose and let him take out the bad guys single-handedly.”

Aria laughed delightedly. “Yeah, he’d be like a juggernaut if he had the same power we do. I’m sure he has a lot of pent-up resentment after so many years of slavery.” She twisted a strand of hair around her finger, looking at Clarice speculatively. “I wonder what our limits are. What would it truly take to kill us? How indestructible are we really?”

Clarice nodded slowly. “That presents another problem,” she said pensively. “What if we’re truly immortal and can *never* die—even if we wanted to? For some, that might be more of a curse than a blessing.”

Aria shivered. “Wow, that’s a scary thought. What happens when the sun dies, or the planet explodes? Would we just drift around in space forever?”

Clarice tilted her head, a smile playing on her lips.

Aria raised a curious eyebrow. “What?”

“Do we even need oxygen?” Clarice asked intently. She went completely still.

Aria stared, realizing her sister wasn’t breathing. Tentatively, she stopped as well, waiting for the familiar burn of oxygen deprivation. It never came. Seconds stretched into minutes, and still nothing.

Clarice’s eyes widened with incredulity when she finally broke the silence. “I guess we only need oxygen to vocalize.”

“Do we, though?” Aria countered. “Calypso sings in harmony with herself; she’s creating sound, but not the way humans do. She might be generating vibrations directly from her energy matrix.”

“Good point,” Clarice said, narrowing her eyes. “This energy matrix that replaced our organs must be doing a lot more than we realize. Calypso must’ve learned to manipulate it through music. We need to watch her heal someone and see what the energy looks like in action.”

Aria pursed her lips, absently pulling another twig from her hair. “Her songs are more than just melodies. They’re like templates, channeling energy through intent—like a musical form of guided meditation.”

“Then what about when she brought that man back from the dead?” Clarice asked, glancing back toward the cabin. “Did she just sing him alive?”

Aria shook her head, her perfect memory replaying every detail. “It was different. She was singing, but she was also speaking these words of power, unlike any human language. The words themselves felt... heavy.”

Clarice folded her arms and rested her chin on a fist. "So, did the words have power because she charged them with energy, or do certain words in some divine language hold power on their own?"

She suddenly grinned, her lavender eyes shining with eagerness. "We have *so* much to discover about what we are. When I was transforming, Calypso said she almost understood what was happening, like the knowledge was just out of reach. I wonder if she's learning to connect to some kind of shared consciousness, a racial knowledge network, maybe something like the Akashic Records."

Aria laughed despite herself, prompting an inquiring eyebrow from Clarice.

"Sorry," Aria said, still chuckling. "It's just wild that we're seriously talking about things like energy matrices and Akashic Records. A week ago, we would've thought we'd lost our minds."

Clarice smiled wryly. "Yeah, no kidding. I'm getting philosophical whiplash. All the stuff I used to dismiss as mystical nonsense suddenly feels plausible. I feel like I have to go back and reevaluate everything I thought I knew."

It finally occurred to Aria that she was standing almost completely naked in the forest, her shirt and pants doing more to accentuate her nudity than conceal it. Her hair was the only thing offering any real cover for her chest. Clarice wasn't much better off. Her bra had snapped open, visible beneath the rips in her shirt, and her pink shorts were torn up one leg, held together by only a few threads of the waistband.

Clarice bit her lip when she noticed Aria's slow blush, her eyes sparkling. They stared at each other silently as the weight of their history pushed at their awareness. Aria licked her lips, wishing she had the courage to voice the feelings she had suppressed for so long.

Clarice's amusement faded, and her eyes softened. "Aria, I've been meaning to talk to you for a while now. You're more than my best friend, more than a sister—so much more. I should've had this conversation ages ago, but I was worried you'd feel pressured. I guess I was waiting for something to happen that'd make crossing this gulf easier."

She paused, watching Aria carefully, her lavender eyes searching Aria's face. She took a deep breath. "Now that Calypso resolved your—"

They both froze when their sensitive hearing picked up the sound of a vehicle in the distance.

"Maybe it's just someone exploring," Aria muttered, glancing down the road. She marveled again at the power of her vision. She could see far past the driveway and down the road for miles.

They waited in silence, the unspoken words between them growing heavier. Aria cursed the interruption. She knew that once Clarice opened the door they had both been tiptoeing around, she would finally be able to give voice to all the emotions she had been holding in check—but Clarice had to open it first. They both knew it had to be Clarice.

A pickup truck rounded a bend, still several miles away. Aria studied the driver as he drew closer. His sparse beard couldn't hide the large jowls that jiggled as his truck bounced on the rough road. His gut pressed against the steering wheel, bouncing with each bump. Dark sunglasses reflected the sunlight, and she could even see the large cowboy hat on his dash reflected in the lenses.

Aria looked back at Clarice. "I'm guessing it's just someone going fishing or camping. Maybe we should find some new clothes before we run into a stranger and get mistaken for wild women."

Clarice snorted a laugh, staring at Aria's almost naked form with frank admiration. She met Aria's eyes with unspoken longing and sighed in frustration, shaking her head in disappointment.

Aria opened her mouth, unsure what she was going to say. Nothing came out, and she closed it, hating herself for being such a coward.

Clarice grinned suddenly. "Race you back." She bolted before finishing the sentence, leaving a wicked laugh trailing behind her. Aria rolled her eyes and took off after her, the force of her first step leaving a deep impression in the dirt as she launched forward.

It took only seconds to reach the large cabin. Spotting her uncle on the veranda, she detoured around the side, launching herself into the air outside her bedroom and landing lightly on the three-story deck.

Clarice stood in the doorway on the balcony of her room next door, a smug grin on her face. "I won."

Aria gestured down at her nudity. "I had to detour to avoid Uncle Devon."

Clarice shook her head, smirking. "No, you didn't. You *chose* to detour. It's not like he'd have seen you clearly at the speeds we were going."

"Quiet, you," Aria commanded imperiously. "I'm going to take a shower."

Clarice grinned wryly. "Who would've thought angels could get so dirty."

Aria smiled sardonically as she went through her bedroom door and said, "Fallen angels."

"You definitely fell," Clarice said, her voice carrying clearly from the next room. "You fell a lot."

Aria shook her head and grumbled, "I'm just going to pretend walls still stop sound."

As she turned on the shower, she reflected on how much they would save on razors, since, as Clarice pointed out, angels didn't have body hair. She definitely wouldn't miss the weekly ritual of shaving her legs. It was the little things.

***

After showering and changing, Aria went down to the veranda, where Emily and Devon were eating lunch in the dappled sunlight, with Clarice already deep in discussion beside them.

"I still don't think Calypso should go," Devon was saying, his face serious. "Her presence is too difficult to conceal. If something happens, she wouldn't fight like I know you two would. She's a gentle soul and not cut out for conflict if trouble finds us."

"Agreed," Clarice said firmly. "I never want to risk her being discovered."

Emily studied her dubiously. "Do you really think you're bulletproof? That's not something we can really test."

Clarice nodded confidently, smiling up at Aria. "Aria didn't even get a scratch after I threw her into dozens of elm trees so hard that she broke through branches thicker than her. She swung a stick at me so fast that it literally dissolved into flaming wood chips. We're essentially indestructible."

Devon rubbed his chin, his eyes calculating. "As long as you wear the sunglasses and Aria wears a hat to hide her hair, I don't think this should be a problem." He paused, looking at them pointedly. "And don't hug anyone. You don't seem to be able to stop the emotional effects of angel embraces, and it'd definitely leave an impression."

Aria glanced at Emily and tilted her head. "So it's just Clarice and me going?"

For the first time, she truly saw her mother's age—the soft creases at the corners of her eyes, the silver strands of hair, and the quiet fatigue that came with age. The realization hit Aria like a physical ache. Her mother was aging, and she wasn't. A spike of urgency pressed in on her at the thought of her mother's biological clock inexorably ticking her closer to the end.

Emily sank back into her chair. "That's the plan. I'm totally content to just relax and enjoy this beautiful cabin. I'll leave the hours of travel to the younger crowd."

Aria and Clarice exchanged a look, a shared concern for their mother's age reflected in their eyes. Somehow, they would find a way to keep their family with them.

Devon stood and fished his keys from his pocket, along with a thick wad of cash and a phone. "This phone is safe to use. Your old phones are just liabilities now. Please stick to the speed limit—and don't draw attention. No flying leaps, no glowing, no... theatrics."

"We'll be good," Aria said brightly, pocketing the money.

Clarice grinned mischievously and added, "'Cause we're angels."

Devon and Emily exchanged a worried look as the two angels rose from the table, radiant even in their attempt at normalcy.

Clarice waved with a cheerful, "See you in a few hours!"

* * *

Emily sighed. "Well, I guess there's nothing to do but wait and hope for the best," she said, her voice tinged with worry. "I really hope they're as indestructible as they think. Maybe I should've convinced them to stay another week before leaving our little sanctuary."

Devon sipped his coffee and sighed contentedly. "At their speeds, I doubt they have much to worry about. If something goes wrong, they can simply run. Honestly, if it weren't so attention-grabbing, they could sprint into town instead of driving; it would certainly be faster. I'm still wrapping my head around the insane speeds they can move."

Emily slid deeper into her chair, resting her hands in her lap. "Knowing what we know now, it really makes you look at mythology differently," she said reflectively. "Can you imagine that kind of power in the wrong hands?"

Devon shivered, and a haunted look shadowed his eyes. "I *can* imagine it, and it scares the willies out of me."

Emily exhaled softly. "I've seen the two of them looking at me speculatively whenever my age comes up. I know they're considering transforming me, and probably you, too. They've likely realized what a can of worms that could open. To be honest, immortality has always frightened me. The thought of never reaching an end feels almost claustrophobic."

Devon nodded empathetically, rubbing his chin. "I missed my chance to have a family," he said with a wistful smile. "Once I got wrapped up in contractor work, that option went out the window. I'm pretty sure angels don't have babies, even if they have the equipment. Now that Calypso cleared the nanobots from my system, that option is available to me, and I don't want to trade that opportunity for immortality—at least, not until I've experienced being a father. Who knows? Maybe I'll change my mind down the road somewhere, but for now, I'd rather not undergo the transformation."

"What do you think, Calypso?" Emily asked, knowing the eldest of the angels could hear her anywhere in the house.

When Devon looked around in surprise, Emily tapped her ear meaningfully, and he nodded in understanding.

A moment later, Calypso entered the veranda. She wore a slim skirt with white dragons emblazoned on a cream background. A sleeveless white button-up blouse with a high neck accentuated her hourglass figure. Her long bangs were pulled back, allowing the rest of her brilliant blonde hair to cascade down her back and shoulders. Large, innocent eyes with swirling violet vortexes watched them curiously as she approached, an inquisitive smile on her lips.

Emily had to continually remind herself that this beautiful woman was twice her age. Her ignorance of so much about the world only added to her youthful persona. While Clarice and Aria might look like angels, Calypso possessed an innocence that made her angelic nature feel truly divine.

"Hello, Emily and Devon," Calypso greeted them warmly, filling the veranda with her loving presence. "What might the consequences be if every individual in the world were to be transformed into an angel?"

Devon and Emily exchanged uneasy glances.

Emily drew a breath, her dark eyes speculative. "I suppose everyone would become immortal and invincible. Resources would no longer be necessary, since angels don't require sustenance. But can angels have children? Would the population remain fixed at seven billion forever?"

Devon leaned back in his chair and reclaimed his coffee. "You have to wonder what would happen with wars and conflict if no one could be injured. Can angels survive in space? If so, would we start colonizing other worlds?"

Emily continued the thought experiment, her wonder growing as she imagined the possibilities. "Think about the economic impact of a workforce that suddenly quit, no longer needing food, shelter, sleep, or vehicles. Manufacturing would grind to a halt. All the pollution produced daily would vanish almost overnight. Technology would probably take a huge hit, without a willing workforce of grunts to do the menial labor. Civilization would become far more primitive unless there was a way to motivate people to continue working."

Devon glanced at Calypso. "I guess it depends on whether angels truly are invulnerable. If nothing can hurt you, law and morality start to lose their teeth. People follow rules because there are consequences. If pain and death disappear, what stops someone cruel or deranged from doing whatever they want? How would you restrain them?"

"The only solution," Emily said, frowning, "would be for other angels to police them—some kind of angelic enforcers keeping the peace, and there would have to be a lot of them."

Devon nodded. "Makes you wonder if that's what the 'war in heaven' was about. Maybe it wasn't good versus evil—just a conflict among immortals trying to control the ones who went rogue. The 'fallen angels.'"

Emily's eyes widened. "Wait! What if *humans* were the fallen angels? What if mortality was the answer? Mortality is just containment."

Devon whistled, eyeing her excitedly. "Now *that* would be an interesting explanation for our religious history, for our fixation on heaven, morality, sin, and hell. What if the angels cast down to Earth as humans were visited by other angels and given guidelines for ascension? It's taken thousands of years for humans to develop a society of justice and ethics that has evolved enough that most people can live normal lives—in some parts of the world, anyway."

Emily stared at Calypso. "That begs the question of how Calypso became an angel. Did one of the ascendant angels decide to see if humans had finally become civilized enough to have a chance at salvation?"

Calypso returned their curious gazes thoughtfully. "Perhaps I am not the first angel to appear. What if such occurrences take place every few millennia, simply to ascertain whether humanity is prepared?"

Emily exchanged a meaningful look with Devon. "You mean, like the story of Jesus?"

Calypso shrugged, her large eyes uncertain. "He did heal numerous individuals and perform what were perceived as miracles, such as returning the deceased to life."

Devon stared at Calypso intently. "That's an interesting idea. He wasn't the first one with such a story either, just the latest. He was killed, though, and you're pretty much invulnerable. I wonder if there's missing information about the story, or if it was altered."

Emily tapped her lips musingly. "If he really was an angel, or part angel, I wonder if his disciples were transformed the way Aria and Clarice were."

Devon frowned. "There's a pretty big difference between how his apostles joined him and how your daughters joined Calypso. Aria and Clarice were solely interested in Calypso's wellbeing and happiness, while the apostles were fascinated with his abilities. They struggled to understand his philosophies for a long time. I have a feeling compassion wasn't very popular at that time. The Beatitudes must have sounded insane to people raised on vengeance and pride."

Emily suddenly laughed, her dark eyes sparkling. "Don't let my daughters hear you refer to them as apostles. They have pretty strong opinions about religion."

Devon grinned. "As I recall, so did Jesus."

Emily nodded, her smile fading. "Good point. I'd imagine if he appeared to people today the way he appeared back then, most religions would shun him."

"Without a doubt," Devon agreed sagely. "He'd be considered a bleeding-heart liberal hippie."

Calypso laughed delightedly, raising the positivity around them by an order of magnitude.

When her laughter faded, she said, "Perhaps he was a hybrid—part angelic, part human. That would certainly explain why he could die."

Emily gazed at Calypso fondly. "Well, whatever he was, he certainly shared your spirit. Your dedication to healing sick children is indescribably amazing; tens of thousands of parents still have their beautiful children because of you."

Calypso blushed, looking down demurely under the sincere praise. "Thank you, Emily."

Emily laid her hand on Calypso's, her eyes shining. "No, thank *you*, Calypso. Words can't express how grateful I am to you for saving my girls."

Calypso's eyes glowed brighter, her smile radiant. "You are so very welcome, Emily. It fills me with joy to see them so loved."

The air hummed faintly with love and peace, an invisible benediction settling over the veranda as their conversation faded into quiet reflection.

8 – CROOKED COPS

Aria reached for her seatbelt but paused as Clarice leaned over from the driver's seat and took her hand, grinning.

"We're invincible now, we don't *need* seatbelts."

Aria tilted her head consideringly. "Yeah, I guess so. But if we *don't* wear them, we'll have to deal with that annoying seatbelt reminder." She pointed to the blinking light on the dash.

Clarice leaned forward and buckled the seatbelt behind her, then leaned back with a triumphant grin. "Ha! Mischief managed."

Aria laughed and copied her sister. "Nobody would ever guess you were a Harry Potter fan," she said wryly.

Clarice shook her head. "I'm a Fred and George fan. Luna was pretty cool too. Harry's kind of a twat."

Aria burst out laughing. "Yeah, he wasn't very likable, was he? I'd definitely pick Fred and George as hangout buddies over Harry."

She grunted as their uncle's Suburban bounced around on the washboards carved into the dirt road. "Uncle Moneybags should have this road paved."

Clarice slowed as they hit a particularly rough patch and nodded vigorously. "Or at least get a grader out here. Then again, we couldn't do this without the washboards." She accelerated, then opened her mouth and sang a prolonged "Ahhhhhhh" that vibrated through her voice.

Aria grinned and joined in. "We are Dalek. Exterminate. Exterminate. Exterminate."

Clarice giggled, a sound of pure delight from her angelic voice. She looked at Aria affectionately. "You nailed it."

Aria smiled back, captivated by her sister's ethereal beauty. She couldn't imagine a better way to spend eternity than with Clarice by her side.

They fell into a comfortable silence. Aria kept finding excuses to look over at Clarice, drinking in her radiant features.

Clarice finally turned to face her with a knowing smile. "I won't judge if you just wanna look. Hell, if I weren't driving, *I'd* be staring at *you*."

Aria flushed and let out an embarrassed laugh. "You're not supposed to call me out on it; now it's just awkward."

Clarice reached across the center console and took Aria's hand. "You're so damn adorable when you get all bashful." She pulled Aria's hand up to her nose and inhaled deeply. "God, I can't get over how good you smell."

Aria bit her lip as color flooded her cheeks. Clarice's hand was warm, soft, and electric. It wasn't the same level of intimacy as an angel's embrace, but it was still thrilling. Energy hopped across the meridians in their hands, making the experience far more personal than it had been when she was human.

Clarice let out a delighted moan as the crosstalk of their meridians coursed up her arm. "Okay, everything about being an angel is freaking amazing."

Aria nodded through her blush. "Yeah, I really like the hugs."

Clarice glanced at her with a wicked smile. "I wonder just how intense things can get."

Aria's face flooded with color as her thoughts went straight to her libido. She cursed under her breath. "Why the hell am I still blushing when I don't even have blood anymore?"

Clarice laughed brightly and squeezed Aria's hand. "Because you're so damn adorable when you do."

Aria ducked her head, letting her hair fall forward to hide her flaming face.

Clarice whipped Aria's hand around. "Hey! Cut that out! Stop hiding the main attraction."

Aria groaned, wishing for the millionth time she could just shut off the blood flow to her face, or whatever the angelic equivalent was.

Clarice released Aria's hand and gently lifted her chin. "No hiding, you goose. Don't you dare hide my sister's beautiful face."

Aria shifted uncomfortably, even as a warm smile lit up her face. Clarice had a way of making her feel both awkward and special at the same time. She could feel the pull between them, almost a physical force. It had grown significantly stronger since they had become angels, making it increasingly difficult to keep her distance.

Clarice smiled softly. “There’s that smile I love.”

Warmth filled Aria’s chest, along with a strange sense of familiarity. Her smile widened as she darted a shy glance at Clarice, meeting lavender eyes full of love. Clarice made no attempt to diffuse the moment, as she always had before.

Aria’s lips parted, the words tumbling out before she could second-guess herself. “I love you, Clarice.”

Clarice’s eyes filled with silvery tears, and she squeezed Aria’s hand again, clearly hearing the deeper intent. “I love you back, Aria. I’m so happy I’ll have you by my side for our eternity.”

* * *

“Do you ever wonder why they put 55 mph signs a few hundred feet before the 45 mph signs?” Clarice asked critically. “Then a 35 mph sign a few hundred feet after that. It seems like a total waste of tax money to put up all those redundant signs.”

Aria glanced over at Clarice pointedly. “If you want to go on a crusade for wasted tax dollars, there are a lot juicier targets than the Department of Transportation.”

Clarice gestured vaguely at the road, her eyes full of righteous outrage. “Yeah, but these are the ones I *see* all the time. There’s even a police car just waiting to pounce on someone who waits until the 35 mph sign to slow down. That’s total crap. Why don’t they put that money into deer fences or something useful?”

Aria couldn’t help giggling at Clarice’s antics. Her sister always had *something* to criticize about the infrastructure when they were driving.

Aria gestured at the power lines paralleling the road. “What about those? I thought you were on a crusade to get them buried?”

Clarice shot a scornful glare at the offensive power poles. “Well, why *can’t* they bury them? They bury the phone, gas, and water lines. Do you know how much money they must spend on tree trimming every year to keep the damn tree branches out of the power lines? And they still lose power every time the wind kicks up.”

Aria arched an amused eyebrow. “Maybe high voltage is dangerous to put underground. What happens when it floods?”

“Nonsense,” Clarice flapped her argument away with her hand. “They could just put them in concrete tunnels with proper drainage, or encase them in proper shielding. They already bury them in some places, so why not everywhere?"

Aria watched her sister with fond amusement. "I'm pretty sure that'd get cost-prohibitive fast."

Clarice narrowed her eyes, spotting Aria's grin. "More prohibitive than constant tree maintenance and lawsuits from wildfire victims? Besides, think of all the trees that would still be alive if they weren't replacing power poles and sparking wildfires."

Aria glanced into the side mirror, waiting for Clarice to finish her tirade before speaking. "That cop's following us. You weren't speeding, so what's his deal?"

Devon had let them use his black Suburban, a twin of Emily's. It had tinted windows he had assured them were below the legal limit. They had all the seats down to make room for instruments.

Aria eyed the cops warily in the mirror. "Just pull into a store or something."

Clarice looked back at the Durango critically, her twinkling eyes at odds with her tone. "Do you know how much taxpayer money it costs to fully outfit a police car?"

"Seriously?" Aria demanded in exasperation. "Just pull in somewhere already and give those two someone else to bug."

Clarice studied the police officers through her rearview mirror. "The dude driving looks like he passed the physical. His partner looks like he's been hitting the donut shop a little too frequently, though."

"*Clarice!* Pull *over* already," Aria begged, anxiously wringing her hands. "They're going to pull us over for some BS probable cause, and then we'll have to show them your ID. I'm pretty sure they're going to recognize us, and even if they don't, our names will probably get run through their computer system and get us flagged by the Agency."

Clarice sighed theatrically, rolling her eyes exaggeratedly as she pulled into a Subway sandwich shop. "Fine. I'm pulling over. Happy?"

Aria groaned as the police car followed them into the lot.

Clarice smirked at her. "Yeah, pulling over didn't help much," she said archly.

She parked in front of the shop and turned off the car. The police cruiser pulled in right next to them, though they had yet to turn on their lights.

Clarice glanced at the cops and spoke softly. "Keep your face turned away. The media fixated on your flamboyant hair, so I'm probably less recognizable. Get out the phone Uncle Devon loaned us and pretend to be busy."

Aria complied, trying to look like a screen-obsessed human. The cops hadn't exited their vehicle; they just sat, watching the two angels.

Aria focused her ridiculously sensitive hearing on the conversation in the car next to them.

"I don't think they're getting out," the corpulent cop said, then belched.

"That's probable cause enough for me," Lean Cop declared, sounding satisfied. "Loitering in a Subway parking lot."

Aria frowned uneasily. "You better go in. I'll wait here."

Clarice was already exiting the vehicle, sunglasses in place. She looked significantly different from what she had in the few online clips from the biker incident.

"Well, never mind... I guess they are getting out," Donut Lord grunted in surprise. "Should we follow her in?"

"Let's wait and see if her friend gets out," Lean Cop decided. "We don't want her escaping while we're inside."

"What if she doesn't get out?" Donut Lord asked.

"We'll grab the other one when she comes out," Lean Cop said. "If her friend tries to leave, we'll be close enough to stop her."

"How much do you think they'll be worth?" Donut Lord asked greedily. "She looked pretty hot. I'll bet they'll pay top dollar, especially if her friend is decent."

"Probably fifteen or twenty G's," Lean Cop replied, sounding satisfied.

"I guess it's just pennies to the people who buy them," Donut Lord said enviously.

Aria's face flushed with rage when she realized what they were talking about.

"Clarice, they're trying to capture us and sell us to human traffickers," she growled, her hands shaking with fury.

Clarice's head whipped around to look at her from inside the Subway, her mouth tightening.

Aria scowled. "I'm not sure how we're going to get out of this without blowing our cover. They're going to try and arrest you as soon as you come out."

Clarice nodded and walked up to an employee, her expression artfully anxious. "Excuse me, can I use your phone, please? It's an emergency."

The employee looked at her oddly for a moment, then fumbled a phone from his pocket and unlocked it before handing it to her.

She smiled gratefully, her voice like melted chocolate. "Thanks."

The employee's neck and face exploded with color, clearly not expecting to be a hero to a gorgeous woman.

She spoke as soon as their uncle answered. "Uncle Devon, there are some crooked cops waiting outside a Subway shop who plan to sell us to human traffickers. Can you think of a way for us to get out of this without breaking cover?"

His deep voice was terse. "What town are you in? Is it a state or local car?"

"Local," she answered, telling him the name of the town.

"I'm calling the local office right now," he said grimly. "If the whole department isn't corrupt, I should be able to put some heat on them."

"Thanks, Uncle," Clarice said, relief thick in her voice.

"Can they see you if you stand at the front of the store?" he asked quickly.

Clarice glanced out the window at the patrol car. "Yeah, they're right outside the front door."

"Walk over to the window while holding the cellphone to your ear and stare at them," he instructed. "Make it obvious you're inspecting them."

Aria watched her sister walk to the window and stare intently at the police cruiser.

"Oh, shit, is she talking to someone about us?" Donut Lord exclaimed nervously.

"Fuck, let's get out of here," Lean Cop snarled. "It's probably a trap."

The police cruiser quickly backed out of the lot and sped down the road.

"They just took off," Clarice told their uncle.

Devon sighed, relief evident in his voice. "Em says you're too damn pretty for your own good."

"Don't I know it," Clarice growled irritably. "I wish we weren't trying to lay low—I'd have a long chat with those cops and whoever they were planning to sell us to."

"It's an ugly world out there, Clarice," Devon said sadly.

"Thanks again, Uncle," Clarice ended the call and took the phone back to the plump young man behind the counter. He had been ogling her whenever he thought she wasn't watching, his expression a mix of disbelief and eagerness. Her tight yoga pants left little to the imagination, and her snug spaghetti strap tank displayed a generous view of her cleavage and flat stomach.

She smiled at the young man winsomely. "Thank you so much. You really helped me out."

He stumbled over his words as he took the phone back with shaky hands. "No, not a problem. Any time at all."

Despite the positive energy coursing through her meridians, Aria still felt an uncharacteristic rage. The thought of the very people sworn to protect them committing such a repugnant crime made her burn with fury.

Clarice returned to the car and studied her face with concern. "You okay?"

"I'm not feeling like a very nice angel right now," Aria grated, feeling the positive energy transpose into righteous fury.

"You need to stop!" Clarice snapped, putting her hand on Aria's cheek and forcing her to look into her eyes. "Let it go for now. Please, Aria."

Aria closed her eyes and took a deep, calming breath and breathed out slowly. She cupped Clarice's hand on her cheek. "I was so angry. The energy switched from benevolent to something else."

"I know," Clarice said gently. "You were glowing."

Aria's eyes shot open. "I was?"

"Yeah," Clarice confirmed, lips curving up on one side. "It was pretty hot."

Aria felt the fury vanish as she dissolved into giggles. "Thanks, Clarice. I really needed that."

"Any time, Aria," Clarice murmured softly. "You're stuck with me for eternity now, so really, any time."

Aria laughed again as Clarice withdrew her hand and started the car. They pulled back onto the highway and continued their interrupted trip.

Aria idly wrapped a strand of hair around her finger. "We should seriously consider the superhero career path in the near future," she mused, glancing at Clarice speculatively. "If we wear masks, we could totally take out some bad guys. We don't really need cars to get around at the speeds we run, and we don't sleep. It's perfect."

Clarice grasped Aria's hand, her eyes full of righteous judgment. "I really want to get those bastards, too, but we've been angels for less than a day and only tested our abilities for a few minutes. We have some growing to do before we go full vigilante."

Aria grimaced. "Do you think the whole police force in this town is corrupt?"

Clarice nodded, her eyes flinty. "I wouldn't be surprised. They couldn't be this brazen if the rest of the force weren't in on it."

Aria grunted, her lips twisting in revulsion. "That's disgusting."

Clarice's mouth tightened into a thin line. "It sure is. You remember the trigger phrase that transformed us, right?"

Aria smiled unpleasantly. "To vanquish evil. Right... it's actually part of who we are now. We *need* to vanquish evil—just like Calypso *needs* to heal people."

Clarice nodded, a slow smile forming on her lips. "Let's discuss our new career path with the others when we get back. We're going to be avenging angels."

Aria smiled grimly. "I like the sound of that."

They arrived at the music store a few minutes later, a surprisingly large establishment for the medium-sized town. As they walked over to inspect the percussion instruments, Aria overheard one of the employees near the front of the store speaking to a coworker.

"Damn, Max, I'm taking this one. Those two are freaking *hot*."

"Okay, Romeo," Max said, her voice dull with the disinterest of the terminally bored. "Go get 'em, tiger—" She cut off when she saw them, sucking in a surprised breath. "Aww hell no."

They both wandered over, looking increasingly dumbfounded as they approached. Clarice turned to face them, smiling warmly.

The two employees struggled to find their words, staring at Clarice with frank admiration. Max had shoulder-length pink hair, shaved on one side, and a cluster of rings on her eyebrows, nose, and lips, and enough black eyeshadow to suck the light out of the room.

"Hey, how's it going?" Clarice greeted the two employees, her riveting voice like a kiss working its way up the neck. "Mind if we put some of these instruments through their paces? We have a pretty long list."

When they just continued staring at her, jaws slack, she exchanged an amused glance with Aria, then waved her hand in front of the entranced employees. When they remained unresponsive, Clarice said, "Aria, smack that cymbal."

Aria hesitated, but when the employees continued staring at Clarice with a kind of reverential awe, she shrugged and picked up a drumstick, then smacked the cymbal.

Max and "Romeo" flinched at the sudden crash, then flushed when they realized they had been staring at Clarice to the exclusion of all else.

Clarice repeated her earlier greeting and question, her lips curving into a small smile that looked more alluring than amused.

Max was the first to find her voice. "Um, we're good," she said awkwardly, nervously stuffing her hands in her pockets. "Feel free to play any of the instruments."

Clarice flashed Max a grateful smile that sent a new wave of color flooding into the girl's cheeks. "Thanks, Max."

The angels spent almost an hour picking out and testing instruments. They played a few of the guitars before settling on two Fenders. Several shoppers had joined the two employees to gawk at them as they put the guitars through their paces.

Aria marveled at how much better she could play as an angel. Complicated finger work was no longer something that required her full concentration and every scrap of skill she possessed. It was almost effortless as her fingers flew up and down the fretboard, playing in sync with Clarice as they stood facing each other a few feet apart.

When they finished playing, a loud cheer erupted, punctuated by a few appreciative whistles. Clarice offered their impromptu audience a dazzling smile while Aria tried to shrink in on herself at the unexpected attention. As they walked away, she overheard one customer say to his friend, "There's nothing hotter than a beautiful woman who can shred a fretboard."

"Go get her number," his friend urged, nudging him.

"Nah, man, she's taken," he sighed regretfully. "Didn't you see the way they were looking at each other?"

Aria's cheeks burned, and she studiously avoided Clarice's gaze as they moved toward the checkout desk. She jumped when she felt a pinch on her ass, spinning to see Clarice winking at her with an alluring smile.

"You are *so* bad," Aria hissed as the people around them gawked at the display.

"Told ya, dude," the man told his friend wryly. "But damn if that isn't hot."

With the help of the two employees, they loaded all the instruments into the SUV. Max dropped a kettledrum in her nervousness, and Aria's hand shot out lightning-fast, catching it before it hit the ground. Max gasped, staring at Aria in amazement as she easily raised the kettledrum, one-handed, and placed it into the SUV. She remembered kettledrums being heavy, but it felt as light as everything else did now.

Max nervously licked her lips, studying Aria with a mixture of fear and fascination. "Are you, um, vampires or something?"

Aria exchanged a look with Clarice, then burst out laughing. She reined in her mirth as Clarice closed the back doors and smiled mysteriously at Max and said, "Or something."

As they drove away, Clarice smirked at her from the driver's seat. "We're not *always* too pretty for our own good. Look at all the help we got loading up."

Aria giggled mischievously, remembering the scene. She had dealt with awkward, tongue-tied people before, but it seemed to have gotten a lot worse since their transformation.

"Anywhere else you wanna go before we head home?" Clarice asked, lifting her sunglasses to rest on her head now that they were in the privacy of their vehicle.

Aria settled into her seat, angling herself to better appreciate her view of her gorgeous sister. She shook her head, putting her own sunglasses up. "We never get hungry, so no, not really. Aside from the little hiccup getting into town, things went pretty well. Nobody recognized us."

Clarice looked at Aria with an appreciative grin. "It helps that our features changed with our transformation. So. Damn. Hot."

Aria sighed enviously. "You still got the cuter face. Can't I have my hair and *your* face?"

Clarice nodded eagerly. "I'll trade you faces any day of the week. Your self-image is seriously warped."

Aria shook her head ruefully, admiring Clarice openly. "Nope. I don't think you realize how stunning you are. You could seriously sit in a booth and charge people to look at you."

Clarice laughed, looking at Aria hungrily. "You're such a sweet talker. I'll have to find a way to express my appreciation—at length."

Aria shivered at the sensual promise in Clarice's eyes. A soft warmth filled her as she realized the wall between them was fading away. A nagging thought clung to her mind, an old fear she had always known would make opening herself to Clarice difficult.

"Um, what about Mom and Dad? I'm not sure they'll look at this, uh, philosophically."

Clarice burst out laughing, her eyes glowing with affection. "They've been asking me why I haven't taken things further with you for years. They're a hundred percent behind us, Aria. Why else do you think Mom would've suggested sharing Calypso?"

Aria gasped, her lavender eyes widening. "Seriously? Oh my god, that's been weighing on my mind for *ages*. I can't believe I've been stressing about that for nothing this whole time."

Clarice chuckled, taking her hand again. "You really are adorable, Aria."

Aria smiled back sheepishly, idly wrapping a strand of hair around her finger and dropping her gaze. "Um, can I ask a kinda personal question?"

Clarice squeezed her hand with a sweet smile. "Anything, Aria."

Aria took a nervous breath, eyes darting up to Clarice's gaze and then quickly away. "I always wondered why you never kept any of your dates overnight. Did I ruin your chance at romance because I'm too scared to do anything?"

Clarice smiled gently. "Not in the way you think. Sometimes I worried you weren't interested, so it was my way of seeing how you'd react. Honestly, I couldn't feel anything but mild affection for other women because you'd already claimed my heart. Nobody else could compare to you, so yeah, you ruined my chance for romance with anyone else by being too perfect. Who could live up to Aria?"

Aria thought she might melt.

Clarice suddenly slowed as they saw police lights in the distance. Aria stared intently, eyes zooming in on the cruiser several miles away. There was a white Ford Focus, and several young women sat handcuffed on the side of the road under the watchful eye of Donut Lord while Lean Cop searched their car.

"Pull over, Clarice," Aria said firmly. They were still a few miles from the incident.

Clarice looked at the determination on Aria's face and sighed. She pulled onto the shoulder and shut off the car.

Aria's anger returned, filling her with righteous fury. "You know what they're going to do to those girls. I'm *not* going to let that happen."

Clarice squinted at her. "Do you think you can do it without glowing? We don't want word of a glowing superwoman popping up all over the internet."

Aria closed her eyes and willed herself to calm down. The glow slowly dimmed as she regained control of her rage.

Clarice gestured at the cops ahead. "What are we going to do? Just throw some rocks and knock them out?"

"They'll just do it again," Aria ground out darkly. "They need to be stopped—permanently."

Clarice blanched. "You're not talking about killing them, are you?"

Aria smiled icily. "No, just making them rue the day they were born. A swift kick in the gonads seems like justice to me, hard enough to end their posterity."

Clarice nodded, the corners of her mouth turning up. "Okay. But *fast*. We don't want anybody seeing anything but a blur."

"Right," Aria agreed, exiting the car. "Let's go."

She pushed herself to high speed and yelped as her shorts began to smoke from the friction. She ignored it, moving in on the cops as they prepared to load the three girls into the back of the cruiser. To her heightened perception, they were completely frozen, as if time had stopped.

She kicked the first cop between the legs from behind, launching him over the car. The second cop was already flying, courtesy of Clarice's kick.

The two angels spun to face the dejected girls in a burst of wind and pinched the handcuffs, breaking the bracelets on each wrist. Aria took a split second to study their faces. The youngest girl couldn't have been older than thirteen, while the oldest looked about seventeen. Tear streaks marked their faces. The sight nearly sent Aria into a glowing rage again, but she managed to mentally clamp down on her anger and ran back to their vehicle.

"That went well," Clarice said conversationally, combing her wind-swept bangs back. "I made sure to fry the hard drives the bodycams record to, just in case they were able to pick anything up."

Aria watched the cops as they moaned on the ground, curled up in the fetal position. The girls stood staring around them in shock. They hesitantly walked to their vehicle, looking back at the cops after every step. When it was clear the cops wouldn't be getting up, they started their car and left.

Aria laughed victoriously. "Yeah, that definitely went well. We vanquished some evil today."

They both felt a sudden stir in the energy matrix inside them as *something* changed. She felt an itch on her back and reached back to scratch it, then froze when she felt the ridges between her shoulder blades.

"I think we might have some wings on the way," Clarice breathed in wonder as she felt her own back.

"Yeah," Aria whispered, her eyes sparkling with excitement. "We're going to be able to *fly*."

Then she saw Clarice's eyes. They were no longer lavender, but a glowing violet, like Calypso's.

Clarice suddenly grinned and played with her phone as she pulled back onto the highway. A moment later, "The Hero!!!" from *One Punch Man* began blasting through the Suburban's speakers.

9 – WINGS

As soon as they exited the vehicle, Calypso flew into their arms, her swirling violet eyes brimming with relief. "I was dreadfully worried!"

Aria gently cradled Calypso's head. "We're invincible now, so we'll always come back safe."

Clarice kissed Calypso's forehead and smiled grimly. "It's the bad guys who'll have to worry from now on."

The air seemed to hum as they held each other close. Aria felt the familiar surge of energy that always came from hugging Calypso—only this time, it was exponentially stronger. The resonance built like a living current, arcing between them in waves until it felt electric.

She shivered as the energy concentrated along her spine, and the faint tingling from before suddenly burned white-hot. Her weight diminished, and pressure built between her shoulder blades, until something erupted from beneath her skin.

With a sound like tearing silk, wings burst from the backs of all three angels. The brilliant white arcs stretched above their heads, the tips brushing the ground. Aria staggered, half laughing, half stunned, as she flexed new muscles. The wings responded as naturally as if they had always been there, blanket-thin and soft as thought.

Emily stepped out onto the porch, her eyes wide and a hand to her mouth. "I guess you really *are* angels."

Aria turned to face Emily, her excited grin charging the space around them with radiance. "I guess we really are!"

Clarice's voice bubbled with excitement. "We're *definitely* going to need a tailor—*because we have freaking wings*!"

"*Wow!*" Calypso gasped, her swirling eyes wide with wonder and a radiant smile stretching across her face. "I can scarcely believe it's truly happened! I've wished to be able to fly since I was a child. This is absolutely marvelous!"

Clarice winked at Aria, looking her up and down. "The goods are spilling out—not that I'm complaining. We might want to get some fabric to wrap around ourselves until we find a tailor."

Aria held her shirt up in an attempt to maintain some level of modesty. Clarice and Calypso were doing the same, their elation tempered slightly by their nudity dilemma.

Emily snorted and turned back to the house. "I'll get some fabric."

"Thanks, Mom," Aria said sheepishly, following her a few steps.

Emily shook her head, glancing at Aria's large wings. "Just stay out here for now. You're going to have enough trouble navigating the house with those wings without trying to hold your shirts up and giving your uncle a heart attack."

Clarice laughed excitedly, her face glowing with joy. "I feel so freaking *light* now. We're as light as you, Calypso. I *really* want to try flying."

Aria laid a calming hand on her shoulder. "Modesty before mobility. Let's wait for Mom to fix us up."

Clarice bounced on the balls of her feet, unable to contain herself. After a few more seconds, she abandoned all pretense of patience. With a powerful leap, she shot skyward, rising several dozen feet before her wings snapped open in a flash of white. Each beat propelled her higher, carrying her to the clouds in seconds.

Aria stared up at her anxiously. "Someone's going to see you, you goose!"

Clarice spread her wings wide to halt her ascent, then dove. Flapping to increase her downward velocity, she shot toward them like a falling star. At a hundred feet, she pulled her wings out and thrust down with a powerful wingbeat that halted her descent. The wind from her powerful wings buffeted them with gale-force intensity, creating a miniature hurricane. Aria pinned her shirt to her body to keep it from flapping away.

Clarice had either forgotten or didn't care to hold her own shirt up. Aria flushed, unable to look away as Clarice gracefully descended the remaining hundred feet. A flood of desire left her shaking with intense need as she stared at Clarice's perfect breasts, imagining what it would be like to have them in her hands. Another gust of wind finally snapped her out of her lustful thoughts, and she called up to her sister, "Pull your shirt up, you trollop!"

"Oh, yeah," Clarice laughed, her face alight with exhilaration. She tugged the tatters of her shirt back up just as their mother returned with some cannibalized fabric and safety pins.

Emily sighed, shaking her head with exasperated affection. "You just couldn't help yourself, could you?"

Clarice giggled gleefully. "Not even a little. You have no idea how *fun* that was!"

Calypso watched her with open delight. The contagious joy in Clarice's laughter pulled a matching grin from her lips. Aria felt it too, the irresistible urge to launch skyward, but she held herself back with visible effort.

When Emily approached, Aria gestured toward Calypso, who looked ready to launch skyward at any moment. "Take care of Calypso first?"

Calypso started to protest, but Emily was already wrapping her in makeshift bands and pinning them in place.

Emily chuckled wryly. "I told Devon to stay inside for a while." She fastened another pin and looked over at Clarice. "So, how did the rest of your trip go? Any... complications?"

"Maybe?" Clarice replied evasively, her eyes darting away. "I guess that depends on your definition of 'complications.'"

Emily turned to Aria. "Spit it out, Aria," she ordered, her tone leaving no room for evasion. "What happened?"

Aria summarized their second run-in with the corrupt cops while Emily pinned the last strip of fabric around Calypso's shoulders.

"Good!" Emily said fiercely when Aria finished, her dark eyes flashing. "They got better than they deserved."

Clarice blinked, clearly expecting a reprimand. When none came, she let out a relieved laugh and shot Aria an incredulous grin. Aria grinned back, silently agreeing that their mother was the coolest woman alive.

Emily looked Calypso up and down in satisfaction. "Okay, Calypso, this should hold until we can get some clothes tailored for wings."

She turned toward Aria and began wrapping her next.

"Favoritism," Clarice complained under her breath.

Emily arched an eyebrow at her. "You already flew; you can wait."

Clarice turned to Calypso. "Aren't you going to try flying?"

Calypso shook her head. "It will be far more enjoyable if we go together."

"I hear that," Clarice drawled, affecting a redneck accent.

Aria gave her sister a level look. "I swear your IQ drops by a decimal point every time you speak hick."

Clarice smirked, and her voice switched to a prim British accent, sounding eerily close to Calypso. “Should I gain points if I strive for a sexy Calypso dialect?”

Calypso smiled awkwardly, a soft pink staining her cheeks, and Clarice’s smirk widened. Aria smacked her sister on the shoulder but couldn’t stop a small giggle from escaping. Clarice had certainly nailed the “sexy” part of that dialect.

Calypso cleared her throat. “So, um, where shall we take to the air?”

“Hold up,” Emily said reluctantly, clearly hesitant to dampen their excitement. “I’m going to be a party pooper and suggest waiting until dark. If someone videos a trio of angels flying around the mountains, it’s going to be hard to keep this place hidden. Cryptozoologists and Calypso fans will be combing every inch of the place.”

All three angels groaned.

Emily sighed. “Fine...but at least get up high quickly and go far away.” She looked at Clarice inquisitively. “How fast can you fly?”

“I’m pretty sure we can break the sound barrier,” Clarice replied, practically vibrating with impatience.

Emily shook her head firmly. “Not if you want to keep your clothes on. Until we get something more fitted, maybe keep it under Mach One. Say, a few hundred miles an hour, just to see how the clothes hold up.”

Clarice grinned teasingly. “Yes, oh wise one. And I say that with only a little sarcasm. You’re brilliant, Mom.”

Emily chuckled, giving her a quick hug before returning to her task. “That’s sweet of you to say.”

Calypso cleared her throat, looking hesitant. “May I inquire about Aria’s birth mother and Clarice’s birth father? I’ve met many families over the years, yet I have never witnessed a stepparent show such devotion to their children as you do, Emily.”

Emily’s expression softened, her hands pausing mid-motion. “It’s all right,” she said warmly. “Aria’s mother died giving birth, and Clarice’s father died in a car accident when she was two. I met Eric about five years later. The girls were the same age and inseparable from the moment they met.” She smiled fondly at Aria. “It’s hard not to love her like my own. She wanted a mother so badly. She pampered me constantly, brushing my hair, bringing me little gifts, and snuggling every chance she got. I think I had my hair brushed more that first year than in my entire life before that.”

“Mine too,” Clarice added, bumping Aria’s shoulder affectionately. “I think she was afraid we’d disappear if she didn’t spoil us enough.”

Aria blushed, her eyes darting around. She opened her mouth, but no sound came out.

Clarice smiled gently. "It's okay, Aria. You can accept some flattery. You're one of the most compassionate and loving people I've met, and I love you for it."

Aria's eyes filled with quicksilver tears. She pulled Emily and Clarice into a tight embrace. "You're the best sister and mom," she told them, her voice thick with emotion. "I really am the luckiest person in the world. I love you both so much. Thank you for making me part of your wonderful family."

Calypso watched the scene tenderly, her swirling eyes glowing with affection.

Emily let out a startled gasp. Aria and Clarice pulled back in alarm, then noticed her glowing neck.

"Oh no," Aria cried out in dismay. "I'm sorry, Mom. We meant to get your permission before we let any angel tears get on you."

Emily's eyes widened as she stared into space. Before their eyes, the gray vanished from her hair, returning to a deep, glossy black. Her few wrinkles softened and disappeared, leaving her skin glowing with youthful vitality. She looked barely older than Clarice and could have passed as her twin when she was mortal.

"Wow," she whispered, touching her face in disbelief. "I feel better than I have in decades."

Clarice patted Aria's shoulder reassuringly. "It's just the seed. She won't actually turn into an angel unless she triggers it with the key words."

Calypso frowned pensively. "I intended to mention that there may be different classes of angels. I don't believe we belong to the same class. I think I am a healer, whereas you two might be more combat-oriented. I'm uncertain what other kinds of angels there might be, but the point is, there could be other phrases that will trigger the transformation."

Emily's lips curved into a wry smile. "So if I don't want to become an angel, I just have to stop talking for the rest of my life?" She gave a small shrug. "Oh well. If it happens, it happens." She smiled and turned to Clarice. "Now hold still, you're next."

Five minutes later, all three angels were decently wrapped and bubbling with anticipation. They exchanged a look that needed no words, then leapt skyward, wings unfurling in a burst of white as they rose together into the sunlit sky.

Aria felt pure exhilaration as the ground fell away beneath her. The wind rushed past her face, tugging playfully at her hair as the world below became a blur of color and motion. She laughed, the sound bright and unrestrained, carried away on the rushing air. Within seconds, they had pierced the clouds.

Clarice's voice carried to them easily with their sensitive hearing. "Keep an eye out for airplanes. Which way should we go?"

"South," Aria suggested, unable to stop grinning.

Flying felt impossibly natural, like her body had always known how. With the faintest thought, her wings angled and adjusted, slicing through the sky.

Emily had been right to worry about their clothes. The air slammed into them like a solid wall as they accelerated, the force trying to rip the fabric from their bodies. They streaked across the sky at near-supersonic speed, laughing as they weaved through the clouds and skimmed over a startled flock of geese that scattered in their wake.

In less than half an hour, they had traveled hundreds of miles. From that height, the curve of the Earth was visible, a breathtaking panorama of gold-lit clouds and jagged coastlines. As the oxygen thinned, the sky shifted from blue to a bruised purple. Their telescopic vision allowed them to discern every detail of distant aircraft far below, even the pilots' eyes glinting in the sunlight.

They slowed, hovering together nearly ninety thousand feet above the Appalachian Mountains. Below, the peaks rose like jagged emerald teeth through a sea of white mist. From so high, it all looked strangely flat, lacking parallax for reference. The sun was a harsh, blinding white disc, unsoftened by the atmosphere.

Clarice shouted, her voice alive with joy. "Let's go down to the peaks!" She hovered in place with easy, rhythmic wingbeats. It required a lot more effort to stay aloft in the thin air, but their tireless bodies made it a trivial matter. The sub-zero temperatures had no effect on their new bodies, though Aria had discovered she needed to vibrate her wings to break the ice off them on their ascent, producing a loud hum.

"Very well," Calypso agreed, smiling as the wind tousled her hair. "I've never stood upon a mountain peak before."

Aria tucked her wings close and dove. The rush of air screamed past her ears as she plummeted through the sky like a meteor, a blur of color and motion through the clouds. A cry of exhilaration echoed across the sky as she dropped. Just before reaching the treeline, she unfurled her wings and banked hard, curving around a narrow ridge before coasting upward on a warm updraft. The sensation was intoxicating—freedom in its purest form.

Calypso glided beside Aria, her laughter carrying over the wind. They spiraled toward a small clearing near one of the peaks, touching down with effortless grace. Seconds later, Clarice dropped from thirty feet, landing in a crouch that kicked up a soft cloud of dust.

She whooped, her violet eyes dancing. "That was *beyond belief* awesome!"

Calypso smiled tremulously, a single quicksilver tear sliding down her cheek. "It was everything I ever dreamed of—and more," she whispered. "I am so very happy."

Aria stepped forward, drawing Calypso into a tight embrace, folding her wings around her like a silken cocoon. "I'm so glad it was so wonderful for you," she murmured, gently stroking Calypso's hair as the angel trembled with joy.

They remained that way for several long, timeless moments, surrounded by the sound of the mountain wind, before a light cough broke the spell.

"Yeah, I'm still here too," Clarice said dryly, crossing her arms. "No need to worry about me. I'm just *fine* being the third wheel."

Aria laughed and unfurled one wing, then used it to reach out and pull her sister into the embrace.

"That's more like it," Clarice purred contentedly, nestling between them with a grin.

Calypso smiled warmly, her eyes wide with wonder as she felt Aria's velvety wings. "I can scarcely believe how soft our wings are. I had imagined feathers, like those in Renaissance paintings—not these silken sails."

Clarice made a purring sound that sent warmth to all the right places. "Yeah, these wings make silk feel rough."

They stood in each other's arms, the intimate exchange of energy across their meridians melding them into one.

In a state of euphoric joy, they watched the sunset, holding each other as the sky melted from molten lava to velvety black. The moment ended when their delicate hearing detected the sound of helicopter rotors in the distance.

Aria sighed and reluctantly stepped back, her wings folding against her back. She squeezed them in tightly, then smiled when the thin membranes flattened enough that they could be mistaken for a cloak.

She turned toward the sound of rotors and focused her godlike vision. Half a dozen military helicopters advanced in formation, two Apache gunships flanking four large transport choppers.

Aria felt far less worried than she would have a week ago. It was difficult to feel fear when nothing could hurt you. "Do you think they've seen us yet?"

"Hmm..." Clarice murmured dryly. "Military scanners, thermal imaging, satellites... Yeah, I'm pretty sure they see us." She finished with a wave at the sky.

"Seriously?" Aria deadpanned, raising an eyebrow at Clarice. "You're *waving* at the people trying to kill us?"

Clarice shrugged. "We don't *know* they're trying to kill us. I'm pretty sure they want us alive."

Aria growled, "Yeah—so they can dissect us." The thought triggered a surge through her meridians, and the shadows around her vanished as her body flared with radiant light. Her violet eyes blazed, followed by an aura of authority that was physically palpable.

Clarice snorted. "They've definitely seen us now. Chill out, okay? Let's find out what they want before we go psycho on their asses. There might be some young, dumb Calypso fans in there who're just following orders. It's not like we can't leave whenever we want."

Aria shook her head. "I'm trying to chill out, but as long as I feel like Calypso is threatened, I'm not going to be able to relax."

Clarice sighed. "Maybe it's just as well." A moment later, she flared into incandescence as well. "At least wait to see what they want."

Aria nodded, holding back the power in her eyes that she knew could vaporize finite matter with a touch.

Moments later, the helicopters reached them. The two Apaches flanked the angels while the transports lowered to a dozen feet above the trees. Thick ropes dropped, and dozens of soldiers rappelled to the ground, quickly forming a perimeter among the trees, their weapons raised.

Aria scanned their faces, seeing a blend of fear, confusion, and awe. Her acute hearing picked up the radio chatter crackling through their helmets.

"The CO didn't say we were attacking angels," an anxious voice spoke into his radio. "There's no freaking way I'm opening fire on an angel; I'm not going to hell."

"I second that," several voices agreed.

"Those aren't angels," a cold voice declared firmly. "They're alien entities mimicking human mythology."

"That's bullshit," a soldier argued. "Look at them! They're glowing just like angels from scripture. I swore to defend God and Country, and this feels like a betrayal of both."

"Unless you want a court-martial, you'll follow orders," the cold voice barked. "Subdue and detain the entities."

"Negative," came the terse reply. "I'll take a court-martial over eternal damnation any day."

"You bunch of religious nutjobs!" another voice sneered, followed by the crack of a rifle.

A tranquilizer dart hissed through the air toward Aria, and her hand blurred, catching it effortlessly between her fingers. With deliberate calm, she pressed the dart into her palm until the needle snapped.

"I don't think tranq darts are going to work," the shooter said weakly. "She just crushed it like it was nothing."

Calypso's voice rang out, harmonizing in an impossible stereo that seemed to come from everywhere at once. "Why are you attacking us?"

"Holy shit, that's NOTESTOREMEMBER," one of the soldiers gasped. "She really *is* an angel."

A new voice boomed from the Apache's loudspeaker. "Lie face-first on the ground with your arms spread out, or we will open fire."

Clarice's voice, cold and resonating with authority, cut through the air. "You don't have weapons that can harm us. We will allow you to leave if you do so peacefully. Anyone still aiming a weapon at Calypso after I count to ten will be judged swiftly and harshly."

A tense silence followed. Then, one by one, over a dozen soldiers lowered their rifles and backed away. The others hesitated, torn between fear and obedience.

"I'll handle the pilots," Clarice murmured. "We don't want anyone dying."

Aria nodded, her glow intensifying until the fresh dew around her glittered. Her aura of authority intensified, bringing with it a wave of unmistakable menace. The remaining soldiers took one look at her blazing form and retreated. Something primal told them that light meant death.

The first Apache opened fire, and Aria wrapped her wings around herself in an attempt to protect her clothing. The roar of thirty-millimeter cannons shattered the air, shells hammering the angels' wings. Metal screamed and ricocheted harmlessly away for nearly a full minute.

Heat fused in Aria's eyes as she stared at the tail of the gunship. A second later, a blinding light shot from her eyes and vaporized the back of the Apache.

As the war machine began spinning, Clarice shot upward like a comet. Quicker than thought, she tore the door free, ripped through the restraints, and pulled both pilots out. The entire rescue, a blur of motion and impossible speed, took less than three seconds. Springing free of the plummeting aircraft with both operators in her arms, she descended to the ground next to Aria and Calypso, gently setting the two operators down, where they immediately collapsed.

The other gunship had been arming its missile bays after observing the futility of machine-gun fire. A moment of hesitation followed when the crew saw their fellow operators kneeling with the angels.

"Are you hurt?" Clarice curtly asked the two soldiers. "I didn't have time to be gentle."

Calypso knelt by the terrified pilots, her swirling eyes studying them intently. "They merely have some bruising," she said after a few seconds. "Nothing appears to be broken."

Aria glared at the remaining gunship. "You should probably get them out of here before their buddies 'accidentally' fire on them."

The transport helicopters had pulled away several thousand feet when the first gunship opened fire.

Clarice smiled wolfishly, glowing brighter as she prepared to attack. "I have a better idea."

The second gunship launched several Hellfire missiles as Clarice's eyes blazed like miniature suns. She vaporized the missiles as quickly as they launched, then targeted the gunship's armaments. When she finished, it was no longer a gunship—just a helicopter. The pilots immediately retreated, struggling to keep the imbalanced craft airborne.

Aria's sixth sense prickled. She looked up and spotted movement high above the horizon—two F-22 Raptors closing fast from the north, their contrails glowing faintly in the starlight.

"We'd better take this to the air," she said briskly. "If those jackasses start firing, these jackasses will get killed in the crossfire."

"Agreed," Clarice said shortly. With a leap that launched her a hundred feet into the air, she beat her wings, accelerating to Mach 1 almost instantly. The wind from her takeoff flattened the grass and sent trees swaying like reeds.

Aria and Calypso followed, streaking skyward like winged missiles. Within seconds, they broke the sound barrier, shockwaves rolling behind them like thunder.

The Raptors were only a few miles away when Aria swung wide to flank them, banking sharply until she flew parallel to their projected path. Clarice signaled to her with a glance and a gesture—*right one's yours*.

Her body ignited once more, incandescent with restrained fury. She accelerated until she was face-to-face with the jet's canopy.

The pilot tried every evasive maneuver in the book, from barrel rolls to sudden dives and hard banks, but Aria matched each one effortlessly.

Compared to an angel's reflexes, even the most advanced aircraft was clumsy and slow.

She hovered inches from the cockpit, her eyes glowing like judgment.

"Turn back," she ordered, her voice resonant with divine authority. "Or I'll fry your machine where it flies."

Through the tinted glass, she couldn't see the pilot's expression beneath his oxygen mask, but she felt his fear and understanding. The jet banked hard away, retreating toward the horizon of its approach. Aria shadowed him for a few seconds, then pulled away to rejoin Calypso and Clarice.

Her sister was just finishing with the second pilot, who was also turning tail for home. Calypso caught up with them easily, and they hovered in the upper atmosphere, the stars blazing brightly above them.

Clarice glanced upward. "I'm tempted to go satellite hunting. I'm not sure I want them watching us all the time."

Aria glanced back north, her eyes tight with worry. "Do you think they've found Uncle Devon's house yet?"

Clarice pursed her lips, following Aria's gaze. "We'll head back and check. Now that it's dark, we should be able to fly lower. I really hate that they can track our movements with satellites when we're airborne, though."

Calypso turned to look down at the site of their earlier confrontation. "Do you think they understood that they are entirely outclassed?"

Clarice snorted. "I seriously doubt they learned that quickly. We're talking about the top of the testosterone pile here."

Aria grinned widely. "I think we can all agree that we freaking *rock*! We just took down the U.S. military without killing a single person."

Clarice returned her grin, thrusting her fist into the air with a victorious cry. "Hell yeah, we *totally* rock. I think we've made it clear we can handle ourselves. I'm not sure how much hiding is still necessary."

Aria paused, looking at her uncertainly. "Really? What about family? They would totally go after them to try and control us."

Clarice sighed. "Yeah, I suppose you're right. But soon, I think we'll be able to return to the world. We only have Uncle Devon and Mom and Dad to worry about, and hopefully, not for long."

Aria chewed her lip anxiously. "Maybe we should split up. What if they go after Dad? They must've made the connection that the angels they fought today are the same people who were with Calypso during the biker incident."

Clarice nodded quickly. “Agreed.” She looked at Calypso. “Who do you want to go with? Do you want to meet our dad?”

Calypso smiled softly. “I have met Eric before, do you recall? But I should very much like to meet him again.”

Clarice laughed ruefully. “Oh yeah. Fifteen years ago seems like a lifetime at this point.”

“Seriously,” Aria agreed fervently. “Who do you want to check on, Mom or Dad?”

Clarice hesitated, then smirked. “I’ll let you check on Dad. I want to see if Mom accidentally transformed herself yet.”

Aria giggled at the thought of Devon’s face if his sister transformed in front of him. “Poor Uncle Devon.”

Clarice burst out laughing. “Poor guy has had a wild couple of days.” She took a deep, unnecessary breath and pulled them into a hug, which worked surprisingly well while flying. “Be safe, okay? Even if we’re invincible.”

“You too,” Aria murmured affectionately into her ear. “I’ll see you soon. Love you.”

“Love you back,” Clarice breathed, kissing her forehead.

With a final squeeze, they separated. Aria and Calypso angled northwest, wings slicing the cool night air. Clarice arced northward toward the cabin, fading into the stars.

Calypso’s smooth brow wrinkled as she flew next to Aria. “Do you truly think they’ll be in danger?” she asked anxiously.

Aria nodded, her wings beating in rhythm with Calypso’s. “We already suspect they’ve been keeping tabs on Dad, probably leaving him alone to see if he’d lead them to us. And Uncle Devon’s cabin? I’m sure satellites are rolling twenty-four-seven with archives; they can probably follow our flight path right back to him.”

Calypso frowned disapprovingly. “That scarcely allows any privacy for anyone.”

Aria shook her head in disgust. “They’ve convinced people to trade privacy for security. Like Uncle Devon said, total control is every government’s dream.”

They flew in silence for a time. From this height, the world unfolded beneath them like a living map. The dark night was as bright as day to Aria’s enhanced vision. Her sense of direction worked flawlessly, guiding her along familiar landmarks.

Calypso broke the silence, drifting a little closer to Aria. "How are you faring, now that you are an angel? I have yet to see you and Clarice share any sort of intimacy."

Aria bit her lip as a flood of competing emotions raced through her thoughts. "My fear of intimacy is gone, but I'm still a shy person by nature, so it's hard for me to initiate anything meaningful beyond words. I know Clarice, though, and she'll handle that part of things when the time is right."

Calypso nodded, smiling gently. "Good. I was concerned the transformation might have restored the barriers I removed."

Aria let out an awkward chuckle. "Nope, I can definitely confirm that the thought of Clarice ravishing me no longer terrifies me."

"Ravishing?" Calypso repeated curiously. "Is that similar to kissing?"

Aria smiled through a sudden blush as she answered. "If kissing is where intimacy starts, then ravishing is where it ends."

Calypso was silent, and Aria glanced over to see her cheeks glowing a brilliant shade of red, enhancing her already gorgeous complexion. Aria nearly laughed as she thought about how long she and Calypso would have struggled with a physical relationship without Clarice. The thought of being with both of them intimately sent her thoughts spiraling into an overheated fantasy of epic proportions. She had to quickly squash her train of thought before she forgot how to fly and crashed through the home of some unsuspecting humans.

At their speed, the trip only took fifteen minutes. They hovered above her childhood home for a moment, scanning for bystanders. When the street below seemed clear, they dropped down and landed lightly on the porch.

Her parents lived in a gated community, with a beautiful two-story home on a sculpted half-acre property. Her mother's life as a congresswoman paid well, but it was her father's work as a business owner operating a chain of cut-and-sew factories that put them in the lower brackets of the wealthy.

Aria glanced around the upper-class neighborhood, knowing they were most assuredly being recorded by multiple surveillance systems as she rang the doorbell.

She heard his familiar grumble from upstairs. "Who in the world could that be?"

A smile tugged at her lips. She had missed that voice.

When the door opened, Eric froze, staring at her in disbelief. "Aria?"

"Hi, Dad," she said brightly. "Got room for your little angel in there?"

He blinked hard. "Is that really you?"

"Yes, it's really me, you ninny," she laughed, stepping forward and pulling him into a tight embrace. "I missed you."

He gasped as her presence enveloped him, flooding his soul with radiance. She finally pulled back and gestured toward the door.

"Come on, let's go inside before someone sees a couple of angels standing on your porch."

The front room was like a shrine to their family history, with pictures covering the walls, cabinets, and bookshelves. There was a clear change in the number of pictures from before their daughters' cancer ordeals and after they were healed, as if being given a second chance had made them realize how precious each moment of life was.

"Hello, Eric," Calypso greeted him warmly as she followed them inside. "It has been some time. How have you been?"

He shut the door slowly, still staring as though seeing a ghost. "Calypso?"

She nodded gently. "I sang to Aria and Clarice fifteen years ago—at the hospital, you see."

He blinked again, then suddenly pulled her into a fierce embrace, his eyes filling with tears. "Thank you, Calypso. I don't think I could have gone on if I'd lost my little girl."

Calypso smiled softly as she returned his hug warmly, saturating his soul with radiance.

Aria's eyes moistened with quicksilver tears. She carefully kept them from touching her father until she knew how he felt about immortality.

He suddenly laughed through his tears. "You know, Emily always believed you were the one who healed our girls. I've always been a skeptic, and I couldn't accept that they were healed by magical music. It seems I was wrong about a lot."

Calypso laughed ruefully. "You are not the only one still learning. Until your daughters discovered me a few days ago, I had no inkling of how renowned I'd become, nor that I ceased aging a century past."

Aria smiled fondly at Calypso. "She didn't even know she was an angel."

Eric took a deep breath and stepped away from Calypso, wiping his eyes. "So, you really are an angel. I've been reading everything I can online, trying to understand what's been going on with my daughters. I've seen a lot of people claiming you were an angel, but I was too skeptical to accept it. How did Aria become an angel, too?"

Aria looked around the room warily. "We shouldn't talk about it here, Dad—I guarantee this place is bugged. We're actually here to take you with us, in case the people trying to kill us decide to use you as a hostage. We had a showdown with a bunch of military aircraft thirty minutes ago. We let them go after making it clear they didn't stand a chance. We figured they'd start going after our loved ones who *are* vulnerable. So far, we think they've just been watching you, hoping you'd lead them to us."

Eric's brows drew down in confusion. "Who exactly is 'they'?"

Aria grinned. "Apparently, conspiracy theorists were right about a lot of things. In this case, there's a shadow government pulling the strings of world governments. They have access to some pretty advanced technology. Uncle Devon used to work for them."

Eric frowned thoughtfully. "Your mom and I suspected he worked for one of the intelligence agencies. So he finally admitted it?"

Aria nodded toward Calypso, who was inspecting the photos throughout the room with a tender smile. "Calypso destroyed the nanobots that prevented him from talking about it."

Eric nervously thumbed his knuckles. "How long do we have to get out of here?"

Aria walked over to the window. A van had just pulled up to the curb a few houses down. "We should already be gone. It looks like they're here. I might have to make a scene to get us through them."

He studied her with a half-smile. "So... what? You're a superhero or something?"

Aria chuckled, glancing at Calypso. "Way more than a superhero. I'm totally impervious to any kind of damage. I have insane strength, speed, vision, hearing, smell, and I can fly. Oh yeah, I can also shoot laser beams out of my eyes."

He started to smile, then froze, realizing she wasn't joking. "You're serious?"

She smiled grimly. "I just caught up to an F-22 Raptor and told the pilot I was going to vaporize him if he didn't scram. Think Superman-like powers, without the kryptonite weakness."

He blinked, then shook his head vigorously. "Am I even awake?"

Aria smiled mischievously. "We'll find out soon. Do you ever have those dreams where you're falling? 'Cause we're not driving to the safe house."

His eyes widened as she flexed her wings. "Don't tell me you're going to *fly* me there..."

Her smile widened. "I'm going to fly you there. Don't worry, we've already had some practice. Clarice pulled some pilots out of an Apache gunship mid-crash earlier."

He nervously chewed his lip. "I really don't like flying."

She smiled reassuringly. "Not a problem, Dad, we'll take care of your fear of flying, too."

Her attention snapped back to the van outside. A group of men in work overalls were moving toward the house, weapons hidden beneath their clothes.

Aria held up a hand. "Hold that thought, Dad."

Before he could respond, she was gone—a blur of motion and wind. She zipped past each gunman, delivering a sharp chop to the side of the neck. One by one, they dropped, unconscious before they hit the ground. She was careful not to break the sound barrier; the neighbors wouldn't appreciate the broken windows. She was equally careful not to kill them, knowing they could be slaves to a swarm of nanobots infesting their blood, just like her uncle had been.

She was back in less than five seconds, hair tousled and grinning. "All clear. Ready?"

"I don't know about this," he hedged, backing away.

Aria frowned, studying his meridians. Something was interfering with them. "Oh yeah, first things first. Calypso, do you know what's going on with his meridians?"

Calypso stepped closer, eyes narrowed as she examined him. "Nanobots," she said in quiet disgust. "Tracking devices, I believe. I'll remove them."

She began to sing. The notes were low and ethereal, vibrating in the air like liquid light. Aria watched in fascination as Calypso's meridians pulsed in rhythm with the melody, forming patterns eerily similar to runes that flashed across her body. Her father's meridians responded, syncing to her frequency. A flash of energy surged through him, burning away the nanobots.

Aria stared, eyes wide. "Yeah, I'm convinced—there have to be different angel classes. Whatever you just did, I definitely couldn't replicate it. Those runes you make... they're formed from sound frequencies, like music turned into language."

"Runes," Calypso echoed softly. "That word seems familiar in some way. It may be connected to a language."

Aria pursed her lips. "Probably the divine language, a way to command matter itself, like words that shape reality."

Calypso nodded slowly. "I do not think about it consciously. I simply... feel the music. Once I am in that state, the light takes shape through me."

Aria scanned the street again. "Let's talk more once we're safe. Time to move."

Her father was still staring between them in disbelief, as though convinced he would wake up any second.

"Come on, Dad," Aria said gently, towing him outside. She wrapped her arms around his chest from behind. "Here we go."

Before he could protest, they shot into the sky. His startled cry was lost in the wind as Aria's aura flared, flooding his body with comfort and calm. She carried him higher and higher, her wings pumping against the night air in deep, powerful strokes. Fortunately, her unlimited stamina made accounting for the extra weight a simple matter of flapping her wings faster.

They flew for nearly an hour, the world glittering beneath them. Mindful of her father's fragile human body, Aria kept her speed low—just under a hundred mph. By the time they reached Devon's cabin, it was nearly midnight.

She touched down lightly in the driveway, lowering her father to the ground. His eyes were wide, but his breathing was steady.

Looking up at the stars, Aria's soul flared with joy. Someday soon, she would fly to them.

10 – NUKED

Aria had barely landed when Clarice shot out the door and embraced their father. A moment later, Emily and Devon emerged from the cabin. Emily approached and waited for Clarice to release him, a look of relief on her now-youthful face.

Devon chuckled wryly, observing Eric's bemused expression. "Looks like they've formed a welcoming committee. Did you run into any more trouble?"

Aria grinned impishly. "Not much—just a van full of gunmen trying to sneak onto the property. I knocked them out before they knew what happened."

Devon slipped his hands into his jean pockets as he studied her. "From what Clarice said, you two sound like an army all by yourselves. It's starting to seem less like you need our protection and more like we need *yours*."

Aria nodded, glaring up at the sky. "That seems to be the case. We were thinking about doing some satellite hunting."

Devon eyed her wings doubtfully. "You think you can fly that high?"

Aria nodded confidently. "I'm pretty sure we can. We don't need oxygen, we don't get cold, and there's still atmosphere up there—at least, far enough up for us to zap satellites. I'm pretty sure our eye beams can shoot stupidly far."

Devon knuckled his chin musingly. "It's the low-Earth-orbiting satellites you need to worry about. Those are the ones with high-resolution surveillance. There are so many of them up there now that you're visible to half a dozen at any given time."

Aria frowned, zooming her eyes in until she spotted one of the internet satellites flying past. "Are you talking about the Startlink satellites? I thought they were just for internet."

Devon snorted in amusement. "Do you really think they'd invest billions so a few rural bumpkins could get broadband? Those satellites provide internet, but only incidentally. Their main purpose is to offer ultra-wideband support for drones and other robotic gizmos that haven't been revealed to the public yet. I wouldn't expect the next attack to include actual humans. You've shown they're no match for you, so expect things to get more exotic."

Aria scowled. "Maybe we need to go visit whoever's in charge and cut the head off the snake."

Devon grunted sourly. "Good luck finding them. They keep everything extremely compartmentalized, so nobody knows who's really in charge. For all we know, it could be an AI that's already taken over. Some of the decisions they've made over the years certainly make that seem plausible."

Clarice gasped, releasing her father. "So we're going to be fighting the Terminator? Angels against machines! How cool would *that* be?"

Aria and Devon laughed. Eric was too busy getting smooched by Emily for either of them to join in.

Eric pulled back, studying Emily's features suspiciously in the dim yard lights. "Did you get younger?"

Devon looked up at the sky distrustfully. "Let's go inside to talk about this. Too many technologies can read lips or pick up sound out here."

They made their way into the front room and found seats. Their parents snuggled into a loveseat and Emily leaned into Eric, her relief at his presence evident.

Devon frowned at the angels standing across the room. "I totally forgot we need to find some new furniture to accommodate wings. Let me get some of the kitchen bar stools."

Clarice held up a hand. "No need, Uncle. Standing isn't the same for angels. We don't get tired, and we have this ridiculous euphoric energy filling us with happiness all the time, so discomfort's a thing of the past."

He hesitated, then nodded.

Eric looked expectantly at Emily, brushing his fingers through her dark hair. "You were going to tell me why you look like Clarice's sister?"

She smiled contentedly as Eric continued stroking her hair. "Our daughters are angels now because one of Calypso's tears landed on their hands.

They aptly called it an angel seed. The transformation only occurs after saying an activation phrase."

He nodded slowly. "Okay. So... angels throw pity parties to reproduce. Interesting mating ritual, but whatever."

Emily playfully backhanded Eric's gut. "We actually have a great theory about just what angels are, but that's getting ahead of the story. We were out talking in the driveway earlier today, shortly after they grew their wings. Things got a little emotional and one of Aria's tears landed on my neck. Apparently, they have a rejuvenating effect, which is why I look twenty years younger."

He shook his head with an appreciative grin. "More like thirty. So you're going to be an angel, too?"

She hesitated, glancing at Calypso. "Not necessarily. I haven't said the phrase that triggered it for Aria and Clarice. Calypso thinks there might be multiple classes of angels, and there may be other phrases. I'm just going to continue as a normal human unless I accidentally say one of the trigger phrases."

Eric eyed his daughters speculatively. "So, angels are the equivalent of Superman, except you don't need to eat or sleep, and Calypso can heal? Is that it?"

Clarice nodded. "Pretty much." She looked at Aria and Calypso admiringly. "And we're super freaking hot."

Aria added, "The laser eyes might be a class-related ability that only Clarice and I have."

Eric cleared his throat. "So, do angels have... I mean, do you still—" he cut off, blushing as his eyes darted around the room. "What I'm trying to ask is, do you, um, still, you know, have—"

Clarice shook her head sadly. "No, Dad, angels don't have a gender."

He frowned, a look of disappointment on his face. "Really? Oh. Well, I guess they got that much right."

Aria smacked Clarice's shoulder. "She's so full of crap. Yes, Dad, we're still *very* female." Aria turned to stare disapprovingly at Clarice. "You're a *bad* angel."

Clarice shook her head vehemently. "Hey, we've been over both of those points already! We can't be full of crap because we don't eat." She patted her narrow waist demonstrably. "And we're angels, so anything we do is, by default, good."

Aria smiled sweetly. "Then you're a fallen angel, and fallen angels *can* be bad."

Clarice's eyes brightened with sudden hope. "Do you need to punish me, mistress?"

Aria laughed helplessly, barely restraining a blush under Clarice's suggestive leer. "You are *too* much."

Emily shook her head, laughing softly. "Tweedledee and Tweedledum are at it again. Some things will never change, no matter how much everything else does."

Eric nodded sadly. "And now it's going to go on forever. I pity the future generations that'll have to endure this endless banter."

Devon eyed Eric and Emily in amusement. "I'm starting to see where they get it from." He looked at the angels, wincing as the thought of leaving them standing around still seemed to bother him. "You know, all angel chairs would need is a divided backrest."

Clarice rolled her eyes. "Stop fussing, Uncle. It's not like we can't sit on our wings."

She demonstrated by sitting in one of the loveseats, tucking her feet and leaning back. Her wings folded beneath her, wrapping around her like a blanket. "See? We can sit just fine if we want."

Devon eyed her doubtfully. "That's not uncomfortable?"

Clarice shook her head firmly. "Not in the least. Like I said, we don't feel discomfort or pain."

He raised a curious eyebrow. "Do you feel comfort?"

She nodded enthusiastically. "Pretty much all the time, and it's not like we build a tolerance to it, considering we no longer have squishy brains. We have perfect memories, so we remember *exactly* what discomfort feels like. We don't need the dichotomy of pain to offset pleasure, since I can recall everything as if it were happening right now, sensations and all."

Emily's eyebrows shot up. "You can relive any experience you want? So if Aria wanted to relive her first kiss, it'd be like she was experiencing it now?"

Aria's face flamed brilliantly as she recalled the memory, feeling Calypso's lips against her own—soft, warm, and incredibly sensitive.

Emily laughed, watching her mischievously. The expression was eerily reminiscent of Clarice, made more pronounced by her regressed age. "I'll take that as a yes."

Eric looked at Aria in dismay. "Hey, I missed Aria's first kiss?"

Emily laughed merrily. "You sure did. It was so intense that it knocked Calypso unconscious."

Calypso blushed a rich scarlet as Clarice and Devon laughed uproariously, but not quite as vividly scarlet as Aria.

"Look at that," Clarice gasped between bouts of laughter. "Her face is the same shade as her hair!"

Eric joined in the laughter, his blue eyes full of affection as he watched his overheated daughter.

Feeling a sense of rebellion in her soul, Aria pulled a blushing Calypso into her arms, her lips meeting Calypso's. Calypso's wings wrapped around her, shielding them from view as she passionately returned the kiss.

"Boo!" Clarice cried out disappointedly. "No hiding the show!"

Aria hadn't kissed Calypso since becoming an angel and wasn't prepared for the intensity of the experience. The energy in their meridians connected with a much denser bridge when their lips were together. Power flooded between the two of them, the intensely intimate exchange buckling her knees. She gasped and pulled back, her eyes alive with desire.

"Wow," she breathed in awe, staring into Calypso's beautiful, swirling eyes. "That. Was. Amazing."

"Yeah," Calypso whispered, wonder in her voice. "Truly amazing."

Aria grinned ruefully. "Sorry to spring that on you. Sometimes I can be a little willful—it's a redhead thing."

Calypso's answering smile was enchanting. "Do you hear me complaining?"

Clarice cleared her throat pointedly. "Are you two aware you aren't touching the ground?"

Aria blinked, then looked down. Their feet hovered several inches above the floor. She reluctantly released Calypso, then sucked in a surprised breath when they remained hovering in the air. She tried to step toward a chair and found herself floating toward it.

Clarice watched her in fascination. "Every time you experience anything intimate, you come away with a new ability. Are you unable to walk now, Aria?"

Aria tried to walk to the edge of the room but floated across the space instead. "I'm going to be pissed if I can't walk anymore," she fumed, trying to move her legs independently.

Calypso dropped to the ground and took a few steps. "You must focus on the distinction between floating and walking."

Aria focused her intent on walking instead of floating, rather than thinking of the destination. She slowly descended to the floor and let out a relieved breath.

She tilted her head with a frown, winding a lock of crimson hair around a finger. “Okay, this one’s a little weird. I can’t really see a reason to float around instead of walk.”

Clarice made a seductive, purring sound. “Then you’re not using your imagination very well.”

“Clarice!” Aria admonished her sister sharply.

Calypso furrowed her brow, looking between the two of them in confusion. “What have I missed? This was simpler when I could still hear your thoughts.”

Aria straightened her shirt primly. “She’s just being dirty.”

Clarice studied Calypso, her eyes wicked. “Can you float horizontally, Calypso?”

“I believe so,” the blond angel nodded, her face going still. She rose into the air again, then slowly rotated until she was lying flat a few feet above the ground. “I am curious whether we might be able to incorporate this into flight. We might not need to use our wings to hover, perhaps not even to fly.”

Aria gazed at her sister disapprovingly. “Clarice, you’re a *bad* angel.”

“I know,” Clarice admitted with a sultry smile.

Calypso looked at Aria inquisitively. “I feel as though I’ve missed the punchline.”

Clarice gave her a slow, sensual wink. “I’ll explain—later.”

Understanding dawned on Calypso, and her face flushed. She quickly rotated ninety degrees.

Emily shook her head in amusement. “You really are a bad angel, aren’t you?”

Clarice smirked, eyeing Aria and Calypso with a lascivious grin. “One does one’s best.”

Aria groaned plaintively. “I feel like I need to bathe.”

Clarice winked suggestively. “I’ll scrub your back.”

Aria finally lost it, giggling uncontrollably at how outrageous her sister was. Calypso smiled fondly as she watched them.

Eric exchanged a look with Emily. “Oh boy, here comes one of Aria’s laughing fits. This might go on for a while.”

Aria struggled to shut off the mirth valve, but it was futile. Once Clarice triggered one of her ‘giggle episodes,’ she usually couldn’t stop until her stomach muscles were exhausted. Now that she was an angel, she wondered if she would *ever* stop laughing. The thought of wandering the heavens while laughing uncontrollably for eternity sent her into another round of hysterical giggles.

She was just getting a handle on her hilarity when she made the mistake of meeting Clarice's gaze. Her sister blew her a kiss, sending her into fresh peals of laughter.

Devon raised an eyebrow at Eric. "So... this is normal?"

Eric nodded, obviously struggling not to grin. "Yep. I guess you've never seen one of her 'episodes.' I don't think they would last as long without Clarice to keep her going. Did they say angels don't ever get tired?"

Calypso answered, her own lips curved into a wide smile. "That would be correct."

Eric rubbed his chin musingly. "This might go on for quite a while, then."

Clarice suddenly jumped to her feet and vanished, leaving a miniature whirlwind in her wake.

The action snapped Aria from her giggle fit. She listened intently, catching the faint whine of tiny servos. The sound cut out, and a heartbeat later, Clarice was back, entering much slower than she had left.

Their parents and Devon were still halfway to standing, eyes wide with alarm.

Clarice scowled, holding up the remains of something that looked like a metal dragonfly. "Looks like we have a Peeping Tom."

Devon studied the crumpled electronics. "Stealth drone. Usually undetectable because they mimic real dragonflies perfectly." He looked up at Clarice. "How did you even know it was there?"

Clarice tapped her ear. "These godlike ears warned me. I could hear the little servos inside."

He blinked. "Your hearing is *that* good?"

"Yep," Clarice nodded gravely. "I could hear a spider fart in Asia."

Aria sighed. "Thanks for the visual."

Clarice grinned. "Any time, Tweedledee."

Emily turned to Devon anxiously. "Do you think we're under attack?"

Clarice shook her head with a grimace. "My sixth sense isn't tingling, though who knows if it'll always warn me. I think we should scout around."

"Agreed," Aria said quickly. She ghosted out into the night, hovering a few feet above the ground, testing her new ability. When she accelerated, her body shot forward effortlessly, with no drag or wind resistance. It felt like thought had become instant motion. She grinned at the realization the wind would no longer tear her clothes off.

It didn't take long to find an anomaly. Several miles from their cabin, she found a semi-truck with a long, matte-black trailer dotted with small holes where more of the micro-drones were entering and exiting.

She swiftly ghosted to the back of the trailer and inspected a door with a combination pad. Activating her righteous fury, her body erupted in light, and she vaporized the door.

A dozen uniformed operatives sat at workstations, their faces bathed in the sterile light of monitors. They scrambled to their feet when they saw her where the door had been, reaching for weapons and squinting against her radiance.

She smiled grimly. "Good. Now that you're trapped in here with me, let's have a chat."

She wasn't sure if it was the knowledge of her own invulnerability granting her the courage she had lacked as a mortal, or if it was whatever Calypso had done to fix her childhood trauma, but she felt no fear or anxiety as she faced a mobile command center full of armed operatives.

At the other end of the trailer, a sergeant shouted, pistol trained on her chest, "Get down on the floor and put your hands behind your head!"

Aria smirked. "Clearly, you haven't heard what happened to the last team who pointed their guns at me. I'll give you three seconds to drop your weapons and start talking."

The sergeant's finger began to flex on the trigger. Before he could blink, she was in front of him, her hand restraining his trigger finger.

"I said it's time to talk," she said dangerously, easily removing the gun from his straining hands. "But first, we'll need to deal with some troublesome pests."

Aria called out in her authoritative voice, "Clarice, can you bring Calypso over here?"

After a few seconds, Calypso entered the trailer with Clarice. The other operatives still had their guns trained on them, but no one fired.

Aria turned to face the two angels. "Can you clean them up, Calypso?"

Calypso nodded and began a low hum. Faint runes glowed in her meridians, and the energy pulsed outward, mirrored by the humans. Within seconds, the nanobots within the soldiers disintegrated.

"There," Aria said, smiling at their relief. "Now that you're free, it's time for some honesty. Are you with The Agency, or regular military?"

The sergeant licked his lips nervously, his eyes a mixture of fear and hope. "The nanobots are gone?"

She nodded with a reassuring smile. "They're gone."

A collective sigh of relief swept through the other operatives.

"We're with The Agency," the sergeant answered, anxiety evident in his eyes as he waited for his heart to stop. When he continued living, some of the fear drained out of him.

Aria maintained her smile, knowing her uncle could have been any of these people before Calypso destroyed the nanobots inside him. "What were your orders here? Just to surveil us?"

The sergeant nodded. "To gather intel."

Aria frowned. "So, try to listen to conversations, map the area, that kind of thing?"

He nodded again, swallowing hard. "Yes... and observe your capabilities."

She looked around the mobile surveillance command center curiously. "Are there any other operatives up here on the mountain?"

He eyed her uncertainly, his face cycling between gratitude and awe. "I don't think so."

"How did they find us here?"

He hesitated. "They didn't tell us, but it was probably satellite tracking."

She grimaced at Clarice. "We need to take those satellites down after all."

Clarice smirked. "There are going to be a lot of pissed off Startlink users."

Aria shrugged indifferently. "They'll just have to deal with it." She frowned, glancing back at the operatives. "You guys can go now. Let your superiors know we're coming for them next if we get even a whiff of anyone snooping around the area. Of course, now that your nanobots are gone, you might want to find a different vocation."

The man nodded, his face thoughtful.

Aria left the trailer in a burst of speed, the lack of wind making it seem like she had teleported away.

Clarice caught up to her and glared.

"Hey! I wanna be able to zip around without affecting the air. That's not fair."

Aria arched an eyebrow, her lips curving into a small smile. "Well... you know how to get the ability now."

Clarice sighed dramatically. "It'll be a hardship, but I'll just have to persevere."

They reached the edge of the clearing near the cabin when Clarice suddenly wrapped herself around Calypso—wings and all. Aria heard unmistakable kissing sounds, and her face heated up. She had been hoping Clarice would kiss *her*. She tried to ignore the intimate sounds, but her self-control failed within seconds. When she glanced over again, the two were levitating several feet above the ground.

"Hey," Aria deadpanned. "You've sucked so much oxygen out of Calypso that you're floating."

The kissing sounds continued for an additional minute. When it finally ended, Clarice unwrapped her wings from Calypso and floated away. Her eyes wide with wonder, she moved around effortlessly, untouched by the atmosphere.

"This is *so* cool. This is going to *totally* change how we fly."

Aria nodded with a wry smile. "Yeah, no need to worry about our clothes getting torn off now."

Clarice winked, making the action more erotic than any wink had a right to be. "I wasn't super worried about that. The speeds we'll be able to move at now are going to be insane. Reaching those satellites shouldn't be a problem anymore either. Let's try it out."

She vanished.

If not for Aria's enhanced senses, she would have thought Clarice had teleported. Grinning, Aria focused on a point far above, and instantly, she was there. She found herself several hundred miles above Earth, the nighttime world a glittering orb below. Stars stretched across the void in ultra-high definition, broken only by the thousands of satellites drifting above.

Calypso appeared beside her, gasping softly. "It's *gorgeous*."

Aria nodded, watching another satellite glide by. "Almost perfect. I think it's time to remove the eyeballs watching us."

Her body flared with light, and a beam shot from her eyes, vaporizing the satellite. She began sweeping through orbit, blasting one after another like an angelic space invader.

Clarice soon joined her, laughing as she turned it into a game.

Aria paused after zapping the twentieth satellite. "This is going to take a while. There are thousands of them."

Clarice raised an eyebrow. "Did you forget how fast we are?" she asked archly. "We don't have to wait for them. Also, I don't think we need to destroy them—let's just tear the cameras off."

She vanished in a beam of light, streaking across the heavens like a meteor. Aria grinned and went the opposite direction, marveling at their speed as they practically teleported to each satellite. Within minutes, she met up with Clarice on the other side of the world. She found it strange that their thoughts seemed to accelerate along with their movements, almost like their minds were overclocked. It took less than a millisecond to remove each camera, then move on to the next satellite.

Clarice watched curiously as a smaller version of a space shuttle flew past. “Is that the X-37? I’m going to check it for cameras.”

She darted away and reappeared a heartbeat later, grinning triumphantly.

“No more cameras. Also, fun fact—there’s a guy living in it. So much for it being unmanned. Talk about boring.”

Aria stared at her in horror. “Seriously? Why would someone want to live in solitary confinement for months on end?”

Clarice shrugged. “Some kind of psychic experiments, I’d guess. It’s probably more effective from orbit or something. Still... freaking boring.”

Aria made a face. “Weird *and* boring,” she said critically, then looked down at the planet beneath them. “Are we done here?”

Clarice put her hands on her hips and slowly rotated, surveying the stars above them. “That should take care of the worst of the surveillance, though I think we may need to take out the geosynchronous satellites above our place, too. They’re a lot higher up, so it’ll be a good time to find out just how far up we can go.”

Aria grinned eagerly. She had be in *space*! Low Earth orbit still felt like Earth, so it didn’t count. “How high are they?”

A matching grin appeared on Clarice’s delicate features. “About twenty thousand miles. You ready to go to space?”

Aria’s grin split her face. “You know it.” She turned to Calypso. “You coming too, Calypso?”

Calypso nodded fervently, her vortex eyes swirling furiously. “I would not miss it for the world!”

Clarice rubbed her hands together eagerly. “Let’s skip back to our side of the planet and go to space.”

She vanished in a streak of glowing angel light.

Aria and Calypso followed, appearing above their mountain in seconds. Grinning at each other, they launched skyward.

They reached a massive satellite within moments. The planet looked considerably smaller than it had from low Earth orbit, almost like a large grapefruit held at arm’s length. It was breathtaking and at the same time humbling to see it looking so small, knowing there were billions of people living their lives on the floating ball of water.

Clarice grasped the large satellite and rotated it so the cameras faced them. “This one’s loaded with lenses. Everyone say cheese.”

“Cheese,” Aria and Calypso chorused.

Clarice laughed mischievously as she tore the cameras off. “I would love to see the analysts’ expressions when they see our faces grinning at them in space—assuming it can see anything at close range. Okay, let's take out a few more in the area."

Aria paused, furrowing her brow. "How are we talking in space? There isn't any atmosphere this high up. Hell, there wasn't any atmosphere in low Earth orbit, but we were talking just fine."

Clarice nodded. "I noticed that, too." She gestured at them. "I can see your meridians generating sound waves as you talk. They seem to intuitively help out when they understand what we're trying to do. They're creating an energy channel between us, almost like beaming a radio wave."

Aria studied Clarice's energy matrix as she spoke. "Wow, that's pretty awesome. Now that I know what to look for, I can see it too. It's just like how Calypso sings in harmony with herself."

Clarice grinned. "You're right! We'll have to try it when we get back to Earth."

They continued dismantling the geosynchronous satellites, carving a vast blind spot over the Western Hemisphere.

Aria flew toward a massive orbital platform. "Hey, come check this one out!"

Twelve sealed bays lined its side. Sensing the dense materials within, she whistled. "I think these are nukes."

Clarice inspected the space silo curiously, slowly orbiting it. A red light blinked, and one of the bays began to open.

Clarice's glow brightened slightly. "I guess it has a proximity sensor. I wonder where they're supposed to launch them when it's tripped."

Aria studied the nuclear station with a mixture of curiosity and concern. "Maybe they're controlling it remotely, and they've decided to just try nuking us."

Clarice glanced at Calypso, worry evident in her voice. "Do you think it'd work? Could a nuke hurt us?"

Calypso frowned. "I rather doubt it, though I know nothing of nuclear devices."

Clarice's glow intensified. "I should probably vaporize it, just in case."

A blinding flash of light erupted from the missile chamber, momentarily turning their vision white. When the light faded, the silo was gone. Aria blinked, realizing all three of them were naked.

She stared at Calypso's and Clarice's naked forms, heat flushing up her neck and into her cheeks as desire ignited like a... nuclear blast.

"Well," Clarice said, smirking as she eyed them appreciatively. "Apparently nukes don't hurt us—but they're hell on clothes."

Aria sighed in defeat. "We're really going through clothing fast lately. We need to find a tailor."

Calypso's face was the same shade as Aria's as she floated in front of the other two angels. She folded her arms self-consciously, avoiding their gazes.

Aria tried to ignore her own nakedness. Becoming an angel had purified her body, making it more beautiful than she could have imagined. It was hard to be embarrassed when she had a perfect body, and with her fear of intimacy no longer a constant worry, the thought of being naked in front of the other two angels was far less concerning. Even so, it was hard to stop herself from hiding with Clarice leering at her. She'd never admit it—not even to herself—but Clarice's open admiration sent a thrill straight to her libido.

"Let's go get some clothes," she suggested as she tried, and failed, not to ogle the other two. "We don't have to worry about wraps or tight-fitting clothes now that the wind doesn't affect us."

"Aww," Clarice whined as they shot toward the surface at hypersonic speeds. "I was really enjoying the show. That's okay, it's just as good from behind."

Aria ground her teeth, her cheeks flaming. Calypso had her face in her hands as they landed on the deck outside her bedroom. The two of them quickly retreated into their rooms.

"Don't be strangers, you two," Clarice called from her room, knowing they could hear. "I feel like the show ended way too early."

Aria knew better than to reply but couldn't resist. "Next time, we're charging admission."

"Only if I get a lap dance," Clarice countered, her voice laced with sensual promise.

Aria heard a groan from Calypso's room and smiled, finding a strange comfort in knowing someone was even more embarrassed than she was.

11 – WARDROBE ISSUES

"Are you three back?" Emily's voice called up the stairs.

"Yeah, Mom," Clarice shouted down, her tone dripping with mischief. "Things got a little heated with the three of us, and we need some new clothes."

A long, considering silence followed.

"Aria," Emily called finally, "can I get a more *honest* version of events?"

Aria's voice was muffled as she tried to figure out how to put on a shirt with giant wings attached to her back. "They detonated a nuke next to us in space, and it vaporized our clothes."

While she could fold the silky wings tightly against her back and pull a shirt over them, they would still hang far below the hem. A slight twitch of her wings would leave her topless and blushing. She finally gave up and settled for a bra, silently vowing to find a tailor as soon as shops opened.

Emily's voice jumped an octave. "They detonated a *nuke* next to you?"

Aria emerged from her room in white pants and a pink bra. "Yeah, they did. We need to find a tailor—today."

From the base of the stairs, Emily looked up at her steadily for a few seconds before her lips started twitching. "Nice bra."

Aria scowled down at her threateningly. "So help me, Zeus, I will fly you into the sun if you mock my wardrobe."

Emily's eyes widened with feigned innocence. "I wouldn't *dream* of it."

Clarice exited her room with an appreciative whistle. "She's rocking the bra look, yeah? Turns out it's *really* hard to make normal clothes work with wings."

She was wearing short denim cutoffs and a revealing black lace bra. Aria quickly looked away before her cheeks could betray her, grateful her angelic nature no longer had a pulse to reveal a sudden spike in her heart rate. She hopped over the stair railing to land lightly beside her mother.

"I'm going to the library to find a tailor," she announced levelly. "This is *not* my new look."

Emily folded her arms and began tapping her lips, her contemplative pose at odds with the mischievous sparkle in her dark eyes. "It's going to take a few days for a tailor to make new clothes," she said in a voice dripping with concern. "That's assuming they aren't backlogged. Could be weeks."

Aria adjusted the shoulder strap of her bra and gave her mother a confident smirk. "When an angel flies into the shop and requests a rush job, they'll *find* time. After the last twenty-four hours, I'm pretty sure the secret about angels is out of the bag."

Emily arched an amused eyebrow. "You're going to just fly into town in broad daylight?" she asked incredulously. "Wearing a bra? Do you *really* want the first YouTube videos of you to be an angel in lingerie?"

Aria waved a dismissive hand and headed to the library. "Luckily, I move fast enough that nobody's even going to see me until I'm in front of the tailor."

"Are my favorite cupids back yet?" Eric's voice called from the veranda.

"Cupids is right," Emily called back dryly. "They're having wardrobe issues."

Tuning out the rest of the conversation, Aria focused on the screen in front of her. Opening a new browser tab, she froze at a headline on the news feed.

ASTRONOMERS BAFFLED BY MYSTERY LIGHTS APPEARING IN THE SKIES AROUND THE WORLD

People across the globe witnessed an inexplicable light show in the skies last night, leaving astronomers scrambling for answers. The lights moved so rapidly that they sometimes appeared as solid lines drawn across the night sky. A brief Startlink outage coincided with the start of the light show, but SpacesX maintains that the events were unrelated.

Jerald McCormick, an astrophotographer who was capturing a comet at the time, managed to take the clearest image yet of one of the light sources (image below). Internet users have compared the object to a winged figure, and although distance and speed blurred the images, one appears to depict an angel.

The light show culminated in a brilliant flash that illuminated the ground over North America. The flash has been compared to the nuclear explosions recorded during Operation Fishbowl in 1962, when the military conducted high-altitude nuclear detonations. However, experts claim this explosion occurred at a much higher altitude than those in the 1960s.

Given the internet's ongoing fascination with Calypso and claims about her angelic nature, many believe she is engaged in a battle with a secret organization attempting to kill her.

Adding fuel to the fire, footage surfaced last night allegedly showing a military encounter with three "angels." Although grainy and distant, the footage depicts three glowing figures, one of whom appears to be firing beams of light that destroy an aircraft.

One entity appears to have red hair, prompting speculation that it is Aria, the woman seen with Calypso on the day she resurrected a biker. Aria and her stepsister, Clarice, previously drew attention when their apartment exploded under what officials called a "gas leak," despite the absence of a gas line to the building. The two women, along with their mother, have since vanished. Many now believe they are living in hiding with Calypso.

A popular influencer known as WorldController has even speculated that all three women are angels.

The Pentagon has declined to comment, with a spokesperson only confirming that an Apache gunship crashed during "routine training" in the Appalachians, resulting in no fatalities.

Meanwhile, televangelists continue to denounce Calypso as a false prophet, claiming her miraculous healings are demonic possessions in disguise. One prominent preacher has even urged that children healed by Calypso undergo exorcisms.

As strange as things have become over the last week, it is safe to say that more surprises are on the way. Check back here, at alicenominas.com, to find out.

Aria absently toyed with a strand of hair after finishing the article. It seemed like a lot of people were already convinced Calypso was an angel. She skimmed through some of the comments curiously.

Borked4life-> Right, so I was out in the garden at the crack of dawn when I looked up and saw lights absolutely tearing across the sky. Proper mental, it was. Honestly thought the bloody Martians were finally invading.

I even spotted this dead bright flash, looked exactly like that massive sci-fi energy beam that brought down the chopper. So, it's either an alien apocalypse, or the angels are currently having a proper straightener up in the clouds.

I feel a right muppet even uttering the words, but I saw it with my own two eyes. Makes you a believer, doesn't it?

DarkTeaTimeOfTheSoul-> I'm one of the soldiers from that video. Our CO never told us we were fighting angels. He claimed they were aliens, but I was twenty feet away from them, and holy shit, the power of their presence was un-fucking-believable. We all recognized Calypso and refused to engage, so now we're facing court-martials, but I'd rather go to jail than hell.

Don't even get me started on the insane power disparity. Nothing we had could hurt them, and they were literally shooting laser beams out of their fucking eyes. They took down one of the Apaches and then saved the pilots before it crashed. It was obvious they could have wiped the floor with us, but they let us live, even after we attacked them.

Believe what you want, but the U.S. military tried to make us attack angels, and we said hell no!

seeingisbelieving-> They saved me and my friend and sister yesterday after we got pulled over by some dirty cops who planted evidence in our car. They arrested us, even my 14-year-old sister, and were putting us in their car when a blur shot past us. Both of those bastard cops suddenly went flying over the top of their car, and it looked like they'd been kicked in the nuts super hard. One of the blurs stopped in front of me for a split second, and I immediately recognized Aria's red hair. She had lavender eyes, like Calypso. I don't know why they were there or why they decided to save us, but if you're reading this, thank you!

Aria smiled, a warm glow spreading through her meridians as she read the latest comment. It was nice to see the girls had gotten home safely. She felt a sudden need to continue helping people, almost like a compulsion. She wondered if this was how Calypso felt about healing people. Maybe it was hardcoded into angel DNA or something.

She glanced at the next comment down and facepalmed.

godisgreat-> I can't believe you have all been fooled so easily! Jesus warned us of false prophets and false angels that would perform wonders.

You have all been deceived! This isn't rocket science, people! These are wolves in sheep's clothing luring you down the path to hell, and you people need to WAKE UP!!! REPENT of your foolish choices and return to Christ. CHRIST IS KING!!!!!!!!

Aria snorted derisively. Apparently, she was a wolf who was pulling the wool over everyone's eyes. She felt a sudden urge to howl. "What a funny world," she murmured with a wry smile.

Shaking her head, she refocused on her task of finding a tailor. She spent the next hour jumping from website to website. Distance was no longer a barrier, since she could travel to any shop on Earth in moments, but that didn't make the search any easier.

Her first problem was the search terms. Every query for "tailor" returned business suits. The image of angels in suits triggered a fit of giggles. She could practically picture uptight, corporate angels in three-piece ensembles, wings tucked through jacket slits, arguing about quarterly miracles. *No, thanks*.

Switching tactics, she searched for "custom costume shops." That finally led her to someone in rural northern California who specialized in custom costume designs. Jackpot.

Gritting her teeth, Aria hit "call," suppressing her introverted panic.

"This is Tamra," a woman's voice answered on the second ring.

"Hi, Tamra, my name's Aria," she said in a rush. "I'm looking for someone who can make clothing to accommodate wings."

A pause followed, long enough that Aria began cursing her overenthusiastic tongue. She was opening her mouth to repeat herself when Tamra finally spoke.

"I can make costumes to accommodate wings," she said cautiously. "How much wear and tear are you expecting? Will you, uh... be wearing it frequently?"

Aria took a deep breath, forcing herself to speak normally. "Pretty much all the time. We'll need three different sizes, with ten shirts in each size."

She heard Tamra's breath catch, and she tilted her head, wondering what she had said to trigger the reaction. Had she spoken too quickly again? Had her tone been too brisk? God, she hated meeting new people, especially when she couldn't see their facial expressions.

"Would you want something exotic or casual?" Tamra asked, her voice a little unsteady. "And how, um, durable would they need to be?"

"Durable, definitely," Aria said firmly. "And *probably* casual, but who knows with Clarice."

"How soon could you come in for a fitting?" Tamra asked faintly.

"Faster than you can imagine," Aria offered hopefully. "Right now, if you'd like."

There was a sharp inhale. "Is this... really Aria?" Tamra asked with quiet awe. "The one with Calypso?"

Aria froze, suddenly realizing why Tamra had been so out of countenance. She must have suspected from the moment Aria revealed her identity—there weren't a lot of Arias out there.

"Um, yeah?" Aria admitted hesitantly. "Is that a problem?"

"No, no, no, not at all," Tamra said, her words spilling out in a rush. "Nothing wrong with that at all!"

"Good," Aria said mildly. "Mind if we stop by now? We're kind of stuck wearing bras for tops until we can get new clothes. A nuke incinerated our last outfits, and now my sister won't stop calling it 'the bra club.'" She kept her tone light in an attempt to put Tamra at her ease.

"That really was you last night?" Tamra asked faintly. "Were you really fighting some shadow organization?"

"In a manner of speaking," Aria acknowledged dryly. "We got tired of them creeping on us with their all-seeing eye, so we took out their surveillance network. Give me a minute to grab Calypso and Clarice, and we'll be right over."

"O-okay," Tamra stuttered, the sudden excitement in her voice bleeding through. "See you soon!"

Aria hung up with a relieved sigh. She had done it! She called a stranger and didn't even need Clarice to rescue her!

Her spirits buoyed, Aria stood and made her way to the stairs. "You two ready to go? Or are you doubling down on the bra club?"

Calypso's reply was immediate, her voice easily carrying from her room to Aria's sensitive ears. "So very ready."

"*Fine,*" Clarice sighed in a put-upon tone, "but only because I'm excited to see what she can make."

As Aria met them on the third-floor balcony, Clarice gave her a calculating look. "Where does she live? And can you find her house without GPS?"

Aria smiled smugly. "That's the beauty of perfect recall! I spent half an hour zooming in and out of Maps, and now I've got half the country memorized. Tamra's about eighty miles outside of San Francisco, in a small rural town."

Clarice grinned at her with open admiration. "You're both smart *and* gorgeous. That's one hell of a sexy combo."

Aria's eyes shifted to Clarice before she could stop herself. She had been avoiding the sight of her sister's alluring body, knowing she needed to stay focused. Unable to look away, her gaze roamed Clarice's long, smooth legs, taking in the short denim cutoffs and their low, teasing waistline. Her flat stomach looked deliciously soft, calling out for Aria's hands to slide up its silky surface to cradle her generous—

"Aria?" Calypso prompted, a note of amusement in her riveting voice.

Aria snapped out of her erotic thoughts with a guilty start, tearing her eyes from Clarice's barely concealed breasts. She forced her breathing to slow as her cheeks flared a brilliant red. She sneaked a peek at her sister and found Clarice staring at her with a look of such sensual promise that she lost control of her breathing again, her chest rapidly rising and falling as her mouth went dry.

Then Clarice winked, slow and deliciously seductive. Heat flooded Aria in a tsunami of desire that made intelligent thought impossible. She couldn't pull her gaze away from Clarice's, captivated by her flawless features and soft, chocolate eyes—eyes that burned with a hunger as hot as Aria's own.

Clarice broke the connection with a sudden grin. "Let's boogie!" she exclaimed cheerfully, then launched herself skyward, shooting dozens of feet into the air before her first wingbeat.

Aria took several long seconds to reel in her overstimulated libido. Clarice had been gorgeous as a human, but it was her personality that took her allure to the next level. Becoming an angel had augmented that combo to mythical levels, making her nearly irresistible. Aria wasn't sure how long she could keep playing the "look but do not touch" game. As the walls in her mind rapidly broke down, her fear of intimacy was replaced by a desperate hunger, borne from years of repressed sexual tension.

She took a shaky breath and followed the other two angels, rising a few thousand feet before accelerating to hyperspeed. They streaked across the continent in seconds, her overclocked mind rendering the ground in exquisite detail, even at these ridiculous speeds.

Tamra's house sat on five wooded acres, complete with a fenced garden. A few chickens wandered the yard, scratching and pecking at the soil. A shimmering pool lay beside the porch, glittering in the morning sunlight. Tamra stood waiting among the trees in front of her house, shading her eyes as she searched the skies. When the three angels descended like bolts of lightning, she let out a startled squawk and leapt back.

"Hi, Tamra," Aria greeted the stunned woman brightly. "This is Clarice and Calypso. It's nice to meet you in person."

Tamra extended a shaky hand, and Aria took it gently.

"Hello, Tamra." Calypso stepped forward and embraced Tamra warmly. "How is Adelle faring?"

Tamra froze in Calypso's embrace, her face radiating contentment as warmth enveloped her.

Clarice stepped beside Calypso. "Did you have a loved one who Calypso healed?" she asked gently.

Tamra's blissful expression faded to sorrow and she stepped back from Calypso. "She healed my... niece," she began, but her voice faltered.

Calypso's eyes tightened with concern and she placed a hand on Tamra's shoulder. "Is Adelle quite safe?"

Tamra shook her head, her eyes glistening. "It's been over a year since she went missing," she said in quiet anguish. "She and a friend were walking to her house to celebrate their fourteenth birthday, but she never made it. We spent months working with the police and the FBI, but they couldn't find a trace. She had only been free of her cancer for a few months when she disappeared."

Clarice's eyes sharpened. "Do you have anything with her scent? Even if it's old."

Tamra's eyes widened with sudden hope. "I have her jacket hanging in the mudroom."

"Take me to it," Clarice said briskly.

Tamra led them to the mudroom and pulled a blue jacket from a peg. "She wore this a few days before she disappeared."

Clarice took the jacket and inhaled deeply before handing it to Aria.

"We'll find her," Clarice promised with quiet certainty. "We'll be back soon."

Tamra glanced at their bras. "Would you like some wing-fitted tops before you go? They're not tailored for you, but they should work."

Aria brightened. "Oh my god, that would be wonderful!"

Clarice sighed dramatically. "Okay, fine. Guess it's time to give up the bra club."

Tamra guided them through several workrooms where rows of automated cutting tables hummed and plotters spat out patterns, until they reached a costume storage area. She selected a soft, blood-red, sleeveless leather shirt and eyed Clarice appraisingly. "This should fit. Might be a little snug in the chest."

Tamra showed her how to detach the shoulder buttons so the divided back wrapped around her wings.

Clarice was stunning. The leather outfit hugged her narrow waist, rising snuggly until it reached her breasts, where a thinner elastic fabric strained over her generous curves, leaving them defined in sensual detail. An oval cutout displayed her cleavage, and a high collar featured a small zipper. Red had always looked amazing on Clarice, and this was no exception.

She whistled at herself in the mirror. "Damn, this looks awesome!"

Aria nodded fervently, flushing when Clarice caught her staring in open admiration. Clarice slowly winked, her expressive lips curving into a seductive grin.

Calypso was silent, biting her lip as she studied Clarice, a faint splash of pink coloring her cheeks.

Tamra turned and fetched another shirt, almost a match to Clarice's, but green instead of red.

Tamra buttoned the sides above Aria's shoulders. The chest was less tight, almost a perfect fit. Clarice gave another wolf whistle as Aria inspected herself in the mirror. The green sleeveless shirt had golden scrollwork that curled around her breasts and up the high collar. She cinched the laces to tighten the waist, admiring the fit as she studied her reflection.

Tamra had a third shirt for Calypso, this one a brilliant white with silver scrollwork around the bodice and a cutout in the chest to display her generous cleavage. Calypso looked angelic in the bright white garment—an extremely sexy angel. She also got a wolf whistle from Clarice, producing a shy smile as she stepped up to the mirror.

When they were all outfitted, Clarice turned to Tamra, radiating confidence. "Okay, we'll be back with your niece shortly. Hopefully her friend, too."

Tamra's eyes brimmed with hope as she led them out of the house. "Do you really think you can find her just from her scent?"

Clarice nodded, patting Tamra's shoulder reassuringly. "You wouldn't *believe* how powerful angel senses are. See you soon."

The three of them took off into the skies and split up, Aria toward L.A., Clarice inland, and Calypso north.

It only took minutes for Aria to catch the scent as she flew over Beverly Hills. She followed it to a sprawling mansion, a frown darkening her features as she stared at the large complex. She decided to fetch the other two before assaulting the place.

She found Clarice within moments. Since becoming angels, she had felt a connection to her sister, allowing her to sense Clarice's location, a sixth sense that drew her like a beacon.

"Found her," Aria said grimly, rage simmering just below the surface. "Let's get Calypso."

Clarice noted the fury in her eyes and laid a hand on her arm. "Where is she?"

"Beverly Hills," Aria ground out. "I have a feeling I know why she's there."

Clarice's eyes hardened, and she nodded.

They gathered Calypso near Seattle and returned to the mansion, landing on the porch. Aria easily tore the locked front door off its hinges and hurled it aside. A large, snarling dog greeted them, crouching to leap at the angels. It met Aria's glowing eyes and let out a pitiful whine before bolting with its tail between its legs.

Following Adelle's scent, Aria found a stairwell leading to a basement. They moved down a long hall until the trail suddenly ended at a concrete wall. She punched straight through the four-inch wall and felt a steel-reinforced frame on the other side. With a deafening bang, she tore the entire hidden door from its casing, leaving a cloud of dust in its wake.

Another set of stairs lay beyond, and Aria could hear the unmistakable sound of crying in the distance. Her normally loving energy field transposed into righteous fury as she guessed the cause of those cries. She shot down the stairs in a blur, taking in the main room at a glance.

A large, chubby man was in the act of rising from a desk at the other end of the room, a handgun raised toward the stairwell. An anxious frown stretched his pudgy face, and close-set, piggy eyes were still widening in fear as Aria blurred across the hundred yards separating them. Before he could blink, Aria removed the gun from his hands, crushing it in her grip as if it were a wad of paper.

Doors lined the room at ten-foot intervals, each one fitted with a slot at the bottom and another at shoulder height. The crying was coming from one of those rooms, though Aria could hear heartbeats and breathing from several others.

Clarice ripped one of the nearby doors clean off its frame, revealing a naked fifteen-year-old girl curled on a thin mat, her body bruised and trembling. The room filled with incandescent light as Aria's fury went nuclear.

"Who else is down here?" she grated, shaking with the need to eradicate the piece of excrement cowering before her.

Calypso knelt and began talking to the girl. She stared up at Calypso in shock, her tears forgotten. Bruises covered her face, and her wrists and ankles were swollen. Calypso's eyes filled with tears as she stared at the state of the girl, suddenly understanding one of the world's cruelest realities.

Clarice didn't wait for the man to answer; in a thunderclap of sound, she tore open every remaining door in under a second, revealing three more naked girls, one as young as ten.

Aria could feel the heat in her eyes building up as she stared at the trembling man in front of her. He towered over her by nearly a foot, but size meant nothing anymore. She knew no justice would be served by leaving him to the court systems. With the wealth these people had, they could buy their way out of any crime.

The heat in her eyes reached ignition, and the man vanished in a burst of light.

"You are safe now, my darlings," Calypso sang softly as the girls stared at the angels with hope-filled eyes.

Aria heard a sound from somewhere in the mansion above, and her fury flared anew. "Calypso, can you do anything for them? I'm going to finish exterminating the vermin."

Calypso nodded as Adelle finally overcame her shock and flew into Calypso's waiting arms. The girl's tears vanished as the overpowering cloak of Calypso's radiance enveloped her.

Aria flashed up through the mansion, her passage as silent as a whisper. She found the owner in the master suite and snarled when she recognized the world-famous actor. Emmy awards lined the shelves, surrounded by grotesque sculptures and paintings that would have made her puke if she still had a stomach.

His face drained of blood as the glowing angel appeared before him. Guilt and fear filled his eyes, and with a desperate cry, he fell to his knees, words forming to beg for his life.

His knees never reached the ground.

There was incandescent flash, and the pedophile was gone, leaving no indication of what had happened—no burn marks, not even a mote of dust.

She listened carefully for any other sounds, but the rest of the mansion appeared to be empty, aside from the attack dog cowering near the back of the house. She zipped through the entire house anyway, just to be sure.

She returned to the hidden basement, feeling no remorse for taking two lives. She didn't even think of these monsters as human.

The four girls sat around Calypso, staring at her in awe as the angel sang softly, her healing light wrapping around them. Runes flowed from her song, mirrored within their bodies, restoring skin and soothing minds. The air glowed with the hum of divine energy, dispelling the aura of pain and humiliation that had seeped into the very walls.

The oldest of the girls had long, blond hair, finely sculpted features, and a face that didn't miss being beautiful. She was several inches taller than Clarice and Aria, with deep blue eyes that had seen too much. Awe and hope left her wide-eyed and trembling as she stared at the angels in disbelief.

The bruises, swollen wrists, and ankles vanished before Calypso's angelic voice. The healer's eyes shimmered with quicksilver tears as she sang, her soul heavy with the weight of the horrors humans inflicted on each other. When she finished, the four girls stood around her in a state of trancelike euphoria.

Aria stepped close to Calypso. "Let's take them back to Tamra's," she murmured in a subdued voice. "We'll figure out the rest from there."

Clarice fell in beside her as they guided the four girls up the stairs and onto the lawn.

"You okay?" Clarice asked softly, her eyes gentle and glowing with compassion. She reached up and tenderly cupped Aria's cheek. "This was pretty bad."

Aria didn't trust herself to speak and just nodded, looking down. Clarice gently raised her chin, so she was looking into her sister's loving eyes. "I'm sorry you had to deal with this, Aria. I wish I could protect you from these horrors."

Clarice pulled her into a comforting embrace, and her sister's loving energy flowed into her, filling her with renewed strength and determination. Aria took a deep breath, and Clarice released her.

"Thanks," she whispered fiercely. "I love you, Clarice."

A brilliant smile lit up her sister's face. "I know you do, Aria. I love you, too."

Aria took another deep breath and addressed the four girls. "We're going to fly you to Adelle's aunt's house. You're safe with us."

The girls exchanged excited glances as they watched the angels expectantly.

Calypso smiled affectionately at Adelle, stroking her cheek softly. "I'll take Adelle and Stacy."

Aria nodded, taking the oldest girl, Lexi, into her arms.

Wrapped in the angels' arms, divine energy poured into the girls, melting away the last of their fear. Aria lifted off the ground, holding her passenger securely as Calypso and Clarice did the same.

She was grateful for their upgraded flight ability, no longer affected by the wind. Rising above the city, the three angels carried their rescued charges high into the sky, leaving the darkness far behind.

It took them only seconds to return to Tamra's house. Their troubled passengers eagerly soaked up the love and comfort surrounding them. Aria couldn't imagine what they had been through. Just the thought kept her glowing with a simmering rage. She had known human trafficking was a reality, but seeing it firsthand made it nauseatingly personal. A slightly different roll of fate's dice, and *she* could have been one of these girls. Until now, she had lacked the power to do anything about the monsters of the world preying on children; now, though... things were different.

Tamra was waiting in her front yard when they landed, her hand over her mouth. She rushed forward with a strangled cry and wrapped her niece in a trembling embrace.

Clarice glanced at the increasingly awkward girls. "I suppose this is the right place for extra clothes."

Tamra nodded quickly and released her niece. "Yes, let's get them some clothes. Follow me, young ladies."

She led them into her fitting room, and soon the girls were trying on clothes. They looked like they had stepped out of a D&D campaign, but at least they were no longer naked.

While the girls were dressing, Tamra stepped closer to Aria and asked in a low voice, "Where were they?"

Aria's face glowed slightly brighter as her rage flared. "Beverly Hills," she said flatly, then told Tamra which actor would never disgrace another screen.

Tamra gasped. "I never would've guessed he could be such a monster." Her eyes hardened. "I hope he rots in a cell, assuming the court system does its job."

Aria smiled bleakly. "There isn't enough left of him to rot anywhere. Or his lackey."

"*Good!*" Tamra growled fiercely. "If only the rest of them could fry."

"They will," Aria promised, her normally expressive voice grim with dreadful intent.

Calypso turned to the eldest girl, her voice soft. "Lexi, could you tell us how you came to be in that place? Might we then make contact with your parents?"

The girl's head jerked up in surprise at hearing her name. Fear flickered across her face at the mention of her parents, and Aria felt the first sparks of fury flare again.

Calypso gently took Lexi's hand. Warmth and love flowed through her touch, easing Lexi's trembling. "Were they the ones who brought you there, Lexi?"

Lexi nodded, tears spilling down her cheeks. "They said it was modeling work... that this was just how the world worked. They told me the money would go toward my college tuition." Her voice cracked. "I never saw them again after they left."

Aria silently vowed to find those parents and ensure they never hurt anyone again.

Calypso pulled Lexi into her arms, holding her close as she continued questioning the others.

Calypso looked over Lexi's shoulder at the youngest victim, a wide-eyed ten-year-old. "Anna, do you know how you came to be there?"

Anna nodded uneasily. "I was walking home from school yesterday when what I thought was a sweet old lady told me she'd dropped her glasses in the back of her van. She said she couldn't reach under the seat and needed help." She paused and let out a shaky breath, her bottom lip trembling. "As soon as I went inside, a fat bald dude grabbed me and stuck a needle in my neck, and then I woke up in that place. They had stolen my clothes, and no one would talk to me. The fat dude hit me really hard when I screamed for my mom."

The girl's eyes were red-rimmed, but she smiled as she looked at Clarice. "I prayed that God would send an angel to save me. I prayed that Calypso would save me. I *knew* she was an angel."

Clarice shared a look of pure relief with Aria. The poor girl hadn't yet suffered the same horrors as the others. It would still scar her, but far less deeply than the other girls.

Aria thought about how fortuitous the chain of events had been that led them to the mansion. She felt an odd sense of gratitude toward the shadow government for nuking her. If they hadn't vaporized her clothing, forcing her to seek out a tailor, that little girl would still be in chains at the hands of the vilest of monsters.

Clarice laid a comforting hand on Anna's shoulder and smiled down at her cheerfully. "Let's get you home to your parents, shall we? Do you know your address?"

The girl smiled and nodded once.

Clarice knelt and opened her arms. "Okay, are you ready to fly again?"

Anna's eyes sparkled as she ran to Clarice, throwing her arms around her neck. "I'm *so* ready to fly again! My sister is never going to believe me when I tell her that I got to fly with *angels*!" She shivered as radiance enveloped her. "I *really* like angel hugs."

Clarice laughed and moved toward the front door. "Yeah, angel hugs are the best."

Anna excitedly waved at Calypso as they exited the front door. "Bye, Calypso!"

Calypso waved, smiling as the door closed behind them.

Aria turned to Adelle and her friend, Stacy, laying a hand on each of their shoulders. "Can you tell me how you two ended up there?"

The hollowness in Adelle's eyes lessened at Aria's touch. "A cop car pulled up and told us we were under arrest," she said quietly, leaning into Aria's hand. "They cuffed us and drove us to a warehouse, where a bald man showed up and... took us. We've been in that place ever since."

Her lip trembled as she finished, and Aria pulled both her and Stacy into her arms, charging them with her radiance. Adelle took a calming breath as the boundless love imparted by an angel's embrace flushed the anxiety from their minds.

"It's time for some housecleaning," Aria said grimly, her violet eyes blazing with anger. "After I take you two home, I'm going to visit that police station and deal with the ones responsible." Her voice darkened. "You'll never have to worry about dirty cops again."

Aria met Calypso's gaze, and a fresh surge of anger flared when she saw the pain in the gentle musician's face. Whoever was responsible for quenching the spark in those soft violet eyes would pay dearly. She longed to hold the gentle musician, to rid the world of the kind of filth that could subdue such a sweet spirit.

Aria turned to Tamra. "Can Lexi stay with you until we return? We shouldn't be gone long."

Lexi stiffened in Calypso's arms, and Calypso held her tighter.

"Of course," Tamra said gently, her eyes soft as she smiled at Lexi.

"We shall return," Calypso promised Lexi, her voice like a soothing lullaby. "As soon as Adelle and Stacy have been reunited with their families."

Lexi gave an almost imperceptible nod into Calypso's shoulder, clinging a moment longer before reluctantly releasing her.

Tamra and Lexi followed them outside to see them off, and Tamra gave her niece a parting embrace. Lexi anxiously watched them leave, hugging herself tightly. Aria regretted leaving the young woman without an angel. Should she have waited for Clarice to return before leaving? She sighed and decided to trust in Tamra. After all, they wouldn't be gone for long.

As they flew, Calypso quietly informed Aria that she had removed the emotional attachment from the girls' memories, making the last year seem like a bad dream. Perhaps Calypso could do more for Lexi when they returned. What kind of hell had the poor girl endured growing up, with parents who were willing to sell their own daughter to pedophiles?

She focused on the present as they dropped into a crowded subdivision and landed at a modest house with an economy car in the driveway. Ignoring the stares of pedestrians and a few drivers pulling over to gawk, Aria knocked on the door.

Adelle tugged Aria's hand. "We don't need to knock, you know—I live here, after all."

Before Adelle could grasp the handle, a wary, middle-aged woman opened it a crack to peer out suspiciously, sucking in a surprised breath when she saw Aria. Then she saw her daughter. She let out a low cry, threw the door open wide and pulled Adelle into a trembling embrace.

"Adelle!" she gasped, squeezing her daughter tightly as desperate sobs wracked her body. She tried to speak but was too choked up to articulate anything intelligible. She grasped Adelle's head and began kissing her forehead, then pulled her in tightly again, squeezing her eyes shut as a deluge of tears soaked her daughter's hair.

Adelle shook in her mother's arms as her own sobs shook her slender frame. "Oh, Mom, I missed you *so* much!"

Aria gave them a minute to cling to each other before lightly touching the woman's shoulder. "We need to talk in private," she said gently, nodding meaningfully at Adelle.

The woman looked at her through glistening eyes as a few more sobs escaped, then nodded and stepped inside, never releasing Adelle as the others followed her in.

Aria gave her a few more minutes before clearing her throat. "Calypso, maybe you can get Adelle and her friend to show you around while I talk to her mom?"

Adelle's mother reluctantly released her daughter and turned her attention to Aria with a look of wonder, taking in her eyes and wings.

Aria stared into the woman's meridians as Adelle and her friend led Calypso away, suddenly seeing the aura radiating from the complex spiritual matrix. She could finally see the mark Calypso claimed contained a person's name. Something must have changed in her understanding of spiritual energy, because it had never made sense before.

Aria stepped closer and quietly said, "Eilleen, we need to talk about what your daughter's been through."

Eilleen's eyes filled with tears again as she realized what Aria was hinting at. She nodded and led Aria into one of the bedrooms, then turned to face her with a look of trepidation. Aria explained where they had found her daughter as gently as she could, but how do you tell a mother her daughter's been a monster's plaything for the last year of her life?

Eilleen fell to her knees with her face in her hands, weeping bitterly. "How could anyone do this to my poor baby after all she's been through?"

Aria's heart broke for the poor woman. "I know this won't change the horror of what they suffered, but Calypso healed their minds as well," she said gently. "Most of what they remember will seem like a bad dream, rather than something with emotional attachment." Her tone lowered to an angry growl. "The local cops are the ones responsible for your daughter's abduction."

Eilleen's tear-streaked face snapped up, shock turning to venom. "The bastards I worked with to find her did this?"

Aria nodded, her body glowing brighter with her own rage. "Yeah. I'm paying them a visit after we drop Stacy off with her parents."

Eilleen eyed her with a mixture of doubt and hope. "What are you going to do? What *can* you do? They're the law, after all."

Aria smiled grimly, her expression as bleak as an executioner's. "Think of me as a *higher* law. They'll share the same fate as the bastards who held your daughter."

Eilleen stared at her worriedly. "Won't that bring trouble down on you?"

Aria raised an eyebrow and fluffed her wings. "You know what I am, right? We've been dealing with much bigger fish than rogue police departments."

Eilleen studied her winged form intently, a cautious light growing in her eyes. "Are you really angels?"

Aria spread her wings out as wide as the room would allow, then snapped them back in. "We are. But we have never served, nor do we now serve, a deity."

Eilleen furrowed her brow. "So, all that stuff about heaven and hell is just made up?"

Aria shrugged. "I assume so. I know that spirits exist; I can see the energy matrix it generates throughout your meridians. However, what happens to spirits after physical death is beyond my current understanding. Calypso might know more, though it's hard to say."

Eilleen sighed with a discontented shake of her head. "Part of me wishes hell existed, so those horrible monsters could burn, but the idea of scaring people into being good with the fear of judgment has always bothered me. Can't people just be nice without the constant threat of punishment?"

Aria laughed, warm and bright. "I've thought the same thing many times, Eilleen." She held her hand out to the kneeling woman and gently pulled her up. "I just want to reiterate that Calypso healed your daughter's mental scars. The horrors she endured are already fading."

Eilleen smiled tremulously, tears shining in her eyes. "Thank you so much for bringing my baby back to me, Aria. I'd given up hope."

Aria pulled her into a warm embrace, and Eilleen gasped as a wave of radiance washed over her. She clung to Aria as her soul hungrily drank in the deluge of love and joy.

Aria held her for several minutes before Eilleen stepped back, a hand covering her mouth as she stared at Aria in awe. "You really *are* angels," she whispered.

Aria's wings reached out and folded Eilleen into another embrace, wrapping around her like a silken cocoon. "Eilleen, we're going to take Stacy to her parents now. After that, I'm paying a visit to the local police station to find out how deep the rot goes. I'm going to ensure your daughter *never* has to fear the cops here again."

Eilleen nodded slowly, her eyes filled with wonder.

Aria pulled her wings back and released Eilleen. "Can you reach Stacy's parents?" she asked hopefully. "We were lucky you were home."

"I'll call them right now," Eilleen said quickly, rushing out of the room to get her phone. "They both work in town and shouldn't take long to get here."

Aria followed Eilleen into the kitchen and waited as she called Stacy's mother.

"Hello, Eilleen, how are you?" a woman's voice asked with a note of concern. Aria could hear the subtle undercurrents in her tone, evidence of a deep sadness.

"Kate, I need you to come to my house right now, no questions asked. Can you do that?"

"What's wrong?" Kate asked in alarm.

"No questions," Eilleen reminded her, unable to keep the jubilation from her voice.

"Okay, I'm on my way," Kate said, a sudden spark of hope in her voice.

Eilleen added quickly, "Tell Ben to come, too."

"Have you," Kate's voice broke, "have you heard something about our babies?"

"Just come now," Eilleen answered, a smile in her voice.

Aria's eyes glowed with joy as she witnessed the long-overdue reunions unfolding. There were so many other desperate parents out there, praying that a miracle could bring their children back to them. Aria hoped she could be that miracle for more families.

Adelle and Stacy burst into the room, their eyes shining with excitement.

"Calypso really *is* NOTESTOREMEMBER!" Adelle exclaimed to her mother. "She played my keyboard and made up a song in *minutes*! It was so...I don't even have the words!"

Aria's soul ached as she realized the girls had been imprisoned before the world discovered Calypso. Adelle had obviously suspected the NOTESTOREMEMBER channel's origins, like so many of the other patients Calypso had healed.

Eilleen smiled at Calypso, her lips trembling. "Calypso, this is the second time you've saved my daughter's life. Words will never be enough, but *thank you!*"

Calypso smiled and pulled Eilleen into a warm embrace. "The finest thing you can do for me is to cherish your beautiful girl."

The sound of honking shattered the moment. Eilleen moved to the front window as the noise continued. Her brows drew down as she gazed out her window with a puzzled frown. "What in the world is everyone doing in my yard?"

Aria narrowed her eyes shrewdly, her heart sinking. "Is there a crowd out there?"

Eilleen nodded with a bewildered glance back at Aria. "There are cars backed all the way up the street and people all over my lawn."

Aria sighed. "Our fault. Quite a few people saw us land earlier, and word must have gotten around."

Sirens wailed as a squad car threaded through the jam. Two officers stepped out, barking orders that no one heeded.

Adelle and Stacy edged to the window, then went rigid with terror.

Aria stepped into view, making herself visible to the crowd. "Were those officers involved in your abduction?"

Adelle nodded, her eyes glued to the cops.

Aria's core ignited with renewed fury, and she burst into light. She stormed out of the house, heat coursing through her meridians as she closed the distance. People stared in awe, phones held high to record.

The cops blanched when they saw her glaring at them like an avenging angel, their eyes widening with sudden fear. Aria could see the filth congealing on their auras, a dark miasma tainting the space around them with putrid rot.

Aria spoke, the authority in her voice warping the air. "Your job is to protect the innocent. You have tarnished your souls with your heinous acts. Selling children to human traffickers is one of the lowest forms of human depravity. Make better choices in your next life."

Her eyes blazed brightly, and a beam of energy shot into the terrified cops, vaporizing them instantly.

The crowd recoiled but surged forward again once her glow faded, awe overtaking fear.

A middle-aged woman fought her way through the crush, struggling to reach the house. When she finally broke through the press of bodies and came face-to-face with Aria, she pulled up short with a gasp.

The moment ended when Stacy came running out the front door with a squeal of delight, tackling her mother in a fierce embrace.

Her mother gaped in shock and stood frozen for several seconds. Then a choked sob escaped her throat as she clung to her daughter, crying and laughing, trying to squeeze her daughter tightly enough that she would never disappear again.

Kate pulled back just enough to look into her daughter's face. "Oh, Stacy, where have you been?" she wailed between sobs. "I never thought I'd see you again."

Stacy smiled brilliantly. "We were saved by angels, Mom! They just tore the doors off our cells and vaporized the men hurting us."

Kate's eyes widened in horror. She closed her eyes as fresh tears ran down her cheeks, pulling her daughter into a much gentler embrace. "I'm so, so sorry, Stacy," she choked out. "I should've been there to protect you."

Stacy stroked her mother's back comfortingly. "It wasn't your fault, Mom. Some cops arrested us and took us to those other guys."

"Which cops?" Kate demanded, her voice razor-sharp.

Stacy pointed toward the cruiser. "They were standing there a second ago, but Aria vaporized them with her eyes."

At the reminder that an angel was in front of her, Kate's eyes snapped to Aria. "You saved my baby?"

Aria nodded with a gentle smile. "We did."

Calypso stepped out with Eilleen, and the crowd erupted. Aria grinned as Calypso froze, staring at the roaring crowd in shock. It was easy to forget that she was the most famous musician in the world.

Calypso gave a shy wave and a smile, producing another roar from the crowd.

Aria leaned in close to Kate, raising her voice over the noise. "We should probably go, but I wanted you to know that Calypso healed your daughter of both physical and mental scars, so the last year will seem more like a bad dream than a real experience."

Kate studied Aria's eyes as her own brimmed with fresh tears. She finally nodded, mouthing a *thank you*, her heart in her eyes. Aria wrapped her arms and wings around mother and child, instilling as much love and hope as she could before walking back to where Calypso was watching her adoring fans, a light blush on her cheeks.

Aria grinned. "I'd say it's time to go. Wave goodbye to your fans."

Calypso glanced sidelong at her, then raised one of her arms high and waved. The crowd whistled and cheered with renewed vigor. The two of them launched into the air at speeds just below the sound barrier. Everyone's head jerked upward to stare after the quickly vanishing angels.

"We are not returning to Tamra's?" Calypso asked as they went in the opposite direction.

Aria shook her head, her face like a thundercloud. "Police station. It's time to find out how far the taint has spread."

12 – CORRUPTION

Aria and Calypso dropped from the sky in a streak of brilliant light, landing soundlessly in front of the police station. It was a two-story antiquated office building that had clearly undergone heavy renovations in an attempt to modernize it. A set of hinged glass doors reflected the light of their glowing forms.

Radiant with fury as memories of Lexi's haunted, fearful eyes replayed in her mind, Aria strode through the front doors like a glowing, angel-shaped vision of wrath.

Gasps and shouts rippled through the marble-floored lobby as the two angels stormed through. The walls were lined with chairs where visitors sat gawking like fish out of water under the stale glow of fluorescent lights. A thick metal door with a fob reader was set in a wall next to a tall counter topped by thick glass, staffed by a short, middle-aged man with a shaved head who stared at them in stunned disbelief. Three of the visitors in the waiting area scrambled to their feet, phones already raised to record.

Aria's lavender eyes blazed against her brilliant red hair, her luminous skin flooding the room with daylight.

"I need to speak with the police chief," she said, her voice carrying quiet, terrifying authority.

The man froze, mouth agape. Aria flared her wings, then snapped them against her back, sharp as a whip crack. "The chief. *Now.*"

"H–he's out of town," he stammered, his eyes wide with awe and fear.

Aria studied him, reading the sparkling lines of energy that traced through his meridians. His aura was untainted, even kind. She nearly smiled, realizing she was beginning to see auras like Calypso. She reined in her anger, knowing this man wasn't deserving of her ire.

Her tone softened. "How long have you been on the force, Jared?"

He swallowed, his Adam's apple bobbing like a jig on a fishing line. "Almost three—three years."

The crippling social anxiety that would normally have left her slinking away from confrontations in embarrassment lay buried beneath an avalanche of rage. Even so, she avoided glancing around at the raised phones recording them, pretending they didn't exist, and let her voice harden. "There are officers here aiding and abetting human traffickers. Were you aware of this?"

The lobby erupted with gasps, and someone muttered, "What the fuck, man, seriously?"

Jared's aura rippled with a blend of guilt and fear. She could see in his eyes that he knew *something*.

She leaned forward, her violet eyes growing cold. "How much do you know? I won't lie to you, Jared. I'm going to kill every one of them unless there's a very compelling reason not to."

Another susurration of gasps whispered through the room, and the same male voice as before muttered, "She's serious."

Jared licked his lips and blurted, "I didn't know it was trafficking. I just knew... they were dirty. There's a clique of fifteen officers."

She narrowed her eyes, feeling a growing sense of authority broadcasting from her aura. "How many of them are here in the office right now?"

Someone in the back offices had finally discovered there were angels in the building, and she heard them going door to door, telling the other employees. She smelled fear from some, stark and rank. The ones without fear quickly gathered in the briefing room and started fighting about who would get to talk to the angels.

Flustered, Jared fumbled his words. "Um, I think, um, maybe eight?"

She gave a small, approving nod. "Thanks, Jared. You're a good cop." Then she was gone.

A thunderous crash shook the building as Aria burst through the steel door connecting to the back offices, leaving a cloud of dust in her wake, a good portion of the wall pulverized.

In less than a heartbeat, Aria had followed the trail of fear through the building, chopping each corrupt officer unconscious before they could move. Eight men down before the echo of her explosive entrance faded.

A second later, she was in the briefing room, a luminous comet flashing into existence before the stunned officers. She studied their auras intently, detecting no malevolence. After two back-to-back incidents with dirty cops, she had been losing faith in the police, so it was heartening to see there were still good ones.

"How many of you knew your coworkers were trafficking children?" she asked grimly, folding her arms as she observed their reactions. She tried to appear stern, an expression that didn't come naturally, but when she saw her reflection in a mirror at the back of the room, she was disappointed to see that she just looked petulant.

One of the women gasped, several others blanched, and a few cursed loudly.

Calypso suddenly appeared beside Aria as if she had teleported, her brilliant blond hair framing her flawless face, the very picture of an angel. Recognition lit up in every eye in the room as the officers stared at arguably the most famous person in the world.

Calypso laid a calming hand on Aria's shoulder. "These are good people; their auras are pure."

A young officer stared at Calypso, almost worshipfully. "You're Calypso and Aria. You really *are* angels." He broke off, playfully punching the officer next to him in the arm. "I *told* you she was an angel."

His friend winced and rubbed his shoulder, ruefully shaking his head. "Okay, you were right."

Aria interrupted, trying to steer the conversation back on track. "Is the police chief involved in the trafficking operation?"

A small, dark-haired woman—Nancy, according to her aura—nodded almost imperceptibly, staring down at her hands. Something about the woman made Aria think of a mouse. "I think so," she said nervously.

Aria smoothed her features and kept her voice gentle. "Nancy, can you tell us what you know?"

The woman flinched at the sound of her first name, as if it confirmed everything she had been told about heaven, angels, and hell. Her voice shook as she spoke.

"The chief ignored too many complaints against certain officers, coming down hard on the rest of us for minor infractions. Their clique made no secret that they were above the law and would arrest women they found attractive so they could grope them while they roughed them up."

Nancy paused, licking her lips. "The chief had too many closed-door meetings with that group. Whenever kids turned up missing, it was always his inner group who handled the investigations. I submitted complaints to Internal Affairs, but they dismissed them as spurious accusations. I think there are more people involved, higher up the food chain."

Aria scowled. "All the way to the top, no doubt."

A few of the officers stared at Nancy in stunned incredulity.

A blue-eyed Leroy stared at her in disbelief. "The chief was a *human trafficker*? But he's a family man! He's got *children*, for God's sake!"

Aria shook her head sadly. "Leroy, there probably isn't a city on Earth without ties to human trafficking, however tangential. There's a whole hidden class of people with malice in their hearts who walk, talk, and act just like you and other good people. They're drawn to power and exploit society's hierarchical structure to exercise their dark and twisted desires in secret. But the time of deceit and aggression is over. We're going to fix this broken world and end the nightmare so many innocent souls are trapped inside, once and for all."

The words welled from hidden depths, like instructions for assembling a kit. She stood, frozen in shock for a split second as she felt the unimaginable vastness of a consciousness hiding just below a thin membrane separating her conscious thoughts from an ocean of potential.

Calypso looked at her appraisingly, lips pursed in a way that looked far too inviting. Aria pulled her eyes away—she needed to stay focused.

Leroy studied her, his face bright with hope. "How do you know our names? Can you read our minds?"

Calypso answered, her serene gaze scanning each of the rapt faces in a moment. "Your names are inscribed within your auras, and although Aria cannot read your thoughts, an aura reveals much of a person's character. You are all good people, and it warms my soul to sense your purity and light."

Nancy slowly deflated with relief as Calypso finished. Aria almost smiled. Another person thinking they were there to represent a deity and dispense judgement. Of course, she *was* there to dispense judgement, to a point.

Aria heard groaning in the other room. As if a switch had been flipped, she went from benevolent to wrathful instantaneously, light pouring out of her as she exited the room and stared at the man slowly rising to his feet.

"Martin Grubbs," she intoned, her eyes flaring brighter. "You have violated children for greed and lust. May you make better choices in your next life."

When she finished, an intense beam of brilliant light arced from her eyes, vaporizing him. In less than a second, she flashed through the building and vaporized the other seven corrupt cops.

"What the *hell* is going on here?" a voice barked from the ruined doorway.

She felt his aura pulse like sickening slime as she turned to face him, a miasma of rot and depravity that clung to him like sewage. He was still climbing over the remains of the door when his eyes fell on her, taking in her expression of utter revulsion. His face flashed with surprise that quickly morphed to fear, skin stretching tight as his mouth opened into a wide rictus. She longed to make him suffer, to feel the same torment his victims had experienced, but she firmly tamped down her darker desires and vaporized him in a flash of light. She wouldn't let them turn her into the same kind of monsters they had become.

"That makes eleven," Aria noted in grim satisfaction. "Four left."

Several of the officers had followed her out to investigate. Their faces were masks of shock and trepidation as they witnessed her burning their colleagues from existence with less emotion than a person would show swatting a fly.

Nancy's voice quavered as she stared at Aria with a fanatical zeal. "Are they dead?"

Aria nodded sharply. "Right. There are four more who need to be dealt with, including the chief. I promised some girls they would never be harmed by these monsters again. What's the best way to get everyone into the station? I'd rather not hunt them down individually."

Nancy glanced at the clock on the wall. "Shift change is in a few minutes; that's why Derek showed up just now."

Aria smiled gratefully. "Thank you, Nancy. I'll wait for them to arrive, then."

Roger nervously rubbed his shaved head. "Is it true you can't be killed?"

Calypso nodded, smiling faintly. "So far, that appears to be the case. We survived a nuclear explosion last night whilst removing cameras from satellites. I am not certain what humans possess that could outclass a nuke."

Aria sighed and muttered, "Too bad our clothes don't survive as well."

She didn't realize she had spoken so loudly. Several officers blinked at her, then seemed to struggle not to undress the two angels with their eyes.

Nancy licked her lips, watching them hesitantly. "How hard is it to get into heaven?"

Her cheeks flushed as both angels turned their inhuman gazes upon her.

Aria kept her expression neutral. "If you don't have wings of your own, you can usually take a jet or other aircraft."

"You can just fly to heaven—" Nancy began, puzzled, but stopped when she saw Aria's lips twitch. "Oh. It *is* real, though, isn't it?"

Aria shrugged. "Heaven just means skies in religious texts. The skies are real. As for the misogynistic, bearded guy who throws temper tantrums—

I'll have to claim ignorance on such an entity. We don't serve a deity. We *do* serve a higher purpose, however. Calypso is a healer; that's one of her purposes. If you want to call this driving force a god, I suppose that word works as well as any other."

Josh eyed them curiously. "What's *your* purpose? Are you a healer, too?"

Aria grinned. "Haven't you guessed? My purpose is to vanquish evil, wherever I find it."

His eyes brightened, and he grinned back. "Wow, that's badass. So, you're an angel cop."

Aria laughed. "Bingo."

Just then, three men pushed their way through the broken door.

"What the hell happened to the door?" the first one, Angelos, demanded in exasperation, pushing past the wreckage.

"Chief's gonna be pissed," declared a flaxen-haired David ominously. "Heads are gonna roll."

"Seriously, did the Incredible Hulk escape or something?" the last one, Dominic, asked in wonder. "How the hell did this door get so wrecked?"

Aria's aura flared—revulsion like acid in her meridians. Their energy was vile, the same black sludge she had come to recognize as soul-deep corruption.

"Hello, Dominic, David, and Angelos. There's no place in this world for monsters like you. Goodbye."

Their eyes widened, and the air filled with the stench of fear. As she spoke, their panic intensified, and one turned to flee. Before he could take a third step, a brilliant beam of light lanced through the air, vaporizing all three.

Aria nodded in grim satisfaction. "Now for the chief. Time to find out where he's hiding."

Josh eyed her curiously. "How are you going to do that? He didn't even tell us where he was going on vacation. He could be anywhere."

Aria glanced around the room. "I need to smell something of his. Is that his office?"

Nancy nodded, speaking softly. "It's locked. He keeps the key with him at all times. There isn't a spare."

Aria pushed through the solid wood door as if it were paper. The deadbolt buckled under her strength. "Sounds suspicious. Let's see if he has any leads to other pieces of shit hidden away in here."

The moment she entered, a foul reek assaulted her senses, like being in a reptile house, only far worse. She glanced around, noticing a safe on a desk. "Why does the chief have a safe?"

Nancy followed her into the office. "He said it's for confidential documents—which doesn't make sense, because we have secure file cabinets in the records room for confidential documents."

Aria flared brightly for a moment and vaporized the safe door. Inside was a thick binder. She pulled it out and flipped through the pages.

"This looks like a ledger—payments received and services rendered, between ten and twenty thousand for each entry."

Nancy watched her intently. "Are there any names?"

Aria flipped through each page, memorizing them. "No, but there are phone numbers and addresses."

She lifted the binder to her nose and inhaled, then recoiled from the stench, so foul she would have vomited if she still had a stomach. Grimacing, she threw the binder down. "Okay, we're done here. Time to take care of the chief. I'll see if I can get some answers out of him before he dies."

Calypso laid a gentle hand on Nancy's shoulder. "Nancy, you truly are a good person. There was nothing more you could have done against the powerful people you faced. Your aura does not deceive, and I perceive a spirit brimming with compassion and purity when I look at you."

Nancy stared at her, eyes wide. "Are you sure you can't read my mind?"

Calypso smiled faintly, tapping her temple. "I said Aria cannot read minds—I did not say that I cannot."

They all stared at Calypso, some in consternation. She blushed slightly and looked at Aria. "I think it's time to go."

Aria smiled at the officers, sincerity glowing in her eyes. "Thank you for being good people."

The two angels vanished from the room at speeds too fast for human eyes to register.

13 – I WILL VANQUISH EVIL

"Whatcha doin'?" Clarice called down in a redneck drawl as Aria and Calypso exited the police station at high speed.

Aria looked up to see Clarice standing on top of an office building across the street. They flew up to land next to her, and Calypso immediately pulled Clarice into a warm embrace.

Aria's eyes hardened. "Keeping a promise to Adelle by making sure these crooked cops never hurt another child. We're hunting the police chief."

Clarice smiled approvingly, patting Aria's cheek. "Good. I'm ready to kick ass and take names." She stepped back and looked Aria up and down. "I've gotta say, Aria, I'm impressed. Becoming an angel really pulled you out of your shell. I like it."

Aria grinned, flushing at the praise. "It's like a smothering weight was removed from my psyche after my transformation. I wonder how much of my fear and anxiety was a result of the squishy brain that burned away when I ascended."

Clarice nodded thoughtfully, stepping forward and sliding her fingers through Aria's bangs, eliciting a shiver of delight. "I liked being your protector, but I also love this new side of you. I'm excited to see where it takes you—but I'm still going to be your protector."

Calypso stepped closer and caressed Aria's cheek. "I very much like this Aria as well. I daresay it has always been there—ascension merely allowed it to surface."

Aria leaned into the caress, smiling at the two angels affectionately. "This all feels so familiar somehow, the three of us together."

Clarice studied her and Calypso thoughtfully. “Yeah, it really does. I can’t help wondering if we knew each other in different lives.” She took a deep breath. “Okay, so, police chief, where is he?”

Aria tapped her nose. “I have his scent. It’s the foulest thing I’ve ever smelled. I just need to track him down.”

Clarice arched her back, running her fingers through her long hair. “We’ll just follow along then. I want to talk to you about something on the way.”

Aria nodded, clamping down on a sudden rush of desire. She launched herself into the air and flew south, Clarice and Calypso following on either side.

Clarice took a deep breath, her voice soft. “I want to bring Lexi back to the cabin with us. She can’t go back to her worthless parents, and the system would eat her alive—especially after what she’s been through. Also, there’s something oddly familiar about her. Maybe she’s another piece of whatever puzzle we’re forming.”

Aria smiled affectionately at her sister, feeling a deep swell of love for Clarice and her compassionate heart. “I think that’s a great idea.”

She came to a sudden stop as her nose picked up the chief’s trail, then looked down at a dairy farm. Large outbuildings, silos, and service roads veined across several thousand acres.

She dropped to a few hundred feet and began narrowing her search. The scent was coming from one of the silos.

They landed in front of the silo door and listened for any sign of occupants. She could hear voices faintly from somewhere inside.

She looked at Clarice and Calypso, frowning. “Someone’s talking in there. It must be extremely insulated or goes really far down, because I can’t make out what they’re saying.”

“It’s so wrong,” Calypso whispered in revulsion.

Aria took Calypso’s hand in concern. “What do you hear?”

Calypso began to tremble, her eyes full of horror. “They are evil.”

“Let’s go,” Clarice said, kicking the door and knocking a large portion of the wall inward.

The smell was awful. Aria stopped herself from breathing as she pushed inside the giant tin can. The door had been reinforced like a bank vault, but they had clearly failed to reinforce the wall around it.

Alarms wailed as they entered. The inside of the silo was almost completely empty, save for a shaft at one end that dropped into the ground. She walked over and jumped down, falling for three hundred feet before she hit the top of an elevator lift. She tore the top hatch off the lift and tucked her wings tightly against herself before jumping inside.

As soon as she landed, white gas jetted from a series of nozzles. Ignoring the poisonous vapor, she jabbed her hands between the elevator doors and pried them open to the sound of tortured metal.

The large room beyond the elevator resembled a horror movie on steroids. Humans were connected to exotic machines clearly designed for inflicting pain. Rows of pods lined one wall, with more humans trapped in stasis. The vile stench that slammed into her triggered an immediate reaction deep within. She lit up like the sun, burning away all traces of darkness.

Several human-shaped entities stood before one of the humans, collecting blood from the tortured wreck of a person trying to shriek past a gag. The entities had red, scaly skin and small nubs protruding from their heads. When they saw Aria, their reptilian eyes widened in shock.

She launched across the distance and slammed her fist into the face of one of the entities. Instead of exploding as she had expected, the blow knocked it back fifty feet, where it broke through a concrete wall. Soil fell through the cracks as the creature pulled itself free. They were far more durable than humans.

Switching tactics, she flared brighter and fired a beam of light at the entity. As soon as the beam struck, it shrieked in agony and began to smoke. Seconds later, nothing remained of what Aria decided was a demon.

Clarice, already blazing with incandescent light, had begun attacking the other three demons. Aria quickly joined her beam with Clarice's, vaporizing the remaining entities.

Moving at angel speed, she quickly disconnected the traumatized humans from the horrific torture machines.

Calypso stared at the scene in shocked horror but quickly pulled herself together and began to sing. Her song used many of the powerful words Aria had heard during the biker's resurrection, pulling from deep within as she sought to heal both the bodies and minds of the ravaged humans.

When Aria could finally focus on the humans, she wept tears of fury. There were *way* too many children in this house of horrors. She choked back the urge to shriek in rage at the creatures responsible for such ghastly acts of cruelty. The *demons*.

Clarice stepped up next to her, wrapping an arm around her shoulders. "The world just got uglier," she said softly. "Demons. The thought crossed my mind when angels became a reality. I hoped there wouldn't be an equal and opposing balance to angels, but apparently the universe is just a shitty place."

Aria nodded, feeling a burning resolve to excise the rotting cancer from the world. "Maybe humans are getting more help in their descent to depravity than we gave them credit for," she muttered thickly, fighting to hold back tears. "One of these demons was the police chief. I wonder how many more are slinking around in positions of power."

Clarice surveyed the room in disgust. "They were pretty weak. We vaporized them with the same ease as we do everything else. I wonder if there are stronger demons out there, or if they're all this weak. We need to evolve if we're going to face more powerful enemies. It might be time for more angels, too. It's clear that agents of evil are orchestrating a lot of the horrors in our world, and three angels probably aren't enough to deal with a scourge of this magnitude."

"Yeah," Aria breathed her agreement. She watched the humans gather around Calypso, soaking in the warmth of her healing presence. There were almost forty of them, ranging from single-digit ages up to the late teens. The demons seemed to prefer the young.

Clarice studied the machines where the humans had been bound. "They were harvesting their blood, and they clearly wanted them terrified while they did it. This looks like a chemistry lab."

Aria scowled at the machines. "Could they be after the adrenaline in the blood? There must be more to it, because they can synthesize adrenaline."

Clarice turned her gaze to the entranced humans. "We need to get everyone out of here. Let's get them to the surface, then we can figure out what's next."

Aria nodded fervently, her eyes filled with loathing as she glared at the demonic lab. "We'll probably need to fly them up one at a time."

Clarice walked over to Calypso, who was struggling to maintain a compassionate presence. She looked like she wanted to break down after witnessing the horrors the humans had suffered. Clarice watched the humans with pity in her dark eyes, and Aria had to marvel at her sister's strength as she took charge.

"Let's start flying everyone up," Clarice said gently, laying a hand on Calypso's shoulder. "I'll stay down here, and Aria can wait at the top while you fly them up. That way, one of us will always be with them."

Calypso's eyes shimmered silver with unshed tears. Clarice pulled her close, her warm, grounding energy flowing into the trembling angel. Calypso clung to her, squeezing her eyes shut. After several long seconds, she let go, offering Clarice a small, grateful smile.

Aria went into the elevator and blasted the roof off with a beam of light, then flew to the top of the shaft. A moment later, Calypso emerged, carrying a frightened child. She set the child beside Aria, who immediately wrapped the girl in a cocoon of love and warmth. The child pressed close to her radiance, and soon others followed, rescued one by one until the ground around Aria was filled with huddled, wide-eyed survivors.

Clarice joined Calypso on her last flight up from the bunker. The children were slowly coming back to life as the open skies and sunlight convinced them their ordeal was over.

Aria pulled Calypso into another embrace, joined a moment later by Clarice. They rested their foreheads together, meridians intertwining as their energies braided into a single pulse. Aria felt one of Calypso's tears splash onto her hand. Each quicksilver drop sparked with light as it touched them, tiny detonations of power snapping through the air. Aria's own tears joined hers, mingling in a shimmer of silver. Clarice gasped when their energies collided and merged.

A golden sphere of light ballooned around them, expanding outward and bathing the field in radiance. For a moment that felt eternal, they hung suspended in the heart of pure energy.

When the glow faded, everything felt changed.

Aria blinked and saw the world differently. Light moved beneath the soil, a molten river of energy threading through the planet. Formerly invisible frequencies shimmered in the air, webs of color crisscrossing the sky.

Clarice stared in wonder. "Am I seeing radio waves?"

Aria shook her head slowly. "I have no idea."

The world of energy and matter overlapped, dazzling in its complexity, a lattice of brilliance enveloping the Earth.

Calypso nodded slowly. "I understand now. This is where the physical meets the spiritual. I can sense the planet's aura."

Aria's eyes widened in sudden comprehension. The glowing filaments weren't random; they were meridians—the planet's energy veins. The Earth itself was alive.

Calypso stepped back, spreading her wings. She lifted her arms, eyes closed in concentration. The air warped, and a shimmer of light tore open before them, forming a doorway through reality. Their cabin stood on the other side, sunlight filtering through the trees.

Clarice gasped, staring at Calypso excitedly. "Calypso, did you just make a gateway?"

Calypso nodded. "I believe my desire to aid these children has influenced my evolution. I no longer place trust in the government to reunite them with their families—assuming their families were not responsible for their current plight. It is evident that there are demons in high places."

Aria grimaced. "Yeah, and now I know what they smell like—so foul. At least I'll recognize them."

They ushered the children through the portal. The transition brought a brief wave of vertigo, then vanished.

Aria let out a relieved breath. They were home. The cabin had already started feeling more like home than her old apartment.

As the group settled on the grass, Clarice excused herself to fetch Lexi from Tamra's house. Aria turned to survey the crowd of forty children, many still staring at the angels in mute fascination.

Aria slipped her arm around Calypso's waist. "We need to figure out sleeping arrangements for forty extra people."

"Well, this is unexpected," Emily commented as she exited the cabin and joined them. She studied the large group of children curiously. "I get the feeling we're going to need more rooms."

Aria drew Emily aside, out of earshot. "Mom, we just rescued them from demons who were torturing them and harvesting their blood," she said quietly, barely holding back a fresh bout of tears. "Calypso healed them, but I'm not sure how much mental trauma remains. Now that we know there are demons in higher places, we can't risk handing them over to the state."

Emily's eyes narrowed. "When you say *demons*... you don't mean that figuratively, do you?"

Aria shook her head bleakly. "I mean actual demonic entities, with scales and horns."

Emily drew her into a protective embrace. "Oh sweetie, I'm so sorry. I was starting to wonder if there was going to be a counterbalance to angels." She sighed, stroking Aria's hair comfortingly. "We should start looking for somewhere to house the children soon. The cabin is large enough, but we'll need more bedding."

Aria squeezed her mother and stepped back, nodding toward Calypso. "She can make portals now. I'll see if she can make a gateway to a store so I can purchase mats and sleeping bags." She eyed the children speculatively. "We can put the older kids in the bedrooms. There are only six who look close to eighteen, which leaves us needing thirty-two mats and sleeping bags. This place is turning into a refugee camp."

Emily nodded, eyeing the sprawling three-story cabin appreciatively. "It's a good thing it's so large."

Aria returned her attention to the children. “Once everyone’s settled, we’ll start finding their parents. Hopefully, they’ll remember phone numbers and addresses.”

Calypso was singing softly to the children, creating a warm, welcoming ambiance. They stared at her, captivated by her beautiful voice as it soothed their souls.

Aria approached her tentatively, not wanting to interrupt. “Think you could make a gateway to a sporting goods store so I can get some sleeping mats and bags?”

Calypso gave a tiny nod. A ripple of light formed in the air and opened into the break room of a store. A young employee gasped as Aria stepped through.

Aria smiled reassuringly. “Hello, Amanda. My name’s Aria. I need to get sleeping mats and bags for some children we’ve rescued. Do you think you could help me?”

Amanda gaped, her mouth moving soundlessly.

Aria suppressed a sigh and placed her hands on the girl’s shoulders, infusing her with radiance.

After a moment, Amanda calmed and found her voice. “You’re the angel who vaporized those cops!” she choked out, half gasp, half yell.

Aria nodded, her eyes hard. “The very same. Such will be the fate of anyone I find harming children. Will you help me with the bedding?”

Amanda jumped to her feet, nodding vigorously. “Yes! Of course! Follow me.”

They stepped onto the sales floor, and it was all Aria could do not to cringe. Shoppers stopped mid-aisle, phones rising, whispers spreading. Focusing on the flow of radiance charging her with joy, Aria ignored the stares.

Shoppers followed her and Amanda around the store while trying to appear casual. Aria had an almost overwhelming urge to go to the shoe aisle and ask to inspect the souls, just to see their reactions. She refrained—she wouldn’t do something like that without Clarice there to appreciate it, too. She made a mental note to try it after things settled down.

Amanda led her to the camping aisle, where shelves of sleeping bags and mats stood. Aria didn’t feel like being filmed hauling armfuls of gear, so she slipped into hyperspeed. In seconds, the shelves emptied, sleeping bags and mats vanishing into the portal as if by magic. Bystanders gasped and pointed as the blur of light flickered across the aisles.

When she finished, she returned to Amanda, hugging her and pressing some cash into her hand. Amanda gasped as the surge of radiance washed over her.

"Thank you, Amanda," Aria said softly.

Then she vanished, moving at speeds too fast for the human eye to track.

Amanda hurried back to the break room, sighing in disappointment at the absence of a magical portal.

* * *

Clarice dropped out of the sky like a meteor, landing in front of Tamra's house, where afternoon shadows webbed the pines. She walked up to the front door and knocked, careful not to break the door.

Tamra's voice carried from inside. "That's probably them right now."

Lexi's voice, thin with anxiety, followed. "What if it's one of those people again?"

Tamra's reply was grimly amused. "Then they're going to have a bad day. I can be pretty mean when I want to be. You can stay here while I—"

"It's Clarice!" Clarice called, her voice warm and clear.

There was the sound of running feet. The door flew open, and Lexi crashed into her arms, shaking with relief. Clarice projected loving reassurance as she held the young woman tightly. Lexi soaked up the powerful emotions like rain in the desert.

"Thank you so much for coming back," Lexi sobbed, her voice choked with emotion. "I thought I would never see you again."

"Shh," Clarice consoled her, gently stroking her hair as she held her tightly. "We're angels—we'd never leave you. We'll always be there for you, whenever you need us."

Tamra appeared at the front door, smiling sadly. Clarice smiled back, her expression confident and indomitable. Things were going to change in this world. They were going to change a lot.

Tamra stared at Clarice, feeling the sheer determination pouring out of the angel. A sudden hope sparked in her eyes as she sensed momentous changes on the horizon.

Clarice spoke softly. "Thank you so much, Tamra," she said gratefully. "You are truly a wonderful person."

Tamra smiled warmly, shaking her head slowly. "Thank *you*. You saved my niece—I can't thank you enough." She paused and smiled wryly. "We still haven't fitted the three of you yet. I know you all have your hands full right now. Come back anytime, and we'll get you measured so we can make you some new clothes."

Clarice grinned mischievously. "We'll definitely be back. Aria and Calypso weren't fans of the bra club."

Tamra chuckled, clearly remembering the two blushing angels.

Clarice nodded warmly, slowly rising into the air as she held the clinging Lexi. "See you soon, Tamra."

They knifed through clouds and contrails, rocketing through the skies, untouched by wind. By the time they landed at the cabin, Aria was a blur, ferrying mats and sleeping bags through a shimmering portal. At a nod from Aria, Calypso closed the gateway and turned to Lexi.

"Hello, Lexi," Calypso said gently. "I am so sorry we left you alone. We encountered some difficulties, and it took longer than we had anticipated."

"It's okay," Lexi whispered shyly, staring at the ground.

Gently, Calypso lifted Lexi's chin until she was looking into Calypso's swirling eyes. "You are in no way a burden to us. We are angels; our very purpose is to serve. Your happiness is far more important to us than you can possibly imagine."

Lexi stared, captivated by Calypso's hypnotic gaze. After a long moment, Calypso stepped forward and embraced her. Lexi closed her eyes and smiled contentedly, her face finally relaxing in the safety of Calypso's arms.

Calypso pulled back and gestured toward the other children. "I wish to introduce you to some other youngsters we have found. They are rather fragile, having endured certain traumas. They'll be staying the night until we can begin the search for their parents tomorrow."

Lexi finally noticed the dozens of children around her, most of them staring in awe at the angels.

A girl in her late teens walked over to Lexi, smiling, her dark eyes bright with excitement.

"Hi, my name's Amber," she said, stepping forward to embrace Lexi. "Can you believe we were saved by real-life angels?"

Lexi shivered as the realization hit her. Clarice watched her eyes widen as she finally grasped that they really were angels.

"I'm Lexi," she told Amber shyly.

Clarice watched Lexi closely. She seemed to have some serious self-esteem issues that had survived Calypso's healing. They would need to handle her carefully until she could put the trauma of the past few years behind her.

"I see you've already started the party without me," a deep voice rumbled, and they turned to see their uncle smiling.

Lexi flinched at the sound, pulling back from Amber, her eyes widening with fear.

Calypso pulled her back into a comforting hug. "This is Aria and Clarice's uncle. He owns this cabin and has been of tremendous assistance to us. He is a good man, one you may trust completely. He has already risked his life many times to ensure our safety."

Lexi slowly relaxed again in Calypso's arms, watching Devon warily as he stared back at her with kind eyes.

She took a deep, shuddering breath. "I'm sorry."

He smiled gently. "No need to apologize. I don't know your story, but I know what horrible things humans can do to each other. I'm sorry for whatever you've gone through to make you fear a man's voice."

She closed her eyes and took another deep breath. "I'm Lexi," she said, exhaling slowly. "I know I'm a wreck. I'm sorry if I offend you with my behavior in any way."

"I'm Devon," he greeted her with another smile. "And I'm pretty much impossible to offend, so you're safe there."

A young girl took Lexi's hand, looking up at her sympathetically. "Did the demons hurt you too?"

Lexi's brow creased. "Demons?"

Calypso nodded, speaking softly. "When we rescued these children, they were being tormented by actual demons. It was a scene of unimaginable horror. I have erased most of their memories of that time in captivity. Some things are far too horrific for the mind to recover from."

Devon's eyebrows shot up at the mention of demons. He studied Calypso searchingly while she held Lexi.

Calypso took a deep breath, her eyes full of pain. "We were pursuing a police chief who had corrupted most of the force and turned them into kidnappers. Aria dealt with the officers involved in the abductions. The chief was not present, so we used his scent to track him down. We discovered him at an old dairy farm, in a silo several hundred feet beneath the ground. He was a demon—scales, horns, reptilian eyes, and all. There were several other demons there as well, engaging in the vile acts typical of folklore. Aria and Clarice vaporized them, and we brought the survivors back here."

Aria made a disgusted sound. "I've never smelled anything so foul. It'll certainly make finding them easy."

"Actual demons," Devon muttered, frowning at the ground as he absently picked at his ear. "So, you're not evenly matched. Good."

Aria's lips twisted sourly. "They were a lot more durable than humans. I punched the first one in the face hard enough to cave its skull in, but it only knocked it back through a concrete wall. Luckily, they had no defense against angel fire."

He raised an eyebrow. "Angel fire?"

Aria shrugged. "I just made it up. That's what I'm calling the beam of light we shoot out of our eyes. It vaporizes anything it touches."

Clarice narrowed her eyes. "I think they were weak demons. I have a feeling there are more powerful adversaries out there. We need to get stronger."

Aria nodded firmly. "Agreed. You were right when you said we need more angels, Clarice. We aren't going to be enough if there are significantly more demons, especially if they're more powerful. If our angel fire works on them, it's altogether possible they'll have something that can kill us."

Emily stared at them silently for a moment. Calypso's eyes widened just before Emily spoke.

"I dedicate my life to vanquishing evil."

Aria and Clarice gasped at the suddenness of their mother's proclamation. They watched the angel seed on her neck spread, building a lattice of new meridians that fused with her mortal body. She began to glow brightly as holy fire consumed her insides, culminating in a blinding flash of light from her eyes. When the light faded, lavender eyes, set in a face as youthful and radiantly beautiful as their own, stared back at them.

Clarice gasped in shock. "Mom! Are you sure you wanted to do this? Wasn't this a little sudden?"

Emily smiled radiantly. "If there are demons threatening my girls' lives, this is the best form for me to protect you." She looked around in awe, experiencing the powerful emotional and physical sensations of being an angel. "I feel *wonderful.*"

Aria wrapped her in a fierce embrace, tears silvering her cheeks. "Oh Mom, I'm *so* glad you're with us now."

Clarice joined the hug, her meridians arcing into the other two angels and forming a super lattice of light. "Mom, you really are *the* best! I'm so glad you chose to become an angel."

Devon's eyes twinkled as he gazed at them fondly. "I feel like I should build a church or temple—one big happy family of angels."

Emily smiled brightly at him. "What about you, Dev? You still want to start a family before making a decision?"

He nodded with a wistful smile. "I missed out on too much while contracted to The Agency. I want to experience more of life before I make the choice to become immortal."

Eric walked out of the cabin, looking around at the gathering curiously. "What's with the light show?"

"I'm sorry, dear," Emily apologized gently. "I need to be able to protect our daughters, and this is the best way. I won't ever risk losing them again."

He stared, slack-jawed. "Emily? Is that really you?"

Emily snorted dryly. "Close your mouth, dear, you'll catch flies."

He blinked, then laughed. "Yep, that's you alright."

Devon eyed the mountain of bedding Aria had piled on the lawn. "I'm going to start getting the children settled."

Clarice reluctantly released her mother, and a moment later, Aria did as well. Calypso immediately took their place, giving Emily a quick embrace.

"Emily, I cannot tell you how delighted I am that you have joined us," Calypso beamed.

Emily pulled Calypso in tightly. "Thanks, Calypso. I should have done this earlier. I can't believe how *wonderful* I feel."

Calypso released her with a dazzling smile, then turned to Devon. "Allow me to fetch those for you."

In a blur of motion, all the bedding vanished as Calypso ran in and out of the cabin with armloads of bedding at angel speed.

"I was going to say I could get it," Devon said mildly, "but I won't complain."

Clarice laughed, shaking her head fondly. "Okay, kiddos, let's show you around the house where you'll be sleeping."

Emily eyed them keenly. "I bet they're hungry. I'll get some food started right away."

Before she could move, Eric pulled her into a quick embrace. "Sorry, dear, I just wanted to grab an armful of this hottie before my wife gets back."

Her laugh was like the sun coming up after a dark night, brightening the mood around her. She pulled him down for a kiss that lasted long enough to make the children giggle. Partway through the kiss, she lit up like an incandescent bulb. When she finally released him, her eyes had sharpened, etched patterns appearing around her lavender irises.

Clarice smirked, a mischievous light in her violet eyes. "Wow, that didn't take long. I can't wait to see what you look like tomorrow morning."

Emily winked, then disentangled herself from Eric, her expression becoming businesslike. "Okay, I'm going to get some food going for the kiddos."

"I'm hungry," one of the children chimed in, right on cue.

"Me too," several more voices chorused.

Emily laughed indulgently. "Of course you are. Let's go see what we have."

Clarice beckoned Lexi to follow her into the house. Lexi had been watching Emily and Eric wistfully.

Clarice smiled warmly back at her parents. "I really lucked out. I wish you could've had parents like mine."

Lexi sighed, looking uncertain and lost. "That would've been amazing. It's wonderful to see the love you have for each other."

Clarice smiled softly. "Well, now you're included in that love. You're my new sister, and I'll tear the world apart to prevent anyone from hurting you ever again."

Lexi snuffled quietly, and Clarice reached out to hold her hand reassuringly.

Lexi cleared her throat. "Do you mind if I ask a question?"

Clarice grinned playfully. "You mean *another* question. Ask as many as you like, Lexi."

"You used to be human, like me, didn't you?"

Clarice nodded with a wry smile. "Yep—two days ago, in fact."

Lexi stared at her in amazement as they entered the house. "Really?"

Clarice grinned, squeezing her hand. "Really."

Lexi studied her with a puzzled crease to her brow. "I thought angels were from heaven or something. How did you become angels?"

Clarice guided her up the stairs to the third floor as they talked, telling Lexi all about their second meeting with Calypso, including how ignorant Calypso was of the fact that she *was* an angel. When she mentioned the angel tears, Lexi stopped her.

"What could make an angel cry? You seem so powerful and untouchable."

Clarice smiled fondly, reliving the memory. "Love made her cry. Calypso spent over a hundred years caring for sick children. She never had anyone to care for her or show her the same compassion she showed others. When Aria and I showed her how much we cared, and how important her happiness was to us, it overwhelmed her."

Lexi's eyes brimmed with sudden hope. "Could *I* become an angel?"

Clarice nodded slowly. "If you want to, sure. I'll need to discuss it with Calypso, Aria, and my mom, but I imagine the option will be there... when you're ready."

Lexi gasped. "*Really?* I could be like you and fight against evil?"

Clarice frowned pensively. "That depends on whether you want to be a healing angel or a battle angel. We haven't discovered the phrase that triggers the change to a healer, only the one for battle angels."

Lexi's response was immediate and fierce. "I *definitely* want to be a battle angel. I want to save people from monsters the way you saved me."

Clarice studied Lexi's meridians, wondering if there was a way to accurately determine someone's age by observing their energy matrices. "How old are you, Lexi?"

Lexi's face clouded. "What's the date?"

A spike of sorrow twisted Clarice's gut as she realized how time had become meaningless for the imprisoned young woman.

Clarice gently squeezed Lexi's hand. "It's April 23, 2026."

They entered one of the bedrooms that had a queen bed and Clarice turned to face Lexi.

"Wow, really?" Lexi asked, her eyebrows rising. "It feels like so much longer. Time didn't seem to move at all in that horrible place. I turn eighteen tomorrow."

"*What!*" Clarice exclaimed, staring at her excitedly. "*Tomorrow* is your birthday?"

Lexi shrugged, smiling shyly. "Yeah. It's not a big deal."

Clarice glared at her with mock severity. "Like *hell* it's not a big deal! You're going to be a *grownup* tomorrow! It's a rite of passage that *demands* a party you'll never forget."

Lexi shook her head, her fair complexion flushing. "You don't have to do that. You have way more important things to deal with than a silly birthday party—"

Clarice raised a hand sharply, cutting her off. "Did you hear something?"

Lexi froze, her eyes suddenly wary. "What was it?"

"It was the sound of you getting a party whether you like it or not!" Clarice crowed with a triumphant smile. "Though it might have to be the day after tomorrow, since we have all these kids to take home tomorrow."

Lexi let out a relieved breath as she realized there was no danger, then glared at Clarice in outrage. Clarice smirked back, one eyebrow raised expectantly. Lexi spluttered for several seconds before laughing helplessly and leaning into Clarice.

Clarice straightened, all traces of levity gone. "Now we have to get serious for a minute, okay?"

"Okay..." Lexi said slowly, reining in her laughter. "What?"

Clarice maintained her stoic expression. "What kind of stuff do you like? What kind of music? What's your favorite food?"

Lexi stared at her blankly, then giggled, swatting Clarice's arm. "You're too much."

Clarice grinned roguishly. "Like I told Aria: too much goodness. I actually have a PhD in awesomeness, so you can call me Dr. Clarice, if you like."

Lexi collapsed back onto the bed, giggling madly as years of living without any humor finally burst through like a breaking dam. She lay giggling for a minute, then looked up at Clarice, who was mimicking a studious expression, chin on fist, sending her into another fit of giggles. Every time she started getting her mirth under control, she would look up and see the laughter in Clarice's eyes and dissolve again. The merriment eventually drew the attention of a few of the younger kids, who came into the room with curious smiles, looking for the source of the commotion.

"What's so funny?" a boy asked.

Clarice raised her hands innocently. "I have no idea. She just keeps laughing every time she looks at me. Is there something on my face?"

Lexi had just started to compose herself when Clarice spoke. She wheezed and toppled over again, laughing until tears leaked from her eyes.

The boy studied Clarice critically. "I don't see anything on your face."

Lexi's laughter was contagious, and some of the other kids started laughing too, not knowing why.

The boy squinted. "Seriously, what's so funny?"

Clarice threw her hands in the air defensively. "I have a PhD in awesomeness, not comedy—I have no idea what's so funny."

He furrowed his brow. "How can you have a PhD in awesomeness?"

This set off a new round of giggles from Lexi, which cascaded down to the other four girls in the room.

Clarice struggled to keep her lips from quivering. "Are you familiar with the term 'honorary doctorate'?"

His puzzled brow deepened. "No?"

Clarice explained, glancing at Lexi, who was holding her sides and taking deep breaths to calm herself. "Normally, you have to go through a lot of academic study to get a doctorate. But sometimes somebody does something so groundbreaking or important that a university will give them an honorary doctorate in recognition of their achievement. In my case, I am so *freaking* awesome that our dean nominated me for an honorary doctorate of awesomeness. So, you can either call me Dr. Clarice, or Dr. Awesome—your pick."

She hadn't even finished speaking before Lexi was on her back again, laughing hysterically.

"Stop!" she gasped through tears. "My sides are killing me!"

Clarice sighed regretfully. "Okay, fine. I'll stop being awesome."

The boy grinned as he started getting into the spirit of the room's humor. "So, I should have an honorary doctorate in coolness because I'm so cool, right?"

Clarice held her hand out for a high-five. "You've got it."

He slapped her hand, grinning widely.

"Dinner's ready!" Emily's voice called from the second floor.

There was an immediate stampede out of the room as all the younger children ran for the veranda.

Lexi smiled wanly. "I really needed that."

She lay back in bed, head turned to the side, watching Clarice fondly.

Clarice smiled softly. "I know you did. There'll be plenty more where that came from in the years to come."

"Well done, Clarice, you freaking rock," Aria's voice echoed from the library.

"You're damn right I do," Clarice replied, smiling affectionately.

Lexi blinked. "You do what?"

"I was talking to Aria," Clarice explained, gesturing out the door. "Angels have ridiculously powerful senses, so we can hear each other from opposite ends of the house."

Lexi's eyes widened. She looked down at the floor, then out the door. "She can hear everything we've talked about?"

"I sure can—and we're totally having a party, whether she likes it or not," Aria's humorous voice confirmed.

Clarice grinned. "She says yes, and that we're totally having a party, whether you like it or not."

"Wow!" Lexi breathed. "You really are like superheroes."

Clarice nodded, grinning widely. "Think Superman without the kryptonite. We're pretty much indestructible, have absurd strength, super-senses, weigh practically nothing, don't need to breathe, can fly, and shoot laser beams out of our eyes. Oh yeah, and in Calypso's case, she can heal and resurrect people, as well as make gateways to anywhere on Earth—maybe other worlds too; we haven't checked."

Lexi stared at her disbelievingly. "You don't need to breathe? You could go into outer space? Or into the oceans?"

Clarice nodded, her eyes bright. "Yep, we've already been to space. We were destroying the cameras on all the satellites so the stupid government couldn't track us anymore. You wouldn't believe how awesome the stars look from high orbit."

Lexi stared at her in awe as she realized how powerful they were. She suddenly furrowed her brow. "What do you mean you weigh practically nothing? With those wings, you must weigh more than me."

Clarice grinned challengingly. "Come pick me up. You'll see."

Lexi squinted, no doubt wondering if it was a prank. She got off the bed and walked over to Clarice, hesitantly reaching for her armpits.

Clarice batted her hands away. "Just lift from the waist; otherwise, I'll be too ticklish."

Lexi dubiously wrapped her hands around Clarice's narrow waist, gasping at just *how* narrow it was under the shirt. She planted her feet and lifted, nearly dropping Clarice when she went upward with almost no resistance.

"Holy crap!" Lexi gasped, holding Clarice above her head with no apparent effort. "Doesn't this violate some science-y rule or something?"

Clarice shrugged, grinning down at Lexi. "Pretty much everything we do violates the natural laws. But that just means humans aren't as smart as they think they are. What they think of as laws are more like guidelines for angels."

"Do you know how badly I want to be an angel now?" Lexi asked excitedly, spinning around in a circle.

Clarice let out a startled laugh as she was twirled. "Yeah, I could definitely guess. Aria, Calypso, Mom... what do you think?"

Emily responded immediately. "I'm one hundred percent behind you."

"We need more angels," Aria noted thoughtfully. "And she doesn't have family to worry about. I think I'm on board."

"Yes, most certainly," Calypso replied, a smile evident in her voice.

Clarice smiled down at Lexi. "Okay, I guess you get to be an angel."

"Really? *Really?*" Lexi exclaimed, releasing Clarice and bouncing on her toes. "Oh my god, I'm so excited! When can we do it? Can we do it now? Please, now!"

Clarice heard the other angels laughing as she smiled at Lexi. "Before we do, I need to warn you about a few things you won't be able to do anymore once you're no longer human. First, we don't eat or sleep. How attached are you to food and sleep?"

Lexi shuddered, her eyes haunted. "I *hate* sleeping. I just have constant nightmares. And I haven't had a decent meal in so long that I couldn't care less about food."

Clarice took a deep breath, growing serious. "Okay, one more consideration. We can't die, as far as we know. And we don't age. Are you okay with the idea of living eternally, with no way to die—even if you want to?"

Lexi paused, her brows drawing together. "What happens after humans die? Are we just reborn or something?"

Clarice shrugged with a wry smile. "We have *no* idea. We know we have spirits, but we don't know what happens to them after we die."

Lexi frowned thoughtfully. "Well, it sounds like we'd just live forever anyway, if we have spirits. Whether we get reincarnated or move on to something else, our spirits probably live forever too, so I might as well live forever in a body I like."

"That's a pretty good point," Emily commented approvingly. "I should have thought of that when I was hesitant to make the change."

"Good point, Lexi," Clarice congratulated her with a smile. "We're also pretty sure angels can't have children. Are you okay with that?"

Lexi nodded fiercely. "I will *never* let a man stick anything in me *ever* again."

Clarice nodded her understanding. "I kind of thought that'd be your response, but I had to ask. Okay, that's all the warnings. Oh, one more thing. All your insides disappear, like your organs. They're replaced by a kind of spiritual energy matrix."

Lexi's eyes brightened. "I won't ever have to go to the bathroom again?"

Clarice nodded with a grin. "Correct. No more number one, two, or three."

Lexi's smile was brilliant. "I'm *so* in. What do we do now?"

Clarice smiled softly. "Now... we make you an angel. Come here."

She embraced Lexi, thinking of all the horrors they had witnessed that day—and all the horrors yet to come. Then she thought of having another sister to fight with them, another member of her family. Her eyes grew damp as she hugged Lexi tightly. "I'm going to love having you as a sister," she whispered, a tear falling onto Lexi's neck.

Clarice stepped back to give Lexi room as her neck began to glow. The circles under her eyes and the anxiety etched on her face faded as the angel seed prepared her body for transformation.

Clarice grinned in anticipation. "Now say you want to vanquish evil."

"I *will* vanquish evil, wherever I find it!" Lexi vowed, her voice ringing with conviction.

Her neck glowed, then the rest of her body lit up brightly. Clarice watched the process in fascination, wondering what the other classes of angel could be. She grinned as Lexi's eyes lit up like high beams, then dimmed. Lavender eyes opened, staring at Clarice in wonder as a smile split her face.

"I can't *believe* how *good* I feel!" she exclaimed excitedly, gazing at Clarice in awe. She flew across the six feet between them in a fraction of a millisecond, embracing Clarice tightly.

"THANK YOU THANK YOU THANK YOU THANK YOU," she cried repeatedly.

"It was truly my pleasure," Clarice whispered, enjoying the crossflow of their meridians. A moment later, Aria and Calypso joined them, wrapping their arms around the two of them.

"Welcome to the family, Lexi," Aria told the newest angel warmly.

"Welcome, Lexi," Calypso echoed, her face glowing with delight.

14 – LEXI

Clarice spoke quietly from the library, surrounded by sleeping children. "Now that we have a fifth angel, we can split some responsibilities."

Aria's voice was little more than a whisper from where she sat in the large living room, where more children slept peacefully around her. "We are stretched a little thin."

Emily lay in bed with her sleeping husband. "What did you have in mind?" she asked softly.

Clarice took a deep breath. "Now that we know demons are real, it's hard not to think these shadow agencies are either controlled by them or heavily infiltrated," she said contemplatively. "They're probably the reason this world has so much wrong with it. If we want to fix it, we have to start there. Even with five of us, we're probably still outmatched—unless all demons are as weak as the last ones. We need to do a lot more scouting to gauge the pervasiveness of the demonic presence. They probably have weapons we haven't seen yet, so we can't assume we'll stay invulnerable—our mortal family and friends definitely aren't."

Aria sighed. "We also need to get these kids back to their parents as soon as possible. I think we'll need to explain what really happened. Considering who we are, I don't think they'll have trouble believing us."

Emily's calm voice grew reflective. "We should look for a secondary base of operations. We need a fallback location in case something happens here, and a larger place to house more people in the event of another refugee crisis like tonight."

"Yeah, it's kind of crowded," Clarice noted dryly, glancing at the sleeping bodies around her.

Aria hummed thoughtfully. "Obviously, those of us who can fly should handle the scouting for now, but once the rest of you have evolved, we can split those tasks up so we all get experience in different areas."

Lexi stood on the widow's walk, keeping an eye on the night sky and surrounding area. "How do we evolve?" she asked, her honeyed voice eager and curious.

A pregnant pause followed as Aria and Clarice tried to think of a way to explain the cause of their evolution without sounding like deviants. Emily rescued them.

"Angels thrive on expressions of love," Emily told the newest angel, a smile in her voice that Clarice just *knew* was a smirk. "When an angel experiences a new level of love, sometimes through intimacy and other times through shared experience, they evolve."

Clarice elaborated, and there was *definitely* a smirk in her voice. "For instance, giving Calypso a shoulder massage triggered her first evolution, but she didn't really take off until Aria smooched her."

"It was not a *smooch*!" Aria hissed vehemently.

"My bad," Clarice whispered contritely. "Let me rephrase that. When Aria *snogged* her."

Clarice could almost *feel* Aria's face heat up as their mother laughed softly. "Snog is an even worse word than smooch!" Aria hissed in exasperation. "Can't you just say I kissed her?"

"I concur with Aria," Calypso said disapprovingly from where she stood outside the guest rooms where the older kids were sleeping. "Snog is far worse than smooch."

Clarice smirked and adopted a British accent. "But snog is from your very own land of origin, my dear Calypso. It's the English way of saying kiss."

Calypso's silence was eloquent.

Lexi spoke up, her voice hesitant. "So, kissing made you evolve?"

"It was one of the factors," Calypso answered softly. "When three of us embraced, that triggered another evolution. There is something about the mingling of three angels' energies that causes it. That is why your eyes changed so swiftly following your transformation."

Lexi's voice vibrated with sudden eagerness. "How long did it take you to get wings? If you've only been angels for two days, it must've been pretty quick."

There was a soft rustle of movement as Clarice appeared beside her in an instant. Lexi gasped at the suddenness.

"I don't have my massage table, unfortunately—it was blown up in our apartment—but since you're an angel, you can just lie down on your belly without getting uncomfortable like a human would. Off to the bench with you."

Lexi smiled nervously and stretched out on the wide stone bench by the railing. Clarice knelt beside her and began to work, her fingers finding just the right pressure.

A small groan of contentment escaped Lexi as Clarice moved from her back to her shoulders and neck. Dawn was staining the eastern horizon when Lexi suddenly gasped. She glowed for a moment, then stood up with a look of wonder.

"I feel so light," she whispered excitedly.

"Let's see your back." Clarice ran her hands over the area between Lexi's shoulder blades and felt the ridges beneath her skin. "Looks like your wings will be here soon. We still need to get fitted at Tamra's. We only have one set of clothes that work with wings. Once it's morning over there, we can visit Tamra and get measured, so you'll have clothes ready when your wings come in."

Lexi looked at her curiously. "What did you three do when your wings appeared?"

Clarice grinned, remembering Aria's hungry eyes roaming her body. She had seriously considered delaying the trip to Tamra's in favor of dragging Aria and Calypso off to one of the bedrooms for the rest of the day.

"We showed up at Tamra's in bras," she answered with a smirk. "I was totally okay rocking the bra look, but Calypso and Aria wanted actual shirts."

Lexi laughed, clearly picturing it. "That would definitely be awkward."

Clarice shrugged with a confident smile. "We're angels. We literally have perfect bodies. We don't really have anything to feel self-conscious about. I remember being a teenager and always fretting about every blemish, not wanting to go out in a bikini in case I had a rash or pimple or *something* to be embarrassed about. As angels, we have flawless bodies. Being seen in a bra certainly isn't going to bother me."

Lexi watched her contemplatively, her cheek resting on the stone bench. "I guess I didn't experience that kind of stuff. My parents sold me off when I was fourteen. I never worried about what I looked like because all it brought me was trouble."

Clarice pulled her into a tight embrace. "I know what you mean, Lexi. My mom always said Aria and I were too pretty for our own damn good. In some cases, she was right. We had a stalker for a while who'd leave notes in our lockers at the gym. We made it clear we weren't interested in men, but he was the type who couldn't accept that. We finally had to get a restraining order after we found him in our room one night. Mom came running down the hall with a butcher knife when she heard Aria scream."

Clarice laughed softly at the memory. "I don't know what the idiot expected, but a butcher knife waved under his nose wasn't it—you don't want to see my mom in momma bear mode." She shook her head wryly. After a moment, her face lost its humor, replaced by disdain. "Boys at that age let hormones do all their thinking. Some grow out of it, while some just get worse with age. Some just get freaking weird. The last time we saw him was the day we moved away to college. He was hanging around one of the neighbor's houses a few blocks away, just outside the restraining order perimeter."

Lexi's mouth twisted in disgust. "That sounds like the creeps I've dealt with—except money makes them worse."

Clarice's eyes grew flinty. "What's your last name, Lexi?" she asked calmly.

Lexi frowned. "White. Why?"

Clarice sighed. "That's going to make things difficult. What are your parents' first names?"

"Trisha and Adam," Lexi replied slowly. "Why do you want to know?"

Clarice groaned. "Adam White. There'll be a million of them."

"Clarice?" Lexi prompted.

Clarice smiled coldly. "I'm going to pay your parents a visit and have a little chat—if I can find them, that is."

Lexi was silent for a moment. "What are you going to do to them?"

Clarice's smile went sub-zero. "Let's just say I'm going to enlighten them."

Lexi didn't say anything, but she did pull Clarice into a tighter embrace.

They stood together until the sun crested the horizon. Clarice sighed and released their newest angel. "I'd better get back to the library before the children wake up."

"Thanks, Clarice," Lexi said softly, her voice barely a whisper. "For everything."

Clarice leaned forward and kissed her forehead. "Happy birthday, Lexi."

Lexi beamed, love radiating out of her in waves. "It's definitely been the best birthday ever."

Clarice dropped down the ladder and blurred through the house until she reached the library. The children were still fast asleep. Calypso had played her harp for them at bedtime, singing a lullaby that sent them into deep, peaceful dreams. Clarice expected at least a few night terrors, but Calypso's magic held strong.

"I'm going to start breakfast," Emily announced. "I'm guessing they'll start waking up soon."

Clarice smiled at the lucky kids. A world-class chef for breakfast wasn't much compared to what they had endured, but every bit of kindness helped balance the scales.

She flipped open a laptop and pulled up the missingkids.org database, typing in the names she saw glowing faintly in the children's auras. The database revealed the cities from which they had been taken, though little else. Hopefully, the kids still remembered their home addresses and parents' names.

An eight-year-old boy named Luther was the first to stir. He sat bolt upright, looking around blankly. Clarice waved at him, and his eyes lit up as he remembered the night before.

"My mom's making breakfast when you're ready," she said softly.

He grinned eagerly and stepped gingerly around the other sleeping kids. Clarice smiled to herself as she watched him make a beeline for the veranda. It was wonderful to see the life in his eyes, free from fear and pain. How could anyone or any*thing* want to harm a child, to extinguish that spark in their eyes?

Soon, the rest were awake, drawn by the smell of food. Clarice joined them on the veranda, gently asking for parents' names, addresses, and phone numbers as they ate. She didn't need to write anything down; her new memory absorbed every detail effortlessly.

"Most live within a few hundred miles of each other," Clarice told the other angels. "The demons didn't go far to snatch them. I'll start calling the parents I have numbers for and setting up meetings."

Aria smiled at her gratefully. "You're so good at the extrovert stuff, too. I'm totally good with taking the kids to their parents after you set up the meeting."

Clarice shook her head. "You should probably focus on scouting, since you can fly." She absently ruffled the hair of a girl hugging her. Some of the children just wanted to feel the powerful love and comfort of angel embraces, and would randomly run over and hug them. "We don't want any surprises popping up—especially with all these kids here."

Aria nodded. "Okay, twist my arm, why don't ya. I'll fly if I have to."

Calypso laughed, running a hand through the hair of two children attached to her like vines.

Aria turned to Emily as she entered with another platter piled high with food. "When's Dad going to become an angel?"

Emily refilled the plates for the teenage boys who seemed capable of infinite consumption. "Sometime today, probably after we finish reuniting the kids with their families."

She looked at Aria and Clarice pointedly. "And you need to find Devon a wife while you're out. He won't make the change until he's started a family, and if we leave it to him, he'll be ancient before that happens."

"Got it," Clarice said dryly. "I'll add 'divine matchmaking' to my to-do list."

Once everyone had eaten and Calypso and Lexi were keeping the kids entertained, Clarice returned to the library to start making calls. She began with the youngest—Julie, a seven-year-old who still knew her parents' number.

"Hello?" a woman's voice answered.

"Hi, Deborah, I'm Clarice," she said, using the authority in her angel voice to ensure she had the woman's full attention. "Calypso, Aria, and I rescued some children from a bad place, and one of them is your daughter, Julie. We have reason to believe the government is involved in the abductions, so we prefer to bring her to you in person rather than involve law enforcement. Is there somewhere we can meet you with Julie?"

The line went silent, then a choked sob broke through. "You... you have my Julie?"

"Yes, she's safe now, but we need to discuss what she's been through," Clarice said gently. "Where can we meet?"

"I'll drive home right now," the woman choked out. "I'll be there in fifteen minutes."

Clarice confirmed the address, then went to find Julie, who was playing hopscotch with Lexi in the dirt outside. "Julie, it's time to go see your mom," she said with a warm smile.

Julie's eyes widened. "I'm ready!" she squealed, running to Clarice excitedly.

Clarice pulled her into her arms. "We're gonna fly this time, okay?"

Julie's eyes went wide, and her smile nearly split her face in half. With a laugh, Clarice launched into the air and rocketed across the continent. Julie screamed with excitement as they traveled at many times the speed of sound without feeling a trace of wind. She landed in the front yard of a small house and waited another ten minutes for Julie's mother to arrive. The street was surprisingly quiet. One car drove past while they waited, but the driver seemed oblivious to the angel near the house.

A white car pulled into the driveway, and a woman about Clarice's age leapt out almost before it stopped, rushing forward with a cry. She took Julie from Clarice's arms and clutched her tightly, sobbing.

"Mommy, I missed you so much!" Julie cried, clinging to her mother's neck.

"I missed you too, sweetheart," Deborah sniffed, stroking her daughter's hair.

Clarice gently touched Deborah's arm. "Do you mind if we go inside before anyone notices me?"

The young mother smiled through her tears and hurried to the front door. She struggled for a moment to get her keys without putting her daughter down but eventually managed to unlock the door.

Clarice followed her inside, noting the large stack of missing posters on an end table. She heard another vehicle pull up, and a moment later the young father also came in. When he saw his daughter in her mother's arms, he rushed forward and pulled them both into a hug, sobbing his heart out. Clarice let them have their moment before speaking.

"I need to speak with one of you in private for a moment," Clarice said softly.

"I'll go," Deborah said, briefly touching her husband's cheek and kissing her daughter's forehead.

Deborah led her into a bedroom, closing the door behind them. She turned to Clarice, her eyes red-rimmed. "Where did you find her?"

"This isn't going to be pleasant," Clarice warned, her voice sympathetic. "You may want to sit down."

Tears began streaming down Deborah's face again as she sat on the edge of the bed, watching Clarice with dread.

"We were following the trail of a corrupt police chief involved in human trafficking," Clarice began, wishing there was a gentler way to tell a mother her daughter had been tortured. "We tracked him to an abandoned dairy farm, where we found forty other children in an underground bunker beneath a silo. The police chief wasn't human; he was a demon. They were hurting the children and harvesting their blood. Calypso erased most of their memories, so they only remember the day they were taken to the silo. They have no memory of the horrible things that were done to them. Calypso also healed their wounds. Deborah, I'm so sorry this happened to your daughter."

Deborah stared at her in horror, then let out a despairing wail. Clarice pulled her into a tight embrace, flooding her system with radiance.

Deborah gasped, feeling the overpowering emotions wash over her, slowly drying her tears.

"She remembers there were demons," Clarice said gently, "and you need to know that they're real. We destroyed the ones responsible, but there may be stronger ones out there. Don't trust anyone in authority right now—the FBI, police, CPS. The demons have likely infiltrated many institutions. We're still learning how deep it goes."

Deborah nodded weakly, clinging to her for the relief she needed to escape the horrors in her mind.

Clarice sighed regretfully. "I have thirty-nine other children to return to their parents, so I need to leave you now. I wish I could stay longer to help."

"Thank you!" Deborah whispered fervently. "Thank you for bringing my baby back to me."

Clarice smiled softly. "You're more than welcome. We're going to fix this broken world."

The small family of three followed her out onto the porch to say goodbye. Julie wanted one last angel hug. Clarice grinned as she scooped her up into her arms again. "You take care of your parents, okay, Julie?"

"Okay, Clarice," Julie accepted with a firm nod.

Clarice kissed her forehead, then handed her back to her mother. "Goodbye, Julie."

She stepped back, unfurled her wings, and launched into the sky, vanishing into the morning light.

15 – REUNITED

Clarice spent the entire day and well into the evening flying children back to their parents. Much to her relief, they hadn't encountered any more cases like Lexi's, where parents had sold their child.

It was an emotionally taxing day, and she was glad she had a nonstop supply of positive energy charging her emotional matrix. Most of the parents had feared their children dead. Some of them had been missing for years, enduring horrors she couldn't bear to imagine. Every time she handed a child back into a parent's arms, her determination to rid the world of evil grew stronger.

Aria landed beside Clarice on the widow's walk, her eyes warm with concern. "How are you doing?"

Clarice breathed a tired sigh. "It's been a day of heavy emotional toll. If I weren't an angel, I think this would've crushed me."

Aria impulsively embraced her, projecting warmth and love into her meridians, doubling Clarice's positive energy intake.

"You did some amazing good today. You don't just look like an angel—you *act* like one."

Clarice closed her eyes and let the radiance charge her soul with hope. "Thanks, Aria. Knowing I'll always have you to count on makes a huge difference. I can't imagine what this must've been like for Calypso, being alone for all those years."

Aria nodded, her cheek rubbing Clarice's ear. "Especially since she doesn't remember being human. We remember what it felt like to be human, which gives us a dichotomy she lacks, allowing us to appreciate being an angel."

Clarice pursed her lips, running her fingers through Aria's thick mane of hair. "I wonder if there's a way to unlock her memories, assuming she ever *was* human. It's entirely possible she's always been an angel, though that seems unlikely since she was a child at one point. That begs the question: who transformed her?"

Aria let out a contented moan as Clarice's fingers slid up her neck and began kneading the back of her scalp. "Either there's an angelic lineage we don't know about, or there's another angel out there," she said, her voice languid. "We've had enough publicity by now that if there *were* another angel somewhere, they should've stopped by to say hi. It's hard to believe demons would be abducting children indiscriminately if there were other angels. Maybe they're like Calypso and aren't combat-oriented. My punch certainly didn't do anything to that demon—maybe angel fire's the only thing capable of killing them."

Clarice's cheeks moved against Aria's as she smiled. "Interesting theory. I know you're a physicist, but you're pretty damn smart."

Aria suddenly giggled. "Says Dr. Clarice, with a PhD in awesomeness."

Clarice's grin widened. "Being awesome is hard work, I'll have you know. I have to remind myself how awesome I am at least a dozen times a day."

They both heard Lexi snort from inside the house.

Clarice grinned and held Aria at arm's length. "Did you hear something? Sounded like a prospective student eager to learn the ways of awesomeness."

Aria nodded, a playful smile curving her lips. "It *definitely* sounded eager. I think we'll have to induct her into the ways of awesomeness with a proper hazing ritual."

Clarice grinned wickedly. "Let's fly her up to low Earth orbit and drop her into the Pacific. It's not like it'll hurt her."

"I'm game!" Lexi's voice called back eagerly.

Clarice's face fell. "You're not supposed to *look forward* to a hazing ritual."

"No, don't make me do it," Lexi deadpanned. "Please—don't drop me."

A surge of light erupted from inside the house, halting their conversation.

Aria stared at Clarice, eyes shining. "That felt like an angel transformation."

"Dad," Clarice whispered excitedly. "There's finally a male angel. I'm not sure how I feel about that."

"Well, you're just going to have to get used to it," their father declared, his voice deep and powerful. "'Cause you're stuck with me now."

Aria and Clarice exchanged a look, then raced into the house at angel speed, bursting through their parents' bedroom door, nearly removing the door casing in their haste.

Their father stood, wrapped in their mother's embrace, looking no older than they did. His eyes were a deep cerulean blue rather than lavender. His face was clean-shaven and stronger, like someone carved from good decisions.

Clarice gasped in mock amazement. "You've got a *man's* jaw now, Dad! People are going to start calling you *Chad*."

He laughed, a booming sound that charged the air with joy. Clarice and Aria joined their mother in a jubilant embrace. Their parents were finally both safe. For the first time since the world went sideways, a slice of normalcy felt possible. She had been terrified a missile would somehow get through their vigilant monitoring, or some other sneak attack. All that remained to worry about was Uncle Devon.

Silver tears tracked down her cheeks as Aria choked out, "Welcome to the angel club, Dad."

Clarice beamed, eyes shimmering silver. "Yeah, welcome to the club, Dad. We're literally going to be together forever now."

A teasing grin appeared on his chiseled face. "Is it too late to revert?"

Emily's arms tightened around him possessively. "Far too late."

Clarice jumped as a golden glow suddenly surrounded them. She looked at Aria and realized their tears had brushed when their cheeks touched.

Eric studied the golden field with a bemused expression. "What's with the ritzy glow? I feel like—" He broke off as intense energy suddenly charged through their meridians like a bolt of lightning.

Clarice blinked as the light ebbed, her eyes feeling distinctly hot. She shared a look with Aria, and they both gasped. Aria's eyes were no longer violet. Golden orbs of fire stared back, lines of energy slowly twisting around her irises.

Eric blinked curiously, looking around. "What are all these energy lines I'm seeing?"

Emily stared around intently, taking in the countless lines of twisting light. "I'd like to know that, too."

"The planet's meridians," Clarice answered absently, still absorbed in her own transformation. "You can even see radio waves."

Aria examined Clarice. "My eyes feel hot. Some of your nodes are a lot brighter." She looked at their parents. "Theirs are, too."

Clarice nodded slowly, studying the bright nodes. "I have a feeling our angel fire is a lot more powerful now. I'm pretty sure if we focus our eye beams at the brighter nodes, it'll do more damage. Remember how it took a few seconds to kill those demons?"

Aria blinked slowly. "I feel like it can go off at any moment now. It used to need a little time to charge. I don't think I need to work myself into a righteous fury anymore."

Eric rubbed his neck. "I feel like I'm on the fast track for promotion. Shouldn't it have taken me longer to evolve?"

Clarice shook her head. "I think all it requires are the right conditions," she said absently. Frowning, she glanced at Aria. "I want to go somewhere remote to test something. You too, Aria."

Emily arched an amused eyebrow. "Is it a secret?"

Clarice snorted. "No, I just want to see if I'm right before I explain it. We'll tell you all about it once we figure out how and *if* it works. Come along, Aria."

Aria shared a wry look with their parents and followed Clarice into the hallway. "You're just so mysterious," she smirked.

Clarice spun and pressed Aria up against the wall in a flash, her arms trapping her on either side. "Mysterious, you say?" Clarice whispered dangerously, her nose touching Aria's, their lips a breath apart.

Aria froze, her eyes widening as her cheeks flushed crimson. She attempted to speak, but it came out as a squeak. Her chest heaved, her breaths coming in quick gasps, causing their breasts to rub together with each inhale.

Clarice leaned forward, pressing her mouth against Aria's ear. "Do you have any idea how bad I want you right now?" she whispered hotly, her lips brushing against Aria's ear teasingly. "The things I want to do to you?"

Aria swallowed, and Clarice could feel her legs trembling.

Clarice lowered her head and lightly kissed Aria's neck, eliciting a whimper. She brought her lips back to Aria's ear. "I'm going to—"

Lexi appeared around the corner, her eyes bright with anticipation. She froze when she saw them, and Clarice let out a defeated sigh, stepping back from Aria and turning to face her.

Aria closed her eyes, her breaths slowly returning to normal, though her cheeks remained flushed.

"What's up, Lexi?" Clarice asked brightly, hiding her searing disappointment. Now that Aria's walls were down, it was increasingly difficult to wait even a moment longer to take their relationship to the next level.

Lexi hesitated, eyeing Aria uncertainly. "Can I... go with you?" she asked hesitantly. "I want to see what you can do."

Aria switched to hover mode, clearly not trusting her legs. She finally opened her eyes, staring fixedly at Lexi.

Clarice winked at Lexi. "Let's get you some wings first. Calypso, can we borrow you for a minute?"

Lexi's eyes widened, and she started bouncing on her toes. "Really? Oh my god, *really*?"

Calypso came out of the music room on the second floor and joined them with a questioning look. When she saw their golden eyes, hers widened.

"You two have evolved again," she marveled, smiling delightedly.

Clarice nodded, her gaze calculating. "We had another angel tear fusing. I can tell my parents are different from us, so I was hoping the three of us could get Lexi some wings."

Without another word, Calypso embraced Lexi. Aria and Clarice joined in, their energy intertwining. To Clarice's enhanced sight, the flow looked like a maelstrom of light. The current stabilized, and Lexi began to glow faintly. A moment later, wings burst through her shirt.

Clarice smiled mischievously. "Oh right—I'd forgotten about that part. Maybe we should visit Tamra first. She's on the other side of the continent, so hopefully it isn't too late for a visit."

Lexi nodded vigorously, clutching the remains of her shirt.

Clarice performed some contortionist acrobatics with her hands inside her shirt, and a moment later, her hands came out with her bra, which she grinningly offered to Lexi, welcoming her as the newest member of the bra club.

Aria's gaze went to Clarice's braless chest, where her nipples were plainly visible through the soft elastic fabric of her upper bodice. Clarice gave her sister a slow wink and her most seductive smile. She was immediately rewarded with an eruption of color in her sister's cheeks, sending Clarice into a fit of giggles. Aria's walls might be down, but she was still the same shy maiden Clarice had grown up with. Now that she knew souls were real, she was almost certain her sister's bashful nature was a core trait.

They exited the house and launched into the air, taking time for Lexi to get a feel for flying. She still had to deal with wind currents, so they couldn't arc across the continent like they normally would.

Lexi whooped, ecstatic to fly slower as she soared high into the clouds, heading west. Clarice deactivated her antigravity and flew alongside her, enjoying the wind in her hair. Even fighting the wind, they managed to stay just under the sound barrier.

They passed within a few thousand feet of a passenger jet, prompting a wave from Lexi when she saw someone videoing from one of the cabin windows. Clarice wondered how long it would be before the footage hit social media but figured that, at this point, one more viral video of angels hardly mattered. World religions could debate all they wanted—she suspected demons controlled most of them anyway.

The sun was just dipping below the horizon when they touched down at Tamra's, three hours later.

Tamra opened the door with a welcoming smile. "Measuring time?"

Aria grinned, nodding at Lexi. "Yeah, plus we have a new angel."

Tamra's eyes widened. "Is that you, Lexi?"

Lexi beamed, her face suffused with joy. "Hi, Tamra. I'll never have to worry about some bastard taking advantage of me ever again."

Tamra gaped, staring back and forth between Clarice and Lexi. "Humans can *become* angels? I thought you came from heaven or something."

Clarice folded her arms beneath her breasts, grinning mischievously. "We *did* just come from heaven—we flew through the heavens from the other side of the continent to get here."

Tamra blinked, then burst out laughing. "So, you're not from some paradisiacal realm of the gods?"

"Nope," Aria confirmed, glancing at Clarice's chest and then quickly away, her cheeks coloring. "If there's a realm of divine beings, we don't know about it."

Clarice stretched, back arching as she ran her hands through her hair in her favorite pose, a blend of casual and erotic. "Or hell, for that matter, unless that's where the demons came from."

Clarice barely restrained a grin when she saw Aria's eyes pulled toward her like a tractor beam. How far could she wind her sister up before her growing lust outpaced her bashfulness? She would have to thank Tamra for finding a top that was tight in the chest.

Tamra eyed them suspiciously. "Demons are real?"

Clarice grimaced, her mouth twisting with revulsion. "So it would appear. We rescued forty children from a bunker where they were being tortured by scaly, horned demons. They were tough, like angels, and could tank one of Aria's punches. We had to rely on angel fire to destroy them. They were harvesting the blood of terrified children for reasons we don't yet understand, but we plan to find the rest of their nests and find out. There's no room on this world for both angels *and* demons."

Tamra shivered, her eyes distant before she shook herself and focused. "Let's get you all fitted. I'll find a loaner top for you, Lexi, until we can get something made."

The next half hour passed in measurements and notes. Tamra logged everything on her tablet, transferring the data to one of her PCs. Her home looked like a miniature clothing factory, filled with plotters, automated cutters, and sewing machines. When they finished, she handed Lexi a simple wing-cut blouse and a leather jacket.

Aria laid a hand on Tamra's shoulder. "We'll send Calypso over with two more angels, if that's okay," she said tentatively, then hesitated. "We'll bring some money next time too. I totally spaced that people don't work for free."

Tamra shook her head firmly. "There's no way I'm taking any money. I'm not going down in history as the person who charged angels for clothes. Besides, rescuing my niece more than repaid any debt a thousand times over."

Clarice eyed her speculatively. "If you ever feel like a career change, let me know. The only downside to being an angel is that we can't have children. We'll probably find out soon enough, now that my parents are angels."

Tamra fumbled the piece of cloth she was folding. "You could turn *me* into an angel?"

"Yep," Clarice said simply. "At first, we only transformed family, but finding out that demons exist changed that. We're outnumbered, and we don't yet know if they can hurt us."

Tamra narrowed her eyes, fidgeting with a tape measure. "I'll have to think about it. I've always wanted kids, and I don't know if I'm ready to give that up."

A sly smile curved Clarice's lips as a thought clicked into place. "Tell me, Tamra—do you like men with deep voices?"

Aria gave her a startled look, then burst out laughing so hard that tears started leaking out the corners of her eyes. Tamra stared at them as if they had gone mad, her eyes askance.

"Sorry, Tamra," Clarice apologized, barely restraining a grin. "My mom made me promise to be on the lookout for a partner for my Uncle Devon.

He also doesn't want to become an angel until he's had a chance to have a family. Are you available?"

Tamra blinked, clearly taken aback at Clarice's bluntness. "I'm not seeing anyone, no."

Clarice smiled brightly. "How about I bring my uncle by when my parents and Calypso come over? He's a good-looking guy with a deep voice and a caring nature. He's the reason we lived long enough to become angels."

"*Sure...*" Tamra drew the word out slowly, eyeing Clarice speculatively. "Trot him on out, and we'll see where the wind blows."

Clarice pumped her fist. "Slam dunk!"

Tamra snorted dryly. "Give me a few days to finish your outfits. Go tell your uncle to start polishing up—I'm picky."

Clarice grinned, waggling her eyebrows playfully. "You got it."

Tamra laughed, making shooing motions with her hands. "Get out of here, you weirdo. My opinion of angels has taken a real hit tonight."

Clarice laughed and gave Tamra a quick hug. "You just wait until you meet my parents."

Tamra's eyes widened as she felt the powerful love of an angel channeled into her. When Clarice released her, she stared at Clarice with new eyes.

"Okay, you've raised my opinion again. I'll see you in a few days."

The angels let themselves out as Tamra returned to her workbench.

Clarice looked at Lexi admiringly. "You're really rocking that jacket, Lexi—it looks fantastic on you."

Lexi shoulder-bumped Clarice, her face lighting up with a pleased smile. "Thanks, Clarice."

"Let's fly, ladies," Clarice exploded upward into the night sky, followed by the other two angels.

Aria flew up next to her. "Where are we going?"

Clarice glanced at her sister and Aria's eyes snapped up to meet her gaze, blushing furiously. "There's a military site in Utah called the Dugway Proving Ground," Clarice explained, giving her a knowing smile. "I figure if they can test their biological and chemical weapons there, we can test our own firepower without worrying about collateral damage."

Aria quickly looked away, staring at the land far below. "Won't they send more troops to try and stop us?"

Clarice raised an amused eyebrow. "So what if they do? They can't hurt us. We just keep doing our thing while they waste munitions. It might be good practice for upping our evasion skills. We can see how many bullets and missiles we can dodge, refine our aim, and even try blasting incoming projectiles out of the air. I want to see how fast we really are. Just be careful not to get your clothes ruined, or you'll be a naked angel."

Aria's eyes were immediately drawn to Clarice before she could stop them. She coughed and quickly averted her gaze, turning to Lexi. "Um, yeah, remember to cover yourself with your wings if you get caught in an explosion. They're great for shielding your outfit."

Lexi's eyes gleamed with a mixture of excitement and awe. She had spent most of her life powerless—now, she was something else entirely. Clarice was curious to see how she would handle the change.

It only took half an hour to reach the testing range. They landed atop a small mountain dotted with junipers and sagebrush. Dirt roads wound through the valleys below, past cracked concrete test bunkers half-swallowed by time.

Aria pointedly stepped in front of Clarice. "Okay, what exactly are we testing? You've got more than angel fire in mind, don't you?"

Clarice held up her hands. "Can you feel the energy potential in your palms?"

Aria frowned, concentrating. "Yeah, now that you mention it. What is it?"

Clarice grinned. "Watch." She spread her arms wide, then slammed her palms together in a thunderous clap, releasing the energy she had gathered.

A brilliant white light erupted outward. The junipers and sagebrush in front of them exploded in a thirty-degree arc as the blast wave tore through nearly a thousand feet of terrain, vaporizing or uprooting everything in its path. Rock faces shattered, shearing ten feet off the ridgeline.

Aria stared, open-mouthed at the devastation. "Holy freaking crap! It's like a freaking bomb went off!"

Clarice observed the devastation with satisfaction. "Pretty much," she agreed cheerfully.

She picked up a rock the size of her head and casually threw it a thousand feet into the air. As it reached its apex, she triggered the heat in her eyes, and a beam of light shot out, vaporizing the unoffending stone.

Aria grinned eagerly. "My turn."

She picked up a large chunk of limestone and flung it skyward. As it plummeted, her golden eyes flashed a brilliant white, and a beam of light shot out, incinerating it.

Lexi practically vibrated with anticipation, bouncing from foot to foot. "How do you *do* that?"

Clarice smiled indulgently at the excited angel. "At your level, you need to channel your positive energy into something more… wrathful. That endless love you feel inside needs to transform into righteous fury. Think about the guy Aria vaporized back in Beverly Hills."

Lexi stood perfectly still for a moment, then her entire body ignited with light. Clarice tossed another rock into the air. Lexi's glow brightened, her eyes flared, and the rock vanished in a flash.

Clarice smiled encouragingly. "You've got it."

Aria took a deep breath, smiling with anticipation. "I'm going to try the angel clap."

She spread her arms and brought them together with far more force than Clarice had. The shockwave blasted outward with a deafening boom. For several seconds, the mountains lit up like sunrise. When the light faded, the slope across the valley was gone—a thousand-foot-wide hole carved into the rock, with debris collapsing inward in a slow-motion avalanche.

"Wow," Clarice breathed, whistling softly. "You really put some power into that one. Apparently, we can blow up mountains now."

Lexi gawked at the destruction, speechless. Aria stared, equally stunned by her own strength.

"We're still practically babies," she whispered. "What the hell can a fully evolved angel do? And I was holding back—a lot."

Clarice narrowed her eyes. "I'd imagine they could destroy the world if they wanted to. I'm starting to understand those old stories. Entire cities wiped out by angels doesn't sound so mythical anymore."

"Yeah…" Aria agreed uneasily. "I'm not sure *anybody* should have this much power."

Clarice folded her arms, frowning pensively. "We might need it soon, depending on how powerful some of these demons are."

Aria turned and gestured to the west. "I guess we got somebody's attention."

Clarice grinned at the distant thrum of helicopter rotors. "Time for some *real* target practice," she purred, rubbing her hands together with a maniacal grin. She turned to Lexi. "Just be careful not to hurt anyone, unless it's a demon. Most of these soldiers are just kids following orders."

Lexi nodded, her violet eyes dancing with excitement and a touch of fear.

Clarice laid a comforting hand on Lexi's shoulder. "Trust me, they don't have *anything* that can hurt you, especially since we don't have pain receptors. The most you'll have to worry about is me leering at you if they incinerate your clothes."

Lexi burst out laughing, and some of her fear faded.

Aria glanced at her, biting her lip, and Clarice remembered the way her sister's presence had flared with delight when Clarice had ogled her after the nuke vaporized their clothes. Aria probably wasn't even aware that her emotions were broadcasting like an LED billboard when she got excited. It was downright adorable, something Clarice would have to avoid telling her about in case she learned to hide the emotional show-and-tell.

More than a dozen Apache gunships appeared on the horizon, with two F-35s sweeping wide above them. The three angels waited as the helicopters drew closer, and Lexi's glow intensified.

Aria nudged Clarice playfully. "Should we glow too? For effect?"

Clarice's lips curved into a grin. "It would be in character."

All three flared with radiance, bathing the desert in molten gold. The Apache formation spread out and held position roughly a thousand feet away.

Clarice blinked—her mind was automatically decoding the radio chatter she could see flickering through the airwaves.

"Hey, Aria, I can understand their transmissions. That happening for you too?"

A curious smile tugged at Aria's lips. "Now that you mention it, yeah."

"*Targets are maintaining position,*" a voice spoke over the radio. "*No hostile intent observed.*"

"*Engage targets,*" another voice replied crisply.

"*With respect, sir,*" the pilot answered uneasily, "*I'd like a reason for firing on what look like angels. I'm not planning to spend eternity in hell.*"

"*These are not angels, Lieutenant,*" the voice snapped irritably. "*They are mimicking the appearance of angels with advanced nanotech. Engage, or you'll be court-martialed.*"

One of the Apaches opened fire, its 30 mm cannon snarling. Another launched a volley of missiles.

Clarice's power flared. Time seemed to slow as her mind overclocked; she saw every bullet and shell as individual points of light. Twin beams lanced from her eyes, vaporizing each projectile before it reached them. To the pilots, it looked like an unbroken stream of holy light. The Hellfire missiles vanished in mid-flight, erased before they cleared their bays.

For five long minutes, the desert shook under gunfire and explosions. When the barrage finally ended, the comparative quiet of rotor blades felt almost peaceful.

Clarice turned, eyeing the mountains across from them calculatingly. "I think a demonstration might be educational. Let's show them what restraint looks like."

Aria smirked. "Something to make clear that we're not taking them seriously."

Clarice turned her back on the gunships and brought her hands together in a clap to match Aria's. Light exploded away from her, slamming into the distant mountain and coring out a massive hole. Dust and debris mushroomed into the air, glowing in their radiant light.

"Holy shit!" several voices exclaimed in unison.

"She just blasted a mountain apart!" another pilot stammered.

Clarice's voice echoed through their transceivers, calm and unmistakably amused. *"Are you finished? We can do this all night."*

"Channel compromised, all pilots switch to alternate channel," came the terse order.

"You don't have any communication mediums we can't use," Clarice informed them sweetly. *"Why don't you pack up and go home now? Playtime's over."*

"All pilots return to base," the same voice commanded, a touch of exasperation in its tone.

"Was there something you actually wanted?" Clarice asked lightly. *"Or do you just enjoy using us for live target practice?"*

"Maintain radio silence," the commander growled.

"Are you really angels?" one pilot blurted, ignoring the order.

"Yes, we're really angels," Clarice replied, floating into the sky. *"Thank you to those of you who refused to fire on angels. We'll remember you when we meet again."*

The radio filled with stunned silence and a ripple of dread.

Aria raised an eyebrow. "You planning to meet them at the pearly gates or something?"

Clarice shrugged. "I just wanted to get some rumors going among the rank and file. It might make future encounters easier if everyone's terrified of shooting at the messengers of God." She glanced up at the F-35s closing in on them.

Aria grinned. "You missed your calling, Clarice," she said admiringly. "You'd make a killer spymaster—psychological warfare's totally your thing."

A missile streaked toward them. Clarice barely turned her head before Lexi disintegrated it mid-air. The second jet fired several more, and Aria zapped them effortlessly.

Clarice sighed discontentedly. “I wonder how much taxpayer money they’ve wasted on us tonight?”

Aria groaned. “Here we go again. You’ve graduated from criticizing the Department of Transportation to the Department of Defense. Besides, it’s not like you even pay taxes anymore.”

Clarice flipped her hair over her shoulder. “That’s because I already paid enough for a lifetime. Each of those missiles probably cost six figures. They’ve torched millions just to prove we’re immune. And considering we already demonstrated that when they nuked us in orbit, I’d say this is taxpayer malpractice.” She paused, then smirked at Aria. “Besides, last time I complained about the Department of Transportation, you told me there were juicier places to criticize. I’m pretty sure the Department of Defense is at the top of the list.”

Aria held up her hands. “Okay, you got me on that one.” She paused and tilted her head. “You’d think they’d try diplomacy after a nuclear failure, wouldn’t you?”

Lexi gasped. “You got nuked?”

“Yeah,” Clarice said casually, vaporizing another missile. “When we were destroying satellites, a space-based nuke went off right next to us. Totally incinerated our clothes. We had to fly home butt naked. At least I came in last and got the best view.”

Lexi looked at her curiously, then hesitated, looking between them uncertainly—no doubt remembering the scene in the hall where Clarice had pinned Aria against the wall. “Um, isn’t Aria your sister? Who checks out their sister?”

“Stepsister,” Clarice corrected airily. “No shared DNA—and she’s *gorgeous*. You’d have to be blind not to notice. Don’t tell me you don’t think she’s hot.”

Lexi rolled her eyes. “There’s no safe answer to that,” she objected.

Clarice planted her hands on her hips. “Sure there is,” she said, turning and eyeing Aria appreciatively. “You just say yes—she’s hot.”

Lexi’s eyebrows shot up. “If I say she’s hot, you’ll ask me if I’m coming on to your sister,” she said levelly.

Clarice whirled back to face Lexi, her eyes flashing with outrage. “Wait, what?” she demanded truculently. “You’re coming on to my *sister*?”

“Yes, Clarice,” Lexi stated flatly. “I’m coming on to your sister.”

Clarice sighed lustily. “Well, I don’t blame you. She’s freaking *hot*.” She paused, and her face lost some of its humor. “And seriously... she’s mine, so don’t get any ideas.”

Aria flushed, and a shy smile flickered across her face. Lexi eyed Aria appraisingly, clearly expecting some kind of objection. Her eyes widened when she saw Aria's flushed cheeks and obvious attraction.

"Wait... you two really *are* a thing?" Lexi asked hesitantly.

Clarice gave a firm nod. "That we are. We starred in The Addams Family."

Lexi snorted. "I certainly don't find that hard to believe."

Clarice grinned, openly admiring Aria. "You should see just how handsy I can get."

Lexi shook her head, watching Clarice in bemusement. "You're kind of shameless, aren't you?"

Clarice flipped her hair over her shoulder and smirked. "I've always had a very casual relationship with shame. I don't bother it, and it doesn't bother me."

Aria sighed forlornly. "I think I'm being replaced as Tweedledee."

Clarice shot her a sly wink. "I'm sure Mom will have some new names for us—The Three Stooges or some such."

Lexi watched the two of them wistfully as they waited for the F-35s to return.

Clarice eyed her suspiciously. "What's that look for?"

Lexi smiled sadly. "I just love how close you are with your family. It's awesome to see how much you all love each other."

Clarice's eyes softened. "You're a part of that family now, too. We love you too, Lexi."

Lexi froze, closing her eyes as quicksilver tears streamed down her cheeks.

Clarice destroyed the next missile, then drifted over to Lexi and pulled her into a warm embrace. "We love you, Lexi. For real. You really are part of our family now."

Lexi pulled Clarice tight and laid her head on her shoulder as more tears flowed. "I've never had anyone tell me they love me before," she whispered, a smile on her lips. "It's amazing how powerful such simple words are."

Aria joined them, kissing Lexi's forehead. "Words have power. I've seen Calypso use words of power, and I think love is one of them. It's criminal negligence that you haven't been shown the love you deserve until now, but we're here for you, and you're stuck with us for all eternity."

Lexi smiled, radiant even through her tears. "Thank you. I love you too."

Aria blasted another missile out of the sky, then tapped into the pilots' comms. *"We're trying to have a moment here—mind giving us a minute?"*

Clarice snorted a laugh, prompting a questioning noise from Lexi.

"Aria just tapped into their radio and asked them to give us a minute because we're having a moment," Clarice explained.

Lexi blinked. "You can tap into their radios?"

Clarice grinned mischievously. "Apparently. We've been carrying on conversations with the pilots while they've been trying to find secure channels. It's petty, but fun."

Lexi giggled and hugged her tighter. "Words can't express how grateful I am. I'm so happy to be here—with you."

Clarice stroked her hair affectionately, letting her love flow into Lexi's meridians. "We know, Lexi. The only good thing about your ordeal is that we ended up meeting you. Life's only going to get better for you every day from now on."

Lexi nodded against her shoulder, tears tracing silver lines down her cheeks as the three angels hovered in the glowing quiet of the desert night.

16 – DEMONS

As soon as they landed on the front lawn, Calypso rushed out of the house and embraced Aria, then moved on to Clarice and Lexi.

"I know you're practically invulnerable," she said, holding Lexi close, "but I still worry when you depart. I am simply relieved that you made it back."

Lexi melted in Calypso's arms, soaking up the warmth she had missed all her life.

Aria smiled fondly at Calypso. "You never have to explain yourself when it comes to hugs. We're angels—we can never get enough."

Clarice brushed her fingers across Calypso's cheek with a wry grin. "Seriously. It's built right into the angel package. We're rewarded with supercharged energy every time we hug."

Aria winced. "Don't call it an 'angel package,' Clarice," she begged plaintively. "That just sounds so wrong."

Clarice stared down her nose at Aria. "Get your mind out of the gutter, you degenerate angel. You'll contaminate the purer-minded angels with your lascivious talk."

Calypso shook her head ruefully. "I shan't even ask. How did your testing proceed? You were absent far longer than I had anticipated."

Clarice gestured toward Lexi. "We ended up flying the slow way so Lexi could enjoy her first time flying: three hours each way, an hour at Tamra's, and another hour playing tag with the military while testing our new powers."

Aria draped an arm around Clarice's shoulder with a mischievous grin. "Apparently, we can hack radio transmissions—even encrypted ones. We had *way* too much fun talking to pilots while they emptied their arsenals on us."

Calypso looked them up and down. "I see your clothes remain intact. I suppose you were too swift for them."

Aria shook her head, laughing with disbelief and wonder. "We were actually zapping them in flight with angel fire. You wouldn't *believe* how fast we can track and fire. We were literally shooting machine-gun bullets out of the air."

Calypso raised her eyebrows. "That is... quite the power boost."

Lexi's eyes were bright and tinged with awe as she spoke. "That wasn't even the impressive part. They do this angel clap that obliterates entire mountains. Aria blew a hole through an entire range—over a thousand feet wide."

Calypso blinked, worry flickering behind her smile. "That is a considerable amount of power. With all the new angels we are incorporating into our group, we must exercise great care to ensure it is not misused."

Clarice nodded gravely. "I think we need to figure out how to unlock some of these other angel classes. Maybe we should limit the number of battle angels. There are five of us now. We invited Tamra to the angel club, but she wants to start a family first. We should start with some of the former patients you healed."

Calypso folded her arms, nodding slowly. "That sounds like a good place to begin. I believe it may be time for another conversation with Jason and Julia to ascertain how matters are progressing—this time in person."

Aria glanced at Lexi. "Just to recap, we've been reaching out to people Calypso healed, building a network of allies who can help organize, communicate, and sway public opinion. If we can make people aware that demons walk among them, we'll have more eyes watching."

Clarice started toward the house. "I'm going to check the news feeds before that call. I bet the media is losing its mind."

Aria cleared her throat and licked her lips, looking at Calypso nervously. "Okay, we'll be along shortly. I was going to see if Calypso wanted to go for a short flight."

Clarice paused and leered at Calypso. "Preferably somewhere far out of aura range; I need to be able to focus."

Calypso's face flushed brilliantly, and she quickly looked away from Clarice's knowing gaze. Aria's face lit up as well, but she ignored Clarice's comment, took Calypso by the hand, and launched into the air.

Clarice laughed delightedly as she watched them fly away. She was so proud of Aria that she thought she might burst. Her sister was definitely breaking down her mental barriers. The thought sent a flare of anticipation straight to her libido. It wouldn't be long now before they could finally move past longing looks and unspoken desires.

Lexi followed Clarice into the house, curiosity burning in her eyes. "Why out of aura range?"

Clarice smirked as they moved to the stairs. "Because when Calypso gets intimate, she broadcasts it like a cosmic radio station. It's hard to concentrate through that."

Lexi's cheeks colored. "Oh." After a moment, her brows drew down in confusion. "Wait a minute—didn't you say *you* were with Aria? Or were you actually joking the whole time?"

Clarice glanced back at her with a wicked grin. "Nope, you heard right."

Lexi stared at her, a peculiar expression on her face. "She's dating *both* of you?"

"Yep," Clarice confirmed cheerfully.

Lexi eyed her skeptically. "You don't get jealous of each other?"

Clarice slowed as they neared the library and met Lexi's gaze. "If it had been anyone but Aria, I would be hella jealous—but it's Aria. We've always shared everything. And there's just something about Calypso that is so... familiar. I don't know what it is, but I feel like I've known her all my life. We aren't whole without her."

"Wow," Lexi murmured, her eyes a mixture of respect and longing. "You really do love each other, don't you?"

Clarice nodded once, a gentle smile on her lips. "I'd cut off my right arm for Aria," she declared, then paused, cocking her head to the side consideringly. "Well, I would if it were possible; being invincible makes that kinda difficult."

Lexi studied her curiously as they entered the library. "So... um, you and Aria really are a thing?"

Clarice smiled, a blend of mischief and affection. "We're getting there. We've been getting there for a long time now, but I think we're almost to the finish line. The way she took charge and asked Calypso to go on a 'private flight' makes me think she's finally broken down the blocks in her psyche that made intimacy so scary."

Lexi tilted her head questioningly. "Why was she afraid of intimacy? Did something happen to her?"

Clarice nodded, smiling sadly. "Yeah. She ended up with cancer when we were eight, and she had to deal with a lot of invasive procedures over the next two years." Clarice bit her lip, and her vision blurred as tears filled her eyes. "I almost lost her." She blinked back the tears and wiped her cheeks, smiling. “Then Calypso showed up at the hospital and sang her back from the brink.”

Lexi laid a warm hand on her shoulder. “That must have been terrifying. I’m so sorry you had to go through that, Clarice.”

Clarice took a deep, cleansing breath. “It all worked out in the end. We’d never have met Calypso if we hadn’t almost died.”

Lexi blinked. “We?”

Clarice nodded. “I ended up with the same cancer a few weeks later. I wasn’t as far gone as Aria, but I wasn’t going to survive either.”

Lexi chewed her lip, her eyes speculative. “That’s kinda weird that you both ended up with the same cancer at the same time. What are the odds?”

Clarice shrugged a shoulder. “Probably a coincidence.”

Lexi didn’t look convinced.

Clarice took another deep breath and glanced around. “Let’s get started, shall we?”

She flipped a laptop open and sat in one of the chairs, her wings folding around her like a cloak.

Lexi moved closer, then hesitated. “Do you mind if I read over your shoulder? I haven’t touched a computer in over four years.”

Clarice reached into a cubbyhole under the desk and pulled out another laptop. “We have plenty for you, too. You should get some practice if it’s been that long. You can just watch what I’m doing, or ask me for help if you have any questions.”

“Thanks, Clarice,” Lexi said quietly, her aura flaring with gratitude. “I keep having to remind myself I’m not dreaming.”

Clarice squeezed her hand affectionately. “Say that again, and I’ll start pinching you every few minutes just to prove you’re awake.”

Lexi snorted and pulled out a chair next to Clarice, folding her wings around her. Clarice unlocked the laptop for her and opened a browser before focusing on her own laptop.

She didn’t have to look far to find news about angels. Half the headlines were about sightings across the country. She skimmed an article describing airline passengers who had filmed three angels streaking past their jet. Laughing, she pointed it out to Lexi.

“It looks like someone *was* looking out the window when we flew past that jet yesterday. I guess we should have flown closer. They didn’t get very good footage.”

Lexi leaned closer, squinting at the shaky video. “Yeah, we barely show up.”

Clarice's eyes sparkled with amusement. "The comments are roasting them. Everyone's calling it a flock of birds. One person says it's mass hysteria—people seeing angels everywhere because it's trending."

She clicked to the next headline.

ANGELS ATTACKING LAW ENFORCEMENT OFFICERS?

Multiple videos have surfaced showing what appears to be an angelic being vaporizing several police officers. There has been no explanation given for the attacks, and people are concerned these creatures are intent on destroying human civilization. There are reports they've been seen abducting children and even attacking military assets.

A U.S. Army spokesperson has neither confirmed nor denied any engagements with angels. However, an official familiar with the incidents, speaking on condition of anonymity, stated that while several Apache helicopters were conducting training exercises over the Dugway Proving Grounds in Utah, they were "attacked by three winged entities." No casualties were reported, and the military has declined further comment.

Several public figures have urged caution, insisting that whatever these entities are, they are clearly hostile and should be avoided.

Clarice snorted derisively. "Yep, demons are in control of the media. At least we know where to look next."

"That's bullshit!" Lexi burst out. "You've been *saving* kids, not abducting them!"

Clarice nodded, a steely glint in her golden eyes. "Like I said—demons probably control most of the media. Honestly, they're probably running everything right now. We should sniff around Capitol Hill soon and clean house."

Lexi calmed slightly as she continued reading. "At least the public isn't buying it. Look at the comments."

Clarice grinned and scrolled.

mysocksrocks442—> Does ANYONE believe what the media says anymore? There are videos all over the web showing these angels rescuing children from human traffickers—like those cops. They're finally doing what we should have done a long time ago and wiping the floor with these pieces of shit!

Morseydorseyclocktower—> My buddy said he was in one of the Apaches in Utah. They were ordered to kill the angels. He said they didn't stand a chance. The angels vaporized every bullet and missile in midair but never attacked back, even though they could've wiped the choppers out. He claimed they even destroyed an entire mountain range, making it clear they could have killed them if they were truly hostile. He said they hacked comms and thanked the few pilots who refused to shoot. I'm not even religious, but something big is coming. If you're a bad person, you might want to rethink your life choices.

Grotekthegrotesque—> If this were a newspaper, I'd be wiping my ass with it. One of my neighbors had her son returned to her by one of these angels after he'd been missing for over a year. The angel said actual demons were pulling the strings in government and media. Articles like this definitely make me think it's true. She said demons were responsible for the abductions as well. A couple of weeks ago, I'd have shaken my head at such nonsense. Not anymore. There's a war going on, and it's going to get crazy, so buckle up!

Clarice leaned back with a smirk. "They haven't been able to lock the internet down enough to prevent the truth from getting out. They've certainly been pushing for more control over the internet for the last decade. I'd imagine if we started this adventure ten years later, you wouldn't see any videos or comments they don't want you to see."

They paused as a powerful surge of energy pulsed through them. With her enhanced vision, Clarice could see the energy wave blasting past, continuing for several miles. She cursed when the laptop went dead. Whatever it was had knocked out the power.

"I wonder if this is one of those unconventional weapons Uncle Devon warned us about," Clarice muttered darkly. She blurred to the front porch and launched into the sky, focusing her enhanced vision on the epicenter of the surge, at least twenty miles away in the mountains. The mental beacon representing Aria was there, right at the center.

Emily called up to her from where she stood on the ground. "Clarice, do you have any idea what the hell that was?"

Clarice dropped back to the ground, eyes narrowing as a sneaking suspicion took root. Her parents were both waiting when she landed.

"I have a feeling your redheaded stepchild did something to trip Calypso's EMP," Clarice said with a slow, wicked smile. "I've seen something similar, on a much smaller scale."

Emily raised an eyebrow. "So, she turns into an EMP when she gets... excited?"

Clarice nodded, her eyes dancing with mischief. "Yep. Given her past experiences, she's probably evolved again, too."

Eric grinned proudly. "That's my girl."

Emily rolled her eyes at Eric, then raised an eyebrow at Clarice. "I'm glad they found some privacy, but it didn't exactly stay private, did it?" She gave her husband a speculative look. "Speaking of privacy, you and I need to find some."

Clarice shook her head, still struggling to adjust to her parents looking no older than herself. Her mother's facial features were so similar to her own that they could have passed for twins.

Lexi frowned, her brows creased in confusion. "I don't understand. You're saying Calypso caused that energy wave because she got excited?"

Clarice waggled her eyebrows suggestively. "When she's excited in an *intimate* way."

Lexi's cheeks flushed. "Oh... That sounds like it could be pretty awkward."

Clarice rubbed her neck, smiling faintly. "Yeah, they really need to find an island somewhere far out at sea to play on." She looked back at the cabin with a frown. "I wonder if the breakers tripped or if she actually fried the electronics. I know the laptop died."

Several electronic beeps signaled the power was back on. She heard her uncle close the breaker panel and start moving their way.

Eric folded his arms. "Well, that answers that. Maybe the laptops will recover, too."

Clarice eyed her parents speculatively. "I almost forgot—we need to get you two over to Tamra's before you sprout wings so she can get your measurements. We'll take Uncle Devon, too."

Devon joined them, raising an eyebrow at Clarice. "Why do I need to go?"

Clarice rested her hands on her hips and affected a British accent. "Tamra is single, beautiful, wishes to have children before becoming an angel, and she is bloody brilliant. We realized we know someone with precisely the same life goals. Does that ring any bells?"

Devon shifted uncomfortably. "I don't think now's the time for dating. We've got too many projects on the table."

Emily turned to Eric, a puzzled frown on her face. "What's that sound?"

Eric tilted his head. "Bok bok."

"Bok bok bok," Emily agreed, tucking her hands under her armpits and flapping her elbows up and down. Eric mimicked her, and they began strutting around Devon, clucking like chickens. Clarice quickly joined in until Devon finally threw up his hands in defeat, laughing helplessly at their antics.

"*Fine*, I'll go," he relented. "You two finally look as young as you act."

Emily was instantly composed again. "Now that the matter's settled, when is she expecting us? Is today too early?"

Clarice smiled. "Today's perfect—before you sprout feathers, metaphorically speaking, since we don't have feathers." She gave her uncle a once-over. "We'll need to get you pimped up."

Devon frowned disapprovingly. "Pimped up?"

Clarice nodded. "You know, make you presentable for your date." A slow smile spread across her face. "Don't worry, Uncle—you're in good hands."

Lexi chimed in, her eyes bright. "That's because we're angels, so they have to be good hands, right?" She looked at Clarice for support.

Emily groaned, burying her face in her hands. "Oh no. Now there are two of them."

Clarice smirked, her eyes glowing with mischief. "Double the goodness."

Devon gave them a long, level stare, then turned and walked away, shaking his head.

"Go get pretty, Uncle!" Clarice called after his retreating back. "There *will* be an inspection later!"

His shoulders hunched, and he quickened his pace.

"You really are a bad angel," Emily said, her approving tone at odds with her words.

Clarice nodded piously. "I'm here to balance Calypso and Aria out. Someone has to provide comic relief, or eternity will get extremely boring."

"Do you think—" Eric began but stopped as the distant thrum of helicopter rotors reached their sensitive ears.

Clarice scowled. "There's going to be hell to pay if they haven't learned their lesson yet. Mom, Dad, if you need to use angel fire, you need to stoke some righteous fury in your soul. Usually, thinking about protecting loved ones is enough to switch the positive energy over to aggression." She paused, looking up toward the mountain. "It would be nice if Calypso were here so she could make a gateway and get Uncle Devon out of here."

Eric attempted to crack his knuckles threateningly but slumped his shoulders when he discovered their new bodies didn't accommodate knuckle cracking.

Clarice looked at him earnestly. "We still think you're tough, Dad—even if you can't crack your neck and knuckles anymore."

He gave her a flat look. Emily patted his shoulder sympathetically, and he groaned. "How's a man to feel macho with you two constantly poking holes in his self-esteem?"

Emily smiled sweetly. "You'll just have to try harder, dear."

A pinwheel of light bloomed nearby, unfolding into a glowing portal. Calypso and Aria stepped through and stopped short at the sight of everyone gathered outside.

Clarice's gaze snapped to Calypso, studying her intently. Something was different. Then she realized—Calypso had no wings, and her eyes were a deep, human blue. Clarice switched to spiritual sight and gasped. The wings were still there; Calypso's appearance was merely disguised.

"You're a shapeshifter now!" Clarice blurted out excitedly. "You're *so freaking awesome*!"

Calypso smiled, her eyes sparkling with amusement.

Lexi gasped. "That's Calypso? What—how—why—" She gave up, spluttering.

Clarice studied Calypso in fascination as she explained, "You need to use your spiritual sight to see that it's really her. We'll need to get you evolved later so you can see spiritual energy." She tilted her head, listening to the approaching helicopters, about five miles out. "Aria, we need to see who's trying to crash the party. Lexi, please stay and help my parents in case anything gets through, since they've never been in combat before. Calypso, can you get Uncle Devon through a gateway to somewhere safe in case things heat up?"

Calypso nodded and immediately blurred into the house.

Clarice studied Aria as she readied herself to launch. Her sister had subtly changed, appearing taller, her shorts riding higher on her lengthened legs. Her eyes still glowed golden, but there was something different in their light. Switching to spiritual sight, Clarice saw what appeared to be an hourglass-shaped funnel, with energy spiraling through both ends, like a coiled spring condensing power into a single point.

"Tell me about your evolution while we fly," Clarice said, launching skyward.

Aria shook her head with a frown. "I'm not sure what it does yet. It feels... dangerous."

Clarice eyed her sister curiously. "That sounds promisingly ominous." A foul scent, sharp and sulfurous, hit her nose. "Hopefully dangerous to demons."

Aria sniffed the air and scrunched her nose in disgust. "So *nasty*. It stinks even more than the other demons we ran into."

Clarice nodded grimly. "Maybe that means meaner. I don't think this is going to be as easy as the first demon fight. These ones are probably battle-class—like us. Did you and Calypso make it to third base before they interrupted, at least? What did you do to trigger Calypso's EMP?"

Aria blinked in surprise at the unexpected question, then coughed nervously as her face went crimson. "No, we were just kissing... for the most part."

Clarice arched an inquisitive eyebrow. "And what was the *less* part?"

Aria gestured at the helicopters moving their way, avoiding Clarice's gaze. "We have more important things to worry about right now."

Clarice flew up behind Aria and slid her arms around her waist and whispered into her ear, "Hey, if we're going to die in a minute, I wanna know details." She slid her hands up Aria's abdomen until she was cradling her breasts. "Come on, what did you do?"

Aria's breath caught and her wings stiffened between them. She finally managed to gasp out, "I might have slid my knee between her legs while we were kissing."

Clarice kissed her neck before releasing her as the helicopters neared. "Not bad, Aria. I'm impressed. Okay, back to demon slaying."

She studied the helicopters as the two of them flew in from above. Her spiritual eyes revealed a revolting conglomeration of writhing snake-like energy melded together into human-shaped bodies. She knew her mind was transposing the energies she was seeing into something familiar, but it was still unnerving.

They were less than a thousand feet away when a blast of blood-red energy shot toward them, forming a vast web. Clarice unleashed her angel fire, tearing through part of it—but not enough. A moment later, Aria flared like a supernova. A pinprick beam of light lanced from her eyes, touching the net. The entire construct unraveled in a blinding flash.

Clarice laughed shakily. "I'm glad you've got a new trick. I'm pretty sure we would have been in trouble if that thing had wrapped around us."

She slammed her hands together in a thunderous clap. A wave of radiant light exploded outward, vaporizing the helicopters. She watched in astonishment as her blast of light disintegrated the demons.

"That was *way* too easy," she muttered, scanning the area with every sense on high alert. Her spiritual eyes found nothing as far as she could see in all directions. "There's no way they went down that easily. Let's get back to the others."

They streaked home and landed on the front lawn.

Emily's eyes tightened with worry when she saw Clarice's face. "What's wrong?"

"It was too easy," Clarice stated flatly. "They wouldn't send demons that weak. I vaporized them with one clap. There has to be more coming."

Emily wrinkled her nose. "They were demons, then? Is that what that horrible smell was?"

Aria nodded, her nose wrinkling in disgust. "Yeah, that's the stench of demons. These ones stank even worse than the others we fought."

Clarice scowled as she began pacing. "This just doesn't make sense. You can't tell me they can't fly like we can. Why did they need a helicopter to bring them out here? Why were they so easy to kill? How did they find the cabin, and why did they wait until now to attack? There are just too many oddities."

Eric frowned, concern in his cerulean eyes. "Did they actually attack you?"

Clarice exhaled with a nod. "They shot some kind of energy net at us." She smiled at Aria. "I shot a hole in it with angel fire, but it wouldn't have been enough without Aria. Her new ability caused the entire thing to disintegrate."

Emily's expression darkened. "What if they weren't trying to kill you? What if they were trying to capture you? It's possible they don't realize how powerful you've become in such a brief amount of time and thought it'd be a quick grab."

"I have a theory," Calypso announced, appearing out of nowhere.

Lexi stared in shock. "Did you just teleport?"

"Indeed," Calypso acknowledged with a quick nod. "I discovered I could do it when I created a gateway for Devon."

Clarice gazed at her in wonder. "Wow... just... *wow!* You're so *freaking* cool!"

Calypso smiled shyly, basking in Clarice's effusive praise.

Emily watched her intently. "What's your theory?"

Calypso stared into the distance as she spoke, her eyes speculative. "What if demons have controlled Earth for so long that they have never faced a genuine threat? What if they have forgotten what battle angels are capable of? How long has it been since angels walked this world—thousands of years, perhaps? Perhaps there were no battle angels before, and their experience is based solely on subduing non-combat classes. In that case, they would have been virtually invulnerable, with every engagement a one-sided war of attrition."

Aria narrowed her eyes, pensively chewing her lip. "If that's true, we're back to the question of where you came from, Calypso. Were you created by another angel, or do you come from somewhere else entirely?"

Clarice began pacing. "It seems plausible that a non-combat angel could remain hidden from the demons. Maybe that's what the witch-hunts were really about: finding a hidden angel. If she could shapeshift like Calypso, she could have blended in with humans. She might even still be around."

Eric grinned wolfishly. "So, we're essentially the worst-case scenario for demonkind. After centuries of conquest, they're facing something akin to cavemen encountering soldiers with machine guns."

Calypso nodded slowly. "That seems quite plausible to me. Perhaps previous angels did not know the proper words to create a battle angel, or perhaps they were unaware that such a being even existed."

Clarice grinned as a spark of hope began to grow. "That would certainly be *our* best-case scenario. Those little shits are way overdue a serious ass-kicking." She looked at Calypso reflectively. "Do you really think they don't have super strong demons after all the time they've had to evolve and become more powerful?"

Calypso shrugged. "I can only rely upon historical accounts, which are rather suspect. Are there any tales of demons possessing powers comparable to those of angels?"

Emily shook her head. "Not that I've ever heard of."

"That's because you're a bunch of ignoramuses," a growling voice that seemed tailor-made to irritate, suddenly cut in from behind Calypso.

Clarice spun and fired a beam of angel fire before her brain even caught up. A small, scaly creature with stubby horns hovered there—then vanished, reappearing behind Emily.

The creature laughed derisively, disappearing as another beam of light shot toward it. "Nice shot, you overgrown pigeon."

The creature reappeared behind Clarice. She didn't even bother turning, knowing Aria was already firing on it.

The creature cackled, continuing to disappear and reappear. "You chumps are what has the Order of Saturn so worked up? They'll have to invent new words to describe how pathetic you are."

"Is that an imp?" Clarice asked Aria doubtfully as they continued trying to hit the squirrely little bastard.

The creature chortled. "Ho ho, look at that—the oversized chicken can put two and two together. Somebody give the laser brain a prize!"

"I think it thinks it's funny," Aria noted conversationally.

"That's right, carrot top, I do think I'm funny," the imp retorted spitefully. "But there ain't nothin' funnier than you bunch of self-righteous pigeon farmers trying to pull your heads out of each other's asses. Seeing you like this makes me wish I had a stomach so I could vomit. You're barely functioning a notch above the demons on this miserable shithole, and that's really saying something."

"Stop firing," Clarice told the others firmly.

"Why stop now, when you were doing so well?" the imp taunted her with another mocking laugh. "I'm sure you'll eventually get lucky."

The others stopped trying to fire on the little devil. As soon as they did, the imp stopped teleporting. It was nearly a foot tall, with malevolent yellow goat eyes, the classic devil's goatee, and little hooves on its nubby legs.

Clarice raised a cool eyebrow. "So you aren't with the demons who were trying to capture us earlier?"

He snorted disdainfully. "Do I look vaporized to you, doll face?"

Clarice smiled coldly. "Actually, you look like a vacuum for intelligence."

"Listen, sugar buns," the imp sneered condescendingly. "There aren't enough brains in that pouty little face of yours to comprehend just how stupid *you* are, but I'll try to give you some perspective. When the first jackasses to incarnate on this dump you call a world were still sucking on their momma's titty, I'd already watched several realms spawn and burn out. You're about as significant as a mayfly and half as intelligent. Your ignorance is matched only by your naivete."

Clarice snorted. "Clearly significant enough for you to focus your vast intellect on," she said dryly.

"The only significance you possess is that there isn't anything more interesting than what's going on in this shithole anywhere else," the imp spat. "Thanks for ensuring an eternity of unending boredom, you naïve pimple stain."

He vanished and didn't reappear.

"So that just happened," Emily murmured in a bemused voice, her lavender eyes twinkling as she looked at Clarice. "I'm not sure if I like him or hate him, sugar buns."

Aria chortled as she stared at Clarice. "I'm totally going to call you sugar buns from now on. Either that or pimple stain."

Clarice grinned at Aria. "Dibs on pimple stain. It's so graphic it tells its own story."

Calypso looked around the area as if she might find the imp hiding nearby. "Do you think this Order of Saturn he mentioned is the group of demons we're up against? I'm not sure we can trust anything an imp says."

Clarice shrugged, watching Calypso with interest. It was so strange to see a human variant of their angel, since they had never seen her before her transformation. She was gorgeous, but nowhere near the transcendent beauty of her angel form.

"It's as good a name as any for them," she said, unconcerned. "I'd be more interested to know if we really did have this Order of Saturn worried. He made them sound like they're weaker than us, which seems to confirm Calypso's theory that they don't actually have any powerhouses."

"Speaking of houses," Aria began, her face filled with regret. "It seems our secrecy has been compromised. They clearly know where we are now. If we stay, we'll probably be under constant attack."

"I may have a solution," Calypso offered, blushing when her gaze fell on Aria. "My teleportation ability seems rather formidable. I believe I could transport the entire house, together with a portion of the yard, to a new location. By my estimation, I can move everything within a two-thousand-foot sphere."

They all stared at her, too stunned to speak. Emily was the first to find her voice.

"You can teleport an entire *property* to a different location?"

Calypso nodded, smiling. "It is more than mere teleportation—it is an exchange. If I move us to a new location, we trade places with the land already present. There is no risk of splitting the house in half mid-jump."

"Just how much *did* you evolve?" Clarice asked faintly.

Calypso's face went nuclear, her eyes flicking to Aria and back down.

Clarice turned to her sister with a slow smile. Aria tried to hold her gaze but lasted only a few seconds before her cheeks also flushed, and she looked away.

Emily rescued the blushing angels. "I vote we relocate before Devon's cabin gets blown up. All that work shouldn't end in splinters."

Eric stepped up behind her and wrapped his arms around her. "Where did you have in mind?"

She smiled contentedly, laying her hands on top of his. "I have no idea. We'll have to do some exploring. I know some angels who can cover a ridiculous amount of distance in very little time."

"Any particular climate in mind?" Clarice inquired, watching her uncle as he walked out to join them. He had put on some nice clothes, and his short beard was immaculate. He had even plucked his eyebrows.

"Hey, handsome," Emily called, giving him a wolf whistle. "Looking good."

He gave a resigned shake of his head. "I'll take your word for it. So, what happened with the helicopter threat Calypso was getting ready to stuff me into a portal over?"

Emily quickly filled him in on the details, as well as Calypso's ability to relocate his cabin. He whistled in amazement as he watched Calypso.

"That'd be something to see. I know a spot in the mountains of southern Oregon: remote, no roads, accessible only by air. Dense forest cover—nobody would ever find us. We'll have to figure out the internet part, though. I suppose you left the Startlink satellites intact, so that's an option."

Aria nodded at Calypso. "She can make gateways. She could just open a tiny portal into a library."

He turned an interested gaze on Calypso. "Could you really make a small gateway and leave it open like that?"

Calypso pursed her lips. "I am not certain. Why do we not find out immediately?"

She stared at a spot a dozen feet away. There was a ripple like a heat wave, then a small gateway pinwheeled open in the air.

Calypso watched with a curious smile on her human face. "Let us see what occurs if I simply leave it open."

Clarice watched her open the portal with her spiritual vision. It looked like Calypso had manipulated some of the planet's meridians. Once the gateway opened, her connection to it vanished.

"So you have to both open *and* close gateways, or they just stay open?"

Calypso nodded, studying her portal with a critical eye. "Indeed. Though I suspect it will dissipate over time—perhaps within a week?"

Devon pursed his lips thoughtfully. "That certainly opens some interesting possibilities. You could basically snipe anyone in the world by opening a tiny gateway in their most secure locations."

Clarice ran a hand through her hair with a wry smile. "She could probably just open the gateway in their brain if she wanted to kill someone, but Calypso doesn't kill. She heals."

Calypso nodded firmly, her eyes unwavering. "I will never harm anyone unless it is a last resort to protect another."

"Even demons?" Aria asked tentatively.

Calypso hesitated, her lips pressed together. "Hurting a human feels utterly sickening. Hurting a demon does not feel good either—I am uncertain as to why."

Emily rubbed her hands together in a businesslike fashion. "We should probably get the house teleported as soon as possible. Calypso, do you need to fly out to the place Devon is thinking of to open a gateway, or can you read his mind to locate it?"

"I can see it," Calypso answered, turning away. Clarice watched her manipulate the planet's meridians again, this time on a larger scale. A full-sized gateway appeared in front of her, revealing a forested mountain. "Is this the correct location?"

Devon walked through the gateway with a bemused expression as he moved all the way across the continent in less than a second. "This definitely looks like the place. I came here by helicopter to go fishing once. It's between a town called Ashland and the coast of Oregon. I was thinking we could put the house right on top of that hill halfway up the mountain."

"Very well, shall I proceed?" Calypso asked expectantly.

"Might as well," Devon replied, walking back through the gateway.

Calypso closed her eyes and began to hum to herself. Several of her accompanying voices began to hum in harmony with her. Clarice stared in fascination as energy gathered along the planet's meridians, building up an incredible charge. Suddenly, a large sphere of energy formed a shell around them. A moment later, the sky shifted—and the shadows changed direction.

"Holy shit," Clarice whispered, gazing around in wonder. The cabin was intact, the fruit trees and a thousand feet of driveway still in place, even the little waterfall on the veranda still tumbled gently over the stones.

"Well, that's what I call a successful relocation," Eric said, grinning proudly. "Nicely done, Calypso."

"Thank you," Calypso beamed. "I am glad it succeeded; I adore this cabin, and I would hate to see it destroyed."

17 – IMP

Aria grinned, watching her uncle shift nervously on Tamra's porch. The entire clan was there. Calypso had left a gateway open, connecting the two properties.

Emily looked Clarice up and down, pausing on her chest and arching an eyebrow. "Lose your bra? Or were you just trying to make a *pointed* statement on womanhood?"

Clarice gestured at Lexi with a smirk. "She lost her last shirt when her wings appeared, so I had to welcome her to the bra club, generously donating my own."

Emily glanced at a blushing Aria, then back to Clarice. "I notice you didn't bother fetching a new bra after returning."

Clarice nodded toward Aria with a shameless grin. "I'm enjoying the braless effect too much to bother donning a new one. I think this will be my new look for my new club."

Aria was trying not to look at her sister, but her treacherous eyes had a mind of their own and continually focused on Clarice's thinly veiled assets, which inevitably sent her imagination into a tailspin of increasingly carnal thoughts.

Emily pinched the bridge of her nose. "Let me guess: the nipple club."

Clarice beamed. "You got it in one!" She turned to Aria and bent forward at the waist, causing her breasts to hang down. "Wanna join my new club, Aria?"

Tamra opened the door, saving Aria from her mother and Clarice's amused gazes. "That's quite the crowd," she observed.

Her tawny hair was half pulled into a loose bun, the rest spilling down her back in soft waves. Her blue eyes swept over the group with polite curiosity, pausing on Devon—the obvious human. After a brief inspection, a small smile of approval appeared.

Judging by her meridians and physical attributes, Aria guessed Tamra was in her early thirties. She was getting better at discerning age by observing the flow of energy through a person; older humans had tighter, more constricted meridian channels.

Tamra flashed them a welcoming smile. "I believe some introductions are in order."

Clarice stepped forward, struggling to repress a grin. "This is my mom, Emily. She's a world-class chef and the most amazing mom in the world."

Aria raised an eyebrow when Clarice failed to mention their mother was a congresswoman. Of course, with how most people felt about politicians, that was probably a good call.

Emily stepped forward with a warm smile and gave her a brief hug. "Hello, Tamra."

Clarice continued, glancing up at Eric mischievously. "This is my dad, Eric. He's not as cool as Mom, but he's a close second."

Tamra winced ruefully as Eric rolled his eyes and bent to offer his own brief hug. "Ouch... brutal."

Eric gave Clarice a longsuffering look. "I know this will come as a bit of a shock, but Clarice is a bit of a tease," he informed Tamra dryly.

Tamra's eyes sparkled as she matched his wry tone. "I would've never guessed."

Clarice gestured to a very human-looking Calypso in an offhand manner. "And of course, you already know Calypso."

Tamra stared at Calypso blankly, clearly recognizing the clothing but not the person inside them. Calypso rippled and distorted before suddenly shifting to her angelic form.

"It is a new ability I have learned," Calypso explained with an apologetic smile. "Clarice persuaded me to appear as a human, as she thought it would be amusing to see your reaction."

Clarice beamed proudly. "She's a freaking *shapeshifter* now! Just how cool is *that*?"

Tamra eyed Calypso critically. "I like her angel form better. Don't get me wrong—you look great as a human—but you look divine as an angel."

Calypso smiled shyly, her cheeks tinged with color. "Thank you, Tamra. I am still learning how to alter my features in the alternate form. It will likely prove useful for moving about freely among humans."

Tamra smiled faintly. "I can imagine."

Clarice gestured grandly at Devon, her grin no longer repressed. "And this is my Uncle Devon. He's the reason we survived long enough to become angels. Uncle, this is Tamra, a world-class designer."

Devon straightened his jacket and smiled pleasantly at Tamra. He offered a hand and spoke in his deep baritone, "It's nice to finally meet you, Tamra. My nieces have spoken very highly of you."

Tamra's eyes sparkled as she took his hand. "So, this is the illustrious uncle I've heard so much about. It's a pleasure, Devon. Please, come in."

Aria shared a grin with Clarice. The chemistry between Tamra and Devon was palpable, and barring any major ideological clashes, this had potential.

Devon continued, his voice full of charm. "We have a gateway on your front lawn that leads to our house in Southern Oregon. Would you care to join me for dinner on the veranda once you finish your work here?"

Tamra blinked, nonplussed. "A gateway? Like a portal?"

He nodded. "Yes, exactly that," he said, gesturing toward Calypso. "She makes them."

Tamra laughed, a sound full of wonder. "Wow, I feel like I fell into a fantasy world." She met his eyes with a small smile. "Dinner sounds lovely, Devon."

Citing her need to prepare dinner for the two humans, Emily was measured first.

It took half an hour to get her parents and Calypso measured and logged into the computer. Tamra showed them her progress on the clothes for Clarice, Lexi, and Aria, much to their delight.

The new clothing was elegant yet functional—reinforced fabrics with tactical durability, flame resistance, and plenty of flexibility for angels who might find themselves fighting midair while trying not to look unstylish.

Emily returned as Tamra finished the last of the measurements. "Dinner's ready."

Devon offered his arm to Tamra as they walked across the front yard toward the gateway. The two had been stealing frequent glances throughout the evening, clearly attracted to each other.

They walked through the gateway, and Tamra slowed, staring at the cabin appreciatively.

"This place is beautiful," she murmured with a dreamy smile. "A little slice of heaven."

Devon chuckled, glancing at the angels walking beside them. "It even has angels hanging around. I wouldn't be too shocked if this place ended up *in* the heavens someday. They just teleported the entire place across the country after the demons discovered where we were."

Tamra came to a halt, her eyes widening. "They teleported the *entire property* here?"

Devon grinned wryly. "See what I mean? The idea of it ending up in the heavens someday isn't so farfetched anymore. They'll probably evolve some ability to imbue antigravity properties on objects or something weird like that."

Clarice's hands went to her hips, and she scowled at Devon indignantly. "Hey, that's not weird—that's *awesome*. Who wouldn't want a floating sky palace?"

Tamra shook her head and resumed walking. "This is so surreal."

Devon laughed. "Welcome to my week."

As Devon and Tamra made their way up to the veranda, Aria wandered around the yard to look out over the valley. Clarice, Lexi, and Calypso joined her on the side of the house.

Aria stopped at the edge of the new property line to gaze out over the valley. "I figured we'd give them the illusion of privacy," she explained, smiling faintly. "Uncle Devon knows we can hear everything, but she doesn't need to."

Clarice's eyes lit up. "Hey, why don't we give them some romantic music to go with their dinner? We just happen to have the world's greatest musician with us, after all. The three of us could come up with something to add some ambiance to the experience." She glanced at Lexi with a mischievous smile. "And Lexi can dance for them."

Lexi snorted. "In your dreams."

Clarice arched an amused eyebrow. "Well, it would be, except I don't sleep anymore." She turned to Calypso and Aria. "So? What do you two think?"

Aria smiled radiantly, hugging Clarice in her excitement. "Clarice, that's *brilliant!* Let's give them the *perfect* dinner."

Calypso smiled happily. "I am always glad to play music."

The four of them went up to the studio, grabbed a cello, harp, and violin, then flew up to the widow's walk.

Aria fit the violin under her chin. "Do you just want to wing it?"

Clarice's lips twitched. "Pun intended?" She fluffed her wings for emphasis.

Aria rolled her eyes but couldn't stop a smile from stealing across her face. "Troll."

Calypso smiled at them, arranging her harp as one might an old friend. “I’ll begin a melody on the harp. Once you feel it, do join in.”

* * *

Tamra studied Devon curiously. "What kind of work did you do before angels took over your life?"

Her angel friends hadn't exaggerated about their uncle. Devon was handsome in a grounded, quietly confident way, with class, wit, and that deep voice. She had poured most of her life into her craft, and now, at thirty-four, she had begun to feel the ticking clock. Family had always been the dream she kept putting off for "later."

Devon smiled wryly. "You know the people who were trying to kill Calypso and my nieces? The Agency? That's who I worked for—until Calypso found me."

Tamra tilted her head. "Seriously?" She struggled to picture the pleasant, well-mannered man across from her as a thug—he seemed more like a James Bond. "What did you do for them?"

He gave an easy shrug. "Tech work. Installing hardware in global server farms so data could be funneled back to intelligence agencies. The Agency liked to monitor everything under the sun. Anytime a new data center went online, my team was sent in to slip hardware into their infrastructure for silent data exfiltration."

Tamra sipped her water, watching Devon over the rim. "Did you retire from The Agency, or did you just walk away when your nieces joined Calypso?"

He shook his head grimly, staring at the table. "The Agency doesn't let you retire. They recruit promising college graduates with talk of adventure and patriotism. Then they inject you with autonomous nanobots that monitor your vitals and can stop your heart if they think you've compromised the organization. Once those things are in you, your life isn't yours anymore. That was the reality—until Calypso cleansed them from my system."

Tamra reached across the table and placed her hand over his. "That must've been a terrible realization. It sounds like slavery."

He nodded, his eyes haunted. "That's exactly what it was." After a pause, his tone lightened. "I never imagined helping my nieces hide a famous musician would turn into a second chance at life. Funny old world, isn't it?"

Tamra nodded with a small smile. "That it is. I've been designing costumes and custom clothing for over fifteen years. You wouldn't believe some of the odd requests I've had, but when I got a call from someone named Aria asking if I could make clothes to accommodate wings—yeah, that topped the list. The name gave her away immediately. It really is a funny old world."

They both paused as a soft harp began to play from somewhere above them. Tamra shivered as the haunting melody brushed across her soul.

Devon's eyebrows rose, a pleased grin spreading across his face. "I do believe we get music with dinner—from the greatest musician on Earth, no less."

Spellbound, Tamra could only nod. A moment later a cello joined in, weaving through the melody, followed by a violin. The three instruments danced together, painting emotion into the air—poignant and impossibly pure.

Then Calypso began to sing. Her voice slipped through the music like light through crystal, each note alive with color and resonance. More voices joined her, and at first, Tamra thought it must be the other angels, but as she listened, she realized they were all Calypso—layered harmonies filling the air from every direction.

A tear slid down her cheek as her soul rose to better observe the sublime sounds caressing her senses.

Two additional voices joined in, harmonizing perfectly with Calypso. Tamra hadn't thought the song could become more poignant, but as the other two angels added their voices to Calypso's, it was as if the world itself stopped to listen. She couldn't move, afraid of sullying the air with vulgar sounds that would detract from the celestial notes warping reality around them.

As the notes faded, reality slowly reasserted itself, and she became aware of her surroundings again. Her cheeks were damp with tears. She looked across the table at Devon and saw his own cheeks were wet.

He smiled at her companionably, wiping his eyes with a napkin. "That's one of the other perks of hosting angels. It feels like your soul is being supercharged with emotional energy when they play."

Tamra let out an awed breath. "I knew Calypso was an amazing musician, but I had no idea your nieces were also musicians. They're amazing."

Devon nodded, dropping his napkin on the table. "They were both healed by Calypso when they were ten years old; they would've died without her. Of course, they didn't know who she was back then. I suspect many of the children Calypso healed with her music have grown up to be talented musicians themselves. It's as if she imprinted music on their souls."

***

"A single tear rolls down my scaly cheek," an irritating voice jeered from the air next to the widow's walk. "Who do you hate so much that you'd torture them with such horrendous noise?"

Clarice let out a cheerful cry. "Hey, the Pimple Stain's back!"

The imp narrowed his goat eyes when he heard his insult appropriated. "I knew you were stupid, but the lack of originality in your insults really spells out how pathetic you giant chickens are."

Clarice turned to Aria, eyes wide. "Bok bok?"

"Bok bok bok," Aria agreed with a nod.

Clarice turned to Lexi. "Bok bok *bok*?"

Lexi shook her head. "Bok bok bok *bock*."

The imp scowled. "What the hell's wrong with you feather-brained lunatics? You really were scraped off the cosmic floor, weren't you?"

"Bok bok," Clarice retorted fiercely.

The imp made a disgusted noise. "You're not giant chickens—that would be insulting to chickens. You're all fundamentally and irredeemably retarded."

Aria nodded her agreement. "Bok bok bok."

Calypso studied the disgruntled imp curiously. "Why are you here? Is this planet truly more entertaining than any other in the universe?"

He seethed, glaring malevolently at the other three angels. "I can guarantee it's the only planet where angels act like poultry."

"Bok?" Clarice asked with a raised eyebrow.

Calypso regarded the imp with hopeful eyes. "Do you know where angels come from?"

"They sprout from cow shit after a rainstorm," the imp snapped, miming someone squatting to drop a deuce. "What kind of asinine question is that anyway? You clearly converted several humans into angels, so you know damn well where they come from, you feather-brained platypus."

Calypso nodded to the others. "That is where *they* came from, but what about me? Are all angels merely former humans?"

He snorted obnoxiously. "Do all chickens come from eggs? Where the hell else would angels come from? Seriously, you are the dumbest celestial rejects I've ever met—and that's *really* saying something."

"Bok?" Clarice croaked with an injured expression.

Calypso’s calm never wavered. “Well, do you know if there truly are different classes of angels? I am the only healer, and it would be helpful to know how to create something other than battle angels.”

"A healer? You?" The imp roared with laughter, rolling around in the air and pounding the imaginary ground with a tiny fist. "You think *you're* a healer?" he continued cackling as Calypso stared at him uncertainly.

Calypso looked at him with a challenging gaze. “If I am not a healer, then what am I?”

He snorted, still watching her with unholy mirth. "Too stupid to tie your own shoes, from what I can see."

Calypso’s eyes softened. “It is quite all right if you do not know. You simply seemed so knowledgeable that I thought you might.”

"Why, in all that shits, would you think you are a weak-brained healer?" the imp snarled, his eyes growing even more disdainful. "How many healers go around singing songs to heal people? Do you see these stupid chickens *singing* to vaporize demons? Warriors kill. Healers heal. What the flying fudge monkey do you think sings, you pustulant wart on a frog's ass? How have you survived this long with this level of ignorance? I've never felt embarrassed in my life, but I'm feeling embarrassed for you right now, you flying flock of flatulent feces. You're a cosmic embarrassment."

"A bard?" Clarice demanded, her eyes wide. "You're saying she's a freaking *bard?*"

The imp slowly turned to look at her, his eyes wide with amazement. "Behold, it speaks! A talking chicken. Bok flocking bok, you uneducated mendicants."

With a final snort, the imp vanished.

Aria shook her head. "I do so enjoy these visits," she said sarcastically. "What the hell does he keep popping into our business for, anyway? He can't be *that* bored."

Clarice grinned triumphantly. "He likes Calypso's music. The little bastard actually wants to hear it."

Lexi frowned dubiously. "That's not the impression *I* got. He seemed pretty critical. He called it horrendous noise."

Clarice laughed delightedly. "Of course he did. Imps can't admit to loving an angel's music. I'd bet my halo that's why he's hanging around this planet at all. It stirs something in his nasty little soul."

Calypso nodded, her eyes troubled. “I had a similar impression. What is this bard class you believe I am, Clarice?”

Clarice explained, eyes bright. "It's the jack-of-all-trades archetype from fantasy lore. Bards use music to do everything—heal, teleport, cleanse nanotech, boost morale, even resurrect. They're lore keepers, too, with access to hidden knowledge. That would explain your intuition—and that feeling you get, like you're remembering something ancient. If that class exists, you're it. Honestly, it should've been obvious. You've been obsessed with music since forever."

Aria grinned eagerly, her eyes sparkling. "You're right. That little punk of an imp just gave us a *huge* advantage. Knowing you're a bard rather than a healer means we have a much smaller subset of phrases to try to activate the class. It'll almost certainly be something music-related."

Clarice folded her arms and studied Calypso contemplatively. "He also confirmed she must have been human at one point. If angels can only be made from humans, then she *must* have had an angel involved in her transformation. I wonder if he's purposely being helpful, in his own irascible way, or if it just slipped out."

Lexi shook her head doubtfully. "Why would an imp help an angel? Can we even trust what he's telling us? Aren't we immortal enemies?"

"Probably," Clarice acknowledged with a shrug, "but that doesn't mean some of us don't have a change of heart somewhere down the line. If he's really as old as he says, he might be bored with the dark side."

Aria coughed a skeptical laugh, absently twisting a strand of red hair around her finger. "That's a pretty big leap. I think he could still be all for hellfire and brimstone but have a soft spot for transcendent music."

Clarice frowned pensively. "Maybe, but I think there's a more complex story behind the little bastard than a simple fondness for beautiful music or being disenchanted with dark deeds. Something about him seems... familiar."

Aria burst out laughing, watching Clarice fondly. "I'm totally going to start a support group called DDDD—for Demons Disenchanted with Dark Deeds."

Clarice chewed her lip thoughtfully. "I'm not sure that's going to roll off the tongue very well. 'I'm a member of D-D-D-D' just sounds like you have a stutter. Maybe shorten it to DDD and just call it the Triple Ds."

Aria stared at her pointedly, her lips quivering. "There's only one thing people are going to associate with a group called Triple Ds. Sounds more like a Valkyrie support group."

"Ah... yeah..." Clarice acknowledged with a rueful smile. "I suppose quadruple Ds wouldn't be any better."

Aria heard their mother laughingly tell their father, "Eternity's never going to get boring with those two around." Remembering there wasn't anything private in a house full of angels, she shared a grin with Clarice.

She tuned in briefly to the veranda below—Devon and Tamra's voices were softer now, warmer. She could feel the spark of something new growing between them.

Clarice flexed her wings. "I think it's time to visit Jason and Julia. We're running a little behind. He's at MIT. We need to find a way to talk with him in person without putting him in danger once we're gone. It's too bad we don't all have Calypso's shapeshifting ability."

Calypso absentmindedly stroked the frame of her harp as though it were a favorite pet. She looked up at Clarice, raising an eyebrow. "Why do I not simply open a portal and invite him here?"

Clarice facepalmed with a groan. "I'm such an idiot."

Calypso took Clarice's hand in both of hers. "No, you are not. It is still a new ability. It may take a day or two for it to integrate naturally into our strategic plans."

Aria grinned as she imagined Jason's face when a portal appeared in his room. "Okay, so we portal into Jason's dorm room and whisk him over here?"

Clarice pursed her lips, eyeing Calypso curiously. "How do you know where to open a gateway? Do you just intuitively feel where you want the other side to go? How does it work?"

Calypso hesitated, regarding Clarice thoughtfully. "There is a kind of informational layer to reality where all the meridians intersect. Just as everyone's name is inscribed upon their aura, these nodes are layered with information that maps their location between the spiritual and physical realms. I can sense where Jason is because I have observed his aura previously. It is rather like how spiders locate insects by the perturbations in a web. I can perceive his energy signature when I place my metaphorical ear against one of the planet's meridians."

Clarice smiled mischievously up at Calypso. "You're getting pretty close to the three O's of divinity with this omnipresence. You've almost achieved omnipresence and omniscience. Once you become omnipotent, we'll need to build some temples for you."

Calypso released Clarice's hands with a frown. "This is scarcely omnipresence."

Clarice glanced at Aria and Lexi calculatingly. "Before we open a portal to Jason, maybe we should start with a micro-gateway. We don't really want to just walk in on somebody without warning. We can take a quick peek, then say hello before opening it all the way."

Aria tilted her head back with a knowing grin. "Ah, I see. You're worried we'll pop in for a visit while he's in the bathroom."

"Or shagging someone," Clarice added dryly. "Yes, I'm attempting to respect some privacy here." She took a deep breath that immediately pulled Aria and Calypso's eyes, eliciting a wink. "We should probably open it down below, rather than portaling him onto the widow's walk."

Calypso opened a gateway onto the lawn and they stepped through. As soon as she closed it, she opened another small gateway that looked down on Jason from ceiling height. He was sitting at his computer, typing furiously.

Unable to keep the grin out of her voice, Clarice spoke. "Hey Jason, are you available for a quick visit?"

"You're a *bad* angel," Aria whispered accusingly, unable to stop an amused grin.

Jason leapt out of his chair and spun around, searching all around his small dorm, his eyes wild. "Who's there?"

Clarice barely restrained her laughter as she answered. "I'm your fairy godmother. I'm here to grant you three wishes."

Jason's eyes narrowed when he heard the mirth in her voice. He continued spinning, searching for the source.

Calypso spoke up, her voice sympathetic. "I am sorry, Jason. Clarice can be rather a tease. Do you mind if we open a gateway into your room?"

"Calypso?" Jason asked in surprise. "A gateway? Like a portal?"

Clarice sighed. "Maybe we should just start calling them portals."

"Yes, a portal," Calypso confirmed patiently, the corners of her lips curving up.

"Yeah, I guess," Jason stammered. "Portal away."

A new gateway opened a few feet away from Jason. He gaped at the four angels.

Calypso smiled gently. "We have some matters to discuss, but it would be far easier in person. Would you care to join us over here? It will be more secure than your dormitory."

Jason stared at Calypso in all her glory, unable to move his mouth or legs. Aria felt a little bad for him. Calypso really *was* awe-inspiring.

Calypso stepped through and took his hand, guiding the shell-shocked young man back through the portal before closing it.

Clarice turned to Aria and Lexi. "He's never going to wash that hand again. Make sure to only shake his left hand in the future, should the occasion arise."

Lexi giggled, staring at Clarice like a surrogate big sister. Aria was glad she had formed an attachment so quickly after her ordeal. Clarice always joked about Aria being the smart one with a physics degree, but Aria knew her mischievous sister was the smarter of the two of them by a wide margin.

Calypso gazed at Clarice with patient amusement. "Do not pay any heed to Clarice. As I mentioned earlier, she is rather a tease."

Jason stared at Aria and Clarice, studying their features intently. "Are you shapeshifters or something? You definitely didn't look like this in the videos I've seen on YouTube."

Clarice grinned, looking at Calypso. "Funny you should mention that... You wanna show him?"

Calypso tilted her head at Clarice, her blond hair cascading to one side.

"Humor me," Clarice pleaded, her eyes sparkling.

Calypso shook her head with a sigh, then distorted and shifted into her human form.

"Holy shit!" Jason swore, staring at Calypso in amazement. "You really *are* shapeshifters!"

"*I* am a shapeshifter," Calypso confirmed, casting an amused glance at the wildly giggling Clarice. "Those three, however, are *not* shapeshifters."

Aria gestured at Calypso with a warm smile. "Calypso transformed us into angels."

Jason gaped at her. "*What?* I thought angels were another species. How does a person just get turned into an angel?"

Aria smiled vaguely. "There are ways."

Calypso shifted back into her angelic form and raised a curious eyebrow at Jason. "Have you had any success in making contact with any other former patients?"

Jason nodded, smiling eagerly. "Oh yeah. I started a few low-key chat boards on some TOR nodes where we can discuss ideas without being flagged by this shadow agency you warned me about. There are almost four thousand of us now. Each person we recruited went out and recruited more. I have the full patient list from Julia available on the TOR site. People have been getting antsy for action after seeing all the news about angels recently. Someone even claimed you've been fighting demons. I would've blown that off as nonsense a week ago, but it's hard to rule anything out these days."

He finished on a questioning note.

Calypso nodded. "We have certainly been fighting demons." She paused, glancing at the other three angels. "Or, more accurately, *those* three have been fighting demons."

Aria nodded grimly. "We believe demons have infiltrated every influential institution and are controlling the world governments. They're probably behind the bulk of the human trafficking incidents. We've rescued some of the children they were torturing, but we suspect there are *far* more."

Calypso nodded toward the cabin. "Come inside and take a seat. We can fetch you some refreshments whilst we go over the details."

He nodded slowly, his eyes a little wild. Calypso stepped forward and pulled him into a warm embrace, flooding his soul with radiance. "It's really good to see you again, Jason."

He sucked in a breath as the emotional overload hit him. His hands froze when they bumped against her wings, a stark reminder that he was embracing an angel.

She released him, and he stared at her in awe, the nervous energy draining from his eyes.

"You really *are* an angel," he said wonderingly. "I was starting to wonder if you were just aliens disguised as angels. I don't think aliens could imitate love like that, though."

Calypso smiled, her eyes full of affection. She nodded toward the cabin, and he shook himself before following her inside.

Aria rubbed her chin thoughtfully as they entered the living room. "We probably need to make another grocery run soon. Of course, now that we only have one person to feed regularly, the supplies should last longer."

As soon as they entered, Emily blurred into the room, eliciting a startled scream from Jason. "So, this is Jason. Give me a minute to whip something up for him."

She exited as quickly as she appeared, leaving a dazed Jason in a half-sitting position above one of the chairs.

Clarice floated into the air and crossed her legs with a grin. "Angels are kind of fast. My mom's a world-class chef, so congratulations—whatever she makes will ruin you for normal food."

"Your *mom?*" he exclaimed disbelievingly.

Clarice shrugged. "Angels are immortal. Who ever heard of an old angel?"

He slowly finished sitting, staring at Clarice curiously. "Is everyone in your family an angel now?"

Clarice nodded, rotating in the air until she was sitting upside down, with her hair hanging to the floor. Her breasts reversed direction as well, resting against her jaw. "Almost—we've got one holdout who wants to have a family of his own first. We hooked him up with a hot date to get the ball rolling. He's upstairs having a romantic dinner right now."

Jason looked around curiously. "Where are we, anyway? Are we still on Earth?"

Aria shared a look with Clarice, and they both burst out laughing. Clarice's giggling upside-down form made Aria laugh even harder.

Calypso gave Aria and Clarice a reproachful look. "Yes, Jason. We are in Oregon."

Jason's laugh bordered on hysterical. "So...on the other side of the continent. No big deal."

Calypso nodded. "How is the hacking project progressing?" she asked, steering the conversation toward a more comfortable topic.

He grinned, regaining some of his former energy. "Pretty well, actually. I linked up with a few dozen penetration testers to help with the project. We should have a proof of concept ready to execute by tomorrow."

"*What* kind of testers?" Clarice demanded, her lips quivering.

He stared at her blankly for a moment, then his face exploded with color.

"Um, uh, that's just a technical term for, uh, people that, um, try to hack computer networks and, um, devices and such," he stammered, struggling to finish under Clarice's suggestive leer.

"You really are a *very* bad angel," Aria scolded her sister while trying to suppress her own grin.

Lexi had to leave the room, her shoulders shaking as she tried and failed to stop laughing.

Calypso buried her face in her hands as Clarice continued grinning suggestively at Jason. "Remind me to hold these meetings without Clarice present in the future."

Clarice's hand flew to her mouth. "That was hurtful, Calypso. Take that back."

"I am so sorry, Jason," Calypso apologized weakly. "We have been somewhat isolated, so I believe she has some repressed mischief merely waiting to find a target."

Aria nudged her floating sister pointedly. "Let's just move past this awkward moment," she suggested firmly. "What do you need from us to facilitate your plans? Perhaps we should start with a rundown of our abilities."

"Like making portals?" Jason asked faintly.

Aria nodded. "Yeah, like making portals. Calypso's the real powerhouse when it comes to abilities. The rest of us are more combat-focused, so if you run into any trouble, *we'll* be the ones to help. Angels are immortal in every sense of the word—we can't take damage. Bullets, knives, nuclear warheads... none of those things can hurt us."

He stared at her in awe, mouthing, "Nuclear warheads?"

She continued, keeping a sharp eye on Clarice. "We're *significantly* stronger and faster than humans. We could fly around the world in less than a second if we pushed ourselves, so if you're ever in danger and can contact us, we can be there almost immediately. As you probably saw online, we can shoot beams of light out of our eyes that we call angel fire. It's a very surgical method for fighting, but we can also destroy things like mountain ranges if necessary."

He stared at her, waiting for a smile or some indication she was being facetious. When she continued staring at him, he swallowed. "Seriously? You can blow up mountains?"

Aria nodded confidently. "Yeah, seriously. When we first became angels, we only had basic immortality, speed, strength, and heightened senses. Certain emotional events trigger ability evolutions in angels."

She faltered when she heard Clarice murmur, "Like molesting innocent Calypsos," too quietly for Jason to hear.

Calypso squeezed her eyes closed as her face flared a brilliant shade of red. Aria glared at her smirking sister and continued.

"We're much more powerful than we were a few days ago, and we're not sure where it'll end if we're this powerful in less than a week."

She took a deep breath, and her voice grew grim. "However, there are demons out there far older than us who've had much more time to learn how to use their powers. We may need to recruit more angels to help in this fight. We'd primarily be looking at people Calypso healed as candidates. As you can imagine, it's a lot of power to trust someone with. We can't risk raising the wrong kind of human into an angel; the fallout could be catastrophic. We suspect Calypso left her mark on our souls when she healed us, possibly influencing the people we've become."

Jason nodded slowly. "I could believe that."

He watched her in fascination, clearly trying to discern the changes she had undergone since leaving mortality behind. Her eyes had grown larger, shifting to a shimmery gold hue that glittered with energy. And then there were the wings.

Clarice's face lost all traces of humor and she rotated back upright. "There's another problem. Demons have been running the show for a while. They're woven into governing and commerce systems. If we hit too hard, we risk collapsing commerce, supply chains, governments—the entire world economy. That could mean billions of deaths. We need a long-term plan that avoids civilizational collapse. That's where your network shines. We need it to grow—and fast. We need people to fill key roles as we purge demonkind."

Jason blanched as she listed the dire consequences of mishandling their mission. He licked his suddenly dry lips. "No pressure, then."

Clarice smiled suddenly. "Exactly. It'll be easy peasy lemon squeezy. We have time still. We aren't going on a rampage to wipe out demons in a week. We won't be doing that for at least two weeks."

He squinted at her suspiciously, catching on to her exaggerated humor.

Aria smacked Clarice's shoulder. "We don't have a set timetable for when we'll assault the demons. We need to gather a lot more intel on their placement and operations."

Jason frowned, his brows furrowed. "Where have angels been all this time? How did demons get so powerful?"

“We do not know,” Calypso admitted, sharing a small smile with Aria and Clarice. “We have not told many people this. When Aria and Clarice visited me the day before my identity became public, I did not even realize I was not human. I was so absorbed in music and healing that I scarcely noticed how much time had passed.”

She told him about her childhood, the hospital circuits, composing around the clock, and her oblivious agelessness.

Jason shook his head. "You seriously didn't realize you looked like you were barely out of high school for over a hundred years? I'm not trying to be rude, but that's a pretty crazy level of obliviousness."

Calypso laughed but nodded. “I have heard Aria and Clarice make that observation several times. Angels do not eat, sleep, feel pain, or experience heat and cold. Having no memory of ever being human, I did not comprehend how different I was. Without such distractions, I was able to become entirely focused on my purpose in life: creating music and healing children. I had no idea I was invulnerable, supremely fast, exceptionally strong, and possessed senses far superior to those of humans.”

Jason eyed her curiously. "And you were the only angel on Earth until you found a way to make more angels?"

Calypso frowned, her eyes uncertain. “I do not know. We are fairly certain that angels are always created from humans, though we are mostly feeling our way through this. If that is true, then an angel was responsible for my transformation. I have no recollection of anything prior to the age of five, so I cannot say whether it was an angel who changed me, or something else entirely.”

She paused, drawing her long, blond hair over one shoulder. She glanced at the other angels before continuing, receiving an encouraging wink from Clarice. “We have a theory that there have not been any battle-class angels on Earth for thousands of years. They are the only angels we know capable of slaying demons. Without battle-class angels to confront them, angels would be at a disadvantage. We do not know whether they still live and are imprisoned somewhere, or if they were slain by other means."

Clarice picked up the thread. "We think the witch hunts were demon-run sweeps for hidden angels. We also think the demons here are far outclassed by battle-class angels. We've fought them twice now and steamrolled them both times. The second group seemed stronger and were just as easily defeated. We don't know why we're so much more powerful, but it's an opportunity if we plan it right."

Jason narrowed his eyes shrewdly. "If battle-class angels are the ones with the power to defeat demons, why did you say Calypso was the powerhouse of abilities earlier? Or is she battle-class as well?"

Clarice bobbed her head back and forth uncertainly. "We believe she's the equivalent of a bard-class, though we aren't a hundred percent sure. She's been gaining new abilities daily, like telepathy, teleportation, shapeshifting, and, of course, her ability to heal and resurrect people. While she won't be involved in any fighting, she is key to making our plans successful. Her ability to motivate and galvanize the population will be a large part of our plan to maintain stability when the purge begins."

Emily returned with a tray of spinach artichoke dip and naan. She hooked her foot around a heavy coffee table, effortlessly moving it over to Jason and setting the platter in front of him.

"You're too young not to be hungry all the time, so eat up," she told him with a motherly smile that was slightly jarring on a face that looked so much like Clarice's. "What would you like to drink? We have water, coffee, and various fruit juices."

Jason smiled gratefully. "Coffee would be awesome. Thank you so much, um—"

"Emily," she said, introducing herself with another smile. "I'll get you that coffee."

As she left the room, Jason looked at Calypso inquiringly. "Okay, so what now? Do you just want me to focus on recruiting as many people as possible into the network?"

Clarice sighed plaintively. "We definitely need a better name than 'The Network.' It's almost as bad as 'The Agency'," she said, making air quotes.

Calypso nodded, ignoring Clarice's observation. "Yes, I believe recruiting should be our foremost priority. However, if you are able to delegate that and continue work on the hacking project, that would also be most helpful. Crippling The Agency by removing a substantial portion of their slave labor force would be a considerable victory. I would still like to play for the children at the hospitals, though I think Julia and her team can oversee that project."

Jason nodded, ignoring his food as he stared at them. Aria remembered how hard it had been not to stare at Calypso in the first few days. It was *still* difficult. While Clarice and the other angels were beautiful and amazing, there was a divine quality about Calypso that transcended normal angelic captivation—an innocence and love that drew the eye.

Then again, she often found herself staring at Clarice with the same infatuation, but she had been doing that for so long that it didn't stand out anymore.

Emily returned with a mug of coffee and set it down in front of Jason with another brief smile.

Jason sighed gratefully, immediately taking a sip. "Thank you."

Calypso studied Jason silently, her gaze calculating. "Jason, would you mind if we left you alone for a few minutes? I need to have a private word with the rest of the group."

Jason shook his head quickly. "No, not at all."

Aria raised an eyebrow at Clarice as they followed Calypso out of the house, curious what their healer—their *bard*?—wanted to discuss in private.

"You're such a bleeding heart," Clarice said to Calypso with a teasing smile.

Aria stared between them in confusion. "What am I missing?"

Calypso smiled fondly. "Jason is far too self-conscious to eat in front of us. I thought we might afford him a little privacy so he can eat in peace. It would be a shame for something Emily prepared to go to waste."

Emily gave Calypso an appreciative smile.

Aria turned to face Clarice with a disgruntled frown. Usually, *she* was the perceptive one. "How did *you* know that's why Calypso wanted to leave?"

Clarice chuckled. "I've dealt with guys like Jason before. He's too self-conscious to breathe loudly in front of five gorgeous women, let alone be the only one eating."

Aria's eyebrows rose. "I know Calypso could read his mind to find that out, but how did *you* know that's why Calypso wanted to come out here to talk?"

Clarice shrugged. "Because I knew Calypso could read his mind. Simple deduction, Watson."

Aria shook her head. "Sometimes you're so clever I want to puke."

"Except you can't," Clarice pointed out critically. "You don't have a stomach, remember?"

Aria threw her hands in the air with a long-suffering sigh. "See what I mean?"

Clarice, Calypso, and Lexi laughed, while Emily nodded in agreement.

Clarice sidled up to Calypso and leaned into her with a contented smile. "What do you make of Jason? You can see inside his mind. Is he responsible angel material? I'm not sure why, but he seems oddly familiar."

Calypso wrapped an arm around Clarice affectionately and nodded. "I believe so—eventually. He has a pure heart and a desire to do good in the face of adversity."

Aria smiled faintly. "I hate to sound like a corporate wage-slaver, but he would definitely get a lot more done if he didn't need to sleep." She paused, her brow wrinkling. "And yeah, something about him *does* seem familiar. All this familiarity with strangers is getting downright weird."

Calypso hesitated. "He is somewhat young. He still has ample time to develop mentally before I would wish to place this sort of power in his hands. Then, of course, there is the matter of family to consider. He may wish to have children."

"You dumbasses think angels can't have children?" a familiar, grating voice demanded incredulously. "Just when I think you can't get dumber, you prove me wrong."

Aria turned to face the obnoxious imp, who was floating between them and the house with a scornful expression.

Emily stared at him, aghast. "Are you telling me I still have to worry about getting pregnant?"

The imp facepalmed with a groan. "So. Damn. Stupid."

Emily shook her head, sounding distinctly disgruntled. "I guess Devon doesn't have to wait to start a family after all."

"Angels can't make angel babies, you drinkers of yaks' piss," the imp lectured in an insulting tone. "Angels and humans are another matter. You should definitely make some more mutts. There's nothing more sporting for demons than a half-human. It takes almost no time at all to turn them into a demon."

Emily's eyes widened. "You're talking about Nephilim—male angels with female humans."

"Somebody bake this lady a cake," the imp crowed triumphantly. "She's got the brains of a jackass."

"What are you doing here, Grodek?" a voice chided from across the yard.

An angel's voice.

18 – MEET YOUR MAKER

Aria stared at the woman walking up the remains of the driveway. She was clearly an angel, though wingless. Switching to spiritual sight, Aria could see that she was using the same shapeshifting trick as Calypso. She was as tall as Calypso and walked with the carefree gait of someone with nowhere urgent to be. She wore contemporary clothes—a simple T-shirt and jeans. Her human façade looked about thirty, but her true form possessed the same eternal youth as the rest of them.

"Did you forget to pull your head out of your ass?" the imp snapped at the newcomer. "Or is that just how you walk now?"

The mystery angel spread her arms magnanimously. "Your honeyed words are music to my ears, Grodek. I've missed your verbal abuse. The demons here just can't seem to grasp the nuance of vividly descriptive insults."

Clarice narrowed her eyes. "Who are you?"

Grodek laughed nastily. "This is the jackass in charge of mismanaging this pigpen of a world. It's been a long time since a Principality fell so low that even the weak-ass demons here are a threat. You won't find a bigger failure in this half of the realm."

Her mouth smiled, but her eyes remained as cold as an arctic gale. "You just lack vision. There's a certain poetry to redeeming a world from complete and utter ruin."

Grodek snickered, shaking his head in disgust. "Is that what you've convinced yourself you're doing? Whatever you have to tell yourself to look in the mirror without weeping."

"The bar for failure's been set pretty low, as you may recall," the woman retorted acidly. "The higher the fall and all that crap."

Clarice's normally mischievous nature was absent as she studied the angel coldly. "Okay, who the hell are you? Are you seriously the one responsible for letting demons take over the world?"

"I know you," Calypso whispered, her eyes wide with sudden recognition. "You were the one who rescued me from the demons."

"Well, isn't this nice?" Grodek drawled sarcastically. "A heartwarming reunion. You finally met your Maker."

"I remember..." Calypso stared at the woman, horror and pain twisting her face.

Aria stared at Calypso in concern as their gentle angel began trembling violently. Calypso closed her eyes, quicksilver tears streaming down her face.

Clarice rushed forward and folded Calypso into her arms protectively, pouring all her channeled love and comfort into the distraught angel. Aria quickly joined her, adding her radiance.

Calypso moaned despairingly. Aria felt Emily and Lexi join them, routing their radiance into Calypso. After several minutes that seemed to go on forever, Calypso slowly stopped shaking, drinking in their radiance like a starving plant sucking in water.

Aria caressed Calypso's wet cheek tenderly. "We're here, Calypso."

After seeing what demons did to humans, Aria could only imagine the horrors Calypso was reliving. Her heart ached at the thought of what their sweet angel had suffered at the hands of those monsters.

They held Calypso in comforting arms as she continued to process her traumatic memories. The vision culminated in a brilliant flash as her entire body glowed incandescently.

Aria and the others drew back in surprise. When the light dimmed, Calypso stood up straight, no longer supporting one set of wings, but two—a nested layer within the first.

Calypso smiled at them tremulously, her eyes brimming with love and gratitude. "So this is the difference between angel and human," she breathed in wonder. "No wonder you were so amazed. This feels... extraordinary."

Aria cupped Calypso's face in her hands. "You remember now? Being human?"

Calypso nodded sadly. "Yes. I was in the hands of demons from six months of age until I was five, when Carcelonia rescued me. She erased my memories so that I would not have to bear those horrors in my mind during my early years."

Aria turned to look at Carcelonia, who had been waiting patiently, a look of supreme satisfaction on her face. Silky, straight golden hair fell to her waist. Her true eyes were a soft lavender, much like Calypso's had once been.

Grodek had vanished shortly after Calypso's collapse. Jason, finally antsy enough to venture outside, hovered near the doorway, watching the group with concern after witnessing Calypso's meltdown.

"Thank you for saving Calypso," Aria said gratefully, studying Carcelonia intently. She had the impression that Carcelonia was extremely pleased with herself.

Carcelonia shook her head slowly. "I was beginning to think she'd never come into her own. I've waited a hundred years for her to find herself. I think it was worth the wait."

Clarice narrowed her eyes. "Why did you leave her alone to find her own way? You could've told her she was an angel from the moment she transformed. You could've been teaching her to evolve this entire time."

Carcelonia sighed. "There were... complications. First, if she saw me in her early years, it would've triggered an instant memory recall, which would've been very bad. Second, I had a particularly foul demon lord hunting me. Demons weren't the only ones she needed to stay hidden from. I've been searching for her for almost eight decades—someone's been hiding her, and every trail I followed dead-ended."

Aria looked between Carcelonia and Calypso uncertainly. "Are you saying another *angel* has been hiding her?"

Carcelonia shrugged one shoulder. "An angel or a demon. Whoever it was has resources beyond our own. Even with her uploading weekly videos, we couldn't trace her location."

Clarice scowled. "What do you mean, 'an angel or a demon?' Why would a demon hide her?"

Carcelonia regarded her with a condescending smile. "You think angels and demons are dichotomous entities, but nothing is ever that simple."

Clarice planted her hands on her hips. "What's that supposed to mean? Demons are monsters preying on the weak and vulnerable. Are you saying angels aren't that different?"

Carcelonia smiled unpleasantly. "That's exactly what I'm saying. You think your friend Grodek is pure evil? Why tolerate him if you believe that?"

Clarice's jaw tightened, but she remained silent.

Aria hesitated, eyeing Clarice appraisingly. "He doesn't seem threatening—and he's given us useful information."

Carcelonia smiled in satisfaction. “Precisely. Not all angels are good—not by a long shot—and not all demons are bad. Demons run almost every government on this world, yet you lived happy, oblivious lives before you learned they existed. Would life be so cushy if all demons were pure malice?”

Aria exchanged a troubled look with the others. Could there really be such a thing as a good demon?

Clarice tossed her head angrily. “Tell that to the tortured kids we rescued from demons.” She gestured at Calypso, her rage flaring. “Or tell it to Calypso, whom you apparently saved from the same monsters.”

Carcelonia waved a hand dismissively. “There are certainly plenty of demons who *are* pure evil, but you’re making broad judgments based on generalizations. Do you know where demons come from?”

Emily’s eyes were troubled. “Biblically, they’re fallen angels.”

Carcelonia nodded, her voice level. “Any of you could become demons, under the wrong circumstances. If you’re ever captured by the demons running this world, you *will* become demons. Given enough time, they can turn even the most virtuous angel.”

Aria blanched, meeting Clarice’s anxious eyes. She remembered vividly the scarlet net of energy fired at them from the helicopter. It hadn’t been meant to kill—it was meant to capture.

Emily narrowed her eyes. “What about the reverse? Can demons become angels?”

Carcelonia shook her head regretfully. “No, they cannot. There’s never been a case of a demon transforming back into an angel. If it were possible, there would be a lot fewer demons. Many angels—broken and consigned to a demonic existence—are unwilling slaves, forever bound to their demon lord. Their will isn’t their own. Their access to radiance is severed, replaced with a hideous hunger for power. Some demons overcome the hunger, just like a human overcoming an addiction, but their access to radiance is lost forever.”

Carcelonia stared steadily into Emily’s eyes, weariness bleeding through. “Demons have more in common with humans than angels, having also experienced loss and pain. Your average angel has no concept of ethics or morals, seeing them as abstract concepts—aberrations to the natural order.”

Clarice folded her arms, her brows drawing down. “And you’re saying this world is run by these ‘moral and ethical’ demons?”

Carcelonia nodded, though her gaze remained on Emily. “To a degree. The most powerful demons rarely visit this world, preferring the more populated worlds near the center of the galaxy. Even so, demons here must meet their agonite quotas or risk drawing the ire of a demon lord."

Lexi's brows furrowed. "What's agonite?"

Carcelonia's mouth tightened with distaste. "A drug for demons, produced in the blood of sentient species while in agony. Very little can alter an immortal's consciousness—agonite is one of the few, simulating the feeling of power. Since the thirst for power is the core drive of demons, the drug is highly prized."

Clarice made a disgusted sound, flipping her hair behind her shoulder. She stared at Carcelonia, her eyes hard, her voice colder than an arctic night. "If I were forced to torture children, I'd prefer death. If these demons have no choice but to harm innocent kids, they'll have to be seen as collateral damage. If there's truly no way to redeem them and they're subject to a demon lord's will, then we have no option but to destroy them. The alternative is to allow them to continue torturing children, and that's *not* going to happen."

Carcelonia sighed, closing her eyes. After a long moment, she opened them. "The only reason Calypso is here today is because the demon in charge of the agonite lab where she was kept smuggled me in so I could free her. There are loopholes in the chains that bind them, and many have become adept at finding and exploiting them."

She shook her head disdainfully. "Furthermore, you don't have the power to kill a demon—only Cherubim can. If you go on a moral crusade to stop the flow of agonite from this world, you'll draw the attention of a demon lord. Their power is beyond anything you can imagine. They will come here and teach you what true suffering is, along with the rest of the world."

"That's not actually true, you bungler," Grodek said from behind Carcelonia. "They could take on all of the demon lords together, if they were armed with the right *instruments*."

Carcelonia sighed in exasperation. "That's a myth. There's no secret weapon for defeating demon lords. Even if there were, it's not like this lot could use them."

Grodek sneered. "You've done a great job of convincing yourself of that, you coward—but your actions make me think you just might believe it after all. Why else would you have activated a Seraph? They could already wipe the floor with Cherubim—a demon lord would be like swatting a fly to them. If they had the instruments, they would snuff them all out like a candle—all the way to the highest light realm. That's what you're really afraid of, though, isn't it? You're afraid of what they'll become and what that'll mean for you."

Carcelonia glared at the imp, her eyes full of hate and self-loathing. Aria blinked, realizing Grodek was right. This woman, whatever she was, seemed to be a coward at heart—and she seemed to despise herself for it.

Grodek laughed grotesquely, malice burning in his eyes. "Yes, I know where they came from, you puckered pig-sticker. Did you think *I*, of all people, wouldn't recognize the Three? You've backed yourself into a corner, like the whipped dog you are. That's what you get for trusting demons, you jackass. Did you really think they gave you a Principality? I know angels are naïve, but you really took it to the next level."

Carcelonia visibly flinched. Her glare dissolved into anxiety as she stared at Calypso, Aria, and Clarice, sudden terror in her eyes.

"What the flying fudge stick is going on here?" Clarice demanded harshly. "What have you done to Calypso? What is this Seraph he's talking about?"

Carcelonia's mouth moved, but no sound emerged as she stared at Clarice's golden eyes, recognition dawning. Panic flooded her face.

Then, she vanished.

Grodek roared with laughter, rolling in the air and pounding the imaginary ground. "What did I tell you? Biggest coward this realm has ever seen."

They stared in disbelief at the empty space where Carcelonia had stood. Had she *really* just scarpered?

Aria forced herself to focus and looked at Grodek. "What are these instruments you mentioned?"

Grodek looked her up and down disdainfully. "Go see the Lore Boar if you want answers. I'm done hand-feeding you answers."

He vanished with a soft pop.

"That little *bastard*," Clarice fumed, glaring at the empty air. "How *dare* he tease us with tidbits, then vanish when we want actual answers."

Emily looked at Lexi, baffled. "What on earth is a Lore Boar?"

"What's a Seraph?" Lexi added, equally bewildered.

Emily turned to gaze thoughtfully at Calypso. "Well, if they're anything like the Seraphim in scripture, they're the highest order of angel, closest to God, surrounding His throne. If she really is a Seraph, I'm not sure we're on the right track with angel classes—there might not be any special classes based on abilities. A Seraph would be able to do anything any other angel could do."

Clarice snickered. "Why does a God need a throne? Does He get tired of standing?"

Emily shrugged, eyeing Clarice with patient amusement. "It's probably symbolic, representing authority."

Aria studied Calypso intently. "So, Calypso's a Seraph?"

They all looked at Calypso, noting the second pair of nested wings.

Calypso shifted uneasily under their gazes. "I am fairly certain I do not wish to be a Seraph. I cannot imagine myself lingering about some god for all eternity."

Emily patted Calypso's shoulder reassuringly. "I'm pretty sure humans anthropomorphized God into something they can understand. I'd imagine your job would be closer to maintaining cosmic balance in the name of a supreme law than serving an actual person on a chair."

Jason edged closer, his eyes darting nervously between them. "Do you mind if I ask a question?"

Clarice winked at him suggestively. "What's on your mind? Gonna teach us some more '*technical jargon*?'"

Jason blinked, then blushed furiously as he recalled their earlier discussion. "No—I just wanted to ask what the *hell* is going on?"

Clarice threw her hands up, laughing helplessly. "Well, get in line, because we *also* want to know what the hell is going on."

Jason rubbed the back of his neck, eyeing her uneasily. "Were you guys talking to a demon? That floating thing that looked like an imp?"

Clarice looked around in bewilderment. "You guys? I don't see any guys here."

Aria cuffed Clarice's shoulder reproachfully before turning to Jason. "We think he's an imp, and apparently his name is Grodek. We tried killing him when we first met, but he's very resistant to dying. He's extremely obnoxious, but he's also given us a lot of information we didn't have."

Clarice held up a hand, her eyes widening. "He didn't stink like a demon," she said in sudden realization. "I didn't even notice before, but there's no trace of demon stench on him."

They all paused, sharing a contemplative silence.

Calypso nodded slowly. "Then it is as Carcelonia said: not all demons are evil. Perhaps their stench is indicative of their nature rather than their power."

Clarice looked at Calypso shrewdly. "She said angels are forcibly changed into demons. Maybe that's why you don't feel right about killing demons."

Calypso met Clarice's gaze and nodded. "Yes, that would certainly explain it." Her eyes were inevitably drawn lower, and her cheeks grew hot. She quickly looked away and found Jason watching her peculiarly.

Flustered, she blurted. "Jason, I was wondering, would you like to have children?"

It took a while to restore order. Aria, Lexi, and Clarice fell to their knees, laughing uproariously as Jason's face exploded with color. He looked ready to faint as he stared back at Calypso, speechless. Emily was slightly more composed, but she still shook with laughter as she gazed between Jason and Calypso.

"Oh, I *am* sorry, Jason," Calypso apologized quickly, wincing. "I meant, do you intend to have children someday?"

He let out a relieved, slightly hysterical laugh. "Oh—um, yes? Someday?"

Clearing her throat, Calypso continued, ignoring the giggling angels. "We were discussing whether to offer you the option of transforming into an angel," she informed him calmly. "We had assumed angels could not have children. Apparently, male angels can, with human women. Any offspring would be half-human and would probably be incapable of transformation. Since you intend to have a family, I would suggest you wait."

Jason's eyes widened. "Me, an angel? You think I'd be responsible enough?"

Calypso nodded firmly. "We do."

Jason combed his fingers through his hair. "Wow... uh, thanks for the vote of confidence, but I think I'd like a family first."

Calypso smiled. "The offer shall remain available when you are ready," she said placidly.

Clarice took an unsteady breath as she attempted to recover from her mirth, then cleared her throat. "Anything else we need to cover?" she asked, clearly signaling the end of the meeting.

"Just to sum up," Jason said, ticking off points on his fingers. "First, my top priority is getting a hack in place to broadcast your channel so we can destroy the nanobots in The Agency's contractors. Second, hand off the growth of the network to others while I focus on number one. Ultimately, we plan to replace demons in influential positions with people from the network. Is that about right?"

Clarice hesitated. "We'll be in touch regarding your second point. If what Carcelonia said is true, we might have less of a nightmare on our hands with demons than we initially thought—especially if we can find a way to change them back to angels. Let's get you back to your dorm before anything else goes pear-shaped."

Calypso opened a gateway to Jason's dorm, giving him a parting embrace that charged his system with love and confidence. He went back through the portal smiling, brimming with excited energy.

Clarice placed her hands on her hips and glanced around their group. "That went... pretty well. He probably saw more than he should have with Grodek and Carcelonia, but I suppose we'll just have to trust him to keep his mouth shut."

Aria stepped behind Clarice and began playing with her hair. She needed to think, and she couldn't do that while her sister's chest was visible. "Grodek seems convinced these demons aren't very powerful. I wonder if we really are juggernauts in the world of angels and demons."

Emily shrugged. "Unless we meet another angel—besides Carcelonia—it's hard to say. But I've noticed a difference between the three of you and the rest of us. I think we're second-generation angels, while you two were directly affected by Calypso's tears. If she really is a Seraph, maybe her tears create stronger angels than ours. Perhaps a new Seraph means a new hierarchy, with those closer to her being more powerful."

Clarice let out a quiet moan as Aria's fingers began massaging her scalp. The sound went straight to Aria's libido, making her shiver as Clarice spoke.

"That would certainly explain why we've been able to destroy demons who are probably thousands of years old without any trouble," Clarice noted languidly, her head sinking into Aria's fingers. "They expected far weaker angels. Maybe that's why this Order of Saturn is worried. Maybe they realize the same thing Grodek has realized and suspect a higher order of angel. We're basically like wrecking balls smashing through anything they throw at us."

Aria let out a relieved breath. "I guess it's not normal to be this powerful. I was wondering how the world was still standing if every angel started out as powerful as us and then just kept getting more powerful. It also explains how the demons managed to take over the world."

Eric blurred over from the house. "There's more to it than you think. Seraphim sit above Cherubim. Any angel they make will *become* a Cherub—theoretically. Aria and Clarice would both be Cherubim in the making, if I'm right. That's just speculation on my part, and might be totally wrong, considering our source of information on angels."

Clarice's eyes sparkled. "You mean we're going to turn into cute little naked babies?"

Eric sighed and shook his head. "That's not what Cherubim are. You can thank Hallmark for that nonsense. Lucifer was supposedly a Cherub before his fall. The baby imagery probably comes from the lack of facial hair. Before shaving was a thing, only younger boys were beardless."

Clarice turned and bowed to Aria, affecting a prim British accent. "Hello, Your Cherubimship, how do you do?"

Aria matched her accent, curtsying. "Not bad, Your Cherubimship, thanks for asking."

Eric pinched the bridge of his nose. "Those two sitting at the top of the totem pole," he breathed in disbelief. "This is going to be a wild ride."

Emily's eyes grew troubled. "That begs the question: should we stop raising mortals to angels? If every angel we make is going to be several orders above Archangels, we should probably be even more picky about who we allow to become angels."

Eric gazed at Calypso thoughtfully, rubbing his "masculine" chin. "I think we need to find this Lore Boar before we do anything else. If that's where we can find more answers, knowledge should be our primary focus. With demons and angels involved, it sounds like things are even more convoluted than we suspected."

Clarice stretched, wings extending and hands combing through her midnight hair as she arched her head backward, chest out. Aria forgot to breathe as she watched the sensual display. Calypso was little better, lips parted as she stared at Clarice hungrily, a light blush staining her cheeks.

Clarice straightened, winking at the two of them when she saw their matching expressions of naked desire. When Eric and Emily started laughing, Aria quickly wrapped her wings around herself to hide her burning cheeks. She left a gap in her wings where she could still see her sister.

Clarice ostentatiously adjusted her shirt, producing a lot of bouncing. "I wonder if there are any other angels on this world besides Carcelonia," she said, her angelic voice like fingers caressing Aria's neck. "Also, how do you and Mom know so much about all this religious mumbo jumbo?"

Eric tapped his head meaningfully. "You forget we were kids when religion was a lot more popular. Before the internet, people could only get their information from books and churches. It was a lot easier to keep people indoctrinated when there weren't easily accessible sources of information available. My spiritual journey started shortly after the advent of the internet, when I really started digging into the doctrine of various religions."

Emily met Eric's gaze with a nostalgic smile. "Your dad and I used to spend a lot of time discussing the disparities in religious doctrine and what the churches actually taught. There are a lot of apocryphal texts that used to be canon and were removed when they didn't fit the current vision of the various religions. That's where most of the information regarding angels exists. I imagine the demons running this world are responsible for removing most of the real angel lore."

Aria lowered her wings and found Lexi watching her intently, her lavender eyes curious. Aria tilted her head as she returned Lexi's gaze. "What?"

Lexi blinked, eyes darting to Clarice and then back to her. "Um, nothing. I was just spacing out."

Clarice's throaty chuckle made it clear her attempt at evasion had failed. Lexi cleared her throat. "So, uh, how are we going to find this Lore Boar thing? I'm not sure search engines are going to be much help. Devon said AI was a thing now, too, so maybe it might know something?"

Aria narrowed her eyes. Lexi avoided her gaze, staring fixedly at Eric and Emily.

Clarice met Aria's suspicious eyes and winked. "We'll talk about it later." Clarice turned to Lexi and grinned wickedly. "We don't need search engines to find the Lore Boar. Let's just grab a demon and grill them for information. They probably have more info than anyone else at this point."

Aria gave her sister a level look. "Just go grab a demon, huh?"

Clarice shrugged, her grin never wavering. "Why not? We've established we're more powerful than demons here. We'll pick one up and shake it till information falls out."

Aria arched an eyebrow. "Where are we going to find a demon? Or should we just post a Google ad for 'Demons Wanted'?"

"We *know* where they are," Clarice reminded her patiently. "Positions of influence. We could walk into any media mogul's or congressional office and sniff them out."

Aria chuckled sheepishly, her golden eyes abashed. "Oh yeah. Pretty obvious, wasn't it?"

Clarice buffed her nails on her shirt. "Being a genius has its moments," she declared airily.

"Smartass," Aria accused, swatting her shoulder playfully.

Clarice grinned impudently. "My ass's IQ is definitely in the high triple digits."

Emily pushed past their banter with practiced ease, carrying the conversation forward. "When do you want to snatch this demon? And where do you want to take it for questioning? Not here, I assume."

Clarice wrinkled her nose. "God, no. The stench would be awful. We'll just portal over to an island somewhere."

Eric knuckled his chin. "Who do you want to go after? Capitol Hill?"

Clarice smacked Eric's hand away from his face. "Stop obsessing over your Chad chin, Dad." Her evil smile returned. "I figure we just start at the top and grab the President."

They stared at her in disbelief as she grinned back.

Aria was the first to recover. "Clarice, that'd be like kicking a hornet's nest," she said anxiously.

Clarice's hand flew to her mouth in mock horror. "Oh no! You're saying they'd start sending demons and the military after us?" She shoulder-bumped Aria playfully, then leaned forward to stare at her pointedly, their noses nearly touching. "Which is different than what they've been doing... how?"

Their parents shared a thoughtful look.

"She's got a point," Emily admitted grudgingly. "It's not like they're going to come after us any harder than they already are."

Aria swallowed as Clarice straightened, her lips no longer millimeters from Aria's. She nodded slowly, warming to the idea. "Calypso could just open a portal behind him, and I could pull him through before he knew what was happening."

Clarice shook her head. "She could just open a portal *beneath* the bastard and drop him in front of us. It doesn't need to be opened in front or behind." She demonstrated a person falling through a portal with her hands.

Aria leaned over and rested her head against Clarice's.

"What're ya doin'?" Clarice drawled. "Not that I'm complaining."

Aria shivered as their meridians began exchanging energy. "Seeing if I can get smarter by osmosis."

Clarice laughed and slung an arm around her shoulders. Their parents and Lexi laughed, the sound charging the night around them with a soft glow. Calypso watched the two of them in amusement, her swirling eyes full of affection.

When they heard Devon walking Tamra back to her house, everyone turned to watch. The two were holding hands as they strolled slowly across the moonlit lawn.

Clarice turned to Calypso expectantly. "So? How'd it go?"

Calypso beamed. "Success. They are greatly attracted to one another."

Clarice let out a loud whoop, high-fiving Aria, and grinned triumphantly.

Emily wore a pleased smile. "I'm glad he's getting his wish to have a family. He's had a rough lot in life with all this Agency nonsense."

Eric nodded wistfully. "I saw the longing in his eyes every holiday. He loved watching Clarice and Aria banter at Thanksgiving and Christmas."

Clarice draped her arm across Aria's shoulders again, smirking. "Who wouldn't? We could charge admission, and people would still line up to watch."

Emily smiled at her tolerantly, an expression more insulting than any words she could've spoken.

Clarice's shoulders slumped. "That was hurtful, Mom."

Aria leaned her head against Clarice's, smiling cheerfully. "Don't worry, Clarice—I still think you're funny."

Emily turned to Eric, ignoring her pouting daughter. "We need to make a grocery run soon. I think I can still pass as human if I wear sunglasses."

Clarice shook off her wounded pride and walked up to Emily, whispering into her ear so quietly that even Aria's super-hearing didn't pick it up. Emily smiled faintly and nodded. Aria was struck again by how similar the two of them looked now.

Eric raised an eyebrow. "Secrets, Clarice?"

Clarice smiled sweetly. "You've been married long enough to know a girl needs her secrets."

He stared at her levelly, but she just smirked back at him. He shook his head with a sigh. "I'm the man of the house. Aren't you supposed to do what I say?"

Clarice's eyebrows shot up. "Actually, *Devon's* the man of the house," she reminded him with a wink. "Nice try, Dad."

He threw his hands up. "Where's the respect?" he demanded of the sky.

Clarice grinned, maliciously cheerful. "Probably hiding with your manhood."

Emily rubbed his shoulder supportively. "You should know better than to cross words with Clarice. Just stop now, while you still have some dignity left."

Calypso and Lexi shared matching looks of quiet contentment. Both had gone without loving parents for most of their lives and seemed to savor the warmth radiating from the small family's playful banter.

Aria fully planned to make up for their lost family time. She knew she could count on her sister and parents to share their warmth with the two angels. The more exposure Aria had to the cruelties of the world, the more she realized just how fortunate she was to have such an amazing family.

Emily rubbed her hands together in a businesslike fashion. "Calypso, would you mind opening a portal to a grocery store? I'd like to get a large stock of food in case we end up with additional refugees. Let's open it in the kitchen, though, to save some trips back and forth."

Calypso smiled warmly. "Of course. I'll accompany you, now that I can pass for human."

Aria studied Calypso curiously as she walked toward the cabin with Emily. Calypso's double-layered wings were similar to theirs—gossamer-thin and shimmery—but they also seemed to have a higher level of dexterity, capable of wrapping around things like a tail. The energy Calypso normally exuded had subtly changed since the return of her human memories. There was an undercurrent of potential accompanying her usual love and compassion, as if the embryo of a sun were growing inside her.

Aria shivered, thinking of the future that lay ahead of them. If she and Clarice really were budding Cherubim, they were probably going to be involved in angel politics on a grand scale.

Clarice's eyes grew contemplative as she idly played with a long strand of her midnight hair. "Grodek mentioned other realms. Do you think realms are just universes? If so, why call them realms?"

Eric reached for his chin, then paused when Clarice raised an eyebrow at him. Shaking his head, he said, "Perhaps our idea of the universe is flawed. You three can fly in zero gravity. You should do some exploring and see how far you can go. Maybe you'll find answers up there. How fast can you fly? Have you pushed your limits yet?"

Aria shared a hungry look with Clarice. "Dad, that's one of the best ideas you've *ever* had."

"I wouldn't go *that* far," he objected plaintively.

Aria turned to Clarice, grinning. "We better take Calypso with us. She'd never forgive us if we went to space without her."

Clarice tapped her lips musingly. "Hmm... you know, she probably *would* forgive us, since she's Calypso—but I get your point."

Lexi stepped in front of them with an excited grin. "Can I go, too?"

Clarice studied her calculatingly. "One of us will need to hang on to you, since you haven't evolved to be unaffected by gravity yet."

Lexi practically bounced with eagerness. "How do I evolve that ability?"

Aria shared a look with Clarice. Her sister lost it first, eyes crinkling as she began giggling hysterically. That triggered Aria, who began giggling madly as she tried to figure out how they were going to upgrade Lexi without... *smooching* her.

Lexi squinted at them suspiciously as they struggled to stop giggling. Eric just shrugged, his azure eyes amused.

When Aria finally recovered, she held up her fist suggestively. "Paper, rock, scissors?"

Clarice shook her head resolutely. "Not with your luck. We'll have to find a different method."

Aria raised an eyebrow. "So... winner does the honors?"

Clarice's eyes brightened. "Damn right." Her lips quivered with the effort of not laughing. "Since you always win, this should be easy-peasy."

Lexi's eyes burned with curiosity. "What are we talking about?"

Clarice grinned impishly. "That's for us to know, and you to find out."

Aria looked at Eric. "Okay, who's got a coin on them?"

He rummaged in his pockets and fished out a quarter—because of *course* he still carried cash.

Aria grinned. "Okay, Dad, flip it, and we'll call it in the air." She looked at Clarice suspiciously, remembering Calypso's ability with dice. "But turn your back to us so we can't see it."

He nodded, turning his back. "You got it, Pumpkin. Call it."

"Heads," Clarice chorused with Aria.

Aria scowled at her in exasperation. "Just one of us calls it, you ninny."

Clarice nodded, smirking. "I know—me."

Aria threw up her hands in resignation. "*Fine*. One more time, Dad."

He flipped it again. "Call it."

"Tails," Clarice called out, eyeing Aria challengingly.

"Tails it is," Eric said, turning back to face them. "I need to mark this day on the calendar—Clarice actually beat Aria at a luck game."

Aria stared triumphantly at Clarice, while the others looked on in growing confusion. Clarice tried to glare a hole through Aria's head.

"If I ever meet the gods—and it seems like I might—I'm going to slap them silly," Clarice declared viciously.

Aria smiled archly, waggling her eyebrows suggestively. "I'm pretty sure you'll be doing something else with them."

Eric cleared his throat. "I'm going to see if your mom and Calypso need any help unloading the groceries," he announced, finally realizing what they were competing over. He tossed Clarice an amused glance and left.

Lexi let out a plaintive sigh. "Are you going to explain what's going on yet? What does it have to do—"

She broke off in shock when Clarice suddenly wrapped her in her arms. She opened her mouth to ask what was going on, just as Clarice's lips met hers. Her eyes widened in shock, but a heartbeat later, they softened, and she leaned into the kiss, letting out a soft moan as her whole body quivered with sudden desire. Aria was pretty sure Clarice was a much better kisser than she, so Lexi probably lucked out with the coin toss—especially since Aria would almost certainly have chickened out.

As Lexi melted into Clarice's arms, Aria felt a surge of jealousy flare so strongly she nearly lit up incandescently. She forced herself to relax, reminding herself it was a platonic kiss. Why was she so jealous when Clarice kissed Lexi? She had never felt even a hint of jealousy when Clarice kissed Calypso, so where was this overpowering feeling of possessiveness coming from?

Disappointment fought its way through the radiance charging her system, weighing her down like a mortal. She had waited her whole life to kiss Clarice, and now a girl who hadn't even known her a week had beat her to it. She knew it wasn't fair to Lexi, that it was her own fault for not overcoming her bashful nature and just taking the initiative. Clarice had certainly given her plenty of opportunities, especially since becoming angels, but Aria had frozen up each time, waiting for Clarice to initiate the actual kiss.

After nearly a minute of sensual heat, the two of them lifted off the ground.

Clarice finally pulled back, grinning. "There—you have the antigravity ability now."

Lexi blinked, looking down at the ground below them in surprise. "*This* is how you get the ability?" she demanded, blushing furiously.

Clarice laid her head to the side and grinned, her midnight hair sliding across her face in shimmering waves. "That's the only way *we* know how to get it."

Lexi stared at Clarice in wonder, her flaming cheeks only enhancing her extraordinary beauty. "I didn't think I'd ever enjoy a kiss," she admitted quietly. "I thought I'd hate intimacy for the rest of my life."

Clarice's eyes softened, and she gently caressed Lexi's cheek. "It makes a big difference who the intimacy is with. You're not broken. By my estimation, you're one hundred percent functional."

Lexi smiled shyly, avoiding Clarice's eyes. "That's a relief. I was kind of worried about that."

Clarice tucked a lock of Lexi's golden hair behind her ear and smiled encouragingly. "We have eternity ahead of us now. They didn't break your will. You just need time to heal, and you'll have plenty of it."

Lexi pulled Clarice into a tight hug, her eyes wet with quicksilver tears. "I know I've said this a lot, but I'm so glad you found me."

Clarice stroked Lexi's hair affectionately as she hugged her tightly, her own eyes filling with tears. "Me, too."

She shifted her cheek until their tears touched. A golden glow suffused the air around them, accompanied by an influx of energy. When Clarice pulled back, she smiled at the golden irises staring back.

"My eyes feel hot," Lexi murmured.

Clarice laughed, a throaty sound full of sensual promise. "I have that effect on people," she said teasingly. "Welcome to the golden eyes club, Lexi."

"Really?" Lexi squealed. "I have golden eyes now too? This is *so* freaking awesome!"

Clarice glanced at Aria and paused, her eyes growing concerned. "You okay?"

"Fine," Aria assured her with a quick smile, knowing there was no fooling Clarice.

Clarice stepped in front of Aria and studied her face searchingly. "What's wrong, Aria?" she asked softly, cupping her cheek in one hand.

Lexi's enthusiasm dimmed at Clarice's concerned expression.

Aria heard Emily return with the groceries and chickened out. "Who's ready to go to space?" she asked loudly, avoiding Clarice's worried gaze.

Lexi's excitement instantly returned. "I'm *so* ready to go to space!"

Calypso suddenly appeared before them. "You are going to space?"

"We were just waiting for you," Clarice grinned, giving Aria a look that made it clear their discussion wasn't over. "Let's go see what's out there."

The four of them launched into the air and streaked upwards, disappearing in less than a second.

19 – SATURN

"These are the files you requested, sir," Drake said quietly, handing a ring to Peter Ladislav, Director of the North American Territories.

Peter slipped the ring onto his finger and pressed the button on its back. "Access files," he commanded. A holographic array appeared in the air before him, displaying images, videos, and documents that scrolled past in orderly rows. The last file was titled: *Targets Exited System*.

He felt a jolt of adrenaline as the footage played, showing four angels blasting out of the solar system at speeds no archangel could even approach. They hit the boundary at the system's edge and passed through without slowing.

"Just what the hell are we dealing with here?" Peter muttered uneasily.

Drake cleared his throat. "Sir, Carcelonia was sighted in Rome about an hour ago. She seemed...disturbed."

Peter frowned. "How so?"

Drake licked his lips, nervously twisting the ring on his index finger. "According to the agent who saw her land, she looked terrified. She was distraught enough to teleport into an open area where our people could spot her, which is very unlike her. We traced her teleport trail to a cabin in Oregon. It appears to be the same cabin that used to be in New York."

Peter blinked. "You think they somehow teleported the entire residence across the country?"

Drake nodded carefully. "After examining the old location in New York, it appears the positions were swapped. There are Oregon pine trees there now, and the geology is consistent with the Oregon mountains. We believe she was capable of initiating a matter exchange, but on a massive scale."

Peter stared at his aide disbelievingly. "That would require power on par with a demon lord. *Beyond* a demon lord."

Drake met his gaze. "That was our assessment as well, sir. Grodek also taunted us again. He seemed extremely pleased with himself."

Peter scowled. "What did that little bastard say? Anything useful?"

Drake grimaced. "Mostly just gloating about 'how fucked' we are, in his words. He was quite gleeful about what a monumental miscalculation Carcelonia had made regarding something."

Peter didn't grin, but he came close. "So, we're finally getting confirmation that she awakened *our* angel—just not the kind of angel she thought it was."

Drake allowed himself a faint smile. "That was our assessment too. It seems she's realized the angel she awakened wasn't a successor."

Peter stood silently, contemplating the future. His plan to capture a dominion before the system killed her off as a child had failed spectacularly over a hundred years ago, when Calypso disappeared without a trace. She had had a century to grow more powerful, yet, as far as they could tell from the elements they had pieced together, she had remained essentially dormant—right up until she had met with the *others*. Since then, her abilities had exploded. Their chances of harvesting a Dominion's power were quickly diminishing.

The mystery of how she had vanished a century ago was like an itch he couldn't scratch. With the technology at their disposal, it should have been impossible for her to remain hidden for so long—especially while uploading videos to social media on a weekly basis for the last seventeen years.

Someone had been helping her.

Peter clasped his hands together. "We'll have to change our plans. It may already be too late to capture her. It's time to set up a confrontation with Azkar."

Drake nodded. "If we can't gather enough power to trap a demon lord ourselves, we can manipulate events so *she* does."

Peter absently rubbed his thumb across his knuckles, a nervous habit he had been trying to break. "I think it's time to send some envoys to these angels. We can't have them disrupting operations too early, or Azkar will arrive before we're ready."

Drake hesitated, chewing his cheek nervously. "About the other angels... The power they're wielding hasn't been seen since—"

"Yes, I know," Peter interrupted with a scowl. "We're going to be dealing with powers far beyond our level, which means we need to convince them of our goodwill *before* they start hunting us down. I'm still not sure how she managed to activate two Cherubim—the odds of two existing on one world are astronomical, and the system not killing them off as children even more so."

Drake coughed nervously. "Um, there are actually *five* of them, sir. It was in today's report. Both their parents were Cherubim, and the girl they rescued is also a Cherub."

Peter stared at him disbelievingly. "How is that possible? Two is beyond belief; five on one world is something else entirely."

Drake shifted, struggling to contain his anxiety. "We're reviewing the logs on the soul trap to see how they all ended up here. We don't think it's a coincidence either."

Peter shivered, eyes staring into nothing. "Cease all attempts at capture. At this rate, we might as well shut down all agonite farms and wait for the demon lords to make an appearance. There'll be no need to trap Azkar or the others—five Cherubim have the power to simply eradicate every demon lord in existence."

Drake frowned. "Should we continue to support this... network they're building?"

Peter shook his head disdainfully. "No, but don't interfere either. The other factions will probably do something rash soon, and it could be that we'll soon have a proper cleansing."

Drake nodded doubtfully. The other faction leaders weren't stupid; they had all seen the footage on social media and would recognize the power of a Cherub. No angel or demon would go near a Cherub if they knew what they faced.

* * *

Aria marveled at the beauty of interstellar space. Stars surrounded them in every direction, as far as even *their* enhanced eyes could see. They flew past the occasional rogue planet as they shot through space at speeds she still couldn't believe.

The real beauty appeared through her spiritual sight. Lines of energy filled the vacuum, weaving luminous threads through the dark. What mortal eyes saw as emptiness was, in truth, a lattice of power—interstellar rays arcing like cosmic rivers across the void.

Clarice furrowed her brows as a star began to grow quickly in front of them. "I thought stars were light-years away. We're going fast, but not *that* fast."

Aria stared at the growing orb of light doubtfully. "I agree. This doesn't make any sense."

Clarice let out a quiet hum. "Hmm, could astronomers have been wrong about the distances in space? How do they even estimate them?"

Aria took a deep breath—or at least, her chest expanded with the appearance of a breath—pleased to have something to sound knowledgeable about. "They use the parallax of Earth, measuring how much the starfield shifts as our planet moves from one side of the sun to the other. It's not perfect, given the scale involved, but even so... I can't believe how close these stars are. Alpha Centauri's supposed to be more than four light-years away, and we've only traveled a fraction of that—a tiny fraction."

Clarice suddenly laughed. "That would certainly make all the supposed alien sightings more plausible if stars aren't actually as far away as they thought."

Aria wrapped a strand of her red hair around a finger as they flew—it helped her think; at least, that's what she told herself. After losing all her hair to cancer as a child, she couldn't stop playing with it now that it was back—Clarice's, too. "Yeah, maybe. If demons and angels are a thing, would aliens be able to just pop into our world without any interference from either entity?"

Clarice darted in front of Aria and flew backwards, facing her with a wry smile. "What makes you think there isn't interference? How many UFO stories end with a saucer shot down by the military? Maybe demons are attacking them when they visit."

Aria held up a hand as a thought took shape. "Wait. Remember how the demons on Earth couldn't fly?"

Clarice's eyes widened. "You think the UFOs are demons traveling between worlds? They're not aliens after all—just demons commuting the cosmos."

Calypso flew up beside Clarice and cupped her narrow waist, gently turning her around. "There is one approaching this way," she warned, nodding toward the star. "Perhaps you can find out."

Aria didn't see anything until she switched to her spiritual sight. Then she saw a classic flying saucer closing the distance quickly.

Lexi watched the saucer nervously. "What should we do if they attack?"

Clarice tilted her head consideringly. "Let's try to get the pilots out safely. We need answers. I doubt they have any weapons that can hurt us."

They stopped and waited for the disc-shaped craft to arrive. It appeared in front of them a few seconds later. It was over a thousand feet in diameter and had an outer ring adorned with colored lights spinning around the inner disc. Aria sensed an intense electromagnetic field and terrific heat radiating from its hull.

She peered through the physical shell at the pilots inside. They were clearly demons, similar to the ones who had tried to abduct them. Their physical bodies appeared to be human, but that was where the similarities ended. They possessed the same spiritual matrix as an angel, but instead of radiance coursing through their meridians, there were writhing, snake-like tendrils of malevolence. The energy seemed far less frenetic in these pilots than in the demons they had destroyed on Earth.

Aria sensed energy charging in a track on the inner disc. "I think they're getting ready to fire on us."

Clarice calmly looked at Calypso. "Can you teleport us inside?"

Aria blinked as she suddenly found herself inside the vessel. The hallway they landed in was sleek and seamless, its walls and floor smooth like sculpted glass. There were no rivets or bolts—just a single, continuous form.

Clarice gestured ahead of them, her expression gleeful. "The bridge is up here. I'm going to have so much fun with this."

Aria exchanged an amused glance with Lexi and Calypso.

Clarice strode through an archway, Aria on her heels. The bridge was circular, with the four demons seated around it. There was no sign of panels, consoles, or other controls. With her enhanced sight, Aria could see that the pilots' helmets linked to the ship through neural patterns, removing any need for physical interfaces.

She was surprised at how faint the demonic stench was. Perhaps these demons were less steeped in evil than the others.

Clarice walked over to the center of the bridge. "We're going to play a game," she said coldly. "First one to answer my questions gets to live."

The pilots leaped from their seats and flipped the front of their helmets up in shock. They waved their hands in front of their chests, and a bolt of light arced toward Clarice. She folded her wings in front of herself, and the energy bolt harmlessly sizzled out.

Aria stared at the small squares on their chests where the light had originated. In less than a second, she blasted the devices, leaving the pilots staggering in surprise.

Clarice blurred forward, yanking off helmets before they could react. Human faces stared back at her, reptilian eyes wide with fear.

Clarice smiled grimly. "Do you understand me, or do I need to *make* you understand?"

"We understand," the tallest of them answered nervously, his accent eerily close to Russian. He slowly reached toward his pocket as he spoke.

Aria flashed forward and emptied his pocket, pulling out a small token with a button on it. "What's this? A distress call?"

The man shrank away, his eyes bulging in surprise at her sudden appearance.

Clarice smiled thinly. "It's time to start our game. First question: what... is your name?"

The tallest demon licked his lips before hesitantly answering, "Rodek."

Clarice's golden eyes bored into him. "What... is your job?"

Eyes riveted to Clarice's golden gaze, he said, "To monitor the system for anomalies or intruders."

Her glare grew more intense. "What... is your favorite color?" she demanded fiercely.

The demon paused, a confused crease appearing on his brow. "My... favorite color?"

Aria sighed in exasperation. "Flying fudge sticks, Clarice, can you be serious for once? Why in the hell are you re-enacting *Monty Python*?"

Her eyes sparkling with mirth, Clarice primly said, "We're on 'the bridge.' You know, '*The Bridge of Death*'? I couldn't *not* ask those questions."

Aria facepalmed, groaning and shaking her head in resignation. "We travel billions of miles from Earth, board a demon-piloted flying saucer, and your first instinct is to spout *Monty Python*?"

Clarice tilted her head, considering, then nodded. "Yep. That's correct."

One of the demons tentatively raised his hands and began clapping demonstratively. "*Monty Python*? With the coconuts?"

"You see *that*?" Clarice crowed triumphantly, pointing at the pilot. "It's such a freaking classic that even alien demons have seen it!"

Calypso turned to Lexi with a bewildered, "Do you have any notion of what is going on?"

Lexi's smile was just short of laughter as she gazed at Clarice. "She's quoting a movie from Earth, I think. I've never seen it, but I've heard of it."

Calypso sighed, shaking her head ruefully. "Of course she is."

Clarice raised a questioning eyebrow at Rodek. "So, do you demons stay in close contact with the demons on Earth? Clearly you exchange pop culture."

Rodek hesitated. "Well... we're not supposed to, but sometimes things find their way between worlds."

Aria nodded in understanding. "Ah... smuggling. What territory are you monitoring—just this system?"

Rodek nodded agreeably. "Yes, that's correct." He clearly wanted to stay on the good side of his overpowered "guests."

Clarice, her voice conversational and her smile that of a cat sharing a box with a mouse, said, "Well, Rodek, we're looking for something called the Lore Boar. Ever heard of it?"

Rodek shrugged. "It's a myth. They say it can answer any question if you provide it with exquisite food or entertainment."

Clarice folded her arms, the act immediately drawing all three sets of angels' eyes to her well-defined breasts. "And this mythical creature lives... where?"

Rodek relaxed slightly as the conversation remained civil. "They say it resides in Eden—where humans were first seeded. Somewhere in the Sol system."

Clarice sighed dramatically. "Figures." She looked at the pilots, her gaze hardening. "I'd suggest you forget you ever saw us. I'm letting you live, since you have good taste in classics—but if I find out you've blabbed our whereabouts to anyone..." she let the silence finish the threat.

Rodek made a show of looking around in confusion. "Seen who?" He turned to his fellow pilots. "I didn't see anybody. Did you?"

Clarice nodded approvingly. "Good man...er...demon." She turned to Calypso expectantly. "Shall we?"

The ship vanished as Calypso teleported them, leaving the vessel hundreds of miles away.

Aria looked at Clarice admiringly. "I'm impressed by your restraint. I thought you were going to kill them."

Clarice frowned, glancing back at the vessel in the distance. "I thought about it. They didn't stink like the others. I think the worse they smell, the more evil they are."

Calypso let out a discontented sigh, her eyes troubled. "It would be most welcome if demons could be redeemed—particularly former angels compelled to become demons. I cannot accept that they are beyond redemption."

Aria gripped Calypso's shoulders and held her at arm's length, smiling confidently. "Then *don't* accept it. You're a freaking *Seraph*. If you want to redeem a demon, that demon *will be redeemed*."

Calypso smiled winsomely. "With the three of you by my side, I am certain I can."

Clarice wrapped her wings around herself and closed her eyes with a contented moan, snuggling into them like a blanket. "Did I ever mention how much I like our wings?" She opened her eyes and took in the vast empty space around them. "So, where do you think Eden is? I haven't studied religions much, for obvious reasons. I'm kind of clueless in this arena."

Aria mimicked Clarice, folding her own wings around herself, smiling dreamily. "Yeah, angel wings *rock*." She let out a satisfied sigh and glanced at her sister. "We could always bug Mom and Dad," she suggested. "It must've been weird growing up before the internet and not being able to research anything without going to a library. I bet it took forever to get anything done."

Clarice floated closer to Aria and wrapped her up in her wings, packing the two of them tightly together. "In ten years, people will talk about how we grew up before AI became intelligent and how long it took to find anything with search engines."

"True," Aria said faintly, distracted by the sensation of two points poking into her back. "Um, okay... back to the cabin?"

"Nah," Clarice declined, sliding her hands up Aria's stomach, the act hidden by their wings. "Let's stop at Saturn on the way. Let's see if this *Order of Saturn* has its origins on the actual planet. They clearly have interstellar travel, so they've probably inhabited other planets."

Aria tried to answer, but her mouth had stopped working, the sensation of Clarice's hands sliding up her breasts robbing her of speech. She bit her lip, trying not to let out a whimper when her sister's fingertips brushed up against her nipples.

Lexi's eyes narrowed. "Hey, you two aren't getting weird under those wings, are you?"

Clarice's husky laugh was like a tuning fork to Aria's soul. "Weird? I was just keeping Aria warm—it's less than three Kelvins out here, after all."

Lexi raised a skeptical eyebrow. "Oh, I see... so Aria's just flushed from the cold, yeah?"

Aria barely restrained a disappointed moan when she felt Clarice's hands slide out of her shirt. Clarice hugged her once before her wings opened, releasing her.

"See?" Clarice said innocently, gesturing at Aria. "She's still dressed."

Lexi snorted. "Because nobody's ever fooled around with their clothes on before."

Calypso was silent, but the hunger burning in her eyes made it clear she wasn't fooled by Clarice's story.

Lexi glanced at the three of them with a small frown. "Are you sure you want to go to Saturn? I can find my own way home if you want some alone time."

"Positive," Clarice said firmly. "Besides, I have a feeling Dr. Aria wants to see Saturn."

Aria's eyes lit up, and she grinned eagerly, firmly tamping down on her overheated thoughts. "Oh, oh, oh, I know! Let's go to the hexagon at the pole! I want to see for myself what kind of weather pattern can form a hexagon for hundreds of years."

Lexi looked relieved, and Aria felt a moment of warmth for the new angel. She clearly didn't want to be alone but had been willing to leave them anyway to give them some privacy.

It took them only minutes to reach the ringed planet. They hovered over the immense cyclone at the center of the hexagon, its clouds twisting endlessly. Through her spiritual eyes, Aria saw ropes of energy spreading out from the formation, shooting into the rings. The debris making up the rings vibrated with the resonance, transmitting a harmonic that pulsed through the entire solar system.

Clarice studied the effect, her gaze calculating. "What's that resonance doing? It seems to be affecting the entire star system."

Aria nodded slowly, studying the glowing grid. "I noticed that, too. It's influencing matter in a weird way—like sand forming patterns on a vibrating metal plate."

Calypso pointed into the vortex, staring intently. "The center of the vortex leads inside the planet."

Aria stared into the cyclone with a puzzled frown. "It's a gas giant—there shouldn't *be* an inside."

Clarice turned to face her, shaking her head ruefully. "I think we need to forget most of what we learned in school," she advised critically. "Either they were completely wrong or purposely obfuscating the truth."

Aria grunted sourly. "Agreed. Feels like I've wasted years learning things I now have to unlearn."

Calypso eyed the center of the cyclone eagerly. "Shall we investigate?"

Clarice grinned, clearly caught up in Calypso's enthusiasm. "Why not? I'm *so* ready to explore another planet."

They shot down into the vortex at terrific speeds, unaffected by the torrential winds swirling around them.

"Ah, shit," Clarice cursed. As they plunged past the hydrogen and into the atmosphere's denser layers, Aria noticed their clothing's colors bleeding out. Though the wind didn't affect their clothes, the temperature and chemical composition of the atmosphere *did*.

Aria sighed plaintively as they plunged deeper. "I hope Tamra has some new outfits ready. I totally forgot what the pressure down here would do to our clothes."

Clarice looked down at her disintegrating shirt mournfully. "We seriously need to evolve the ability to protect our clothing. I really liked the way this shirt showcased my best asset. Hopefully, the new shirts are similarly designed." She suddenly brightened. "At least I'll get a good show."

Aria shook her head in resignation, resisting the urge to cover herself in the face of Clarice's sudden leer.

"Hey, that's cheating!" Clarice yelled bitterly at Calypso.

Aria laughed when she saw that Calypso had used her shapeshifting ability to appear clothed. "Okay, we don't need to evolve to protect our clothes—we just need to become shapeshifters."

The last remnants of their clothing disintegrated as they plunged deep into the cyclone, where the pressure dramatically increased. The vortex was a thing of beauty, with shades of gold, amber, and cream swirling around them. Sunlight filtered through the top, producing dramatic shadows and light rays that grew hazier as they descended. She could see flashes of electrical discharges in the distance.

Clarice held her breasts up and grinned at Aria and Calypso. "Hey, now you get to see what my shirt was almost hiding."

Aria bit her lip, fighting the urge to do more than look. She glanced over to see a similar struggle on Calypso's face.

Lexi snickered. "I'm not sure what the big deal is. We all have boobs—I thought it was just guys who went nuts over them."

Clarice released her breasts and turned to face Lexi. "It's evolution, ya know? It doesn't matter if you're a boy or a girl; you need milk when you're an infant, and that creates a hardcoded psychological attraction to a nice pair of knockers. The attraction can be more obvious for dudes because they've been programmed by nature to seek out mates with the greatest chance of nourishing their offspring—which is why dudes are more obsessed with size. Chicks are attracted to tits as much as dudes, but size only matters to some chicks."

Calypso was already shaking her head before Clarice had finished speaking. "That is simply not true, Clarice. I have examined both male and female bodies whilst healing humans, and attraction to breasts is almost entirely rooted in attraction to the female form, with very little influence stemming from an infant's need for milk. One of the things I learned during my time in hospitals was that humans are the only species to possess permanently visible breasts outside the context of childrearing. In that sense, breasts serve as a sign that a female has reached reproductive maturity, hence the attraction to them from an evolutionary standpoint. Females who are attracted to other females are often more likely than males to find breasts appealing, possessing an innate understanding of their sensitivity."

Clarice stared at Calypso in surprised silence for several seconds, then performed an elaborate floating bow. "I bow to your superior knowledge, Calypso. I certainly learned something new today."

Aria eyed Calypso suspiciously. "Were you just leading me on the night we first kissed? Since when did you become an expert in sexuality?"

Calypso blushed and looked away guiltily. "I spent some time studying Emily's thoughts on the matter once I became capable of telepathy. I was concerned I might prove an inadequate partner for you and Clarice, and so I sought to educate myself on the subject."

Clarice burst out laughing, swooping over to hug Calypso. "Oh, Calypso, I do love you—even if you ruthlessly pillage other people's thoughts for hanky panky pointers."

Calypso was in the process of turning red as Clarice's nude form pressed into her own naked body. While Calypso had cloaked herself in the illusion of clothing, she was still naked, capable of feeling every curve and crevice as Clarice held her tightly.

Aria racked her brains for a reason to embrace one of them while she was so strategically equipped to enjoy it. Her amorous thoughts were derailed as the atmosphere changed.

The tempest abruptly calmed and the heat spiked. They slowed, descending toward a massive metallic platform thousands of square miles in size.

Clarice released a flustered Calypso, studying the metallic surface in fascination as they landed. "Well, looks like *someone's* been here. I'd bet my halo this thing's responsible for the vortex."

Aria switched to her spiritual eyes, gasping when she discovered the powerful electrical currents rotating below them. The platform was shaping and amplifying the electromagnetic currents, weaving them into a spiral pattern.

"Somebody created this to generate the resonance we observed pinging the rest of the solar system," she said musingly, studying the electromagnetic field below. "This giant circuit seems to be manipulating the planetary magnetic field to produce that vortex. I wonder what would happen if we turned it off."

Clarice frowned, crouching down to feel the surface with her hand. "I'm not sure that's wise," she said cautiously. "We don't know if this is the work of demons, a creator, or some alien species. For all we know, it could be keeping the Earth safe from something dangerous."

Calypso quickly shook her head. "I do not believe so. This is a demonic construct. I can feel the dissonance it is creating—it is wrong."

Clarice brightened. "That makes things easy then. Let's vaporize it."

Calypso nodded slowly. "I believe we should."

Clarice grinned at Aria, looking concerningly enthusiastic. "Okay, let's get vaporizing. Aria, you've got the biggest blaster. Let's see what those hourglass eyes can do to this thing."

Aria grinned back at her sister, then rose several dozen miles. She relaxed the restraints on the condensed energy inside her eyes.

A wire-thin beam of light shot down, striking the platform. She fired continually, moving the beam from one side of the enormous platform to the other. After a minute of nonstop firing, she paused to observe the effects.

The platform rippled like a heatwave as it underwent demolecularization, the chemical bonds unraveling in an expanding chain reaction as the entire platform sublimated. The process completed within a few minutes.

"It looks like the vortex is undergoing cyclosis," Aria observed in fascination as she watched the planetary electromagnetic field blast upward without being transformed by the macro circuit. The swirling funnel of hydrogen and helium was no longer maintaining its intensity; it slowed even as they watched.

Aria shook her head slowly. "This doesn't make any sense. The vortices are powered by thermal gradients, not EM fields. How did removing that oversized antenna shut the vortex down?"

Clarice raised an eyebrow. "That would depend on the other trace elements in the atmosphere, wouldn't it? I read an article about cloud seeding where they dropped barium in the atmosphere and then zapped the sky with powerful EM fields to ionize the atmosphere."

Aria shook her head, brows creased. "This is hydrogen and helium, not oxygen and water. There are trace hydrocarbons in the atmosphere as well, but that still shouldn't account for this dramatic change in the cyclone's decay. Something else must have been going on with that circuit to create the vortex in the first place."

Clarice grinned sardonically. "Okay, Professor, we can solve the cosmic physics later. Stop flexing your degree and let's head home. I'm curious to see if this affected Earth."

Aria sighed, reluctantly following as they ascended the weakening vortex. "*Fine*. I suppose we should go straight to Tamra's house."

"Yes," Lexi agreed quickly. Her face had been varying shades of red since their clothing disintegrated.

Clarice gave a sultry laugh that set Lexi to a deeper shade of red, but didn't argue.

It took them less than a minute to reach Tamra's. All the lights were off except the porch light, and Aria realized it was late—though "late" didn't mean much when you had perfect night vision and didn't sleep.

Lexi hesitated. "Should we wake her up? I don't want to ruin her sleep."

Calypso suddenly blushed crimson. "She is not sleeping."

Clarice grinned wickedly. "Don't tell me—she has a *friend* over."

Calypso nodded, avoiding Clarice's eyes.

Aria smiled slyly. "They didn't waste any time, did they? Remember when I told you what a horndog was, Calypso?"

Calypso ignored Aria's question. "I suggest we go back to the cabin and make do with some of our old clothes until morning."

Aria sighed in mock exasperation. "*Fine*. We won't interrupt the lovebirds *this* time."

Clarice grinned at them lasciviously. "I'm totally fine waiting."

A portal opened on the third-floor balcony, and Calypso stepped through without a word, Lexi right behind her.

Clarice gestured grandly. "After you."

Aria snorted and shoved her sister through the portal. "Not likely, you perv."

Clarice stumped through with a sigh, pouting. "You're no fun."

Aria turned to move toward her balcony door, but Clarice caught her hand. She turned to face her just in time for Clarice to pull her into her arms, leaning her forehead against Aria's. Their breasts pressed together, nipples rubbing with each breath.

Aria's breath caught as pleasure surged through her like a lightning bolt. A soft moan escaped her throat before she could stop it.

"Don't be a stranger," Clarice murmured silkily.

Aria stared into her sister's golden eyes, arousal flaring with an intensity that left her legs trembling. She could see the same naked hunger in Clarice's eyes she knew was in her own.

Clarice kissed her lightly on the lips, then pulled back as Aria leaned in for more.

"To be continued," Clarice whispered, then gave her another feather kiss before releasing her and stepping away and moving to her room.

Aria stood on the balcony, naked and trembling with need. "Clarice, you're a shameless tease!" she hissed, disappointment and frustration washing through her in waves. She was finally capable of intimacy, and Clarice was winding her up just to make her wait! She was tempted to storm into Clarice's room and tackle her onto her bed, despite knowing the other angels could hear everything they did.

Sighing in annoyance, she went into her own room and began hunting for clothes.

Emily's voice drifted from several rooms away. "How was outer space? Did you lose your clothes again?"

Aria barked a defeated laugh. "Yeah. We seriously need another upgrade that protects our clothes from damage. Either that or get Calypso's shapeshifting ability."

Clarice added with a smirk, "Tamra won't be available until morning, so we're stuck with sheets or bras again. Personally, I vote bra club."

Eric's voice carried up to them, his tone suspicious. "Did you girls do anything...extreme...about twenty minutes ago?"

Aria's brows furrowed as she pulled a bra over her shoulders. "Why? What happened here?"

Eric paused, his voice uncertain. "We're not sure. It's like something fundamentally changed, almost like a blanket of negative energy was removed, and I hadn't realized it was there until it was gone."

Clarice was smugly nonchalant. "We stopped by Saturn and destroyed a giant antenna inside the pole. It seemed to be sending out some kind of resonance to the rest of the solar system, but we weren't sure what it did."

There was a long pause before Eric spoke again. "You went to *Saturn*?"

Clarice laughed brightly. "Oh, we went a lot further than Saturn. We went all the way to Alpha Centauri."

Eric's voice grew plaintive. "Is your sister messing with me?"

Aria grinned as she picked up a brush and began untangling her hair. "Nope—but it's not as wild as it sounds. Alpha Centauri isn't actually four light-years away. Either astronomy's been catastrophically wrong, or someone's been lying about the distances."

Eric drew in an excited breath. "Was it populated?"

Aria studied her reflection in the mirror, a curious expression on her face. Her golden eyes looked out of place for some reason.

She shook her head, refocusing on their conversation. "We didn't actually go to any of the planets. We ended up boarding a flying saucer piloted by demons." She shook her head with an exasperated laugh. "Your daughter started spouting Monty Python at them."

Eric was silent for a moment. "I'm going to need more context than that."

Her voice dripping with innocence, Clarice answered, "We were on the bridge of the ship, so I asked them three questions they had to get right to live."

Silence stretched for several seconds, broken by a groan from Emily.

Clearly struggling not to laugh, Eric asked, "So what was their favorite color?"

Clarice sighed bitterly. "Aria interrupted before they could answer." She brightened. "But one of the demon pilots had actually seen *Monty Python*. It's such a classic that it's even popular in other star systems."

Emily chuckled, the sound soft and vibrant. "What happened to your clothes this time?"

Aria made a face. "I forgot about the extreme pressure the cyclone on Saturn would have on clothes. On a brighter note, the astronomy community's going to have a lot to talk about once they notice the hexagon's gone."

"You broke Saturn?" Eric asked, his voice level.

Aria snorted. "No, Dad, we didn't break Saturn—just some demon construct inside the pole. It was about the size of a city and responsible for the hexagon. I vaporized it because it seemed like a good idea. No big deal."

Eric sighed sadly. "It was bound to happen eventually. The power's gone to her head."

"Yep," Clarice agreed cheerfully. "It shoots out her eyes."

"Just let it lie, dear," Emily warned.

Clarice cleared her throat. "So, Mom, did you get everything set up?"

Emily's reply radiated satisfaction. "I sure did. Why don't you girls get dressed and come down to the library? If any of you need help getting wrapped up, holler."

"Clarice?" Aria prompted, her tone expectant. "What's going on?"

"Hard to say," Clarice said airily. "Maybe we should just do what Mom said and take our cute little butts down to the library."

Emily snorted. "I don't remember saying anything about cute little butts."

"I'm just rephrasing what you meant, rather than what you said," Clarice explained helpfully.

Aria quickly slipped into some shorts, then blurred down to the library. She burst out laughing when she saw the giant HAPPY BIRTHDAY LEXI letters hanging from the ceiling. Board games were set up on several tables, and a movie projector displayed a streaming service on one of the white walls. Party streamers and balloons decorated every inch of the room.

She turned as Lexi entered the library. Lexi's eyes widened as she took in all the festive decorations and activities.

Emily smiled softly. "Happy belated birthday, Lexi. We're a little late, but here we are."

Lexi froze for a heartbeat, then tears welled in her eyes. She rushed forward and threw her arms around Emily. "Thank you," she whispered, her voice trembling with emotion.

Emily kissed her head, squeezing her tightly. "It was my pleasure. This was Clarice's idea. She asked me to get all this stuff while I was shopping earlier."

Clarice joined Emily, embracing them both. "And as you can see, she's the best mom in the world."

Lexi nodded, her voice thick with emotion. "Yeah, she really is. You're the most amazing family in the world."

Clarice grinned. "In the cosmos now. Happy birthday, Lexi. We're so glad you joined us."

Aria smiled, watching her sister with quiet pride. She really did have the best sibling in existence.

She turned as Calypso entered the library, then froze. Power radiated from the beautiful musician, her presence exponentially stronger than it had been just minutes ago. It was as if she had been missing a large piece of herself this entire time, and now she was whole.

She had brought her own harp, her eyes shining with happiness as she set it down near the table.

"I realized I could simply teleport to the storage unit to retrieve my instruments," she explained, her smile radiant. "This harp has always been especially dear to me. I feel as though I have just regained the use of a missing limb."

They all stared at her, mesmerized by her supercharged aura.

She tilted her head questioningly. "What?"

Clarice slowly walked up to her. "Calypso... you feel... I don't know—complete. What did you do?"

Calypso blinked, then her radiant smile returned. "I have no idea. I simply grasped my harp and suddenly felt like an entirely new person—as though I had been living only half a life before."

Aria stared at the harp curiously. It was made from a type of brilliantly white wood she didn't recognize. "Where did you originally get that harp?"

Calypso fondly stroked the frame. "My father found it a few years before they found me, resting at the base of the very same tree. That was one of the reasons he returned to that particular spot so often—it was almost a sacred place to him."

Aria stared at the luminous instrument in fascination. "What kind of wood is the frame made from? I've never seen a harp made from wood that color."

Calypso raised her hands, smiling helplessly. "I have no idea. I have never actually played it. My father would not allow me to touch it, and when he died, I decided to honor his wishes. I kept it in the crate where he had stored it. However, I have a new family now, and I believe tonight's celebration calls for some rather special music."

Aria grinned with anticipation. Listening to Calypso play was always magic. "I couldn't agree more."

Emily studied Calypso and the harp with narrowed eyes. "I have a feeling we're in for a treat."

Clarice embraced Calypso tightly. "You really do feel whole. Welcome back, Calypso."

Calypso smiled softly, resting her head against Clarice's. "It feels wonderful to be back, Clarice."

The next several hours overflowed with laughter, games, movies, stories, and warmth. Near morning, they finally convinced Calypso to play her harp.

Calypso watched them shyly. "I am not accustomed to playing before people who are not children."

Clarice grinned mischievously. "Just imagine we're all in our underwear. Oh, wait—we are."

Lexi laughed uproariously, wiping tears from her eyes. It had been an emotionally charged night for her as she soaked up the love and cheer.

The room grew quiet with anticipation as Calypso arranged the harp. With another shy smile, she began to play.

Aria felt a rush of tingling energy climb her spine as the first notes vibrated through her spiritual matrix. The sound wasn't merely music—it was communion. Each string seemed to pluck at her soul, the tone resonating through every molecule of her being. Clarice and the others froze, awe washing over their faces.

Calypso closed her eyes and began to sing.

Power surged through Aria like a dam breaking, energy cascading in torrents and brilliant colors flashing like living auroras. Light flooded her soul until it ached, her meridians reshaping into lattices of multidimensional runes. Her wings shimmered and split into two gossamer layers like Calypso's, as power hummed through her hands and feet, and raw, divine authority etched itself into her soul.

The lines of power connecting the world unfolded before her eyes, overlaid with higher-dimensional paths leading to other realms she now instinctively knew she could reach.

The world could have turned to dust, and Aria wouldn't have noticed. She was a frequency in a sea of creation, remade in real-time.

When the final note faded, she realized every angel in the room glowed with radiant light.

Calypso stood motionless for a moment, her expression rapturous. Then she opened her eyes and blinked at the sight of them—transformed and trembling, with tears streaking their faces.

"I... I..." Clarice tried to speak, but couldn't.

"Are you quite all right?" Calypso asked, suddenly concerned.

"Calypso," Aria whispered in awe, "that was divine."

The others nodded slowly, their eyes filled with reverence.

Calypso looked gratified, her face lighting up with a pleased smile.

Aria licked her lips. "I think that harp might be one of the instruments Grodek was hinting at. I've never felt so much power, not even close."

The others recovered slowly, Clarice finding her voice last. "Yeah, that thing was reaching into my soul and mining for gold. I feel like I just went through twenty evolution cycles."

"I'll bet you did," the snarky voice of an imp laughed. "That harp was made from the Tree of Knowledge."

20 – SERAPH

Drake hurried through the sprawling office complex until he reached Peter's suite at the back, his hands trembling as he knocked on the heavy door.

"Enter," Peter's voice came from the wall speaker.

Drake scanned his ring across the reader and entered the large office. Peter stood with his back to the door, gazing out at the city through the high-rise windows. The office was tastefully monstrous—expensive sculptures on pedestals and priceless paintings under pretentious track lighting. Some of the art was exactly what one would expect from a demon of his status: children with their hands tied behind them, expressions of despair on their faces; a woman with no eyes groping for a light switch. Drake loathed them almost as much as Peter did, but such ambience was expected of a demon in his station.

Drake approached the vast desk near the windows. "I have reports from the agents stationed near the residence. I assume you've reviewed the Saturn feed."

"I have," Peter confirmed, his tone steely. "It raises more questions, however. How did they know we were modulating the moods of mortals with apathy programming? Is this Grodek's doing? How much has that little bastard told them?"

Drake put his hands in his pockets to hide their shaking. "It's possible she's evolved enough to sense the modulator herself."

Peter shook his head disdainfully. "The whole reason we buried it inside Saturn was to make it undetectable," he snapped. "Not even a Cherub could have sensed it."

Drake tried, and failed, to keep the tremor out of his voice. "We were able to debrief Carcelonia before I came here."

"And?" Peter prompted impatiently.

"She said Grodek claimed Calypso was a Seraph," Drake said hoarsely. The word seemed to drain the air from the room.

Peter whirled around, eyes wild with sudden fear. *"What?"*

Drake elaborated, licking his dry lips. "Grodek was ridiculing her for trusting demons. He claimed what she activated was a Seraph."

The Director clenched his jaw, staring through Drake into a future where all hell broke loose. "That would explain the worldwide power surge. What did the agents near the site report?"

Drake shifted nervously. "They said the skies lit up with auroras and the entire cabin glowed like an incandescent bulb. They also claimed to hear what they think was a divine instrument. It nearly destroyed them."

Peter shook his head in disbelief, his composure beginning to crack. "A Seraph with a divine instrument. On Earth. This is going to draw attention from the realms of light. They won't leave a Seraph alone if they think they can stop her before she fully ascends."

Drake rubbed the back of his neck, a note of cautious optimism in his voice. "The divine instruments were supposedly destroyed. If she possesses one, they may not dare to challenge her even at her current level."

Peter sighed in exasperation. "I want to know how Carcelonia ended up with a Seraph. I was personally involved in the arrangements with Carcelonia a hundred years ago, and the data showed a Dominion—definitely a Dominion. The four Seraphim were annihilated long before that. How was there even one left to awaken?"

Drake took a deep breath, straightening his suit. "I assigned some of the AIs to parse satellite archives from the last hundred years. The only anomaly they found regarding the data transfer was a brief flash near the archive room a few days before the meeting. We picked up one frame of a certain imp. We also found evidence that the soul trap had been tampered with."

"Grodek," Peter snarled. "What game is that little monster playing?"

Drake ran a hand through his dark hair, his unease deepening. "Carcelonia claims he wasn't always an imp. She seemed more open once she realized what he'd done to her. She said he was demoted by a Seraph for violating one of their tenets. Apparently, he was once either a Seraph or a Cherub. He tried to hide the divine instruments from the remaining four Seraphim after they destroyed the Three. He was declared fallen, but instead of being unmade, he became... this."

Peter began pacing. "We need to make contact—soon—before those angels start killing anything that smells like a demon. But whoever we send can't be too tainted. If they sense demon rot on our envoy, it'll be a massacre."

Drake nodded quickly. The idea that a *Seraph*—a being as mythological to angels as God was to humans—currently shared his planet was terrifying. He shivered at the thought of one of the god-like entities responsible for creation residing on the mortal realm.

Peter sucked in a breath. "Wait! If she's one of the Three... what do we know about Aria and Clarice?"

Understanding dawned on Drake, and he gasped. Fear pulsed through his meridians, raw and visceral. "You think all three might be here?"

Peter clasped his shaking hands. "Someone hid Calypso from us for over a hundred years. Aria and Clarice survived childhood, which shouldn't be possible for anyone above an Archangel. Too many coincidences. Too many Cherubim surviving to adulthood. Whatever's happening, it's not random chance—it's by design."

* * *

"The Tree of Knowledge from the Garden of Eden?" Emily asked disbelievingly.

"No, you brainless butterfly," Grodek retorted caustically. "The Tree of Knowledge from the garden of slug slime. How many Trees of Knowledge have you heard of to ask such a stupid question?"

Emily scowled. "You don't have to be so insulting about it," she muttered in an injured tone.

Grodek leered at her. "You are correct—it's by choice that I do so. And the Tree of Knowledge isn't *in* the Garden of Eden, moron."

Eric's eyes widened. "Does that mean the tree was chopped down?"

Grodek sneered condescendingly. "How much wood do you think is needed for a harp, genius? A tree the size of a mountain isn't going to miss a harp-sized splinter."

Calypso stared at Grodek intently. "How can I change you back into an angel?"

He froze, taken aback by her non sequitur, his eyes narrowing as he stared at her with an unreadable look. "You haven't the faintest clue what you're asking."

"Yes, I do," Calypso said steadily, meeting his gaze. "I will *not* accept this nonsense about fallen angels being beyond redemption. I can feel how profoundly wrong the idea is within my soul. It is not a question of if, but of *how*."

He stared at her in silence, the mockery draining from his expression. "It's not that it can't be done," he said finally, his voice low. "It's that only an ascended Seraph can do it. I'm not a demon—not like these other jackasses. You don't have the knowledge to do it yet."

Calypso narrowed her eyes. "Why do I feel as though I know you, Grodek? Who are you?"

Grodek looked away, his expression unreadable. "You need to see the Lore Boar," he muttered. "I'm done here."

With a soft pop, he vanished.

Clarice eyed her mother, struggling not to laugh. "Mom, you should probably cover up." Emily had lost most of her shirt during Calypso's divine-instrument performance. Both parents now sported wings and golden eyes.

"*Oh!*" Emily gasped in surprise, then laughed as she quickly left the room. "See how powerful your music is, Calypso? You can undress people, and they won't even notice."

Calypso blushed as the others broke into laughter.

Eric grinned at her retreating form appreciatively. "I wasn't complaining." His shirt was also in tatters, but he didn't seem to care.

Calypso cleared her throat meaningfully. "There is a demon on the doorstep," she informed them calmly. "I believe she wants to talk."

Aria cursed her inattentiveness. She had heard footsteps approaching but assumed it was her uncle. She should have noticed the difference in gait.

She and Clarice blurred to the front door, ready to fire at the slightest hint of aggression.

A dark-haired woman with striking features stood on the doorstep, shock painted on her face. Reptilian eyes stared at them hopefully. She was a few inches shorter than the two angels and wore a simple blue summer dress.

Clarice raised a questioning eyebrow. "How much did you hear?"

The woman's voice trembled with a mixture of fear and desperate hope. "Can she really change demons back into angels?"

Aria's gaze softened. She must be one of the angels who had been turned against her will. Aria realized another reason they hadn't noticed her—the stench of demon was practically nonexistent on the woman. There was something about the demon's presence that seemed familiar. Had they known each other in another life? "What's your name?"

"Arturiel," the woman answered nervously. "I was sent as an envoy from the North American Territory."

Aria shared a look with Clarice before turning back to the demon. "An envoy, huh? What is it you want to discuss?"

Arturiel spoke carefully, her eyes darting away from their golden gazes. "I was instructed to answer any questions you have and to negotiate a truce between you and the North American Territory."

Clarice sighed, gesturing her inside. "Well, come in, then."

Arturiel swallowed hard and stepped forward, freezing the moment she caught sight of Clarice's double-layered wings.

"What?" Clarice asked, glancing over her shoulder.

Arturiel flinched away from Clarice's curious golden eyes as if they were laser beams—which, of course, they were. "It's just... I've only seen someone from the upper triad once," Arturiel answered in what would have been barely audible for a human. "I never thought I would see one on this world, let alone two."

Clarice's eyes glinted with amusement. "They didn't tell you what we are?"

Arturiel shook her head, licking her lips nervously. "Just that you were newly awakened angels whom I needed to treat with the utmost respect. Are you really newly awakened?"

Aria looked at Clarice inquiringly. "I think today's our one-week anniversary, right?"

Clarice smiled brightly. "Yep, happy anniversary, Aria."

Aria grinned, winking. "Right back at ya, Clarice."

Arturiel blinked. "How have you become so powerful in such a short time?" she asked faintly. "I didn't think even Cherubim could awaken this fast."

Clarice shrugged, pointing toward Calypso as they entered the library. "That's probably her fault."

Arturiel froze the moment she saw Calypso standing beside the harp, her eyes widening in terror. She spun to flee, but Calypso was suddenly in front of her.

Calypso pulled her into her arms, closing her eyes as she studied Arturiel with her spiritual eyes.

Arturiel went rigid, dread etched across her face. Calypso tentatively wrapped the demon in her aura of love. Arturiel's shoulders hunched in sudden pain as the angel's loving energy brushed her meridians lightly.

Calypso retracted her aura, and the wince of pain vanished. Eyes closed, Calypso hummed a poignant melody. Aria could tell she was searching for answers, using her music to open herself to the intuition that guided her healing.

Arturiel's wide eyes darted around, searching for a way to escape. Calypso's melody became soothing, almost hypnotic, and Arturiel's frantic gaze slowed as the beautiful voice calmed her soul.

Aria and Clarice studied Arturiel with their spiritual eyes as Calypso sent probing tendrils of light into the woman's meridians. Aria frowned, noticing for the first time the tethered network inside a demon's soul. There were nodes at the chakra points linked by currents that emptied into a vortex near the navel. Calypso's tendrils reached toward that vortex, cautious and measured, and then one disappeared into it.

Calypso stood unmoving for nearly an hour, eyes closed, pulsing faintly with light. Arturiel remained still, no longer afraid but uncertain.

Emily rejoined them, her shirt held together with safety pins. She watched in fascination as Calypso worked, her golden eyes curious.

Calypso suddenly ignited into pure radiance—so bright that Aria couldn't look with physical *or* spiritual eyes. A torrent of unwavering authority surged down the luminous tendril into the vortex of Arturiel's core.

Arturiel opened her mouth to scream, her eyes wide with sudden horror. Just as the scream began, it shifted to a gasp of wonder. Calypso's loving aura wrapped tightly around Arturiel, charging her with radiance. There was no sign of pain this time. Instead, she gasped again and began to glow, brighter and brighter by the second. The entire library was devoid of shadows as both Calypso and Arturiel glowed like two suns.

The light slowly faded, revealing Calypso and Arturiel locked in an embrace. Arturiel sobbed in shock and joy, overwhelmed as she felt her restored connection to radiance. She clung to Calypso desperately, her face buried in her shoulder.

Aria beamed at Calypso proudly. "I knew you could do it, Calypso."

It took a long time for Arturiel to stop weeping, though she smiled the entire time. To be an immortal angel with the constant cord of radiance charging your system with love and hope, then have it severed and replaced with malice you were told was for all eternity... it was a hell she wouldn't wish on anyone. Aria couldn't imagine the relief the redeemed angel must be feeling.

"Thank you, thank you, thank you," Arturiel whispered over and over, tears of liquid silver streaming down her face.

"Arturiel," Calypso whispered gently. "It's all right. You're safe now. You can't become a demon again."

Arturiel pulled her head back and stared at Calypso with wide, reverent eyes. "Never?"

Calypso shook her head with a gentle smile. "There's nothing anyone could do to turn you back into a demon. You'll never have to suffer that fate again."

"How?" Arturiel breathed, her eyes searching Calypso's face.

Calypso frowned disapprovingly. "There's a mechanism in the spirit that allows for a reversal in the type of energy that flows through your meridians. I removed the part that makes that reversal possible. I believe it was implemented by whoever created angels in order to revoke their power. It was flawed, however, and didn't just revoke an angel's power—it turned angels into demons when it should have turned them into mortals."

Grodek suddenly reappeared, sneering in disgust. "That was by design. Too many angels enjoyed harming mortals, so Lucifer altered angels to transform into demons if they harmed mortals. The boneheads mismanaging the program *ostensibly* didn't grasp that making immortal demons would result in demons eventually figuring out how to defeat angels and turning them as well."

Clarice's face darkened. "Why didn't the higher-ranking angels do something about it? Why would they leave angels who'd done nothing wrong in the hands of demons?"

"Because it's political," Grodek spat bitterly. "Mortality's a prison for undesirables."

Emily's eyes burned with curiosity. "Who decided to make angels incarnate as mortals?"

Grodek eyed them peculiarly. "The first three Seraphim. The angels originally lived in the light realms, but there's a hard limit to what you can experience in an infinite realm, where time and pain don't exist. The Seraphim created the mortal realm to experience a new aspect of reality, constrained by time and driven by passions incomprehensible to immortals. There was a mutiny, though, and shit got ugly. Mortality became Alcatraz for anyone on the wrong side."

Aria was beginning to grasp just how powerful a Seraph truly was. They had created the mortal realm? As in, the entire universe? It was hard to reconcile that cosmic authority with the gentle woman standing before her.

Calypso looked at the imp. "Are you ready, Grodek?"

"Nope," the imp shook his head grimly. "I'm not a demon, so that won't work on me. You need to find the Lore Boar first—wherever he's hiding these days. Nothing else matters."

Calypso looked at him hopefully. "Do you know where Eden is?"

Grodek sighed in annoyance. "It doesn't stay in one place. Go bug the demons begging you for a truce—and take sunscreen."

He looked at Calypso with something close to respect before disappearing with a pop.

Clarice beamed. "I knew you could do it, Calypso." She crossed the room and drew both angels into a hug. "Welcome back to angelhood, Arturiel."

Arturiel smiled radiantly, leaning into the three-angel hug. "Thank you, Clarice. Words can't describe how good it is to be back."

Emily gazed at Arturiel musingly. "So... how will this affect your relationship with the North American Territory now that you're an angel? I'm assuming there are more demons who'd like to become angels again?"

Arturiel laughed ruefully. "You wouldn't *believe* how many. The Director has been masquerading as an evil demon for centuries, trying to mitigate the horrors demons inflict on humans. He's weeded out most of the truly evil demons in positions of power. There are a few angels we maintain regular contact with as well. They have to stay hidden, given how many demons are constantly on the lookout for angels."

Aria studied her curiously. The difference in power was stark. Arturiel felt only slightly stronger than a human. It made sense how demons had taken over the world; average angels were closer to Arturiel than to the flying weapons Calypso had raised.

Clarice raised a questioning eyebrow. "So, what now? Calypso, would it take you this long to heal each demon worth redeeming?"

Calypso shook her head. "Only a few seconds. Most of my time with Arturiel was spent trying to understand the mechanism that transformed her in the first place."

Clarice looked at Arturiel hopefully. "I don't suppose you or anyone in your organization knows where to find Eden?"

Arturiel nodded hesitantly. "There are demons who are essentially religious scholars. You might get some answers from them."

Clarice looked at Aria questioningly. "I suggest Aria, Lexi, and I search for Eden while Calypso transforms demons into angels. What do you think, Aria?"

Aria stared at her parents—now winged, golden-eyed killing machines. "Mom and Dad, you'll need to watch over Calypso while we're away."

Emily's eyes hardened. "You can count on us. Anyone looking for trouble will find it."

Eric gave an easy smile. "I'm a peaceful guy, for the most part." His gaze sharpened. "But if anyone threatens those I love, I'll do whatever it takes to keep them safe."

Clarice nodded, a satisfied smile on her face. "Okay then. That takes care of everyone here. Arturiel, can you introduce us to those religious scholars? Do you need to report back first, or are you done with the envoy gig?"

Arturiel shifted, looking guilty. "I was very tempted to abandon the title, but I can't leave them now that I know they can be redeemed."

Calypso smiled reassuringly at her. "If they attempt to keep you against your will, we'll come for you."

Arturiel blinked, startled. "Can you hear my thoughts?"

Calypso nodded, her smile lopsided. "Yes. I used only to hear humans. Apparently, I can hear certain angels now as well."

Arturiel looked down at the ground, her cheeks pink. "Oh."

Calypso rested a comforting hand on her shoulder. "Now that I've connected with you, I can sense where you are and the state of your mind. If there is even the slightest hint of trouble, we'll open a portal and allow Aria and Clarice to stretch their wings."

Arturiel looked up, her eyes glistening with quicksilver tears as she smiled gratefully at Calypso.

Calypso nodded firmly. "Yes, they truly are that powerful. Aria and Clarice could lay waste to most of this world in less than an hour. There is no one here powerful enough to stop them."

Arturiel stared at Aria and Clarice in awe, trying and failing to imagine the level of destruction they were capable of.

Aria had been watching Calypso as she listened to Arturiel's thoughts. She noticed an ethereal thread connecting the two of them, with information passing in one direction. Tentatively, she tried forming a weave of her own. She smiled when the weave formed, then connected it to the same node. Her eyes widened when she heard Arturiel speak without moving her lips.

"I still can't believe how good it feels to be an angel. I can't wait to tell the rest of them they can be angels again." Aria heard Arturiel's thoughts as if spoken aloud.

Clarice had watched shrewdly, and Aria realized her sister had already made the connection.

Aria narrowed her eyes. "How long have you been able to do this?"

Clarice's eyes widened, her whole face radiating innocence. "Not long."

Aria suddenly noticed a tendril connecting herself to Clarice. *"Clarice! How long have you been listening to my thoughts?"*

Clarice's innocence vanished to be replaced by a mischievous smirk. *"Remember the demon flying saucer? Well, after seeing their thought interface, it all just kinda made sense, ya know?"*

Aria scowled, uncertain of whether to be angry or happy. No wonder her sister had been so willing to push past Aria's boundaries—she'd had a bird's eye view of Aria's comfort level the whole time. The thought made her smile, knowing Clarice would never abuse such an ability.

Calypso observed Aria with quiet satisfaction as she picked up the psychic weave.

Aria refocused on Arturiel, curious if it was possible to channel her own thoughts to the redeemed angel. *"Can you hear me, Arturiel?"*

Arturiel looked at her strangely. "Yeah, I can hear you."

"Did she say something that I missed?" Arturiel thought frantically.

"You're not being rude," Aria assured her with a smile, *"I just wanted to make sure you could hear me telepathically."*

Arturiel gasped when she realized Aria's mouth wasn't moving. Clarice laughed with delight, and Aria felt a thread reach out to Calypso.

"I guess the gig is up," Clarice declared eagerly. *"Get ready for some embarrassing thoughts!"*

Aria facepalmed and groaned. "Clarice, you keep your dirty thoughts to yourself."

"Oh, I will," she promised, grinning like a Cheshire cat, *"if you say it like you mean it."*

Aria bit her lip, unable to deny that she really *did* want to hear Clarice's dirty thoughts. Her cheeks lit up when Clarice's smile deepened, her sister clearly observing her inner dialogue.

Emily adjusted her pinned-together shirt and addressed Calypso. "If Seraphim are the highest order of angels, where did a seed come from to create another one? Or is she one of the original Seraphim?"

Aria shared a look with Clarice, frowning at the implications before turning to a distracted Arturiel with sudden interest. "Arturiel, how old are you?"

Arturiel blinked, refocusing on their conversation. "I'm sorry, what was that?"

"How old are you?" Aria repeated, stifling a grin. Having someone else blush more than she did felt empowering for some reason.

"I'm immortal," Arturiel replied, nervously adjusting her dark hair. "I've been around for millions of years. Why do you ask?"

Aria gazed at her intently, realizing they had someone who could give them some *real* answers. "Who sits above Seraphim in the order of angels? Are you an ascended human, or were you an angel to start with?"

Arturiel answered slowly, as if it should be obvious. "God sits above the Seraphim. And no, I was never human. Like I said, I've been around for millions of years."

Aria couldn't hide her doubt after a lifetime of refuting the existence of a deity. "Have you met God?"

Arturiel laughed weakly. "Me? Heavens, no. I'm at the bottom of the totem pole. Only Seraphim can speak with God."

Their parents drifted closer, eyes bright.

"Is God a person?" Emily asked eagerly. "Or is God some kind of cosmic law?"

Arturiel shifted uncomfortably under their intense interest. "God isn't a person, like angels or humans. God is the source—where life and this energy in our meridians comes from. Regular angels like me don't know much about God, since only the Seraphim can commune with it."

Emily glanced at Aria and Clarice speculatively, then turned back to Arturiel. "What do you know about the different Seraphim?"

"Not a lot," Arturiel admitted. "There are only a few Seraphim who interact with the Cherubim directly. I've heard of the Three who remain apart from the other Seraphim and almost never interact with angels. If the stories are correct, they spent all their time learning from God. Most of the stories claim Seraph Rendimus created the light realms and angels, but I overheard Azriel speaking a long time ago about how the Three were the first beings to exist, aside from God. Azriel is a Cherub, so you'd think he'd know. However, most of the stories claim Rendimus created the other Seraphim to help him create the light realms."

"What else do you know about those three?" Emily pressed, a peculiar look on her face.

Arturiel sighed. "Almost nothing. When I overheard Azriel speaking, it was long before the mortal realm existed. He said the Three were working on a place where angels could go to learn how to experience new sensations. Now that I think about it, I'm guessing he was talking about the mortal realm. Azriel said the divine instruments were made by the Three."

Emily was silent for a moment as she chewed her lip. "What were their names?"

Arturiel shrugged helplessly. "We were never told. You have to understand; the Seraphim were viewed with the same reverence that human religions reserve for God. Only Seraph Rendimus, Seraph Grodekkan, and

Seraph Lucifer interacted with angels regularly, and even saying their names is taboo."

Eric held up a hand, his eyes growing wide. "Wait... Seraph *Lucifer?* I thought he was a Cherub."

Arturiel shook her head wryly. "That's what the local religions teach, but they know even less about the Seraphim than angels do."

Eric glanced at Clarice speculatively. "Were all of the Seraphim dudes?" he asked Arturiel, his curious gaze remaining on Clarice.

"Dudes?" Clarice repeated, arching an amused eyebrow. "As opposed to dudettes?"

Eric shrugged, grinning. "Exactly."

Arturiel shifted awkwardly, clearly uncomfortable at applying *dude* taxonomy to cosmic beings. "Um, no. According to the stories, only six of the nine were male in appearance. Seeing a Seraph was *extremely* rare. Compared to you mortals, I'm old on a geological time scale, but I'm just a baby compared to the Seraphim. They've supposedly been around for billions of years. Some say they didn't even have a beginning—they were just always there. Considering how many angels there are, it's not very strange that most of us have never seen a Seraph. It's rare enough to even see a Cherub. The Seraphim almost never leave the highest light realm, and only Cherubim and Seraphim can go there."

Emily stared off into the distance, absently twisting her wedding ring. "So, there were three female Seraphim."

Eric raised an eyebrow at her. "What are you thinking about? I know that look—you've thought of something."

Emily blinked, her eyes snapping back into focus. "What? Oh, nothing much. Just wondering about life before mortality. I've always been curious about how much access we have to things like soul memory." Her gaze drifted over Calypso and her daughters, frowning pensively.

"So how do Seraphim talk to God?" Eric asked, steering the conversation back to Arturiel. "Is it a sentient entity?"

Arturiel raised her hands helplessly. "All I know is based on speculation. There's a reason only the Seraphim can communicate with God. It's such a complex and multidimensional entity that only beings closer to that power and complexity can hope to communicate in a meaningful way."

Aria's eyes sparkled with excitement. "So, Calypso will be able to speak with this God thing?"

Arturiel slowly turned to Calypso, comprehension widening her eyes. "You're a Seraph?" she whispered, equal parts awe and horror.

Calypso nodded, smiling gently. "Yes."

Arturiel dropped to her knees, pressing her head to the ground, her hands shaking. "Please forgive my arrogance, Seraph."

They all stared at Arturiel in shock—Calypso in visible dismay. Calypso knelt and gently took Arturiel's hands in her own. "Arturiel, I do not know what you have been taught regarding Seraphim, but I neither require nor shall ever require any such obeisance. Please, stand and treat me as you did before. I am merely a person, just as you are—only far more ignorant."

Arturiel slowly raised her head, awe and fear still present. Calypso stood and pulled Arturiel up with her. Arturiel looked as if she might faint.

Calypso sighed and embraced her, flooding Arturiel's meridians with radiance. Arturiel gasped as power charged her soul, purging the anxiety and fear. Calypso had to repeat the process several times; each time she released Arturiel, the angel reverted to a state of brittle apprehension. By the third time, however, she finally stopped shrinking away in fear.

"I'm scarcely over a hundred," Calypso said gently. "You are millions of years old, with untold knowledge and experience in that beautiful head of yours. If anything, I ought to be bowing to *you*."

Arturiel's eyes widened in horror at the suggestion, prompting a snigger from Clarice.

Calypso drew a deep breath, her tone patient. "Do you see what I mean, though? Regardless of my station or power, I am but an infant compared to you."

"She really *is* a babe," Clarice agreed lustily. "I've been saying that from day one."

Arturiel gasped, her face blanching.

Clarice shook her head and squared her shoulders. "There's only one way we're going to get this thought through her head," she declared, her eyes sparkling with mischief. She stepped between Arturiel and Calypso, then pulled the Seraph into a sensual embrace, gluing her lips to Calypso's.

Aria didn't think Arturiel's eyes could get any wider, but they did. She made choking sounds as her mind began misfiring. The kiss lingered, full of passion and desire. Warmth suffused Aria's body as she watched with interest, hoping to learn something.

When Clarice finally pulled away with a smile and a wink at Calypso, Arturiel seemed to have finally come out the other end of her crisis. She stared at the two angels in awe—and a touch of curiosity.

Calypso's cheeks flamed, and her eyes swirled rapidly. She stared at Clarice with naked longing, her breaths coming deep and fast.

Arturiel watched them with a troubled frown. "I've never heard of Seraphim engaging in sensual acts before."

"Then they do not know what they are missing," Calypso breathed with a rapturous smile.

Arturiel burst out with a nervous laugh, her lavender eyes wild.

"Listen," Calypso said soothingly. "Most of what I do is by instinct—perhaps intuition, soul memory, or simply the manner in which Seraphim hear God. Whatever it may be, it tells me that things have gone terribly wrong and must be set right. No angel ought ever to feel fear in the presence of a Seraph. My purpose is to heal, to protect, and to love. There is no place for fear in that."

Quicksilver tears brightened Arturiel's eyes. "I can't believe I'm speaking to a Seraph," she said with a disbelieving laugh, "and one that treats me as an equal."

"We most certainly *are* equals," Calypso insisted firmly. "Our duties may differ, but we both feel love, sorrow, joy, and the desire to help others. I know myself well enough to say that there will never come a time when I see myself as anything other than your equal."

Clarice glanced at Aria, lips pursed. *"I'm pretty sure this God entity is doing some house cleaning. How else could a Seraph end up on Earth? I think it's decided to shake up the management team."*

Aria nodded. *"That seems to be where things are headed, unless Calypso is one of the original Seraphim and has incarnated for some reason."*

Clarice's eyes narrowed. *"Now that's an interesting thought. What if she* did *come down here to fix things, but has to start with the same rules as all mortals, having the memory of her former life blocked or something?"*

Aria frowned doubtfully. *"Maybe. If that were the case, shouldn't she remember her old life, since she's an angel now?"*

Clarice glanced appraisingly at Calypso. *"Maybe the memories are returning slowly. She keeps getting hints of them, after all. Maybe she'll eventually have full recall."*

Aria nodded slowly, her eyes thoughtful. *"I wonder how long full recall would take, if that's true?"*

Clarice shrugged uncertainly, then turned to the rest of the group with a bright smile. "And on that note, let's go find Eden and redeem some demons."

Calypso stepped forward to open a gateway, but Clarice held up a hand with a wink. "I've got this."

Aria watched with curiosity as Clarice linked to Arturiel. Aria mirrored her sister's actions.

"Picture where you want to go," Clarice instructed Arturiel.

Arturiel nodded and an office appeared in Aria's mind. A moment later, Clarice opened a gateway into the center of the office. A man sat at a desk, flicking his fingers through the air as holographic images and files scrolled past.

"Dang, you guys have all the fancy tech, don't you?" Clarice remarked enviously.

The man jumped to his feet in surprise. Aria wrinkled her nose at the stench. It wasn't as bad as many of the others, but compared to Arturiel, it was definitely noticeable. When his eyes fell on the two angels, he froze. He felt their power and his shoulders slumped in defeat.

"I didn't expect you to start cleaning house for a few more days," he said conversationally. Aria could see the tightly controlled fear in his eyes. There probably weren't very many things that could kill immortal beings—facing two of them must be unnerving. "So did you kill Arturiel already?"

"No, Peter," Arturiel answered, her voice bright. "They did something much better."

He finally noticed Arturiel, staggering when he recognized her angelic form. "How?" he asked, dumbfounded.

Clarice gestured toward the portal. "Calypso redeemed her. While you stink a lot more than Arturiel did, she says you're a good person. Are you ready to become an angel again?"

He gaped at them, his eyes wide with disbelief. "That's *impossible*! Demons *can't* be turned back to angels."

Clarice nodded toward Arturiel. "Tell that to Arturiel. Are you ready?"

Suspicion narrowed his reptilian eyes as he looked at Arturiel. "What did I tell you about demons when we first met?"

Arturiel smiled. "That demons are just like humans with an addiction to power, and that we could still be good people if we didn't let our addiction rule us. I've shared that sentiment with others many times over the centuries."

The suspicion slowly faded, replaced by a sudden, painful hope. "Can she truly redeem demons?"

Arturiel nodded, her voice thick with emotion. "Yes, Peter—and I can't tell you how good it feels to be an angel again. I'd always taken this benevolent energy coursing through me for granted. Being redeemed was like coming back to life."

"What do I need to do?" he asked simply.

Clarice gestured behind her. "Go through that gateway. Calypso will do the rest."

He slowly walked around the desk toward the gateway, staring at Arturiel in awe. Calypso was waiting for him on the other side, with Eric and Emily flanking her protectively.

"Hello, Krajen," Calypso greeted the demon, causing him to falter at the sound of his true name. "This will only take a moment."

He stopped in front of her, hope radiating off him in waves. Calypso's eyes grew brighter, then she burst into blinding light. When the light dimmed, the demon was no longer a demon.

He gasped as radiance flooded his meridians. His elongated pupils shrank to circles, and his irises turned a deep blue. Calypso pulled him into an embrace and burst into light again, supercharging him with radiance. His shoulders shook as he wept with intense relief.

"What has been done cannot be undone," Calypso said gently. "You will never be turned into a demon again."

While the process to change a demon back into an angel was fast, the emotional aftermath was lengthier. He returned through the gateway ten minutes later, his face alight with bliss.

"I need to gather the rest of us," he announced excitedly. "She said she can redeem us in groups."

Arturiel smiled, quickly embracing him. "I need to take Aria and Clarice to the theologians. They're looking for Eden."

Krajen nodded, releasing her. He had a constant grin and an excited energy mirrored by Arturiel. "I'll get Dorian and Remus up here right away. They'll be your best bet for information on Eden."

They waited over an hour as dozens of demons gathered in the open space outside Krajen's office. He hadn't told them why he was gathering them, and the group was abuzz with chatter as they discussed the possible reasons for their summons. Aria found it odd to see so many entities she had thought of as pure evil just days ago. They seemed so normal, like everyday office workers waiting for their boss to address them.

Krajen finally opened the door and stood before the crowd. They quieted, staring in astonishment as they took in his angelic form and presence.

"Some of you may be aware that a Seraph has awakened on this world," he began, an irrepressible grin on his face. "Calypso is that Seraph. She's discovered a way to redeem demons. If there are any among you who wish to remain as demons, please leave now."

You could have heard a pin drop. He turned back to the gateway behind him and nodded at Calypso. She walked forward, the power of her presence flowing out in waves as she entered the building. The demons watched her with a mixture of fear and hope as she stopped in front of them. With a gentle smile, she burst into light. Dozens of ethereal tendrils shot out, seeking and excising the part of their spirits trapping them in demon form.

Gasps and cries of amazement filled the room as the dark energy filling them reversed, and radiance flooded their meridians. Calypso blazed incandescently as she pushed her aura out into the crowd, charging them with radiance at an accelerated rate.

Aria smiled at Clarice as they witnessed the turning of the tide in the demons' rule on Earth. The redeemed angels embraced each other, laughing and crying as they basked in the positive energy they had been denied for so long. The room glowed with raw, wild, emotional energy.

When things calmed down, Krajen introduced Remus and Dorian. The two angels were difficult to talk to, as they continued rejoicing in their unexpected redemption. After nearly twenty minutes of patiently watching them revel in their restored angelic forms, Clarice pushed the conversation forward.

"Remus, Dorian," Clarice said crisply. "We need to find Eden. Do either of you have any idea where to look?"

The two angels grew serious, watching her warily. "We know a little," Remus hedged cautiously.

Aria immediately made a telepathic connection to the two angels. They were terrible actors, and they clearly knew more than a little. Clarice also linked with them, then connected with Aria as well.

"We were told we need to find the Lore Boar to get answers," Clarice told them intently. "We were led to believe it was in Eden, which is supposedly somewhere in this star system."

"We swore to never reveal the location of Eden to anyone else," Remus thought. *"But a Seraph? There must be some kind of exception."*

Aria held up a hand. "You don't need to tell us if it means breaking an oath. We'll find another way."

They stared at her in shock.

"Can you hear our thoughts?" Remus asked in amazement.

"Yep," Clarice confirmed with a nod. "Aria's right. If you're under oath, we'll find another way to locate it."

They shared an uncomfortable glance. Remus finally spoke hesitantly.

"Well... our oath was to never speak the location to another person," he said slowly. "If we just happened to think of it, our oath would remain unbroken."

Aria smiled ruefully at their logic. "Only if you're comfortable with it," she insisted, eyeing them gravely.

They didn't answer, but their thoughts did. Aria blinked when she saw where Eden was located.

"On the freaking sun?" she thought to Clarice in astonishment.

"Their thoughts indicate the sun isn't hot," Clarice replied, just as surprised. *"Apparently, another piece of science we've been misled on."*

"But the freaking sun?" Aria exclaimed, unable to reconcile the impossibility.

"I'm guessing by the looks on your faces that you have what you need from us," Remus noted with a chuckle. "You two were humans before you became angels, weren't you?"

"Yeah..." Aria replied faintly.

Dorian laughed, shaking his head. "All angels know the sun isn't hot, but of course humans are taught it's the opposite of a thermonuclear bomb."

"But I can feel the heat from the sun all the way on Earth," Aria protested, her face baffled.

"You're just feeling photons interacting with the atmosphere and creating heat from friction," Dorian explained with a shrug. "It's the same temperature on the surface as it is here. Only the corona is actually hot."

Aria gawped at them, her mind unable to unlearn that the sun was an inferno of mating hydrogen atoms.

"Come on, Professor," Clarice said, pulling her away with a wry grin. "Thanks a lot, Dorian and Remus."

"But it's the *sun*!" Aria spluttered insistently.

"Yep," Clarice nodded agreeably. "We should probably get some clothes from Tamra now that it's daytime. You realize we've been in our bras this whole time, right?"

Aria looked down at her chest and blushed furiously, staring around in sudden embarrassment. "Flying fudge sticks, let's go."

Calypso's shoulders shook with laughter as she followed them through the gateway. Aria shook her head in exasperation. Clarice was rubbing off on the Seraph. Two days ago, Calypso would have been blushing as much as Aria was. Of course, Calypso was projecting her own clothes with her shapeshifting ability, so *she* wasn't walking around in her underwear.

"You're so cute when you blush," Clarice told her with a naughty grin.

"Shut up, Clarice," Aria muttered, closing the gateway behind them.

21 – EDEN

Aria stood in Tamra's living room, talking with the others as they waited for their new clothes. She was conflicted, enjoying the sight of Clarice in a revealing bra, but unhappy to be in the same state of undress. She secretly hoped Clarice's new top was as alluring as her old one had been. At a wink from Clarice, she remembered there *were* no more secrets—not with her sister spying on her thoughts.

She wanted to feel indignant about the clear invasion of her privacy; instead, she felt a spike of arousal at the thought of Clarice seeing past her bashful nature and to the erotic theater of desire she didn't have the courage to voice.

She pulled her thoughts back from perdition after another wink from Clarice and focused on Arturiel.

"How much do we need to worry about The Agency now that the demons in charge of this area are angels?" she asked.

"They don't actually lead any of the human agencies or militaries," Arturiel answered, watching them with even more fascination than they watched her. "They place demons in influential positions within those organizations and pull the strings from the shadows—mostly through the use of secret societies."

Arturiel was struggling not to be overwhelmed by the presence of the powerful angels. Her thoughts were even more entertaining than her warring expressions of awe and fascination.

"I still can't believe she actually kissed a Seraph!" Arturiel thought wonderingly. *"I feel like I should be punished for how much I enjoyed watching, but they seem so relaxed and accepting that I can't bring myself to feel too guilty."*

Aria and Clarice could have won trophies for not reacting. Occasionally, Arturiel would suddenly remember they could hear her thoughts. Each time, her face would freeze and then turn bright red. The three of them would pretend not to notice, and she would soon forget again.

Clarice folded her arms, immediately drawing Aria's eyes. "What about the President?" she asked, waggling her eyebrows at Aria before returning her attention to Arturiel. "We'd planned to borrow him to get some answers right before you showed up."

Arturiel's eyes widened. "You were going to abduct the *President*?" she squeaked.

Clarice shrugged nonchalantly, an action Aria found particularly distracting. "We were just going to drop him through a gateway. Is he a demon?"

Arturiel nodded faintly. "We rotate masks for that role. Different demons wear the face."

"Why should I be surprised they'd abduct the President?" Arturiel thought hysterically. *"With the kind of power they have, they can literally do whatever they want."*

Aria sighed, looking at Clarice with defeat. Her sister was staring at her triumphantly, lips curved into a victorious smile. "Okay, Clarice—you were right."

Clarice giggled, her golden eyes sparkling with delight. "You're damn right I was. I've said for years the President was just a pile of asshats in masks. It's not even hard to notice—half the time they're different heights."

Aria studied Arturiel curiously. "I couldn't help noticing you don't have wings. Did you have them before you were turned?"

Arturiel looked down, her cheeks tinged with pink. "Only archangels and higher ranks have wings."

Aria's eyes widened with sudden realization. "*That's* why demons are using helicopters and flying saucers—because they didn't have wings as angels. We thought it was a fallen-status thing."

Arturiel nodded, looking back up. "Exactly. Demon lords have wings and can portal. Most of them were archangels, though two were Dominions."

Lexi stood with her arms folded self-consciously, clearly dissatisfied with her membership in the bra club. "How powerful are archangels compared to regular angels? Carcelonia made it sound like they'd wipe us out as soon as one showed up."

Why was Lexi so uncomfortable in a bra when she was surrounded by other women? Based on their earlier conversation, she had assumed Lexi wasn't attracted to women, but she spent a lot of effort staring fixedly at their faces and avoiding their chests for someone who wasn't interested.

Arturiel shifted uncomfortably. "There's a significant power gap between an archangel and an angel."

"And they're not nearly as forgiving if you don't show the proper respect," Arturiel thought, briefly reliving memories of being reduced to a quivering wreck for not bowing low enough or answering with the proper amount of respect in her voice.

Clarice's expression darkened. "If I ever see an archangel treat an angel like that, there'll be one less archangel."

Arturiel blushed, avoiding their eyes as she remembered, once again, that they could read her thoughts. Aria could sense her guilt at feeling mildly resentful at the archangel's frequent rebukes.

Aria rested a warm hand on Arturiel's shoulder. "You should feel a lot more than a little resentment. Nobody should *ever* be made to feel less than another person. If he's still around, he has a day of reckoning in his future."

Arturiel closed her eyes as quicksilver tears glistened on her lashes.

"How different would things have turned out if we had leaders like these three," Arturiel thought warmly. *"Is this why we were sent to the mortal realm? To learn humility and vulnerability?"*

Lexi licked her lips. "How would an archangel or demon lord compare to a Cherub?" she asked tentatively, clearly concerned about their eventual arrival.

Arturiel barked out a laugh as she shook her head. "There *is* no comparison. Cherubim are the tools of judgment—the only class of angel who can kill an immortal. No demon lord, archangel, or *any* other class of angel would come near a Cherub if they knew who they were facing."

Clarice moved behind Lexi and began massaging her shoulders. Lexi stiffened at first, but relaxed after a moment of uncertainty, a soft smile lighting her face.

Aria met Clarice's gaze and smiled. *"You're such a softie."*

Clarice shrugged, her eyes holding Aria's. *"I figured it was time for another example of what being around people who love you is like. She's never experienced physical contact in a positive environment, so we have our work cut out for us."*

A different kind of heat warmed Aria's soul as she watched her compassionate sister with a mixture of love and pride. The flame of attraction was still there, but accompanying it was something much deeper and infinitely more powerful.

"Are there different classes of Cherub?" Clarice asked Arturiel. "Aria and I were directly transformed by Calypso, but my mom and Lexi were transformed by us. My dad was transformed by my mom, so he's three generations down from Calypso. We all have laser eyes, so I assume that makes us all Cherubim, right?"

Arturiel nodded, forcing herself to meet Clarice's golden eyes without flinching. "That's my understanding. There are three levels of Cherubim. The only difference I know is that the lower tier can't kill the higher tier, but the reverse isn't true. As for who raised them… it shouldn't make a difference—your class doesn't change after incarnating. Whatever your class was in the light realms will be your class when you awaken."

Clarice grinned at Lexi. "I guess I can talk all the smack I want without worrying about Lexi frying my ass then."

Lexi's eyes were soft and full of affection as she turned to stare back at Clarice. "As if that would ever happen. No amount of smack talk could ever make me want to harm you."

"Aww, come here, you," Clarice purred, drawing her into an embrace.

Lexi's face lit up with contentment as she melted into Clarice's arms.

"The bonds of love between these angels are unbelievable," Arturiel thought, her eyes moistening again as she witnessed the beginning of a new order of angels based on love and kindness. *"It feels so right, like this is how it was always meant to be. What a difference the lens of mortality makes."*

Aria once again felt that nagging sense of familiarity she had experienced when first meeting Arturiel. "Arturiel, there's something so familiar about you. Did we know each other before I incarnated, or something?"

Arturiel blinked, looking at Aria curiously. "No, I didn't know anyone from the first triad, but I've felt the same sense of familiarity with all of you. I don't understand it."

Clarice and Lexi looked at Arturiel in fascination, both of them nodding.

Clarice frowned. "That's pretty weird. It's like an itch I can't scratch. I noticed the same thing as soon as we met you, Arturiel. I felt it with Jason as well."

Aria tilted her head, studying Arturiel intently. "What was your life like before demons took over the world? Did humans know you were an angel?"

Arturiel nodded with a hint of a smile. "There were places where people were aware of us. Common angels who've never been mortal, like me, only appear to humans if they believe, so a lot of it was based on cultural traditions. There are some references in history to the time before demons took over, though most of it is highly inaccurate."

She paused, brushing a strand of her midnight hair behind her ear. "Most Greek and Roman mythology was based on archangels and demon lords. They had an uneasy truce, but there were constant betrayals on both sides. The ascended angels were also breeding with mortals a lot during that period, resulting in hybrid angels. They were immortal but not invulnerable. They thought creating hybrid humans would help bolster their numbers in the fight against demons. It turned into a disaster because it was so much easier to turn a hybrid angel into a demon."

Clarice frowned, resting her head against Lexi's. "How *do* they turn an angel into a demon, anyway?"

Arturiel shivered, her eyes bleak. "It's not pleasant. They lock us in a room where they torture innocent humans, then give us the option to torture one ourselves, or be forced to watch while they torture them one after another until we give in. Harming a mortal with malicious intent is the trigger that transforms an angel into a demon. They continue harming innocents while forcing you to take agonite."

She paused, looking sick. "For an angel, agonite doesn't produce the same high as it does for a demon. It floods our minds with doubt and confusion, leaving us vulnerable to psychological manipulation. We can be convinced that harming innocents is enjoyable. It takes years for some of us to break. The longer it goes on, the more despair sets in as endless lines of innocents are tortured before our eyes. When the change occurs, your moral compass shatters, and you no longer have a sense of right or wrong. The only thing that matters is power."

Calypso walked over and pulled Arturiel from her chair, embracing her comfortingly, her swirling eyes brimming with tears.

Aria blinked. Calypso's tears were no longer quicksilver—they were gold.

"I am so terribly sorry you endured such horror," Calypso choked out, her voice thick with emotion. "I cannot even begin to imagine suffering such cruelty."

Clarice looked sick, her eyes shimmering with unshed silver tears. She was always so strong and unflappable that it was easy to overlook the deeply compassionate soul hiding behind her snark and humor.

Arturiel's eyes widened with ecstasy as Calypso's overpowering aura flooded her meridians with radiance. A streak of gold trickled down Calypso's cheek and landed on Arturiel's head.

There was a blinding flash of light, and a shimmering golden sphere enveloped them. Energy shot out from the sphere and into Arturiel, causing her body to spasm in Calypso's arms as if she were experiencing a seizure. She began to glow brilliantly, banishing the shadows from the room.

Aria's eyes widened as she watched Arturiel's nodes morph and expand, dramatically increasing the flow of energy in her meridians. A tearing noise could be heard over the resonant hum of energy as wings sprouted from her back, ripping through her shirt. They were more birdlike than the wings Aria and her group had started with, resembling the winged angels from Renaissance paintings.

"What... happened?" Arturiel panted, her eyes wide and rapturous. "I feel so much more *alive*."

Calypso gently caressed her cheek. "You are now an Archangel of the First Order. You are precisely the sort of archangel this world is in need of."

Arturiel gasped, her brows arching in disbelief. "Me? An archangel? But angels *can't* change their class."

Clarice snorted. "And demons can't be redeemed, right? If Seraphim really are the creators, then I'm pretty sure altering one of their creations isn't a big deal."

Arturiel laughed wonderingly. "I can't believe how different this feels. I thought being an angel felt wonderful after being a demon, but this..."

Clarice laughed, releasing Lexi. "Yeah, we totally get that. During the first few days after our ascension, it was all I could think about. I'm still in disbelief at how good I feel all the time."

Aria frowned at Arturiel. "Didn't you say harming humans with malicious intent was the trigger for transforming angels to demons? We've definitely killed several humans, and I was absolutely feeling malice when I did it. Shouldn't I be a demon now?"

Clarice made a purring sound that tickled Aria's libido. "Oh gods, Aria, I've got this sexy image of you with devil horns and a tail in my head now."

Clarice shared her mental image of devil Aria, and Aria tittered awkwardly at the erotic scene depicted in exquisite detail. Her face felt like it could be used to cook on as Clarice inserted herself into the scene and began doing things to Aria she had only dreamed of. Aria trembled, overcome by a nearly unquenchable desire to drag her sister off somewhere private.

"Oops," Clarice said unconvincingly. "Too much?"

Aria stared back at her, breaths coming fast and a growing tension crying out for release. She was a breath away from taking Clarice right then and there, but was interrupted by the arrival of Tamra.

"Let me guess," Tamra deadpanned as she joined them with an armful of shirts. "You need another set made."

"Maybe?" Clarice admitted in a wheedling tone. "We seem to be multiplying. You're going to have to add a dovecote for us to hang out in."

Tamra laughed good-naturedly as she began handing out clothing. "Clarice, only you would compare angels to pigeons."

Aria put the brakes on her runaway lust and took the offered shirts from Tamra, excited to see the finished product. "We know an imp that compares us to a lot worse," she commented as she set all but one of the shirts down.

Aria paused in the act of pulling her shirt on to stare at Clarice. The new shirt was similar to the last, but if anything, it showed off Clarice's assets even more blatantly. Shaded a deep red, the shirt was a snug, lightweight fabric that cut high across her chest like a second skin, with an open back held together only by a thick band at the waist and two wide straps over her shoulders.

Clarice eyed herself critically in the mirror, then slipped the shoulder straps off so the face of the shirt fell forward, allowing her to remove her bra before sliding her arms back through the straps. She smiled at her reflection in satisfaction as the fabric molded to her breasts, leaving almost nothing to the imagination.

She turned to find Aria staring at her with open admiration, frozen in the act of putting her own shirt on.

"Judging by Aria's reaction, you've outdone yourself, Tamra," Clarice purred, sensuously running her hands down the fabric beneath her breasts.

Tamra chuckled, eyeing Aria with amusement. "Honestly, this is a common design you probably could have found in regular clothing stores, considering how popular high-neck crop tops are these days."

Clarice grinned. "Yeah, but when Aria said she was going to find a tailor to design some custom-fitted shirts, I decided to keep my mouth shut and see what you came up with—I've never had anything made to fit."

Aria turned a dangerous gaze on her sister. "You *what?* Are you saying you already knew there were styles that would work with wings?"

Clarice shrugged, her chocolate eyes sparkling. "I might have. But would we have met Tamra and Lexi if I'd opened my mouth?"

Aria frowned, her gaze flicking to Lexi and Tamra. "Yeah, I guess. You're such a freaking troll."

Clarice held her hands up defensively. "Hey, it's not my fault you hated anything to do with fashion growing up. Mom even has a crop top back home, so get mad at her if you want to blame someone."

Aria narrowed her eyes. "Hmm... you make a good point. Why *did* she stay silent?"

Clarice shrugged, gesturing at Aria's chest. "You going to put that thing on, or just stand there holding it?"

Aria blinked, then glanced at an amused Tamra with a rueful grin. She had to step into the shirt from the ground and pull it up, slipping her head through the neck loop on the front.

Clarice gave a loud wolf whistle. "Damn! You look SO. DAMN. HOT!"

Aria bit her lip as she looked at herself in the mirror. It was almost the same design as Clarice's, showcasing her breasts with a thinner nylon fabric in the chest. She had retained her bra, so her nipples weren't popping out to display her arousal status to the world like a teenager on social media. She had always been extremely sensitive as a human, and that hadn't changed with her ascension. When she was human, she had worn nipple pads with her bra as an extra precaution, much to Clarice's amusement.

She took a deep breath and turned to Tamra with a grateful smile. "These look amazing, Tamra. It fits *perfectly*."

Tamra orbited her, inspecting the fit with a professional eye. "You're stunning, Aria. The fuchsia works beautifully, since your hair is actually true red."

Calypso nodded, eyeing Aria appreciatively. "I concur—she is truly stunning."

Aria shyly smiled, drinking in the sight of Calypso in her white shirt of the same style.

Lexi, in a shade of royal blue, turned away from her mirror to smirk at Aria. "People are going to either think angels always have big melons, or that you're only accepting humans who are well-endowed." She paused, tilting her head. "Actually, I never thought to ask, but what *did* you look like as a human? Were you always this developed, or was it due to your ascension?"

Clarice sidled up to Aria and draped an arm around her shoulders. "She's always had a nice pair of knockers, but she tried her damndest to hide them," she told Lexi dryly, hip-bumping Aria. "She used to buy these thick sweaters that seemed tailor-made to turn your body into a cylinder, as if she were afraid someone might notice she's female."

Aria scowled but couldn't deny it. She had *always* been self-conscious about the size of her breasts and the attention they attracted. They were an introvert's bane, making high school a special kind of hell as boys lined up to be disappointed when Clarice informed them her sister was gay.

She surreptitiously glanced over at Clarice, wishing she could do more than just *look* at the goods on display. Thoughts of what she wanted to do to Clarice paraded through her mind, winding her ever tighter.

Maybe she could take Clarice and Calypso to an uninhabited island somewhere for a few days and put everything else on hold while they got to know their new bodies. Years of fearing intimacy had created a reservoir of unrequited need, and now that the dam had finally burst, she could scarcely think about anything else.

"All in good time," Clarice's thought interrupted her fantasy.

Aria's face lit up like a cherry as she remembered, too late, that Clarice could see her thoughts.

Clarice turned her head to grin at her playfully. "You're getting a little warm around the ears, Aria—I didn't think angels could get sunburned."

Aria scowled, futilely trying to will herself to stop blushing. "You're a bad angel, Clarice."

Clarice smirked, looking Aria up and down hungrily. "Hey, I don't blame you for fantasizing—we're crazy hot. Tamra really outdid herself."

Tamra looked at her pointedly. "I suggest going topless if you find yourself heading for a black hole or another planet with superstorms. Otherwise, I don't think I'll be able to keep up. Where are you going next?"

Clarice adopted an exaggerated British accent. "Funny you should ask. It just so happens we are off to the Sun."

Tamra snorted. "I wouldn't put it past you. You three have been jumping out of the frying pan and into the fire since I first saw your angelic little faces on YouTube last week."

Clarice looked at Aria archly. "She thinks I'm kidding, doesn't she?"

Aria glanced at Tamra playfully. "We could tell her we have it on good authority that the Sun isn't actually hot."

Clarice smirked, glancing sideways at Tamra, who had a sickly grin on her face. "I don't think she'll believe us."

"It really isn't hot," Arturiel assured Tamra confidently. "It's just a myth created to keep humans from trying to go there."

Tamra stared steadily at the new archangel. "Even if it isn't hot now, it will be when they get there, mark my words."

"Damn right it will be," Clarice crowed with a sly grin. "'Cause *we're* so freaking hot!"

That seemed to be the last straw for Arturiel. She burst out laughing so hard that she had to hang on to Calypso for support. Lexi joined in, gazing at Clarice as if she were a favorite superhero.

When the laughter subsided, Tamra inspected Arturiel with a practiced eye. "Arturiel, I probably have a shirt that'll work for you until I can make something to your measurements. Follow me, and we'll get you fixed up."

Arturiel's shirt hadn't been torn to the point that the front detached, but it was close.

"Thanks, Tamra," Arturiel said gratefully, smiling warmly at the rest of them as she followed Tamra.

Clarice eyed the other three appreciatively. "I suppose we should get going. Four hotties ready to party it up on the sun."

"Arturiel, there's a portal to our cabin on the front lawn," Aria told the new archangel, knowing she could hear them from the back room. "I'm guessing you plan to do some flying now that you have wings. Make sure to go with our parents in case you run into trouble. I know you're an archangel now, but better safe than sorry."

"Thanks, Aria," Arturiel said brightly, her voice charged with excited anticipation.

They walked out to the yard and turned to face each other.

"Portal?" Clarice asked, raising an eyebrow and looking up at the sun.

"Portal," Calypso agreed, opening a portal to the surface of the sun.

Brilliant light flared out, but there was no inferno of heat scorching the Earth—or their clothes.

"So far, so good," Clarice said cheerfully, gazing at the shining portal eagerly. "At least it didn't instantly cook the planet."

Aria went through first, her drive to protect Calypso pushing her to scout the alien landscape. She looked down in surprise when she felt soft soil beneath her toes. No longer requiring shoes had been a nice perk of being invulnerable. The ground glowed under her feet, sinking only a little beneath her diminished weight. The luminous soil stretched as far as even *her* eyes could see.

"Either the gravity on the sun is a lot weaker than it should be, or angels are immune," she commented, digging her toes into the soil curiously.

Looking up, she marveled at the enormous ropes of magnetism arcing through the sun's atmosphere. She flew high above the glowing plain, magnetic filaments warping around her as she stared down at the surface. There was a coronal hole not far from their portal, and to the south, she spotted a large sunspot bubbling with magnetic froth.

The others joined her, eyes wide with wonder. Aria felt like she was in a dream as she viewed the alien landscape in awe.

Clarice looked around, a small smile on her face. "The sun's a big place. It might take a while to find the Lore Boar."

Aria absently twined a strand of hair around her finger as she thought. "Grodek said Eden was constantly moving. What if that's because the sunspots and coronal holes are some kind of entrance to an inner world? Sunspots are constantly opening and decaying."

Clarice held up a hand. "Wait a minute, Grodek told us to bring sunscreen when he sent us to talk to the former demons. He obviously knew Eden was here, so why bother sending us to ask Krajen and the others?"

Aria's eyebrows shot up. "Hmm... that's a good point. I wonder if there's something preventing him from giving us direct answers."

Calypso frowned. "Perhaps so."

Aria took Calypso's hand and was rewarded with a warm smile. "We can figure out what's going on with Grodek later."

Clarice gleefully thrust her fist into the sky. "Let's go explore some sunspots."

The four of them shot toward the nearest sunspot, its edges resembling colossal Grand Canyons collapsing into a gaping hole. Burning with curiosity, Aria plunged in.

The reality was nothing like she had imagined. Rolling green hills and enormous oceans spread out tens of thousands of miles beneath the sun's outer shell. Mountains soared dozens of miles high, their peaks stabbing into the air, jagged and rocky.

Clarice whistled, gazing into the distance. "I guess it's the hollow Earth theory, but for the sun—a whole world hiding inside our star."

"A freaking *huge*-ass world," Lexi added in amazement. "Isn't the sun a million times bigger than Earth?"

Aria nodded. "The outer shell is. However, we dropped down about eighty or ninety thousand miles, so it's a bit smaller here."

Lexi spun in place, eagerly taking in the alien world. "Where should we start?"

Calypso scanned the horizon. "We are meant to be searching for a garden," she said thoughtfully. "Let us conduct a swift survey of the world and gain some sense of what exists here."

"Good idea," Clarice said, congratulating her with a quick hug. "Sorry, Calypso—I just realized I haven't gotten a hug from you in almost four hours."

Calypso smiled, caressing Clarice's cheek affectionately. "Never apologize for hugs. I do not believe I could ever have enough of them."

"I hear that," Clarice agreed, moving on to Aria with a grin and pulling her into a hug. She held her for several seconds, and Aria realized this wasn't just affection—something was wrong.

"What's the matter, Clarice?" Aria whispered, holding her tightly and stroking her hair tenderly.

Clarice trembled in her arms, a sob escaping as she attempted to speak.

"Shhh," Aria whispered soothingly. "We're here for you. I'll always be here for you, Clarice—no matter how crazy things get. I love you."

Aria held her sobbing sister until the weeping storm subsided.

"I'm sorry, Aria," Clarice said thickly. "It all just hit me like an eviction notice written in lipstick while I was admiring the beauty here. They tortured children so they could turn angels into demons. I saw it in her thoughts—the endless torment and anguish. Innocent angels like Arturiel. It happened across the entire world, and they've been stuck in that neverending nightmare for thousands of years. What kind of god would allow this to happen to their angels? What kind of god lets demons defile angels and turn them into abominations?"

Calypso flew over and wrapped her arms around the two of them, pulsing with love and sympathy. "I am so sorry, Clarice," Calypso whispered sadly, kissing her forehead. "I do not know what led to this horror, but I promise you this: I shall set it right and never allow it to happen again. I only wish I could take your pain away, dear one."

Lexi slowly drew closer, her eyes full of sympathy. She tenderly caressed Clarice's cheek, wiping away her tears. "I don't think there is a god, Clarice. I think it's just all of us—one giant mind unable to comprehend individual suffering on a small timeline. Something arranged for us to fix the sickness in our collective mind. *We* are the cure. We're going to fix this mindfuck and make everything right again. I promise."

Aria smiled at Lexi, impressed by her abstract reasoning. She had the equivalent of an eighth-grade education, making it easy to forget the intelligent mind hiding behind that beautiful face. Captivity had given her plenty of time to weigh the world's injustices and reflect on the harsh realities of life.

Clarice took a deep breath, soaking in their love. "Thank you. I knew that was going to surface soon. It's been writhing under the edge of my awareness for a while now."

"You'll be dealing with mine soon enough," Aria warned, giving her a peck on the forehead. "But I know you'll be there for me. We've got each other for all eternity."

Clarice closed her eyes as a few more tears leaked out. "Aria, I'm so lucky to have you. Eternity seems less daunting with you by my side."

"Not just Aria," Lexi said firmly. "I'll be right here with you, every step of the way. As will Calypso. You'll never face anything alone."

Calypso's arms tightened around her in unspoken agreement.

Clarice smiled tremulously. "Okay. I think I'm ready. Let's go find a boar."

Aria squeezed her tightly once more and let go. She knew Clarice's mischievous nature and humor masked a deeply compassionate and vulnerable soul. The horrors they'd witnessed this past week would have crushed them if they hadn't had each other to lean on. She made a mental note to give Clarice more time to decompress later; she clearly needed to talk through some of those traumatic memories.

"We're going to talk more when we get back," Aria promised.

Clarice nodded, smiling back with pure love.

"I see something," Calypso announced, pointing at a speck in the distant sky.

"Let's go investigate," Clarice suggested, smiling eagerly as she shot forward like a falling star, streaking through the sky.

Aria flashed to her side, flying shoulder to shoulder.

"It's a floating island," Clarice breathed in awe. "Guess it never heard of the law of gravity."

The underbelly of the floating isle was a jagged canvas of rock. From its periphery, thunderous waterfalls plunged, weaving a shimmering, vaporous curtain below. The top was a canvas of untamed, kaleidoscopic life. Hues of lavender, crimson, sapphire, and emerald adorned strange, flowering trees—a living tapestry woven from every color in the spectrum.

At the center of the enormous sky island stood a tree that staggered the mind with its immensity. It was the size of a mountain range, towering hundreds of miles into the air. Small huts and crude buildings dotted the ground around the base near the center.

Clarice whistled. "If this isn't Eden, it must be Eden's older sibling. That is one big-ass tree."

"Big-Ass Tree of Life," Aria corrected with a grin.

Clarice grinned back, all signs of her meltdown gone.

Aria began descending toward the crude city. "Shall we go see if the locals know where the Lore Boar hangs out?"

"Oink oink," Clarice replied with an exaggerated snort.

In the center of the primitive city was a clearing where a circle of stones stood—an intact version of Stonehenge, Aria decided. People walked along dirt roads, dressed in colorful garments that seemed designed more for beauty than practicality. Their clothing left plenty of bronze skin visible on bodies that looked sculpted for Olympic altars. At first, Aria thought they were angels, but as they descended, she saw human meridians—at least, partially human.

"I think these are hybrid angels," Aria said as they landed in the stone circle.

Several people noticed their arrival. A small cluster of locals cautiously approached.

"Hello!" Clarice called out cheerfully, waving with a friendly smile. "I don't suppose you speak English?"

The puzzled stares were answer enough.

Aria extended a tendril of energy to the thought node of the nearest woman—a tall blond with a lithe figure and brilliant blue eyes.

"I thought the angels were only myths!" Zerune thought in amazement.

Aria frowned, wondering how the woman's thoughts translated to English in her head. The thoughts were just impressions, but her mind seemed to be reconstructing them into a structured language she could understand, as if her brain had a companion app for translation.

"Hello, Zerune," Aria thought to the woman, eliciting a startled squawk. Zerune took a step back, watching Aria warily. *"My name's Aria. We mean you no harm."*

Aria used her aura to send an accompanying wave of radiance with her words.

Zerune's eyes widened as she felt the powerful flood of euphoric warmth wash over her.

"It's nice to meet you, Zerune," Aria thought, offering her a friendly smile. *"We're from a place called Earth, searching for something called the Lore Boar. Do you know where we can find it?"*

"You're speaking into my mind?" Zerune asked uncertainly.

"Yes. We don't speak your language, so we'll need to communicate this way," Aria explained. They weren't words, exactly, but the intent behind thoughts.

Zerune frowned, trying to grasp the idea of multiple languages.

Clarice smiled wryly. "I guess if they've been here for who knows how long, it's no wonder they don't even know what a foreign language is."

Zerune's eyes flickered with comprehension when she heard them speaking English.

"You are from a place called Earth?" Zerune asked in confusion. *"Is it up in the sky?"*

Aria nearly facepalmed, realizing they were about to spawn a new round of religions with claims of being from somewhere beyond the heavens. She suppressed a sigh and patiently sent mental images of the cities and humans populating Earth. She showed the memory of their journey via portal to the surface of the sun and the inner world beneath the light shell.

Zerune stared in amazement as the memories flooded her mind. When the thought of a sentient boar flashed across the mental link, Zerune's eyes lit up with recognition.

"It lives inside the tree," Zerune informed her, frowning dubiously. *"It's a very... unusual creature."*

"How so?" Clarice asked curiously.

"It's very... flatulent," Zerune admitted, making a face, *"and kind of disgusting. It doesn't make very much sense most of the time."*

"We were told it responds well to delicious foods and entertainment," Clarice said. *"Is there any truth to that myth?"*

"Oh, absolutely," Zerune chuckled ruefully. *"It's very vocal about substandard food and music."*

More people had gathered around Zerune, gawking at the angels in amazement. When Zerune laughed, the other Edenites stared at her in confusion.

"Would you mind explaining to the others who we are and what we're doing here?" Aria asked, casting a friendly smile at the growing crowd.

"I'll try," Zerune responded dubiously. *"It will be difficult to explain in a way they can understand."*

"I'll take care of it," Calypso announced, her eyes scanning the crowd. A moment later, golden threads of energy unfurled and connected to the Edenites. She transferred a condensed stream of memories and impressions, just as Aria had done.

The Edenites froze as the visions ended, then gazed at them in reverence.

"Having more of your neighbors understand what we are and where we come from should make it easier for you to explain matters to the others," Calypso told her gently, smiling at the curious gathering.

She pushed her aura outward, filling the hybrids with radiance. Gasps and tears spread through the crowd as they basked in her aura.

Clarice winked at Calypso. "Let's go see what the Lore Boar thinks of divine music."

Calypso winked back, earning a delighted giggle from Clarice. Calypso's personality had continued to soften since regaining her memories of mortality, growing more nuanced and mature.

They rose into the air and followed a wide path leading from the city to a vast fissure in the trunk of the Tree of Life. The colossal white surface gleamed with fine veins of light that formed intricate patterns across its face.

They landed at the opening and entered the illuminated corridor. It wound deep into the Tree before opening into a cavern the size of a stadium. Smaller trees grew along the walls, their white fruit glowing like lanterns. In the center of the chamber sat a massive, house-sized boar, its crossed legs dangling over the edge of an even larger stump. Its tusks curved upward from a broad snout, and its intelligent blue eyes watched them through a pair of spectacles with curiosity. Other creatures sat in a semicircle before it, as if attending a lecture.

"I guess we found it," Clarice murmured in fascination. "It's *huge*."

Shock coursed through Aria as she stared at the beast. There was something so *familiar* about it, a powerful connection to the giant boar she couldn't make sense of.

"Greetings, creators of the light," it boomed, its voice shaking the trees. "It has been some time since I've seen any of your children."

"Hello," Calypso greeted it with a curious smile. "You speak our tongue?"

"I speak all languages," it replied. A sudden blast of flatulence thundered through the cave, causing a few glowing fruits to fall from their branches.

Aria glanced warningly at Clarice, but it was futile. Her sister's shoulders were shaking as she desperately covered her mouth. At Aria's glare, Clarice lost what little restraint she had and laughed hysterically. Calypso watched with a patient smile while Lexi covered her own mouth to hide a grin. Just when it seemed Clarice would recover, another thunderous blast of flatulence erupted from the Lore Boar's backside, sending her into another fit of uncontrollable giggles.

"Sorry about Clarice," Aria apologized to the giant boar with a resigned sigh. "She's still an adolescent at heart."

"I'm accustomed to this reaction," it boomed gravely. "Many in Eden react similarly."

Calypso looked at it curiously. "Do you know why we have come to see you?"

"Do *you* know why you've come to see me?" it countered, raising one large brow.

"Primarily because Grodek instructed us to seek you out," Calypso replied, her expression growing thoughtful. "However, I have questions which I am told you may be able to answer."

It lowered its head to peer at them sternly. "What have you brought in exchange for these answers?"

Calypso reached into a tear in the air and withdrew her harp. "A song, if it pleases you."

It studied the instrument, its eyes narrowing. "With that harp?"

Calypso hesitated. "If that is all right? I can use another, if you would prefer."

It closed its eyes and let out a gusty sigh of relief that blew the leaves off some of the trees. "All things must come to an end," it breathed in a quieter voice. "Play for me, Seraph."

Calypso stared at it in concern. "Will this cause you harm?"

It smiled, weary but serene. "It will complete me."

Calypso hesitated, studying it with worried eyes. She was clearly seeing something more than Aria as she inspected the boar.

Aria activated her spiritual sight and gasped at the dizzying array of nodes and energy lines connected to the enormous creature. It looked like a microchip connected to uncountable energy distribution points. A large number of the points were directly linked to Aria.

"Please, Seraph," it implored, its tired eyes filled with longing. "Play for me."

Calypso nodded slowly, compassion in her gaze. She lifted the harp and began to play, her fingers coaxing out a melody of pure light. The Lore Boar closed its eyes, and the world itself seemed to listen.

The room reverberated like a bell with each plucked string. Power flooded the space as the glowing walls of the tree blazed with light. Calypso began singing, her voice intertwining with the harp's melodies, and the room became a cyclone of power, spinning around them like a giant maelstrom of light. Aria knew if they'd been lesser angels, the power would have scoured their immortal bodies to dust.

The beauty and power of the song surpassed anything she had ever heard Calypso play. She dropped to her knees and closed her eyes as the transcendent music reforged her spirit. Her nodes expanded, connecting her to distant repositories of knowledge and light. The song flailed reality until the room became nothing but overwhelming emotional essence.

Calypso blazed brighter than the sun as she once again rewrote reality. Aria felt as though her soul had been completely saturated by the sublime power raging in the maelstrom.

As the final notes died away, she opened her eyes. Calypso stood before her harp, golden tears spilling down her cheeks. Where the Lore Boar had once sat, a golden tin whistle now rested on the stump. Aria felt an immediate connection to it—as if something long missing from her soul had just called her name.

Clarice rushed to Calypso, pulling her into a comforting embrace. Distracted by the new divine instrument, Aria hadn't realized how distraught the Seraph was. Calypso trembled, golden tears streaking her face, sorrow radiating from her in waves as she buried herself against Clarice's shoulder.

Aria stepped closer and laid a hand on Calypso's shoulder. “What is it?”

“I destroyed it,” Calypso sobbed, her voice heavy with remorse.

“No, you didn't,” Aria assured her gently. “It's still here.”

Aria flew up to the stump and stood before the tin whistle. The call grew stronger as she drew closer. When her hand grasped it, she felt a shockwave ripple through her fractured soul. An inverted boom shook the sun, shaking the Tree of Life like a sapling, as power flooded into her. Beaming with indescribable joy, she returned to the others. Calypso stared at her hopefully, her tears slowing to a trickle.

“It transformed,” Aria explained, unable to restrain the brilliant smile lighting her face. “It was always a part of my soul. I don't know how my soul was divided, but it's *finally* whole again. I feel so *amazing*.”

Clarice stared at her, wide-eyed, lips parted in wonder. “Oh, Aria... you're whole.”

Aria flashed Clarice a radiant smile, then lifted the tin whistle to her lips and began playing the melody of her soul. Bittersweet power washed throughout the room as her divine instrument manipulated and warped the fabric of reality. Golden light bathed her and the other angels as she played, binding them together ever tighter, linking their souls with an ethereal bond. She could feel their emotions as if they were her own, their hopes and fears—their love.

They stared at her in wonder as the bond took form. Lexi's eyes widened, finally sensing the intensity of their love for her. Never again would she doubt that she was loved. A deep wound in Lexi's soul filled with light and sealed shut as she became conclusively convinced of her own worth.

Clarice grinned mischievously at Aria. “So, you've been a Gemini this whole time? I'm going to start calling you my little piggy.”

Aria glared at her threateningly. “Not unless you want to go to market.”

Clarice threw her head back and laughed, filling the air with joy as her aura arced outward. She surged toward Aria, pulling her into a loving embrace. Tears welled in Aria's eyes as she felt the depth of Clarice's love through the bond, burning like a supernova. How could anyone love her so much?

She could feel the same love from Calypso, a fierce devotion that stunned her with its intensity. They had only known each other for a few days, but there was an unseen connection hinting that their shared history had outlived the stars.

"How much did we evolve?" Aria asked softly, studying her angel family fondly.

Physically, Aria couldn't see much of a difference in the others. The only visible change was a steady glow emanating from beneath their skin, softer than the incandescent blaze that occurred during battle. The less visible changes were far more dramatic. She could now feel a direct link to all the realms, including the higher light realms.

"I think we can travel to all of the realms now," she noted absently. "I also feel a connection to the intuitive knowledge base Calypso described. I think I speak every language now, too."

"It's so weird seeing you like this," Clarice breathed, her eyes wide. "It's like you've been hiding part of yourself all these years, and now I can finally see it. Your power's jumped through the roof. Makes me wonder if there's a missing piece of me out there, too."

Lexi stared at them with a wondering smile. "I think I could find any of you blindfolded now. You feel like part of me."

Clarice grinned impudently. "Like a wart."

Lexi laughed, eyeing Clarice affectionately. "I can even feel your emotions."

"Found you," a malevolent voice growled in satisfaction. "And you even led me to Eden."

Aria wrinkled her nose as an overpowering stench of demon rot filled the air. Across the chamber stood a winged demon lord—seven feet tall, with ram's horns curling from a scaly head and legs bent backward into hooves. Bright red eyes with slit pupils gleamed triumphantly as he smiled cruelly.

"You found us, alright," Clarice agreed, wrinkling her nose and fanning the air. "Dude, you stink worse than a dead fish in a hot tub."

"I like an angel with spirit," the demon lord purred, his cruel smile widening. "You'll be so much more fun to break."

"Did you really just say that you like a girl with spirit?" Clarice demanded in disgust. "Is that line in the villain starter pack? Because that's cliché, even for a snake-eyed goat kisser."

The demon flashed across the room, his hand lunging for her throat. His eyes went wide as Clarice caught his wrist mid-strike and hurled him into the wall, leaving a demon-shaped crater.

“Do we want to offer to turn it back?” Clarice asked Calypso reluctantly. “Or can I just kill it now?”

The demon lord rose, eyes narrowed. He gestured, and a thick black mist filled the air. The reek of agonite struck Aria's nostrils, and she immediately stopped breathing. The demon smirked as he advanced, but Calypso plucked one sharp note from her harp, and the mist vanished in a flash. The demon lord screamed, clutching his head as the sound of the divine instrument tore through his soul.

Aria blurred forward and caught him by the throat. He struggled to break free, but he might as well have been an insect for all the good it did him.

“What the hell *are* you?” he rasped, fear bleeding into his glowing red eyes.

“Not impressed,” Aria told him, fury flooding out of her in a torrent. This *thing* was responsible for the agonite farms. It had just filled the air with the blood of tortured children. She loathed herself for not immediately vaporizing it. “I'm going to make you an offer, and you have one chance to accept it. Do you want to become an angel again?”

His face twisted with hate, his lip curling in disgust. “Fuck you and your god. I’ll be back to feast off your despair as we slowly suck the virtue out of your sanctimonious soul.”

He flickered but failed to vanish, repeatedly trying to teleport out of her grasp. Aria smiled grimly. “Goodbye, Azkar.” She fired a beam of golden light into the core node of his neck. He had time to widen his eyes in terror before the intense beam vaporized him.

“One less demon lord to deal with,” Aria declared, turning back to the others with satisfaction.

“He was one of the original fallen Dominions,” Calypso said with a frown.

“How can you tell?” Lexi asked curiously.

“After seeing Arturiel’s meridian bandwidth, I had some notion of what to expect from a demon lord who had once been an archangel, but his were vastly greater,” Calypso explained, sighing regretfully. “I had hoped we might save him.”

Aria winced. “I'm sorry. I should've asked you before vaporizing him. Maybe you could've changed him whether he wanted it or not.”

Calypso smiled reassuringly. “I am not second-guessing your choice. I am fairly certain he would have made a dreadful angel regardless. Arturiel said that two Dominions became demon lords. Which means there is still one more somewhere.”

Lexi walked over to inspect the demon-shaped crater in the wall. "How do you think he found us?" she asked, tentatively running her hand along the luminous heartwood.

"We *did* just play two divine instruments," Calypso pointed out thoughtfully. "We evolved considerably as well. Our nodes were forming a great many connections to other realms. I would imagine that caused rather a great deal of noise."

"It made a *lot* of noise," Grodek growled, appearing atop the tree stump. His scaly skin was blue, rather than the red she remembered. "You'll have some celestial visitors before long."

Aria eyed him warily. "Will they attack us?"

"Unlike that jackass you just atomized, the higher triads can sense the power of divine instruments," Grodek said disdainfully. He barked an ugly laugh. "Those worthless politicians will be too terrified to attack you outright. They'll try guile, or a metaphorical dagger in the dark. They want those instruments and would sell their own Seraph to get them—not that it matters; only a Seraph can play them."

"How did you know part of my soul was here?" Aria asked, feeling a sense of gratitude to the ugly little imp for pushing them to find this place.

"Maybe someday you'll remember," Grodek shrugged indifferently. "Or maybe not."

"So what now?" Lexi asked curiously. "Are two instruments enough?"

Grodek shook his head, his expression sour. "You need the other two instruments if you plan to fix reality. You'll have to find them quickly, too. I'm sure the other Seraphim have finally taken notice of you. They'll be preparing nasty surprises to stop you from changing the status quo. You *definitely* don't want them to find the instruments before you do."

"Is it just me," Clarice asked dryly, "or is it messed up that the ones we have to worry about most are the ones who supposedly stand for truth and justice?"

Grodek sneered. "The only thing they stand for is maintaining their own power. You're dealing with beings who've never felt pain or loss. They're emotionless monsters militaristically obsessed with order and control, and they're terrified of death. You'll find no sympathy, empathy, or grace in the light realms. The only difference between demons and angels is that most demons don't enjoy the suffering they cause."

"Not for long," Calypso said softly, her eyes hard with resolve. "If I must make Seraphim experience mortality in order to understand virtue, then so be it."

Grodek stared at her appraisingly. The way she spoke didn't sound like a threat; it sounded as inexorable as gravity. There was an undercurrent of authority that even the imp seemed to find compelling.

Clarice looked at Grodek hopefully. “I don't suppose you have any ideas of where to look for the other instruments?”

Grodek shrugged. “Earth. They aren't in one piece, though, and nobody knows where all the pieces are. A foolish monk in a cave near the top of Everest has a part of one. Another piece is in Madjack's possession. He's a regular jackass who roams the Rocky Mountains, playing pranks on unsuspecting humans. Just follow the stories of people claiming to see Bigfoot or getting abducted by aliens. After that, you'll just have to find the rest yourselves. If you're lucky, the pieces will have a resonance you can use to find the others.”

Aria stared at the imp curiously. He'd completed an entire conversation without mocking them. Something had changed drastically in his opinion of them since their first meeting. Was it Calypso and her natural innocence that had softened his little demon heart? Then again, he was blue now—maybe he had a friendly twin, and this wasn't even the same imp.

He vanished a moment later, no farewell or final quip.

“Is it my imagination, or has he gotten a lot nicer?” Lexi asked, a small smile playing on her lips.

“I think Calypso won him over,” Aria responded, smiling fondly at Calypso. “It's hard not to love her.”

Calypso returned the smile, her eyes shining with affection. It was strange to think they'd only known her for a little over a week; it already felt like a lifetime.

“Let's check on the family,” Clarice suggested, opening a gateway back to the front lawn of their cabin. “I want to make sure no demon lords have tried to invade while we were gone.”

“Good idea,” Aria agreed, moving quickly toward the gateway. Before she could step through, the edges of the portal warped and twisted, bouncing in place like a bubble about to pop.

“Hey, no free rides,” a petulant voice complained—from the portal itself. “You think I'm just here to cart your butts around for free?”

Aria froze, sharing a startled look with the other angels before turning back to the buoyant gateway.

“Did the gateway just talk to us?” Lexi asked disbelievingly.

“I'm a portal, not a gateway, you troglodyte,” the portal snapped peevishly.

“So... you're sentient?” Aria asked faintly.

"Well, are you talking to me?" the portal shot back. "Are you in the habit of asking self-evident questions?"

"I guess I am," Aria admitted slowly. "This is getting so surreal."

"Hey, portal, we have places to be," Clarice declared imperiously, hands on her hips. "What do you want?"

"I'll settle for some experiences," the portal said slyly. "If you're willing to part with some of your experiences for a little while, you can go through."

Clarice glared at the talking aperture. "Aria, make another portal."

Aria narrowed her eyes, tracing the meridians she needed to form a new portal. "It's got all the connections tied up. I can't open another."

"Then we fly," Clarice decided. "I don't trust this thing even a little. Talking doors never end well. Douglas Adams 101."

"Fine, fine," the portal huffed, its tone edging toward desperation. "You can go through if I can just *look* at your memories. I won't take them."

Aria eyed it doubtfully. "Why do you want them?"

"Do you have any idea how boring it is being a portal?" it whined. "Nothing but travelers whining about distance. I just want a little stimulation."

"I say we fly," Clarice insisted, eyeing the portal distrustfully. "We're essentially trusting that thing to warp reality enough that we can step across insane distances in an instant. If Douglas Adams taught me anything, it's that adding personalities to things like doors and portals always turns out badly."

The portal sighed in defeat. "Okay, I'll just look at *one* memory."

Emily's voice called from the other side. "Are you four coming through, or are you planning to stand there all day?"

They all looked through the portal to see Emily walk out of the cabin and approach the glowing oval.

"Our portal came to life and is bargaining for passage," Clarice told her in exasperation. "Flying seems safer."

Aria grinned. "You fly back—I'm going via portal. I'd rather not lose all my clothes again flying through the sun's corona. We're Cherubim—what's the worst that could happen?"

Clarice snorted. "Now that you put it that way," she said dryly. "Just about anything."

Aria flashed her a grin and stepped through. On the other side, she turned and waved. "See? No problem."

Clarice glared at the portal, clearly arguing with herself. Calypso patted her shoulder and walked through, then turned, waiting patiently.

"*Fine*," Clarice grumbled, gesturing for Lexi to go ahead.

Lexi hesitated, eyeing Clarice with concern. "You sure? I can fly with you if you'd prefer."

Clarice sighed and shook her head. "It's too late now. Might as well see what happens."

Lexi frowned, but went through and turned to wait for Clarice expectantly.

Clenching her jaw, Clarice stepped across the threshold. After exiting, she turned to stare at the portal distrustfully.

Emily studied them curiously. "Looks like you four have changed a lot. You feel... immense. And you're glowing."

Clarice turned to face Emily with a mock glare. "You're looking pretty fat too, Mom."

Emily gave Clarice a long-suffering look and shook her head. "I see you haven't changed *that* much. Did you find the Lore Boar?"

Clarice immediately dissolved into a fit of giggles, bent over with her hands on her knees.

"I take it there's a story there," Emily said dryly.

Clarice straightened, gesturing grandly toward Aria. "I present to you—the Lore Boar!" she announced before dissolving into giggles again. "This little piggy went to market."

Emily sighed with a rueful shake of her head. "She's lost it, I see."

Taking pity on Emily, Calypso quickly explained the encounter. Emily stared at Aria curiously, clearly sensing her daughter's increased presence.

"The price is paid, the contract complete," the portal declared formally, then dissolved.

"I want pancakes," Aria said suddenly, turning imploring eyes on her mother. "Please? I can help."

Emily stared at her, nonplussed. "Aria, you don't have a stomach. What would you do with the pancakes?"

"Can I paint my room black?" Clarice asked hopefully. "I want to try the gothic look for a while."

"What on Earth has gotten into you two?" Emily demanded.

"I want to get a nose piercing," Lexi declared eagerly. "Do you think it hurts?"

Calypso frowned, concern creasing her brow as she looked at the three of them. "Aria, how old are you?"

"How could you forget my age?" Aria asked, sounding injured. "I'm almost eight."

22 – ADOLESCENCE AGAIN

"Uh oh," Emily groaned wearily. "I don't think I can handle adolescence again."

Lexi looked down at Clarice shyly. "Hey, Clarice, do you wanna go to the movies with me?"

"How old are you, Clarice?" Calypso asked patiently.

Clarice rolled her eyes dramatically. "Still thirteen. Did you think it was going to change overnight?" She looked Lexi up and down. "Sure, I'll go to the movies with you."

"And how old are you, Lexi?" Emily asked tiredly.

Lexi grinned proudly. "I just turned fourteen a few days ago. I'm old enough to go on dates now."

"Sure you are," Emily muttered, pressing a palm to her forehead.

Eric blurred out to join them. "What's going on out here? Because it sounds pretty weird, so far."

Calypso frowned. "It would seem that portal scrambled their memories. We must find some way to undo it."

Aria tugged on Emily's sleeve, her eyes wide and hopeful. "So, can we make pancakes, Mom?"

"Sure, honey," Emily replied, her voice troubled.

Aria let out an enormous blast of flatulence, and her voice suddenly boomed loud enough to shake the cabin's windows. "Their minds have been trapped in childhood objects. Find the objects and destroy them to free their memories."

Calypso turned to Emily and Eric. "This must be the fragment of Aria's soul that inhabited the Lore Boar." She turned to Aria, pointedly ignoring

Lexi and Clarice, who were rolling on the ground with laughter after Aria's flatulent explosion. "Do you know why that portal became sentient?"

The Lore Boar's voice boomed out of Aria. "The divine instruments are tools for shaping reality. Ripples from their use can affect reality in the world around them."

Calypso narrowed her eyes. "Why did it not affect me?"

Sorrow filled Aria's face. "It only has access to mortal memories. It shied away from your only memories of mortality."

Calypso nodded in understanding, receiving a comforting hug from Emily.

Calypso looked at Eric and Emily hopefully. "Do you still have any of their things from childhood?"

Eric rubbed the back of his neck sheepishly. "I always meant to donate them. They're boxed up in the attic."

Calypso opened a portal into the living room of their old home. "Show me."

Eric led her upstairs and pulled down the attic ladder. Moments later, Calypso opened another portal to the lawn, whisking every box out of storage in seconds. Aria waited nearby with Emily, but Lexi and Clarice were missing. Calypso followed their new spirit bond and found them behind a tree, their lips locked together.

"Well, that did not take long," Calypso muttered, her cheeks flushing as the empathic bond between their souls conveyed everything.

When the boxes were piled on the lawn, all three adult angels turned expectantly toward Aria.

Aria pointed at a pink stuffed animal and boomed, "The elephant feels connected. Destroy it to restore her mind."

Emily hesitated. "Clarice gave this to her when she started going downhill. She always kept it with her, right up until Calypso healed her. If I ever run into that portal again, it's going to be sorry." Emily sighed sadly, then vaporized the elephant. They glanced expectantly at Aria.

Aria furrowed her brows. "Why are our old toys on the lawn?"

Emily studied her intently. "How old are you?"

Aria narrowed her eyes. "Is that a trick question? I'm twenty-five, Mom. You have perfect recall as an angel, so I know you didn't forget."

Aria's parents sighed with relief, confusing her even more.

Aria scowled at them. "What's going on? And why in the hell are Clarice and Lexi making out like teenagers?"

Calypso took her hand soothingly. "You were trapped within a memory of yourself as a nine-year-old." She blinked, feeling jealousy burning through their bond. It seemed so unlike Aria. Did she feel this way when Clarice was with *her*? "The memory trap was bound to one of your childhood toys. When we destroyed it, you returned to normal. Do you know what Clarice's favorite possession was when she was thirteen?"

Aria flushed as the bond continued to feed them increasingly intimate sensations. "She's thirteen right now?"

Calypso nodded through her own blushes. "Yes, and Lexi is fourteen. What did Clarice treasure most at thirteen?"

"Her phone," Aria replied dryly. "She also liked the stationery kit with the wax stamps. If I didn't love Lexi so much, I'd vaporize her right now."

Calypso tilted her head, studying the crimson-haired angel uneasily as Eric and Emily rummaged through the pile. "Are you all right?"

Aria shrugged, offering a tight smile. "I'm good."

Calypso raised a doubting eyebrow as the bond continued to burn with jealousy. Her anxiety spiked as she began questioning whether Aria really was okay with a three-way relationship.

"Hey, none of that now," Aria said gently, stepping closer to Calypso and pulling her into a soft embrace. "It's different with you. I don't know why—it just is."

Calypso felt the truth of her words resonate through their bond. She let out a relieved sigh, smiling into Aria's golden eyes. "Very well. So long as you truly are content with our arrangement."

Aria smiled warmly. "More than okay—it'd feel wrong without you."

There was a flash as Emily vaporized the stamp kit.

Ears burning, Aria shook her head. "I don't think that was it—unless she decided to keep fooling around after her memory was restored."

Emily eyed the two of them curiously. "Why are you two blushing so much?"

Calypso cleared her throat, fighting to keep an embarrassing moan from escaping. "Our souls formed an emotional bond in Eden. We are able to feel one another's emotions and, apparently, physical sensations as well."

"Oh," Emily glanced back toward the large tree where the sounds of kissing continued. "That's either going to be a lot of fun or really embarrassing."

Eric snapped his fingers. "I thought her guitar was her favorite object at thirteen."

Aria snapped her fingers. "Right! I wasn't even thinking of instruments."

Emily hesitated. "Are we really going to destroy her first guitar? She really loves that guitar."

Calypso opened a small portal into the cabin and pulled the guitar through. "Let us try severing the strings first and see whether that proves sufficient."

She quickly removed the strings and let Emily vaporize them.

"What the hell?" Clarice gasped in confusion. "Lexi?"

"What?" Lexi asked, her voice full of insecurity and dread.

"Were we just making out?" Clarice demanded.

"Yep," Lexi replied warmly. "You're an amazing kisser for a thirteen-year-old. Been practicing?"

"Thirteen?" Clarice repeated in a mystified voice.

"Just go along with it for the moment," Calypso sent the thought. She quickly explained the last hour's events to a shocked Clarice. *"Finding something belonging to Lexi is likely to be the most difficult, so she may remain trapped in her fourteen-year-old mental state for some time."*

Clarice spoke gently. "Let's slow down a little, okay, Lexi? I don't want to ruin things by moving too fast."

Lexi's face burned with shame. "Okay."

"None of that," Clarice said firmly. She pulled Lexi forward, kissed her again, and released her with a playful smile. "I just mean slow down a little and get to know each other more. Okay?"

Lexi smiled back, her rejection forgotten. "Okay."

Her voice burning with interest, Clarice asked, "Lexi, what's your favorite possession?"

Lexi blushed and looked down at her feet. "It's silly."

Clarice lifted Lexi's chin and brushed a stray hair behind her ear. "I'm all about silly. So? What is it?"

Lexi smiled shyly. "It's a fictional book I reread once a month. It's about a goddess disguised as a girl who rescues another girl from her horrible parents and takes her on adventures all over the world."

Clarice kissed Lexi's forehead sadly. "That sounds pretty amazing. Where do you keep it? Is it on a bookshelf in your room or something?"

Lexi shuddered. "God, no—my dad would freak out if he ever found it. I keep it hidden under a floorboard."

Calypso opened a portal to the house from Lexi's memory, and she and Aria stepped through. Using her spiritual sight, Calypso quickly found the hidden compartment, and Aria lifted the board and retrieved the book.

Aria flipped it open. "I'm going to scan this to memory so she still has a copy."

Calypso nodded as Aria quickly flipped through each page, adding them to her endless memory banks before vaporizing it.

Aria smiled sadly. "That's that. We'll have to find her another copy somewhere."

Calypso took Aria's hand and squeezed it. "I'm curious now. You'll have to read it to me later."

Aria returned her squeeze, smiling. "Sounds like a date, then."

Footsteps sounded in the hallway. A balding man in his fifties entered, a gun trembling in his hands. His eyes bulged at the sight of two angels.

"You were Lexi's father," Aria said coldly, her meridians flaring with violent light. "The one who sold her to traffickers."

The man bleated in terror. "I did my Hail Marys! I've been forgiven! Jesus forgave me!"

"He might have," Aria snarled, "but *I* haven't."

Calypso laid a restraining hand on Aria's arm. "I believe you should bring him with us."

Aria glanced quickly at Calypso and saw the steely glint in her eyes. She nodded, casually snatching the gun from the man's hands and crushing it. A loud pop echoed as several bullets exploded in her grip.

She glared, fury feeding her light until she shone incandescently. "You're coming with us, Henry."

He tried to back away, but she flashed forward, grabbing his arm and hauling him toward the portal. "There's a special place in hell for parents like you, Henry."

"Mercy! Have mercy!" he begged pathetically as Aria dragged him through the portal.

Fury twisting her features, Aria growled, "Like you had mercy on Lexi? Is that the kind of mercy you want?"

His legs gave out, and Aria towed him across the ground, ignoring his whimpered prayers.

"What have you got there?" Clarice asked eagerly from where she and Lexi stood with Emily and Eric.

Aria released Henry and he collapsed into a sniveling ball of poor life choices. "We thought our goddess of the forsaken might have an opinion about this miserable bastard," she replied darkly.

Pitiless gazes stared down at the man from six pairs of angelic eyes. Lexi stepped forward, her face a mask of loathing. "Hello, Dad. Did you get my college tuition paid for yet?"

Henry gaped at the sight of his daughter. She stood in all her angelic glory, both sets of wings arched out, her golden gaze burning into his terrified eyes with disgust. She glared down, on a knife's edge of obliterating him. Calypso felt Lexi relive the horrors of her childhood, then the hell she had endured after being sold off to a pedophile. After a moment of intense struggle, she finally turned her face away in disgust. "He's not worth the stain on my soul."

"Fuck that," Clarice snarled, flashing a brilliant white as rage suffused her meridians. A beam of light shot into the man, and he was gone.

Lexi staggered, then flew into Clarice's arms, sobbing bitterly for her stolen childhood. Clarice held her tightly, wings folded around her, whispering soft words as she pulsed with love through their shared bond.

Eric stood, shell-shocked. "Clarice doesn't play around."

"Good," Emily growled, her voice burning with quiet fury. "If she hadn't done it, *I* would have."

"Or me," Aria added grimly.

Calypso felt a tremor ripple through her psychic web—one she recognized instantly. A node tied to her had just suffered trauma. Without hesitation, she opened a portal and stepped through.

* * *

Protective instincts flaring, Aria shot after Calypso.

"What's going on?" she asked, scanning the crowded university campus.

Her nose wrinkled in disgust when the stench of demons filled her nostrils. She blurred toward a nearby walled dumpster enclosure and ripped the gates off their hinges, tossing them aside. Two demons had Jason pinned to the wall. The larger one—nearly seven feet tall—was choking the life out of him. Jason's face was red, his eyes bulging.

Aria fired a beam that vaporized the demon's hand and part of his forearm. Jason collapsed, coughing violently, as both demons whirled to face her.

Aria smiled brightly. "What do we have here? A couple of bullies."

The demons stared in dawning horror at her golden eyes and nested wings; they were pinned with no escape.

"If you try to run, I'll vaporize you before you can say *Beelzebub*," Aria warned conversationally. "It's time to start talking. Why were you attacking Jason?"

The smaller one licked his lips nervously. Behind Aria, students were already gathering, phones raised. Fortunately, Calypso drew most of their attention as she walked slowly across the quad.

Aria connected to their thought nodes. No need to make them talk when she could make them *think*.

"She's going to kill us either way. There's no point in talking."

"You have two options," Aria informed them calmly. "You can answer my questions and live, with the option to become angels again, or... you can die right now."

"What's she talking about? That's impossible."

"You two stink, but I've smelled worse, so I don't think you're unredeemable," Aria said brusquely. "Do you want to be angels again?"

The taller demon watched her warily, not speaking. Fortunately, he didn't have to.

"This must be some kind of trick. What kind of sick angel would use the hope of being redeemed as leverage to make us talk? Does she think we were born yesterday?"

"I want to be an angel again," the shorter demon blurted weakly.

"That's impossible, you idiot," the taller demon growled disdainfully. "She's taunting us."

"Calypso, I believe both of them would like to be redeemed," Aria announced, never taking her eyes from the demons. "You'll need to regrow the arm on the tall one, though—I vaporized it to stop him from choking Jason."

Calypso quickly connected to the vortex near the demons' navels, then flashed into brilliant light as she burned out a part of their spirit. The crowd of students flinched back from her sudden radiance in shock.

The two former demons gaped as the darkness drained from their meridians, replaced by a flood of radiance. Silver tears ran down their cheeks as the emotional overload slammed into them.

Aria moved past them and pulled Jason to his feet. He was still struggling with his windpipe, which had been partially crushed by the demon's powerful grip.

Aria lifted and carried him to Calypso. "Jason needs healing."

Calypso sang three quick words of power. Jason inhaled sharply, relief flooding his features as his crushed windpipe reformed and the bruises faded.

"Thank you, Aria and Calypso," Jason panted gratefully. "I thought I was a goner. I guess I really *can* just pray to you if I'm in trouble."

Aria snorted. "It's not prayer, you goose. And she didn't hear you—she felt your distress."

Jason's gaze shifted to the two trembling figures nearby. "Did she really just turn those demons into angels?"

Aria nodded, a pleased smile on her face. "She did. I'm glad they were redeemable; we killed a demon lord earlier today who wasn't."

Jason's eyebrows shot up. "Wait—you killed a *demon lord*? I thought they were insanely powerful."

Aria shrugged. "Depends on your basis of comparison. The one we killed was supposed to be one of the strongest in existence, but it was like stepping on a bug. More importantly, Calypso discovered how to redeem demons. We've already redeemed close to a hundred."

While Aria spoke to Jason, Calypso continued talking with the newly redeemed angels, who were slowly recovering from the emotional storm that followed their redemption.

Aria raised an eyebrow at the two. "Would you mind telling us why you were attacking Jason?"

Eyes still glowing with joy, Drejan answered quietly. "We were ordered to rough him up to within an inch of his life. They didn't tell us why, but we believe they were trying to send a message to you—that your friends would be harmed if you didn't stay away from The Agency."

Before Drejan even finished speaking, Calypso had opened a portal to the hospital where she had once healed Aria and Clarice, stepping through without a word.

Julia shot to her feet in shock as Calypso emerged from the shimmering gate.

Aria followed quickly, the stench of demon corruption thick in the hospital air. She blurred up to the third floor and grabbed a demon who was aiming a small crossbow over the balcony at Julia. He gasped when she appeared, his finger squeezing the trigger.

Time slowed as Aria overclocked her mind and shot down to the main floor, snatching the crossbow bolt out of the air just before it reached Julia.

She let out a small scream as Aria suddenly appeared in front of her, hovering in the air and holding the bolt inches from her nose.

Aria opened a portal beneath the fleeing demon's feet, dropping him onto the floor in front of her. He sprang back up, attempting to run, but Aria grabbed him by the back of the neck, rooting him to the spot.

Julia stared, eyes wide. "What's happening?"

Calypso scowled, the expression looking strangely out of place on her normally placid features. "Certain demons were ordered to harm those we love. We are ensuring that does not come to pass."

Around them, more than a dozen phones were already filming. Aria sighed. *Great. Another viral headline courtesy of demon-run media.*

She addressed the struggling demon in her grasp. "Would you like to be redeemed as an angel? You reek of corruption, but there might still be something worth saving."

A feral scream was the only reply.

Aria pulled the human mask from his head, revealing a red, scaled demon face with small nubs dotting his head.

Julia gasped, recoiling in horror as murmurs and frightened cries rippled through the spectators.

Aria met Calypso's eyes. "I didn't want to vaporize him while he looked human—not with all these cameras."

Calypso's eyes softened with sadness. "We'll redeem only those who are willing."

Aria didn't hesitate, vaporizing the demon before she could second-guess herself. Startled exclamations erupted from the spectators.

"Who else do we need to check on?" she asked quickly.

Calypso turned to Julia, her voice layered with urgency. "Julia, where are James, Malek, and Latecia? Simply picture their locations in your mind."

Julia gave her a strange look but complied.

Calypso opened three more gateways. Aria sniffed at each one for a whiff of demon stench but smelled nothing. Malek gave her a startled look from his home office when he saw her stick her head through the portal.

"No time to talk," Aria told him shortly. "Just making sure there aren't any demons around. We'll chat soon."

She did the same with James and Latecia before Calypso sealed the portals.

Jason had followed them through the remaining gateway and stood awkwardly in the hospital lobby as curious students on the other side filmed the glowing portal. A few intrepid students poked their hands through experimentally.

Another gateway shimmered open nearby, and Lexi and Clarice stepped through, their wings folding as they scanned the area for danger.

"Do we know who ordered the hit?" Clarice asked, her voice cool and steady.

"No," Aria said, shaking her head. "The two we redeemed at MIT were grunts—no intel on their command structure."

Clarice grunted. "Well, I know someone who can probably point us in the right direction. I think it's time to visit Krajen again. I'll bet he'll have some intel on where to find those responsible."

Calypso smiled down at Julia, her swirling eyes glowing with compassion. "Julia, how many ill children are here at present?"

Julia brightened, hope flashing across her face. "Three. Could you... visit them while you're here?"

"Of course," Calypso agreed, smiling warmly. She opened her spiritual sight, scanning the hospital for the faint, flickering auras of illness, then opened a portal to the nearest one. "Thank you, Julia. And should you ever find yourself in danger again, we shall be there before you know it."

"So I noticed," she replied with a strained smile.

Aria followed Calypso through the portal into a small hospital room. An eight-year-old girl sat in bed, hunched over a phone. She was hairless and pale, her cheeks hollow. Her eyes went wide when a glowing Calypso stepped through the portal.

***

Calypso smiled warmly. "Hello, Melany. Let's get you healed."

Melany's eyes lit up with excitement and awe when she felt the overpowering presence of Calypso's aura wash over her. Calypso walked up to her and sang a few words in the language she now recognized as divine instructions for healing. She no longer required entire songs to heal. She couldn't remember her life as a Seraph yet, but some of her dormant knowledge of how to use her authority had awakened.

Melany glowed brightly for a moment, her eyes growing bright with vitality. Unlike previous healings, which only resulted in removing the illness, she now had a much greater command of her powers. Melany's hair sprouted, spilling down in waves. A moment later, her hollow cheeks filled out with a healthy glow.

The door burst open and a woman rushed in, then froze at the sight of her healthy daughter. Calypso held out her hand to the girl, who stood with an exuberant smile.

"Melany?" her mother whispered, tears sparkling on her cheeks in the fluorescent hospital light.

"Mom!" Melany cried excitedly. "Calypso healed me!"

Calypso smiled as Melany's mother rushed forward, pulling her daughter into a tight, emotionally charged embrace. Calypso embraced them both, filling their souls with radiance.

"It was lovely to meet you, Melany," Calypso said with a tender smile. Stepping back, she opened a portal to the room of the next ill child.

"Thank you!" Melany's mother sobbed, clutching her daughter tighter.

It felt wonderful to be healing children again. Calypso felt a sense of nostalgic contentment as she healed the last child—an eleven-year-old boy fighting a flesh-eating bacterium that had already claimed his legs. She left him with new legs and a heartwarming embrace.

She sighed, thinking of the countless other children who needed healing throughout the world. She portaled back to the lobby and found Julia at her desk, surrounded by people who were peppering her with questions about her relationship with the angels. When they saw Calypso and Aria return, they fell silent and retreated from Julia's desk.

Cognizant of the watching eyes and phones, Calypso leaned closer to Julia. "How soon before the project is ready?"

Julia straightened, an eager light in her eyes. "Within a few hours of your signal. We finished preparations last night. Everyone's ready."

"Let us begin, then," Calypso decided, feeling the millstone of time grinding the lives of mortals inexorably towards their end. "Will eight o'clock Eastern time suffice?"

Julia nodded with an exuberant grin. "That should give us plenty of time. We'll have everything ready."

Calypso beamed. "Wonderful. I'll see you later this evening, then."

She turned to Jason with a smile. "Jason, would you come with us, please?"

He stood awkwardly off to the side, clearly unsure of whether he should have followed them through the portal. With a small sigh of relief, he nodded and followed.

Emily and Eric were waiting with Clarice and Lexi on the other side. Sunlight glinted off the lawn in the late afternoon.

Emily took one look at him, and her mothering instincts took over. "Let's get you some food, young man." She blurred away into the cabin, leaving him blinking at her afterimage.

He smiled in bemusement. "It's strange being called 'young man' by someone who looks younger than me."

Eric laughed, nodding. "I'm still having a hard time adjusting. It's been thirty years since she looked this young."

Calypso turned to him, her eyes bright. "We'll be broadcasting to every hospital tonight. Once that is done, we'll be ready to destroy the nanobots—whenever you give the word."

Jason rubbed his hands together, grinning. "It's pretty much ready. We've got a team of over four thousand people working with us on this operation, all people you healed. Some of them work *in* the intelligence agencies and gave us access to the backdoor trojans they use. I'd suggest we do it right after you finish with the hospitals, so they don't have time to react."

Calypso smiled warmly. "Well done, Jason."

Clarice leaned toward him and leered. "Did you just say backdoor trojans? Is this more... tech jargon?"

Jason's ears turned crimson. "Um, yeah, it's another technical term."

Aria shook her head, struggling not to laugh. "Just ignore the adolescent, Jason."

"Come on in, Jason," Emily called from the veranda. "You'll think better on a full stomach."

Jason smiled expansively. "I won't say no to that. She really is an amazing cook."

Eric nodded, smiling wistfully. "Kind of ironic she can't eat anymore."

"Fortunately, the tradeoff is *well* worth it," Emily noted from the veranda.

Now that Calypso could remember being human, she firmly agreed. Bliss pulsed through her every second—a soft, divine current. Her heart ached for the fallen ones still trapped in shadow, forced to remember light they could no longer feel. *That* was hell—recalling the light and being unable to feel it while being compelled to commit atrocities by a demon lord.

They went up to the veranda, finding spots where they could enjoy the view without appearing to watch Jason. She remembered how self-conscious he was when eating in front of beautiful angels.

Aria joined them near the edge of the veranda, overlooking the front yard. "I have the invite ready to send out to everyone later this afternoon. Hospitals will have the kids watching in conference rooms or on tablets they distributed to the bedridden."

Calypso smiled gratefully. "Thank you for arranging everything, Aria."

The fretful mountain air danced among the windchimes, producing an oddly calming melody that spoke of hope and renewal. Calypso couldn't help wondering how long the calm would last after tonight's performance.

23 – ASSASSIN

Aria sat down across from Jason as he finished eating, her wings folding around her like a cloak. Clarice had taken Calypso to some billionaire's cabin she had stolen and relocated to the sun. Aria would have felt abandoned, but with access to their new bond, she could feel just how deep Clarice's love and attraction burned. She was sure her sister had a good reason for not including her.

She glanced across the table, focusing on Jason. "Things might be a little weird for you when you get back to campus," she cautioned.

Jason thanked Emily as she took his dishes away, then turned a questioning frown on Aria. "Weird how?"

Aria looped a strand of hair around a finger, watching Jason speculatively. "Half the student body filmed Calypso redeeming those demons," she explained. "Since it's obvious we're in close contact with you, I imagine your face is all over the internet as people try to puzzle out your connection to the angels."

Jason facepalmed and let out a groan. "I can't believe I didn't think of that. Yeah, I'm definitely going to get mobbed by my dormmates when I get back."

Aria winced apologetically. "It'll probably be a lot more than just dormmates. We've experienced this before, and things have only gotten more intense. You're probably going to have media corporations, influencers, religious figures, and every other flavor of chaos seeking you out to learn more about the angels."

Jason groaned again. "Oh my god, you're right. I wonder if I should take a short break from school."

"Mind if I join you?" came a hesitant voice from the edge of the veranda.

Aria turned and smiled welcomingly. "Arturiel! Not at all. Did you get a chance to try flying yet?"

"*Yes!*" Arturiel beamed, her eyes sparkling with excitement. "I can't believe how fun it is. I've done a lot of fun things in the last few million years, but this still rates in my top ten."

Aria grinned back at her. "I know, right?" Aria gestured at Jason. "Jason, meet Arturiel—the first demon ever redeemed, and the first angel to change her class. Arturiel, this is Jason."

Jason nodded at the beautiful angel, his cheeks coloring. "Nice to meet you."

"Poor Jason," Aria thought with an amused smile. *"He's surrounded by beautiful angelic women on every side."*

Arturiel greeted him with a warm smile. "Hey, Jason. I've heard so much about you."

Jason blinked. "About *me*?"

Arturiel nodded, gesturing at Eric. "They told me all about your project to purge the nanobots from Agency contractors. It's a monumental undertaking—probably the biggest hack in history—and *you're* going to be the star in the history books."

Jason's eyes widened. "Wow. I guess I never saw it from that perspective."

Aria playfully kicked his foot under the table. "That's because you're a good person, Jason. You've focused on the outcome of this project rather than personal glory. You did this to help Calypso."

Arturiel sighed with an impish grin. "If I were mortal and a few million years younger..."

Jason coughed nervously. "Uh... um, didn't Aria say that mortals and angels could, you know..." he made vague gestures, his cheeks reddening.

Arturiel smiled playfully. "Yeah, but rumor has it that you want a family. If you slept with an angel, you'd never be satisfied with a mortal woman."

Emily snorted dryly from the doorway. "How thoughtful of you to point that out. He'll be busy fighting off suitors after those videos go viral—especially when people realize mortals can become angels. I've already seen people suggest the possibility, after internet sleuths revealed that Aria and Clarice lived perfectly mortal lives before meeting Calypso. You'll be the new gateway to immortality."

Jason looked sick, seeming to realize just how crazy life was about to get.

Aria exchanged a curious look with Arturiel. "I'm going to check it out. I want to see if Jason's already trending."

Jason's focus sharpened as Aria reached through a small portal and pulled out a laptop. "How far can you make a portal to?"

Aria opened the laptop and quickly logged in. "There isn't a limit. We can travel to the highest light realm. I could open a portal to Proxima Centauri b if you want to take a peek at an alien world."

Jason leaned forward excitedly. "Is there *life* around Proxima Centauri b? Are there really aliens?"

Arturiel shrugged. "Of course. There's life everywhere in the cosmos."

Aria smiled wryly. "But they aren't as far as you've been taught. We flew over to Alpha Centauri the other day, and it was *way* closer than four light-years."

Arturiel folded her arms, her eyes thoughtful. "That's the hardest lie for demons to maintain. If people actually thought about how far light-years are, they'd realize that stars should constantly be winking out of sight. At those distances, a microscopic dust particle would be large enough to blot out the closest star. With so many rogue planets, space dust, asteroids, and comets, you wouldn't see stars at all. One of the demons in charge of psyops came up with the flat-earth theory to discredit anyone asking questions about the distance of stars. It keeps search engines from showing anything relevant and just shows flat-earth propaganda."

"Seriously?" Jason asked, dumbfounded. "So stars are actually close enough to travel to?"

Arturiel tilted her head consideringly. "Well, it would still take a long time if you were flying rocket propulsion vehicles," she said critically. "But if you used EM propulsion vessels, then yes, they're easily within range."

Jason laughed giddily. "My mind is blown. Why aren't we seeing aliens all the time then?"

"You do," Arturiel said dryly. "It's called 'swamp gas.' In this quadrant, the only thing traveling between worlds is demons. Earth isn't the only world they've overrun. The fact that angels can be turned into demons made it a battle of attrition where angels would inevitably lose—until now, that is. Everything changed when Calypso began turning demons back into angels."

Aria froze, suddenly *vividly* reminded that she shared a bond with three other angels. Her face burning, she staggered to her feet and hurried toward her room. "You two carry on... I'm going to... to... go lie down for a bit."

Arturiel and Jason watched her, their concern turning to confusion as Emily started laughing wickedly.

She heard Lexi staggering toward her room as well. This was *definitely* going to get awkward.

***

Jason looked at Emily inquiringly. "What was that all about?"

Lips still twitching, Emily explained. "The four of them went to the Garden of Eden on the Sun earlier and ended up with their spirits bonded in such a way that they feel each other's emotions, and to some extent, sensations."

Jason held up a hand, eyes wide. "Wait, the Garden of Eden is on the *Sun*? How is it not burnt to a crisp?"

Arturiel started laughing, watching Jason with amusement. "The Sun isn't hot, Jason. The light is a result of electrical currents traveling through channels of plasma that connect star systems. There's a habitable world below the shell of the Sun. The only part that is hot is the corona."

Jason looked like a fish out of water, his mouth moving silently, eyes bugging.

Emily patted his shoulder. "You'll have to unlearn a lot of what you've learned in a world of angels and demons."

Arturiel leaned forward. "So, what's affecting Aria so strongly that she had to leave? Is one of the others in danger?"

Emily's grin widened. "Clarice and Calypso are having a... moment."

Arturiel blinked, then shook her head in disbelief. "A Seraph... being intimate. I still can't quite picture that. They're supposed to be distant—cosmic arbiters, not... people."

"Maybe that's the whole problem with the cosmos," Emily said thoughtfully. "If Seraphim experienced a touch of mortality, they might learn compassion. Empathy doesn't grow in perfection."

"Are there really only four other Seraphim?" Jason asked, feeling a sense of awe that he was interacting with a being who would one day sit at the top of the ruling class in the cosmos.

Arturiel nodded. "There were nine originally, but only four remain in the light realms. I still can't believe I have *actually* been talking to a Seraph. They're never seen outside the higher light realms."

Jason pursed his lips. "Do regular angels and archangels live in the light realms?"

Arturiel smiled wistfully. "We lived in the lower light realms once—before the mortal realm was created. It's such a wonderful place. Thoughts influence reality, allowing you to bring ideas to life. Rules are so restrictive in the mortal realm. I wonder if we'll ever be allowed to return. The majority of angels still live there, but some of us were selected to oversee the mortal realm."

Emily gazed at Arturiel shrewdly. "Arturiel, why haven't the Cherubim and Seraphim dealt with the demon problem? If they sent you here to oversee mortals, shouldn't they be concerned that demons have overrun the mortal realm?"

Arturiel frowned uneasily, as if it weren't the first time the thought had occurred to her. "I don't know. I spent thousands of years thinking we would be rescued somehow, but it became apparent that wasn't going to happen—until Calypso suddenly appeared."

Eric rubbed his chin contemplatively. "I get the feeling significant changes are coming now that Calypso's ascending. Whatever force arranged for my daughters to become intertwined with Calypso seems to have a motive that involves a changing of the guard. I wonder if there are any other Seraphim like Calypso that'll arise in the cosmos."

Emily smiled mysteriously. "I think there just might be."

Eric raised a suspicious eyebrow. "What's with the mysterious act?"

Emily smiled sweetly. "If I told you, I wouldn't be very mysterious, would I?"

Arturiel gazed at Eric thoughtfully. "I definitely feel like we're on the brink of great change. The appearance of a divine instrument is both terrifying and extraordinary."

Jason finished his egg bite with a satisfied groan and looked at Arturiel. "What's the significance of divine instruments?"

He felt both overwhelmed and excited by the sheer amount of knowledge he was gaining about how the cosmos actually worked and the true history of life. Questions competed for priority as he stared at a being who had been around for more centuries than he could imagine, a being with answers to some of life's biggest questions.

Arturiel's face was almost reverent as she explained, "The divine instruments are tools for altering reality. I'm still agog that I've actually seen one. Only the Seraphim can use them, and anyone lower than a Cherub won't survive hearing them played. The power unleashed by fully ascended Seraphim is too powerful for lesser beings to withstand. That's probably the main reason there haven't been hordes of invading angels. All Calypso would need to do is play that harp, and it would wipe out all but the Seraphim and possibly the Cherubim."

Eric stared at her intently. "Does it require all four instruments to rewrite reality, or could they do it with just the two?"

"Just the *two*?" Arturiel asked, startled. "They have *two?*"

Emily burst out laughing. "Oh, you haven't heard about Aria yet, have you?" she asked, her lips quivering. "It's too bad Clarice isn't here to tell the story. Anyway, the Lore Boar had the other half of Aria's spirit. I get the feeling she was at least a Cherub before mortality, and that her spirit couldn't be contained in one mortal body. When Calypso played a song for the Lore Boar with that celestial harp, it transformed the Lore Boar into a divine instrument and merged with Aria. She now possesses the tin whistle."

Arturiel stared, eyes wide. "There are *so* many things in that explanation that boggle my mind. First of all, the Lore Boar was *real?* I thought it was a *myth*."

Emily nodded. "That's why they went to Eden. It was inside the Tree of Life. You can thank Grodek for putting them on that path. He kept insisting they needed to speak with the Lore Boar. He must have known that Aria's other half was there."

Arturiel stared into space, her eyes troubled. "And *Aria* is the one in possession of the other divine instrument?"

Emily nodded firmly. "She is. She's the one who forged their spirits together with it. Why? Is that unusual?"

Arturiel chewed her lip. "I thought only Seraphim could play divine instruments. I'm almost positive that's the case."

Eric leaned back in his chair, hands resting behind his head. "You should have been there when Calypso played the harp the first time. We ascended more than twenty levels as a result."

Jason looked at Eric curiously. "What are these ascension levels you're referring to?"

Arturiel answered, glancing at Emily and Eric appraisingly. "When a mortal is raised to an angel, they don't reach the peak of their power immediately. There are triggers that cause bursts of development, increasing their powers and abilities. It usually takes angels much longer to ascend, but my only metric is angels and archangels. Perhaps Cherubim and Seraphim ascend much faster."

Jason raised a finger. "Or perhaps they're developing at the same rate, but their power is just so much greater that it only appears quicker. Maybe they're still fairly weak compared to what they'll eventually become."

Arturiel nodded approvingly. "That's a sound hypothesis. I've heard stories of Cherubim leveling star systems. It's hard to gauge scale when everything they do is apocalyptic."

Eric shivered. "That's a terrifying thought. I'm not sure I want that kind of power."

Emily stepped behind him and began massaging his shoulders. "It's a bit late to make that decision, Honey. Besides, that's exactly *why* you should have that power, instead of someone who *would* want to destroy star systems."

Jason nodded. "Power in the hands of those who seek it is the last place it belongs."

The words had barely left his mouth when all three angels suddenly froze, their eyes widening. A heartbeat later, the sky outside darkened, then exploded into auroras. Ribbons of green and rose shimmered above the trees.

The angels turned toward the inner cabin as one.

"Well," Emily said dryly. "I suppose there are *some* perks to a unified consciousness."

Arturiel blushed faintly as she met Jason's confused gaze.

He looked up at the auroras, still washing the skies with vivid ribbons of green and pink, in mild alarm. "What's going on?"

Arturiel's cheeks dimpled as she smiled. "I expect the sun just had the equivalent of an X-50 solar flare—judging by the sounds from the cabin, anyway."

Jason frowned, forgetting angels had super-hearing. "Is it something we should worry about?"

Emily smirked. "No, but I suspect Calypso and Clarice will have some new powers when they get back. Maybe even Aria and Lexi."

"Oh," Jason said awkwardly, finally grasping the context clues.

"That's my girl," Eric declared proudly, his eyes sparkling.

Emily slid her arms around his neck. "You and I might need a little portal trip to the sun ourselves."

Eric met her eyes with his own smoldering gaze. "We certainly do."

Jason looked at Arturiel uncomfortably, trying to think of something to change the subject. She watched him with a knowing smile, her eyes sparkling with amusement.

"So... do we need to worry about any of these other Cherubim showing up?" he asked, desperately trying to fill the silence.

Arturiel sighed, shaking her head slowly. "I haven't the faintest idea. As a lowly angel, the movements of the mighty were too far removed from my station for me to know what they might do." She paused, studying Jason intently. "I'm getting the strangest sense of familiarity with you, Jason. I had the same thing happen with the others here. It's getting bizarre."

Emily nodded curiously. "I've been feeling the same strange connection, as if our souls have history. But you'd remember us, wouldn't you, Arturiel? You never incarnated, so your memory was never wiped."

Arturiel nodded slowly. "Exactly. That's what makes this so bizarre. There's no way I could have known a Seraph or any Cherubim."

Devon walked through the semi-permanent portal on the lawn and began making his way up to the cabin. Jason had never met the man but knew he was postponing his ascension to angelhood until he experienced parenthood. He was whistling as he walked, a cheerful expression on his face.

Jason gestured toward the yard. "Where does that portal go?"

Arturiel smiled indulgently. "To Tamra's house. The two of them hit it off pretty well."

Jason frowned. "Should I know who this Tamra person is?"

Arturiel gestured at her form-fitting shirt. "See this shirt? Tamra's our tailor. She makes costumes for various theaters and movie production sets. These tops were custom-made to accommodate wings."

Emily chuckled. "Before we met her, the girls were constantly pinning their clothes together—or, as Clarice put it, 'joining the bra club.' They've had their clothing destroyed on multiple occasions, so if you ever see them running around in bras, you'll know they've burned through all Tamra's outfits."

Jason tried *really* hard not to imagine the gorgeous angels running around naked, but he failed spectacularly. His face turned red, and he started reciting code syntax in his head. Emily's low chuckle didn't help.

Devon's voice called out from the doorway, saving him. "What did I miss?" He spotted Jason and moved toward him with a welcoming smile. "I see we have a guest. I'm Devon, Em's brother."

Jason stood to shake his hand, glad for the distraction. "I'm Jason. I've been working on the hacking project to kill off the nanobots when Calypso sings to the world."

Devon shook his hand with a firm grip. "It's nice to finally put a face to the name. Thank you for putting this project together. It's personal for me."

Jason nodded, recalling his first conversation with Calypso almost a week ago. "That's right, you used to work for that shadow agency, didn't you?"

Devon grimaced, clearly unhappy with the reminder. "Indeed, I did. It'll be great to give other people the chance I had to put it behind them."

"How far is—" He broke off as a tall angel suddenly appeared behind Emily, radiating power. Twin layers of wings flared, golden eyes igniting like miniature suns. A beam of white fire lanced toward Arturiel.

Jason recoiled as Aria flashed between Arturiel and the angel, her entire body flaring like a nuclear blast. Her eyes blazed with incandescent fury as the beam of light slammed into her chest and fizzled out. The angel stumbled backward in surprise. Before he could react, Aria fired an intense beam of light into his neck, reducing him to motes of light that dissipated in the wind.

Eric spun around in shock. "Who the hell was *that*?"

Aria growled, still blazing with righteous outrage. "Someone who thought they could whittle down our numbers."

"That was a *Cherub*!" Arturiel exclaimed in shock. "You just killed a Cherub like it was *nothing*!"

"It *is* nothing," Aria grated, her eyes shining like spotlights as she scanned the surrounding area. "Now. Just like anyone else will be if they try to harm my family."

A flare of light heralded Clarice and Calypso's arrival. Clarice was glowing like a small sun—and wearing a half-donned shirt that left her chest open to the world. Jason looked away so fast he nearly strained something.

Aria frowned, still scanning the area for threats. "It must have been a second or third order Cherubim. Otherwise, I wouldn't have been able to kill it, right?"

She addressed the question to Arturiel, but Calypso answered.

"It was a First Order Cherubim," she declared firmly. "I can sense the lingering residue of its essence."

Aria's brows drew down. "So, Cherubim of the same order can kill each other?"

Arturiel shook her head firmly. "They'd have killed each other long ago if they could. The first order Cherubim are the oldest angels besides the Seraphim *because* nothing can kill them."

Clarice grinned in satisfaction. "Until now, anyway." She rushed over and hugged Aria tightly. "Thanks for reacting so fast."

"Of course," Aria replied softly. "Nobody's getting past me. Also, finish pulling your shirt up before Jason dies of asphyxiation."

Clarice laughed, breaking the tension as she quickly ducked her head through the neck loop.

Jason let out a breath he hadn't realized he was holding. He decided Arturiel probably wasn't being facetious when she said she didn't want to make mortal women a letdown for him. Angels all seemed to be formed to perfection.

Aria narrowed her eyes. "I guess we know the other angels are aware of us now. That was a pretty cheap shot, trying to teleport in and assassinate one of us on the sly. I guess it wouldn't have actually harmed Mom and Dad, but the others could have been killed. These angels really aren't much better than demons, are they?"

Arturiel smiled up gratefully at Aria. "Thanks for saving me."

Aria returned her smile. "Of course, Arturiel."

Arturiel pulled her long dark hair over one shoulder, frowning as she continued. "There's a reason the mortal realm was created. It was supposed to be a kind of school where angels could learn what compassion and empathy were as they experienced pain and loss. Unfortunately, only a few angels from the higher triads were sent here."

"Oh my god," Jason breathed, a sudden realization dawning on him. "Was I one of the angels who was an asshole? Is my spirit bound to constantly reincarnate here until I learn my lesson?"

Arturiel nodded with a look of compassion. "I'm afraid so. I should point out, though, that the first triad was very indiscriminate about who they consigned to mortality."

"You can say that again," Grodek snorted, materializing beside them with his usual disdain. "Mortality was just a weaponized prison for inconvenient angels."

He turned to Jason, studying him. "I remember you, Jason. You were one of the decent ones—too decent. Always questioning orders. So they dumped you here to stop you from interfering."

Jason stared at the blue imp in fascination, a fleeting sense of familiarity washing over him.

Grodek smirked. "They didn't plan for a Seraph to wake up and gather a host immune to their authority. The upper triads are screaming like spoiled children right now. Demons culling angels was part of their plan to make sure no human ever ascended again."

Aria frowned. "Why was I able to kill that Cherub? Calypso said he was the same order of Cherub as me."

"Maybe there's more to you than you thought," Grodek replied cryptically, then chuckled darkly. "The remaining Cherubim are going to be a lot more cautious when they find out Kadmiel's no longer with them. They thought they were untouchable until now. It's going to be glorious to see the fear on their faces when I tell them Kadmiel's no more."

Arturiel gasped, staring at Grodek with wide eyes. "That was *Kadmiel*?"

Grodek laughed evilly. "*Was* being the operative word."

Arturiel swayed, staring at Aria and Grodek in disbelief. "He was one of the first to turn on his Seraph, Lucifer, before Lucifer was cast out. He was one of the most powerful Cherubim of the first triad."

"Oh, I remember well when he turned on Lucifer after gathering so much support for him," Grodek snarled, rage twisting his features. "The little weasel thought he could stop the revolt if he pulled the rug out from under him. The little snake was always slithering through the ranks, poisoning the minds of anyone who didn't fall in line. He's responsible for more angels being sent to mortality and consigned to demonic assimilation than any other person—and that's a picnic compared to what he's done to the mortals on the worlds controlled by angels."

Calypso sighed regretfully. "There shall be many more who join Kadmiel before we are finished. I am not certain there is any means by which they may be redeemed, even through mortality."

Grodek grunted. "Good riddance. Every horror you've seen down here on this world can be laid at their feet. There are billions of other worlds far more disparate. A quick end is a mercy they don't deserve."

Grodek vanished with a pop.

Jason rubbed his temples, trying to process everything. Just a week ago, he had been a grad student debugging code and cracking ciphers. Now, he was apparently a reincarnated angel sent to a cosmic penal colony. The idea that his soul was trapped in an endless loop ignited a new, unfamiliar flame within him—righteous fury.

Aria broke the silence with a grin. "Time for the show." She turned to Calypso. "You ready?"

Calypso nodded, her eyes shining. "Absolutely." She turned towards the theatre where her instruments awaited, her voice electric with purpose. "Let us go and heal the world."

24 – HEALING THE WORLD

Aria opened the video conference link Julia had sent her earlier that day. Once the video window loaded, she centered the camera on Calypso. The Seraph stood on the small stage with her harp, looking into the camera, her swirling violet eyes hypnotic and intense. Her wings shimmered beautifully under the track lighting, framing her white-clothed form and giving the scene a magical ambiance. With her brilliant blond hair tumbling down her shoulders, she was the perfect embodiment of an angelic being.

Aria briefly tranced out, captivated by the beautiful Seraph. When Calypso winked, she finally broke free of the enchanting spell and joined the video call.

Her eyes widened at the number of viewers. People from hospitals all over the planet were watching the broadcast, not just those in her own country. Julia had clearly seized the opportunity to heal people worldwide.

Calypso smiled radiantly into the camera. “Hello, everyone. I only wish I could be with you all in person. Since I cannot, we shall heal you, and perhaps we shall have the opportunity to meet properly another day.”

Without further ado, she began playing Aria’s harp. Aria quickly fell under her spell as the beautiful music filled her soul with light. Calypso’s voice joined the shimmering notes, and it was immediately obvious she had evolved again while on the sun with Clarice. Her voice rippled with waves of magic, washing through the soul like a tsunami. Aria heard words of power interwoven throughout her song, strangely familiar, like a phrase on the tip of her tongue.

Aria could tell, without being able to see the patients, that a sea of vitality was washing the taint from millions of bodies. A growing feeling of connection was building inside her, almost like a character in a story glimpsing the chapters ahead.

Calypso's large, expressive eyes were filled with emotion as she serenaded the world with healing love. She was beautiful, her face a masterpiece of passion and joy. Aria melted inside as she watched the musical healer fulfill her life's goal.

When she finished singing, she briefly closed her eyes as a golden tear ran down her cheek, then smiled angelically. "I've wanted to reach more of you for so long," she said in a voice trembling with emotion. "I'm so glad this opportunity finally came. Goodbye for now, dear ones."

Aria ended the stream. Emails flooded the inbox of the account she had used to host the event—people sending selfies of their healthy loved ones and short messages thanking her profusely for healing them.

Aria stared at her excitedly. "It looks like it worked. You did it, Calypso! You healed the world!"

More golden tears streamed down Calypso's face as she smiled brilliantly back at Aria. Hearing her finish, the rest of the group came into the theater and began offering their congratulations. Clarice pulled Calypso into a tight embrace, golden tears running down her own cheeks.

"Calypso, you really are the most amazing person ever," Clarice whispered, holding her tightly. "Do you know how many parents you saved from losing their child tonight? I'm so glad we met you, my sweet musical genius."

Calypso closed her eyes as she embraced Clarice, her emotions filling the cabin around them with love, gratitude, and joy.

Aria joined Clarice, feeling a sense of radiant wonder that the plan they had enacted what seemed a lifetime ago was a success. Lexi joined them, and they stood in each other's arms for several minutes, basking in their shared accomplishment.

Clarice finally broke away with a reluctant sigh. "Okay, we'd better move on to the second phase of the plan before they shut down the internet."

Calypso glanced at the laptop. "Where are we to do it? Here?"

Clarice chuckled mischievously as she stepped back from Calypso and looked at her father. "Dad, is everything ready?"

Aria looked at Clarice in sudden concern, feeling the bubbling excitement mixed with anxiety in her sister's emotions. "Clarice, what have you done?"

Clarice grinned at her wolfishly. "Did you ever wonder what Dad's been up to for the last couple of days?"

Aria raised an eyebrow pointedly. "I've been too busy to wonder what he's been up to—and so have you, as I recall."

Clarice opened a portal onto the side of a stage. "We're going to do our live broadcast on stage."

There were dozens of musicians on the stage, including a full orchestral ensemble and choir. A large drum set sat center stage, and several electric guitars sat on stands with headsets attached.

Clarice grinned at them. "Dad put a band together with the information Julia gave us about former patients. It turns out every single one of them is a musician of varying skill. I sent them the songs Calypso made here at the cabin. I figure we can play the new ones and kill the nanobots, heal anyone we missed at the hospitals, then move on to her older content."

"And you didn't think giving us a little *warning* would be a good idea?" Aria demanded, her stomach churning with butterflies—which didn't make sense because she didn't *have* a stomach.

Clarice laughed impishly. "Hell no, I wasn't going to warn you ahead of time—you would've chickened out."

The musicians on the stage were just finishing a song and hadn't noticed the small portal. Several people in the audience had noticed, however, and craned their necks, trying to get a better look.

Clarice grinned as the song finished. "Come on, Tweedledee." She grabbed Aria and Calypso by the hand and dragged them through the portal.

Aria blinked, looking out at the crowd. She thought it would be a small audience hall, but it was a full-sized concert hall with thousands of seats full of Calypso fans.

They clearly weren't expecting Calypso to make an appearance. The cheering cut off abruptly as Clarice dragged the two reluctant angels forward. The audience stared in stupefied shock as the three approached the guitars. You could've heard a pin drop. The musicians looked as stunned as the audience when Calypso hesitantly picked up a guitar and pulled the strap over her head.

Clarice reached out to place the headset on Calypso, but the Seraph shook her head with a small smile. "No need."

"Dad posted a live event for Calypso's YouTube channel right before she played for the hospitals," Clarice explained as she slung her own guitar strap over her shoulder. "There are probably hundreds of millions of people watching right now. Don't let them down, Calypso." Clarice grinned.

Calypso drew a deep breath, looking out at the crowd watching in reverent silence. "Hello, everyone. Shall we begin?"

Her voice effortlessly carried to every corner of the concert hall. There was a pause, then a wall of noise flooded the room as the audience surged to their feet and roared with excitement.

Clarice beckoned the woman who had been handling lead vocals before they arrived. Rather than try to talk over the noise, she made a telepathic connection. *"Do you mind switching to accompaniment and letting Calypso take over lead vocals?"*

The tall brunette stared back and forth at Clarice and Calypso disbelievingly, her eyes wide with shock.

"You still with us?" Clarice asked her with an encouraging smile.

"Um, yeah," the woman nodded, still looking dazed. "I'm just going to sing accompaniment with Calypso."

"You've got this, Lori," Clarice told her with another encouraging smile.

"Living the Tale," Calypso announced to the musicians, her voice easily carrying over the roar of the audience.

The musicians snapped out of their daze and readied themselves. Calypso nodded to the woman at the piano, and the first notes began, followed almost immediately by the orchestra. Clarice joined in on the guitar as the rest of the musicians began to play. Calypso's voice rang out above the instruments, easily carrying to every corner.

Shockwaves of power radiated around the room as the instruments provided the substrate for Calypso's transcendent voice to shake the world with her tale of beauty and triumph. The concert hall was charged with so much positive energy that small auroras spontaneously erupted throughout the space above them. The audience was completely gripped by the sublime riptide pulling them deeper into a world of fantasy and wonder. Calypso's music reached deep into the soul and refined whatever it touched.

Clarice could hear the words of power woven into Calypso's words, wiping out any nanobots within range of her voice. Words of healing rippled through the air, curing anyone within range of her broadcast of their illnesses.

As the first song concluded, the audience remained silent, too entranced to react. The musicians watched Calypso in reverence. They had all heard her sing in the hospital at some point, but the difference when playing with a full ensemble was a life-changing experience. Her skill in weaving each instrument and note into a formula that achieved transcendental perfection was nothing short of divine.

Slowly, the crowd awakened from their trance and erupted into wild cheers. Aria noticed a child struggling to see over the heads of the adults in front of him. With her spiritual sight, she saw a prosthetic in place of his left leg.

Calypso noticed him as well. She opened a portal directly in front of the child, beckoning him and his mother forward with a welcoming smile. The child didn't require additional prompting, hurrying through to stand in front of Calypso with an excited grin. The woman followed hesitantly, glancing self-consciously over her shoulder as thousands of eyes watched them.

"Hello, Caleb," Calypso greeted the child warmly, dropping to one knee. "Would you like me to mend your leg?"

"You can do that?" Caleb asked in awe.

His mother gasped, her hand flying to her mouth, staring at Calypso with naked hope in her eyes.

"Yes," Calypso confirmed with a nod. "All I ask in return is a hug."

Caleb grinned and threw his arms around her neck. Calypso blazed brightly and spoke several words of power. The prosthetic fell to the ground as a fully formed leg replaced it.

Caleb released her and looked down at his new leg in astonishment. He lifted it and twisted it about experimentally before looking up at her with a huge smile. "Thanks, Calypso!"

"You are most welcome, Caleb," Calypso smiled, rising to her feet. She looked towards the astonished mother and smiled warmly. "You are a wonderful mother, Anna. I am very glad you came tonight."

Anna blinked back tears as she smiled. "Thank you so much, Calypso. You really are an angel."

Calypso winked playfully. "Was it the wings that gave it away?"

Anna laughed, tears spilling down her cheeks.

Calypso smiled radiantly at the two of them. "I do hope you both enjoy the rest of the show."

Anna and Caleb went back through the portal, and Calypso closed it. The audience had watched the miracle unfold in silence. Tears sparkled in thousands of eyes as they regarded her with something close to worship.

"200 years," Calypso called over to the musicians.

Intense emotional energy ruled the night as Calypso sang her vision of reality. During the second song, she opened her aura, flooding the audience with her love and hope. The concert became a deeply moving religious experience for the enraptured audience. When the performance finally finished several hours later, localized auroral-like discharges arced throughout the concert hall, twisting the air with colored ribbons. It would be a night to tell their children and grandchildren about.

At the end of the concert, Calypso looked out at the rapt faces, her eyes bright. Then she unfurled her aura, broadcasting a tsunami of radiance on waves of seraphic power. Gasps erupted across the audience when they felt the joyous energy fill their souls with light. Calypso held her hand up high in farewell and created a portal back to the cabin. The three of them exited the stage, faces glowing with satisfaction.

"I told you you'd do great," Clarice said smugly as they entered the front room.

Aria had lost all sense of self as she played, completely in the zone. The audience barely existed for her, pulled into Calypso's divine music.

Calypso looked up as Devon entered the room. "Do we have any confirmation that the nanobots were destroyed?"

He nodded, smiling broadly. "I've been receiving messages from contacts for the last two hours. Some of them just happened to be near someone whose phone started playing the song, and it still healed them. I think what you did tonight will cripple what's left of The Agency. There are a *lot* of contractors who'll never look at The Agency again. Some organizations will actively attack them when they discover their weakness."

"I would like to offer my congratulations as well," a smooth voice said as a demon lord appeared in their living room.

Aria stared at him, waiting for the barest hint of aggression to fry him.

"Lucifer," Arturiel greeted the demon lord with a deep bow, her voice filled with respect.

"*Lucifer?*" Aria gasped in amazement. "Like *Satan* and *Beelzebub*?"

"The very same," Lucifer replied with a wry smile. He turned back to Arturiel. "You need not bow to me, Arturiel. I have never stood on formality."

Aria sniffed the air curiously, detecting no trace of demon. There was something deeply unpleasant, but it wasn't the foul stench she had come to loathe. "Did you learn to hide the demon stink or something?"

"The stench is metaphorical," Lucifer said with a half-smile. "You're sensing the state of their soul and interpreting it as a foul smell. Demons who've embraced their nature will smell a lot worse to you than demons who fight their nature."

"I see the party's already started," Grodek noted as he popped into the room next to Lucifer. "Do you have the piece?"

Lucifer pulled the body of a violin out of a small portal in the air. It was missing the neck but was easily recognizable as part of a divine instrument. It was a brilliant white that had an inner glow. He offered it to Clarice, who stared at him curiously as she slowly reached out and took the broken instrument, her hands shaking.

When her hands touched it, an inverted shockwave rippled inward toward her, shaking the cabin. Her eyes widened, and her lips parted with a gasp. Aria could feel *something* twist around her sister's spirit, wrapping tightly before melding into it. Her presence expanded dramatically as she became more... whole.

"You lucked out," Grodek told them gruffly. "We happened upon this while searching the demon vaults in the former North American Territory headquarters."

"Are you ready?" Calypso asked Lucifer intently, her eyes showing a sense of familiarity.

He nodded, his eyes bright with anticipation.

Calypso connected to his core, flashing with incandescence as she removed a portion of his spirit. He closed his eyes as light radiated around him, filling the room. His bat-like wings shimmered like a heatwave, morphing into double-layered Seraph wings. Then his eyes blazed for several seconds before dimming to a glowing sapphire blue. Nearly seven feet tall, he stood radiating a palpable mantle of authority.

"Thank you, Calypso," Lucifer said in a deep, powerfully enchanting voice. He was awe-inspiring to behold.

Grodek suddenly cackled madly, his eyes full of evil glee.

Lucifer watched him with a smile, though the amusement never seemed to reach his eyes. "I take it there were some ripples?"

"More like a tsunami," Grodek sniggered malevolently. "They all felt your return. A general panic is washing through the ranks of bootlickers and toadies. Azriel said Michael's petitioning the Seraphim for a full-scale attack, trying to get them to leave the realm and come down here. He's not having much luck. Leaving the higher realms isn't pleasant when they're used to radiance several orders of magnitude greater than the mortal realm offers. Now that there are more Seraphim here, and *with* divine instruments, the other Seraphim are probably shitting their metaphorical pants."

Emily studied Lucifer with a troubled frown. "How did they turn a Seraph into a demon?"

Lucifer glanced around the room appraisingly. "That answer requires some background," he said carefully, glancing at Grodek with an unreadable expression, and Aria had the sense that he wished the imp wasn't present. "There were nine of us in the beginning. We shaped reality and created the other realms according to instructions from what you think of as God. When we shaped reality and seeded life with the triads of angels, we remained in the highest light realm, where only Seraphim and their

Cherubim can survive the high levels of radiance. We studied our work from afar, trying to puzzle out the mysteries of the GoD."

He gestured around them. "This mortal realm is a finite place with finite laws and rigid rules governing reality. It would be difficult for you to comprehend the limitless nature of the light realms without remembering your time there. After more time than you can comprehend with your current memories, there was discord in the lower light realms."

Lucifer nodded at Arturiel. "Angels are immortal entities who cannot die. Some grew disconsolate with their existence and began tormenting others. We Seraphim granted Cherubim the power to extinguish life for those who wished for an end as boredom robbed them of reason. We also instructed them to maintain order when angels preyed upon the agency of other angels."

Lucifer paused, frowning. "This worked well, for a time. Eventually, however, more angels grew bored of eternity, and the number seeking death became alarming. We sought answers from the GoD."

He paused again, gazing at Calypso, Aria, and Clarice consideringly. "The solution was to create a mortal realm and allow angels to incarnate their spirits into physical bodies. There, they would forget who they were for a time and experience the dichotomy of pain and pleasure, fear and joy, love and hate—alien concepts to us at the time—to better cope with eternal life."

He smiled, though Aria didn't see it reach his eyes. "This was a partial success. Angels who experienced mortality found a renewed passion for eternal life. With memories of mortality and the emotional growth it imbued, they no longer took the positive energy filling their immortal bodies for granted, and eternal life became a place of beauty and passion."

He sighed, shaking his head sadly. "However, not all angels were willing to experience mortality. They feared the loss of their power and memories, as well as the pain and suffering it inflicts on the soul. Only about a third of all angels had experienced mortality when a group of Cherubim convinced four of the Seraphim that mortality should only be for angels who disrupted the agency of others."

Lucifer pointed at himself as he continued. "I was one of four Seraphim to experience mortality at that point. The four who hadn't experienced it believed mortality should be a prison for the unruly until they were rehabilitated. It was clear to me and the others who had experienced mortality that this system was ripe for abuse."

He paused, looking at Grodek inquisitively. The imp made an impatient gesture to get on with it. Lucifer snorted wryly and continued. "We organized the angels who'd experienced mortality and made it clear we wouldn't accept this system. We suggested *everyone* undergo at least one mortal incarnation. The four Seraphim—poisoned against us by their Cherubim—became convinced we were attempting to remove them from power. Using the divine instruments of creation, they tried to kill us but ended up transforming us into demons and mortals when the instruments wouldn't allow our unmaking."

Lucifer grimaced, his face tinged with disgust. "The Seraphim sent undesirable angels down to monitor humans, knowing the demons would assimilate them. They ordered the demon lords to make humans suffer, believing it would result in more compliant angels when they ascended. They left their Cherubim and Dominions in charge of the operation, and the Cherubim made sure the angels sent down to protect and guide humans were eventually converted into demons, turning mortality into a prison realm, ensuring the angels in the mortal realm would never return to the light realms."

Arturiel stared at him with as much astonishment as the others. She had clearly believed her mission to the mortal realm was to help troubled angels become respectable angels. Anger ignited in her eyes as she realized she had been deceived, purposely subjected to the horrors of becoming a demon, just so that some Cherubim could avoid experiencing mortality.

Clarice nodded slowly. "That explains... a lot. How did a Seraph seed end up in Calypso if you were all sent down here at the same time? Where do you even *get* a Seraph seed?"

"There's no such thing as seeds," Lucifer answered with an ironic smile. "At least, there are no class-related seeds. Only the transfer of angelic essence that reawakens who you already were. Calypso was a Seraph, as were the two of you." Lucifer nodded at Aria and Clarice.

"Uh, we're clearly Cherubim," Aria corrected him matter-of-factly. "Note the golden eyes and laser beams we shoot to vaporize things."

Amusement flickered in Lucifer's eyes. "Do you really think a Seraph cannot do the same things as a Cherub? You awakened the abilities you believed you needed to protect Calypso. You are both Seraphim."

Arturiel stared at them disbelievingly. Their parents didn't look nearly as surprised. Eric looked satisfied, while Emily looked smug. Calypso's face was full of affection, but no surprise. Aria wondered if she had known or at least suspected. Lexi was grinning without any sign of surprise; she probably expected no less of Clarice. Aria glanced at her sister and found no astonishment there either. Had Aria been the only one not to suspect she was a Seraph?

Aria huffed. "What was all that talk about warrior and bard classes earlier, Grodek?" she demanded suspiciously. "If classes don't even exist, why'd you tell us she was a bard?"

Grodek grinned slyly. "*Did* I tell you she was a bard?"

Aria rewound her memory, studying the conversation with Grodek. She frowned as she realized he hadn't even shown any kind of affirmative reaction to Clarice's question.

"You said healers heal, warriors kill, and singers sing. What the hell else were we supposed to make of that?"

Grodek smirked, looking extremely self-satisfied. "You were supposed to think of yourselves as warriors, that's what. The last thing you two needed was to start developing healing powers when demons were trying to capture you."

"You were just manipulating us then?" Aria asked critically.

"Yep, that's exactly what I was doing," Grodek agreed pleasantly.

"What about the phrase you have to say to activate it?" Aria asked intently. "Is it just the same for everyone? They have to say they want to vanquish evil?"

Lucifer nodded. "The mortal realm was designed, in part, to rehabilitate angels who were troublemakers. When you say you want to vanquish evil, or any similar variant, after receiving an angel tear, you're declaring your virtue and desire for righteousness. The angels tasked with assisting mortals were instructed to use their judgment when deciding if a mortal was ready to ascend. Since an angel can't be compelled to cry, angel tears were chosen as the method to initiate the transformation."

"Who's this fifth Seraph?" Clarice asked shrewdly. "It's you, isn't it, Grodek?"

"Give the girl a gold star," Grodek drawled sarcastically.

Aria grinned triumphantly. "So, it's not four Seraphim against two—it's four against five. Is that why they haven't attacked?"

Grodek snorted. "They're just a bunch of cowards. The idea of leaving the higher light realm to do battle in the mortal realm and risk dying terrifies them. Nothing can die in the highest light realm, so they're hiding there like the cowards they are."

Clarice narrowed her eyes. "Lucifer, you said only four Seraphim had experienced mortality. Who was the fifth Seraph who remained? Grodek?"

"Correct," Lucifer nodded, a grim smile on his face. "He wasn't opposed to experiencing mortality eventually. Once Rendimus and the others thought we were unmade, Grodek took two of the divine instruments and hid them in the mortal realm. He bound the tin whistle to the Lore Boar for safekeeping and embedded the harp in the Tree of Knowledge until he moved it to the tree where Calypso's father would find it. When the other Seraphim discovered what he'd done, they tried to unmake him with the remaining two instruments, but the instruments broke in the process. The pieces appeared in the mortal realm, scattered across planet Earth. By some quirk of fate, he ended up as an imp instead of being unmade. He remains unconstrained by the mortal realm and can still visit the higher light realms."

"What about the fourth instrument?" Emily asked curiously. She and Eric had been listening to the conversation with rapt fascination. "Who'll possess the fourth divine instrument now that Aria, Clarice, and Calypso are in possession of three of them?"

Lucifer pulled out the neck of a guitar. "I have part of the guitar. I believe Grodek gave you some clues on where to look for the other pieces. Finding them is the most important task right now. Once the four instruments have been restored, we won't need to worry about the other Seraphim. We will have the power to rewrite reality, consigning them to mortality if we so choose. Calypso has already rewritten reality several times on a localized level, one of those times being when she raised Arturiel to an archangel."

"She doesn't need all four instruments to rewrite reality?" Emily asked in surprise.

"Not for small events," Lucifer replied with a shrug. "You only need all four to rewrite the foundations of reality, such as turning a Seraph into a mortal."

"I *knew* changing classes wasn't supposed to be possible," Arturiel declared with a grin.

They all paused as Aria's sixth sense flared with alarm. She teleported above the house and saw hundreds of fiery missiles raining down from the sky. Lucifer appeared next to her and spoke a single word of power, and all the lights in the sky winked out of existence. There was no angel fire or destructive wave, just a single word that tickled something in the back of her mind—or perhaps her soul.

Clarice and Calypso had also teleported with her. Arturiel rushed out of the cabin and flew up to them, the others not far behind.

"It looks like the demons of the other territories panicked and thought a full nuclear strike would accomplish something," Lucifer observed with a shake of his head. "They're not thinking very clearly if they think nukes can harm immortal beings."

Arturiel frowned uneasily. "They might not be targeting us. They might be trying to plunge the world into chaos by starting a nuclear world war. It might be their only way to prevent society from galvanizing against them, especially now that Saturn's apathy modulator is gone. Humans will revolt against their governments as they regain their sense of passion."

Aria looked at Arturiel in surprise. "Is that what that thing on Saturn was? We weren't sure what it did, but Calypso was sure it needed to go."

"That was *you*?" Arturiel asked, staring at her in amazement.

"Yeah. We were doing a little exploring since we were able to travel through space at ridiculous speeds. I've been wondering what it actually did."

Arturiel shook her head, still staring at Aria in amazement. "It's hard to imagine just how much more powerful you are than the average angel."

Aria looked at her pointedly. "You're pretty powerful too, you know. Weren't you the one who told me archangels were significantly more powerful than angels?"

Arturiel smiled ruefully. "Oh, they are. I'm an army ant to a sugar ant, while you're a human compared to both ants. Your power's not even comparable to ours."

"Army ants are pretty freaking scary," Aria declared fervently. "Drop a human in an army ant nest and see what happens."

Arturiel bit her lip anxiously. "We should probably make sure there aren't any nukes dropping elsewhere in the world."

Aria opened a series of twenty different gateways into the sky, each one covering a different part of the globe. "I don't see any above any of the major European or Asian cities." She opened a few more gateways in Russia and the Middle East. "Looks like all the major nuclear powers are in the clear."

Arturiel stared at her in awe as she closed the portals.

"What?" Aria asked curiously.

"You just open up portals like it's nothing," Arturiel breathed. "I've seen archangels spend up to an hour trying to open a single portal correctly. I've heard Principalities and Dominions can open them quickly, but you just opened *dozens* at the same time."

"It's just a matter of connecting the correct nodes in the cosmic meridians," Aria explained, shrugging self-deprecatingly. "It just takes a little while to get used to using your spiritual vision to see the hidden world of energy overlaying the physical plane."

Arturiel covered a small smile as she looked around. "I'll take your word for it." She slowly flapped her wings to stay aloft, reminding Aria how useful it was to be able to hover effortlessly.

Clarice pursed her lips. "Maybe it's time to rid this world of nukes. It wouldn't take us very long, and it'd eliminate a lot of future threats if nobody had them. Since we can vaporize them, it wouldn't even leave any radiation behind."

Lucifer chuckled at her suggestion. "That would certainly have far-reaching geopolitical ramifications if it became known that nobody had nukes anymore."

"Why bother?" Grodek asked caustically. "Who cares if they have nukes when your ultimate goal is to return them to the light realms. This is just a prison, and the more time you spend on distractions, the longer people suffer."

Lucifer stared at him flatly, a hint of anger flashing through his eyes, then vanishing just as quickly.

"I think it's time for Calypso to show us how to redeem demons," Aria announced firmly. "If we really are Seraphim and have that kind of power, we should start redeeming any demons we come across while we're hunting down those instruments."

Emily faced Aria, her hands on her hips. "If you don't mind showing us how to open portals, your dad and I would appreciate it."

Hiding a grin, Aria turned to Emily and showed her a slow example of opening a portal. It took her a few minutes to wrap her head around the concept, but she eventually got it. "Now you and Dad can have some alone time somewhere off planet."

"Thanks, Aria," she said dryly.

"Well, I'm off to gloat," Grodek announced with a chortle. "I don't want to miss any of the gnashing of teeth going on upstairs right now. It's going to be the highlight of the millennium."

Grodek vanished with a pop, leaving a chuckling Lucifer behind.

"What are you going to do?" Aria asked Lucifer curiously. *I'm questioning Satan. This is just too freaking surreal.*

"I'm going to start redeeming demons I know," Lucifer answered thoughtfully. "There are a lot of demons who've unjustly suffered long enough."

"You know how?" Aria asked in surprise.

"I'm the one who created the design for the energy inverter in the first place," Lucifer said with a faint smile that never reached his eyes.

"Oh yeah," Aria said with a frown. "That's right, Grodek said it was by design. I guess I'll see you around, Satan." She couldn't *not* say it.

Lucifer threw his head back and laughed. "Take care, Aria. I know you don't remember me yet, but when you reach full ascension again, your memories will return. Enjoy your ignorance; you'll look back on these days with fondness."

25 – EXFENESTRATOR

"It feels like this puzzle is finally forming a coherent picture," Clarice mused, floating cross-legged above the veranda pond.

Aria arched an amused eyebrow from where she stood near the railing. "So that's your replacement for furniture?"

Lexi grinned and copied Clarice, folding her legs beneath her. After a moment of contemplation, her smile grew. "Honestly? This works better than chairs."

"I know, right?" Clarice spun lazily in midair, her hair whipping behind her before settling into loose waves. "Anti-gravity rocks."

Aria stared at her with a soft smile, her eyes entranced. Clarice felt her burning attraction through their bond and winked. Aria blushed shyly and quickly averted her eyes. She was so damn adorable. The spiritual bond they now shared made hiding their feelings from each other impossible. Learning that the three of them had been together for billions of years had changed Aria's feelings toward Clarice. What had been a steady increase in attraction had become something far stronger. Clarice knew what remained of that particular wall would soon crumble. She had time—lots of time.

Clarice glanced at Calypso, her other favorite piece of eye candy. She was standing next to Aria, gazing down at the verdant valley. The changes to her character since recovering her memories of mortality were subtle but significant. Her emotional depth was more nuanced and intense, enhancing her already radiant personality and making the gentle angel even more attractive and lovable.

The beautiful musician had grown more confident since their tryst on the sun, giving Clarice hope that Aria would similarly benefit from a crash course on how the various sensitive erogenous regions of the female body worked.

Calypso folded her arms, softly tapping a finger on her bare arm. "Lucifer's explanation aligns disturbingly well with what Emily and Devon were theorizing whilst you two were out hunting for instruments. I wonder how much of what they surmised came from buried soul memory."

Emily eyed them thoughtfully, the burble of the stream exiting the pond adding a serene ambiance to the veranda. Her eyes fell on Lexi, who floated close to Clarice like a lost puppy. Reaching into her purse, she pulled out Aria's brush, moved behind a surprised Lexi and began to brush her long, silky strands.

Silver tears reflected in Lexi's eyes at the motherly action, and the bond glowed with a powerful surge of love. "Thanks, Emily."

"Of course, Lexi," Emily said gently, squeezing her shoulder.

Clarice met Aria's gaze. *"We really do have the best mom in existence,"* she thought at Aria with a faint smile. Her smile grew. *"Even if our mom is younger than us."*

Aria stifled a giggle. *"Hey, you're going to send me into a giggle fit."*

A warm glow of love flowed through the bond as Clarice regarded her sister fondly. *"I'm always up for one of your giggle episodes."*

Aloud, Clarice said, "It's kind of funny when you think about it. If we're really Seraphim, the answers to everything we've been searching for are already buried somewhere in our memories. We just don't have access to them yet because we haven't finished ascending. Maybe that's what this intuition Calypso's pulling from is."

Aria shook her head disbelievingly. "I still can't believe we're Seraphim. We had this entire character class we'd convinced ourselves we belonged to that was limiting our growth this whole time."

Arturiel breathed out an incredulous laugh. "I can't believe I'm in the presence of not one, but *three* Seraphim." She stood near Calypso and Aria, watching them with a look of wonder. "You're literally the ones who created me and all the other angels. There was so much I thought I understood that was wrong."

Aria suddenly laughed.

Clarice raised an eyebrow, her lips curving into a small smile. "What're you laughing at, Tweedledee?"

Aria grinned at her admiringly. "You were right about Calypso from the start, Clarice. She *was* an amnesiac angel—twice. First, because Carcelonia wiped her memory, and second, because she got stuck in mortality. She won't remember everything until she finishes ascending."

Calypso shared a look with Clarice, and they both burst out laughing.

Clarice gazed at Calypso affectionately. "Sometimes the first observation is the correct one," she commented sagely.

Aria stretched lazily, her gorgeous red hair draping across her shoulders. "Do you realize we've been going nonstop for a week? And I still feel like I just woke up from a perfect night's sleep. Immortality has its perks."

Clarice smiled wryly, shaking her head as she thought about how far they had come in such a short time. "It *has* been a busy week, hasn't it? We floundered so much at the start. Grodek's riddles certainly didn't help."

Aria gave an exasperated laugh. "That little shit sent us on a wild goose chase looking for class activation phrases."

Clarice grinned ruefully. "And we were scared of making mortals too powerful—turns out it just depends on who they were before they got dumped in this prison. I suppose the fact Lexi, Mom, and Dad are Cherubim contributed to that mistaken belief. What are the odds of two Cherubim and two Seraphim being in the same family? Then, the very next angel we raised is *also* a Cherub."

Lexi blinked. "Wait, how many Cherubim *are* there?"

Arturiel's eyes widened. "Seventy of the first order," she said slowly, her brows creasing. "That really *is* a coincidence of cosmic proportions."

Lexi frowned. "How many angels are there?"

Arturiel's wings shifted as she exhaled. "Quintillions. The odds of your family ending up together like this are beyond chance. Something—or someone—arranged it."

Clarice's mind reeled. *Quintillions*? There was no way it was coincidence. Some outside force had to be orchestrating it all. But who—or what?

Aria absently wrapped a strand of hair around her finger. "According to Lucifer, a third of angels have gone through mortality. I wonder how many actually learned compassion from it. Are some still incapable of empathy? Or just... really slow students?"

"Hmmm..." Clarice's brow furrowed, then her eyes flew open wide. "Oh, wow."

"What?" Lexi asked intently, leaning closer.

"This really *is* a prison," Clarice whispered, the realization dawning like lightning. "Why are we leaving *anyone* mortal? Every human we meet is trapped here—just like we were—cycling endlessly through incarnations. Shouldn't we be helping *all* of them ascend?"

Aria hesitated. "What about the angels who were sent here because of their behavior? Or the families still raising children?"

Clarice narrowed her eyes. "I don't buy the 'sent here to learn lessons' story anymore. Even if it's true, they've had more than enough lifetimes to learn them. Anyone who hasn't developed empathy or compassion by now probably never will."

Calypso turned to face them, leaning back on the rail. "It may make more sense to create an exit upon death," she said thoughtfully. "If everyone were suddenly to ascend, this realm would collapse. Society is far too dependent upon its machinery and supply chains to survive without billions of mortals maintaining them."

"I'm not convinced," Clarice countered, shaking her head. "You ascended as a *child*, Calypso. That means it's possible to raise kids to angels. They would still grow up, just without needing food, money, or shelter. Enough angels would stay to help those who choose mortality, and we could easily clean the planet—industrial waste, pollution, everything. Are we really going to walk free while billions remain trapped?"

Aria leaned into Calypso, slipping an arm around her waist. "We need to know how angels are consigned to mortality," she said with a pensive frown. "If less than half have gone through it, we'll have to make sure the rest do, willingly or not. What's forcing our spirits into human bodies? When does it happen?"

Clarice sighed. "Oh no. This is going to sound like a pro-life argument, isn't it?" she asked with a smirk. At Emily's sigh, she sobered. "But seriously, something's hijacking angelic spirits and stuffing them back into mortals. We need control over that mechanism."

Arturiel cleared her throat. "Spirit transfer happens in the lower light realms," she said slowly. "Every world has a soul trap—a mechanism that intercepts returning spirits and reincarnates them as mortals."

Lexi looked at Clarice doubtfully. "Won't it take a crazy amount of time to free all the people trapped here? And what about all the other worlds?"

Clarice made a triangle with her hands. "Think pyramid scheme. Each ascended angel frees another, then another—it snowballs. Within weeks, everyone here could ascend. Other planets would be trickier. We'd need archangels or higher to open interplanetary portals, and even then, it'd take ages."

Aria gave an uncomfortable cough. "What about people like Uncle Devon? He wants to stay mortal and have kids. Do we just tell him, 'Sorry, you'll thank us later'?"

Clarice gestured at the sky. "Remember, there are still plenty of angels up there who need to experience mortality—all the assholes who sent us here in the first place."

Aria nodded slowly. "Then we talk to Grodek and Lucifer first. They'll know how the soul trap works and what freeing everyone would look like."

Clarice frowned, feeling inexplicably hesitant at the idea of confiding in Lucifer. They could worry about that later. "In the meantime, I say we stop being selective," she suggested firmly. "People like Julia are fair game now."

Calypso leaned into Aria's sideways embrace with a contented smile. "I have a feeling we could restore everyone using the divine instruments," she said musingly. "There is a great deal we may one day accomplish with them, and it shall require very careful thought. We have lived within the mortal realm for untold iterations across several thousand years. Perhaps there are changes we might make to the way things function which would still grant people the growth they require, without the horrors this world has inflicted upon so many of us."

Aria's arm tightened around her protectively, the bond between them burning with shared empathy. Rage coiled in Clarice's chest, seething as she thought of the Seraphim who had consigned Calypso to this fate. How much had they known? How much had they *planned*? According to Lucifer, a lot.

"You okay?" Lexi asked anxiously.

Aria and Calypso looked at Clarice with concern, feeling her fury blaze through their shared link.

Clarice's eyes filled with dreadful promise as she grated out, "If I find even a hint that the other Seraphim had a role in your ordeal, there'll be tales of the horror they'll suffer echoing into the halls of eternity."

The air itself seemed to shudder. Aria's aura flared with fury, her eyes turning to frost. "Yes, there will be."

Lexi nodded fiercely, her skin igniting with wrath.

They all froze when a tripwire in the psychic node that linked them to Jason flared with panic. Without a second thought, Clarice teleported, time slowing as her mind sped up.

Jason was already falling, hurtling over the edge of an eight-story building. Clarice dove and intercepted him twenty feet above the ground, angling their descent to soften the impact as she pulled him close.

She smirked at him as she landed and stood him on his feet. "You sure do get into trouble a lot. What happened?"

Aria and Lexi burst through a shattered window on the top story moments later, razor-focused. Jason's eyes were wide, and his breath came in ragged gasps. "I really thought I was a goner this time!"

Clarice affected a look of wounded pride. "We told you we'd keep you safe—where's the trust?"

Jason nodded toward the roof, his voice unsteady. "Somewhere up there. How the hell did you know I was in trouble?"

Clarice tapped her forehead. "Think of the people we watch over as members of a psychic web. We can feel spikes of adrenaline or intense fear."

They both looked up to see Lexi dragging a man out of the window and dropping him toward them.

Jason let out a laugh that wasn't *quite* hysterical. "So, you're omnipresent?"

Around them, a cluster of students had gathered, phones already held high. Angels were trending in real time.

Lexi landed at their feet, one hand clamped hard on the back of a burly man's neck, holding him with enough force that any attempt to flee would result in a broken spine. Clarice couldn't smell demon on him, but his face twisted with pure hatred.

Clarice poked the man in the shoulder. "Is this the guy who shoved you?" He had several thin scars on his cheeks and looked knuckled-down and mean.

Jason threw his hands up helplessly. "I have no idea. I was just walking down the hall, and someone shoved me through the window." His hands were trembling from the adrenaline burnout, but his breathing slowed as he regained his composure.

Clarice planted herself in front of the man, hands on her hips. "Well, Thomas, what do you have to say for yourself? Is there a reason you decided to exfenestrate Jason?"

"I'm still intact," Jason objected indignantly.

Clarice shifted her attention back to Jason, lips curving into a slow smile. "What do you think 'exfenestrate' means, Jason?"

Jason stared at her, his cheeks coloring. "Oh. It means something else, doesn't it?"

Her expression didn't change. "What did you *think* it meant?"

"It doesn't matter," Jason mumbled, awkwardly brushing a hand through his hair.

Her smile widened. "You must have thought it meant *something*."

Aria suddenly appeared beside her, playfully smacking her shoulder. "Leave Jason alone. Besides, exfenestrate isn't a word. You're thinking of 'defenestrate.'"

Clarice lifted her chin and stared down her nose. "Nope, I'm just correcting the morons who used the wrong concatenation of Latin words to come up with nonsense. Defenestrate just means to fill up a hole in a building. *Ex*-fenestrate would be more appropriate."

Aria dragged a hand down her face. "Oh, Clarice... I don't even have the words."

Clarice snorted. "Neither did the pretentious jackasses who came up with 'defenestration.'"

Aria sighed and gestured at Lexi's captive. "What's the story with Thomas here?"

"We hadn't gotten that far yet," Clarice winked at Jason. "We were exploring the English vocabulary."

Aria sent a probing tendril of energy into Thomas's thought node. "So, he's a member of Opus Dei? I guess it was just a matter of time before the world religions started sniping at us. I wonder if he's here as a result of humans or demons."

"Probably demons," Clarice guessed with a shrug. "They know they can't get close to Jason without us detecting their stench, so they probably decided to send a human."

Jason's brow furrowed. "You can tell if demons are near me based on their stench? Wouldn't *I* be the one smelling them? Or can you smell through my nose?"

Clarice tapped her nose. "It's a metaphorical stink. Their souls are rotten. You won't notice it with your nose, but your spirit will certainly recognize one and alert us."

Aria looked at him curiously. "I thought you were studying cybersecurity. Why are you in building 36?"

"Um, a friend invited me to see a lab," Jason answered, wisely avoiding Clarice's gaze and missing the sudden leer.

"Oh, is it a *girl* friend, Jason?" Clarice asked archly, looking around for said girl in the growing crowd of students and faculty gathering around them.

The students close enough to hear their conversation stared at Clarice, nonplussed, clearly not expecting teasing banter from angels.

"Yes, she's a girl," Jason admitted defensively. "And yes, she's a friend."

Clarice tried to rise into the air to look for said girl...friend, but Aria grabbed her wing and pulled her back down.

"Focus, Clarice," Aria said crisply. "What are we going to do with Thomas? If we let him go, they'll probably just kill him. Should we just turn him into an angel?"

Thomas had remained stoically silent for the entire exchange, glaring at them with hate-filled eyes. As soon as Aria suggested turning him into an angel, he began thrashing wildly, almost breaking his own neck as he struggled to escape Lexi's grip.

"Damn fundamentalists," Clarice growled in exasperation, raising a hand to knock him out, but Calypso's palm rested gently on her arm.

"Thomas, we shall not turn you into an angel if that is not what you desire," Calypso told the flailing man gently. "As far as we are concerned, you are free to go, though I rather suspect the local authorities may not prove so lenient."

As Calypso finished speaking, campus police burst through the crowd, tasers drawn. They froze at the sight of the angels.

"Release the man and get on the ground, arms out, palms up," the lead officer barked. She couldn't have been older than nineteen, her hazel eyes fierce under a cap that barely contained a bun of brown hair.

Her two partners weren't nearly as brave; their tasers wavered and dipped the moment they realized exactly who—or what—they were pointing at.

Clarice tilted her head at Thomas. "So, what'll it be? Their custody or ours?"

Thomas spat at her, eyes full of venom. She didn't bother dodging, vaporizing the spittle midair with a short blast from her eyes.

The officer took that as her cue and fired her taser. Clarice's hand blurred as she snatched the prongs out of the air, holding the wires between her fingers. She shook violently for several seconds before stopping and grinning at the officer.

"Sorry, I couldn't resist. Did you really think a taser was going to do anything? Honest question."

The woman narrowed her eyes and dropped the taser, replacing it with a handgun.

One of the other officers nervously licked his lips. "I don't think that's a good idea. You're going to get yourself vaporized."

"Grow a pair," she snarled, flipping the safety off and aiming the gun at Clarice. "Don't make me ask again. Get down on the ground with your arms out, palms up."

Clarice almost complied. "I am *so* tempted to actually do it, just to see where things go, Mary," she said with a slow, seductive wink. "You could do the whole sexy woman in uniform theme, then we could move on to a dominatrix act with those cuffs when things heat up."

Aria covered her eyes. "I'm not related to her," she told the officer. "Seriously—we just happened to bump into each other a few minutes ago."

Lexi was struggling not to laugh as she continued holding Thomas by the back of the neck, her back to the officers. Calypso looked like she was just along for the entertainment as she watched Clarice with a small smile.

The officer licked her lips and increased pressure on the trigger. Clarice could tell by the look in her eyes that she knew it wouldn't do any good. She clearly had a chip on her shoulder with angels and wanted to settle some kind of score.

"You can shoot," Clarice told her encouragingly. "I'm just going to vaporize the bullets out of the air, so you might as well get it out of your system—whatever *it* is."

"This isn't right," Mary thought as seeds of doubt took root. *"They're not acting anything like I thought they would. If they really do serve that bastard of a god, they aren't acting like the angels in stories. But if angels really exist, why couldn't they save Alexis?"*

"We don't serve a god," Clarice told her gently. "Your Alexis isn't really gone."

That was the wrong thing to say, Clarice reflected, as she vaporized bullet after bullet while Mary screamed. When Mary finished emptying the clip, she launched herself at Clarice with a cry of rage.

"Where were they when Alexis was sold off like cattle?" she raged inwardly, hammering futilely on Clarice's shoulders and chest, even kicking her ankles. Clarice just stood there and let her unleash her rage.

"How can they strut around like gods while letting predators steal children all over the world?" Her thoughts were knives of grief and rage. *"They weren't there for her when she needed them most!"*

Clarice saw the image of the girl Mary was thinking of—a fourteen-year-old Lexi with eyes still full of innocence. Aria and Calypso had clearly been listening to her thoughts as well; they shared a stunned look, then turned to Lexi.

"What's going on?" Lexi asked in sudden concern as she felt their shock.

At the sound of Lexi's voice, Mary froze. "Alexis?" she whispered disbelievingly.

Aria walked over and took charge of Thomas. "I think you have an overdue reunion," she said gently.

Lexi relinquished Thomas to Aria and turned to stare at Mary in shock. "Mary? Is that you?"

Mary blinked rapidly, tears forming as she stared at Lexi in disbelief. "Is it really you?"

Lexi's eyes widened, and a moment later, she blurred over to Mary, drawing her into a tight embrace. Sunlight reflected in the quicksilver tears that pooled and ran down her cheeks. Mary gasped as the power of Lexi's radiance suffused her soul. Her knees weakened as the spiritual overload overwhelmed her mortal body. Then her neck began glowing as a silver tear landed softly, producing a gasp.

Clarice deadpanned, "Looks like we're going to have one more giant chicken."

Calypso dissolved into a fit of infectious giggles, drawing Aria into her mirth. Love from the two of them flooded the bond as they gazed at Clarice with fond amusement. She had never heard Calypso giggle like this before—it was *adorable*.

"What happened?" Mary asked Lexi wonderingly. "How are you an angel?"

"They saved me," Lexi nodded at the three of them, her expression filled with love. "They stormed the mansion and vaporized the bastards holding us captive. They gave me the option to become an angel and help fix this broken world."

You could have heard a pin drop in the crowd as the drama unfolded. Clarice felt a wild urge to shout '*BOO!*' just to see what would happen.

"Come back with us," Lexi urged, glowing with joy. "I'll tell you all about it. Some of the things I've learned are so crazy, it's seriously going to blow your mind."

Mary turned to Clarice apologetically. "I'm sorry for attacking you. You saved my best friend—I'll never be able to repay that."

"Bring those cuffs along, and we'll see," Clarice suggested with a waggle of her eyebrows.

She dodged as Aria dropped Thomas and tried to tackle her, laughing as she teleported back to the cabin.

A moment later, a gateway appeared, and Calypso came through, followed by Jason, Lexi, and a dazed Mary. Clarice glanced around warily, then yelped when Aria materialized above her, tackling her to the ground and grinding her knuckles into Clarice's scalp.

"You are a *bad* angel," Aria declared, laughing helplessly.

The gateway snapped shut behind them, leaving a dozen phones recording the sight of one angel pinning another in the grass, both laughing like maniacs.

***

Scott blinked, trying to process what he had just witnessed. The man the angels had been restraining bolted the second Aria released him, but no one moved to stop him. The cops were frozen, staring at the empty space the portal had occupied moments ago.

"Man, what the *hell* just happened?" Scott's roommate Chet finally said, his thumb hitting *stop* on his recording app. "I don't even know where to start with how messed up that was."

Scott scanned the crowd. "Anyone get the whole thing?"

A Japanese student raised his phone in acknowledgment. "I was filming campus footage for our virtual tour project when that Jason guy came flying out the window," he said, his voice tight with excitement. "That crazy hot angel just popped out of thin air and caught him while he was falling."

"Which crazy hot angel?" Scott deadpanned. "They all looked like celestial supermodels."

The man grinned. "The flirty one. If heaven's like that, I'm repenting right now."

"Did I hear her say they don't serve a god?" asked a lanky guy wearing a periodic-table T-shirt that read "Can I lick it?" above the elements.

"Yeah, I got that part," a woman said excitedly, waving her phone. "I can't believe we just saw actual angels. *Calypso* was here!"

"Did they offer to turn the guy who threw Jason out the window into an angel?" a woman asked. "Why would they want a murderer as an angel?"

Before anyone could answer, a pretty blond woman with terrified blue eyes burst from the building. "Where's Jason?" she demanded anxiously, searching the area. "Is he alive?"

"Freaking angels saved him," Chet told her reassuringly. "One appeared out of nowhere and caught him mid-fall."

She sagged in relief. "Is he hurt? Where is he?"

"He went through a portal with them—" Chet broke off as another portal flared open.

Clarice strolled out, grinning like she had just stepped off a runway. "Hi, Susan. Can you follow me, please? Jason's freaking out about leaving you to freak out."

Susan's mouth dropped open. She stared at Clarice in shock, then at the portal behind the angel.

Clarice grinned playfully. "It's totally cool; you only end up with your legs on backwards about half the time when you go through a portal."

"Jason's with you?" Susan asked hesitantly, studying Clarice's beautiful features nervously.

"Yep. My mom's getting some food for him as we speak," Clarice said with a chuckle. "It's a rough life for a chef in a house full of angels who don't require food."

"Hey, Clarice, you single?" a voice called out from further back in the crowd, emboldened by the press of bodies between them.

Clarice blinked, looking toward the source of the voice. She narrowed her eyes. "No, Derek, I'm with Calypso and Aria. Sorry."

Scott watched Derek blanch when he heard Clarice say his name.

A ripple washed through the crowd as people began talking excitedly.

"I thought God hated gays?" someone called out derisively.

"God doesn't love or hate," Clarice replied dryly. "God just *is*. Don't take any of that religious mumbo jumbo seriously. You'll understand soon enough." She turned back to Susan. "Shall we?"

A student called out, "Is heaven real?"

Clarice paused, then flashed a mischievous smile. "Yes, Jeremy, the sky is real."

She led Susan through the portal, and it snapped shut with a soft pop.

Scott snorted. "'The sky is real.' That's gold."

Chet elbowed him, lowering his voice. "Did you catch what Lexi said earlier about being rescued from a mansion? Sounds like they wiped out some traffickers."

Scott's grin faded, his jaw tightening. "Good. Someone needs to take out those pieces of shit."

"They seem to be able to turn anyone they want into angels," Chet said quietly. "She also said we'd 'understand soon enough.' Do you think they plan to turn *everyone* into angels?"

Scott blinked, glancing at Chet curiously. "Why would they turn everyone into angels?"

"Maybe it's like the Borg—some kind of holy assimilation thing," Chet muttered with a shrug. "I don't even know where that thought came from."

A few students nearby nodded thoughtfully.

Scott smiled eagerly. "Honestly? I'm *so* ready to be a Borg."

* * *

Jason glanced across the table at Devon and Tamra, and he immediately recognized the doting stage of a new relationship. Tamra was leaning into Devon with a contented smile while they waited for Emily to finish cooking.

Tamra met his gaze, her brown eyes briefly sharpening when she saw him observing them. She was always pleasant, but he sensed a layer of steel beneath her normally affable personality. He didn't want to see what happened when that genial nature vanished.

She nodded to Emily with a grateful smile when the angel brought a steaming plate of teriyaki chicken to her. Emily smiled back with warm satisfaction, clearly approving of the relationship.

"One of the perks of being with Devon is access to the best food on Earth," Tamra noted appreciatively. "You wouldn't believe how fast she preps food at angel speed."

Devon smiled after Emily. "Her cooking's actually improved since the upgrade—super smell results in super seasoning, apparently. She really spoils us."

Tamra nodded firmly. "She won't even let me cook my own meals anymore. You can imagine how sad that makes me."

Jason chuckled with Devon as the other angels laughed. The arrangement sounded pretty awesome to him.

He inhaled, his stomach growling in response. "That smells *so* freaking good."

Devon sighed. "I may never leave mortality if it means I can keep eating Em's food. Having my nieces around is great, but let's be honest, the kitchen is the true highlight."

"You're such a glutton," Aria said fondly, hovering beside Lexi and Calypso, all three of them seated on air. "As an angel, I'm obligated to mention that's one of the seven deadly sins."

Hearing Susan's voice from the front yard, Jason jumped up and hurried to the veranda railing. Clarice stepped out of a portal with Susan in tow. His friend—who was a girl—took in the cabin, then spotted him and smiled, relief bright in her blue eyes. He waved back, wearing the world's dumbest grin.

"We have a lot to talk about, Susan," Clarice was saying as they crossed the bridge.

Jason met them at the top of the stairs. Susan had that wide, radiant smile she was insecure about—which was absurd because it was the best thing about her face.

"...she's been dying to cook for more than my uncle and Tamra," Clarice finished as they came up. "So, you two are a—" she smirked "—godsend."

Susan's smile faltered. She hauled Jason into a tight hug, a tiny sob escaping. "I thought you were gone. I'm so glad I get another chance to do this right."

"Do what right?" he asked, bewildered.

She took a breath, then kissed him. He froze, brain-buffer spinning, until Clarice gave him a discreet shove. He kissed back, heart hammering. He had never had the nerve to risk the friend zone.

She pulled back, her eyes bright. "That."

"Oh," he said eloquently. The grin crept back, and she laughed, pulling him into another embrace.

"Almost losing you made me realize what I was about to miss," she murmured.

"I see our plus one is here," Emily noted, bringing two large platters of food through the door. "Hello, Susan. I'm Emily. It's wonderful to meet you."

"Hello, Emily, it's wonderful to finally meet you," Susan replied warmly. "I can't thank you and your daughters enough for saving Jason."

Emily smiled fondly at her daughters as she set the food down on one of the tables. "They're pretty good at saving the day. Come have a seat and dig in. I'll fetch you some tea."

Susan smiled gratefully as she sat down next to Jason. "Thank you, Emily."

"Is Mary staying for dinner?" Emily asked, placing the kettle on the burner with a clink. "Or is she leaving mortality before dessert?"

The angels all went still for a moment, listening to something Jason couldn't hear. Emily nodded, smiling. "Fair enough. We'll be going over a lot with Jason and Susan. Bring her down when she's ready."

Jason looked at Emily expectantly. "Super hearing?"

She nodded. "Yep. Just remember, there's nowhere within a mile of the house you won't be overheard by the rest of us, even if you're whispering."

Susan watched Emily in fascination. "Jason mentioned you have super senses. Is that how you knew he was in trouble?"

Calypso smiled welcomingly at Susan and said, "That was more akin to a psychic link. Now that we have met, we have cataloged the resonance of your spirit. We are all connected through a web of energy within the ethereal realm, so if we sense fear or danger disturbing the threads that bind us, we shall be there before you know it."

Susan smiled ruefully. "Angels must have a serious mental boost. I can't imagine keeping track of all those threads."

Aria tapped her temple meaningfully. "Being an angel *definitely* upgrades the mind."

"So, tell me about the two of you," Emily said, pouring Susan's tea, her motherly tone at odds with her youthful features. "How long have you known each other? How'd you meet?"

Jason chuckled as she bustled about them, her maternal manner putting him at ease. "I spilled my coffee all over her during my first week at MIT. I was looking the other way, went around a corner, and ran right into her."

"He totally ruined my shirt," Susan complained playfully. "He was so mortified that I actually felt sorry for *him*. He insisted on buying me a new shirt and tried to give me money for it right then and there. I told him he'd have to come help me pick it out."

Clarice dissolved into giggles. "I can only imagine how red his face must have been. Jason is the quintessential computer nerd, with all the social awkwardness that entails. Please tell me you decided to get some underwear while you were shopping for shirts. I can just see his poor face combusting while you were picking out panties and a bra."

Susan laughed as Jason's face burned. "Yeah, he looked like he was going to faint. As far as the actual shopping trip... yeah, his head would've exploded." She smiled softly at Jason. "Some girls find the confident smooth-talkers attractive—I've always been a sucker for earnest and awkward."

Clarice grinned, turning to Calypso. "We know all about that. Calypso's always had that earnest innocence and adorable naïveté that makes her irresistible."

Calypso's cheeks flushed at Clarice's words, eliciting a delighted laugh from Clarice. "See what I mean?"

Susan laughed merrily, her eyes alight with curiosity. "Did you two just meet when all the excitement started a week ago, or have you been together longer than that?"

Clarice smiled reminiscently. "Aria and I visited her the day before that Redditor exposed her identity. It feels like a lifetime ago. When we talked to her at the hospital after watching her heal some children, she was so full of innocence and love that you couldn't *not* fall in love with her. She spent all her time helping others and had no one to care for her. It was like watching her emerge from hibernation into the warmth of spring when she finally had some friends to reciprocate the love she so freely offered everyone else."

Calypso smiled at her, love shining in her large eyes as a golden tear traced a path down her cheek. Clarice and Aria returned her smile, their own eyes filled with affection.

"So... um... uh, never mind," Jason stammered, cutting himself off with a mental wince and a blush. Susan looked at him questioningly, and he winced outwardly, too.

"Yes, we both love her," Clarice said, a hint of laughter in her voice. "I wasn't about to lose Aria for Calypso. Aria's been my best friend since we were seven. We've been there for each other through some of the worst life has to offer. We'll be together forever now, and Calypso will be right there with us."

Susan sniffed, dabbing at her eyes with a napkin. "That's beautiful."

Aria's cheeks flushed as she stared at Clarice, her eyes glowing with love. Emily watched the three of them affectionately, radiating quiet satisfaction.

Aria suddenly glanced around. "What's Dad up to? Is he playing secret agent for Clarice again? I thought the two of you would be gone longer than a few hours."

Emily floated up into a sitting position, hovering across from Aria. "He's portaling Arturiel around to a few of the North American Territory offices. Arturiel's still learning to make portals by herself." Her voice softened, and she smiled fondly. "She is such a sweetheart; I'm glad she joined us."

Her smile faded, replaced by a look of annoyance. "Clarice, we have to find a better place than the sun for a vacation home—or at least a better place *on* the sun than where it was. There were a bunch of megafauna in that region. Turns out, megafauna like lumber. They tore the cabin apart, gorging on the logs like they were grass. Luckily, we weren't wearing our clothes when they stepped on us, or we'd be waiting on Tamra for new shirts. There's an angel-shaped impression in the ground where something brontosaurus-adjacent stepped on us."

Clarice and Aria were giggling madly by the time Emily finished, joined by Calypso a moment later. Tamra and Devon laughed uproariously, shaking their heads as they gazed at Emily affectionately.

"I would have paid good money to see that," Clarice gasped, golden tears of mirth in her eyes. "Can we time travel? Because if we can, I am *so* going to watch that."

"Why didn't you move?" Aria finally managed to ask, her eyes also shimmering with tears of mirth.

"We were... busy... in the moment," Emily grumbled, a slight blush rising on her cheeks. "We figured they'd just bugger off after tearing the cabin apart. We didn't expect them to stomp on it."

Clarice dissolved into another fit of giggles, watching her mother with fond amusement.

The three angels' laughter abruptly ceased, their gazes fixed upward.

"What did I miss?" Jason asked, looking in the direction they were staring with a puzzled frown.

"There's a new angel in the household," Clarice purred, her eyes alight with curiosity. "I wonder what she'll be."

"Is it that police officer, Mary?" Jason asked, curious to see her transformed appearance.

"Yep," Aria grinned eagerly. "Bring her down and let's get her charged up, Lexi."

A pause hung in the air, then a blur as Lexi rushed into the room. A moment later, Mary followed, accompanied by a gust of wind. She was much faster than a human but moved at less than half the speed Jason typically saw the other angels move. He wondered if she was deliberately moving slowly or if the difference was due to her lower rank and power level.

Her police hat was gone, and her hair had been freed from its bun. Rich, glossy brown hair tumbled down to her shoulders in waves, and large lavender eyes stared out of a sculpted face filled with euphoric joy.

As she came to a stop next to Lexi, Clarice walked over and pulled them both into a warm embrace. "Welcome to the club, Mary. We're ecstatic to have you. Don't get weirded out when I pull the back of your shirt up—we don't want your wings tearing it apart."

A small flash of light enveloped Mary for a moment. Clarice continued to hold them both as a golden tear ran down her cheek. Clarice pressed her cheek to Lexi's, where silver met gold. A sphere of gold flashed brightly, surrounding the three of them. As it faded, a pair of wings sprouted from Mary's back. They were different from the wings of the other angels—a brilliant white that looked smooth and velvety. While noticeably thicker, they were smaller than the Seraphim and Cherubim wings.

Clarice finally stepped back, a grin on her face as she observed the two of them. "I'll leave you to take care of the remaining upgrade."

Lexi's face went incandescent. She stared back at Clarice with wide eyes, her mouth working soundlessly.

"It can wait until later," Calypso announced, moving over to embrace the newest angel fondly. "Welcome to the family, Mary."

Aria joined her, wrapping her arms around the two of them. "We're so happy you've joined us, Mary. Tamra will have a shirt you can use that'll accommodate wings."

"I can't believe how *good* I feel!" Mary exclaimed in amazement. "Is this how good the rest of you feel *all* the time?"

"It sure is," Clarice laughed, winking at Calypso. "Sometimes we feel even better."

Susan watched Mary intently. Jason eyed Susan thoughtfully, revisiting his choice to wait on starting a family before ascending.

Clarice cleared her throat. "Okay, now that we're all here, let's explain to Mary, Jason, and Susan some of the information we've discovered. It'll probably heavily influence your decision on when to become angels."

"Way to psyche me up," Jason commented dryly.

"You'll see," Clarice said mysteriously.

26 – REALITY REWRITE

Jason still couldn't wrap his head around it: Lucifer. *The* Lucifer. And apparently the so-called boogeyman of religion was less "dark overlord" and more "cosmic whistleblower."

Susan frowned. "So, as far as the other Seraphim are concerned, we're just locked up in this mortality prison indefinitely?" she asked, narrowing her eyes. She had taken the information a lot better than he had expected. Of course, he had been sharing a lot of what he learned with her back at MIT.

Clarice nodded grimly. "Pretty much. We don't know how hands-on they are with the demons, but if they've had any part in the torture racket, there's going to be a reckoning. Lucifer made it sound like they were heavily involved."

Jason's jaw tightened. He had already heard about Calypso's captivity under demon control before Carcelonia found her. The thought of that happening to anyone—much less her—made his vision go red for a second.

Clarice's gaze swept over him and Susan. "So, knowing all that, do you want to stay in the prison, or do you want out?"

Jason met Susan's eyes, already seeing her answer forming there. His own hesitation felt smaller by the second. He had always imagined a family, the cliché house-and-kids picture, but it was hard to cling to that dream when he realized the whole setup was a cage.

"Jason," Calypso began, her eyes full of understanding as she watched him fondly, "I ought to remind you that there are a great many children in need of parents. One need not be a biological father in order to be a parent. You could be both an angel *and* a parent."

Devon and Tamra traded a look, hope flickering behind the hesitation. Jason felt something click into place. He actually laughed, rubbing a hand over his face. "I can't believe that never crossed my mind. Of course, we could adopt."

Susan laid her hand on his, her eyes glowing with warmth. "You'd make an incredible father."

Jason grinned, turning toward Clarice. "Guess we're ready."

Jason flinched as Clarice suddenly jumped into the air, thrusting a fist up high. "Wahoo!"

Aria grinned exuberantly. "At least you got one last meal before you changed. It's going to be so nice to no longer worry about assassins or freak accidents."

"I'm *really* looking forward to that part," Jason declared, grinning so wide his face hurt. The tension he had been carrying dissolved, leaving him lightheaded and eager. He was really doing this—ditching time, stepping into forever.

Across from him, Susan looked just as exhilarated.

"What do you think?" Devon asked Tamra speculatively. "I hadn't even thought of adopting. We can discuss it privately if you'd like."

"It's the best of both worlds, isn't it?" Tamra murmured with a slight smile, gazing at Devon with barely repressed excitement. "Calypso, you're a *genius*. I don't know why we didn't think of this before."

Devon's nieces and sister stared at him with sudden hope, unconsciously holding their breath. He finally nodded. "Let's do it."

At Devon's nod, they erupted—three glowing blurs colliding mid-air and landing in a laughing heap. Emily recovered first, tackling her brother in a fierce hug before pulling Tamra in, too.

Emily smiled at them with tears in her eyes. "It's going to be such a relief to no longer worry about someone killing you in a sudden skirmish." She bent down, touching her cheek to Devon's forehead, then Tamra's.

Their foreheads glowed for a moment, faces transforming into younger versions of themselves. Tamra gasped when she saw Devon, a slow smile spreading across her youthful features.

She grinned teasingly. "Not bad... for an old man."

He laughed, shaking his head in wonder. "I haven't felt this good in *decades*."

Clarice smirked, her eyes sparkling. "Oh, you think *that's* good? Just wait till you sprout wings."

Calypso moved over to Jason and Susan, pressing a tear-stained cheek to each of the students. The changes were more subtle for the younger humans—a tightening of skin in the stomach and thighs.

Practically vibrating with excitement, Clarice said, "Now say you want to vanquish evil."

Jason chorused the words with the others, then shuddered as tingles spread through him. Searing, painless heat swept through his body, peeling away mortality like old paint. His flesh hummed. Then, light burst behind his eyes, and everything human burned off in a blaze of incandescent joy.

He gaped at the rush of intense positive energy saturating his system. He caught Susan's gaze—and forgot how to breathe. The woman he loved was still there, only impossibly refined, her every feature sculpted from radiance.

Clarice clapped her hands, eyes shining. "Welcome to the family! One big, shiny, happy angel clan!" She pounced on Devon and Tamra in a laughing hug, then moved on to Jason and Susan.

Jason was still staring at his hands, flexing fingers that glowed faintly. "We feel this good *all the time*?" he asked in disbelief.

Clarice laughed delightedly. "Now you know why I'm so relentlessly cheerful. These bodies run on love and light. Imagine living like this—then swap the charge for venom and despair, and you get a taste of what Arturiel endured as a demon. That's why we're redeeming as many as we can."

Susan shivered. "That would be horrible. I can't imagine losing this wonderful feeling now that I have it."

Calypso smiled, her eyes growing contemplative. "Even this is diluted. The mortal realm's energy field is but the faintest layer. The highest light realm is so intense that only Seraphim and Cherubim are capable of existing there. The other Seraphim will not even leave the highest realm for fear of losing access to the greater energy field. According to Grodek and Lucifer, nothing can die within the highest light realm."

Clarice pursed her lips, her eyes alight with curiosity. "He also said the Seraphim existed alone in the universe before we created the angels and light realms, following directions from this god-thing. Apparently, most Seraphim didn't even understand what God is, and the three of us spent most of our time studying it. If fully ascended Seraphim don't understand God, it seems unlikely we'd comprehend it in our limited state. Even so, I'm very, *very* curious."

Jason narrowed his eyes, speculatively eyeing the other angels. "Are we sure this isn't just a computer simulation and God is the helpful AI or something? I mean, it sounds like the Seraphim consult it for information the same way I'd consult one of our primitive AIs. Before technology evolved here in the mortal realm, would the Seraphim even have any concept of what a computer simulation is?"

Clarice frowned doubtfully. "Interesting idea. However, Grodek made it sound like we had been around for billions of years before we created the angels. It seems like the concept of a simulation would've come up in all that time. Arturiel also talked about the light realms being extremely malleable, allowing them to create their own worlds from ideas—which sounds a lot like what we think of as simulations. I wonder if God's beyond our current level of comprehension. Remind me to ask Grodek if they had things like computers in the light realms next time we see him. The more I think about it, the more I agree with Jason on this."

Aria nodded slowly. "Considering we hacked encrypted military comms with our minds, I'd say there's definitely advanced tech baked into our biology."

Jason squinted at her. "So... can you tell what class I am now? How far down the hierarchy did I land?"

Aria sighed. "There it is. I knew that question was coming."

Jason hunched defensively. "Hey, I'm surrounded by Seraphim and Cherubim. You can't blame me for wondering if I'm the office intern of Heaven."

Calypso smiled at him reassuringly. "You are a Dominion, Jason. All of you are Dominions, with the exception of Devon and Tamra—they are Cherubim."

Jason exhaled in relief. He hated to admit it, but the thought of being cosmic cannon fodder had bothered him.

Aria looked at Calypso curiously. "How can you tell?"

Calypso pointed towards Jason. "It is part of their energy signature. You can see that his meridians possess lower bandwidth than Devon's or Lexi's. Furthermore, if you look closely at their nodes, you'll notice a specific rune imprinted upon them. I am not entirely certain how I know to identify them, but his denotes a Dominion of the First Order. Devon's and Tamra's runes signify Cherubim of the Second Order, whilst Lexi's marks her as a Cherub of the First Order."

Emily studied Jason in fascination. "So, Jason's one step below Cherubim. What am I?"

Calypso smiled, gazing into Emily's golden eyes. "Must you even ask? You and Eric are both Cherubim of the First Order."

Aria stared at Calypso intently. "Now that you can identify rank, can you confirm we really are Seraphim?"

Calypso nodded, a small, knowing smile playing upon her lips. "I have known for quite some time."

"Wait, *what*?" Aria squawked.

"*How* long have you known?" Clarice demanded, her golden eyes accusatory.

Calypso glanced up toward the ceiling thoughtfully. "Ever since we discovered that I was a Seraph, most likely."

Clarice spluttered in outrage for a moment before suddenly laughing. "You're learning from the best, Calypso. I'm so proud."

Aria shook her head, smiling. "Why didn't you tell us?"

"I was not entirely certain at first," Calypso said, eyeing Clarice with a playful smile. "When Aria obtained a divine instrument, it confirmed my suspicion, since only Seraphim are capable of using them. I confess I rather wished to see how long it would take you to work it out for yourselves. I could tell Emily had realized it the moment she began questioning Arturiel about Seraphim. I have a feeling Clarice has known for some time as well. I believe she may be rubbing off on me somewhat. Lucifer rather spoiled the fun by telling you."

Aria shook her head, laughing softly. "You know, I *thought* you looked a little too blasé when Lucifer told us. I'm glad we provided you with some entertainment." Aria broke off, staring at Clarice in bewilderment. "Why in the world do you find that freaking hot?"

Calypso shifted awkwardly as everyone looked between her and Clarice curiously.

Clarice shrugged with a coy smile. "She's my innocent angel being naughty—it *is* freaking hot."

Calypso's blush swept up to the roots of her hair as Clarice's grin widened, becoming suggestive. Aria and Lexi's faces flushed bright red as well.

"You're a *bad* angel," Aria accused Clarice, a trifle breathlessly.

"Does anyone know what's going on?" Jason asked in confusion, looking at Susan's blank expression and finding no help.

"I see you already forgot their emotions are linked," Emily noted dryly, shaking her head at Clarice. "That bond's going to be interesting with Clarice tied to your spirits."

Jason's eyes lit up with understanding as he stared at the trio of blushing angels. He had forgotten about the emotional bond the four angels shared. Clarice was basically running an empathy prank on divine broadband.

Susan caught his eye and raised a questioning eyebrow. He bit back a smile and muttered a quiet, "Later."

Mary watched Lexi's blushing face curiously. Before she could question her, a portal opened, and Eric came through with Arturiel.

The new arrivals stared around in surprise as the portal closed. Eric's eyes widened when he saw Devon and Tamra looking no older than twenty. He grinned broadly and quickly pulled Devon into a warm embrace.

"I can't tell you how happy I am to see you transformed," Eric declared happily, trading Devon for Tamra. "I was afraid I'd be the only male angel for the next twenty years."

"Lucifer's male," Clarice pointed out dryly.

"Okay, the only male angel in *this* group," Eric corrected, rolling his eyes.

"He *is* in our group," Clarice said sweetly.

Eric sighed in exasperation. "Fine... the only male who's related to you within two generations. Happy?"

"You have no idea just *how* happy I am," Clarice purred, winking at Calypso and Aria.

"Don't start that again," Emily warned her daughter sternly. "If they blush any harder, the cabin's going to combust."

"Oh, hey, Jason," Eric greeted him with an enthusiastic smile. "I see you've finally joined the club. Who's this lovely lady?"

Jason's brain jammed. "Uh—this is Susan. She's my... my—"

"She's your *girlfriend*, you ninny!" Clarice exclaimed with a wide grin. "Now say it!"

Jason blushed furiously, darting a look at Susan's amused eyes as she watched him flounder. "Yeah... she's my girlfriend."

"Woot!" Clarice cheered, punching the air triumphantly. "Jason's got a girlfriend!"

"It's nice to meet you, Susan," Eric grinned down at her, his eyes twinkling with amusement. "Don't mind Clarice; she has a mental condition that prevents her from taking anything seriously."

"It's called being ridiculously awesome," Clarice declared airily. "You should try it sometime, old man."

"And she's a Seraph," Arturiel murmured in a bemused tone. "I feel like reality's about to take the road less traveled."

Aria eyed the new angels with a calculating gaze. "We should probably get everyone ascended as much as we can. I think most of them can handle their own growth after we get them started."

Clarice started toward Jason and Susan with a predatory gleam in her eyes, but Emily grabbed her wings and pulled her back.

"We'll handle this, Tweedledum," Emily announced firmly. She stepped forward and pulled Susan into a warm embrace. "You too, Jason. I won't bite."

Jason laughed nervously and tentatively put his arms around Susan and Emily. He felt the flow of positivity from the other two begin exchanging energy with his own meridians. It was a surprisingly intimate experience, making him glad Emily had taken Clarice's place; he wasn't sure he could've kept his composure with her leering at him during such a personal experience.

Around them, Aria joined Devon and Tamra, while Clarice paired with Mary and Lexi. The energy built, humming through every particle of Jason's being. His meridians pulsed until light rippled under his skin, and he felt an odd itch between his shoulder blades.

"This next part requires tears," Emily said softly. "Can either of you manage one?"

Jason frowned, unable to think of anything that could make him feel sadness while being flooded with intense loving energy.

"I can," Susan whispered, her eyes shining with quicksilver tears.

"Good," Emily smiled, a quicksilver tear of her own running down her cheek. She pressed her cheek to Susan's, and as the tears touched, a golden sphere flared around them. Energy surged through Jason like a living sun, and his meridians expanded, reshaping.

Then—rip.

Wings tore through his back, spreading wide and knocking several chairs over.

"Oh shit," Emily sighed in exasperation. "I totally forgot to give you one of Tamra's wing-friendly shirts." She stuck her hand into a hole in the air and pulled out a shirt, handing it to Susan. "We're about the same size, so this *should* fit well enough. Follow me, and I'll show you how to put it on around the wings."

A portal opened into one of the bedrooms, and Emily led a blushing but ecstatic Susan through.

Jason flexed experimentally. His wings moved like a second pair of arms. He couldn't wait to try flying—with his girlfriend. He grinned stupidly at the word.

He looked around the room and noticed Tamra had learned from their experience, pulling the back of her shirt up before her wings appeared.

Then dizziness hit—sharp and sudden. The air vibrated, and they all staggered as the world tilted.

Calypso gasped. “It is a rewrite! Aria, Clarice—do not believe any—”

EPILOGUE

Aria sat up in bed, her heart pounding. The familiar shadows of her room surrounded her.

"How is my room still here?" she whispered. "The apartment blew up."

She threw off the covers and ran to Clarice's room. Even as she moved, the memories began to fade, slipping through her fingers like sand. She clenched her fists, forcing them to stay.

"Clarice?" she called, pushing the door open.

The memory struck her like an icicle to the heart: her sister's death, the doctors telling her it was a psychotic break, that her mind had invented angels to survive the loss.

She dropped to the floor as grief ripped through her.

Tears burned her cheeks—ordinary tears.

A sound tore out of her, half scream, half sob, raw enough to scrape her throat. The future stretched before her, an endless night without her sister's laughter, without her light.

The pain was unbearable, as if her soul were being torn in half, leaving her a wailing, broken wreck. "Clarice! Oh gods, Clarice! I can't... I can't..."

She desperately shook her head, moaning, "Please, oh please, not this, not Clarice. *Please, not Clarice!*"

She lay on her sister's floor for hours as time melted away like the last rays of a dying sun.

When the front door opened, she barely noticed. Footsteps echoed through the empty apartment.

"Aria? Are you here?"

Emily found her curled on the carpet and knelt, wrapping her arms tightly around her. She didn't speak. There was nothing to say.

Eventually, Aria looked up, her red-rimmed eyes desperate. “Was it all fake?” she whispered. “Calypso, the angels—everything?”

Her mother met her gaze, tears running silently down her face, and managed a small, broken smile.

“I’m so sorry, Aria.”

END OF BOOK 1

Books in Mirrors of the World

Return of the Fallen
Rise of the Seraphim
Author's Respite
The Last Circle of Dominion
Rhapsody of Light
Aeri Awakening
Glitch in the Shell

Other books by Kai Stormhaven

A Shudder Before the Beautiful
Tethered

ABOUT THE AUTHOR

I'm a techy by day and a fantasy author by night. I've been writing since I was a teenager, primarily for the sheer joy of exploring new worlds. I'm still on the fence about whether the universe is a high-fidelity simulation or just a very elaborate prank, a concept I explore at length in some of my novels. I live in a beautiful, forested region of the Pacific Northwest, not far from the giant redwoods. My stories are heavily influenced by my intense love of music—symphonic metal—an element that often manifests within my stories.

I grew up on a steady diet of Pratchett's wit and Jordan's epics, often skipping school so I could dive into the adventures of my favorite characters—looking at you, Granny Weatherwax. I like to craft stories that balance existential questions with irreverent humor, focusing on a blend of urban fantasy and lesbian romance. When I'm not debugging the metaphysical architecture of my latest fantasy world, you might find me hiking through ancient redwoods, rollerblading at questionable speeds, or losing imagination-based skirmishes to my favorite twelve-year-old / coauthor.

www.ingramcontent.com/pod-product-compliance
Lightning Source LLC
LaVergne TN
LVHW030915080826
845145LV00013B/2897

* 9 7 8 1 9 7 2 0 6 5 0 2 0 *